THE LUCKY STAR

Also by William T. Vollmann

You Bright and Risen Angels (1987)

The Rainbow Stories (1989)

The Ice-Shirt (1990)

Whores for Gloria (1991)

Thirteen Stories and Thirteen Epitaphs (1991)

An Afghanistan Picture Show (1992)

Fathers and Crows (1992)

Butterfly Stories (1993)

The Rifles (1994)

The Atlas (1996)

The Royal Family (2000)

Argall (2001)

Rising Up and Rising Down: Some Thoughts on Violence, Freedom and Urgent Means (2003)

Europe Central (2005)

Uncentering the Earth: Copernicus and the Revolutions of the Heavenly Spheres (2006)

Poor People (2007)

Riding Toward Everywhere (2008)

Imperial (2009)

Imperial: A Book of Photographs (2009)

Kissing the Mask: Beauty, Understatement and Femininity in Japanese Noh Theater (2010)

The Book of Dolores (2013)

Last Stories and Other Stories (2014)

The Dying Grass (2015)

Carbon Ideologies I: No Immediate Danger (2018)

Carbon Ideologies II: No Good Alternative (2018)

William T. Vollmann

VIKING

VIKING
An imprint of Penguin Random House LLC
penguinrandomhouse.com

LIBRARY OF CONGRESS CATALOGING-IN-PUBLICATION DATA

Names: Vollmann, William T., author.
Title: The lucky star / William T. Vollmann.
Description: New York : Viking, [2020]
Identifiers: LCCN 2019032256 (print) | LCCN 2019032257 (ebook) |
ISBN 9780399563522 (hardcover) | ISBN 9780399563539 (ebook)
Classification: LCC PS3572.O395 L83 2020 (print) |
LCC PS3572.O395 (ebook) | DDC 813/.54—dc23
LC record available at https://lccn.loc.gov/2019032256
LC ebook record available at https://lccn.loc.gov/2019032257

Printed in the United States of America
1 3 5 7 9 10 8 6 4 2

DESIGNED BY MEIGHAN CAVANAUGH

In memory of Jean Stein,

gentle benefactress and beautiful friend.

I will never forget you.

Since there are so many *literal* gaps in the tattered texts with which we are dealing, in effect all readings of Sappho are really fictions of Sappho.

JANE MCINTOSH SNYDER, 1997

And that is how Madhavi was born, with a pubis like a cobra's hood.

PRINCE ILANGÔ ADIGAL, *ca.* 171 A.D.

CONTENTS

IV

V

THE LUCKY STAR

Because thy lovingkindness is better than life, my lips shall praise thee.

PSALM 63:3

You Who Were Loved Above All Others

I, the servant of God, am thankful to Him that no one can help falling in love with beautiful women, and that no one can escape the desire to possess them, neither by change, nor flight, nor separation.

SHAYKH UMAR IBN MUHAMMED AL-NEFZAWI, *ca.* 1400

1

Not until Selene's wedding, when the fan's three blades winged slowly round and round while green ribbons twitched from the light bulb, did the transwoman, resurrected from another crying spell, meet her for whom she must have been meant: the lovely quiet one who could help her, the adorable one with the pubis like a cobra's hood—the lesbian. On this glaring afternoon, no less fortuitously because the procedure had been conceived and undertaken in Selene's honor (her cheeks excitedly pinkening), the transwoman, whom younger and therefore crueler ladies called sloppy, fat, unclean or just plain lazy, had so painstakingly constructed herself that at least here in this dark lounge she might have been female to the core. The retired policeman whom she dated once a week liked to compare her to a suspect who can nearly pass his polygraph examination. She had long since persuaded herself not to be hurt by repetitions of this compliment, which, since he did regularly hire her, expressed his tastes as much as her womanliness. The last time she had looked half as good, which was on Easter, when she, Shantelle and Selene availed themselves of the cosmetics liquidation sale in Chinatown, she'd swished into his room and said: Maybe now you'll agree that you've seen something, to which he replied: You ain't seen nothing until you've seen a girl take a bullet right through her smile and down her throat.—During their appointments, which terminated with what he called a climax, she frequently drank comfort from a lovely fantasy of surrendering to an unknown man who hid his face while penetrating her over and over, this act being observed by a crowd of flint-knapped faces that would have included the retired policeman no more than some gynecologist whose invasion has been rendered safely invisible to the patient through the childish magic of a surgical drape. Her clients, sweethearts and *special friends* tended to be male; many of them she actually liked, but her heart's desire was to be a woman with a woman—and now right here among our tall and smooth-skinned drag queens who smelled of powder sat the lesbian in a green blouse, her shoulder smoothly sparkling like Venus's marble breast.

2

Last year or maybe the year before, a different goddess had set her own unanswerable tone. When she first saw that girl's black curls shining so wide around her shoulders, and when the girl's white teeth and lustrous eyelashes consequently commenced to illuminate us, the transwoman lost her ability not to watch the breathings of the girl's breasts in their white, white blouse; how she longed to slide her face down the girl's brown arms, which shone as only young female flesh can! Unlike those misdirected lovers who push their own cause, the transwoman adored the girl's self-assured voice, which was sleekly insistent if not domineering. Possession being impossible, she aspired merely to parasitize. Sometimes she ordered an extra bourbon and ginger ale (six dollars), stirring its lone ice cube round and ever round in hopes that the girl would uncross her legs. No matter what, such efforts were never wasted, thanks to that sleek voice within the stunning white smile—because (most fortunately for all worshippers) the girl, whose name was Letitia, liked nothing better than to speak of herself. Her long yellow-pale fingers were always gesturing to explicate who she was not, why others miscomprehended her and what she refused to do. Fascinated, the transwoman tried to memorize her smell.

I know exactly what you mean, said the girl, because everyone has these conceptions of me. If all that people think about me are certain conceptions, she smilingly continued (not realizing that several degenerates, Francine the barmaid for instance, thought nothing whatsoever about her), then that shows a willingness to simplify me so they can deal with me quickly.

The transwoman nodded avidly, licking her lips.

I found it interesting, remarked the girl, that you could only imagine *that.* That you couldn't move beyond it.

Watching her crossed legs, the transwoman mouthed the prayer *open, open, open.*

The girl continued: I smile every time people say, *the thing about black women is . . .*

Oh, yes, well, that's right, said the transwoman, almost sick because at any moment Selene's best friend Samantha would come in, and then she would no longer have Letitia to herself. Fortunately, Letitia and the transwoman's frenemy Shantelle hated each other. Shantelle, who liked to inflict spitefulnesses interspersed with lovey-doveyness, sat contentedly enough on the dark side of the bar, doing business with Francine.

Do you have any understanding of the point I'm making?

Well, I guess so, but . . .

I'm ready for a refill. Only up to here. Otherwise it gets too watery.

Francine, could I please get a round for Letitia?

Six dollars.

But just up to here.

Yeah, Letitia; I'm not deaf. What about you, hon?

Oh, what the *hell,* cried the transwoman in high self-delight. Make it a double.

Thirteen dollars total. Thank *you.*

And then, Letitia continued, they gave me a rose quartz necklace. It went extremely well with my white gold earrings. Of course they're not responsible for that. And I don't blame them for not understanding that I'm allergic to sterling silver.

I'll bet it's real pretty on you. Why don't you model it sometime?

The thing is, I wanted to give them the opportunity to see how it looked on me while I was managing the project.

I'll bet you got compliments. *I'll* give you compliments—

Actually, I didn't, because what the marketing team failed to consider was that Stage Four might go over budget. They probably didn't feel comfortable with the analysis design. And yet they expected me to get the business panel on board!—You don't understand any of this.

Just as an old school lesbian separatist would have turned away from an otherwise comradely woman who occasionally fucked boys, Letitia drew the line at the transwoman for being simply *impure.* But she was too perfect to tell her. And so the transwoman got to stare at her in unalloyed delight.

Judy, are you even listening? That's why they pushed it over to me, to sabotage me, but it backfired because I actually expanded the project base.

Is your drink okay? asked her adorer. You're not touching it.

Do you have any idea what a product base is?

I'm sorry but I can't quite picture it. I wish I could. Do you want to explain it to me? I mean—

I like to think you're just lazy. But maybe it's something more mindless or even vicious, said the girl. I could use another cigarette.

Rushing across the street to buy her a pack of filter-tipped high-tar Carolina Naturals, the transwoman had thought to desire Letitia throughout her life, but the lesbian's appearance removed that impulse, not just then but retroactively. And yet it would not be fair to label our Judy's emotings as any more insignificant than the shadow on an old sandstone relief, whose kings and goddesses appear deliberately outlined for an eternity which is actually but one bead on a necklace of alterations—and why is this tallheaded figure's face now shaded while the paw of that eroded lion glares out so self-importantly?—Random or subtle as may be, imperceptibly restless, the shadow never fails to make pretty embellishments. Whatever the image may be at any instant, it presents a perfect reality, as was the case with Letitia—who, however, got bored and disappeared.—That stars do get overthrown is the first law of celebrity astronomy, as we saw in 1983, when the seventeen-year-old underdog Kathy Horvath came up against Martina Navratilova at the French Open. The young challenger decided to be aggressive in the very first set, *by hitting deep* (thus the printed account) *to Navratilova's backhand*, and won by six to four, then lost the second set zero to six, but in the final set hit a deep forehand crosscourt, which her opponent, narrow-eyed, her wheat-colored bangs sweat-glued to her forehead (Francine licked her lips), clenched her muscular arms and swung at, but failed to float, so that Kathy Horvath won again, six to three, locking Navratilova out of a Grand Slam. But Letitia's case was different. Having triumphed over us, she departed to continue her own Grand Slam. Sincerely desperate, the transwoman begged the retired policeman to track her, which he did in less than three minutes while she sucked him off, which required nearly twenty: Letitia had career-hopped to Atlanta; she wasn't even dead yet!—The transwoman rushed to cry this news. Foreseeably, Francine couldn't care less (when she lay all alone at night, she longed to be crushed between the thighs of the black tennis star Serena Williams), and Selene uttered two catty remarks, but we most important regulars began once again to sicken with loneliness. (As Xenia said: It must be something I've seen on TV, watching men and women be in couples.) We could not bear the lack of any adorable someone, being unable to adore ourselves. So the transwoman started trolling right away for a new idol—first fixing on gentle, blonde-banged little Erin, whom thanks to a mismatch in street medications she had once perceived as sneering at her, hence another memorably public detonation into tears, at which Erin had hugged her, kissing her cheek with a reassuring *awww!*; Erin had furthermore said: But, Judy, I *love* T-girls!* There was one that helped me put my luggage on the bus last night. She had this long blonde hair down to *here*, and she had long hands and huge fingers and she was tall and slender and I *love* tall and slender people! I just saw her for two seconds and I wanted to cream in my pants.—After this, the transwoman began hoping to make Erin one of her *special friends.* Why not? Hadn't Judy Garland found herself a lucky star? But as for the rest of us, especially Shantelle, when we entered the bar in late afternoon, the thing we hunted had not yet wafted down any spoor, so we sat drinking adulterated liquor out of superficially washed glasses, waiting for whatever might come in the night.—In came the lesbian.

3

While broadshouldered longhaired ladies laughed in bass voices, shotglasses clinked and the minister beamed over his clipboard, the lesbian sat unaccompanied, drinking gin and tonics. For several weeks she had been growing famous in our bar, admired not only by the men and women who desired her, but also by the high-class impersonators young, slim and beautiful, who could dance like nymphs and lip-synch without error (you would never guess). They all began to drink her in as if they were spectators at her fatal car crash. Without knowing why, Selene sometimes daydreamed of watching her sipping from a silver cup; while Shantelle acted out, Francine smiled despite herself and the straight man frowned as if a fist were beating his breastbone. Now even the transwoman had heard of her.

It had happened the previous Sunday at the wake for Al's boyfriend Ed. First Francine and then Sandra dropped a name: *Neva*, so of course we regulars took notice even though any number of important people received comparable

---

* A T-girl is a transgender woman. A G-girl ("genetic girl") is a woman who was born into a female body. An L-girl is a lesbian. Some people consider these terms offensive.

consideration—Judy Garland, for instance, after whom the transwoman had named herself; and when Michelle Obama appeared on the muted television, teaching underprivileged children how to weed carrots in the White House garden, our Selene, who most often incarnated herself as a big-shouldered blonde with vast eyelashes, was riveted, at which Shantelle informed her: Honey, you ain't never gonna have ten percent of what *she* got, but I love you anyway, to which Selene replied: Then you can still be my number ten bitch.—Francine by calmly asking who was ready for a shot of what headed off *that* fight, mostly for the sake of Selene, who never got violent; as for Shantelle, who had already been eighty-sixed twice, Francine would just as soon have cracked her over the head, but then the police might have degraded the occasion; hence business best be served itself by preventing Shantelle from going off, and just maybe Francine loved Shantelle. High above the top row of woman-waisted bottles, Ed's snapshot now occluded the faded old postcard of a breast with pink spectacles balanced on it. Al sat silently wiping his eyes with a napkin. Unlike me (I appeared svelte in extra-large) Al was too obese to fit into any T-shirt; his belly resembled three sideways buttocks. Francine kept reminding him that today all his drinks were on the house; he said no thank you and tossed down a tequila without noticing, so she topped him off. The retired policeman, who missed Ed but would never admit it, absorbed another shot of Old Crow in order to explain: No, Francine, it was that homeless case. They were being shot in the head while they slept. I got to talking with some people in the neighborhood who said, you know these kids up in the street, they're always out shooting their guns, and so I went up and located shell casings in the dirt by their door, and we actually matched them to the murder weapon.—Meanwhile Samantha sat apparently praying (she was actually keeping in practice, lip-synching to Barbra Streisand); and although she had promised herself to oversee her waistline, the transwoman could not stop gobbling meatballs, potato salad and those *cute, cute* miniature roast beef sandwiches with the toothpicks stuck through the buns; oh, my, she simply *could not* stay away from meatballs, even ones which were frozen in the middle; thus she honored the memory of Ed, who had cheated on Al with her lowpaid semiprivate assistance from Christmas Eve until three months ago, when Ed became too sick to fuck; aside from Francine and the retired policeman, nobody else (especially not Shantelle, thank God) had detected their romance, although it grew peculiarly disheartening the way that Al so often frowned at her; just now she felt ashamed to meet his bloodshot gaze, not that she had ever felt half as connected to Ed as to the retired policeman, who had apparently stopped dating Melba the G-girl bitch.—Just then Xenia was explaining to Francine: I feel like what I have is *feminine intelligence.* When I pick out the customer who wants a good conversation . . .—at which point Francine had to mix up my usual: six dollars. It was late afternoon going on evening, and after Al drank eight more tequilas and stumbled away sobbing, the red light-fixtures over the bar kept sweating through their glass scales: on summer days the Y Bar invariably sweltered with beer breath and estrogen sweat. A discreet aroma of marijuana approached me from the middle-aged German G-woman who sat sucking on her custom-modified electric cigarette, moving her dark-painted lips as if singing to herself; while three old men in shorts who had known Ed at least as thoroughly as Al kept kicking their glossy legs to the country music; then Selene's best friend Samantha came in and hugged almost everybody; she was a vast woman in a red wig, with blood-red spangles on her zipper-pull-like earrings; with these formalities safely over, the transwoman ate two more meatballs. (In those days she and Samantha still loved to torture each other with the anecdote about the studio writing Judy Garland out of *Showboat* because she had grown too fat to film.) Without asking, Francine mixed Samantha's usual: a wine cooler with a maraschino cherry and two ice cubes. Smiling, the latter blew her a thank-you kiss. As for Shantelle, she wished the straight man would come; he was the only one who didn't mind when she cheated at liars' dice. Meanwhile the three old men went home hand in hand, and Xenia was telling Sandra: My best friend who's now passed away, he got beat one time on the street, he and his buddy who was super feminine; they got beat up, chased; he handled it well; it didn't stop him from being comfortable with his gayness . . .—Wondering whether or not to eat the last four meatballs, the transwoman sat eavesdropping on two longhaired young G-girls with perfect teeth and ring-hoards on their fingers; cradling their beers, they told us jokes about red-hot redhaired drunk chicks; they both desired the same librarian, who claimed to be straight, and were debating with Francine whether they should try to do her together. The transwoman would have given everything if she could have looked like either of them. She fantasized that Letitia would soon come in and insult her one more time, just a little, and maybe slap her cheeks five or six times while everyone laughed and spat on her; that gave her an erection. Well, why not another meatball, or else a furtive handful of potato salad? Bored and sad, she longed to go home and chew up three sleeping pills—but just then she overheard

Shantelle and the two G-girls gossiping about the lesbian, who had been destined to suffer and cause suffering.

4

On Tuesday night she nearly met the lesbian, whose crumpled cocktail napkin became Shantelle's prize, at which Francine stood rolling her eyes; Xenia ironically applauded the new possessor's assaults upon the lipstick-stain: lusty licks and loud smacking kisses accomplished their effect, and bits of napkin clung to Shantelle's mouth, reminding sardonic Francine, who aspired to be asexual, of the first time she had tried cunnilingus (her reward a tongueload of pissy toilet paper); while Al, whose spirits had improved from desperate to morose, finished drinking his first tequila, and the retired policeman told me: Well, yes and no. The whole thing was that finding him doing the same thing was circumstantial. There were no items of evidentiary value at the scene. The other problem was, he had some really bad mental issues . . .—On Wednesday the lesbian was absent but the straight man was there because he could see underground; on Thursday I bought Xenia her usual (Old German Lager), in exchange for which she repeated what she always did: I've been a dancer for seven years, and I'm twenty-nine and a half. (She might have been fifty.) My plan, she assured me, is to keep on at the Pink Apple for another year, until next July. I think then I'll go back to Australia, and work there for three seasons, because you wouldn't believe the tips. (Last month she'd sworn that she never once left the good old U. S. of A.) I have a friend that lives in Laos; he runs a resort there. So after Australia I'll go to Laos and . . . I wouldn't mind just being a slave at some beautiful hotel, and just, you know, be there. There's boredom and there's contentment . . .—while Selene and Francine bent toward each other over the bar, recalculating the cost of hors d'oeuvres and deciding where the minister would stand.—On Friday the transwoman skipped her doctor's appointment so that she would not have to inhabit her body while the intern sliced another skin cancer from her back—she was getting old and nobody loved her!—which was why she picked a fight with the retired policeman and refused to let him beat her; on Saturday I accidentally sat next to Xenia again, and this time she swayed on her stool while telling me: I wanna get out of this and just . . . I'm smart; I'm ahead of the game; I'll get busted out in July . . .—Then came Sunday, wedding day, with a ringed, jeweled glitter-bracelet caressing Selene's sparkly wrist and the fan's three blades winging slowly round and round.

(Holly whispered: Oh, no, darling; bleeding might be a cancer sign.—Hunter replied: But Victoria says that Selene put in that vaginal ring and then she got a rash on her face . . .)

The bride stood even taller and wider than usual; her vast blue eyelashes were weapons.—Sweetie, said Francine, sit down and relax.—Shantelle pulled Al to his feet, but he declined to dance, although a vast unknown T-girl with rouged cheeks, blood-red lips and blue eyelids began slowly nodding to the music, like a Buddha in an earthquake. Shantelle shouted: *Yeah, bitch!*—at which Francine raised one eyebrow. The minister arrived, escorted by Samantha, from whom he bought his marijuana twice a week, and they both hugged Selene, who had grown sufficiently nervous that Francine poured her a stiffer drink. The retired policeman stayed home with a fit of gout, so he could hardly exercise control over the transwoman's asocial behavior; accordingly, while everyone else waited for the groom, who was late as expected, she chewed pink goofballs in the ladies' restroom, then seated herself demurely at the bar, drinking rum and tonic with the straight man's on-again-off-again ex, her not quite *special friend* Sandra, who answered: Umm, I don't know which one came first. I remember this house that's not the one I grew up in, so it must have been a different house, and I remember my parents sleeping and I was up before them, because it must have been my birthday; they had gotten me a plastic tea set and I really wanted it. I must have picked it out at the store and then they bought it and said you can open it on your birthday.

Well, I wish *I* could have had a tea set when I was little! cried Judy, starting to feel good and high. All I ever got was cap guns and goddamn cowboy hats and all that Indian-fighting bullshit they thought boys had to have . . .

And I remember the neighbors' porch, said Sandra very slowly; I remember being there and it being late afternoon sun and then it being very shady.

Yeah, said Judy, I remember sitting on the porch, all right, because they wouldn't let me into my room; they wanted to toughen me up, but when I tried to make friends with the other boys they could see right away that I wasn't their kind, so they—

Ready for another? asked Francine, hoping to save her from bursting into tears.

Could I take mine straight up? said Sandra.

Straight up the ass, said Francine. Judy honey, are you finished playing with your ice cubes?

Not quite, said the transwoman, who worried about rent money.

Yes you are, said Sandra. Sweetheart, let me buy you a round.

Are you sure?

Of course I'm sure. Aren't you my girlfriend? Aren't you my very best friend?

The transwoman began smiling, because she truly did love Sandra, but then it happened: As soon as she laid eyes on the lesbian, she knew with the certainty of the utmost faith, never mind any prior certainties, about for instance Letitia, that here was a green-bloused someone *from whom she could not bear to go away*, someone whom she longed to be near forever, even if merely to spy on her; if the lesbian never spoke to her it would still be perfect, if only she refrained from going away!

Francine, pour it strong, she said. Hey, who's that stunner in the green blouse?

But Sandra was saying: And I have one very strong memory, but I don't know if this is really about my body or not. You know, at nursery school the kids have to keep shoeboxes with extra clothes inside, in case what they're wearing gets dirty. And I remember—

Sandra, who's that gal in green over there?

Who? I said I remember always wanting to wear dresses and being forced to wear corduroys. One day I got to wear this really, really beautiful dress and it was a sailor dress; we did fingerpainting that day and I got paint on myself and had to change into my corduroys. I remember feeling desperate. I know you can relate. And, Judy, I couldn't stand it! I must have thrown a tantrum.

You must have looked pretty cute at nursery school.

Thank you! But I don't remember how I looked. I'm remembering back to old photos. Francine, do you have any photos of yourself when you were little?

My house burned down, said the barmaid.

That's horrible! You never told me—

It don't matter now. Selene, let me top you off. This is your big day.

Francine, I'm *so sorry* about your house!

Forget it. Samantha, how about another?

Judy, do you think I hurt Francine's feelings? I really never knew—

Of course not, sweetie—this assertion being uncharacteristically emphatic, in order to keep on track, because just as if one were to ascend Jones Street past the Hotel Krupa and all the way up to Sutter Street, which for its part presently slopes gently down into the playpen of banks and insurance towers, so, thanks to those goofballs, Judy was rising *up* and *up*, which meant that if she allowed herself to be at all tentative she might forget what she was saying, maybe even disgrace herself, so she insisted: Francine *loves* you! Now, when you think of yourself as a little girl, what do you see?

Well, when I picture myself as little, I am picturing myself as sepia toned . . .

Having paid politeness its due, the transwoman returned to the fundamental issue: Do you know that girl over there in the green blouse?

Now Sandra felt hurt, but her favorite thing in the world was helping others and pleasing them, so she merely said: Of course I do. You mean that you don't?

That's right.

She's really, really nice. Her name's Neva. Even Francine's attracted. Would you like to buy her a drink? I think she likes gin and tonics—

First I have to buy you one, because you just bought mine.

Never mind, said Sandra. Go sit next to her if you feel like it. Excuse me, Francine, but I think Judy wants to buy someone a drink.

Sandra, you're the most gracious lady ever. And I do mean *lady.*

Well, I don't know about that.

And I'm sorry I . . . I mean, I wish I could see one of those sepia-toned photos from when you were little.

Oh, that's just a manner of speaking. Look! Did you just see Neva smile at you?

What'll it be? said Francine.

I, well, a gin and tonic. For—

Seven dollars. Richard, once I make this can you walk it over to Neva?

Embarrassed now, Judy laid her hand on Sandra's wrist and said: Tell me the rest of the story.

Which story? Oh! Well, said Sandra, I was going to be a lady from the first. I remember again, and this must have been nursery school since I went to a different school for kindergarten because I remember the parking lot, and the night before, my mother and I had watched the first part of *Camelot* the musical and got really obsessed with it; so when my mother picked me up from school, she had gotten me some pink plastic jewelry in a case, and my mother told the teacher, right in front of everyone, that the reason I could have it was so I could watch *Camelot* with her and be Guinevere. And I felt so proud! There was this sense that I had, probably because my mother did, that being little I was very precocious, until at some point I *wasn't* anymore—and then in some way I fell behind. My mother was very good with little children and she still is. She taught four-year-olds for years and I have seen her be very tender and understanding . . .

The transwoman was staring at the lesbian. Just as she would have been loyal to the child whom she could never bear, so now meticulously and irrevocably she fixed her loyalty upon Neva, riveting herself to her with every invisible glory of subservience.

5

Please, a moment of silence.

What is this, a funeral?

Let's have Selene sing the wedding song.

No, Francine, I told her track number two . . .

And the vast bride in her silver spangly net-dress and her immense crown of blonde hair commenced singing or actually lip-synching to Judy Garland: *Somewhere over the rainbow,* as her Latino groom stood beside her with a flower on his breast and his painted eyes closed. Suddenly he winked and laughed at Selene, while Samantha slowly groomed her wig from behind. Meanwhile Xenia kept weeping, tasting the lesbian with her eyes.

The minister said: Let us lift our hearts together in jubilation at the marriage between Selene and Ricardo, and Samantha finished smoothing out Selene's wig.—We are blessed to open our hearts to their love. Let us each dedicate ourselves to the love in our own lives, while the bride stood as majestic as a planet, Francine beamed from behind the bar and another middle-aged T-girl sat dabbing at her left eye.

Isn't this sweet? said Sandra.

Oh, yes, said the transwoman, struggling not to watch the lesbian, which is to say thirsting to drink from the promise of her, perhaps the only promise in Judy's life which would ever be kept; for Neva, the one who could love without shame or limit, would have sinned against that love had she not fed it to anyone in need, even to leeching Judy who so perfectly reminded me of myself; soon the lesbian would be lovingly embracing that sad fat woman, rubbing her breasts against hers, running her fingers through her partner's long hair while Judy, naked and submissive, gazed stupidly ahead; after which the lesbian would go wide-eyed and motionless beneath me as she gave herself, so as to be towering over us all, and the minister said: Marriage is the essence of human relationships. It challenges us to be in accord . . .

Shantelle burst into tears. She was black, smooth, young and skinny, with hair like ferns and waterfalls. Francine kept grinning proudly behind the bar.

As the bride and groom recited their vows, Samantha began to look soft, old and gentle, the groom now repeating after the minister: *May our love forever remain and keep us strong.* Francine had helped dream that one up.

Selene kept dabbing at her eyes, and other smiling T-girls and G-girls were blowing their noses. Ricardo repeated after the minister: *I give you this ring as a sign that I choose you as my lover, my partner and my best friend for all the days of our lives.*

(Shantelle side-whispered: You're gonna say, *that's okay, lover.* You just have to remember who to say it *to.* See who the fuck you wake up with . . .)

The minister said: It gives me great joy to pronounce you husband and husband!—at which everyone began clapping big echoing hands.

Samantha said: She beat me to the altar; I was too damn late!

I *look* like I cried, said Xenia, but I didn't actually cry.

I'm gonna shake it *up!* shouted the wide Nigerian T-girl in the green executive sweater.

Shantelle called smirkily: Congratulations to my old back sister, my *old, old* back sister!

Fuck you! shouted the bride in a bass voice.

The wedding cake appeared to be a vast cushion of flowers and whipped cream.—Miffed or maybe just teasing, Selene shouted: Eat *that*, damn you!

Lemme give a hug. Whoo-ha, whoo-ha!

Oh, just cut the goddamn cake, bitch!

The bride went into the men's bathroom, locked the door and came out five minutes later in a green dress and a spangly silver collar, having armed herself in another great yellow wig which resembled a Valkyrie's helmet. Xenia felt called upon to defend Selene against me, as if I could ever have grown sufficiently active to object to anything; I kept nodding dizzily and Xenia was insisting: If they feel that they are a woman then they are a woman. I don't believe in discriminating against another person, because I know what it's like to be discriminated against. I will never understand why they do it, to go through what they go through, and now dear old Selene . . .—Francine dropped ten quarters into the jukebox, and so the dancing started, with the disco ball's rainbow rays whirling across lovely girls' faces. By now Sandra was in the corner, soul-kissing another G-girl. Xenia chose a crewcut white man with an earring in his right ear and a T-shirt across whose breast a tank upraised its great gun at a target which proclaimed **SUPPORT OUR TROOPS** while an American flag waved over each galaxy and all of us who had ever been spat on. The newlyweds were having fun; they chuckled, whispered and cha-cha-cha'd. The G-girl boasted to Sandra: I've had girls lick my vagina and say, *oh, wow, that's real!*—As for the transwoman, who had applied flower lashes like the drag queen Leeza Monet, in high delight she rushed onto Xenia's stool, so that she now sat a mere two places from the lesbian, to whom she said: I'm Judy, and I brought you this piece of wedding cake . . .—Not long ago Shantelle (who herself was snakelike) had told her that her eyes were too small; therefore she widened them as much as she could whenever she gazed at her prey, trying not to blink, which led Shantelle to consider her quite the freak. Now Xenia was slow-dancing by herself. With the black gap of her mouth, those sad lovely eyes and that crumbling makeup, she emblematized the beauty of ruins. I got up and took her for a spin. Then I sat and sized up the lesbian, whom I had first seen standing in the doorway as if she were nerving herself up to something. I won't deny that she lit up my heart in neon lights! She was even lovelier than Letitia, and, unlike her, never looked at herself in the mirror unless she needed to put on lipstick. Meanwhile the bride performed her best lip-synch dance, to the opening number of the movie *Cabaret*; her golden beehive became so incandescent that it seemed about to catch on fire. Wild, gleeful Ricardo snatched up the transwoman, who would much rather have sat staring at the lesbian, but did what she was called upon to do, showing off her new red dress, smiling blankly whenever Ricardo squeezed her ass; and now polite men were handing dollar bills to Selene.

Whichever regulars happened to be high grew ever more amazed at the blending of the rainbow disco ball into the screeching microphone once the fat man in the rhinestone-silvered suit began to dance, Xenia enthusiastically singing along although one could hear only the black girls who kept breaking off to kiss one another on the mouth. Free of Ricardo, the transwoman rushed over to gobble more wedding cake, returning to her wonderful lesbian, who smiled and made room right beside her! Earrings were glittering; men in suits kept hugging T-girls. The bride towered over the groom, who whispered naughty things into her shoulder. The straight man kissed the plastic orchid in the hair of the Honolulu T-girl, who refused to play liars' dice with him, and the ever-giving lesbian in her green spangled blouse began to sway to music; never moneyless, she had quietly bought drinks for everyone around her, murmuring to Francine amidst the excitingly deep voices of the T-girls. Xenia with her ruined face and her crumpled black-red mouth felt a duty to work extra hard; she dragged Al to his feet and made him dance. His eyes were red; he didn't want to, but she hissed: Do it for Selene!

Shantelle, who loved to take everything upon herself, was explaining to Sandra: When you get yourself married in the eyes of the community, it's *our obligation* to keep the love alive!—while Xenia kept dancing and retelling the plots of all the Hollywood movies she once starred in, some of which remained unseen in directors' secret vaults, and Samantha, who used to work in one of those mid-level establishments where the strippers all wipe the catty pole clean with the same rag, and now made a vocation if not a career of displaying the boundary line between a cheap wig and a sweaty middle-aged male forehead, sat at the bar's last stool, blotto, clapping her hands whenever Selene kissed shy fat Ricardo, who would need to leave within fifteen minutes to avoid getting fired from the furniture store. The minister had said: *I pronounce you husband and husband,* and the sentimental transwoman wept without knowing why. *And the cloud of the hymen is like a shining emerald,* whispered the straight man. Samantha kept weeping exhilarated tears and the transwoman, who had swallowed even better pills, felt happier and happier for Selene (not for Ricardo, whom she had never met before, and suspected of meditating abandonment)—happier still because the lesbian was smiling, sometimes at her but usually at Selene.

Eager to hear the lesbian's voice, the transwoman wondered how to coax it forth; what if she herself were to sing? . . .—but everyone said her voice was awful even when she sang hymns in church. Unable to turn away from her, she longed to say: Neva, what do you sound like?—The lesbian (she who caused everything to happen) kept silent, but at each toast to the wedded union of Selene and Ricardo, she did touch shotglasses with the transwoman, who rapidly fell in love.

6

In the lesbian's time songs were customarily bought and sold from machines, which may explain why no songs got sung about her even after she died; old lovers gave up speaking about her, firstly because the machines expressed ever newer topics onto those tiny rectangular telephone screens over which we bent, stroking words and pictures as if these were jewels; and secondly because since death was not supposed to happen, it needed to be forgotten as quickly as possible. Hence the young disdained the old, whose sallow wrinkles called into question expectations of eternally increasing happiness; as for the dead, their unclean state might be contagious—for what if our very own many-colored dramas, whose stories promised perfect pleasure, someday betrayed us by coming to an end? Death was an ill-mannered cough at a concert, a bad smell at a party; it meant running short of money just when someone had expected to buy herself the present that she really, really wanted. So when the lesbian died, our happiness refused to close. New-beloved beauties swam into our ken like the wriggling slate-diamonds of manta rays, but my own longing for Neva resembled the slow-pulsing translucent parasol of a jellyfish. In my soul I called her *you who were loved above all others.* Here came a shoal of rays swimming together, then other jellyfish like mushrooms, and the long narrow spear of a manta's tail. If you have ever heard the ancient lyric in which long-dead Anacreon asked his Muse which metal-worker could have fashioned the sea with its shining silver waves, you may have wondered about this other sea in which our swimmers swarmed, doubling back on lives, or circling around them, so that they would never get beached at the end. Here in this bar where our lesbian once lived, the fan's three blades shone vaguely silver, and all the fish kept wriggling toward happiness because the jukebox played new songs. Some of us might have feared that if we mentioned her too much, she would climb back out of her grave, naked and rotten, to torture us with the horror of her end; we could not understand that she had already shucked off her flesh just as the transwoman once did in her last boyhood years, pulling out the semiliquid prosthetic breasts she'd carried all night inside her slinky pinky party dress, and hiding them against the daylight as if they were slaughtered things. By day she had concealed herself from the truth; while day and night the lesbian now lay in darkness. We no longer speculated as to what she might have seen, won or suffered, to make her the way she was.

I could tell you how in her arms our lovemaking so often ceased being what rape prosecutors refer to as "goal driven"—everything being equally present and perfect, as when we rubbed our tongues against hers for hours and hours. But my certainty that it felt that way for all of us may be misplaced. If I weren't such a loser I'd have kept quiet.

Two months after the memorial service, I did speak her name right here at the Y Bar, at which two lesbians and a lonely old queen smiled sadly, not looking at each other; no one blamed her for dying, but since she was dead, it seemed better that she should stop coming around—for there were new women's names on our lips. (We all have our war stories, said Francine. But you know what? Making love with Neva, feeling tied up in knots about her, we all got through that, because we had to. But this part I don't know how to get through—so *shut up*, and let's . . . oh, what the hell.) So I too gave up mention of Neva, which made the secret all the sweeter in its sadness.

Then late one night at Amanda's Spot the transwoman and I were getting drunk for no reason (I forget where the retired policeman was), and when the fat T-girl in the spangleblue skirt came stamping out onto the stage and flashed her strap-on so that lesbians in the audience all screamed for glee, *our* lesbian, the dead one, came back for both of us, perhaps because she was the only universally loved woman we knew who had actually been born with a vagina; Judy and I protected our memories from each other but we did agree that Neva had been graceful, lovely, awfully nice although how nice exactly remained disputable. The transwoman resumed weeping. She must have said something to Selene or Samantha, because after that Neva's name rose back up into mention at our bar, much as the bloated corpse of a drowned victim returns to the surface. Remembering how we used to desire her, some desired her still, while the rest collected adequate gratification from the memories, which might as well have been lovely irregular coins bearing images of vulvas, insects and hydras. She who used to sit just past the edge of us, smiling at us, never at herself, remained our treasure.

7

Sandra once said in reference to some dead movie star, probably Marlene Dietrich, that to be perfect must be a burden and a sadness, at which the lesbian rose up in my mind, because to be such a one as her who was a promise to so many might have become an outright horror. When the transwoman first told him about her, saying *ohmigod, what a stunner,* the retired policeman chased the lesbian's smile on his computer, partly for laughs but mostly because watching and hunting any person, especially someone unknown, reminded him of how he used to be; before the transwoman had even finished rinsing her mouth in that hotel room sink for which they both found so many uses, the lesbian's face was filling his screen from corner to corner, shy but proud, with her lips painted red and her teeth so white and clean, as if she were offering herself to him; his sated penis tried to stir, doing its due diligence, and so eventually did he, even showing up at the door of my room at the Amity Hotel, where I no longer live because the night manager and I disagreed on the subject of an underaged visitor of mine. Anyhow, I told the retired policeman some of what I knew, keeping back the best parts for myself, and after twenty-odd minutes the transwoman, obviously following instructions, rang my buzzer, so now there were three of us, and four forty-ounce cans of malt liquor in her purse: two for her and two for me (not our usuals); *he* stayed faithful to his Old Crow. So I stretched out on my bed, halfway enjoying the novelty of company here where I generally lay alone, Francine being my favorite exception; and he sat wheezing in my one chair, with Judy in his lap, while we talked about the lesbian, almost as if there had been no time to do it while she was still alive, with the *idea* of her face floating over us, a perfect mask of serenity like the anciently-carven *zo-onna* of a Japanese Noh actor; he was good at asking questions while pretending not to, while I for my part kept coaxing and complimenting the transwoman, less because she might say something I hadn't heard than because it was a way of getting back at him who if he wasn't going to make straight up inquiries deserved nothing; as it happened, in the end they did both tattle out new stories; a week later Francine excreted three more secrets; then through the retired policeman's steely kindness I met the lesbian's former neighbor Catalina, who had never gone to the Y Bar. That brownhaired brown girl, current and former resident of Room 545, now sat across from me in the window niche of a juice bar, daintily, thoughtfully reaching her fingers into the past: I'm getting a bunch of memories, all right. Which one to pick?—And she sat thinking very seriously.—Okay, resumed Catalina, I started having some super intense dreams about her, and that was when I knew this was gonna be different. I dreamed about my mom giving Neva a key . . .—Scratching away mascara-clots, Xenia for her part said: All right, here's what I recall. Her body couldn't bend more than mine. Somewhat flat-chested, but decent tits; pretty brown hair, very innocent or maybe even blank brown eyes, and a beautiful little-girl body, very cute pussy . . .—What about her personality? I asked.—She said: She reminded me of this Rebecca whom I did sex work with for maybe four years; we were hand job whores together; we were fucking together and she was very possessive, but she claimed not to be a lesbian . . .—Interrupting, I insisted that Neva had never been possessive, to which Xenia replied: You think so because you don't understand the difference between fucking as a man and fucking as a woman . . . !—at which point I went my ignorant way.—Samantha refused to discuss the lesbian, but Sandra gave me a poem she had written about Neva and herself as mermaids on a white bird-island somewhere in the North Sea; even Shantelle pissed out a few of her stinking recollections; then late one afternoon I woke up recollecting and possibly even understanding certain aspects of the lesbian, and those lost memories I now dribble through my fingers, enjoying their cold silveriness and the soft sweet clickings when they touch each other.

Child Star

Association with women is the basic element of good manners.

GOETHE, 1809

Well, Judy Garland isn't sophisticated. There's only one way to put it—
she's nuts about her mother.

JAMES CARSON, 1940

1

A Finnish woman once told a tale of another Finnish woman who got regularly called away from her woodcutter husband to become a wolf-wife in the swamps, fragrant with mud and bilberries, lusting to tear heifers to pieces, howling with delight whenever her wolf husband penetrated her. About her new fanged and hairy shape the tale explained: *The Devil may shape a witch into a wolf or a cat or even a goat, without subtracting from her and without adding to her at all. For this occurs just as clay is first molded into one, then shaped into another shape, for the Devil is a potter and his witches but clay.* Exactly thus the murderess regards her victims. Between the one daughter whom her twisting ligature will make famous and the other daughter, poised and pretty, who knows nothing until she is awakened by the downstairs neighbor's screams, nothing can be added or subtracted, because each girl is a hunk of the common clay. Likewise works the mother, squeezing and twisting her offspring into the most finished shape; and should the daughter evince distress, never mind, for thermodynamics proves that nothing can be created or destroyed! The awful question: *What color was your daughter's hair?* should be calmly answered: *The same as it always was and will be,* because the child never existed in and of herself; the mother gave her birth (as could be said about whatever the Goddess creates) only for her own pleasure, separating out of herself her own substance, which at whim or will returns to her. How can mere busybodies who exhume the dead girl to pluck a hair sample comprehend that? Goddess, forgive them; they know not what they do. It took four strong men to hold down the woodcutter's wife when the police carried her daughter's corpse away. But the wolf's wife, cross-examined in court, sat utterly calm even though her fingers kept drumming on the table. Whether the official cause of death would be set down as throttling, or aspiration vomiting from being throttled (or vomiting from being tortured, raped or simply frightened), the wolf's wife knew that her prey never died because it never lived nor was anything but her own projection invented to feed her dream of hunger. This mother had beautiful claws. On the witness stand she turned them over and admired them. Just as Judy Garland used to envy Joan Crawford for her *long, glittering fingernails,* so even the woodcutter's wife, whose hands were roughened by housework, could not help but wish she had fingernails like her enemy sister! And now, on a tiny oval velvet pallet, a resurrection man carried in the choicest of the daughter's relics. *Her hair is a little lighter with just the right touch of gold to enhance those lovely eyes that feature dark curling lashes.* Those eyes and lashes were rotten, of course, so to help the jury visualize them, the accused woman smilingly indicated her own.

2

The mother's biography begins in the easy days between wars when America promised to grow forever better, at least for clean-thinking right-colored sorts who worked hard; needless to say, the retired policeman told it worse than it was, with searches, and then dried blood inside a cupboard, which caused somebody's mother to be arrested, but there were no bloodstains in the lesbian's story, as even the compliant transwoman remarked out loud; unembarrassed, the retired policeman kept picking my brain about Neva's childhood, but I pretended not to know anything; to get him off my back I started quizzing the transwoman, who said: And just then I looked out the window, I don't know why, and I saw Neva . . .—Glaring into my eyes, the retired policeman demanded: You mean to tell me that even when she was in the crapper, you never snooped through her purse?—Correct, I lied.—By then they were both pretty sure that I had no information to swap; on the other hand, since I was one of them, having loved the lesbian, and since I never blabbed to anyone else but Francine, who also dwelled in our inner circle, it gratified them to expose me to some details. Moreover, the retired policeman knew that I was nearly as intelligent as he; whenever he gifted the transwoman with his famous bedtime lectures on historic criminal cases, all she did was gape admiringly; if it weren't for his other peculiar requirements, he would rather have dated a soul mate. On a certain faraway occasion when I treated him in the Cinnabar (Carmen had not yet been fired for embezzling the till) he had demanded whether or not I believed that old-time flypaper could have been soaked in water on a soup plate for several days, and the resultant arsenic infusion employed for murder purposes; I replied that arsenic was an effective poison based at least in part on its solubility. He liked me then. He could see I was good for something. To reward me, he bestowed on me one of his knowledge-pearls: Arsenic eaters tended to undergo a speedier postmortem decay than the rest of us.—I'll drink to that, I said. So now all three of us were drinking to the lesbian's mother, at my expense, in my room at the Amity Hotel: a twelvepack of Coonhound malt liquor in the extra-tall bullet-shaped cans. My guests felt so comfortable with me that neither one even closed the bathroom door whenever it came time to go piss it out, so here's a knowledge-pearl for *you*: Judy stood up to pee just like the rest of us.

Back to the lesbian's mother, whose image to me then was as a noseless woman's head of speckled clay, staring at what I could not know; by now the retired policeman's amateur prosecution had traced her back to her own mother's years when Indiana steel mills still smoked and flamed as if for all time, and the generation begotten by quietly married demobilized soldiers was in its own turn pairing off, happily disinterested in great causes, so that bungalows, duplexes and ranch homes swelled quickly up in the new thickets of opportunity called suburbs, budding off the latest attachments and releasing seeds of automobiles so that boys could go meet girls and have *fun*—kiss-kiss!—which goal derived from that dream long ago enacted by dead or silent uncles: the chimera of salvation from fear, which had been accomplished no less nobly than temporarily, for victory in time discredits itself not unlike defeat; survivors fatten and fail, laying burdens down; hence for the sons and brothers who had not, for instance, squatted in some jungle foxhole, counting the flashes of incoming Japanese shells, it seemed wonderful to turn away from everything but money and happiness. When their own trouble came, some blamed it on the money, and others on the happiness, but the white collar men who rode to work and back on commuter trains, and the stay-at-home wives in those mortgaged houses, never wondered which other lives they could have lived, because to ask would have been to advertise doubt, which is suspicious. Certain women blamed the men for leaving them too much at home, while some men disliked to find their wives resentfully stale in those little mortgaged bungalows that every year seemed less and less like castles, so that they joined secret lodges to worship the dove of Mary, the lily of Mary, or else, it being a decade too early to parachute into that doublepage spread of Natalie Wood who in a dark outfit posed behind the open door of her white Thunderbird (a present for her sixteenth birthday, paid for from her earnings, of course, and soon wrecked, after which she got a pink Cadillac), they simply stopped at a bar with colleagues, while on those same long, long days the newer wives might visit one another, waiting, complaining and confessing dreams that the radio had taught them. When all they needed to carry was a baby or two, those visits could still be enjoyed, but there came a time when babies grew into children, after which there were other babies, so that for years a mother's entire time went for laundry, buying dinner and cooking dinner, with the children often sick or naughty or else fighting, and no comfort ever but the television: *somewhere over the rainbow*—until finally, thank God, the babies stopped coming, which meant the women were no good anymore; all the children were at school, which proved unexpectedly sad; the bungalows were sagging and one's hair was greying, by which time visiting one's good old gal pals was less fun than formerly, they too being worn out, excepting only those rare secret part-time wolf-wives who kept the thrill alive (I remember for instance a woman with bruise-colored eyeshadow who stared out from the police photograph: pretty and feral, young and reddish-blonde, blue-eyed, tight-lipped, leaning slightly forward as if to bite the officers as she had bitten her six-year-old daughter); and without children getting in the way, everything seemed too quiet; besides, those housewives' thoughts had been interrupted so many times for so many years that it felt easier not to think. Besides, what was there to say? Shirley knew everything about Geraldine that Geraldine knew about herself. So they went shopping in their big cars, then watched the soap operas and the big bright shows whose heroines were all incarnations of one beautifully distraught soprano in her long white dress, after which it came time to set out snacks for the children and start making dinner. The children ruined life. Before they came, marriage had been exciting. Their husbands loved them more. It was pretty swell to greet them at the front door, perfectly made up, with a cold highball in hand and fresh lingerie under the welcome-home dress. But often now the husbands came home late, so that the highball was spoiled. And when they did arrive, they, too, were tired after a long day's drudge. And the little brats always crying, couldn't they shut up? Even in their secret societies of train, bar, office and Masonic lodge, the husbands never admitted how much they disliked their children. Once upon a time there had been just a husband coming home to a wife who adored him. Then suddenly the baby came, and the wife loved her husband less. She was always weary and angry. If the baby even whimpered once, that had to be attended to, but if a husband grumbled about his rights, well, you should see the wife put him in his place! Had the husbands confessed their jealousy, it would have sounded childish. So instead they stayed late together, telling jokes about the follies of women. After they got used to expecting little from their families, the colleagues they drank with all the time became their real brothers. Sometimes they joked about running away from their wives, seducing a secretary and doing it all over again. And the women kept dinner warm for them in the oven, wondering when they would get home.

3

The lesbian's mother was born into one of those families. Being there was not as bad as remembering it, because at that time the prefabricated little houses that all faced each other were still new. Those lost memories which might as well have been lovely irregular coins with images of vulvas, insects and hydras I now dribble again through my fingers:

Now tell me this: What do you want to do when you grow up to be a great big girl?

I want to be a singer, Mr. Beery. And I'd like to act, too.

Now the little lady standing here beside me isn't exactly a celebrity yet. She's only twelve years old.

Judy was actually thirteen. And this radio show was already so ancient that they rebroadcast it only late at night, in that silence between the return of the jury and its pronouncement of verdict, when frogs sang in subdivisions and middle-aged mothers imagined being teenagers again.

Wait until you hear her sing. All right, Judy, whip along!

And Judy sang "Somewhere Over the Rainbow."

Judy Garland, child wonder of the screen. She's the cutest little dancer and blues singer that's ever been seen or heard. She is only thirteen.

She was fifteen, in fact, and the years kept wounding all the sentimental women who wished that they had married someone else.

4

The lesbian's mother yearned to be another person. Any real goddess's love for us would have known that our love for her was never meant to be permanent; once she had taught us how to love, she needed to go away and die, to give us hope of adapting to dimness and darkness, so that we could love each other. Not being a goddess, this person tried to be a 1950s nymphet in saddle shoes and a button-down cardigan sweater. She wanted to be the girl whom everyone loved.

Once she found herself to be a woman, she rose up and looked about her at the brightly inescapable question: How long had she been living in this way, which was so different from what she had expected? She answered: As long as she could remember. (I envision a marble female head with orange tear-stains on its cheek.)

Without compassion the next question illuminated her: Would her loneliness continue forever?

To save her, a man named Mr. Strand proposed marriage.—I do, she said. And just as we place the rings, watches and other such relics of murder victims in numbered envelopes, next affixing counterpart numbers (usually engraved on metal plates) to each corpse, so he attached a token of rescue to her finger. Kissing him, she went into the bedroom, closed the door, sat on the bed for a moment, then rushed into the bathroom and vomited.

5

Once the lesbian came along, once upon a long ago happily ever after time among the Mission style houses of Vallejo, California, during the era of what the retired policeman referred to as *crime control*, which terminated among those dreamy 1970s Mardi Gras balls whose most perfect princess might wear her feather dress up tight against her neck (along for example with wide feather earrings and platinum bangs pulled down just over her eyes, and why not, just because one can, long dark eyelashes?), the Strands christened her Karen, contentedly unaware of what she would become. (The Lotus Sutra relates that at eight years of age the daughter of the Dragon King became a Buddha; do you suppose that disgusted her dragon family?) Until then, like Judy Garland, she was a child star. In other words, she who was born to be loved resisted her destiny until she had been broken to it like a horse.

She was a laughing little baby who delighted her grandparents; they clapped their hands and sang to her; to her parents they said: That kid has it all!—Why she presently became watchful nobody thought to wonder; she was a good little girl who could be safely left alone, so the grandparents began saying that she *had sense.* When her parents realized that this child might be beautiful, they felt proud, even self-proud, as if they had bestowed extra effort upon her conception, and perhaps they loved her better than before; of course they also turned anxious, for we found it eternally profitable to purvey news of rape and child abduction. (The transwoman enjoyed it when her master told her what each murderess wore at her sentencing; sometimes he could even show her pictures.) A little girl learned early to watch out; her mother turned unkind eyes on strangers who merely smiled at her child star.

Well, how are Judy Garlands perfected? There are so many ways to be good! You may remember how the ghost of the Queen of Spain persuaded the youngest of three sisters first to lure in the young man for the love of whom the Queen had died and gone to hell, next to poison him and then to lock him in a secret chest beneath the Queen's flaming-eyed corpse, which the girl faithfully did—yes, she was good!—as a result of which she and her two elder sisters grew rich and lived happily ever after.—Karen was schooled in another sort of goodness.

Considering the times, not to mention their socioeconomic class, her mother dressed her dazzlingly. She could not help longing for the triumph when her daughter would be the prettiest; and there was even the time when she took her to the beauty parlor to get turned into a blonde, just for fun, although the family really couldn't afford it, and Karen looked so *cute* reading a comic book with her baby face titanically helmeted by the electric dryer.

When, as grew necessary most of the time, her husband left them alone in that old Mission style house with the green, green lawn, the mother sometimes helped herself to chemical improvements. Other mothers did it—women she knew, who felt bored and abandoned; in those days the doctors wrote prescriptions when a housewife complained of feeling fat and sluggish. These pills came in different colors, and they were inexpensive. When certain wives got together, pills brightened an afternoon watching the children at the playground, or a pin-the-tail-on-the-donkey party where someone's little boy kept getting bullied, or the shared cocktails at naptime when they whispered to each other thrilling tales of adultery and divorce.

The girl began to grow up just a little. The neighbors still called her their little child star. You could almost call her the talk of Triumph Drive. Sometimes her father and her uncle sat in the back yard of that Mission or maybe not quite Mission style house with the red brick stairs, complaining about welfare and crime, while her mother nursed a martini in the living room, smiling at the shadowed face of the beautiful soprano. *That's how I see Hollywood,* said Judy Garland, *as the place that gives everybody a chance.* The conductor kept waving his dowsing-rod as if he had extra joints in his neck and shoulders. The next door neighbor slammed a window shut, but Karen's mother was humming her way along ledges of white and gold, while the soprano glided through orchestra music, haunted by the faraway tenor, stretching out her pink hands, caressing herself, knitting her brows, embracing pillars, opening her mouth so prettily. Smiling, Karen's mother poured more gin into her glass to celebrate that reddish-golden fruit on white trees glinting in stage-light.

It grew dark outside. Through the sliding glass door Karen, who sat still on her bed, hugging a plushy zebra toy with magic powers, could hear her father open two more beers. She heard the men clink cans together.—Down the hatch, said her father.—Her uncle, who had been an old man as long as she could remember, had shipped out from Guadalcanal with dengue fever. His latest affliction was the Japanese family that had bought the corner store: *Slanteyes out of America!* And he retold Karen's father (the child could hear every word) exactly what he had seen and smelled after the Japanese had machine-gunned Australian nurses on Banka Island and bayoneted hospital patients on the Malayan Peninsula. Karen tried to sing a song to her zebra. It was very hot; the bougainvillea was growing up against the house again.

Unappreciated at work, her father came home angry. Her uncle knew what to do about that, because sometimes after too many recon patrols the regimental surgeon used to take a hard look, slip a fellow a bottle of gin and some little white pills, oh, God, those *sweet* little white pills, and say: This'll settle you down.—So Karen's uncle stopped by with rye whiskey; the child could hear two drinks getting poured. Her mother turned up the television. It was oh, so cool and pleasant in the living room with the curtains drawn and nothing allowed but singing, dreaming, hoping and wanting. The girl tried to sing to her zebra, but the television was louder. Then came another back yard gift: a manly bottle of pills.

Karen's uncle was doing pretty well. In the back yard he explained to Karen's father how the Japanese would pretend to surrender and then reach for their grenades. That was why you could never trust a goddamn slant. He described what Japanese looked like once they died of blackwater fever. Sometimes he dreamed about a certain Japanese who had wrapped himself around a grenade and tapped it until the fuse went off. That night in his sleep he heard again the screams of a sick Japanese when the boys were shooting him in his hammock. When he woke up, he remembered that he had given his pills to Karen's father, so he blew his brains out.

6

Karen's father threw the white pills in the garbage. He started drinking more.

As for Karen's mother, she occasionally swallowed a pink pill or two whenever she felt especially alone. It felt lonelier than before with her little girl in kindergarten, and sometimes ever so tiring when her little girl came home; sunny afternoons daunted her, especially when followed by the possibility that her husband might be disagreeable. And there never stopped being laundry to fold and drag upstairs, with dinner and breakfast to think about, and she felt so unloved!

Your Mommy loves you, she kept saying to the little girl.

The child nodded.

Won't you give Mommy a kiss?

I don't like that game.

What do you mean, you don't like it? Why don't you like it?

No, Mommy; I don't like it.

But Mommy loves you! Don't you love Mommy?

No.

Why, you bad girl! Mommy's going to spank you.

No!

You come here *right now.* Mommy needs to spank you.

But when she had caught the shrieking child and pulled down her panties, an unexpected excitement infused the jaded mother.—Who can blame her? Consider the case of Shirley Temple, whom they called "Little Miss Miracle": Even the department store Santa Claus in Los Angeles, once he got her on his lap, wanted that child star's autograph.—And Karen's little buttocks were so smooth and pink—so fun to squeeze whenever she wasn't slapping them.

There came to be times when she just loved to slip her hand down inside her daughter's underwear. Had she owned a little puppydog that tried to get away, she might have yanked it by the leash, so it would learn to mind; something like that most definitely needed to be done to Karen! And if the naughty child complained or tried to twist out of her grip, then the mother, all the more rejected and unloved, might pinch rather sharply, in order to carry her lesson. She so much wanted Karen to be a good girl! But Karen didn't love her. She didn't love her own mother! This much she sometimes let drop to other dissatisfied wives, at which they (secretly appalled) agreed: They're all brats.

One time she overheard the girl saying to one of her little friends: I like my Daddy better than my Mommy.

This seemed to the mother the most painful and untoward thing that she had ever experienced. She felt that she could never love her child in the same way again. Too humiliated to tell her husband, and therefore all the more isolated, she swallowed more pills.

Eventually she said to herself: Well, if that's how she's going to be, I can certainly do what I want.

7

It was not at all the case, at least not at first, that touching the child's vulva brought her gratification, but because the girl had been so strictly toilet trained, she knew her little peepee to be a nasty place, and it shamed her if anyone even saw it. Well aware of this, the mother found occasion to dominate her precisely there, poking, grabbing, inserting and hurting, all the while insisting: Mommy *loves* you.

No! Let go of me—

Then you really don't love Mommy. Say you love me. Say it *right now.*

The girl did her best never to think about those times, which might or might not have led to her becoming shyer and quieter, and somehow less beautiful than her parents had thought. Sitting up in bed, with her sweater pulled tight across her chest and her long hair lank, she stared like a sick child. By now her plushy zebra had grown ratty and smelly, so her mother threw it out.

8

Losing his job gentled her father. He loved Karen more and more. She wanted to do whatever he did.

9

The girl's biography requires mention of the fat tabby cat named Princess who mostly hid, and who for the first three years after they had taken her in from the street would hang limp and silent in anyone's arms, so that they called her brain damaged; the next phase was when she grew confident enough to hide, which was how she lived out most of her life, but when Karen sat all by herself in the kitchen, Princess sometimes glided to the doorway, then, after she had decided that it might be safe, slid across the linoleum floor and under the table, looking silently up at the child with her somewhat wolflike greenish-yellow eyes. Formerly she had meowed for food, but if Karen set down a tiny scrap of fat or cheese she would simply look at it. Raising her voice, Karen's mother said: *Don't ever do that again. All you've done is make a mess.*—But when the mother was away, Karen would go into the laundry room where Princess watched from on top of her artificial tree, then drop a tidbit into the metal bowl. And Princess would watch. As soon as Karen had left the room, the cat would plop fatly down to the floor and gobble up that treat. In time she picked up sufficient courage to descend while Karen was still in the room. And so the time came when Princess would stalk all the way to the kitchen and look up at Karen, coldly, lovelessly waiting for something good to fall her way, which she would eat without apparent fear, or interest in Karen—until footsteps approached; then the creature would rush back to the laundry room, at which Karen must pick up the food and rub the grease off the floor with her napkin before her mother could punish her.

Late at night, creeping through the darkness without waking up her parents, pretending that she was a monster or perhaps Princess or maybe even an angel, Karen thought she might be happy. And why not be more kinds of herself than one? One might compare her to Natalie Wood, who was "Woman of the Year" at ten and "Child of the Year" at eleven.

10

Just think how God feels, said the nun. He's our best parent. He loves and provides for us. Then we reject Him. And even then He goes on offering His love! He wants us to be sorry and return to Him so that He can embrace us and forgive us. He waits and waits for that to happen. Sometimes He waits all our lives. And then do you know what happens?

We go to hell, the girl whispered.

That's right. And, Karen, it's very appropriate, the way you whispered such a bad word. Now, why do you suppose we go to *that place*?

Because . . . because it's too late.

Good girl.

Sister Mary, if He wanted to, couldn't He forgive us even then?

Of course He could. And He feels sorry for us when we sin. But once we die, our souls can't change anymore. So if we die rejecting Him, we're trapped in rejecting Him forever and ever. What would heaven be like, if He allowed those people to stay there? What if you had a birthday party, and one boy was really mean, and kept hitting all the girls? Maybe your father would ask him to apologize and behave. If he didn't, what kind of father would he be, to let him keep hitting you and your friends, so that your birthday party was ruined? Do you see now?

Yes, Sister Mary.

Do you love your father?

Yes, I—

And you love your mother, don't you?

11

Her father found another job. He took her out for ice cream, after which for a half-hour he inhabited her room with her, correcting his expense accounts while she did her homework. Now he was sitting on her bed with the cat watching him from atop the dresser, while she worked at her desk. They were happy together. Then he had to go. An hour later he came in to wish her goodnight, and there was a vomit smell. He murmured into his wife's ear, asking what they should do. The wife stormed into the girl's room. She was one of those who disguised her alarm as anger; as for him, he sat listening to the girl's denials, literally worried sick.

The doctor explained that Karen's potassium levels were alarmingly low. Confronted by both parents, she whispered that she had been sick to her stomach two or three days before; that was all. Her mother sent her outside to throw away the plastic bag of evidence.

12

Shortly after a vacation with her parents, who in spite of one or two long quarrels in restaurants both considered the week a success, and finally even went on the town without their daughter, who preferred to stay in at the hotel, the girl began to lose weight. For years her mother had been telling her she was too fat. Dazzled by their own miseries, the parents failed to notice the disappearance of her first ten pounds. She must have weighed about a hundred and thirty by then. A month later her father seemed to see, not without vague pride, that she was looking glamorous, svelte. His best friend said: Something's going on with Karen. I didn't recognize her when I saw her.—The father finally began to pay attention. The mother, so she said, was losing sleep. She told the father: I don't know what to do. She eats and eats, but she's losing weight.

The father took another business trip. On his return he felt alarmed. His daughter's shoulder blades stuck out. When she came to sit on his lap, she was far too light.

He was proud that he and Karen kept a perfect understanding. They always had. Entering her room, he stood over her, asking whether anything might be wrong. She said no, not really. He asked her point blank if she was making herself throw up. She promised that she wasn't. He informed her that he was worried about her weight, and she said surprised: You are?

Much relieved that his daughter had not endangered herself, he told her mother: I believe her.—Her mother kept worrying, so he said what any American man would: Do something about it. Weigh her every day, then write it down.

Day after day, the girl weighed exactly a hundred pounds.

She was eating ice cream and cookies with her father. One night she came to hug him and his heart began to pound with dread because her breath smelled like vomit, but then he realized that it was just the sugar in those cookies which had ketoned in her mouth.

The next day her mother screamed in rageful panic. She had caught the girl trying to smuggle a bucket of vomit into the back yard. The mother was shouting: *There are shadows under your eyes!*

The father hunted for his child. She was neither in her room, nor in the kitchen, nor in the car where her mother was waiting. She lay pallid on the living room sofa with her eyes closed, and the television singing "Somewhere Over the Rainbow." As gently as he could, the father said: Sweetheart, I'm not angry about your lie; I'm worried.

I wish you were angry, the girl whispered. You should be angry.

The father said: Try and think about why you're doing this. I won't ask you to tell me, since now it's clear that I can't help you. Mama can't help you. I'm going away on a business trip. If your weight's not up by next Saturday, I think we should take you to the doctor.

Karen nodded compliantly.

13

Pouring himself a triple slug of bourbon to relax his nerves, he thought back on the time not long ago when he got three sobbing messages on his office answering machine, two of them at midnight, the girl crying and crying because her mother was shouting at her and shaking her, so the girl weepingly claimed; she had finally pushed her mother out of the bedroom and stood there holding the bedroom door but her mother got back in, then grabbed her and slapped and yelled at her, said the girl.

In a calmer moment, the girl had asked her father to please delete those messages without listening to them; anyhow he had not yet heard them, having been away on business; one thing the girl had said was that she wished he were around more.

He asked Karen how he could help her. Neither of them could think of anything. Feeling noble, he said: Go as far away from your parents as you can.

14

He called a ladyfriend of his, an elegant fortyish black woman, who after saying she was sorry about Karen remarked: We don't usually admit this, but I learned how to do that in high school. And even now, if I'm out having a big dinner with some girlfriends and then I have to go to a party and my dress feels tight, I just go into the bathroom and make myself throw up. There's nothing to it.

15

A few days before her mother caught her carrying out the bucket of vomit, the girl got into a car accident in a parking lot. It was her fault. A woman accused her of trying to run away but the girl wept to her parents that she had only been parking. Her father believed her, of course; her mother didn't.

The mother insisted that Karen pay for the damage herself. The next day the father tried to slip the girl two hundred-dollar bills (all the cash he had), saying: This is too much for a teenager to pay.

The girl refused to take the money. She insisted on not taking it. She hugged her father, who was very touched.

16

She longed to please her mother, who was never satisfied with her. She did not like her mother to touch her, but even that she would have borne for the sake of her mother's love. However, just then her mother would not touch her.

Had she been a good girl like you or me, she would have felt fulfilled by her mother's love. But since she kept disappointing her mother so terribly, what on earth could she expect?

As for her father, no matter how tenderly she loved him, that disgraced and timid nonentity was hardly the sort to whom anyone ought to turn.

Innocently she strolled into the bathroom at the end of every meal. The door locked, the toilet seat clicked up, the sink began running until the toilet flushed, and then she came out with sour-bitter breath to wash the dishes. The grieving father, caressing his skeletal daughter, wondered how soon she would be lost to him.

17

After her parents divorced, her father kept calling her mother to say: *I wish I could see you; I wish I could please you again*; but her mother never wanted that.

As for the daughter, presently there was an older girl who taught her what gifts she possessed: true beauty, and the ability to make others love her.

Her mother was snoring, with a bottle of gin and a bottle of heart-shaped red pills beside her. The girl tiptoed up and down the hall, telling herself long secret stories in which she utterly believed. Then she met E-beth. She entered into motion. Across her heart's silver medallion, a golden chariot, driven by a golden-winged, high-breasted, gilt-robed Victory whose silver face smiled across the rearing horses, now halted, and the girl's life-pulse froze.

Victory would have been beautiful enough—but beside *her*, shaded by a silver devotee's golden parasol, stood divine Cybele, facing sideways, gazing straight out of the scene, into the third dimension . . . and if she could only have turned Cybele's head, causing the goddess to love her, she would have won everything—and Cybele's head did turn, and Cybele chose her, so that the girl became a lesbian.

When an Innocent Girl Abandons Herself

When an innocent girl abandons herself to the voluptuous lovemaking of a promiscuous lesbian, she gives little if any thought to the consequences. The same girl very often becomes adept at seducing others . . . It is this kind of cycle or chain of seduction that accounts for the increasing incidence of lesbianism in our midst.

Frank S. Caprio, M.D., 1954

Nobody ever taught me what to do on a stage.

Judy Garland, 1951

1

Of course the girl could have now developed in any number of ways, none of them conventionally "good," not that convention retained much shaping power over her inner nature; she had been altered, and the change must remain secret. Had anybody wise and decent (she knew no such people yet) read the secret right through her clothes, then asked why it could never come out, she would have answered (had she replied at all: an impossibility) that nothing harmful had been done to her, so why raise trouble?—and if that nonexistent decent seer convinced her (another impossibility) that she had in fact been permanently injured by her mother's actions—which perhaps wasn't so—then she would have fallen back to her inner line of defense, which was: I'll never hurt my mother!— And the girl remained proud of this. Why not? A good daughter is praiseworthy beyond all the emeralds of this dying world. In that sense she was conventional indeed—all the more so if we admit to consideration the masochistic pieties of love, sexual and otherwise; of beauty as the rest of us defined it; most of all, of craving to please, the pleasure being localized behind curtains and walls on that front lawn of perfect rectangles mown almost down to the white sidewalk. The direction in which most child stars developed entailed the discovery that pleasing, whether pleasant or not to *them*, could enlarge them into future power.—Karen, unfortunately, never learned to be selfish.

I grant that from the outside she resembled most any other goddess: The face of a glowing young movie star wears an infantile neutrality. The capability that it possesses (of being cared for) appeared inexplicably, and very recently; now it seems inexhaustible. And so the star gazes on our world serenely, from afar. We are all new to her. She perceives us in catlike fashion—which is to say, not without, but *beyond* understanding us. (Stare into a cat's eyes, and what consciousness stares back?) And Karen, once she came into her mirror-eyed prime, would presently regard us with just such haunting awareness. We grew divided as to whether her gaze was babylike, seductive, omniscient, dreamy, or contemplative.

But in those years of old knucklebones and lovely greenish round gamepieces she remained merely Karen, the unprimed one who minimized her exposure to mirrors, for shame at her own ugliness. How could she realize that she would become like no one else, the loveliest ever? At school she never received excellent or unacceptable grades. Sitting on the flagpole's plinth, staring out at the two well-kept palms, too shy to make friends, but in her final days of unobjectionability, she rarely drew down upon herself the other pupils' cruelty. She continued going to church. She used to kneel down and pray to be more loving and grateful to her mother.

Then came the time when she had to admit to herself that another girl was watching her. It always happened in the interval between classes. Karen lacked time even to visit her locker and switch out textbooks, there being only five minutes. But this other girl was never in a hurry. She stood outside the door of Karen's biology class, and looked her in the face. Sometimes she smiled, and once she waved.

Karen came home, and her mother grabbed her and gave her a slobbering kiss.

2

She returned to school, and there was that girl again, her face as carefully perfect as if some master mosaicist had made it out of a galaxy of shining tiles, each one uniquely cut and painted for its purpose. She was short and thin, with crewcut hair like a lush silver fox pelt. She wore three black studs in each ear, black nail polish, coveralls and many-laced and -grommeted boots that reached her knees.

She said: Your name's Karen, isn't it? I'm E-beth. Are you a sophomore?

The girl flushed and nodded.

I'll save you a seat at lunch. Look for me by the snack machine—

And Karen felt as happy as little Judy Garland had been when she received a cream-colored makeup kit from Norma Shearer!

Even then she could not have explained why the one for her was E-beth. I who am cynical because I outlived her offer this for a reason: She was ready, and E-beth came along. Of course to Karen there appeared to be something about the other girl which could not be imitated. Whatever she said, even if others had said it before, had never been said that way. But when two women go dancing, and one takes the other into her arms, whence came the once upon a time?

So she met E-beth in the cafeteria. They ate lunch together every day. Hardly able to believe it, looking discreetly straight ahead, she followed instructions, slipped her hand beneath the table, and when E-beth took it answered: Yes.

3

I'm not really a senior, said E-beth.

Oh, said Karen.

I'm actually a bit older. Since I don't look my age, I can get away with wandering the halls. I know when each period begins and ends.

So you . . . Why?

To catch pretty girls like you! whispered E-beth, licking the inside of Karen's ear. And do you know what?

I—

Don't take the bus today. I'll drive you home. My apartment's around the corner.

4

At first it was not so different from when her mother came into the department store's fitting room, making sure that each prospective high school blouse fit just right around the breast. But within a few moments it grew evident that E-beth, rather than dominating, *adored* her, longed to please, and knew just how. That first time was wonderful only for being the first time. In retrospect, when she was alone in her bedroom and could remember it over and over, it grew perfect.

As she unzipped her skirt she was looking into the mirror, not at herself but at E-beth undressing. She felt terrified, nauseated, excited. And suddenly, shockingly, there was E-beth, tanned except for her bikini line and goggling breasts. The light went out. E-beth touched her. She almost threw up. E-beth was holding her, and she insisted to herself that she needed to love this. E-beth was on top of her, lustfully panting, riding and rubbing her. Even though she truly did love it, Karen could not help being anxious until it was over. Then she could treasure it. She had closed her bedroom door and was happily masturbating, thinking of E-beth, when the knob turned and her mother came in, saying: Karen, honey, I heard something. Is everything all right?

5

Her mother watched her going in and out. Something was going on, for a fact. The girl looked happy and expectant when she departed, and came in appearing satisfied. The mother said: Karen, sometimes I think that you don't care about me.

6

. . . And without a word she followed E-beth into the bedroom, then as usual stood in the doorway not knowing what to do, until her lover stalked toward her with that triumphant smile. The girl felt like prey—how she wanted to be eaten!—as indeed she would be.

E-beth's mouth burned against hers, E-beth's nipples were hard, E-beth's cunt drenched with excitement, and E-beth was screaming and screaming as she rubbed her clitoris against the other girl's—until finally, suddenly and for the first time, she, Karen, achieved relief in another person's arms.

Now she was ecstatic, because she would be loved forever. She was in bliss, like a little child empowered to eat every last marshmallow. (We wisely sour old love addicts could do the same, but our palates are too sophisticated.) The best part (she told E-beth) was that her mother had no idea. Already accomplished at hiding her emotions from herself, the girl now made what she supposed to be ever more successful forays at concealing her actions. It was easier than she had nervously imagined, because as long as her mother kept getting what she wanted, she didn't care what her daughter did—bad grades or unpleasant rumors aside.

She came home and her mother was up waiting for her, tipsy on gin. Her mother grabbed her and kissed her mouth. The daughter locked her teeth. The mother's tongue pushed and thrust against them. Unable to enter, it angrily slimed the girl's lips.

Can't I even kiss my own daughter? she demanded.

Detecting her opportunity, the girl pulled free. But as she backed away, her mother rushed furiously after her, and caught her again. The girl could scarcely endure the loathsomeness of that embrace. Freezing into stiffness, she permitted the sallies of her mother's tongue against her closed lips.

My Karen doesn't love me, the mother wept.

7

Suppose that a child refused to listen to her mother and skipped out into Nebraska Street, where a passing car almost runs her down. I can dream up any number of unfortunate psychological outcomes. Here are three. In her fear, which for many parents easily catalyzes into rage, the mother shouts at the girl and maybe shakes her, causing her to believe herself despised. Alternatively, suppose the mother quietly reasons with her, explaining why she must be more careful, and from this what the girl takes away, because what affected her most dramatically was the squealing of the brakes and the exclamations of other people, is that her mother has failed to show sufficient psychological affect, so that she seems fundamentally indifferent to her. Or finally, what if the mother were to embrace the scared child and weep over her? Why couldn't the child link this expression of affection to the trauma that precipitated it, in which case she might engage in risk-seeking behavior, or perhaps masochism, in order to potentiate a feeling of being loved, which discharges itself in a climax?—With such thought experiments I used to construct my hypotheses as to how we all became whom we were. None explained her, let alone myself.

8

For E-beth's birthday they checked into a motel. It was only for the day; Karen had to be home by dinnertime or her mother would worry.

We need one bed, said E-beth.

You mean one bed each, said the desk clerk, who was a watchful, bitter-looking lady of a certain age.

No. One bed. One *big* bed, said E-beth. We're a *couple.* We're *girlfriends.* Do you get it?

That's disgusting, said the clerk.

There's nothing disgusting about it. I suck her pussy and she sucks mine. You have a pussy, too. Now, will you rent us a room or not?

I need the manager.

Fine, said E-beth.

The lobby seemed to be full of people, who were all listening. (As Lana Turner once said: *It's very difficult, growing up in public.*) Oh, how ashamed Karen was . . . !

The manager emerged, plump and worried.—What's the trouble here? he said.

We want one bed, said E-beth. Your employee wants to rent us two beds, but we want one bed.

One bed, repeated the manager, as if he could not understand.

To all the people who were waiting in line, the clerk now said: I'm sorry about the inconvenience. We're trying to get this straightened out.

The manager said: You know, I don't really—

We're *lesbians*, said E-beth loudly, at which Karen blushed. And we have a right to be accommodated. Now, will you rent us a room with one bed, or do you want a lawsuit?

We don't have any more king suites, said the manager. All we have left is one queen in the smoking section.

Fine, said E-beth. I smoke—

It's not ready yet, said the manager. It won't be available before three.

E-beth said: My girlfriend and I are going to keep standing right here. And if we see you rent a double room to any of these other couples, we'll report you for discrimination.

Miss, I'll tell you what. Please let me wait on all these other folks and then I'll see what I can do.

We're at the head of the line, said E-beth.

The manager said: I'm sorry, everybody. We're trying our best to get this sorted out. It's not our . . . All right; I'll need to see identification from both of you. Your *friend* appears to be under eighteen.

Fuck you, said E-beth, and she took Karen by the hand and led her out. They got into E-beth's car. E-beth laughed shortly, and drove them down the street to another motel.—Wait in the car, she said.

In ten minutes she came out smiling, waving a brass key in the air.

9

From E-beth she learned that to love and be loved was beautiful. As a favorite lover once said of Judy Garland: *Christ Almighty, the girl reacted to the slightest bit of kindness as though it were a drug.*

10

Because she had woven protective fantasies around herself from a very early age, her pain had not degraded her into self-pity. Indeed, she never understood the sadness of her situation. And now in E-beth's arms it seemed to her that she might finally be living the effortless life of a mermaid even here in sight of the high school's long white buildings with their grid of not quite square black windows. E-beth's wide red Pontiac Conspiracy 76 was parked in front of the swimming pool. One Saturday night they drove to a basement club in Berkeley where she got to meet slender tall T-girls in black vinyl suits, black beehive wigs and huge dark sunglasses, and there E-beth taught her how to smoke marijuana. Two women danced, one with her hand around her partner's neck while the other embraced her waist, and they swung back and forth in each other's hands like rocking horses, longhaired and young. Their joy in each other brought tears to Karen's eyes, not that E-beth noticed.

Then they were at home together. E-beth yawningly paged through magazines while Karen scrubbed a sinkload of dishes. Just as she was untying her apron, E-beth came running up and kissed her.

At five in the morning E-beth dropped her off at her other home, where her mother sat waiting up for her.

11

Her purpose (although she could not have expressed it so) was to love and be loved "purely" and "truly"—which, like most things said about love, sounds shopworn—but when we love, it matters very little to us that others have done the same. Perhaps if I labeled her mother's love for her impure, and went on to propose that she needed E-beth's love to be the opposite, that might attach some individuality to her "purely" and "truly"—but why not less parochially assert that she sought to experience an *eternal secret intimacy* warmed by inexhaustible desire and illuminated by ever-altering joy? This she had found.

Perhaps she was partly to blame for what happened, because she thought to become mermaids with E-beth without any renunciation.

12

After they caught her kissing E-beth, the other girls liked to chase her to the bus stop, shouting: What the fuck is that thing?

Karen tried to keep it secret from her lover, but the next time it happened, E-beth was there, throwing rocks at the cruel girls until they ran away screaming.

On the bus, when she was alone with them, they started calling her *the lesbian.*

13

What are you so fucking ashamed of? said E-beth. Stand *proud.*

Marcie told the science teacher I was touching her. She called me a pervert.

Then what?

The teacher asked me . . . and I said no . . . and a week later Marcie complained again.

I'll put a stop to it, said E-beth. What's the teacher's name?

Honey, please don't.

Then what will *you* do about it?

I don't know. I feel so bad—

That's just your internalized homophobia. You need to feel better about yourself.

Haven't you ever . . . ?

I've experienced a variety of things, said her lover with that same crooked smile she wore while making herself come.—I've been called awful names. I have been called pit bull dyke and like that. I've probably been discriminated against without my knowing it, just because I'm a woman. I've been sexually assaulted—

The girl wondered how much E-beth knew or guessed about her case. Instead she asked: How did you handle it?

Like every woman. You laugh it off, Karen. With the name-calling and the stares and threats, well, before, I felt embarrassment and shame, and then it evolved into anger and frustration, and now I'm just tired of it, and ignoring it the best I can. When the really bad things happen, the first thing you're thinking is your career. You immediately think survival.

(Karen was thinking the same.)

I was unemployed when it happened, her lover continued. He was using that power over me. I thought I had to keep quiet. Most women do. They try to play around it; they end up protecting him. I forgot it, too, to be real frank. Until now.

And silently, protectively, E-beth touched up the other girl's eye shadow.

14

E-beth began to grow her hair out, so Karen did the same. She loved to comb her sweetheart's long brown hair, which smelled like lavender and smoke.

She set out to be more beautiful for E-beth. The key was to lose weight. Once her mother got up to clear the dinner dishes, Karen quickly swept her food into her napkin. Then she went to the bathroom, shook the napkin into the toilet, hid the napkin at the bottom of the wastebasket beneath her mother's stinky old, hairy old menstrual pads. Whenever that was impractical she locked the door and made herself vomit.

Karen? said her mother, rattling the doorknob. Karen, I heard something! What are you doing in there?

In the morning Marcie was waiting in the hallway with three other girls.—We all know you're queer, Marcie said.

The girl tried to run, but they encircled her and pushed her against the bank of lockers. She closed her eyes and pretended to be somewhere else while they slapped her face and spat on her. Finally Janet, who was Marcie's best friend, began to get squeamish. She laid out her position: I'll say one thing for the bitch. She's never ratted us out. Isn't that right, Karen?

The girl nodded.

Then how come your lezzie friend threw rocks at us? demanded Marcie.

I never told her to.

I believe that, said Janet. But I've seen her spying on us. What's her lezzie name, queer?

Who is she? said Emily.

The girl would not answer.

You know what? said Janet. She's got heart.

She does not, said Marcie. Didn't you see her lick our spit off her face? She's disgusting.

Janet said: How about this? There's Justin over there. Hey! Hey, Justin, c'mere.

We've got a bitch for you. Stick your tongue in her mouth and make her like it. Karen, open your mouth. You two give each other some tongue. Then we'll leave you alone.

And Karen did it. She always aimed to please.

So Justin thought to be her boyfriend. He gave her a sweatshirt with the high school colors: Go, Apaches! Go, go, Valley Joe! And two years departed. Each and all those nights cut themselves into her bones, like the white picture-incisions on the back of a bronze mirror. On her special days Karen waited and hid in the grove of young redwoods by the stadium, until E-beth rolled up in her red Pontiac.

15

When they entered the bar, which from the outside looked derelict, it seemed to the girl that E-beth had brought daylight in with her, for the regulars, hitherto noiselessly unmoving, being middle-aged at least—extremely old to her—now all (excepting the tattooed muscleman in the tank top who played pool by himself, racking them in by means of sniper-perfect single shots) looked up in delight, chaffing E-beth on the new tint in her hair and on the young thing she had brought with her. E-beth sparkled politely back; Karen was thrilled to see her starring over everyone.—Still the same! cried some geezer, shaking his head in a gleeful mimicry of disapproval.

The establishment was called Jingle's. Creeping toward them, the ancient barman inquired concerning their pleasure, and E-beth said: Two Hot Bitches on the rocks.

You like what you like, he tittered, mixing up those famous sweet pink cinnamon-fired concoctions, then sliding them inch by inch across the wraparound Formica bar with its cracked vinyl armrest. Karen felt very special that E-beth had ordered for her without asking. She began to drink the first Hot Bitch of her life—what a red letter day!

E-beth pointed out the black-painted cinderblock ceiling.—It's like the night sky, she said, a remark which Karen found beautiful. She looked up for an extra second. Since this place pertained to E-beth, the girl tried to love everything about it.

Now the glow around them subsided, much as when Karen's mother killed the porch light switch on summer nights and the incandescent filament slowly faded, releasing moths from their orbits of unwholesome attachment, the oldsters wilting ever lower over their beers and cocktails; at which E-beth turned back to the only face which still yearned toward her, and began to complain about a certain someone who had mistreated her at the Country Women's Festival in Mendocino.—I want you to take her something from me. If she sees me she'll close the door in my face.

Not daring to ask: Do you love her?, the girl said: Okay.

The thing is, she won't know you, E-beth repeated. Once you get inside and give her this letter, look around for signs of someone else. Do you understand me, Karen?

No, said the girl.

Just pay attention and tell me what you see. Don't mention me. I'm counting on you.

The girl nodded, staring across the shining bloody reflections on the bar. Out of nervousness she had drunk her Hot Bitch too quickly, and now she was feeling tipsy-sick. Fortunately, E-beth would teach her how to drink.

Are you ready? Then let's do it.

E-beth left a dollar on the bar. The barman said: Good hunting, killer!—and E-beth gave him two thumbs up.

Now they were in the car, turning left by the Electric Shaver Center, then left again on Tennessee Street, and E-beth was saying: You wouldn't believe it. I mean, she's so sweet on the outside, but then . . .

Where did you meet her? asked Karen in a whisper.

What's the difference? Stanford.

At once knowledge came to the girl, like one of those hallway slaps which she had learned to expect at school. A month before, when they were turning E-beth's mattress, she had discovered a color snapshot caught between the boxsprings. E-beth, her view blocked by the upraised mattress, failed to see her take it. They remade the bed; then Karen went straight to the bathroom and locked herself in; E-beth never disturbed her there. The subject was a young woman with long brown braids who sat on some other bed, outstretching her arms and opening her fingers almost like some Indian goddess, with solarized likenesses of the Beatles on the wall behind her. On the back was an inscription in ballpoint pen: *Waiting for E., Stanford '74.* Karen hid it in her bra, transferred it to her schoolbag, looked at it when she was alone, then slid it back under the mattress.

It's that blue house over there, said E-beth. Give her this envelope.

What if she doesn't answer?

What do you think? Bring it back.

Numbly, the girl crossed the street. The night was cool. She wanted to throw up. First she rang the bell, then knocked. When no answer came, she returned apprehensively to the car where E-beth sat in the driver's seat with the lights and engine off.

I did my best, she began, at which E-beth said: I know you did. Come give me a kiss.

16

Trying to slink away down Nebraska Street, Karen got all the way to the stadium before they caught her. They hemmed her in, pulling her hair, spitting on her and bitch-slapping her face. They advised her: What you are, it's illegal and it's sick. They should lock you away.—She stood still, while their spittle ran down her cheeks.

Then she went home, where her dear mother waited to bestow her kiss.

17

So now she had E-beth's place, the red Pontiac, and the long wilting string of red lights over the mirror at Jingle's, where sometimes a certain sweet, harsh-voiced old barmaid with tinted bangs looked at her so gently and lovingly. How thrilled was Karen there to sit next to E-beth, underage! (At Jingle's nobody cared about such trifles.)—Later they started taking their beers to the round hightop in the corner, where they could whisper in the dark.

E-beth taught her myriad ways of giving and getting pleasure, of gratifying oneself by fulfilling the other, of turning self-denial and even pain into joy. One might point out that anyhow the first lover is by certain criteria *necessarily* the best, but I who never met her prefer not to underestimate E-beth's talents. The joy when Karen's young fingers learned to know the long thin lips of E-beth's vulva, which she stroked up and down, on command up and down forever, with E-beth's tongue in her mouth and her heart pounding and her nipples so hard they ached, might be chalked up to mere novelty, but Karen was soon presented with a more advanced curriculum requiring all-night stays, toward which her mother grew surprisingly permissive (my Karen has her little *secrets*!) In short, she learned both to magnify her senses and to suffocate herself in desperately delicious acts of submission. Sometimes E-beth liked to bite her nipples, and when that was very painful Karen cried out. That made E-beth very hot, and soon they were *clashing clamshells*, as the Japanese might put it. Sometimes E-beth controlled her seeing, her urinations or even her breaths; such was Karen's gracious teacher, with coolly careful fingers around a sweetheart's throat. (I who was not there cannot be prevented from insisting on the difference between Karen and E-beth: the difference between joy and pleasure.) And sometimes, after Karen had washed the dishes, started the washing machine and scrubbed the kitchen floor, when she used to lay her head in the other woman's lap, E-beth would tell a fable to beguile her, murmuring of an island where only women lived; and all those women were in love.

18

Another year went, so that she could stay away at night no matter what her mother said, which was now almost nothing, although Karen slowly grew yoked to the conviction (which she told herself had oppressed her from the first) that during their most intimate acts E-beth was imagining other women—because there always came the moment when E-beth would go away, possibly to play with someone else—lovely, smiling E-beth, whom no one and everyone knew. But, oh, how alluring her smile, which yearned and promised rather than demanding!

Then came that other smile, when Karen had done her job, and E-beth's eyelids began to close, but her neck-tendons stood out and she was grinning crookedly; she seemed to be concentrating on a funny little story that the girl had told her long ago; and in joy she cried out. This made Karen happier than anything.

She used to ask what if anything could be singular in E-beth's love for her; she had given E-beth permission to love as many others as she chose, even to love them more than she loved Karen—but only if there were some specific way that she loved Karen alone! Of course whatever E-beth said to reassure her, however strikingly and even beautifully it might be stated, lost its vibrancy even before the goodbye kiss—because our Karen resembled her mother! She could not prevent herself from wondering whether her lover's declaration was luminous precisely because she had grown accomplished at whispering it to others . . .—and so E-beth, realizing that no words could satiate Karen's hungry sadness, grew annoyed.

Tacked to the wall of E-beth's bathroom presently appeared a photo of a woman in boots and garters, spreading herself from behind.—Who's that? said Karen.—Oh, my ex.

There came the morning when E-beth remarked that although she still loved her best (in proof of which she now tattooed their initials in a heart on the back of her ankle), there happened to be a nameless girl, whom she had kissed two months ago, then slept next to for three nights, not that Karen should imagine that she and the other girl had done the special things that she and Karen did, even though, come to think of it, she had climaxed once, not that she cared to tell exactly how that had been achieved. E-beth next explained that whatever she did with the other girl would be secret; Karen was never to ask about it, not that she should worry—although a week later, E-beth stopped reasserting the fact that she loved her best . . . so there were angry tears, mostly on Karen's side, because E-beth also said that she was in no mood to lie down with Karen; nor did she especially want Karen to give her advice on her personal life.

Eventually they got back to making love, as a favor to Karen.

That night, after the girl had slowly, carefully licked E-beth's pussy even though it tasted bitter-stingingly of contraceptive jelly, and E-beth had happily climaxed, they fell asleep; then it was very early morning and she heard E-beth climaxing in the bathroom.

They went out to the All Star Diner, E-beth's favorite, for breakfast. Karen's sadness swelled almost past bearing. Ever more caught up in her delicious longing to lick E-beth's groove, whose complex dark lips she now knew so well, she sincerely believed that given one more chance, just one, she could boomerang her sweetheart's affections sizzling back! Who am I to say that it would not have been so?—Halfway through their omelettes, E-beth went out to the phone booth in the parking lot. Karen crept to the restroom to throw up. When E-beth returned, she wore her irresistible old smile. Perceiving her lover's expression, she instantly grew angry, and said: I've told you not to ask about that.

And so Karen, whom almost everyone, her mother most definitely excepted, now called *the lesbian*, resolved to be more loving and compliant with E-beth than ever before.

You Seem a Little Sad

And Virgo, hiding her disdainful breast,
With Thetis now had laid her down to rest.

THOMAS SACKVILLE, EARL OF DORSET, 1563

Ah, Catulla, dearest, that you were less lovely or less vile!

MARTIAL, 1st cent. A.D.

1

You seem a little sad, said E-beth.

Maybe a little.

You'll feel better when I hold you tonight, won't you?

The lesbian scarcely dared to look at her. It came easier to stare straight ahead, watching the sunlight retreating up the hills. The highway was already in shadow. E-beth drove fluently, rubbing her slender gentle fingers across the lesbian's knee. For more than an hour they sat silent. Now only the summits of the forest hills remained bright. From the corner of her eye she caught E-beth twisting a strand of hair around her thumb.

It was the last night of their vacation. The lesbian sat on the edge of the bed. Standing by the window, E-beth said: All right, then, Karen. If you really want to know, it's because you haven't been discreet.

About what? You're the one who taught me not to be ashamed—

I don't care who knows that I like girls. But our relationship was supposed to stay secret.

I swear I never told anyone your name . . .

That's what *you* wanted.

But now I don't! I'm proud of our relationship!

Well, I'm not. It's over.

What you're saying is—

You know what I'm saying.

The girl had risen. Slowly, she sat down again, struggling not to feel. Looking at her hands, she whispered: This doesn't make sense to me, because—

If it doesn't, it doesn't, said E-beth, lighting a cigarette. Anyway, it's time for you to find somebody else.

The lesbian could not speak. When her cigarette was done, E-beth, her body smooth as marble as she leaned back on her left arm, her small breasts perfect to hold in some lucky girl's hands, exhaled and laid the smoking butt in the ashtray. She looked out the window. Then she said: I'm restless. I might be out all night.

A vacuum surrounded the lesbian. Everything from and to her had been somehow interrupted.

'Bye, said E-beth.

For a considerable time the lesbian could hear her descending the concrete stairs to the parking lot. She could not hear when the car drove away.

Standing up, she drew the curtains, unable to cry out. (I who tell my corrupt version of her story years later assert that precisely what she needed in order to become the one whom we would love above all others was E-beth, cruel and rejecting. But the retired policeman credits Karen's mother.*)—The bathroom door was open. E-beth had left the light on. Very slowly, the lesbian approached the mirror, as if discovering whether or not her face had changed would teach something that would save her. What she saw could have been a woman's marble semblance wide-eyed upon her own sarcophagus.

Beside the plastic-wrapped cake of motel soap stood a jar of ear-cleaning swabs. She withdrew one swab. Each end was a cotton ball. Slowly she knelt down on the cold tile floor. She raised the toilet seat. She bent over the bowl. Then she opened her mouth. Probing with the swab, she found the correct place almost at once, tickling her tonsils so that she vomited. The feeling was almost sexual. Then she began sobbing.

After a long time she rose and returned to the sink. When she bent over the tap, rinsing the foulness out of her mouth, she saw vomit in her hair.

---

* If you find her or any other lover in this tale immoral, then pray to Zeus, the god of suppliants, who heartily abhors the killing of a man, and yet as heartily befriends the killer.

2

The reason for her great pain was this: Once E-beth rejected her, Karen could no longer deny that she was, and always had been, alone.

3

Needless to say, she had grown so accomplished at not feeling whatever pain inhabited her that even while she was weeping and vomiting up E-beth's cancelled promises, her experience consisted of *shock without emotion.* Once this ending settled into her bones with the undeniable conviction of illness, she began to exist without hope, but thankfully also without feeling, so that if she were to die it would not signify; even bodily anguish while dying might be easy, on account of her indifference.

Meanwhile she reasoned with E-beth—this being an entirely rational matter. She promised to improve herself. She also pleaded.

No, said her ex-lover. I've told you that we're done.

But what should I do?

Find another girl.

I don't want to!

Good for you, said E-beth.

All I want is you.

Karen, the reason you're making this so difficult is because I was the first to make you climax. You might not even be gay. Sometimes you act like a closeted heterosexist.

I'm not!

Then I'll take the credit.

For what?

E-beth lit a cigarette.—If nothing else, she said, I was the one who brought you out.

Excuse me just a second, said the lesbian. Locking herself into the bathroom, she ran the water loud, bent over the toilet and tickled her tonsils with a paper clip until everything came up as easily and powerfully as if she had won some kind of relief. She kept retching thin brown mucus. Her throat was burning. She flushed the toilet. Looking in the mirror, she wiped the vomit off her face. Then she swished and gargled two capfuls of E-beth's mouthwash, just in case E-beth might care to kiss her.

4

There was a bandage over E-beth's ankle tattoo. She explained that new work was being done on that area.

5

Nowadays E-beth never answered the phone. They saw each other less and less. One Sunday morning they met for coffee; E-beth was late and grumpy. The lesbian said: There's something I want to ask you.

As long as it's not the same old thing.

That time I went down on you, and tasted, well, I thought it was contraceptive—

E-beth raged coldly: First of all, I told you not to invade my personal business. Second, how would *you* know what spermicide tastes like? Third, I'm leaving right now and don't call me.

6

It seemed, as in such situations it always does, that she would never get over E-beth. (Unlike the Madonna, who could restore the sight to any princess whose eyes had been pecked out by a magic bird, all the lesbian could do was to love and love.) Sometimes she used to go past E-beth's apartment, and it almost maddened her to think that her ex-lover might be in there, *without her*, and presumably with someone else. As most of us do, E-beth had "moved on." In one of their final meetings, she explained to the girl—who by then would have done anything, even moved next door merely to see her walk in and out with her other women—that she needed to grow up. Not only was she no good in bed, she was spoiled, and afflicted everyone around her with her impossible attitude. Moreover, she never felt good about herself.—You don't realize how hard I've tried, said E-beth—who was right as usual.

So the lesbian went home to her mother.

7

Her mother was worried, so she took her to a therapist.

The therapist said: Karen, this is all between you and me. You can trust me.

Thank you, said the girl.

Your mother's concerned about your weight. Do you know what bulimia is?

I think so.

You may be bulimic.

I don't want to talk about it. I'm fine.

Karen, your mother said something about another girl.

She . . .

Do you want to talk about that?

No. I told you I'm fine.

Karen, is anything going on at home?

What do you mean?

Is there anything you want to tell me?

The girl shook her head.

The therapist, who was greyhaired and had some sort of palsy, laid her trembling hand on her other trembling hand, smiled and said: Don't worry, Karen. You're not a lesbian.

8

What is it? said E-beth at the fourth ring.

I wanted to hear your voice once more.

Karen, please listen to me. I'm trying to say this nicely. I wish you love and happiness in your life. What you and I did together, that's over. It's never going to come back. If you don't let go of your need for me, you won't ever have anything, because I'm not there for you. Do you understand me, Karen?

But I still don't understand why.

We've talked this through, over and *over.* Karen, please don't contact me in any way. Not in a year or twenty years or ever. Karen, this needs to be our last conversation. If you send me a letter, I won't open it. If you call me again, I'll report you for harassment. If you see me on the street, we *do not* know each other. And now I'm ending this. Goodbye, Karen.

The lesbian was standing on the sidewalk. Her chances of indefinite remission were small. Hanging up the heavy black receiver, she left the phone booth and, quietly as she could (imagining E-beth's face so fixed and cold), reentered Jingle's Bar and ordered another Hot Bitch straight up. It stung her throat. She watched the unmoving wind chimes and the plastic dragonfly which dangled on wires from the ceiling. Locking herself into the ladies' restroom, she raised the lid of the reeking toilet, bent over it, and expertly sicked up her liquor, which burned even more on the way out. Then she sorted through her ring of keys, found the sharpest-ended, and stabbed it into her palm. Outside, someone tried to turn the door handle. She flushed the toilet, spat vomit into the grimy sink, and cupped tapwater in her hands, but just as she raised it to her mouth someone kicked the door sharply, and her heart pounded. She went out.

You were in there a fucking long time, a woman said.

Sorry, said the lesbian, feeling tipsy or maybe dizzy. Making a fist to conceal her bleeding hand, she sat down at the bar. Then she stood up.

The bartender looked her up and down. He was the old man who used to like her. He asked: Did you get sick?

I didn't make a mess; I cleaned up everything.

That's what they all say. And I'm the one who—why don't you go home? Hey, where's your *friend*?

Sorry, said the lesbian. I'm really sorry.

I can't serve you anymore.

At the corner store she bought mouthwash. She swished and gargled in an alley.

The Island

It is more than a coincidence that inverts have a fondness for islands.

FRANK S. CAPRIO, M.D., 1954

And from this moment on I shall strip myself that I may clothe myself.

THE APOCRYPHON OF JAMES, bef. 314 A.D.

1

When someone longs for "the past," what she truly pines for is *return into her vanished self*, bearing all knowledge of what she has since become and lost, because how could this awareness not embellish the cherishing of that ancient hidden jewel of happiness now restored to her? But she also wishes to be spared this selfsame loss and knowledge which must shadow the jewel's green flame. Hence what she wishes is to unify a contradiction, without which the more trivial impossibility of time travel would be no good to her. That treacherous face she still adores, if she could make it love her again, all the while remembering its present readiness to turn away, wouldn't that be saddest of all?—Nostalgia is nothing more or less than a drive to square a circle.

So the lesbian, unable to convince herself either that E-beth might possibly let her back into her heart or that E-beth had shut her out forever, lay sweating in bed, with her clothes on. It was two in the morning. She heard the doorknob begin to turn. By the time her mother crept in, she was already on her feet and looking out the window.

I thought your light was on, said her mother. Wasn't your light on just a minute ago?

No, Mother.

Then why aren't you in bed?

I'll go to bed soon, I promise.

Karen, why are you so upset?

I don't feel well.

You're upset at me, aren't you?

No, Mother.

You know, sometimes I get the craziest notion. It almost seems that you don't love me, said the mother, gliding steadily forward. The girl could not bear to look into her eyes.

2

She had of course written letters and torn them to shreds; don't we all? If she could persuade E-beth to once more kiss her, why wouldn't they dwell again within that green jewel whose fire nourishes and whose faceted infinities hide intimacies from the world, so that the past could be present, forever?—But the intervals between her and the older girl began to weigh her down like those sweaty blankets now pressing on her heart and snaking around her throat. E-beth probably wore a different look now. She was a different person. And even if she had not changed, how pleasant would it feel to be rejected by her again—to suffer that again, seeing E-beth's face so fixed and cold? So she tried and failed to square the interior circumference of her skull.

Again she crept into her room to lie down; but this time, perceiving her ministrations to be rejected, the mother took offense and hounded her back onto her feet, which might not have been the worst result. The girl did her math homework, counting and recounting zeroes. E-beth came into her dreams, in order to reject her again and again, until Karen could believe in it; week by week the incision deepened, as if the other woman could actually be bothered to be present, in order to keep sawing into her heart.

3

On what she correctly suspected to be her last visit to E-beth's place—for its stated purpose was for her to gather and remove her belongings—she had entered the bedroom while her ex-lover sat on the living room couch, smoking a long cigarette and jigging her booted toe in the air. Concealing her tears in order not to provoke further annoyance, the girl searched dresser, closet and nightstand for any of her own relics, and, finding none, continued her researches in the bathroom. Discovering that her half-used lipstick had been purged, she felt something far less definable than resentment or grief—indeed, something *secret*, which impelled her to do another secret thing; so she returned to the bedroom and from under the mattress stole that snapshot of the long-braided young woman sitting on a bed, with the solarized Beatles on the wall behind her. In the doing, this act consoled her. But on her return to her mother's house, when she took the photo out of her billfold she could not fathom why she had desired it. She thought to tear it to pieces—or mail it back to its owner—or take it to the blue house where its subject presumably lived. In the end she hid it behind the encyclopaedia volumes in the living room bookcase. Then she forgot it.

4

When a woman whom we love has died, it is difficult in the first interval after interment not to dwell on her lonely putrescence right *there* underground; but there comes a time when the bond of empathy, like the corpse itself, withers away, and we withdraw our thoughts from the beetle-jeweled skeleton in the box. Likewise, when a woman whom we love has left us, for some days and weeks as we live beside the silent phone we think on her thinking of us, defined, unlike us in our desperation, by pity, disgust, anxious avoidance, or some other feeling equally alien to the former affection, her attachment to us rotting away more rapidly than ours to her, although ours must eventually undergo a kindred process, until there comes the relief of dissolution. It is an ugly time, the time of sending out thought-waves to meet decay. And through this time the resistless girl was now carried.

The rest of us, brutally healthy, evacuate our hearts' dead stuff, retaining bitterness or woodenness. Karen was different.

5

After E-beth ended the relationship, the lesbian began yearning for a place where only women lived, loving each other equally without jealousy. (Judy Garland for her part had told *Movieland*: *I'd like to have been part of that life where all women were glamorous, all men romantic, everything was exciting, and no one was ever dull or lonely or sad.*) But of course there had never been anywhere like that, not even E-beth's candle-lit bedroom back when Karen still excited her. Had there been such a place, it might have lain in Oaxaca, Hiva Oa or eastern China. But once she had proved her obedience by no longer calling E-beth's cell phone over and over, the other woman suddenly out of pity sent her the address, which referred to an island in the Northwest. The retired policeman, who as you will presently read voyaged there with the transwoman for a detective-style honeymoon vacation, found nothing where my story posits something; well schooled by his broken-spined old true crime paperbacks, he reminded me that everyone lies, so that Karen Strand, alias Neva, was living a lie, therefore, what the fuck should I expect? Because I failed to hide my belief in the lesbian's story, he laid more of his wisdom on my shoulders. Once upon a time, which is to say nineteen years before he retired, he was out on patrol when the dispatcher radioed a low-urgency call concerning a certain schizophrenic all too well known to the department as a result of entering trouble on his fourteenth birthday, which was when he forced his twelve-year-old sister, or by his account allowed her, to give him a blow job; and here the retired policeman inserted: Never worked a day in his goddamned life; supported by his parents; preying on God knows how many young girls; somebody should have shot him in the ear!—When he threatened his parents, the father called the police, telling them only that he was *sick.* The retired policeman and his partner, knowing him for violent, ascended in a combat-ready state of mind, which turned out to be warranted, because the young man stood there threatening them with a shovel. They advised him to drop it, but he construed their guidance as intimidation, so the conversation speedily became an argument, which agitated him to the point of snapping off the shovelhead, letting that clang down the concrete stairs while he stood cursing, weeping and gripping the handle, which could have accomplished gross bodily harm; and to save us all from any such eventuality the retired policeman loomed before him while the other officer went behind, after which something off the record but surely discreditable to the subject took place, resulting in the discharge of a pistol into the crown of the suspect's head; he would live but was never going to be pretty; the rearmost officer deposed he had to fire in order to protect his partner, the retired policeman, who told me: Yeah, I'm grateful.—The mother, so he heard, came to the lawyer's office in a low-cut outfit; she was as beautiful as a model. Her house was filled with garbage. What the parents actually expected to get in their lawsuit was unclear; if they won anything, it would only be transferred from one line item of the state budget, public security, to another, indigent medical care. Once the lawyer spread his empty hands, the mother tracked down the retired policeman at home, her proposal being that if he perjured himself and denounced his partner she would split the settlement fifty-fifty (plus or minus fifty, of course), and she would also take him to bed. He stood there with his hands in his pockets, enjoying her figure, her desperation and most of all her lies—why, she was sicker than that fucking schizo son of hers! The way she spun it, she and he would live happily ever after. The husband was a detail; she'd get rid of him. Maybe she even believed it. She asked to come in, just to give him a taste. Sure he wanted her . . . !—All fucking lies, he repeated, belching in my ear.

6

In her island fable, the lesbian travelled first by train and bus, then ferry, finally by trail, descending root-stairs through the luxurious gloom whose evergreen wind smelled ever more of the sea; and there the ancient lady, sitting down slowly, took her sweaty young hands, looked her carefully in the face and asked why she was so sad.

The girl answered, resting her chin in her left hand, telling the story in a slow voice, as if she herself were old.

Leaning forward, opening her long weaver's fingers, the old lady said: If somebody calls me and needs me, I always try to come. But we sure could use more of our members. And, dearie, you should . . .

The lesbian did not comprehend. The old woman said: And when I come to anyone, you know how I travel? On my broomstick! That's our joke around here, because we . . . But most of the time what's *said* is not what's most important. What's your name?

Karen.

What a pretty name. But you're not going to keep it. You won't want it once we break it.

The old woman waited awhile, then remarked: But not all people like to talk; they don't . . . necessarily . . . like to . . .—Do you mean to join?

Staring into that frail, trembling face with the deep-sunk dark eyes, which seemed to see from out of their skull into any other woman's, the lesbian nodded desperately.

7

The old woman wore bluejeans and a sweater. She had knitted the beret she wore. Gesturing toward a wall hanging, she said: And then the lady who gave us this, I don't really know the full story about her. I think she was associated with some school in Oklahoma. After she joined, she started her own thing down there. You know, spread the love. Sometimes they remember us. Well, they've been real generous, and they're gracious. Do you understand?

No, ma'am.

And if you'd been here last—last month, I should say . . . we—everyone got a big kick out of it, and that little nymph . . .

A young woman had been standing in the darkness behind her. Presently she came out. She knelt down, gazing at the girl. And the wise one rested her wrinkled old hand on the shoulder of this darkhaired young Jewish lesbian in the cableknit sweater whose sleeves were far too wide for her slender white wrists. Slowly the Jewish woman leaned back, closed her eyes, and rested her head on the old lady's breast. Then she went away, to stir the dyepot.

The girl hesitated. Then she, too, knelt down.

That's right, honey; that's the way to . . . That's what E-beth did, when she first . . . Now give me a little kiss.

The old woman knew exactly what to do with her wrinkled hand and her tired grey tongue. Before she knew what she was about, the lesbian was screaming in ecstasy. Afterward, she knelt down and gratified the old woman. You see, she had had plenty of practice. That was how she joined the organization.

Now tell me more. So E-beth broke another heart, did she? Oh, dear. Well, from what you're telling me, dearie, there's only one way to go forward. Open your legs again; that's a good girl. Let me . . . That's right. Now I'm going to listen to your heart. Yes. Yes, I'm afraid you do have the power. Oh, my. My poor dear girl. Kiss my breast. Yes, that's how it is. Here's a blanket. Find yourself somewhere among those trees. No eating, and try not to sleep much. Come back tomorrow morning.

She returned at sunrise, and the old lady, who seemed as if her face had become sandstone and then someone had attacked it with hammers, said: Sweetie, I'm not going to cure you. I wouldn't if I could. I'm going to make it worse. Do you accept?

Slowly the girl said: If it gets worse . . .

No, you won't do that yet. Someday you may. Now, Karen, it's better if you don't ask why. Are you ready to get hurt without knowing why?

Yes, the girl said.

The old woman smiled and said: Dearie, I'm so proud of you. Now come in and have tea.

Too numb to feel afraid, the girl went in and sat on a low stool while her hostess put the kettle on. Sometimes she hoped that this magic would kill her, or bring back E-beth. The darkhaired Jewish lesbian came in, stroked her hair and said: Karen, I love you.

The girl did not know how to reply. The Jewish woman embraced her, then walked out onto the ocean path.

What did your mother do to you? Tell me everything.

The old woman listened without turning around. She nodded. She said: Then that's exactly what I'll do to you.

Now the kettle was boiling, and the old woman poured it into a single cup. Smelling the steeping of unknown herbs, the girl felt dizzy. At last the old woman faced her. She lowered the cup. She said: Drink it down. Good. That's right. Is it all gone? Right. Soon you'll need to vomit, but you're an expert at that. Now give yourself to me. Say it now. Say that you give yourself.

I give myself, to . . .

For my full use . . .

For your full use . . .

To be disposed of in any way, even unto death. Say it, Karen.

The gulls were calling, and the girl said: . . . Even unto death. Now I feel sick—

All right, honey. Be brave.

The first time she vomited was not painful, although her ears rang. The old woman held a bucket for her. She allowed her to rinse out her mouth, then made her drink more tea. All day and night the old woman kept leading her slowly and expertly into desolation, gripping her face and breathing into it a breath that grew ever fouler. By sunrise the girl hardly knew what and where she was. Again the young Jewish woman came behind her and briefly held her, then departed. And in the morning the old woman's tranquilly enormous face grew and grew, shining down on her.—Drink water, she said. The girl swayed in the chair. Again came those same ancient pains, but what the old woman did to her was or became somehow more abstract or schematic in its inflicted sensation.

Sleep in the corner, said her hostess, and before she knew it, three women she had never seen before were slapping her awake. They appeared to be sorry for her. A different tea, very black and bitter, was brought to her by someone who might have been the Jewish woman; whenever Karen closed her eyes, women slapped her, and then beautiful sparks made circles in the air. She began to feel warm all over and her heart was striking painfully, as if she were afraid again.

The old woman, who had not yet slapped her, said: Karen, today I want you to suffer as much as possible. Do you want to suffer?

No.

What if I told you that if you didn't want to, I wouldn't love you anymore?

You said you'd always love me.

I'm turning away from you. How does it feel?

No, don't—

Then if you can do a little something for me, a *very* little something, you'll have me back again. Do you see this needle? Take it and prick it all the way into your tongue. Then I'll make something out of you.

Things were done to increase her smothering anguish bit by bit, as if someone were treading on her breastbone. The girl kept weeping and vomiting until she could barely breathe. She thought they were burning her, but later there would be no scars. And then they kept making her climax, which felt worse than anything. How many of them were there? They gave her broth to drink, and led her to the toilet. And she slept, but not enough. Again they were slapping her; then came very familiar sexual things.

The old lesbian treated her with the steady thoroughness of the nurse who as she examines the raped woman explains to her what she is finding: a rectal tear, two bruises where the violator's hands have gripped, foreign pubic hairs, a crust that tests positive for semen—so that the woman understands what is now being done to her and what *was* done while she was in shock or unconscious. But for a long time Karen did not understand, because there came no explanation in words. With slappings, lickings, chokings, pinchings, beatings and penetrations they made love out of nothing—or, if you like, but two memories only: of E-beth and, well, yes, of her mother; because *love can be taught*, and her mother was her first teacher. (To remember love is to create and recreate it.)

I who was not there propose that by exercising her in acts of love, the old lesbian meant to free her from what her previous two possessors had done to her. But no such acts would have freed *me.* So perhaps what the old lady intended was that the girl would be a chosen instrument of hers to carry her love before woman and man; the preparation began with showing her how much she must suffer for the sake of what would now be put on her.

Now you need to thank me, said the old lady.

Thank you.

Again.

Thank you—

Did anybody ever spit on you before?

Yes . . . Four girls . . .

Who else?

I don't know. Sometimes more, and once there was a boy . . .

Then all thirteen of us will spit in your face, and you're to thank us. Say thank you.

Thank you.

Say you're a bitch, a stinking little bitch.

I'm a stinking little bitch.

Good girl. Dearie, I love you so much. Now say you're a goddess.

I'm a . . .

Go on. We're making you into a goddess.

I'm a bitch.

Good girl. We'll beat you some more. Now open your mouth. That's right; that's right. Hate yourself so we can love you.

It continued until she could begin to feel those things without distaste, and then, presently, to feel them in her own way, down within a certain darkness far deeper than not believing in herself. And the old lady cut away from her the things which should be cut from her, Karen's self dissolving like a cedar cone half gone in the moss of that tree's own root.

One morning the girl, who had been starved, penetrated and injured until she repeatedly soiled herself, opened her eyes to ask: Am I a bad person?

No.

Why has my life been so sad?

You never deserved it, but now you need to live it.

She was in her mother's house, that low dark place where all that she could see was the past.

Be patient, honey, said the old woman, recommencing to slap and beat her.

8

Honey, who are you doing this for?

I don't know. For you.

Who else?

For them.

Who are they?

All of you . . . I don't know—

Why not for you?

When I do it for them, I'm doing it for me.

Because it makes you feel good?

I don't know.

Dearie, I don't know, either. Maybe every generation has things visited upon them by their parents. I certainly had things visited on me.

But what those things were the old lesbian kept to herself, because this was Karen's time. So the women of the island kept ripping open and raping the wound that her mother had inflicted, as if out of ritual cruelty, but in fact to teach her that whatever she could not cure in herself she must enlarge.

I need more blood, said the old woman, and the young Jewish lesbian asked: Karen, do you feel the changing?

I feel anxious, because everyone's looking at me. Please . . .

They are, said the old woman. That's what the power does. Now bend over and close your eyes. This won't be bad. That's right; there it goes. Hold still. Breathe in. Hold still. That's done. Dearie, you're the bravest! Now turn over. Don't open your eyes. This will hurt, not too much but for a long, long time. I'm going to put a mark on you between your breasts. It's not the devil's; it's the women's mark, and most women won't be able to see it. Hold tight. Hold my hand.

After a long time the old lesbian censed her, then said: *Grant what no woman has seen and what has not entered into any woman's heart.* Murmuring and whispering secret things with many examples, she rocked the girl in her arms, simultaneously teaching and comforting her. She said: Because your mother loves you . . . ! You were born to be loved. Honey, you're the most loveable person in the world.

9

When the old lady had done away the offensive thing which had been on the girl, when she had entirely removed the pain that was in her, replacing it with a brighter deeper one, she bathed her and fed her. It was dawn. They lay down in the moss together.

She said: I was kind of a tomboy, dearie; I didn't like to dress up, and my Daddy said, you want to grow up to be a lady like your Aunt Ethel, and I said, I'd really rather not.

The lesbian was almost asleep.

The old lady said: I think I first heard about sex from my Cousin Sadie. She said, oh, I didn't know where babies comes from, but a guy has these worms and they crawl outside of him when they hatch inside of you. No, dearie, just close your eyes. What I did to you is all done. We're all proud of you. And nobody will call you Karen anymore. But, dearie, you're always going to be alone. Just rest, honey. I'm talking you to sleep, because I love you. When you wake up we'll all play. You haven't played enough. In my time I played mostly with boys. I was kind of one of those boys. I was flat-chested, and then when everybody started developing, my girlfriend and I stood in front of the mirror raising and lowering our arms to see who had the biggest tits. It was very concerning to me to see that everybody else was more developed. And then my best friend and I became lesbians. You still awake? Go to sleep, dearie. And I didn't get my period until between my freshman and sophomore year, and there was this guy who was really interested in me and would take me out in a sailboat, and I fell down the steps and got my period, and I said, oh, shit, I think I'm bleeding internally, and my girlfriend said, oh you're not, you idiot. And my mother said you'd better go to bed and put your feet up. My mother didn't want to talk sex really. I wanted to talk about masturbation and she wouldn't. Later she said, of course we did it but we never talked about it. I said, oh, I thought there was something wrong with me. What is this thing about sex anyway? Why should it be controlled? Well, honey, you'll never get away from it now. Yes, that's how it is. Some will love you as jealous lovers, and some like children, you see, unconditionally but without knowledge, and some like sinners hoping to hide inside you, and some to justify themselves over others, saying Neva loves me but not you. Neva's going to be your name. I'll tell you again when you wake up. And you're going to love them all the same, but the ones who will love you as broken things are the ones like you. Well, now you've joined and we're all proud.

And the girl fell asleep.

10

You who are now reading this fable may have been warned that giving your heart, body or self to more than one other will cause you sorrow should your true and predestined sweetheart later appear. And if you never find your soul mate, the result of promiscuity will be a kind of numbness. These warners insist that if you accept love too lightly, your lover may go away; and the same goes for your own self, of which too free a giving resembles too free a taking. Thus counsel our virginity-wardens, monogamists, deacons and lifelong spouses, not to mention those dirtyminded busybody hotel clerks in lonely little towns where no other sleeping-places may be hired:—these I deem purity's frog-eyed angels, who refuse to check potentially unconsecrated couples into a double room with a single bed, or at the very least demand deposits and identification from both parties, all the while exuding an unwinking disgust whose appropriate recompense is hatred. To them I say that whoever interferes with the giving and taking of love between adults should be *damned.* But I do admit that giving or taking love in excess may lead to sorrow. And since the same may be said of unrequited or miserly love-giving, why not let lovers follow each other's inclinations? Nobody could say that the lesbian didn't have a "choice."

11

She awoke at dusk, feeling cold, with the entire coven sitting in a circle around her. Embarrassed, she sat up quickly.

The old lady drew a quilt around the girl's shoulders and said: You're prettier than ever, dearie. We all want to love you.

Thank you, the lesbian whispered.

But you don't want to be a social worker. I really like sex. I have no problem with that. In high school we combed each other's pussy. It's just I don't go off with people to fix them. What about you? I said, honey, what about you?

What do you mean?

The old lady smiled. Then everyone rose and went away, except for the beautiful young Jewish woman, whose name was Belle. She led the lesbian into a thicket of blueberry bushes and opened herself. The lesbian had never felt so desired. At first she imagined that Belle (who was only her fourth true lover) was particularly skilled and enthusiastic on her account, as well she might have been, but as soon as Belle had finished, here came Lucia, jealously anxious, and after her, all the other members one by one, but for the old lady, who sat at home behind the open door, spinning lamb's wool thread while the cat purred between her ankles.

The lesbian finally had the gift now. When others first opened themselves to her, all the more exciting for being unknown, she flew from one to the next, like a petted child who flits from lap to lap at a party of tipsy adults whose indulgence she gladly mistakes for unconditional love. The brilliant pleasures of faces and forms, not to mention previously unimagined erotic habits, saved her (at least then) from commitments, and certainly from systematic categories. When she truly realized that she could make almost anybody love her—or rather, that she could hardly prevent anyone from loving her—then she became perfectly herself; in other words, she lost her freedom forever.

From her mother she had learned how to be strong in submission and endurance; from E-beth, how to suffer the loss of love. From the old lady there came no concealment; yet what the new witch, if that is what she was, got from her lessons is hidden from me. (I think of a Bible verse: *She shall have no inheritance; I am their inheritance.*) But aren't so many first fruits unknown? And who but the straight man can see underground, knowing where roots reach? (My heart still hungers for her traces, even for the dirt in which she lies.) The retired policeman unfailingly pegged her as dull, neutral, almost less than human; while I believed the contrary; certainly no one ever taught her the queenliness which overawes others. So much else is dark to me!—not least the women's mark, which as a man I can describe only by hearsay.

They taught her how to listen to any woman's body in order to pleasure her. This was the gift, the gold, the shadow on the lily.

What it was that made us love her remained as inexplicable as the capacity of certain American flags to draw a tear from the retired policeman; it might have been biochemical; and when Judy Garland, drunk and bloated, wearily told posterity: *I have a machine in my throat that gets into people's ears and affects them*, that must have been the same; whether Judy shouted in despair or sang in controlled commercial wistfulness, what she and the lesbian had, or what had them, could neither be aped by others, nor coaxed to stay. The adorable little girl who could have been a child star, the shining-eyed young man whom everybody loved to be around, the actress who could have really been something if she hadn't drowned, or maybe stayed almost something because she had drowned, these cold cases make me wonder whether (as the television whispers) charisma most often incarnates itself in youth—but shamans are charismatic, as Tecumseh and Sitting Bull must also have been even as they aged; likewise top-ranking Japanese geishas and Noh actors; and that ancient island woman whom the lesbian once served is another instance, if an incomprehensible one.

It was dawn again. They grilled bread and fish over the campfire. The lesbian sat alone, with her head in her hands. The old lady laid by her spinning. The lesbian went to the outhouse. On her way back she heard Belle and Lucia in a thicket quarrelling.

The old lady stood in the doorway.—Come in, she said. They're fighting over you.

What should I do?

That's a mess, honey. I like Belle, and I don't dislike Lucia, because she's a good person.

I just want everyone to be happy . . . !

And what about you?

I'm happy; I really am, sobbed the lesbian.

Sit down. I think you're on the road to perdition. Sweetie, being absolutely unloved is pretty darned bad. But being absolutely loved, well, that's not necessarily . . .

The lesbian hung her head and said: What am I supposed to do?

You have to love them back.

Why?

Because that's how you were made. But you think you're gonna take care of everybody. You'd better cut back on that. If you can't, well, but I *know* you can't.

Belle asked me to be her girlfriend.

What did you say?

I said okay. But then Lucia was just as in love with me, so I—

You should have been really straight with Belle from the beginning.

I didn't know how—

Oh, I can see that, said the old lady very sadly. She got up and chopsticked three fish heads into the cat's bowl. The lesbian wished to die. Returning to the rocking chair, her hostess said: Your name is Neva, okay? I wanted to give you the loveliest name.

Okay.

Say it.

Neva.

Now I've named you, we won't touch you anymore today. And remember: Don't be a social worker.

Isn't that what *you* are?

Well, well. Where would I be if I took my own advice? Cheer up, honey; give me a kiss. So you're breaking hearts already, just like E-beth! That's . . . But you have more power and more pain, so more people will love you. And you'll never be unkind like her. So nobody will understand you. It's going to get worse and worse. Our mouths will praise you. Would you kindly fetch me my knitting bag? Thank you. And one more thing, dearie: You're not necessarily a . . . No, don't be anxious; this isn't as bad as the rest. Let me hear your heart. Breathe in my mouth. No, you're not a lesbian. Do you know why? Because you're a social worker, like me, so you can't turn anyone away. Neva, you're going to be the best social worker ever. Give me another kiss. Oh, that's wonderful. Go into the house and sleep. I'll keep the members away.

When she woke up it was noon, and the old lady sent her over the hill and down the road to buy sugar.

The store owner burst into tears. The lesbian asked her if there were anything she could do, and the woman said: I want to marry you.

Presently the store was closed and locked, and the other woman was opening herself with both hands for the lesbian's tongue, sighing: This feels so relaxing.

The woman's pussy was as salty as tears.

12

The old lady said: Neva, did you want to?

She wouldn't even take money for the sugar. I felt so sorry for her.

That was why you wanted to?

Yes.

That's right, dearie. We're all proud of you. But when we pray, how often do our prayers get answered?

I don't know. Not all the time.

So you don't have to say yes all the time.

But I want to.

That's why you're a goddess. Now you know. They're going to come to you with offerings. And the very best they give you is, oh, my. Well, sweetie . . .

Defiantly, the lesbian told her: I remember what you said. You said: *If somebody calls me and needs me, I always try to come.*

That makes me a social worker. Now, dearie, what about your mother?

Maybe now she—

Silly girl, she couldn't keep her hands off you before! How can she resist you now? So what will you do?

With her?

It's up to you. You rest now. Go sleep in my bed. Tomorrow I'm sending you to her. Then come home to us.

13

So she made that turn after the tenth brick step, with seven more to go; the blind in the big grey window stirred, and then the door opened by itself. Once more she embraced the mother, the stone Etruscan woman who contains human ashes within herself. (Karen, where have you been? What's happened to you? I just don't understand why you reject my love. What have I ever done to you?—Nothing, Mom.)

When she returned to the island, her sisters led her up the hill. They stripped her and made her lie down upon the white and glowing gold of a bobcat skin. For a moment she believed that this had never happened to anyone but her. They penetrated her slowly and carefully, in much the same way when the tide goes out, unseen clams begin to squirt from under the mud; sometimes their jets go waist-high, sometimes only inch-high. This time the lesbian understood what they were doing to her. And it seems to me that what she must have learned was how to stop letting anything simply happen to her or be done to her, and start believing that she was *meant* to live a certain way, which was exactly the way she would ever after be living.

Belle and Lucia were holding hands.

14

The old woman, who had already given herself, even to the point of allowing herself to go frail, arthritic and dependent, now expected the lesbian to live with her. The lesbian promised to do this. There were shifting reddish-brown branch-shadows on the green moss. She led the old woman up the trail, while the others sang behind them. The old woman was palsied and trembling. They undressed each other. Wearily the old woman lay down and opened her legs. The lesbian began kissing and touching her. The old woman cried out in joy. Then she slept. No longer was she Neva's healer and shaper, but a mere worshipper. After the others had carried her home, the lesbian remained alone, reclining on top of the mountain in a rocky hollow of dry moss, gazing alone at the pale sky and milky-green sound and the many low hazy islands—yes, there at the top, waiting for something to be borne in that steady wind far below.

A day later the old woman, who was now more wife than mother, summoned another daughter of hers, a poet named Reba; and Reba, her white hair tied tightly back, squinted down at the lesbian, with the necklace of wooden beads barely rising and falling over her heart. Reba taught her a song of names to sing, so that she could always be again with every woman she had loved. And the question of what to do went peacefully away.

Reba, kiss her, said the old woman, and soon Reba's hand was entering her like a blue dragonfly darting through mossy darkness. Reba began weeping, astonished at the lesbian's power.

Although the fires of the 1960s and 1970s were ashes, and Neva met with no group which would have illuminated its members' common political interests, her sisters sometimes brought up what could be described as ideology; they explained that as the black lesbian poet Audre Lorde once said, if we failed to define ourselves for ourselves, then others would define us to suit *their* ends. But although Neva's power possessed its own intelligence, she was not one who thought in sociological or even moral terms. Does a goddess in fact define herself, or simply endure whichever misdefinitions our passionate lonelinesses project upon her? To never be alone again . . . ! and never be unloved! To make others happy, to love and be loved as all of us are meant to do . . . !—Such was now her state: the loneliness of being loved. And when she began to think on *why*, the darkening sea splashed against tongues of volcanic rock.

She stayed faithfully with the old lady until the end, meanwhile loving all the rest. It took not much longer than a summer. (Never forget your feelings, the old lady had warned.) Now the mourners were coming out onto a rock-walled promenade of dark moss, shaded by logs and Pacific madrones whose peeling-barked, reddish-brown skeletal arms clicked and rustled as the lesbian looked out at the blue-green sea and hump-backed forest hills. Swaying, she wept a trifle—because she could never help getting attached. Perhaps she should have wept more, but how could any goddess emote in proportion to her powers? (With a smile that might have been a grimace, E-beth had said: You'll never cry over anyone else the way you're torturing yourself over me. You know why? I was your first; that's all. —And Karen tried to remember how much she had cried over her mother.) The other women held her up and drew forward so that they all kept walking steadily to the edge of the grave. Reba led them in singing the song of names as they stripped the old woman's corpse. Each of them kissed it. Then they gently lowered it into the mucky wormy hole.

And then Neva had to go her own way. Most of them entreated her to stay; Lucia and Belle were already quarrelling over her again. Reba wanted her even more, but said what was right: We have each other. She didn't make you for us. Go where you're needed.

Oh, yes; the lesbian felt attached! If Reba hadn't sent her away, she would have stayed—especially because she loved Belle and Lucia so much—but then, come to think of it, didn't *we* love her?

Reba was the question-knower. She asked: Neva, are you still prepared to suffer?

And Neva nodded—wondering that she felt less about that than Reba seemed to. Thus the spending of a life, and the losses that could never be made good.—As for any other spending, the old woman had left her a sealskin pouch full of hundred-dollar bills. Belle said: Don't worry; it will outlast you.

Reba said: The more they love you, the more they'll take, until you're hollowed out. But that's what you were born for, to love and be loved.

The lesbian smiled at her. She had heard this many times before. She said: When I'm tired to death, I'll come back.

Please don't, said Reba, walking down the path. Probably she was crying. Neva's heart ached. Then she wondered what else to feel. The other members came to kiss her; they were likewise sad, but had not been born to suffer.

Now they had all gone away. Charged with the power of the one who is loved, she set out in late morning, ascending above the oak-shade and spruce-gloom until at last she was sitting on a wide pubis of yellow grass, with below her a great tranquility of islands in the calm sound. She was looking all the way to snowy-peaked Canada, the piney cool wind blowing up from the trail, and she was wishing to die.

15

In those days the lesbian had shoulder-length brown hair with blonde stripes in it. She appeared very fresh and young, especially when she smiled. Her teeth were perfect. Some women claimed to find her brown eyes a trifle small, but they used her just the same.

It's All Been Wonderful

It's all been wonderful.

Judy Garland, 1945

There is no law prohibiting a person from being a sex deviate, or queer. Perverts may roam at large providing they do not practice certain prohibited acts.

John P. Kenney, Ph.D., and
John B. Williams, LL.M., M.S. in P.A., 1968

1

Consider by contrast the transwoman's namesake. Born Frances Ethel Gumm, in place of the hoped-for son who would have been called Frank, she first opened her eyes in Grand Rapids, Minnesota, but transferred that event to Murfreesboro, Tennessee, the latter birthplace being *more glamorous.* Presently she also changed what they called her: *It occurred to Frances that Judy was an interesting name, and she promptly adopted it.* You see, Frances was not yet *interesting.* How could this anxious child star get ahead? She needed attention. Hence she thrust herself forward, learning how to look pretty and when to fawn. What matters "truth" once the makeup goes on? When she was almost eighteen they called her sixteen. By then she might have believed it. And so she dressed herself in sincerity. *"I meant every word of that song I sang to Clark Gable in my first picture," Judy seriously confided to me as she slipped off a little blue wool dress with the white lace petticoat trim showing two inches below the hem.*

Unlike her, Neva (a *more interesting* name than Karen) owned nothing but obligations. Power is a burden, no matter how it might be spent. But I cannot say that power is not sweet. And I would not deny that she felt some kind of rapture, to be so honored and raised up into what she now was.*

2

No longer shielded from the lusts of women and the brutalities of men, she began to fulfill her purpose. Well, what of the role itself? How authentic was it? Just as the Hollywood actress, whose true tasks are to take direction in embodying the commercialized fantasies of others, and to be the submissively unattainable object of public yearnings, falsely appears to be her story's subject—spoiled, enriched, ravishable, envied and petted—so anyone whose doom is to be *seen* must keep drudging away to sustain her "look"—anyone, that is, except for the lesbian, whose beauty went bone-deep. Again she confounds me. From where they came, those allurements and involvements of hers, or even from what substance or energy they had been extruded, I can tell you no better than I can make sense of those pleated woman-robes flowering outward from the black center on the underside of a Greek drinking cup.

E-beth had been made apparently irrelevant, like a former church-window's roundness now filled in with stones so that its ovoid sill of paler pebbles remains inexplicably. It seemed that her mother could no longer hurt her, and of course she would never or always be lonely. Her new life already fitted her with almost ominous ease, as if she lacked anything to renounce. To be sure, she, resisting, still occasionally believed herself to be unloveable; but she had been well taught to take the wills of others for her own—and there were so many wills! As Reba had explained, if she only did good to herself and others, there was nothing else she would need to do; and if she removed herself from consideration the work would be even simpler.

On the ferry from the island she stood on deck, breathing in rain and gripping the railing, until a middle-aged lady in a suede jacket came to stand beside her. The lesbian found herself instantly understanding what this person was longing for her to say, so she said it, the lady opening her brown eyes and commencing the

* It could have gone the other way: When Shirley Temple outgrew her charm and got fired at age twelve, she fell out of the paradise of *sure-fire numbers, hot babes* and *real hits*, but for all I know she got to eat delightfully wormy mouthfuls of repose there in anonymity's graveyard.

languid swaying of a wounded Amazon; presently the landing-horn moaned; they crossed the gangplank into the city and went to bed.

Next came a stronger woman who also needed to get something out of the girl.—

What would any of us have aimed for, if we could have been her? I who hope for nothing but to maintain the altars of my seven addictions cannot imagine. For Judy Garland, success was like candy. *She reads all the fan magazines. She is a Ping-Pong champion . . . She makes fudge . . . She is a husky, hearty little girl with a huge appetite . . .* And at the end she was shouting into the tape recorder: *I'm not something you wind up and put on the stage; I wanted to believe and I tried my damndest to believe in the rainbow that I tried to get over and I couldn't. So what?*

As for Neva, before her beginning she had already reached the end. What the old woman had done to her restored her to indifference . . .—or one might say that she took on a stately and almost vegetal placidity, much as when Apollo's prey turned herself into a bay-tree so that the god could rape her only by plucking her many leaves.—How could a bodhisattva be troubled by anything? Smiling and ready, she loved us.

3

Certain dooms arise from their victims' own deeds, and many result from accident, but some are simply magical, as when a pretty young soul named Luz Hernandez-Chavez, persuaded by the public defender, pled guilty to third degree felony battery, which then, *because it was a hate crime* as Judge Hempel explained, enhanced itself most miraculously into a second degree felony even as the public defender was patting the defendant's shoulder and latching shut his briefcase, so that she had to swallow a decade in state prison. To be sure, Luz tried to spit it out like a rapist's cock; although the tired public defender was already on vacation, she wept and cursed until his colleague agreed to move for a withdrawal of the original guilty plea *on the grounds that she did not know she was pleading to a hate crime*, at which point the case rose brightly (appealed against her by the district attorney) all the way up to the Second District Court of Appeal.—Well now, sighed Judge Luther, wasn't this crime motivated by some kind of hate? And he walked into the courtroom, so that everyone had to rise.

The district attorney explained: Christina Rojas is a declared lesbian and therefore falls within the statutory protected class.—The public defender's colleague began searching for something on the old trial transcript, but it ducked into hiding, so that the district attorney could not be checkmated and therefore continued joyfully: Luz Hernandez-Chavez, in combination with Ramon Lopez and Maribel Kingslee, drove together from Vallejo to Stockton for the sole and admitted purpose of beating up the victim, who was in a rival gang.—Judge Luther looked at the defendant over his glasses. His niece had been raped by gangsters, so he wished he could send Luz to the gas chamber. The district attorney was now saying: The gang to which the assailants belonged stigmatized homosexual activity, and because the victim was a lesbian, this woman and her friends assaulted her.—At last the public defender's colleague found the page for which he had been longing. He smiled delightedly, but the district attorney was already poisoning our minds: Specifically, Your Honor, the arrest warrant stated that Luz Hernandez-Chavez continuously beat the victim until ordered to stop and that the victim was thereafter transported to the hospital due to her injuries . . .

Objection, ventured the public defender's colleague, not for the first time, but she got overruled, and so Judge Luther said: We affirm the conviction of Luz Hernandez-Chavez, and the denial of her motion to withdraw the plea.—Both other judges concurred; poor Luz therefore served every moment of her stipulated ten years, passing the time by dreaming of smashing in the face of the first stinking bull dyke she would meet outside.

At last they dismissed her. Strutting gaunt and angry down the street, she met the opener of all our locks, the one who existed without us, the lesbian. Right away Luz was sobbing sweetly in her arms.

In the morning Luz said: I want to be honest and I want to be loving. With *you*.

Thank you, said the lesbian, running her hand through the other woman's hair. Soon she went away.

4

Once upon a time Judy Garland confided to the press: *I have a private instructor in my dressing room. It's loads of fun . . . I'm taking a postgrad course on my favorite subjects, music appreciation, art appreciation and French. I'm learning oil painting, too. I've been at it five days.* Sometimes the lesbian must also pretend to have fun. That is how celebrities gratify us little people.

For both of them, as for any of the world's other sweethearts, it would all be wonderful. Both their mothers schooled them to lie; Neva was even better than Judy at keeping secrets . . .

But I Feel Like a Terrible Person

> Dr. La Forrest Potter of New York believes that "once a woman is seduced by one, it is almost impossible for any man, husband or lover to win back his wife or sweetheart from the fascinating toils of these perverts. No man stands any chance against the active Sapphist . . ."
>
> FRANK CAPRIO, M.D., 1954

> What we're really scared of is that your love will go dead on us; that you will leave us.
>
> JUDY GARLAND, 1955

1

Another day came when she stood in a motel bathroom beside a stranger. A fullgrown woman she was then, smiling and tilting her head, without a stitch on but for that moss-lush towel of new white terrycloth wrapped round her hips, with her breasts nearly as white as that, a trifle tawnier maybe, and her teeth yet whiter, and golden-white glows of light running down her tawny-pink thighs, which would only turn snowier in those last years. Her thick brown hair hung down her shoulders, half before and half behind her as she smiled, shyly gripping her right hand in her left, snugging in the towel against her crotch; the hollows of her throat caught more light, and those soft round breasts of hers, just ripe, just firm, shone out from the rest of her like ripple-twinned reflections of the Arctic sun in some fjord when it is late on a midnight summer night and the water glows ever so faintly pink while two suns go on being soft, soft white, almost weak, or maybe just mild; one never tires of looking at them and wondering about them.—Smiling, the lesbian let fall the towel, exposing the issue of her life: what she would do with the loves of others.

That was summer; in the autumn she would wear her hair in bangs like an

Austrian ski champion whom she once glimpsed through a restaurant window. She had not yet perfected all her manifestations, such as that certain way (learned from E-beth and then unpracticed for all that time on the island) in which she would gaze at her cell phone when it rang, with that expression which showed each of us that another lover was calling.

In place of E-beth's smile, which as I said yearned and promised rather than demanded, the lesbian's, which demanded nothing either, was loving and sad.

She released the towel. The stranger adored her; then she broke his heart. (Another way of stringing together these facts would be to imagine that she found herself desiring to be held while slowly stroking his back, but he was all business, so business was what she gave him. I myself don't believe she desired anything.)

Each of us experiences anxiety in a specific part of the body. When something made Karen nervous, she got a stomach ache—happily cured with a pipe cleaner between her tonsils. If she stayed nervous, she got diarrhea. Neva was supposed to no longer get nervous; on the island they had polished her heart until it was as shiny as the linoleum on the poolroom floor at Jingle's Bar. Had she lived as long as I, she might have come down with acid reflux; as it was, by the time I met her she showed distress in swallowing, as if the food stuck in her throat. Did that signify nervousness, repression, desperation or ordinary middle age? Once or twice I've wished that our former goddess Letitia had been in the same room as Neva, because as the former had so often advised our transwoman Judy: I'm an empath. I can see everyone's emotions. I know you better than you know yourself. (She babbled on and on without ever asking a question. Her self-delight was sweet in its way.)

Neva felt guilty; Neva felt sick. She had not fully come into her power.

I know there have been other complications, she told the stranger, but don't you know that I love you?

Indeed she did . . .—but he raged; he called her a liar—because she'd do it with anybody! After leading him to the understanding that the center of her heart could hold any number of souls, Neva closed herself into the bathroom, feeling nauseated, and this time nothing came up.

2

The next time she visited her mother, a photograph was lying face up on the coffee table. It was already late at night.

Who's this *E.*? inquired her mother. Is she a *special friend* of yours?

The lesbian fell silent.

And who's this girl with the braid?

I never met her.

And yet this picture does belong to you.

Yes, Mother, said the lesbian.

Waiting for E., Stanford '74. What does that mean?

I don't know.

I found this when I was dusting the bookcases, her mother explained. At first I thought it had something to do with your other *friend.* But you don't see her anymore, do you?

No, said the lesbian.

Karen, how long has it been? Since you . . .

Years, Mother.

And what have you been doing all this time? How do you live?

Some friends have been helping me.

But you can't live on charity all your life! What do you plan to do? Is it something to do with your *friend*?

Not really, said the lesbian.

I gather you had some kind of falling out. But you won't confide in me. You never do.

The lesbian looked down at the rug.

So you won't tell me what this is about?

Don't worry, Mom.

But why did you *hide* this picture? Karen, what's your little secret? It must have made you very, very sad.

I think I'll go to bed, said the lesbian.

In the morning the photo had transferred itself to the counter of the breakfast nook. Turning it over, the lesbian gazed at the brown-braided girl whom she had never met but who might or might not have dwelled in that blue house on the night that E-beth sent her out of the car to deliver an unknown letter. In the sunlight the snapshot's highlights showed yellow, while the girl's red mouth had gone pale pink. Her hair was now tinged with wine, and the solarized faces of the Beatles on the wall behind her were even more deliciously lurid.

The lesbian hesitated. She heard a door open upstairs. Quickly she hid the photo in her overnight bag, in hopes of never again discussing it.

Her mother came slowly downstairs. She looked astonishingly old. She said: Karen, will you still not tell me?

Swallowing, the lesbian said: What am I to tell you?

Where have you been all these years?

3

I adore you so much, said the lesbian, and if it got to the point where you just couldn't stand my other people . . .

That was how Sandra talked, at least in my hearing. Neva was nearly fullgrown now; everything she said would soon ring (at least to the retired policeman and me) slippery, enigmatic.

The man considered the meaning of *where you just couldn't stand my other people.* Into his chest came a sour-sweet feeling, not quite sickness, sorrow or dread. Improving himself, he determined to tolerate anything, if only Neva would keep loving him! For her part, she learned what not to say while he was adoring her. The island's emetics and whippings had refined away her shame; almost all her new actions she did rightly, and the rest erased itself along with her inexperience. What she needed to do would happen even of itself, carrying her with it under disguise of being done by her. Her bangs were in her eyes, her head was bowed and her eyes shining sideways. Again she wondered how she could possibly endure this dreadful state of being. Meanwhile, the man in the motel bathroom, looking at her smoothly stubborn little face and especially at her lips, suddenly conceived a vision of her anus—because this organ, after all, is nearly independent, semi-sentient, as determined to keep shut as a clam, which opens only when it chooses; soon the lesbian was crying out with pain as he penetrated her from behind, her moans indistinguishable from those of pleasure; he was fondling her face, stroking or choking away her tears, until finally she wished to sob: *I don't like this*; but it was nothing compared to what the island witches had done to her, so she kept quiet, and soon enough, remembering how E-beth used to scold her for failing to *always* feel wonderful about herself, figured out how to make the best of it, as if anal penetration presented her with some kind of promise; soon one of their so-called favorite things was when he would be licking her pussy, rubbing the rest of it with a finger, and sliding two fingers deep and quickly in and out of her anus, the anus that resisted but in his interpretation hungered; and this hunger was what he so conveniently perceived in her face.—Shantelle, as haughty-looking as one born to the crown, her unsmiling eyes disdaining us from beneath deep-arched eyebrows, would simply have said: Okay, let's get it over with.—But Neva said what the witches did: I love you.

Next she pleasured the man's brother, his niece and his nephew. Her vulva was as rich as a bowlful of fresh quartered limes.

I who cannot be female will never know whether it was true what Xenia once told me: Between women the sex can be very hetero. Everybody wants to be fucked, so it's simply a matter of how are we going to accomplish this. Between women there are more options.—Anyhow, none of the men went away ungratified.—But no matter whose hand she held, they called her *the lesbian.*

4

The retired policeman once told us the tale of the nuclear physicist who because his wife had stopped loving him slipped radium into their son's pillow. (Francine grew fascinated that he lovingly dubbed her Francium.) The boy already felt sick by the time that burns began to express themselves on his face—at which point the father considerately concealed more radium in the mattress. By the time he was arrested (he pled insanity), their child had leukemia.—To reduce the probability of suchlike retaliations, *the lesbian must never stop loving anyone.*

And now her story enters in upon its purpose, which is to establish whether the one can ever love the many as perfectly as the many are called upon to love the one. We are instructed to love God, the ruler, or the Motherland, and each of these is said to love us all faithfully and even uniquely in return, to the extent of that entity's perceived omniscience. But for a member of the many to love as if *she* were the one, well . . . ! Some of the many despise that, knowing themselves incapable of doing the same, so that they brand her immoral, selfish, hypocritical. Naturally, they will change their opinions once she descends to love them.

5

Her bangs grew out. She became ever more softspoken. Everyone could watch the shinings of her long hair.

When her expressions and procedures were perfect, she bought a bus ticket, paying cash from that sealskin pouch or billfold, which looked and smelled as had E-beth's hair in that first year when she butch-trimmed it into a silver pelt (the driver said: If you do what I ask, then we'll be friends), and not many years before the Cinnabar got darker, narrower and more hollowed out (the new barmaid would insist that it had always been that way), when hardly any homeless tents had risen up on Ellis Street, she who dawned above us passed into San Francisco, with shadows slanting up the granite facade of the Golden State Mall on Market Street, accompanied by streetlamp trios glowing like bronze, flickerings of people's legs and of bicycle wheels, clatters of wheeled suitcases being dragged down toward the stairway'd pit of the underground rapid transit, and the amplified prophet's voice: *Jesus said I am the first and I am the last; Jesus, Jesus, Jesus: He trusted us with the judgment that . . . Christ's door and Jesus is Lord and God raised from the dead so that we will be saved. See, there's no more guessing.*

On Civic Center Plaza a black man dressed in black slumped on a bench, with a white blanket pulled up to his waist. Seeing Neva, he slowly straightened, and his eyes began to glow.

In a tiny dark apartment on Hayes Street she pleased a married couple all day and night. Then she inhabited snapshots of other women one after another, the colors muted, the women smiling or sometimes sleeping. Almost around the corner from the Y Bar rose the Hotel Reddy, where she paid in hundred-dollar bills for Room 543, which was centrally situated between Catalina's place and Room 541 where we guests of Neva often heard a man beating a woman; her lover-to-be Victoria lived with a sister Helga in Room 547—and all this lay convenient on the third floor, catty-corner from the stairwell. She loved us all without preference—although most of us turned out to be women.

Neva

She still takes her Teddy Bear to bed with her. She puts her dolls to bed every night of her life.

GLADYS HILL, 1938

I never played with dolls, *never*.

JUDY GARLAND, to Gladys Hill, 1940

Mom wants me to be safe . . . but I don't think that's at the top of God's list.

KATHRYN SPRINGER, 2014

1

Judy Garland once said: *I think women get themselves mixed up by making too many promises. There is something so romantic about promising your heart forever to a person.* Whether or not the lesbian made outright promises is a matter I resist weighing in on, but that soul of hers and her pubis like a cobra's hood both approximated promises, being perfect. (I used to imagine her upside down on the catty pole, with her legs wide, wide apart.) And she kept being Neva, loving without pitying us—or did she? (My reconstruction of her, or if you like my projection, requires me to humanize the superhuman.) She apparently felt that any loving (or pitying) was beautiful! When it pleased us to deceive her, she agreed with all our childish lies. When she smiled, it was as if nobody had ever smiled that way, as if she had either overcome or completely become herself; in short, they perceived her as she once perceived E-beth.

Francine once told me (in dirtier words) that all the lesbian's relations with us—her entire career, if you will—could be characterized as *reactive and defensive.* But I had had my own experiences of Neva, which is to say my own ecstasies. Even if a disproportionate allocation of her efforts did go to overcome a certain bad dream that was as simple and gruesome as a promontory of black bones, why should that concern us? Hadn't she been raised to serve others?

Not long before she left home she'd said: You know, Mother, I keep having nightmares.

Well, replied Mrs. Strand, you have no idea how difficult it's been for me.

Now Neva was dead. The transwoman bought me a drink and announced that the lesbian had never felt sufficiently loved. But how could that be? Judy and I, not to mention all the rest of us, certainly gave her most of whatever love we had, dishonestly promised her the rest, and pleasured in pleasing her, even as she fulfilled herself (at least apparently) in fulfilling us. So what did she need nightmares for? As for us, some learned better than others, but even the most selfishly, dangerously desperate felt better when we had lain down in her arms.

And since I was there, I can swear that this was all true, the truest thing you ever could imagine; truth was when the Y Bar's front door swung open, and her silhouette began to come in from the glaring light.

2

Shantelle, Selene and Xenia, sitting in a row, turned their heads toward her like three snaky-haired Furies silently inviting some mortal to drink from a cup of steaming poison; then she came in out of the light for them to see her, and they loved her.

Who We Were

> And in my case there is no question of performance—my job is solely to remember lines and positions and rattle them off as quickly as possible never mind the meaning etc., etc. All the time I think it *must* be my fault, but really I know it isn't.
>
> JENNIFER JONES, to David Selznick, 1953

> It is natural that when one thinks of sex and wants to feel aroused, one thinks of one's own sexual experiences.
>
> HILARY ELDRIDGE, quoted in *Female Sexual Abuse of Children*, 1993

1

Of course the retired policeman's broken-spined true crime paperbacks, priced in cents rather than dollars, would one and all have received her into their stories, eroticizing her into a perfect victim or manipulator—since from the very first even Francine was widening her nostrils, sniffing after the lesbian!—Correction: I meant to say, she who for professional reasons had become the best of us at seeing, if not necessarily remembering (although Francine *was* excellent at remembering who had broken which rules), saw over, past and through our titillated attentiveness to conclude without effort that here was someone worth paying attention to.—So we crowded into the Y Bar to smell Neva, thirsting for her, most of us not yet daring to desire her (the retired policeman, stronger than anyone, sought to take our minds off her by explaining, supposedly only to Francine: We had a jury say that even though he confessed to it, he's frickin' nuts. It was kinda one of those cases. We knew he was involved. Even the jury could see it. But they were thinking, well, the judge put fear in us and you have to look at the fuckin' evidence. So they made it attempted homicide, which was fine with me, because it got him off the street and we never had that type of homicide since . . .)—but within two winks and three drinks, he limped home, after which love reinfected us, the kind of love that perpetually craves any animal scent of its object, be it her sweat fresh or stale, or the hayfield fragrance of her hair, the excitingly sharp odor of her armpits, or the smell from inside her shoes. And all this happened so quickly that even to me who was there it grows ridiculous in the telling, and therefore wretched, hence almost without interest, like some young girl's lies about really truly seeing Wonder Woman. We came wide-eyed unto her:—Just as a dead woman's corpse attracts flies both male and female, so our lesbian, now in fullest flower, drew us without distinction. Were you to ask whether Letitia in her day had exercised a comparable gravitational pull, I would have said: Let me see Letitia's picture!—But even if those two had sat side by side in real life, how could I have compared them? Just as the most spectacular orgasm decays into a glow, which sublimes away, leaving but a residue of vague fondness, so feminine allure passes on, and all we fans and ex-lovers retain is a wavering impression as of electromagnetic force (represented at the Y Bar by Francine's washed out old postcard of the giant breast with pink spectacles on it, a tasteful memento which every now and then fell off the shelf). I could tell you what Judy Garland's wide white forehead once meant to me, but my descriptors would be placeholders. I could even try my best to represent that sweetly sad and white, white face of the young Judy Garland in the transwoman's old silver gelatin photoportrait: her airbrushed skin enrolls her in that soft marble pantheon whose retouched pubises are hairless, slitless mounds of perfect whiteness, and whose armpits are smooth white hollows; as *Screenland* magazine explained: *She looks healthy and happy and wise without being sophisticated.* But what could I convey beyond rippling echoes?—Regarding Neva, there was something about her cheekbones that we adored, and maybe something about her top front teeth when she smiled, but what about the color of her eyes, which only I would have sworn were brownish-green?—We all sought out her secret, in useless hopes of copying it. (Although we pretended to be unaware of it, we knew all too well that the lesbian, our goddess, was *she who suffers.*) Our investigations briefly flowered into a perverted game, which we could equally play alone in our beds or sitting on our stools at the Y Bar, discussing her with one another until she walked in. But because we could never establish any cause of her effect, we tired of this, stared at her almost in misery. Then we simply stared.

You might have tried to tell me that she did not belong here, being too good for us, as was certainly true, but my sole reply is that precisely on that basis, oh, how she belonged here! We desperately gave ourselves over to her—another way of stating that she was our slave, our thing, whom we had now captured and intended to use most avidly.

No, said wise old Xenia. No matter who has which genitals, there's always one in the couple that's more of a top; there's a catcher and a pitcher. I admit it can switch back and forth. Sometimes the butch is more the pitcher, but oh, it can switch.

What about Neva? I asked.

What about her?

Is she a top or a bottom? We need her so much, and yet she does whatever we ask . . .

What's Judy?

A bottom, obviously.

So what's Neva?

That's what I'm asking.

I need to piss, said Xenia.

By then I had other questions. Why Neva, and not for instance Shantelle, who practiced both intuition and science in her varied manipulations? (Shantelle said: Neva's special, sure. There's some kinda magnetic energy around the bitch who got chosen, *because she got chosen.*—But *why* was she chosen? I asked.—That shut her up!)

Since what had been done to her on the island still remained unknown to us, Francine and I, who both failed (exultantly) to resist her, sometimes posited to Selene that Neva's magnetic power was nothing more than coincidence between our need to worship and her presumable craving for adoration—a marriage cemented by coincidence. Hoping we would like her better if she agreed with us, the transwoman quoted an appropriate scripture from Judy Garland, who warned each and every actress who would come after her to never lay aside humility: *If she loses her sense of perspective, she may begin thinking how great she is, when actually her success may be just a matter of luck and a few pretty close-ups.*—And with Neva, she said, maybe it's just the way she looks at us or something.

Or something, said Francine. Six dollars.

2

The first time I myself saw her stride in, which as you know was at Selene's wedding, I remember that she stood just within our darkness as if she were waiting for her pupils to enlarge so that she could see us in our boredom and numbness, showing off our shallow friendships, petty cruelties and filthy jokes, not knowing that we illuminated ourselves far more distinctly than that through our various lonely self-tortures. (Al sat toadlike in his chair, shaking his head back and forth, while another man with folded arms stood smilingly shaking *his* head.) She looked, not long but long enough—she who would soon take my hand. After that one time, she never paused when she came in.

3

Now I had better introduce some of us (the rest will not hesitate to insinuate themselves): half-secretive addicts and dreamers, greyhaired little boys who suffered without knowing why, because they never worked out that they should have been girls; women stained with a need which they told themselves was simple femininity; souls who hated themselves for being neither fish nor fowl—not to mention all of us who no matter how "enlightened" our self-acceptance trudged the night streets in dread of having our skulls smashed in. In absolute terms we were not such wretches as all that, but who could be anything attractive in comparison to perfect Neva? Anyway, we all had meteoric pasts:*

> (1) Sandra, most innocently gentle of us all, was nearly but not entirely a G-girl. She projected the silky, faraway little-girlness of Natalie Wood.
>
> (2) The straight man was a recent graduate of one of those vacations which begin in a double bed and end in two single beds, each party lying silent, rigid and desperate, longing for the other to be the loving angel of yesterday, dreading the next sound, wishing it could be over.

---

* If emptiness is sadness, then the past must be sad, even if it was happy back when it was full: Beneath some eminently present city, up one of whose alleys a redhead in a blue goosedown jacket slowly wanders, peering down at the screen of her mobile phone, while a blonde cycles past, a brunette in the doorway of a cosmetics shop optimistically greets and beckons to passers-by, an old man stops to rub his eyes, a tourist couple clears the way before them with their matching lime-green wheeled suitcases, and two curlyheaded ladies meet to share a cigarette, there lie the crypts and foundations of the past—mere shells and channels now, dye-vats barely marked with the vestiges of pigment; cloacas whose foulness has cleansed itself into dust, mean nubbins of labyrinths for people whose language is forgotten and whose skeletal remnants proclaim them to have been smaller and less significant than we—as must be so, since we are not dead like them.

When Madeline came out from the shower, he saw with horror that she wore a towel around her and quickly dressed with her back to him. Soon she was saying so bitterly: You don't know how it's been for me with you not seeing me for six months and me all alone and remembering the last time when you said we'd never live together, so I got resigned, and now you say, well, maybe we can live together, but that's just because you don't like the idea of me living with someone else. I think you're pretty damned insensitive.—Then she left the straight man, who accordingly longed to ejaculate his loneliness into someone else. Fortunately, he had Sandra.

(3) Shantelle, lacking the benefit of Natalie Wood's driving mother, was the kind of lover who would only suck you with a condom on, and never let you taste her, "for health reasons," but who fake-moaned softly (for considerations of discretion) and plausibly, in hopes of hurrying matters along. Of course the foregoing rules went by the wayside in cases of lust, anger or profit. She knew that some women looked down on her for being a hardcore double *bitch*, but *fuck* them! Her favorite thing of all (aside from being with Neva) was losing her temper. The delicious smell of her rage often exalted Judy into a yearning to lick her armpits.

(4) Holly, blonde and barrel-shaped, was a one-oh-one-percent out lesbian whom we hardly knew; with Neva now in the picture she swam into the Y Bar more and more. First she looked intrigued to be among us; then she started getting sadder and sadder.—Or am I imagining this? Sometimes I make up stories, to help me feel more alive; and it could well be that all my fellow drinkers at the Y Bar were just as happy as I; they often imply that I am stupid, upon which I go inside myself and pretend.

(5) Xenia, who back in her speed freak days used to shave her head, effecting some kind of androgyny, but nonetheless never eschewed long eyelashes and leopard prints, kept pretending to be twenty-five. If I could turn into a woman, but not into Neva, maybe I would hope to resemble Xenia. Unlike me, she was always up and doing. She moonlighted at the Pink Apple, about which establishment she said: You get to the stage and do your thing, and the people are very happy, and

you look behind you, and they're taking their money back . . .—She readily entered into love but flinched at inevitabilities. Rich in stories and advice, she knew what to say to those who suffered, so long as they looked up to her wisdom while allowing her to be young. (Well, Xenia kind of feels a notch above, said Francine. Most of us aren't like that. When I text her I do say I love you.) She intended to leave us anytime, thanks to her superior options.

(6) Hunter, formerly a shy child who collected pictures of kd lang to put on her bedroom wall, was or possibly was not a part of Xenia's departure plan; we avoided her because she was beautiful and unavailable. Sandra once told her that she embodied whatever lesbian chic might be, at which she smiled. The transwoman was nearly through with hoping to imprison her in adulation forever. Like the rest of us, Hunter yearned to kiss the lesbian, but most certainly loved Xenia in some strange and noble way which could not be explained.

(7) Waiflike Erin was almost gratuitously kind to Judy, who thirsted for stories about being a little girl or being a woman, which the retired policeman referred to as *all that phony first period crap.* Sometimes when she told Judy about something that had happened to her long ago, Erin could not believe herself. Preferring not to cry in front of others, she went outside and improved her day by forgetting. She never wanted us to find out where she lived, although I guess Neva must have known. Now Erin was forty; she tried to go on being a waif but that was getting more difficult.

(8) Francine got through life by refrigerating her own desires. She so well knew what each of us drank, and followed those data into our mouths and up into our skulls, to discover how we thought (answer: not in words), and even what we lived for, which is to say, how we each went about ruining ourselves: most of us going fat and diabetic from alcohol, our truest medicine, whose grace, entering our blood one shot at a time, allowed us to tolerate the lesbian's infidelities.—Francine's coolly careful affect invariably (and I submit unfairly) put the retired policeman in mind of a certain well-tailored, motherly old landlady he had once arrested who advised the court: And I would like to point

out that I was never in the deceased woman's room alone.—*That* bitch got convicted, of course. But Francine remained at large.

(9) I was a nothing; I existed, if at all, for no good reason. My most distinguishing characteristics being foreknowledge and passivity, I realized that when my wife Michelle began to stare silently at me for half an hour at a time, weeping silently, that I should hold her or leave her; so I did neither. But when it dawned on me that her flat of birth control pills had remained three-quarters full all month, I took charge; which is to say that the interrogation extruded from her a denial so shamefacedly false that why I failed to pull out of our connubial activities is a mystery, especially since I then had two other women on the side, the nasty little addict and the tall gaunt thief; but at least the pills resumed their one-by-one diminution—down the toilet, no doubt. Since Michelle had now missed two periods I determined to suggest an abortion, in consideration of the lukewarmness of our attachment; so I got drunk and watched the shadows changing on the wall. Once Cassandra was born, I certainly should have shown how much I loved her, but I blamed her mother for dishonesty, which was why I spent even more time in the beds of other women. And so Michelle's silences developed a more scheming quality. Half poisoned with dread that she would run away with the child, I fled to the city of Martinez for a three-day cocaine weekend with a young lady who had found me adorable. Upon my return I found mother and daughter gone, along with most of their clothes; for a souvenir they had left me a sinkload of dishes now invested by a regiment of German cockroaches. Since I had lived off Michelle, and the rent would be due on Wednesday, I skipped out, parasitizing a man and his wife who failed to keep their promise to have my likeness appear in a sex magazine. Michelle must have gone to her mother. I rang up the old lady, who called me a monster and warned me never to contact her or her daughter again. Thus assured that I was correct as usual, I called Michelle ten times an hour until finally she answered, coldly verifying my hypothesis. The mother died; after some years Michelle contracted an incurable illness, as I had been hoping she would, at which point Cassandra, whose heart they had inculcated against me, went to distant

relatives in Morgan, Minnesota. Thus my glowing career. I have folded down the corner of this page in order to more easily rehearse my accomplishments.

(10) As for Victoria, she had married the boy next door, then just before turning fifty decided that she was a lesbian. She was tall and a trifle overweight; unlike Judy she never cut her wrists, because whatever happened to her had actually happened to someone else. She came to our bar irregularly, in part because she lived a few doors down from Neva but also because she feared Shantelle, who was not at all the sort who would let a nobody such as Victoria come between her and her pleasures.

(11) No one much cared about Al although we tried to be nice to him. Ditto for Samantha.

(12) The retired policeman was not only a diabetic sadist, but the brainiest of us all. One of his life lessons: *I think the community policing should be limited to gang detectives in uniform.* The reason that no one liked him (not that we didn't love him) was his sour outlook—a common result of having dealt with human beings for decades. He believed that we would all lie, steal, rape and kill whenever we thought we could get away with it. The wife-beaters who pulled guns on him denied the fact and abused him in court; so did several wives, who in the interest of domestic harmony blamed their bruises on him. He remembered the middle-class young man who had enjoyed dangling from the ceiling while wearing women's panties; when he accidentally went too far it was the not yet retired policeman who, delighted by *manual strangulation* and *injury to the deeper structures*, defied the father's threats and the mother's slimy vituperation for not hiding those circumstances from the newspaper. He claimed to see us better than we did ourselves; I grant that he knew us more than we knew him. Judy's basest actions rarely surprised him. It was partly for him that we acted out our stories, especially there at the Y Bar; while he mostly stayed in, sitting or lying on his bed, wheezing. To be sure, I sometimes met him at the Cinnabar; Al sighted him at Jojo's Liquors; before his disease entirely paralyzed both legs he was known to do business in certain watering holes of Chinatown and even North Beach. From

his throne of voyeuristic knowledge he presently (as will be told) interested himself in the case of the lesbian, who opened heart and legs to all without ever showing her mind.

(13) Meanwhile the transwoman longed to be abject, and sometimes succeeded in eclipsing even such perfect practitioners as the Mexicana I once met when I came out into the light, leaving that kind of hotel where when somebody spits the happy product of fellatio into the sink, ants immediately arrive:—Having parted from the longhaired Indian girl with the tight little cunt which like Shantelle she declined to let me taste, I (who, not having yet met the lesbian, actually wanted more than anything to lie down in stillness forever) descended stinking stairs and met a wretch lying on a sidewalk which I would have judged was almost too hot for naked flesh to endure; her bare feet were black with dried filth, her eyes like two deep-dug graves. She stretched out her leathery hand, into which I placed ten pesos, at which she murmured some inaudible formula of thanks, blessing or malediction. How could her lowliness compete against Judy's? Being aware, self-contained and almost regal, that sidewalk woman declined to be mortified. In a way she was as coolly divine as the lesbian—while the transwoman exemplified this ancient Christian admonition: *Show yourself so submissive and humble that all men may trample over you and tread on you like the mud of the streets.*

4

If, like me, you are so enlightened as to advocate for human extinction, this catalogue of all us mortal shitbags will have wearied you, so I now end this chapter. Pop yourself open a can of Patriot Dry Lager, swallow three pills, and lights out forever!

What She Did to Us

God, the magnificent, has said: "Women are your field. Go upon your field as you like."

Shaykh Umar ibn Muhamed al-Nefzawi, *ca.* 1400

Unhindered by any ambiguity, she spoke openly, and what she spoke of was not love but sexual satisfaction, and this, of course, referred to the only sexual satisfaction she knew, the pleasure she took with a woman.

Colette, 1941

1

Now that you know us, let me tell you how the lesbian snagged Shantelle.

When Judy Garland, born in Grand Rapids, Minnesota, explained: *I was born in Murfreesboro, Tennessee, in case anyone is interested,* she showed us all that we could remake ourselves—like Shantelle, for instance—although I who never bought the privilege of fucking *her* can only begin her biography in the faith that she was a G-girl straight from her mother!

When that failed to work out, she swam through other vicissitudes until she found the Y Bar.

The lesbian came in, and that was when I heard Shantelle sigh without knowing or meaning to, like a child of poverty who has just seen her first department store window when they deck out its temptations for Christmas season.

2

Neva's near neighbor at the Reddy Hotel was Helga, Room 547, who lived with a sister named Victoria who was big-boned and silent, with close-cropped red hair. Yes, indeed, this was the same

(10) Victoria, who just before turning fifty decided that she was a lesbian.

At first she never even said hello to Neva, who accordingly assumed that here was one person in the world who disliked her—a relief.

One morning after Helga had slammed the door to her apartment, hastening to work, the lesbian went out into the corridor, meaning to go downstairs and pay her monthly rent. Helga's door had silently opened. The room was dark, and Victoria was sitting in it, staring out through the doorway.

Hello, Victoria, said the lesbian.

Victoria remained silent.

Closing but not locking her own door, the lesbian paid her rent in hundred-dollar bills (the greybearded little window clerk could not stop admiring her, because her bangs were precious and her head was bowed, her eyes shining sideways), zipped shut that famous sealskin pouch, then came back upstairs. Her door had opened itself. Entering her apartment, she found it as dark as she had left it. She came into the kitchenette and turned on the light. Victoria was sitting there.

Hello again, said the lesbian.

Victoria did not answer.

The lesbian opened the refrigerator. She took out the plastic milk jug and set it on the counter. She tilted the glass jar of cereal until her bowl was two-thirds full. Then she poured the milk in, returned the jug to the refrigerator, removed a spoon from the drawer, took spoon and bowl, and sat down across the table from her guest, who remained as silent as a cat.

The lesbian began to eat her cereal.

Victoria said: Will you or I break the silence?

Go ahead, said the lesbian brightly.

I want to deepen our relationship, said Victoria.

Okay, said the lesbian.

Victoria stood up. She approached the lesbian and said: You're irresistible.

Thank you, said the lesbian.

I love you, Victoria said. She clasped her arm around the lesbian's neck.

Smiling sadly, the lesbian stroked the other woman's hand.

Thank you, Victoria whispered.

The lesbian knew that she must now love Victoria.

Am I annoying you? asked Victoria.

No.

Good, said Victoria.

The lesbian stood up slowly. She caressed the back of Victoria's neck. Victoria moaned.

The lesbian finished her cereal. Then she took a shower. Victoria stayed at the table.

What will you do today, Victoria?

Victoria laughed.

I've got to go out now, explained the lesbian.

Victoria walked out, weeping silently. The lesbian went by rapid transit under the Bay to Richmond, where she kept her car. Then she drove to Vallejo to visit her mother.

When she came home, Victoria was sitting in Helga's darkened room with the door open.

Hello, Victoria, she said.

Victoria did not answer.

The next morning the lesbian got up early. She could hear Helga or Victoria in the shower. When she opened her door, Victoria was already sitting there staring out. Victoria looked at her. The lesbian smiled and waved. Then she poured herself a bowl of cereal. Victoria came in, stood over her and announced: I love you.

I love you, too, said the lesbian.

Her guest continued to seem sad, so the lesbian laid a hand on her breast.

After that Victoria became a regular at the Y Bar.

3

Some people say that the gospel of truth is joy, although we usually believed the opposite, which explains why we were, if not alcoholics, at the very least medicinal drinkers; shot by shot, we blurred away truth's sadness into something warm. And then here came the lesbian, whose *je ne sais quoi* proclaimed the cosmic I am. We couldn't get enough of her!

She was telling Shantelle something about rent and the cost of toilet paper. Judy listened open-mouthed. Francine stood behind the bar watching the lesbian's lips and imagining that they were closing and opening around each of her nipples in turn, first the right, then the left, after which she would return the favor. Xenia, who would far rather have been chatting with the lesbian, stood on the dark side of the bar reporting in to Hunter on her little magenta phone: And at the Pink Apple last night there was this guy who was visiting his parents, and his fiancée was coming to be with him in five days. Well, he kept going on and on about how much he loved her. Meanwhile he got me to shove my titties in his face! Then he wanted to date me. I said, why do you want to mess up that good thing that you have? He said, oh, he loved her so much, but he just couldn't wait, not even five fuckin' days. Come on, Hunter, don't be like that. That's right. That's right, honey. Of course I do. No, Neva's not here. Of *course* I'm waiting for you.

I strolled across the street to buy a pack of condoms, just in case. (Nobody ever trusted that I lacked any disease.) When I got back the transwoman was saying: And if I could, Neva, I'd buy you and me matching pairs of metallic shoes, and then when we went out . . . Have you heard of wax-coated jeans? That's what the high-class models wear.

Shantelle, quite sure that their *tête-à-tête* failed to advance her interests (just as a chief executive officer brought in from a different kind of business will most likely seek to impose what prospered him there upon the unfamiliar realities here—for instance, choke the suppliers into submissive half-suffocation—so Shantelle supposed that when the time came, she, too, could bullshit Neva), said: Come on, Judy. Since when did a model have fat hairy legs? You'd better go puke up some pounds, girl. Go upchuck that greasy life of yours! And get a shave, *Frank*.—Did you hear that, Neva? I said to that bitch, I said . . .

The lesbian looked at her sadly, at which she started flicking the wheel of her cigarette lighter, making the flame thrust up and then go down to nothing, over and over because she was ashamed.

4

Francine had finally paid forty dollars and received her very first medical marijuana card, so she wished to know which strain was the strongest.

Birthday cake, said the transwoman, delighted to know something useful.

Birthday cake ain't *shit*, said Shantelle. What you want's red dragon.

Well, one toke of birthday cake . . .

At the other end of the bar, Hunter was informing unenthusiastic Victoria: And he stuck a five-dollar bill in her G-string, and then he wanted *change*! Can you friggin' believe it? So Xenia posted a picture of this guy on Diddle.com, just holding his money, and she added giant tits and a giant dick. That's how she punished him. And when *I* found out who he was, I texted him—

Unable to endure the rest of us, I went out. The retired policeman was just emerging from Jojo's Liquors with a paper bag of something cheap. He said: Going home?

I don't know.

Have a drink?

Not at the Y Bar. I'm sick of that place.

So we went to the Cinnabar to pay more for the same booze we would have drunk at the Y Bar. He said bitterly: I guess Judy's busy right now.

I haven't seen her dating today, I assured him, not only because it was true but also because I thought to reassure him. Why not? I'm a nice man.

He said: Neva's sure rocking it. She'd look good in anything.

5

I told him my fantasies about Neva, and he said: I don't trust her.

6

He'd bought the first round, so I bought the second. To tell you the truth, I had meant to abstain until tomorrow, or at least bedtime, and the first shot (his favorite: Old Crow) went down badly, burning my esophagus and fizzing my stomach most nauseously, but the second shot killed that, and just when I was fixing to go he said: Carmen! Hey, Carmencita *mi amor!* A double apiece! . . .—which it would have been rude to refuse.

He asked me, which made me sad: So Judy's not dating?

Not that I've seen.

To my surprise, he looked worried. He said: We gotta fix her look.

She looks good, I told him (because what else would I say)?

He said: Don't bullshit me. She's over the hill. Is Neva cutting into her business?

Well, from what I know, she's not in the market.

I said don't fuckin' bullshit me.

She isn't.

A virgin, he sneered, and I said: Maybe the opposite. But here's one of those *facts* you like. Neva pays for all her drinks with hundred-dollar bills. I mean, when she gets change she pays with the change. But then she breaks out another hundred.

What does Francine say?

Tells me to butt out of Neva's business.

He began to sweat, fished in his shirt pocket, and swallowed two white pills with lint on them. That took care of his double, so I ordered us each a triple, and he said, as if he were a real man of the world: I used to believe in nymphos. Now I don't know.

What don't you know?

He breathed in my face. He said: Is Neva a nympho?

I replied: I hope so.—By then I yearned to go home and drink alone.

He said: Does Judy mean anything to you?

She's a good person, I said. I'm not sexually attracted.

I could care less if she blows you. Just tell me if—oh, forget it.—He rushed off to the men's room, wheezing and clutching at his chest. I sat finishing my drink. With Carmen as with Francine, we mostly settled up in advance, so there was no tab to pay; I could have just left. I considered stopping in at the Y Bar just to sit near the lesbian. Maybe I could accidentally on purpose sniff her hair. Instead, I went to the men's room. The door was locked. I tapped on it and called: J. D., are you all right?—As I waited I wondered whether he were dying or dead, in which case would it be right to tell Carmen? For I had a pretty good idea that he wanted to be out of all this. Then I heard his weak voice: Go home, Richard. Piss off and let me be . . .

So I did, feeling pretty good to have acted righteous without incurring sorrow or inconvenience.

I said goodnight to Carmen, who was too well-bred to inquire why my companion remained so long behind that locked door, and went out. Right away I found myself craving the lesbian.

7

Since he and Judy were the happiest couple ever to be disequilibrated by her, not that I lacked my own claims, let me now relate their once-upon-a-time:

A certain Danny Rivas, now deceased, happened to be driving the transwoman and one of her johns to Martinez where they could all go in on a family-sized baggie of semiprime crystal meth; and Danny, being drunk, was weaving on Interstate 80, so the transwoman grew anxious and begged the john to drive, to which he replied: Why don't *you* drive, bitch?—She said: I haven't driven in fifteen years!—at which the two men started yelling: *Shut up and drive!*, so she did, until just outside of Richmond, a black-and-white* began to flash its light discreetly behind them, and they pulled over.—I know you folks are drug dealers, said the officer, who could have passed for some huge, sullen XYY-chromosomed murderer.—I'm no fuckin' dealer! shouted Danny. Can't you fuckin' see what I am? I'm a fuckin' *drunk!* Ain't that rich? I'm a *drunk*, man!

Get out of the car, said the other cop. He had short blond hair.—Over there, he said. Hands on your heads. No, not you, ma'am. Show me your license.

I don't have a license.

Great. Out of the car, but away from them. Over here. Hands on your head.

The transwoman was wearing a hot pink tank top and a black bra underneath it. The officer whistled. He pulled her top out of her shorts and lifted it up to her armpits.

To her friends she cried: Do you *see* what he's doing?

Shut up, said the cop. Then he plopped her breasts out of the cups one by one. He gave each breast a squeeze.—You must be a double D, he said.

The transwoman began weeping silently, loving the humiliation. The john stared away. Danny was on his knees throwing up.

I'm going to book you for possession, ma'am.

Possession of what?

Of *these.* You have any ID?

In my purse, officer.

Where is it?

On the floor, on the passenger side.

You call that piece of crap a purse? Well, it's a free country. Now, is there any sharp or dangerous object inside?

No, sir. My identification's in my billfold.

All right. Oh, I see. *Frank*, your name is. A he-she. Well, you had me almost fooled, but you wouldn't have made it to the polygraph. Double D, Frank! You over there, what's your name?

Reggie Peters.

You have identification?

In my wallet.

---

* Police car.

Take it out. Slowly. Anything but a wallet comes out, you're dead. That's fine. We'll run a check. Now whose car is this?

His.

Sir, what's *your* name?

Daniel Bailey.

Danny boy, I want your ID right now, and don't fuckin' puke on it. Good job. Now, Mr. Peters, is that he-she your special pal?

No, sir.

I saw him winking at you. True love, dude.

No, sir.

Did *Frank* suck you off today?

No, sir.

What about Danny boy over there?

He can't talk no more, officer. He's practically passed out.

Convenient for you, isn't it?

What do you mean?

Don't try to smartass me, you sonofabitch. Now, I know you don't want your little *it bitch* to go to jail.

No, sir.

So what's up? Where's the shit at?

What?

Where's the dope?

We don't have none of that.

You're about as convincing as *she* is.

They searched Danny's car three times. Then the blondhaired officer said: You're not convincing at all, but me and my partner are about to get off, so tonight's your lucky night. *Frank*, you get your faggoty ass in the squad car.

But, officer, I was only driving for ten minutes!

Without a license. Get in the back and don't move. Now, Mr. Peters, your buddy Danny boy's not going to drive this car, because he's intoxicated. I'll overlook the false statement he made about his surname, which is a criminal offense; what do you say about that?

Nothing, sir.

Good boy. And do we let him drive?

No, sir.

What about you?

I won't lie to you, officer. My license—

Correct. Suspended. Driving under the influence.

Yes, sir.

You know what that means?

No, sir.

The he-she goes to jail, and you two compadres start walking. It'll be good for you. Here's your identification, Mr. Peters. And here *you* go, Danny boy. *You!* Up and at 'em! Car's staying here. Now you boys listen: Every time I see you, I'm going to *jack you up*, and next time I see you, you're going to jail. Go on now. *Move.*

The blondhaired officer sat in the driver's seat of the squad car whistling. When Reggie Peters had disappeared around the block and Danny Rivas knelt down to vomit again, the officer turned around, winked through the wire mesh and said: You'll love it in jail, Frank. Plenty of guys who don't care which hole they stick it in.

Licking her lips, her face tear-streaked, the transwoman readjusted her bra. Then she tucked her pink tank top back into her shorts.

While his partner called in her identification card, the blondhaired officer and the transwoman came to an arrangement. Right away he got fat and lost most of his hair. Then he became the retired policeman. That was eight years ago.

8

It was when he reminisced about his greatest arrests that the retired policeman reentered a most perfect equilibrium with himself. There is an element of dreariness in hearing someone repeat a story. Either he tells it as he did before, in which case he bores us, or else he alters the details, which is worse. But the transwoman (I would never dare to guess how many times she'd watched *The Wizard of Oz*) was that rarest of people, an unfailingly appreciative audience. You see, she could never remember any joke well enough to tell it. If someone began to relate what happened to the whore with the glass eye, Judy recollected right away that she *loved* this story, just loved it, although the punchline (*I'll keep an eye out for you any time!*) hovered just out of reach; she could hardly wait to hear the whole thing through again, in order to laugh and laugh! So it went with her master's stories. She listened with shining eyes, feeling so lucky to be in on the doings of authority; and because her receptivity allured him out of his brooding soliloquies, which accordingly became performances, he even found his penis beginning to stir. Usually they were lying side by side in his sagging queen-sized bed. At this juncture she would slip out from under the sheet and kneel on the floor. As he continued, she would continue her pretense of listening—sparing an instant, I admit, in order to fret about her part time position of considerable importance in the restaurant industry (her gaunt old boss, Mr. Salazar, craning forward lizardlike over the cash register, while through the narrow corridor to the kitchen she could perceive the silvery flashing and clapping of a cleaver), because Mr. S. had yet again expressed dissatisfaction with her efficiency and cleanliness—and all the while she awaited the rise of the retired policeman's erection beneath the sheet, which she would then peel back, upraising herself just far enough to worship his crotch.

9

In the Y Bar it was show night again, with the orchestra crackling at high volume and low fidelity, ten seconds into the one and only act of Samantha, who (she said on principle and we said by disposition) never learned anything new; by now I must have seen her routine fifty times. She resembled an ancient Queen Elizabeth I, draped in stinking folds of royal red velvet, who just happened to be lip-synching to Barbra Streisand and pointing up at heaven while she flipped her hips, strutting slowly up and down the narrow aisle with her hand out for dollar bills. Al gave her two, Judy gave her three and I gave her one. The Europeans gave ones and fives. Then came the applause and whistles, with loyal Judy making the most noise while the Germans clapped ironically and filmed it. A man got grabby, Samantha slapped away his hand and then Francine poured me my usual. Lacking a sitting place, I paid and stood waiting for the lesbian beneath the smiling cartoon blonde on the placard that said **CASH ONLY**.

Next starred an almost naked gartered creature of immense doughy breasts and buttocks, who came on waving her long green polyester mane, which hung all the way down to the crack of her ass; Francine informed me that her name was Sunshine and that she came from Wyoming. I wish I could have looked half that good. Shantelle made a face but the Germans simply couldn't get enough Sunshine—who parked her earnings in her cleavage, slipped a banknote to Francine and walked out; I never saw her again.

Just as a pigeon stares expressionlessly (at least to us) out of the side of its bobbing head, so the transwoman, now nodding and fatly tottering in her too-tight high heels, laid her hairy hand on my arm and said: Richard, why don't you ever participate? You'd look *sexy* in a dress. I mean it. You really would.

Since she was ordinarily so shy, I gazed into her eyes and like a good detective verified the hugeness of her pupils. No wonder she was happy.

Guess what? said Judy.

You're pregnant, I proposed.

No, I got a raise! I got a motherfuckin' *raise*!—the truth having to do with the event which she had in truth expected while anxiously wiping each crooked napkin dispenser in hopes of making its stainless steel gleam all the way into Mr. Salazar's approval . . .—but unless she rubbed *really really* hard, the fingerprints remained even if the crumbs came off; and when she addressed that latter problem, the overcrammed napkins, already gripped in place by only three corners, began to leap out, so that Mr. S., turning his head to frown on her, bit his lip, preparing to scold as soon as the line should thin out. Another napkin dispenser without any failure! Judy began to relax. Here came Mr. S., kinder and sadder than usual: Judy, you're too slow. I'm letting you go now. You're a nice gal; I'm sure you'll find something else—

I'm sorry, I'm sorry! Judy sobbed. Oh, Mr. S., I'm so worthless . . . !

Mr. S.'s nephew reached past her to clear away a dirty plate of rice and salad. Mr. S. said: Well, I'm sorry, too. Why don't you go home and rest? I'm paying you for a full six hours, and he opened the register.

But Judy, sickened at the idea of taking advantage, ran away howling.

Mr. S. stared after her. To the others he said: If she comes back, lock the door. That gal's a nut job.

That's not a gal, said the nephew; that's an *it*.

We're all God's creatures, said Mr. S. Now get ahold of Ilona because we need someone for the afternoon rush. If you can't reach her, try those two new applications from Tuesday. What a life.

I had my own news for Judy, but knowing how terribly easy it was to shoot her down, I decided to wait until the end of her act.

Shantelle was on and ready, wriggling her enchanting bottom, raising one leg and flicking off the blackness of her bra; now she was playing with her black, black G-string. Judy would have done anything, I mean *anything*, to look two percent as hot as this star, who now belted out the obscene Marianne Faithfull number "Why D'Ya Do It?" while we laughed and clapped; one Austrian girl even gave her ten dollars. For an encore, hanging upside down from the catty pole, which she gripped with her ankles, twisting as slowly as the fan, she rubbed her breasts round and round in time with the music, flickering her tongue like a snake. We all assumed that she would win tonight's "Most Popular."

Now came poor Judy's turn. I who rarely failed because I kept doing nothing would have saved her if I could, so Francine topped me off and I raised my glass to good intentions. When I looked again, Judy was wriggling her pinkish-red buttocks while her hair whirled around her throat, so that Al and some man I didn't know leaned forward, staring into her prosthetic snatch, and the retired policeman smiled vaguely like a loving father. When Judy Garland starting singing "Somewhere Over the Rainbow," our Judy lip-synched along until the recorded track skipped, then went silent; Francine spread her hands with comic ruefulness, but Judy kept right on slinging us double servings of her big ass and belting out the words in her best hoarse falsetto.

We all clapped, Francine the hardest. Shantelle wanted another turn, which was granted by German acclamation. When Judy came out of the bathroom, dabbing her sweaty face with wads of toilet paper, I said: J. D.'s at the Cinnabar.

Oh! Is he okay?

I think he's unwell.

How bad is he?

Well, he didn't come out of the men's room. He told me to go away.

Withdrawing from that immense handbag her so-called *sensible pumps*, she dropped them on the floor, leaned on my shoulder, switched those for her heels, which she swept up into the handbag, swigged at my drink and informed me: You're a darling.

Thanks, I said.

Then she left. For some reason my double rum and sodapop stopped satisfying me, maybe because my teeth were getting rotten, so I set the glass on the bar, waved to Francine, who didn't see me because it was time to program the jukebox for Xenia's act, gave Shantelle a dollar and went home. If any of my gentlemen readers have ever been fellated (for instance by Shantelle) through a condom, they will appreciate what it was like to live out my story thus far: not unpleasant, with arousal slowly increasing, and the possibility of a climax brightening one's situation, which all the same remains sad and inhuman; because any excitement swells in perfect proportion with miserably insulated isolation.—At least I was free from fixed ideas.

That night the lesbian continued absent. We all craved more, unsuspecting that our best and deepest intimacies with her might merely resemble owning a gemstone and holding it in one's hand until it grew warm, then wanting to be closer to it, *perfectly* close, and necessarily failing. No, to us it seemed simple.

II

The Stream of Pleasure

And first, upon thee lovely shall she smile,
And friendly on thee cast her wandering eyes,
Embrace thee in her arms, and for a while
Put thee and keep thee in a fool's paradise . . .

Sir Thomas More, *ca.* 1505

Authorities and investigators are not in complete agreement upon the point when desire rises to its highest point. This undoubtedly varies in different women, according to age, climate and general environment.

Margaret Sanger, 1926

1

When Judy Garland's ghostwriter visited her at the Doctor's Hospital in 1959 and discovered that her great, hypnotic brown eyes had dwindled into dark spots sunken into the fat and bloat of her face, true love required the absolutely unvarnished transmittal of this condition to us, the adoring public, because we lived for our sadistic satisfactions; and after that gruesome overdose (rigor mortis on the toilet seat, a fittingly disgraceful end to her whom we had jilted for Elizabeth Taylor and Sophia Loren), certain ever-loving fans wandered around humming: *Ding-dong, the Wicked Witch is dead!*—Resisting cynicism, I strove to disbelieve that once the lesbian washed up we would act as nastily as other human beings.

My specialty had always been anticipating final acts. As soon as I first saw Neva, I began wondering how long she would last. Her act was immediately imperiled by her hope of managing us without needing to explain—a planless strategy which actually succeeded for more than a month, thanks in part to our awe of her, not to mention ordinary human incuriosity about the means and causes through which our pleasures got fulfilled; as long as we felt loved, what mattered why or how?

(Anyhow, explanations would also have brought Neva down. To tell one of us anything would commence an unraveling without end.)

So we were already whirligigging down the stream of pleasure—and, keeping in expert practice, I kept watching out for trouble: dreading it, because all change was for the worse; hoping for it, because it would be exciting; and doing absolutely nothing.

In my own vision of the lesbian I who then barely knew her focused most on her mouth. I imagined kissing it for hours. When I thought of her lips slowly opening and her tongue gliding into my mouth (this movie looped over and over inside me), my penis always stiffened. It was just as her predecessor Letitia used to say: we all "objectified" each woman in this or that way. What it was about Neva's mouth I could not have expressed, and when Shantelle discoursed about her buttocks, or Victoria murmured of rolling her over and slowly exploring her back, they became my sisters in obsession.

2

How far her allurements actually extended (or, if you like, what "powers" she had) would make for postmortem gossip whose entertainment quotient approximated that of such questions as who *really* killed President Kennedy and whether Hillary Clinton had ever emulated us; that is, partaken of lesbian love; in any case, Neva's effects and works have been exaggerated. For instance, the retired policeman successfully exploded the legend of Mr. Hamid Iqbal of Larkin Street, who, unable to avoid learning that his wife was a longtime massage parlor prostitute who had married him solely for citizenship, divorced her in outrage but without violence, upon which she filed a restraining order, which led him to reciprocate, impelling her to file a police report the prize of whose inventions was that he had made physical threats against her, which (ours being a just world) led to his arrest, followed by forty days in jail—but for some reason the court dismissed her complaint, so what could the poor ex-spouse do but accuse him of violating the restraining order, in her apartment building, at night, with a nonexistent gun?—This measure proved so magical that Hamid got re-arrested and even re-jailed, if this time for merely thirty-six hours because his loyal brother Hassan wired money all the way from Pakistan to bail him out, and soon that complaint fell likewise into defeat. Fortunately for justice, by then an undercover police officer was getting superb blow jobs from the ex-wife, and therefore marched badged and uniformed into Hamid Iqbal's liquor store to arrest him for the third glorious time! Now Hassan flew to the United States to bail him out in person, and the charges fell away as usual, after which Hamid, concluding that enough was enough, decided against Hassan's urgent advice to murder his ex-wife. Not long past four-o'-clock on that summer morning when he pocketed a knife and set off for his lurking-place across the street from her massage parlor, which would close before five, he happened to look up and—here comes the allegation which the retired policeman so triumphantly disproved—met the gaze of the lesbian, who stood at a third-storey window of the Reddy Hotel, with an unknown woman's arm around her, and instantly, so he is said to have sworn, Hamid Iqbal felt so *loved* by our Neva that he walked away from murder. From what I learned at the Cinnabar over several shots of Old Crow, this much-wronged individual, so he swore by God to the ever-trusting retired policeman, never fostered murder in his heart anyhow; nor had the ex-wife's client, member of the force athough he proudly was, been the hero who accomplished Hamid's third and final arrest; besides, the retired policeman assures me that on the night in question Neva was at my place, and he surely knows me better than I do. The ex-wife, who was as pretty and flexible as our Shantelle, married a drywall contractor from San Bruno; meanwhile it came out that while consoling, counseling and lending money to his brother, Hassan Iqbal had also coached a cousin to lie about a six-month sojourn in Pakistan, which is why both Iqbals *and* their cousin (whose visit had to do with a dying father and whose lie derived from a misapprehension about losing his place in the dreary electronic queue for American citizenship) currently await separate federal trials on terrorism charges.

3

The Y Bar's fame had recently swelled among European tourists, who took selfies there, posing with those overweight American drag queens and T-girls whom they loved to mock but secretly considered more "authentic" than the familiar transvestites of Stuttgart, Lyon and Stockholm; in short, our sleek inheritors began to patronize the place, laughing at how inexpensive were those watery drinks. They ignored our most convincing trannies, the rare mermaidish Filipinas rich in bangs and long hair who favored sequin body suits. Eschewing the laughing, kissing G-girls (who, naked pink and then naked blue in the lights, not to mention obviously high on goofballs—which was why they made the mistake of auditioning here instead of at the Pink Apple—kept whirling round the pole, gaping their mouth in silent laughter while gaping their legs, so triumphantly offering themselves), the Europeans consumed the sadnesses of our homegrown T-girls.

(Why they were also fans of the beautifully serpentine Shantelle, who had so well remade her story, must be explained by her hard greed and violence, which enthralled them like the glamor of Marlene Dietrich.)

It got so crowded on show night that the Y Bar began charging a three-dollar cover, although Francine still let in us regulars for nothing. The Europeans may have noticed, but never complained, because three dollars was nothing for them. And so three dollars became five.

Just before the presidential election, the Y Bar's owner, whose name was a secret held only by Francine and the other barmaid, Alicia, with whom I was indifferently acquainted, decided to remodel, increase prices and stock pricier liquor. (How would he have decorated the place? Imagine a marble Roman tomb teeming with Muses whose masks leak darkness.) I suppose he understood that his success would have driven away us regulars, not that we constituted any loss even to ourselves. As for the Europeans, I'll bet they would have also fled the place in search of grimier holes to slum in. Once our election fell to an uncouth nationalist, they stayed away anyhow, and six months after that, the Y Bar went bankrupt. But in the time of the lesbian there were still foreigners to make cell phone movies of Shantelle, our tall one who could lip-synch so well onstage, her wide mouth and dark dark lips and greenish curly wig towering over the curtain of rainbow tinsel as she sang out: *How many of you are from Sausalito?* None of them ever were. (Tottering drunk, Xenia opined: It's refreshing and it's really nice to see these millennials, as open-minded as they are.—Then she popped two Zingo-Bingo caffeine pills in order to moonlight at the Pink Apple.) *You gonna drive home drunk tonight?* continued Shantelle while Francine dialled down the amplification. *Those cops don't cut a bitch no slack. You wanna just go home with me? Get on top of me? Or ain't that how you* Aryan *bitches do it?*

The Europeans were delighted. How hilariously American that *they* were in our country, sitting in our best seats, while Shantelle couldn't imagine any farther than Sausalito!—Meanwhile, the transwoman became a special comical pet of theirs.

4

After years of trying to pass, Judy still felt something like terror whenever she went out in the street. Being unemployed certainly fertilized her self-hatred. The fact was, even at the Y Bar, where we sometimes tried to love her, she would probably do something else wrong. As it happened, her next mistake might be no demerit at all to her gender performance, which actually tended to surpass her miserable self-evaluations: She was blessed with pretty hair, and once the retired policeman had gotten attuned to her deep yet nasal voice, it became no less feminine to him than any G-girl's. Francine was used to her; Sandra reassured and maybe even believed in her; as for me, the more friendly Judy and I became, the more womanly I found her.—But her loving public watched her mostly for sport.

The lesbian might drop in, wearing, for instance, a snow-white blouse and milk-white jeans, at which the transwoman would say: I wish I could wear white pants. But the trouble is, I'd spill something on them.—This remark would be electronically twitted and twatted all the way back to Germany, with such captions as: UNSERE LÄCHERLICHE HUNDEFRAU KOMMT WIEDER! And when they laughed, she cried, which made them laugh some more. Half the time, she was too far gone to perform her act.

She kept wishing for herself the tilted black-and-white child-face of Judy Garland, whose skin was so smooth and silvery-white, whose eyes knew how to fix on a fellow (or a gal) and whose lips knew how to part as if she were shyly preparing to kiss us all. Unfortunately, that was not how she looked.

But exactly *why* this sex appeal from, you know, Judy Garland? inquired a bespectacled German girl. Because, honestly, I don't feel it . . .—to which Sandra (waiting on the lesbian's arrival) goodheartedly replied: Well, she is a figure that you are introduced to as a child because of *The Wizard of Oz*. For a long time when you're a kid you just know of her as Dorothy. Then you realize that there are other songs and other movies with her in it, so she is a figure that you can age with. There is always an appeal that a tragic movie star has. There's a romance . . .

Sure is! piped the transwoman, wrapping Sandra's long red hair round and round her big hands. (My dominatrix ex-girlfriend once called Judy *invasive*, but Judy really couldn't help it!)—What turns me on about Judy Garland, she continued, speaking far more rapidly and fluently than usual, is *addiction* and *brilliant dishonesty*—

Honey, said Francine, you're flying on goofballs.

I am? And *degradation*, and, uh, *beauty*, and—

Calm down, said Francine.

And did I say *addiction*?

Sandra, is she bothering you? Xenia inquired.

Well, not really. Maybe a little.

I'll get her paranoid. This'll be fun. *Hey, Judy!* I'm telling a story about something that could happen to you. Two gay guys were coming out of the Dive Room in Laguna Honda and they got beat with pipes filled with sand. One died. The judge in the case pretty much congratulated the abuser. And maybe tonight when you're swishing home . . . Oh, but that was back in 1990 or 1991, so don't worry. Nobody's *ever* gonna call you a stinkin' old he-she—

Stop that, said Francine.

Too deep in her groove to be scared, the transwoman continued: And for sure *enslavement* and, and I'm *tellin'* you, *decay*! And above all the *sadness*; ooh, how I love that! And don't forget her groveling for pills from the makeup girl, and hitting on other actresses so she could, y'know, suck their little—

Well, said Sandra with a grimace, I admit that what you're saying could be true, but I find those details something that I don't want to dwell on. Judy, honey, you're messing up my hair. I see the sadness part of it as pure folly and preventable. Judy, would you *please* . . . ? The only thing that I find appealing when I think about the tragic parts, as in Juliet or Guinevere figures, well, there's a certain appeal to children who are overwhelmed by what romance is. I mean, Judy Garland and Marilyn Monroe, and . . .

And *Neva*! cried the transwoman with shining eyes.

Getting excited, Francine butted in: Yeah, I mean, people who had to deal with the casting couch and public adulation and were survivors . . .—Then she flushed and recommenced washing glasses.

Survivors of *what*? demanded Judy.

Well, said Xenia, anyhow there's something infantile about Judy Garland and all those fuckin' stars . . .

The fat transwoman in her smelly spangles, thrilled that the conversation was about *her*, pouted her lips like a baby. She was supposed to be lip-synching to "Somewhere Over the Rainbow" in forty-five minutes, but in half an hour it would take a noose around her neck to keep her upright. Longing to star in one of those establishments in which men would "make it rain" by throwing up one-dollar bills in the air to then precipitate all over the wriggling girl and the stage she twisted on, she forgot all about the lesbian, because Sandra was so beautiful and so smart, and ever so patient, that why couldn't she become Judy's *special friend*?

Sometimes when a customer ejaculated on her face, Judy pretended that his semen was money; when the applause was sufficiently oceanic she might need to lie on her belly and reach under our seats to pick up all the dollars until her personal assistant (perhaps Francine) came onstage with a pushbroom to gather in farther-flung tips. (When she was still a boy her science teacher once said: Frank, do you ever come out of your dream world?)

No, said Hunter, I predict a war between Neva and Shantelle. You see how they look at each other? And Shantelle's gonna win, 'cause she fights dirty.

Don't be preposterous, said Xenia. Neva won't fight.

Judy turned her dizzy head just in time to hear Holly say: Well, now Francine is counseling me. And she gives real good advice, because she—

Gives head, said Shantelle.

You *wish*, said Francine.

When I think about women and movie stars of that generation, continued Sandra (while Judy sat longing to lick up every drop of Sandra's education), I prefer Lauren Bacall, who made a big splash for being sexy but changed with the times; you see, she was somebody who was not a tragic figure but had talent and kept honing her craft—

Gimme *tragedy*! the transwoman shouted, and Sandra laughed and hugged her—which led Judy to forget herself, becoming so grabby with Sandra that Francine had me take her home. She vomited on the way.

5

Whenever she failed to soil herself, one of us could be counted on to insult her. We were not so nice; we led her on. Just as the Wicked Witch of the West was the true friend who slipped Judy Garland her amphetamines on the set of *The Wizard of Oz*, it might fall out when Francine declined to play savior that Snake Goddess Shantelle supplied the other Judy with just the right happiness pills, thereby profiting not only in cash, but also in entertainment, because when the transwoman got high enough, whatever humiliations her loving public inflicted quickly slopped out of her consciousness, so that the fun could continue all night, in the spirit of children torturing a small animal for hours, careful not to let their victim escape into premature insensibility. To tell you the truth, this was more fun than Judy's so-called act.

As for the lesbian, although we longed for her to attend show night, well, strange to say, she most often appeared in mid- to late afternoon, when the clientele consisted of losers like us, with maybe one of those hunter-looking men whose beard and moustache blended together across the bottom of his face like muskrat fur, and his hair clung down his forehead; his dark eyes were alert and somehow gentle, as is characteristic of many hyper-aware people; while our Europeans stayed out on their beautiful bicycles, ascending and descending San Francisco's hills without getting tired, and the affluent bachelorettes and L-girls did time at the office, replying to e-mails, generating "content," selling, creating trends, inspiring motivation and electronically "reaching out" to vendors, clients and hipsters. Longing to help, so that she would truly love me, I warned her: Neva, you're missing the big time! Those evening people could do a lot more for you, because *our* dumb crowd . . .—to which she replied by laying her hand on the back of mine; at which Shantelle signalled that *she* was overdue for attention and Sandra leaned over to whisper: Oh, Neva, with you I can't think straight . . . !—Then Neva went into the dark side of the bar with Xenia.

I wanted Neva back; oh, did I want her! (My own reason for loving her was that I felt we might be related. Having been adopted out for money, I never knew my real kin, but something about her face made me hope that it might be mine, if only around the skull. If after so many years I now began to notice my own face, that was thanks to her. Why she troubled over me I never understood, and the rest of us wondered the same. What we all disagreed about was whether she was easy to love. I mean, we loved her because we could not help it, but how that made us feel was a variable matter.) After she had sipped at Judy's outthrust drink, and compliantly presented an ear to Shantelle's obscene whispers, she returned to me—at which I felt as if everything were burning! My gaze burned; my sense of smell was on fire to inhale her; my thoughts glowed red and yellow with lust. And this fiery feeling kept me company even after I came home to my dinner of microwaved ramen and lukewarm orange soda, after which, too impatient to brush my teeth, I lay down on my unmade bed and happily masturbated, thinking of the lesbian—who presumably still sat in the Y Bar, with her hand on her purse—for how could I imagine her as living in motion without my gaze? (Xenia must have felt much the same when she insisted: Neva, nobody matters but you and me.)

She reminded me of the woman who lap dances some businessman, resting her head on his shoulder even while grinning encouragingly at the couple in the next row . . .—but that didn't stop me from touching myself, while within my closed eyes she smiled eternally like a stone Virgin. By now the outsiders must be striding in, itching to buy Selene a drink or catch Judy crying or post Sandra's saddest mermaid story *ever* on the SpiderWeb. But how could even those jaded entities ignore the lesbian?

6

No, said a Belgian girl who was nearly in Shantelle's clutches. I . . . in fact I feel very nervous. Can't we—can we talk?

A Japanese asked Francine how he could buy a used pair of the lesbian's panties for fifty dollars.—Ask her, she replied. Or else I'll sell you mine for forty-nine ninety-five.

But you're too old, he said.

All right; forty-eight sixty-six, rock bottom price. You can take 'em off me yourself.

But either the humor did not translate, or else he could not be bothered. So Francine opened another Old German Lager for Xenia.

Judy, asked Al, what exactly is a *hot celebrity tip*? You seem like the kind of gal who'd know.

Judy, said a G-girl from Stuttgart, I'm sorry, but on you that's not a good look.

By then Erin was indulging Judy again, unfolding girlhood memories for her to wrap around herself. (Her auditor, especially enchanted by the way that Judy Garland used to prevaricate to her psychiatrist, once thought that she too could get comfort by telling stories to others—Erin, for instance—but could never think of any. So she kept sucking them up like a hungry vacuum.) Like Sandra, dearest Erin could rarely say no to anyone. Truth to tell, she might turn out to be a Plan B *special friend* for when Sandra and the lesbian were both busy. She always hugged Judy hello and goodbye, and sometimes kissed her cheek.

Let's pretend I'm you, said the transwoman. I want to be a teeny little Erin and . . . am I grossing you out?

It's okay, said Erin.

It turns me on to think of you and me as two little girls playing doctor . . .

I had enough of that, said Erin.

What do you mean? I'm sorry. Did I disgust you?

Never mind.

I know I'm disgusting, she blubbered. I'm no good!

Judy, you're my friend, okay? But pretty soon I need to go to work.

Then *tell me* . . . !

About my childhood? Then I have to go.

Anything!

Well, running around in my back yard, said her *almost-special friend*, that's the one I think about most. I used to make mudpies, and we had a chicken coop. I had three little girlfriends in the house on the side of us and one little girlfriend in the house in back of us. They were about my age, about four, five and six. I liked digging in the dirt. We just liked being with each other. Little kids have their own language; they have their own worlds. The little girls on the side of us, they were Mexican; they had dark hair; and then the little girl behind, her name was Maureen; she was just a little girl who looked more like me. You know what's funny is I've had two sets of friends who were in two houses. There's been two sets of three sisters in my life. I got in trouble once, because the three sisters asked me to crawl through the fence and play makeup with them. I said, well, I can't, and they said, well, just come through the fence, so I went missing, and I came back through the fence, and I got a spanking for that. We just put lipstick on; it was just fun. I was four years old; I was beautiful all the time.

You're still beautiful, said Judy.

Oh, *thank you*! whispered Erin.

I wanna be beautiful all the time, said Judy, and then kindly Sandra rescued Erin by asking her to dance.

Xenia, who liked to play hard all-knowing Superdyke, now put her oar in: I'd never take Neva's job. It would be tough; I'd need a break. If I was her and any bitch came swarming around me the way you all do, I would tell her to *slow her roll.* I'd say, bitch, I don't need anybody to behave desperately around me. It's too much.

Francine said: Neva doesn't mind. She loves us.

No, insisted Xenia, it's something else. Who turns down Neva? Not *anybody.* So how can you know what love is if you don't know what rejection is?

That was unanswerable, so we shut up. Pushing away the empty bottle, Xenia rose triumphantly; I think she was hunting for Neva.

7

The cash settlement for my automobile accident four years ago came through, so I bought Francine a drink. (At that stage I still kept supposing that she was somehow trying to use me, not that that offended me.) I looked her in the face. I asked: Have you been with her, too?

Three times.

Okay, I said. (Somehow that made me sad.)

She sipped carefully at her nondescript brown potion (four dollars), which I suspect had nothing to do with alcohol. I asked: What do you get out of it?

She said: For me, being with a woman, I don't care what she has going on downstairs. I'm attracted to her mind.

Since in those days I knew almost nothing about Neva's mind, let alone anyone else's, that slammed the conversation shut, so I said: I guess I'll have my usual.

Special promotion, she said. Two dollars.

I was too surprised to thank her. She winked at me.

8

Her first time had arrived on the day before Halloween. She wore a white latex nurse's outfit with a red cross over each breast.

Now *that's* cute, said Shantelle.

Thank you, sweetie.

You got a medical fetish?

I've been nursing customers all day. Now, have you met Stacey? Look at her! Stacey's *built.*

Men in drab kept hugging and kissing each other. The straight man, who in this tale will be a kind of late-bloomer, sat almost vertical at the bar, with his fingers straining against his sweating forehead, wondering how to make Neva stop torturing us; the torture was making us believe in true love.—Selene was telling Francine: I've had that experience where people just assume you're friends and they wanna give you two beds or whatever, but it's never really been an issue. But there's always like that awkward silence, or that awkward look. When you're getting it all the time, whether it's at the grocery store when you're shopping and holding hands, or down the street and you get those catcalls, it's very draining.—Eight dollars, replied Francine.—Most of the time, wept Shantelle, drunk, I get in trouble, because I . . . , and the transwoman rubbed her shoulders (she was the first of us, and probably the most sincere, whose love drove her into snooping round the lesbian's secrets). Beside them sat a slender young bearded man in a slip, showing the beginnings of breasts.

Francine in her red wig leaned majestically against the bar, while the television offered footage of glowing fried shrimp and fried chicken more orange than a tropical sunrise, after which the lesbian came in.

Yeah, *darling*, said the barmaid, as if to herself.

T-girl Stacey chugalugged her drink, eyeballed the lesbian from hip to breast and said: Francine, you got a *sweet* woman here! You got a sweet woman . . .—and the straight man, staring straight ahead, kept nodding to the music, with his hands on his knees.

What'll you have, Neva?

How about a kiss? said the lesbian, and then Francine's long ovals of cheek blush began to glow like lava.

Well aware that at the Y Bar she possessed friends of a sort, thanks to her power of pouring free extra shots or cutting anyone off from liquor, Francine—who was the only one of us who knew (although all the rest of us should have understood) that once we had sucked Neva dry, she would go away forever, if she were smart and lucky, after which someone else would take the job, until we had sucked *her* dry—had persuaded herself to believe that she lacked any need to be taken seriously, but carried with her as many secrets, needs and talents as any other person; for instance, she had been raped on a high school date, then deliberately gained weight so as to appear less attractive, took up drinking and deliberately accentuated the appearance of middle age. (Now she *was* middle-aged, so I call her a success.)

The way she saw life, there were only hopes and accidents—which is to say that there were many accidents but perhaps only one nameless hope, even though it might appear that a person gave off hopes as numerous as soap bubbles; since all hopes were nameless even when they pretended to carry names, who could count them once they had burst? Why pretend to a diversity of illusions? But if there turned out to be but one single hope, then its seeming murder and reflorescence made for a comedy repeated endlessly . . .—and what finally happened? The desire was achieved, or not. Either way, it silently exploded and was gone. For all Francine could tell, failure and fulfillment echoed exactly the same. Then came the lesbian.

Neva asked what movies she liked and in particular which actresses and performers allured her—for instance, was she enamored of Judy Garland?—Francine was.—Neva asked where she lived, whether she had children and what she thought of Alcoholics Anonymous.

Francine said: There's a restaurant I sometimes go to. It's just plain food, you know, but if you ever want to go there . . . ?

Sure! laughed the lesbian, smiling at her.

And once she finally allowed herself to believe that she was achieving some sort of success with Neva, Francine poured herself a triple shot of cinnamon-flavored brandy, all the better to explain: And me and the other girls used to go to opening nights, when one of us would get in line two or three hours before the movie place opened, so that she could get us four seats right together, and then . . .

Hey, called Shantelle, when the fuck are you gonna freshen my drink?

At five past five, Francine clocked out, and Alicia, nicknamed Bubbles, who was actually less effervescent than jittery, spiderlegged herself behind the bar. Shantelle tried to hoax a free drink out of her, insisting that she had paid Francine, who had for her part withheld satisfaction.—Well, Fran? said Bubbles.

Bullshit, said Francine.

I give up, said Shantelle.

Everybody watched in envy when the lesbian took Francine's hand.

Where the Y Bar stood, partway up the gentle slope of lower Jones Street, one had a decent view down toward Market Street, although the angels and monsters who used to be so plentiful were almost gone now, thanks to the incomprehensible electronic network that allowed prostitutes to offer and accept appointments out of police view if all the more in police records, and thanks also to Stinger and Arthropod and all those other "technology" firms that kept buying up space at imperial rates so that whores like us couldn't compete.

They went out to the plain food restaurant. Francine was too nervous to eat most of her dinner. The lesbian ate almost nothing anyhow. She paid with a hundred-dollar bill.

An old tan and yellow streetcar with rounded corners went hissing and clattering up Market Street where the amplified prophet spoke of myriads of detailed certainties and a man in an old-time hat whose brim was a perfect halo frowned and glided away. The prophet said: *In the end, when we step off this planet, there is going to be a resurrection. Jesus said, all those who are in the grave will hear His voice.*

In a small voice Francine asked: Do you think that's true?

Maybe we're already in the grave, said Neva. But that wouldn't be so bad because we're used to it.

A man in sunglasses and a hooded sweatshirt ambled between pigeons, attached to his cell phone by headphones as the prophet continued: *Jesus said, you know, Jesus said . . . But they threw the bad fish away. That's how it's gonna be on the Day of Judgment. The Living God of the Bible is the God of Love, but He is also the God of Burning.*

Let's burn! said Francine. Then, fearing her joke might not be appreciated, she got quiet, at which the lesbian took her hand, leading past the hooded man who pushed a shopping cart overflowing with blankets, flags, bins, cans and a broom, and so back into the Tenderloin. Finally they went through the Hotel Reddy's steel-ribbed gate and up three flights of carpeted stairs to Room 543; next door Catalina peeked out and waved. Victoria must have been out. Then, oh, God, oh, God, sucking all the spit out of Neva's mouth (every drop as sweet as rainwater), touching her, *touching* her—how could she ever stop?—kissing her ever more breathlessly (or, to tell the story from the lesbian's point of view, *ah*, *ah*, with this new woman's mouth open as were so many of ours, and from its darkness the moist breath of lust panting out) . . . ! And then finally, when Neva undid the first snap of her jeans, Francine squeezed her desperate fingers in, working them down the smooth downy roundness of Neva's belly until she . . . and all the while she and Neva kept kissing happier and hotter as if life would *never* get cold!

At dawn the lesbian promised her: You and I will always remember the things we did to each other.

9

Then it was Xenia's turn.

I'm pretty bad at receiving oral sex, she instructed Neva. I don't get off.

What will we do?

We'll use toys, and our hands and our straps.

Okay, said the lesbian.

10

You only want me to visit for a short time because you're very very busy and not because you don't love me, right? said Sandra.

That's right, sweetheart, said the lesbian.

11

When she first met the lesbian, Sandra had flushed red like Judy. Without knowing how she knew, she understood straight away that Neva was the mermaid of her dreams. In that first stage of infatuation, when what fills us is sheer desire for the beloved in her mysterious coherence (what she might think or need becomes no part of the picture), Sandra, again like Judy, could barely keep herself from fondling and embracing her prey. And Neva smiled. Here came their first time, and their tenth. Later she could scarcely remember what the lesbian had done to her.

Like many lonely people, Sandra longed to offer herself completely, and sometimes made the mistake of submission to self-sufficient or even selfish people who used her without respect. Worse yet, once she had committed herself, she feared inflicting pain; so she kept her lovers, then cheated. (I was much the same.) But with Neva her luck came up quadruple sevens. And when I consider her greater role, as yet unknown to her—but let me whisper that it would be thanks to her and the straight man that Neva finally escaped over the rainbow—I can only sing *Amen.* At this time Sandra merely noticed—gratefully!—that here was someone as bountifully, inhumanly selfless as she herself had tried to be. And so her dreams enriched themselves.

Frank S. Caprio, M.D., that great heterosexual who knew everything about female inverts *(Hostility is an emotion common to lesbians. I knew a lesbian who threatened to kill a roommate if she continued to go out on dates with a certain man)*, would have diagnosed her adoration as a dangerous case of lesbian-thespian complex. Imagine, for instance, our shy, lovely and unloved Sandra being invited backstage to the *real* Judy Garland's dressing room . . . ! You'll remember that Judy went both ways! Then what? Oh, those Judy Garland eyes, and that smooth white Judy Garland skin, and . . . *The young aspirant to a career in the world of the theatre,* explained Dr. Caprio, *may overtly express her extreme admiration of her idol and invite an intimate relationship. Conversely, . . . the successful actress finds narcissistic gratification in assuming the maternal role towards a beautiful young girl who worships her. The relationship becomes a neurotic one and serves to gratify unconscious, incestuous wishes by the young girl to feel secure and close to a mother surrogate. At the same time, it affords the actress an opportunity to gratify her neurotic, narcissistic need to be adored and loved.* Oh, my! *Unconscious, incestuous wishes!* Not to mention *assuming the maternal role*! Didn't that capture everything about our sick, sick

Neva, who was so infected and hence so dangerous? I promise that this will be a cautionary tale—

Sandra dreamed of oceans, and of a great rock which snowed birds upward and downward. But she was not allowed to visit the rock just yet. It was near enough to be seen from shore, as a greyish-beige mountain on the ultramarine horizon. She discovered that she was a little girl. She wanted something, but what was it? On that cloudy summer evening under a vast chestnut tree, there came the thrilling stately skirl of pipes, and her mother stood in the grass with her little Sandra on her shoulders. Sandra wished not to be so little, and so just as the drums commenced clattering she became one of six young girls in tartan skirts who began to twitch their slender legs, enthralled into dancing. The easy freedom of this change delighted her. Looking up through the chestnut leaves and into the white sky, Sandra sought something, maybe a bird, but nothing came to her. And then, straight ahead of her, through the bars of the wrought-iron fence she saw Neva gliding near, flexing her wrists as would a seal her flippers, and the coolness came up from the grass as drumbeats descended like grapeshot while Sandra and the other young girls bent their knees, jigging up and down on the grass, courteous and stately, with their topknots always vertical, facing each other. Neva passed through the fence, and the grass did not bend beneath her feet. Now the young girls upraised their white arms and opened their fingers, leaping so beautifully and carefully when Neva came (but in her dream Sandra leapt the best); then the drums ceased and a seagull cried thrice while a wood pigeon cooed glottally. Neva took Sandra in her arms. The girl felt so loved and safe, so warm, maybe just a trifle aroused—and hopeful, yes; everything good could happen! Drums rolled; bagpipes blared and wailed, and Neva carried her up into the air, beyond the white arch, past the herb garden and the aviary over the long path through the wheatfield that led round and round the volcanic cone called the Law, past the wild horses and into the fragrance of the sea-wind. Below and behind them, some girl, maybe Judy, was tittering like a gull, while cumuli oozed over the high-grassed dunes. Sandra's life had become perfect. Easily and rapidly she rode in Neva's arms. Crossing the boundary-strata of blackened kelp and then such soft sand as one could have happily laid a head on, they flashed across the sea, toward that great bird-rock which grew taller and whiter with nearness. And the sea went green, with its great bird-rocks going likewise green ahead of them and the wind freshening; while Neva carried her higher and higher. Sandra tried to kiss her mouth, but Neva's face was far away. Seagulls boiled around them in the white sky. Now they began descending into the pissy stink of the guano-whitened gannet island, where it snowed birds upward and then downward into the dark blue sea and a fat white seal waved his flippers. Neva was rushing down; their hair shot straight up over them, and they landed in a narrow dark cove. Again Sandra tried to embrace her lover, but Neva slipped silently right through her, hurtling high to vanish among the gannets and gulls. And everything felt suddenly so cold, and Sandra had lost everything! Comprehending that the dream could change at any minute—Neva might even return to her—the abandoned girl tried to be brave. And now from the receding sea, in the softness of the reddish-tan sand, a naked mermaid arose, wide-eyed. She was beautifully outstretching her arms to Sandra, but she was not Neva.

12

Shantelle, watching the lesbian's long pale hands, used to fall speechless. (I remember Shantelle on the bus, shouting on her cell phone in order to be heard: *No*, because I just didn't realize that the bus schedule got cut back, so I . . . *No*, I just told you that's the reason I'll be late, because when my case worker said . . . *No*, that's not acceptable; I can't miss a visit with my kids. Yes, ma'am, I do admit that last week I was five minutes late, but that was because . . . *No*, I already said I can't help the fact I'm gonna be half an hour late, because this motherfuckin' bus . . . But how can you *do* that to me? That ain't right. You know what? That just ain't right, to keep me from meetin' my kids. Well, whatever. I'll talk to my case worker. And, ma'am, I just wanted to say to you, *you* are a fuckin' *bitch*.) Al and I both agreed that the blue spangles on the lesbian's black dress scintillated like magnified galaxies, burning our eyes. (*Her* eyes seemed to love everyone!) All of us wished to approach her more closely, and perhaps to lick her arms and shoulders—although Al's bravery left him whenever he acted on it. Neva allured us with the shocking brightness of a gold coin in a silver hoard. Sooner or later we each succumbed, like the Nebraska farmer who was sent tantalizing pedophilic mail-order catalogues by disguised entities of the United States Government until he finally signed up for one of their offerings, and got convicted.

We all busied ourselves at arranging our ideas of her, mostly in secret but sometimes with each other's convivial help, into more distinct icons to adore, these being less accurate likenesses of her than thrilling first impressions, but more substantial all the less, on account of their gilded frames: Neva and her narrow-lipped shining slit . . . and Selene with her arms and legs laid out limp around her . . . and Shantelle slapping her own face involuntarily or not . . . and Erin, who usually did not want the lesbian to put anything inside her; she sat up straight in her little black nightdress, which was pulled up above her navel, and could not stop licking the corner of Neva's half-opened mouth, round and round and round with her head lolling back and her eyes not entirely closed, while the lesbian licked Erin's slit, up and down, up and down, until quite soon and suddenly Erin screamed. From the lesbian's point of view it might have been tiresome when we got so exalted that we kept repeating ourselves and then forgetting the punchlines of our stories, expressing our unique loves less brilliantly than we imagined, stinking up Neva's mattress with our sweat. But when we compared notes in the Y Bar we felt like collectors trading rare and beautiful stamps from Central Africa.—It is from these discussions (so many of them thanks to the retired policeman) that I know so much about how we all loved—and whenever I arrived at my quotidian ignorance, I'd lie, fantasize, invent, as I would certainly need to do if I worked in pretty Raquella with her choker of plastic pearls, her plastic pearl earrings, her black scarf, her bustier striped silver and gold and her black hair waved just so. Francine called her *a real class act*; why she said so is beyond me; I saw Raquella at the Y Bar only half a dozen times, in that first July and August, then never again; I do remember that unlike Shantelle, she could not refrain from reaching out to caress the back of the lesbian's hand. But I never learned much about the shape and quality of Raquella's love . . .

13

Once Francine took in the effect that the lesbian was having on us all, she felt, in her words and Judy's, *disgusted*; on the other hand, as she presently confided to me most ruefully: Well, even before my first time I could already imagine going down on her, just licking and sucking and sucking and *licking* until . . . Seven dollars. Actually, sorry, I mean eight dollars.

I paid, and Neva came in.

Seven dollars, said Francine.

Okay, said the lesbian, withdrawing a hundred from that sealskin pouch.

Here's your change, hon.

You keep it, said the lesbian.

Francine put it away, saying nothing. Neva was taller than she had seemed, and maybe not as young, not that it mattered. Francine poured herself a bourbon and soda. Samantha's drink did not yet require attention; that lady sat lip-synching to Barbra Streisand. In the corner, a bald Dutchman was negotiating a date with Judy.

Earth to Francine! cried Shantelle.

What?

Gimme a triple.

Fourteen dollars, big spender.

And less ice. You're rippin' me off with that ice.

The rule is two cubes. If you want one cube, you'll get more air.

Just for once, why not go less stingy with your booze?

It's not mine.

Then why the fuck do you care? Come on, Fran. Pour it up to the top.

That's four extra shots, and I'm not Fran. Twenty dollars.

Forget it.

Then you want a triple and an ice cube. Fourteen dollars.

Then gimme all my ice.

Two cubes?

No. I want three.

There you go. Fourteen dollars, said Francine.

Then the transwoman looked up and abandoned her Dutchman. Seeing Neva, she felt as happy as Judy Garland on morphine.

14

Because she loved the fair sex even more than I do—enough to become a member—the transwoman is one of my heroines. Moreover, what the lesbian did to her, not that I entirely understand it, was so extraordinary that her story might as well come first as well as last. Besides, I heard its most salacious details from her, so why not infect you with the virus? Although neither of us drinks as much as when Neva was alive, we still toast each other now and then, usually at the Cinnabar. I think of her as my little sister, and she thinks of me as someone who would be better off dead.

From what she later told me, I gather that she meant at first not to tell the retired policeman, who anyhow also kept or at least used to keep Melba, that old diva who could still smile fetchingly although it cracked her paint to do it; for a drink and a stinking kiss she aided him in his projects, which was why Judy vengefully concluded that a girl's dates were her own business. In short, she confessed no sooner than she had to.

Meanwhile, like the stripper who wears a T-shirt and nothing else, squatting over the jukebox to choose the toniest accompaniment for her act, while coincidentally marketing her low-hanging fruit, our Judy now most thoughtfully schemed out her debut with Neva—because sooner or later it had to be her turn!

First of all, she had hopes that the lesbian would be allured by the broad shoulders and male strength of transwomen, and perhaps just a little by their masculine smell—because wasn't Neva attracted to anything?

Judy could barely decide what to wear, much less how to act. Unlike Erin, she had never been beautiful all the time. But Himmel's department store had agreed to try her out on Monday, which thickened her confidence. So why not get her hooks into Neva? In the end, she followed the advice of her namesake: *Most of all, on a date I think a girl should be* herself . . . *I've had my moments when I thought I'd try to act like Marlene Dietrich or even Garbo. And then I'd figure that it was my natural self, such as I am, that attracted my date in the beginning . . .* Whether her "natural" self possessed any exchange value whatsoever is a sterile question, by which I mean that Judy Garland couldn't have answered it, either. But that famous photograph of Martina Navratilova at Wimbledon in 1978 was another confidence-builder: that face was unafraid of *anything*! If Judy could only lose weight, be beautiful and make muscles like Martina's . . . !

Hating herself as usual, she could not even introduce herself, but it so fell out that Victoria, who owed her twenty dollars and moreover was growing more night-social, almost chatty, finally (while the rest of us merely laughed at the way Judy kept trying and failing not to look at the lesbian, much as she so often unsuccessfully essayed not to steal our pills), took her hand, led her up to the bright side of the bar, and placed her hand in Neva's. Neva smiled then. She kissed Victoria's forehead. Victoria flushed and turned away.

Hi, said Judy.

Hello again, said Neva.

Do you remember the first time we met? I bought you a drink at Selene's wedding, and . . .

Her idol smiled a little, squeezing her hand.

I've heard about you, said Judy. I mean, I've heard even more. And, gosh. People say things . . .

Oh? said the lesbian.

That you're wonderful and everybody loves you. Are you beautiful all the time?

I'll try, said the lesbian.

At Selene's wedding the transwoman had been spared any obligation of describing herself, her lonely employments or her sad life. What now? She longed to stroke the fine hairs on Neva's arms.

Literalizing what she romanticized, she had pictured her idol as dwelling somewhere as high up the hill as Mason and California, where one can gaze down into a narrowing canyon of lights all the way to Market Street and the light-riddled ridge of darkness behind it, all the while half-listening to the cable car wires scraping like knives on whirling whetstones; and the Fairmont Hotel would be, at least in her expectations and recollections, eternally decked out in rain-glossed Christmas lights.

In fact, as do most divinities, the lesbian lived practically around the corner.

15

And so Neva took her upstairs, sat her down and asked her what she would like to do, or possibly have done to her.

It was not so much what Judy replied as how she said it that stimulated her hostess's intuition; within a twinkling she knew exactly what needed to be done, and did it, folding her new sweetheart into her arms.—Judy, of course, began to weep silently. She said: Oh, Neva, I—I feel so loved! . . .—which at that point meant *seen*.

And the lesbian kissed her lips. The transwoman was ashamed to open them, but the lesbian kept gently, patiently licking between them, until she finally let the lesbian's tongue into her mouth.

16

Judy's mouth stank. The lesbian endured that, because she needed so much to make this sad person happy!

17

A certain half-great writer who was also a half-great Fascist used to divagate about this wave of pleasure or that stream of pleasure; when it rained pleasure his characters got drenched right to their bones; when pleasure seeped out of the sewers it invaded them through the soles of their feet, creeping up their legs in an inverse of the way it left them when they had finished being high on ecstasy pills; and so once upon a time a nubile heroine of his experienced a *stream of pleasure rising up her arm and spreading across her chest and insinuating itself into her most intimate fibers*, as if pleasure were an electroid current, composed of clitoral electrons, conducted from one body to another, through human tissues. Certain apoplectics have described their attacks using comparable tropes.—It started in the fingers of my left hand, said an old fellow who used to be me, and it rushed up my left arm, into my shoulder and up my neck; I was talking on the phone with my lesbian friend, and once that feeling reached my head I couldn't speak, or understand what she was saying . . .—Just this experience now took hold, with coruscations of pleasure rushing from the lesbian's fingers into the transwoman's upper arm, down into her fingers and back up into her shoulder, the current presently dividing in order to tingle inside her breasts until her hardening nipples seemed to be spewing out sparks in the manner of Roman candles.

Too good, it seemed—a divine visitation, which at any moment would leave Judy high and dry forever. But it stayed inside her, every moment she was with the lesbian! After awhile it even began to be hers. *And then I'd figure that it was my natural self, such as I am.* I liken her to some casual swimmer who, gulled by those smooth green waves which seem perpetually available to return anyone and everyone to the sandline, faces outward, approves of the horizon and breaststrokes toward it for the merest moment or two, then back-floats, enjoying the clouds . . . only to realize that she is now far, far away from the cove where her friends lie happily on their towels; already she has passed the wide-lipped lava caves; she is being carried out to sea! So she turns back toward shore and begins to swim, not too hard at first, because she had better not tire herself out with nobody here to help her; nor does she verify her progress often, in case its slightness would discourage her; but after, say, a thousand strokes it would be reasonable to raise herself up—and she has gone nowhere! A little anxious now, she rolls over and backstrokes, which she knows she can keep up for a long time, thanks to the happy buoyancy of big-breasted chubby people. She gently sculls and determinedly kicks, trying to keep calm. After all, she isn't getting out of breath. After five or six thousand strokes she looks up again, and now the beach is closer, but not much . . . and in this one moment she has already begun to be pulled back out to sea. Knowing better than to panic, she rolls over once more, backstroking steadily and resolutely, sculling more powerfully, kicking faster, and after a very long time, worrying and tiring, she looks up; this time the shore is sufficiently close for her to see the miniscule silhouettes of waders and sunbathers. Thus encouraged, she gets on her back again and keeps at it until she is nearly out of breath. Now she can see the colors of people's bathing costumes; she is almost as close in as the farthest surfer. All but one of the lava caves are seaward of her. But she needs to swim more powerfully, because here the undertow is very strong, so she resorts again to the breaststroke, putting her heart into it until she gasps. She should be close enough now to touch bottom with her feet, but she isn't. Dispirited most of all by the monotony of the work, she pants on. Much later than she ever would have imagined comes the moment when she can stand up in the surf. For awhile she rests there, while the green waves strike between her shoulders, sometimes almost knocking her down. Then she begins to wade out of the ocean. With each step she grows safer but also heavier, and when she finally reaches dry sand, with seawater rushing from her hair and her bathing suit, she feels as if she were sinking into the earth.

So it was for the transwoman when, having embarked on a deceptively easy swim into the currents of womanhood, she finally came back home into the lesbian's arms.

Two hours afterward, in the miraculously eternal present which would shelter her whenever she was with the lesbian, they lay side by side with their legs wide open, and as she whirled her middle finger round and round the little hard bullet of the lesbian's clitoris and the lesbian began to pant and lick her lips even as her right hand slid sweetly up and down the transwoman's towering penis, there came one of those moments so familiar to devotees of recreational drugs; and just as a military veteran rarely confides his memories of horrific killing and dying to anyone but another veteran, so the psychedelic veteran locks his insights away from sober people, whose inability to understand too often expresses itself in laughter or contempt; indeed, these experiences lie nearly as far beyond the reach of verbalizing as any color does; whoever has never seen red can by reading multiple descriptions achieve a practical intellectual understanding—it is associated with, for instance, blood, lips, vaginas—but to experience a steady laughing warmth around one's heart after seeing the lesbian's mouth would exemplify an entirely different order of understanding. And so it is with chemically induced realizations, hallucinogenic spiritual visions and extreme sexual experiences. What the transwoman felt when she and the lesbian were masturbating each other would have seemed if stated directly as drearily quotidian as a shimmering pebble withdrawn from the brook and left to dry into dullness; so I must now fail unless I can somehow write beyond or around myself, but let me try: It seemed an absolutely certain fact that even as she felt the lesbian's clitoris and the tiny V-shaped wall of flesh above it and the shining smooth wet plain of pink skin below it, she felt what the clitoris was feeling; she experienced the lesbian's pounding heart and happy rushing urgent excitement as that middle finger graced her faster and faster, and she could feel what the lesbian's right hand was feeling as it so tenderly and correctly caressed her penis's smooth skin; she and the lesbian had become each other even as they continued to be themselves, although all there was to both of them was moving hands and excited sex organs; mouths, eyes, breasts, hearts, brains and straining thighs existed only in some subsidiary sense; in short (and here is where the glistening pebble goes dry), she felt an absolute if deeply narrow oneness with the other woman. You or I can shrug. How often have we dismissed such portentous assertions? My friend, unless something like this happens to you, you will never believe. The transwoman did, of course, and their union went on and on. They neither climaxed nor needed to; what they felt was less intense than an orgasm, but *wider*: a steady and apparently endless stream of pleasure.

18

Once they separated, Judy decided to break her date with the retired policeman so that she could lie down in her room alone, thinking about the lesbian.—What normativizers might consider a weakness, namely, her tendency to dream herself through life, was actually her help and strength, because why not sidestep the so-called "real questions" if their answers would only prove one's helplessness? For instance, the lesbian's beauty, instead of discouraging her, made her thirsty to try to lick it up—as if that were possible!—For a long time she felt a remnant of that strong and steady bliss which had warmed her in the lesbian's arms and lingered as a kind of peace. It seemed as if she could stay awake all night, taking stock of what she had made of herself and who she ought to be. That feeling lasted on and on, as apparently durable and reliable as a wide stone ledge. She went out into the hallway, raised the greasy windowshade, which was smeared with commemorations of bygone houseflies and cockroaches, and looked into the darkness. The feeling was still there; perhaps she could trust it. Although she had begun to feel cold, her hands and face still glowed, because they had been so close to the lesbian. After awhile, she returned to her windowless room, locked the door and stared into the mirror above the sink. She granted that she was ugly, but at least she was trying to be who she was. Her temples began to ache. She lay down on her back, remembering the lesbian. Her feet felt colder, and perhaps that trustworthy feeling had lessened a trifle, or somehow descended. Her hand still smelled like the lesbian's cunt, and that comforted her. Her certainty of union remained, but the sensation of bodily transference had gone to join all her past climaxes: schematically remembered at best, the unique feeling gone forever. Now she felt cold around her heart. Undressing, she brushed her teeth, moisturized her face, hands, shoulders, legs and chest, combed out her hair and shaved her bristly chin. She was sweaty, but her body might still retain the lesbian's scent, so she declined to shower. Her nightgown had once been bridal white; now it was grey. She pulled it over herself. Just then her phone began buzzing. It was the retired policeman, so she let it ring. When it stopped, she turned it off. Then she got under the sheets. Staring at the ceiling, she touched herself, pretending that her hand belonged to the lesbian, but it didn't feel that way. She switched off the bedside lamp. After a dismal five minutes she switched it on again, sat up, pulled her purse off the vanity, snapped it open, and felt around among the tissues new and used, the old bus passes, the keys and condoms, until she found the retired policeman's bottle of tranquilizer pills, two of which she dry-swallowed. Then she turned out the lamp again. It took a long time before she began to feel sleepy, but when that sensation came it was delicious.

She woke up late in the morning, with a headache, shivering, nauseous and desperate. Unable to endure herself, she sat on the toilet weeping.

By noon the retired policeman had given her a black eye in the interest of *crime control*, after which they made up, by means of her opening herself and receiving pain like a true woman; then she arranged a second date with the lesbian.

19

Next came Hunter's turn. She sat nursing her usual (a double Slambang over ice), while Selene was telling Francine: We also had this understanding that when we were grocery shopping at certain places, we wouldn't hold hands. With a lot of Latinos around or children around, we wouldn't. If we were with friends, it was okay. If we felt that we weren't safe, then we wouldn't do it. We would wait until we got home and to the car. Even with family we weren't intimate.

Eight dollars, said Francine.

I'm more open about it now, said Selene. I think if it makes more people uncomfortable, too bad. We give heterosexual couples the liberty of doing what they want. Now it's about, if it's little kids, they need to see that that's normal.

Hunter finished her drink. She drummed on the counter. Finally the lesbian came in.

Xenia would fuck anything, which made Hunter bitter and jealous; this first time with Neva had been intended foremost to punish Xenia—who of course was simply proud that they would both get to compare notes, as if they were sharing a likely seafood dish at the Cambodian restaurant on Hyde Street.

The bathroom door opened, and the lesbian came in, saying: Here's a nice clean towel.

Admiring the sweet rounding of her abdomen, Hunter wondered once more whether or not the lesbian was herself or performed herself, and if there was a difference.

As for Neva, when she had undressed the other woman, she found her plumper and still more fairskinned than she had appeared in her leopard-print dress, and the nipples on her big breasts were charmingly small and pink without any areolae; one by one they hardened on the lesbian's tongue. The two of them started kissing. With her habitual quickness the lesbian realized that Hunter wanted first to kiss more than be kissed, so she opened her mouth and let Hunter very shyly explore it with lips and tongue. She slid her middle finger between Hunter's legs. Hunter was still wearing her leopard-print panties. The lesbian glided her finger back and forth on the smooth polyester until it was dripping wet.—Please, Hunter, she whispered, let me eat your pussy now . . .—And in the sweetest possible frenzy, Hunter jerked her panties down and threw them onto the floor. Her vulva was compact and small-lipped, with a short blonde fringe on either side. Happily closing her eyes, the lesbian began to do as her mother had taught her. Soon Hunter, who reminded me of the violated woman who above all indignities never forgot coming downstairs from the rape crisis center as the mailman ascended, looking up her skirt, was sighing as if from far away, and when she climaxed the noise she made was what a child would hear in a seashell.

Although few would dare accuse the gods of misleading us, given the disparity between us and them in knowledge, not to mention mortality, who would deny that they withhold nearly everything that we foolishly long to learn? I for one feel grateful to go on in ignorance of my death-particulars; and if awareness of my shabby love-destinies fell upon my upturned head, would I be better off? In any event, when we beg, assert, declare and declaim to the Goddess, she most often replies with a smile of heartbreaking neutrality. And exactly that smile now met Hunter when, lying sleepily in the lesbian's arms, she asked: Neva, do you mind if I ask you something?

Go ahead, honey.

How many other lovers do you have?

And the lesbian smiled.

I mean, if it makes you uncomfortable . . .

Not so many. And I don't love any of them the way I love you . . .

. . . Which was to say (expressing the matter in purely physical terms) that whereas most of the other women were best fulfilled at the very beginning, by cunnilingus, Hunter needed extra time and *gentle* time, multiple acts of penetration, usually begun by her sitting astride the lesbian, riding the big dildo up and down, slowly moaning, bending down to kiss her, and then, forgetting everything but the motion, sitting straight up to feel the sensation most deeply, while the lesbian gripped her breasts and sucked her nipples or her throat just the way she liked it; her moans would enrich themselves and she would be smiling; then she would get tired and it would be the lesbian's time to lay her down on her back and ride her missionary style, kissing and kissing her gaping mouth, while the first climax came. They would rest awhile, cuddling and whispering, and then the lesbian would do it again, on which occasion Hunter would get quickly to the point, crying out: oh, my *God*!

And after many sessions, Hunter had overcome her shame so that she too could enjoy cunnilingus. More than nimble, she now embraced Neva with the seemingly boneless flexibility inherent to ballerinas.

They arose that morning, just about the time that Judy was dressing up for her tryout at Himmel's department store, and while Hunter was in the shower the lesbian was already stripping the bed; she had two more pairs of sheets, but the mattress needed to air out before her next lover came. She got everything in the laundry hamper just as the bathroom door opened. How soon she would again be giving and giving of herself was not for Hunter to know. The transwoman was titillated by knowing, while the retired policeman and I both collected facts of all kinds for a hobby; but for just the same reason that I preferred not to foresee my death, so Hunter would rather not face the details of her own non-uniqueness.

Well? said Xenia.

Oh, my God, said Hunter. It was so unbelievable. My clit is still vibrating . . .

Didn't I tell you? I'm always stressing the *sexual emotion.* That's the key about being with women, and Neva—

Are you saying I don't know about being with women? The truth is—

Why get pissy? said Xenia. You fucked her; so did I; now come over here and we'll fuck each other.

Hunter said: I don't know which of you I'm more jealous of.

Double-thickening her mascara, Xenia smiled and said: I think jealousy's *hot.* And power and desire will always be hot—

20

We called Neva the bodhisattva—or, if you prefer, the saint who after dying and being rewarded with heaven could not endure to stay there, but, true to nature, set out straight for hell to be with the eternally afflicted and oppressed. But why? Maybe her childhood defined her, in which case she was merely masochistically twisted.

Aquinas distinguishes between love as an appetite and love as a willed act. What the lesbian offered was the second.

So far the retired policeman lacked a theory as to who or what she was. But for a fact, he disbelieved in bodhisattvas. Not one had ever submitted to a polygraph test.

The first suspicion that his bitch might be changing on him descended on a hot Sunday afternoon in early September at the vegetarian Chinese restaurant on Kearny Street, where he, ordinarily carnivorous, sat drinking jasmine tea and picking over his cashew-decorated mock chicken, watching the doorway's tiled tunnel across which a tall old grey-clad Chinese gentleman whose shoes appeared much too large for him slowly crept, with his cane outstretched before him at a rigid vertical.

As the cars trolled by, the translucent glass horse on the windowsill temporarily darkened.

The cashews in his chicken dish were nearly as rare as semiprecious stones in a sack of highway gravel.

He felt irritated that Judy was late because now they would miss that midafternoon rerun of a certain forensics television show that he liked to watch lying in bed with his upper half raised by pillows to a forty-five-degree angle and Judy beside him, nestling her head in his armpit while he explained that the episode of the man who for cash had faked his wife's suicide by stabbing her (afterward for the sake of orderliness shooting the supposed rapist whom he and she had invited over to play at bondage threesomes) could not have happened as presented, in proof of which he referred her to the bloodstain patterns, never mind that the supposed double murderer from the way he used words and his manner of very slowly blinking must be saddled with a low IQ.

The instant he took his first swallow of tea, his belly began to ache. Although he chewed the brown rice, celery, carrots and vegetarian chicken very slowly, his ankles rapidly swelled, tingling icy-hot as they so frequently did now; something must be seriously wrong with him, so fuck it.

When Judy became an hour late, he went home.

The dread or anger he felt rose up inside his throat, in the form of hot acid. (But I do have a long slow fuse, he congratulated himself.) Without looking, he fiddled on the bedside table, groping for his stomach tablets. His hand was a fat grey-haired crab decorated with age-spots. Encountering the paper-wrapped tube it had sought, the crab squatted down, pinched out three pills and clawed them into his mouth. He chewed and chewed with commendable patience. Finally he swallowed. Now he could forget about his throat.

Groaning, he bent over to tie his shoes. This operation made his waistband cut into his paunch, so that he had to hold his breath.

He found his keys, turned out the light, double-locked the door behind him and limped downstairs. Actually his feet were scarcely puffy at all just yet; what a wonderful life. Conquering the limp, he strode into the Y Bar just as little Erin skittered out. Alicia, the junior barmaid, was on shift.

Where's Judy? he said.

I don't know you, sir, said Alicia. Are you a regular?

Looking around, he saw Shantelle, who was dancing in the corner, with her earbuds in. He diagnosed methamphetamine. Hobbling toward her, he crooked a finger.—She lifted away one earbud; some kind of blues thumped tinnily out of it like the heartbeats of an insect robot. She knew what he wanted, and he knew she loved to tattle.

Your old lady's out and *about* with Neva, she informed him. And you know what, J. D.? I don't trust either one of them motherfuckin' bitches.

Who would? he said.

Sir, said Alicia, if you want to stay here you have to order something.

I order you to suck my cock, he said, which gave Shantelle a fit of the giggles. Wavering over to him on skyscraper heels, she said: *I'll* suck your cock for twenty dollars.

But are you a virgin?

Oh, baby, I am!

Now what do you have against Neva?

What call does she have to keep doing her business for *nothing*?

Sir, said Alicia, you need to go now.

Glad to, he said, because Shantelle had as usual concisely and constructively analyzed the situation. Now his mind had something to do.

He plodded up the hill to Pho Truong and treated himself to a bowl of brisket soup with cilantro and sprouts. After two bites he remembered that he had just eaten vegetarian chicken and that his belly was no good. Then, as a reward for having done something healthy, he went to Jojo's Liquors, where the Palestinian clerk slid over his fifth of Old Crow. Then he started creeping home.

Hey! called Shantelle, clattering toward him like an untuned Model T.

Hey, what? he said. You're out of your zone. Won't broad daylight kill a girl like you?

Help me get that motherfuckin' Neva off her. That would be good for you, I swear—

Don't pretend you care about me.

C'mon, babe, you know I do.

When you lie, you look even more like a goddamned vampire.

She started whining.—I want Neva to myself! Judy keeps hogging my turn, and I want—

Honey, I need to lie down, he said, and Shantelle, amazingly, read his grey face and comprehended that he did.

He had almost reached the front grating of Empire Residences, which is to say home, when she came dancing back.—*Please*, J. D.! Pull your bitch off my bitch.

How? he said.

Talk to Judy. *Tell* her! Beat her flabby ass.

What's so great about Neva? Just curious.

Just tell your Judy to lay off, 'cause I—

Get back to your graveyard, he said. Oh, Jesus, my head hurts.

Wisely he proceeded upstairs by elevator. Then he lay down on his back; the bed creaked. The headache kept savaging him. Fortunately, he had preserved half a Narcocaine (a purchased souvenir of Francine), so he chewed that up and waited. He kept waiting.

Finally he dialled up Francine.

John Daniel, she greeted him. That's what it says on my caller I.D. So that's what your initials stand for. I always wondered—

I've called you before.

You did? Well, I'm getting old.

When do you come to work?

Four-thirty.

I need to buy something from you.

I'm out.

Well, who has any? My headache's killing me.

I'll ask around.

Thanks. Francine, why's everyone so hot on this Neva?

What do you mean?

She must be a real good fuck. *Right?*

Try her and see. Look, J. D.—

Have *you*?

Have I *what*?

Tried her.

Oh, you dirty old man! she chuckled. (She sounded happier and more tolerant than she used to.) Look. I'll scout around, and maybe I'll be able to help you out, but right now I'm scraping aluminum foil off a frozen pizza.

All right, he said, frowning.

So what *was* it about Neva? Was it something secret, or something just plain different? He unscrewed the cap of his Old Crow: volume reduction time. Then he waited some more. The headache barely moderated, so he gave up on that and began waiting for Judy.

21

She was having a bad day at Himmel's department store, where a streamed, amplified and electronicized girl-voice kept singing *break free and love me* and *it really really hurts* while Judy, who longed to give the lesbian more than everything, pretended to concentrate on lining up the shoes so that they all pointed just so, and for extra fun stole peeks at couples going up and down the escalators; after five minutes her feet hurt and after ten it felt like an hour. A young man with long sandy hair came and flicked Judy's line of shoes into disorder, one by one, nudging each shiny toe over the edge of the shelf. Judy smiled at him. He turned his back on her and went to work his magic on another shelf. Judy carefully, carefully readjusted each shoe.

Looking furtively toward the wide counter beneath the big glowing screen where the high-power nosy girls lorded it over the others, she found that zone temporarily clear of the enemy, so she sat down, sighing.

Judy, said the sudden, startling voice of Trina the middle manager right into her ear, you need to be on your feet. Get up *right now.* Sitting down between breaks is a firable offense.

I'm sorry, Judy whispered.

Is something wrong?

No, I just, my feet hurt.

If you continue on with us, said Trina, you should definitely invest in some rubber-soled shoes. And of course if you purchase from Himmel's you'll receive a twenty percent discount.

Oh, said Judy.

Now go over to Area Eight and get busy. You're not to sit down until your lunch hour.

Okay, said Judy, knowing that here too she would soon be terminated.

22

The retired policeman's best friend, whom he hardly ever saw, was a black security guard who always wore sunglasses so that no one could see his emotions. Whenever he mentioned his beloved Mama who raised him in the fear of the Lord and used to knock him upside the head for disrespecting his Napoleonic little stepfather or for expressing a wish to join the Black Panthers, he would sooner or later refer to her death, then remove his sunglasses and excuse himself while the tears rivered out.—She was my best friend, he would say, at which the retired policeman would think: Well, I'm your best friend now.

The security guard lived on the third floor of Donohue Towers. Four times a year, he and the retired policeman met for drinks at the Buddha Bar. The security guard said: Thank God my Mama raised me in the fear of the Lord. You know, there's so much evil in the world.

Amen, said the retired policeman very cynically.

And you know, the security guard continued, nowadays, women who live on the first floor, they get raped all the time. I can hardly believe it. Sometimes they break the kitchen window, and sometimes they come in through the bathroom. Now the way my Mama raised me, if a woman's lying in her own bed, I would never think of forcing myself on her.

Amen, said the retired policeman, pouring himself a shot of Old Crow.

The Lord gave us bigger bones and bigger muscles, said the security guard. That's so we can protect women. I would never even intimidate a woman by calling her a bitch or a ho. Back when I was still in the world, if a woman would yell and scream at me, I'd never hit her; I'd never yell back. I'd just say to her, excuse my language, I'd say: Remember, you've got the pussy but I've got the dick. And then I would leave. Because I was raised in the fear of the Lord.

Amen.

And then I would call her, and I'd say, if you wanna be nice, you can call me. And then I'd hang up. And they knew better than to call me back. My friend Bobby, one time he said to me, don't you ever hitch up with a woman, because she be angry, she set all your belongings outside and change the locks! And I listened. That stuck with me. So I never lived with a woman. I never married.

Smart move, said the retired policeman, because it was time for another shot.

And I'm proud that I never once hit a woman. How about you, brother? Did you ever hit a woman?

What for? said the retired policeman.

Amen! cried the security guard.

Feeling sad, the retired policeman popped three blue pills. He wanted to go home and beat the transwoman. But she wouldn't have been there. She was fucking the lesbian, screaming with joy.

23

Sometimes when he was feeling especially well, the retired policeman would come into the Y Bar, holding the transwoman's hand, and her face would flush because she was proud, ashamed and titillated to enter the Y Bar so obviously *belonging* to someone, while he would yawn or belch and then wink at Francine, the only person on those premises whom he respected—not that he'd ever let *her* know it.

One time when Judy, wishing she could always feel as she now did, was running her hand through Xenia's hair, he proposed a threesome, mainly to make Judy jealous (for a fact, she looked surprised), but Xenia said: The thing is, J. D.—well, how can I put this in a way that won't lacerate your little ego? Men, I have found them to be disappointing in terms of they're emotionally limited, and they're bad communicators. They also tend to be duplicitous. The sidewalk kind of ends and then I'm looking off the edge of a cliff.

Honey, he said, that's just short of where I want you. Judy, get the fuck over here.

And after he ordered his drink he would stand by the ladies' room door, watching people and saying nothing, until the transwoman would come beside and slightly behind him, reaching out her sticky sweaty hand for him to swat away.

The security guard was saying: In my time, we were raised to be nice to women. But these knuckleheads nowadays, they call 'em *bitch* and *ho.* That reduces their self-respect, so they'll be intimidated.

Amen, said the retired policeman. Pumping fists with his friend, he set out for the Y Bar, but the transwoman remained absent. (Victoria had described her as *one of those chicks who, you know, whatever you tell her to do, she'll do it.*) He dialled her cell phone, but the call went to voicemail, while Francine, as unhappy as an actress, stood patiently answering a foreign tourist: I come, well, not from San

Francisco exactly, but from a little place maybe a hundred miles from here. You haven't heard of it, probably.

What it is called?

Stockton.

Stockton, yes, I have heard. Is origin of stock market.

Amazing, gushed Francine. You are so *educated!* Fourteen dollars. J. D., you want your usual?

No, said the retired policeman, who gratefully went home, took off his shoes and had another drink.

24

We now find him ingesting a watered-down shot of Old Crow straight up at the Buddha Bar, sitting as far back as he could get, guarding with his back the humming refrigerator case of beers most of which still lived in their cardboard six-packs and pretending to study his almost obsolete cell phone while he in fact cased that narrow establishment all the way from his end of the smoothworn wooded bar beneath the cheap red paper lanterns to the doorway in the middle of which glowed a pedestrian sign's prohibitory orange hand: No criminals; only suckers. What the fuck did he care about the lesbian? On the other hand, who or what *should* he have cared about? A young couple sat closest to him, snuggling in together on their barstools. He inferred that they would play it safe; they'd never need an autopsy. Then there was a delicate, beautifully dark young African American fellow who was as wiry as a jockey and sat rubbing his breast shirt pocket, picking at something inside or behind it, maybe some hidden wire. With luck he was already in trouble. The Chinese barmaid had charged nearly ten dollars for the retired policeman's drink, but liked the dollar tip sufficiently to leave him alone. On the far side of the jockey, an elegant woman who looked like Julie Andrews was telling an interested gentleman: I did, you know, like a couple of shows. I didn't really want to do topless. That wasn't for me, so that ruled me out straight away. I just didn't want to get my boobs in. They had a gymnastic line; they were covered. I'm five-six, and they asked, who will go topless, and that's what they were looking for, for the line. But I don't think when I was cast for something or rejected I was ever told why.—Considering murdering the lesbian, the retired policeman listened to the cash register printing with the sound of a winning slot machine, and the barmaid's wrists flickered over change and glasses while country music expressed itself with orchestral foreplay and choral orgasms. Why not one more Old Crow, maybe a triple? He swallowed it desperately. For a second it felt nearly as good as the slow sweet sinking into a warm bed after the third codeine tablet kicks in. Now it was getting on six p.m. that Saturday night, with a dozen drinkers in there already, a healthier-looking crowd than at the Y Bar; maybe they could even take booze or leave it. The barmaid wore a sequin-brimmed baseball cap; as she bent to make drinks or trundled back and forth behind the bar it sparkled like the flank of an immense carp while Julie Andrews explained: For the Cat Show, you know what they're going for. They want long legs, and long hair; it's all about the dancing. The whole hair thing, for me, I grew my hair; I got extensions. There was a certain stereotype for so many things. When they had American superstars in London, all the teenaged English girls would have the same makeup.—A young man in spectacles, looking like a techie or broker in his glasses and pin-striped shirt, sat down three stools from the retired policeman and very sincerely leaned into sight of his little phone, then tapped something, sipped his beer, read the label, and never noticed the retired policeman watching him. Maybe he was texting some hot fourteen-year-old decoy; it would be satisfying to send him to Vacaville, Mount Pleasant or maybe even San Quentin.

The retired policeman's ankles barely hurt, so he got up, limping against nature to Grant and Washington as if there could possibly be anything worth walking to; he longed for a fatal stroke, just a big headache and then to hell with the world and Judy in particular. This was a long walk for him. Passing the Chinatown post office at the Stockton corner, he saw so many balding old Chinese ladies holding shopping bags; and young blonde white girls bowing over their cell phones, there on the anniversary of the Chinese Republic. Maybe he should get rid of Judy, just fire her, change the lock and send the bitch about her so-called career—while a neon **OPEN** sign kept modestly blinking at Feng Ca Trading Co. beneath two storeys of curtained apartment windows, in one of which trembled the Chinese flag's reflection. Why care what she was up to?

The sun was already too low to brighten the gilt ideograms of the King Chow Temple. He descended the ramp into the Stockton tunnel, brushing past pairs of tiny Chinese maidens. As a matter of fact he used to date Judy not at the Y Bar but right here on Stockton and Sutter, just for thrills; he'd dial up her crackfaced cell phone, and she'd be looking behind her at the low wide mouth of the Stockton tunnel, within which a row of lights receded on the right and another on the left, and there he was. Yeah, there I fucking was, and for what? Should have strangled the bitch.

His phone rang, but it was only his ex-submissive Melba.

The Green Door was open for massages, while the new chain pharmacy store was either not open or else freshly out of business, with butcher paper inside all the windows, although yellow light oozed out around the edges. Erin and Sandra stood inside the Japanese candy store, holding hands; they didn't notice him. He turned west into the block of opticians, boutiques, fast food, busily glowing garages, mailboxes and art galleries by the Sir Francis Drake Hotel on the far corner at Powell. Sutter had become too tarted up, so when he got to Jones he crossed the street at the intersection, wishing to shoot the tall young man in headphones who stood rudely unconscious of him, then down the grey sidewalk to Cosmo Alley and the Taylor Hotel, right on Post, skirting a huddle of Japanese girls on the corner who smiled into their cell phones; then four pairs of tourists came rolling their suitcases up the sidewalk.

He went left, and down into the valley of grey streets and ancient red lights. He came home to Empire Residences. Then he sat wearily on the edge of the bed, holding his belly in with both hands while the transwoman knelt happily on the grubby carpet, trimming his toenails for him while humming "Somewhere Over the Rainbow." His ankles ached. Unable to make up his mind whether he was in the mood for a blow job, he stared down at the grey roots of her hair.

25

To get Neva out of his business he'd find the dirt inside her, and for the sake of his ethics it had better be real dirt, since he had never been one of those milk-fed officers who plant a pistol on a suspect's corpse. Real dirt meant real dirt. He could compassionate pathetic crimes and criminals, like the West Virginian who went to jail for stealing a storage tank and selling it to a junkyard. The ones who had to be stopped were those who misused the higher feelings of others. Fortunately, every soul was packed with moral fecal matter anyhow, rendering the game a theoretical win every time; but some people were better at covering up, although he for his part was awfully good at digging down.

From his point of view the plot did thicken, but what could actually nail the lesbian? Reba had taught her that song of names to sing, so that she could always be again with all the women she had loved. But she never sang it in his hearing. And of course she had her women's mark and her sealskin pouch of banknotes. There might be more incriminating souvenirs.—When asked where she came from, Neva would say: Honey, c'mere and give me a kiss!, after which the transwoman backed off, in dread of being prohibited from enjoying her favors.

Judy's body was singing against the lesbian's, her mouth sucking and avidly swallowing the lesbian's spit, the lesbian's fingers sizzling against her breasts; then the stream of pleasure shimmered down into more widely spaced gold and silver electrons; and after a long happy sigh Judy said: Neva, I want to see it. Where is it?

The lesbian smiled sadly.

I mean it, said the transwoman. I want to see your women's mark.

Here it is.

Oh! It's—

But try not to tell anyone.

I promise.

While Judy bit her earlobe, Neva lay wondering when to next visit her mother, and whether she was needed by brownhaired Catalina next door. Judy was licking her neck. She said: I want to look just like Judy Garland. Don't you think that's crazy?

Sweetheart, you can't be her, the lesbian gently replied. But guess whom you could be: a tall strong woman like Martina Navratilova.

Oh, do you really think so?

As the lesbian carefully penetrated her and gently, sweetly rode her, Judy's mind likewise wandered, because her partner was being so gentle; she heard the couple in Room 541 arguing ever more loudly, after which the woman shrieked three times very quickly while something crashed; then the woman screamed again and again, rhythmic screams that excited the transwoman, bringing her back to the lesbian's dildo inside her; now she was almost climaxing but then something shattered against the wall of Room 541 so that she couldn't help but worry about the woman in there, but comforted herself by imagining that it was *she* in there, getting beaten to death by a big tall ferociously handsome male brute who hated her, was raping her and would smash her head in. The lesbian's hair smelled like flowers. Perceiving what she craved, the lesbian gently laced fingers around Judy's neck, penetrating her faster and harder until Judy suddenly climaxed, surprising herself with the soft joy of what went on and on and on, the lesbian taking expert possession of what Judy had never known she had; not a maidenhead because she was too unclean and false to have ever been a virgin, but at least there was a womanhead of velvet inside her, and the lesbian in claiming it brought it alive.

The woman next door fell silent. A man's voice muttered and growled to itself. The transwoman lay weeping in the lesbian's arms. Then it came time for them to part, and the familiar anguish of separation intoxicated her. She walked home singing *girlfriend, girlfriend, girlfriend!*

Meanwhile the lesbian dreamed that she was back in the house of her childhood, lying on what she always called her *girl bed*, with her old dolls and stuffed animals still around her, when suddenly the doorknob silently began to turn, the door to swing inward, and she woke up with her heart pounding in terror.

26

The Y Bar was closed for the night. Xenia, *wired* from having just been voted most popular of the Pink Apple's dozen girls in black bras and undies and gaiters—no, maybe eight or nine, pumping those pale buttocks, crossing their legs, sitting in each other's laps, showing off their breasts—had blown in and out, after which some chunky young blonde in a striped sweater swished her bottom, swayed and said: *oh yeah,* oh *yeah!* and then came last call. Shantelle was in bed snorting crystal and masturbating because her dance routine had been voted most glamorous, with Samantha most definitively edged out. In those weeks even Shantelle, who was certainly far from monogamous, remained re-persuaded that the lesbian's other activities robbed *her* of nothing significant; to her our Neva had spoken in the hard straight language of facts, which (so prostitutes love to assure their clients) have absolutely nothing to do with our hearts' realities. Instead of insisting, as people so often do when forced to admit to some unloving betrayal, *you know I love you!*, the lesbian began by saying very sweetly, with that steadfast, half-lowered gaze that the other woman could never resist: Shantelle, I know you love me . . . !—Those words calmed Shantelle: She merely needed to pretend a little bit, and then all would be pleasant; Neva would venture lovingly into Shantelle's pretend world, and *then* . . .

Meanwhile lucky Francine was sleeping in the lesbian's arms, while next door Catalina lay sadly alone. Hunter was in bed with Xenia, holding her desperately.

On Turk Street a man was smashing bottles and screaming, while on all four television screens above him two glamorous women sat kissing. People lay in dark doorways, wrapped up like garbage.

As for Judy, what should she be doing with her life? Longing to receive some portion of Neva's form, or even just to drink any woman's spit or sweat and keep it inside her forever, she tried to remember last night's dreams and looked ahead to the now; keep it simple, Judy, she told herself.—For once she wasn't hungry; nor did she feel up for moneymaking, even with Al, who rarely turned her down. Meanwhile Sandra's phone was turned off, it being her time to snuggle with her dogs, drinking wine and turning her mind to the lesbian, who outshone all others. What about the retired policeman? (We all used to laugh at the way that Judy could not get enough of him and even imagined that they were similar people.) She could hardly wait to tattle about the women's mark on Neva; he'd pat her head and say: Not bad for a girl.—But maybe it was better to save her information for when she needed to get him out of a bad mood. Suffice it to say that she clip-clopped home. When she got there it was dawn, and she found beneath her door a flier meant to aid her, which said:

> Near Jericho in Israel is a place called Sodom and Gomorrah . . . This entire area should be a testimony of GOD to all people, especially those perverts who practice homosexuality and lesbianism. After observing all this, you will know that GOD is not a kidder.

She washed her face, chewed up three yellow pills, brushed her teeth and lay down to think about the lesbian, whose long legs had first reminded Francine of the supermodel Gigi Hadid's.

27

What was Neva to her but a divinity at whose feet she could lay down her entire self—and from whom she could meanwhile take love endlessly? Having modeled her femininity first on her mother and her sister, who had both been disgusted by her, then on blurred bygone footage of Judy Garland pretending to be a little girl, pretending to be a happy wife and mother, giving and giving until she broke, the transwoman had until now constructed herself into a vessel of putrid meat which she despised even while offering it. As a model, the lesbian might be less false than these others; she was certainly more available.

28

Now it was Victoria's turn. Wondering if the lesbian might be sleeping or maybe eating breakfast, lonely, but not meaning to impose, Victoria decided, of course, to impose. It was ten a.m. Smiling, the lesbian opened the door. Victoria instantly felt what she would later describe to Francine as *lightning between her heart and her cunt.*

As soon as they had sat down on the lesbian's couch Victoria blushingly said: What I want is full body contact—you on top of me. And them we can give each other a *small* massage. After that you'll tell me what to do; make me beg you . . .

All right, honey, said the lesbian. Something about this woman's hands, shoulders and laughter reminded her of her mother.

Turn over, said Victoria. I want to explore your body.

The lesbian lay there, trying not to shrink, while her guest gently touched her, kissing the calluses on her heels, parting her buttocks, stroking her back, and all the while she felt ashamed and violated, because she could only please, not be pleased; whenever anyone touched her it was like her mother touching her.

Let me eat your pussy, she said as seductively as she could, to which Victoria sadly replied: But then you're so far away . . .

For once disregarding another's whim, the lesbian inched down to the foot of the bed and placed her mouth on the other woman's cunt. Then she began to lick so gently and sweetly and skillfully; any minute now Victoria's vagina would begin to pulse and Victoria would be moaning, but Victoria only said: Do I taste okay? and then: This is so relaxing . . .—which is to say that under this procedure Victoria would never come. So Neva did what she had to do, which was to grant Victoria's wish—and Victoria was grateful, oh, so grateful.

You're so gorgeous! laughed her guest. You're brave and beautiful like me . . . —and the lesbian felt ashamed . . .—The headboard receded from her. Victoria rushed backward to clamp her mouth between the lesbian's legs. The lesbian gripped the headboard, shuddering and crying out as if for help. Fearing that she had begun to squirm away, Victoria slithered forward, seizing her hips. The lesbian fell silent, held her breath, began trembling deep within her belly, then suddenly screamed.

At this, Victoria, feeling desired, began to be more aroused than before, and finally climaxed.

They lay in each other's arms. Again and again the lesbian gratified Victoria's large smooth body. Victoria kissed her and said: You were utterly adorable.—The lesbian kissed her back.

Neva, do you love me?

Yes, honey.

I love you. Who are you? You don't want me to know. I love you anyway.

29

Shantelle, who must have turned several extra tricks in order to do so, showed up for her date as elegantly black-clad as Marlene Dietrich in *Shanghai Express*. The Y Bar's single television was on mute, which did not in the least impair its ability to transmit the way that the latest young Vegas nightclub sensation would pose in a corner wearing unlaced sneakers, showing off her shining thighs and gazing ingenuously out of smoky-painted eyes.—The retired policeman was there, so Shantelle informed him: One of you pigs broke into my place last year and tied me up. They was searchin' for a suspect but it was mistaken identity. No warrant, no fuckin' nothing.—Honey, he replied, you know why I love you? Because you're a *hot mean bitch*, and I can tie you up anytime.—Shantelle had to laugh.—Xenia, who liked men to talk to her during penetration (she also liked to lose control), sat in the corner checking her text messages and sipping Old German Lager. Her phone rang. As she walked toward the toilet I could hear her say into it: Honey, I want that, too.—Samantha was practicing her lip-synching to an absent Barbra Streisand; none of us could ever decide whether she loved that song so much that singing it was her way of masturbating, or whether she needed to rehearse over and over because she was somehow, you know, limited.

Francine poured the lesbian a free drink, and they were clinking glasses over the bar. Shantelle waited, smiling away her jealous rage.

Catalina flashed in to kiss the lesbian. Shantelle waited.

You look fancy, Francine finally said. Your usual?

You know it. Hi, Neva.

Seven dollars.

Bolting down her Peachy Keen, Shantelle got straight to it: Neva, will you step outside with me?

Sure, said the lesbian, setting down her gin and tonic. Francine looked sad.

They went behind the garbage can, and Shantelle said: Show me how you lure them in. I give it up to you, bitch: You sure know every fuckin' trick—

There's nothing specific that I—

Don't bullshit me.

I won't, said the lesbian.

Then will you come with me?

Right now? Okay.

So Neva allowed herself to be led down Eddy Street, into Martinka Alley, through the wrought-iron gate and up the grubby carpeted stairs that smelled of dust, pet dander, urine and cigarette smoke. When Shantelle released her hand in order to get the key from her purse, the lesbian saw her trembling. In the next apartment or maybe the one below a mother and child were arguing. As soon as they were inside the apartment, Shantelle slammed the door behind them and desperately seized the lesbian's face, slamming their mouths together and growling deep in her throat. Pulling away at last to catch her breath, she dragged the lesbian into the bedroom, shoving her down on the bed, tearing at her clothes. Closing her eyes, the lesbian lay still, letting herself be handled. Right now Francine was slowly pouring one gin and tonic down the sink. Shantelle pulled open Neva's shirt, snapping off half the buttons. Neva rolled onto her stomach so that Shantelle could unhook her bra; she was in a hurry, and ruined one of the hooks.

Turn over, she said.

The lesbian turned over.

With an exultant grunt Shantelle sat on her crotch and began feverishly kneading her breasts until they were purple with bruises.—I'm gonna rape you, she said.—Go ahead, said the lesbian.

While most of us experienced our intimacies with Neva as magnified analogues of loving, trusting, snuggly trips on ecstasy crystals, Shantelle's time resembled marathon intercourse fueled by chewing a handful of speed tablets. (The first time she ever played doctor, at five years old, an older boy said: I see a need in you that nobody should have.) Undressing in an instant, she flung herself down onto Neva, grabbed more and more of her, faster and faster; she needed more hands! She kissed her, squeezed her, snarling: *Look* at me, bitch!—Crouching below her, greedily licking her slit, she worked four fingers inside. Neva was not at all wet, but soon began to moan and tremble. Shantelle gloated; they were both on the verge;

she had never felt so excited in her entire career. Panting with desire, she grabbed the lesbian's head and pulled it down against her, possessing her lower lip with happily furious jaw-snaps until the other woman's chin was dripping with blood. Neva, crying out, began frantically fingering her clitoris, her vagina contracting against Shantelle's fingers until she climaxed in a series of screams. Then Shantelle slithered back up on top of her, taking her own orgasms through grinding frottage, and all the while thrusting her tongue into Neva's mouth. When Neva turned her head away to catch a breath, Shantelle clapped both palms tight against her temples, biting her lips, tonguing her tongue and sucking the spit right out of her. They both came again, or at least Shantelle did; who really knew about the lesbian?—As for Shantelle, she invariably opened her eyes whenever she climaxed, to make sure that the lesbian was still watching her.—She slammed two fingers up the lesbian's ass, meanwhile twisting and pinching her nipple as she kissed her, because that would have felt good to *her.* More and more transported, she kept using her, so high on pleasure that she would have loved it if Neva for her part were beating her to death; as for the raw-rubbed lesbian, she, as the transwoman's therapist would say, *dissociated.* And Shantelle, growling tigerishly, licked her face all over.

30

Then my turn came. I among a few faithful others mean to keep the lesbian's secrets, so I will not tell you (at least not until I can't help myself) what she did to me and I to her, and how with her help I, even I, came into heaven.

Although I tried to remember everything about her, by the time I was going downstairs her perfect face had already become a timeworn two-dimensional image whose closed eyes gazed at something *other.*

31

All the same, at the Y Bar I must have been radiant. The transwoman, ordinarily so shy, smiled joyously to see me so; before I could react, she sweetly hugged and kissed me. She might have been the only one for whom there was no why.

Francine smiled at me, saying nothing. It was then that I first began to consider her my friend.

You, too, said Xenia.

I nodded.

Welcome to the fan club.

Six dollars, said Francine.

Well, said Xenia, don't think you can appreciate her the way I can.

How do *you* know what I appreciate?

As a man you're walking around with a boner and you're looking for a place to put it. With women there's this emotional heat that can only happen with another woman. And when we use our hands, and our toys . . . !

That annoyed me, but Francine winked and poured me a free refill.

For years her bluntness and apparent coldness had prejudiced me against her, she being one of many who rarely troubled herself to reply when I greeted her or asked how she was, so I fell out of that habit. Presently I began to perceive her silent kindnesses: She never poured out short measure, and sometimes did the opposite, gratis, even for those who were not regulars. She gave respect to sadness, and help to sickness, being always good for a few pills. Because I expected nothing of anyone except for the retired policeman (and now Neva), it felt almost painful to deepen my acquaintanceship with Francine, especially since at first I could not fathom what she wanted, and then I could not tell what she saw in me. I now suspect that the lesbian's effects upon us were so strange and wonderful that Francine needed to exclaim. She needed to tell someone that whenever they were making love it seemed as if Neva were singing a song that Francine had always known. So I became the latter's audience.

From our intimacy I learned that Francine sincerely loved Judy. And in time I began to love them both likewise. It also caught my notice that although the retired policeman apparently scorned her, Francine never failed to refer to him with respect.

32

And you made plans to meet her again, he said.

Yes I did.

How much is she paying you?

It's not like that.

I get it. True love.

While she ran water in the bathroom, thinking about the lesbian, who was just then pulling up the long hairless lips of Holly's slit, one forefinger on each, then spreading them open just before beginning to breathe ever so lightly on the rising clitoris, he lay on his back reading the *National Enquirer* and muttering about *willful misconduct, fraud, misrepresentation* and *suppression of fact.* The President was an extraterrestrial. Judy Garland had engaged in incest with her homosexual father. Oh, and just as the ancient Spartan poet Alcman knew the tunes of all the birds, so this motherfucking Neva knew every woman's song. Judy had said as much; likewise Sandra and Francine. Meanwhile Jennifer Lopez was pregnant for real. Venus Williams had been seen holding hands with Martina Navratilova in the same ballroom where Elvis Presley had cross-dressed with Dwight Eisenhower. China was subverting the United Nations, after which it came time to rendezvous with his sweetheart in the shower. When he stood up, for once his ankles forgot to give him grief. First he pretended to call Melba, just to keep Judy in her place. She pretended to be devastated. Fishing under the pillow, he found the vinyl strap. Now he began to feel in the mood. Judy, grunting and groaning with excitement as he carefully beat her, finally wet herself, which was almost literally the climax for both of them; then he yawned and opened the faucet.

What next?

Longfellow used to say that *the thoughts of youth are long, long thoughts*, so the retired policeman must have still been young.

It was not as if he intended to injure the lesbian, although he certainly relished the process of law, which may be defined as follows: link by link, to chain the accused to her public guilt and doom. Such constructions being imperishable and ideal, who wouldn't adore them? In his next life he'd become a forensic prosecutor, whose collected treasures would include the dark stairs of dreams, and the pallid sack under them, with twisted white feet sticking out. In the last drabs of this life he improved his mind, playfully exposing Judy's clumsy inconsistencies, dissecting out stupidities and misstatements to bare the coldly shining darknesses of the lies within. Had she been true to him, he would have gotten far less fun out of her! And for all I can say, she wanted and needed to be caught. Both considered the advantages and disadvantages of admitting certain stories as evidence.

He enjoyed the thought of puncturing whatever secret the lesbian possessed, then laughing at the shock on her face. But for now it was best to ignore the truth.

He knew about Ed and he knew about Al. He thought he knew about me. Unscrewing a bottle of Blissodex, he shook out one tab for her and two for him. She pursed up her lips and air-kissed him. He said: Judy, if you give me a disease I'm gonna fucking kill you.

Her Name in Lights

Let me fly like a hawk, let me cackle like a goose, let me slay always like the serpent-goddess Neheb-ka.

The Egyptian Book of the Dead

If I'm such a legend, then why am I so lonely?

Judy Garland, 1967

1

Shantelle was what the Japanese would have called *a natural born poison woman.* Of course, like any poison woman, she did not see herself as such. She had bad luck, worse parents, you name it. Everyone was against her. Like all the rest of us, she'd been molested. In court she invariably pled innocent.

We read that Natalie Wood's mother impressed on that precocious starlet *the importance of cataloging her career by keeping meticulous scrapbooks containing virtually every magazine article, advertisement and photograph featuring Natalie since she was five years old.*

As for Shantelle's mother, she said: You don't have no Beverly Hills brothers and sisters, and, Shantelle, that's just a fact of life.

Not *my* life, thought the girl.

Later she remembered the time when her best friend Karissa began to go to Christian school, after which Karissa was forbidden to invite her over; and she remembered waiting in the street for Karissa to sobbingly confirm Shantelle's exclusion from her twelfth birthday, at which Shantelle began hating on everybody, her sullenness as ready to release itself as any shock-sensitive explosive.

She did what she did because she required success. (They owe me, said she. I'm gonna get what's mine.) I can almost see her stepping on the gas, speeding down the on ramp by the Tropicana, past Thai Town and Sunset Boulevard, rushing curvily beneath the overpasses and past the Hollywood Bowl, a white cross glowing high in the night, flying down the freeway, smoking crack behind that tall metal fence on Maplewood, and then, after her first paid blow job, running into Celebrity Burger to wash out the taste with a big cup of soda from the machine. After a few more blow jobs, spitting was good enough for our Shantelle.

A customer called her *niggah trash*, and Shantelle pretended to swallow down that insult, but when they were in his car she positioned herself just right, so that when he was inside her and sucking on her titty like an overgrown baby she popped out his shitty little stereo and hid it in her purse.

For her first mug shot she slouched back in her striped fuck-me blouse, giving both deputies the evil eye, with her long black hair arranged just so on her shoulders, and whatever effect of cobwebbed eyesockets she gave off was only because she was sleepless and high, not anxious in the slightest. Once again prosecution was waived, and after several stern intimidations they returned her to her mother, who was drunk when Shantelle came home, which made it all the easier to lift everything of interest, including a wallet and house keys, the lack of which might delay any chase. The girl now owned seventy-nine dollars in cash, a checkbook, three credit cards and her mother's driver's license, so she had made a pretty fair start. Deploying her hair into tall narrow two-paired antlers as if she were a Chu Era tomb guardian, she caught the bus to the south side of town.

Her boyfriend DaShawn demanded to be informed where she was going now.

Don't get all juiced up about it, nigger, 'cause it ain't nothin' so good. But you know I love your ass.

I said where you goin'?

I really don't know, and I really don't give a shit. Point is, stop fuckin' with me.

He tried to stop her, so she stabbed him, not to kill but just to get away. She left him bleeding and cursing on the floor. He was a goddamned motherfucker.

Shantelle caught the night Greyhound bus for Las Vegas.

She colored her hair copper-red, crimsoned her lips, blushed up her cheeks, hooked on the longest jingly dangly earrings she could get, and practiced looking narrow-eyed while half-smiling over her smooth bare shoulder, but even then she failed to approximate the showgirl Noella Neighborly. But at four in the morning, with curtains drawn against the looming dawn and air conditioning first pretending to freshen the casino's cigarette smoke, then moving it round and round the room, her client (since compliments were cheaper than tips) promised that she had what it took to be a showgirl. And she believed it! Just as when one comes from a blinding July afternoon in the Central Valley down into a foggy never-never dusk in Carmel or Monterey, whereupon another and maybe better form of being seems achievable, with the future as wide and soft as a powdery beach, so our Shantelle looked ahead and saw herself making it *big.* Sleep would have inconvenienced her plans, so at midmorning she set out. Nothing in her life had ever appeared as empty as the palm-shadowed stairs of the courthouse—until finally a pretty woman leaped out of a taxi and ran up them for some appearance for which she was apparently late. Shantelle stood there, high on goofballs. After awhile two bulletheaded U.S. marshals, one black and one white, descended the stairs and turned left toward Casino Center while a fat lady came, trusting in her cell phone, whose synthetic robot voice assured her: *your destination is on the right,* and so the fat lady went upstairs. Shantelle proceeded to the ladies' room of the coffee shop on the corner of Lewis and Casino Center, did two lines of meth and then set off for the Strip. That afternoon she scammed her way into a show and watched how that chorus line kicked its legs!—. . . not to mention the front row audience girls screaming *oh my GOD!* when the acrobat in the bathtub blew water out of his mouth, or the almost naked male acrobat one-handedly lifting another male acrobat above his head: slow muscles and perfect balance in the light! Fans shot up their loving arms in tribute to each star as she entered the attention of the whole world—while the ringmaster insulted everyone. The front row girls screamed until everyone's ears rang.

Shantelle strolled to the nearest bar and picked up a retired dancer who said: Now thin and tan is hot shit. I quit because I thought I was old . . .

Shantelle was thin and tan. Indeed, her new friend was fucking *old.*

At the top of the cast is a principal, the retired dancer explained. A lead. In my time there were four principal girl dancers, and a couple of principal boy dancers. It's kind of weird how it all works. You should see this girl with her makeup on. I mean, she's a pretty girl. But onstage, she's just captivating. But certain people, they just have something else.

Well, what the fuck is it? Shantelle demanded.

What is *what*?

That *something else.*

I think it's confidence.

I've sure got that, said Shantelle in her purring, snarling voice.

I love to be looked at but I hate to be looked at, the other woman went on, not understanding that only Shantelle mattered. Who gave a fuck about this dogeared bitch?

The other woman said: I think that anybody that's onstage is like me in that way. They may have some physical attributes that makes them . . .

What about me?

Slow down, honey.

Shantelle's audition might have gone better if she hadn't kept swaying.

2

With the lesbian, as you have read, she put on a better performance, taking pleasure over and over. She was the sun and Neva the moon.

Sensing from her lowered yet determined eyes that Shantelle had now begun considering more strange and ambitious possibilities of intercourse, if not necessarily of love itself, the lesbian said: Next time, you're invited to my place.

That was how Shantelle first ascended the carpeted stairs that the rest of us were coming to know. The lesbian closed and locked the door. There were clean sheets on the bed. Smiling at Shantelle, she stood waiting to be kissed or raped.

When Shantelle realized that her heart had gone out to the lesbian she felt angry and wanted to attack her, all the while shouting *why are you doin' this to me?* but instead clutched her tight, then wept.

Cradling her head, the lesbian began to kiss her face. For a long time Shantelle sobbed loudly. But Neva slipped two fingers inside her tights. Drawn together by what pretended to be the same intention, she and Shantelle presently, propelled by the super-terrestrial gravity of their approaching orgasms, plummeted into each other, exploding in each other's hearts and cunts, then trapped together by tenderness.

The lesbian, exhausted, fell asleep. Shantelle lay watching her, feeling so alone and so rejected.

3

You see, she was a competitor, just like the Olympic figure skater Tonya Harding. As soon as Tonya snatched the gold medal from Kristi Yamaguchi and Nancy Kerrigan at the Minneapolis Nationals, her situation brightened, but the Olympics remained nearly impossible. Then at Munich she vanquished both rivals again. Now that the correlation of forces had altered to her advantage, certain risks grew more justifiable. Kristi turned pro, which removed her from the competition. That left Nancy, who had been training hard; the rumor was that she might have improved her game. Hence it definitely paid to smash her in the leg, ensuring that Tonya would win the figure skating championship in Detroit. No one ever proved that she planned the assault. After she pled guilty to interfering with the prosecution, they banned her from the Olympics for life.

Deerlike Judy intuited nothing. The retired policeman said: Wake up, bitch. You're my little Nancy Kerrigan. And Shantelle's your Tonya Harding, so watch out.

Judy nearly asked which skater Neva was, but fortunately swallowed her tongue.

And so Shantelle called the lesbian and left the following message: Hey, baby, I don't know if it's okay to love you and sometimes it's so hard. I don't know where you are or who you're with right now, but I believe in what you promised me so I know we'll talk soon, and I just wanted to call and tell you I'm thinkin' about you.

I Guess I Just Like Nice People

It does you no harm when you esteem all others better than yourself; but it does you great harm when you esteem yourself above others.

THOMAS À KEMPIS, 1413

Don't yield your leadership. Don't hand us the reins.

JUDY GARLAND, 1955

1

Remembering the white party dress that Judy Garland put on for the Academy dinner when they gave her an Oscar Award, the transwoman dressed in white, because she had decided to *find someone to take care of her*, much as the previous generation sometimes married for safety. Never mind Sandra and Erin; who could that someone be but the lesbian? She went to ring the buzzer for number 543 at the Reddy Hotel, but nobody answered. Neva must be fucking someone.

Give it up, honey, said Francine. You'll never be as pretty as she is.

The transwoman's eyes began shining with tears.

That don't mean you can't be pretty. That don't mean you don't already have a beautiful soul. Judy, I believe in you as a woman. I love you as a woman.

The transwoman blushed and said thank you.

And that's a lovely white dress, said Francine.

Judy ran her finger around the rim of her glass, took a breath, chased her ice cube with the tiny red cocktail straw and asked: Have you seen Neva today?

2

It was almost midnight. Returning to the Reddy, she rang number 543 a second time, and no one buzzed her in, so she rang number 545.

Yes? came an insectoid distortion of Catalina's voice.

It's me, Judy—Neva's friend . . .

The gratinged door made a bumblebee noise. Judy pulled it open and rushed upstairs, gloriously gleeful at being able to invade the unknown domicile of one of Neva's women. She felt good because she looked good; she might even be nearly as pretty as a kiss-hematoma on our lesbian's neck.

Catalina said: She goes out sometimes all night, so I don't know—

Hi, said Judy.

Are you here for Neva or for me?

I'm trying to be a woman, and I want to be a lesbian.

Catalina smilingly said: I love trans people. My cousin is in the process right now, and that's a whole story. But they, I mean, our family accepts them totally. And if you . . .

Do you love Neva?

I have no choice. Neither do you. Now why are you here?

I want to ask you: What if you had Neva's power? Would you . . . ?

Catalina said: That sounds overwhelming. If I had like an actual power, I would wanna just erase the obstructions that men act this way and women act this way. I want men to be able to cry and there would be no more categories.

She yawned.—I think you're not here for any reason, she continued. You made some excuse, in case Neva might come. But I have to work tomorrow in the supermarket. Goodnight, Judy.

Goodnight, Catalina. I mean, I, are you a lesbian?

The other woman nodded, waved once and closed the door. Judy went home and masturbated, thinking of Catalina. Long before her climax, Neva took over.

3

Mr. Khalid accepted her for the eleven a.m. shift at his Nepalese restaurant because that was where his probationers failed or not, with minimal risk to him. She arrived at ten-thirty, a hateful predawn hour which should never have been invented. What she heard first, last and in between was the singing hum of the fan in the fume hood over the grill. Mr. Khalid set her to sweeping the kitchen floor. Then he had her check the table settings. One knife and fork had switched places. Thus his standard trick, to monitor the carefulness of waitresses. Expecting to be tested, Judy spotted and corrected that anomaly.

Okay, said Mr. Khalid. You can eat.

Judy raided the buffet. Some things tasted strange, and many were fiery-spicy, but everything must be good for her. Why, how long had it been since she had eaten any vegetables? Proud of her new healthiness, she loaded up on salad and pickled plums.

What are you doing? demanded Mr. Khalid. Look now! Customer is here!

Judy leaped up. Nobody told her where to take her plate, so she left it there in hopes of nibbling at it. Above her dreamed a fat soapstone Buddha whose eyes had rolled up in his head like those of her ex-girlfriend Mikayla after she had smoked too much shatter. The noise of the fan increased in both pitch and volume.

Welcome, sir, said Judy. Please sit anywhere you like.

The customer picked a naugahyde booth. He sat down. Judy darted off to fetch the pitcher of water.—No, said the customer. I want beer.

Here's our list, said Judy.

Taj Mahal, he said. Big size.

Judy rushed off to tell Mr. Khalid.

No Taj Mahal today, he said.

Returning to her customer, Judy said: I'm sorry, sir, but we just ran out. What's your second choice?

Oh, forget it, he said. Give me water.

Now the air conditioner began throbbing loudly in a series of sickly strainings that tired Judy. The lights appeared to flicker, although when she glared at them straight on they turned into steady planetoids.

Here you go, sir, she said. Now have you decided?

The customer looked her up and down. He shouted: Hey, you, Khalid!

Yes, Mr. Mansoorian, he said, whitehaired and white-shirted.

What do you mean, sending this he-she over here? You serve me yourself. Get this faggot away from me.

Judy smiled and stiffened.

4

Being nearly as unjealous as I, the retired policeman initially felt more than pleased with his sweetheart's new confidence, and once actually said: Judy, you're not only more feminine, but sometimes I even think you might amount to something—not like you'd pass your pussy polygraph; but *whatever*, bitch, *whatever*.—Needless to say, his praise delighted her, so she went on doing what she was doing—the perfect course, all of us would have said, except just maybe for the fact that what she was doing differed from what her patron and master supposed. Just as her namesake once married the known homosexual Vincente Minnelli in order, runs her biography, so that *she could continue to have romantic flings with other men without feeling any guilt*, so the transwoman began to erect a cloud-high dream castle of passions, employing the retired policeman as her safe cornerstone. And he began to get out of bed more; he hobbled all the way to the liquor store and back, as if he were five years younger!

They went to see *Phantom of the Opera* at the Castro Theatre, and while she sat there in the dark holding his hand she wished some monster would carry her away just as in the story. As it was, Neva would be her lucky star. The lights came on, and the organist took a bow. When everyone else began applauding, the retired policeman put his hand on her ass and said: Bend over like a good little bitch.—She did, and he clapped away: both palms on both buttocks. A gay couple raised their eyebrows. Now he was really whaling on her; somebody laughed and three boys grew uncomfortable and an old man proposed calling the police; it was almost as wonderful as the crowds and lines that waited to stare at Judy Garland and Andy Rooney in New York after *The Wizard of Oz.* But then he started getting those neuropathic pains in his legs, so she caught them a taxi and helped him upstairs. Soon she was unlacing his shoes and pulling off his pants while he lay on the bedspread, groaning with misery. Promising to be right back, she clipclopped over to the Y Bar to borrow three codeine pills from Francine.—Judy, he said, you're the best girlfriend I've ever had, and I mean that.

She sobbed happily.

No, take one for yourself, he said grandly. Pour us each a triple to . . . First I'm going to chew mine up; I'm—oh, god*damn* my fucking legs! Lie down next to me, Judy. Put your head on me. That's . . . that's so . . . No, pour me another shot.

That thrilled her . . .—and in time she even got to hear from both Victoria and Shantelle that some of us (I, for instance) *envied* her for the durability of that particular arrangement.—What's your secret, girl? inquired Francine.

The transwoman thought awhile.—Because I'm never dissatisfied, I—

Because you *know* you're a *worthless stinking bitch*! said Shantelle. Francine, honey, fill me up—two ice cubes *max*. And top off her poison. Judy, you skanky-ass crybaby, I'm *teasin'* you! I'm pullin' your fat old hairy old leg! I'm—

So you're buying Judy a drink or not? said Francine.

You fuckin' heard me.

Well *well.* Six and seven, and then you want extra Peachy Keen instead of ice? Yeah? So that's three, so it comes to sixteen dollars.

Oh yeah? Then here's twenty, and keep the change, because you know what? You'd better start saving for a face lift.

Francine looked sore. Then she laughed. Judy clinked glasses with Shantelle. Then the lesbian came in, deploying a hundred-dollar bill.

5

You're drinking a lot, he said.

So are you.

Look, Judy, I don't give a shit about your liver; I'm just curious as to how you can pay your tab.

Shantelle bought me a drink today.

Tell me another one.

But she *did*!

Why not? Everyone makes mistakes. And one stinkin' drink was all you had?

She looked away.

Hey, bitch. You look at *me.* Now what about Neva?

She . . .

She's dating you, so she's paying you. *Right?*

J. D., I swear—

Shut up, he said. He sat up to recommence some of his world-renowned drinking and thinking, while she knelt before him, awaiting orders.

No, he said happily. There has to be some kind of fraud.

Why?

Because there always is. For instance, when you lie to me—

Honey, I only—

No. You cheat on me and steal from my wallet just because you can. We're all the same. Don't tell me Neva's not one of us.

She isn't! You don't know her.

Not like *you* do! How big's her tongue? All right, Sherlock. What's your shitty little hypothesis?

She . . . She doesn't want anything.

From you? Come on. *What does she want?*

To make me happy, said his lover with dignity. He burst out laughing.

6

Neva has no parents, she told him.

Did she run away from home or bump them off?

They died.

Expressing nearly as much affect as a headless seated figure enveloped in stone robe-folds, he said: Let me guess. In a car crash. That's the usual story.

Don't you pick on her! I don't have parents, either.

Of course you do. It's just that they hate you for being a faggot, Frank.

Please don't call me that name.

But that's your legal name. You just get through life by lying about it.

I'm Judy now. *My name is Judy!*

Whatever. And your parents are dead and rotting, except that they live at 73241 Jacinto Way in Oxnard. Fish out that phone from between your phony she-male tits and call 'em up. I dare you.

I don't want to.

All right, Frank. Let's say they died in a car crash. Holding hands, when some big fat homosexual broadsided their bathwagon—

She burst into tears. Laughing, he took her by the ears and pulled her head into his lap. She began to suck his penis mechanically. He closed his eyes, waiting to feel something.

7

And she bears the women's mark, she said. I promised never to tell you—

Then she wanted me to know, *right*? Who keeps secrets worse than you? So what the fuck's a—

Only a woman can see it. And what it looks like, well, it's kind of a little—

Stop. You saw it?

Yes, she said.

But you're not a woman, Frank, so don't that invalidate her bullshit?

I'm a woman.

Because Neva says so? And she buys you drinks. And she buys everyone drinks. What's the fuckin' world coming to? Now this witch mark, is it (lemme guess) a spiral, a fish, a Venus symbol or a—

A triangle, point down, with a—

Vertical line inside it. *Right?* Do you have any *idea* how old that game is?

8

Just as the lesbian in childhood could not bear to consider who she was, which is to say what was being done to her, so Judy had never constructed what the rest of us would call an independent self. The memory-stories of Sandra and Erin helped her; she could never get enough of little girls! (Even Judy Garland professed to believe in little-girl fairytales whenever she was corseted up.) And since Judy's heart's desire *was* girlhood, she cunningly pretended to babyness.

Until Neva's appearance she had existed most vividly when seen through the contemptuously titillated gazes of others. But now that she possessed the beginning of a secret (the secret of happiness), she needed to conceal it in order to better cherish it, so she felt a vague drive to sequester herself. The petty impersonal dishonesties by means of which we all lived at the Y Bar, stealing each other's pills, intercepting dates and paying out malicious accusations for what we hoped was true gossip, had in her case remained transparent or at least translucent to others—for how could a young girl more deliciously humiliate herself than to ensure that her friends' parents caught her pulling down her pants? Had her frauds ever attained to slick proficiency, she would have missed out on the thrill of punishment. But as her Judy-ness finally began to cohere, she needed to feel it, in order to better believe in it. Around all of us she grew ever so slightly more quiet; that was all. Around the retired policeman she had behaved carelessly; now he was sniffing after her all the time, but so what? He could go fuck himself, because she had Neva, Neva, Neva!

She awoke so happy and confident, on account of Neva, that it seemed right to take herself out for coffee. Moreover, she had the day free, since Mr. Khalid had politely let her go. (She ran to Neva, who comforted her with a hundred-dollar bill.) That afternoon she might or might not apply to be a clerk at the Pack'N'Grin.—Smiling as widely as she could (and sweating with anxiety), she ordered whatever would taste sweetest—a buttered double chocolate latte with coconut syrup—and the middle-aged Chinese behind the counter, who looked to own the place, dropped the change in her hand from a distance of two inches. Well, that's just how Asians are—extra clean, said the transwoman to herself. Who can blame them, when that's how they are and I'm disgusting?—Once her dark and sugary drink appeared, she thanked the barista, who did not reply, and carried it to a long high table. She set her purse at her feet. Almost at once an elegant young woman whose T-shirt celebrated the technology company Smargle approached the adjacent seat.—Let me know if my bag's in your way, said the transwoman, wishing so much to prove that she was good and decent and friendly.—I will, said the woman. She sat down, arranged herself, then said, as if she were bestowing some favor: You're fine.

Now the transwoman was feeling the tiniest bit humiliated.

The young woman from Smargle said: Excuse me, but I see my friend. Would you mind moving, please?

But, said Judy, this chair was free, and you said—

Wrinkling her nose, the young woman said: I don't have anything against the homeless. But you need a bath.

Judy turned red. She gulped her coffee and stood up. The young woman was calling to her friend: Lainey, Lainey! Over here! This seat has just opened up.

There being no other seat, Judy stood before the counter, wondering whether she was obligated to order another coffee as the price of taking up space. The young woman and her friend were talking about something intellectual. Judy stood eavesdropping:

When Louise Allen talks about lesbian idolification . . .

But when Judith Butler writes about what it means to her to *speak as a lesbian*—

. . . If there is actually such a thing as consumption of cultural reproduction—

Well, did Judy Garland perform *our* sexuality or not?

Escaping from that place, then not knowing what else to do, she crossed the street to the station, bought a ticket and boarded the underground train. It was commuter time. Seeking a niche where she would not overly obtrude herself on others, she swam between two women, at whom she politely avoided looking, then reached up and across them to grab hold of a sticky wooden bar. Wondering whether she could someday really truly, as Neva had intimated, learn to resemble the tall and mannish tennis star Martina Navratilova, whose sweaty light hair flew up whenever she slammed the tennis racket forward in her big hand, the transwoman felt pride and pleasure in her own grip. Now the train began to hiss and hoot along. At the next station, a crowd oozed in like a syrupy colloid whose elbows, briefcases and purses resembled broken objects of a flood's intentions, and so a short young woman had to place herself below the transwoman's arm. She looked uneasy. Judy wondered: Is it my imagination, or do I stink, or is there something about me that's just *ick*?—To distract herself, she looked leftward, discovering a pretty woman who stood squished in place, within touching distance as a matter of fact, and her pink young ear glistened and shone so deliciously that Judy entertained herself by imagining licking its inside whorls, round and round, devouring every atom of wax that she could; this restored her to good spirits, and at the next stop she squeezed her way out, with many an unacknowledged excuse me.

I must actually stink, she told herself. That's why nobody's nice. I should be dead.

But she did not want to *feel* dead.

She decided not to try out at the Pack'N'Grin. Piggy's Pack and Ship was hiring at ten dollars an hour, under the table. Xenia had charitably shared this intelligence. The transwoman, whose own public demeanor expressed a certain waxiness, which many people found more repellent than pathetic, making her all the more isolated, forced herself into the attempt, flushing red even before the manager said: Judy, we've filled the position.

So she continued down her quotidian career path. In other words, she asked the retired policeman for money.

He pulled off his spectacles.—How much do you need?

I don't know; I'm sorry; I'm *sorry*!

Will you default on the rent again?

Maybe. Unless—

Unless you put more life into those blow jobs. And you know what? Your breath stinks.

Actually, I feel like I stink all over, and that's why people—

Gimme a goddamned break. You hit me up for money, and I also have to be your psychiatrist? Judy, why don't you move in with me?

You mean, you still want me?

Yeah.

Even even after I . . . ?

Shut up.

But, J. D., the thing is—

You do stink. All over. Get down on your hands and knees and crawl. I mean it. Crawl around like a fat little Judy bug. You ugly cockroach!—her thighs quivering as he spanked her.—Here's eighty dollars. That's all I've fucking got. Scuttle off and spend it on your Neva bitch.

Oh, J. D., I can't—

You *will*, sooner or later, because when money talks, Judy listens. Now get out; *get out, get out*—

9

You like it? It's got real spices in it. I heard that in the commercial.

Thanks, Judy; that was so sweet of you.

When I cook for J. D., he won't even taste it. He takes his plate and scrapes it down the sink.

Is he really good for you?

Why can't you try to understand him, Neva? He's a sick old man who needs love—

No, honey, I didn't mean to upset you . . .

Can't you like him at least a little?

I love him, said the lesbian.

Neva, will you marry me?

We're already married.

Please . . . !

Come here. Come sit on my lap and give me a kiss . . .

Tell me a story.

Isn't that Sandra's job? By the way, I hear you came to see Catalina.

Oh, she's so nice! And Erin's made it her job sometimes. I mean, she . . . Have you made love with Erin? I know you have. You have, right?

I'll make love with you, said the lesbian.

10

Since the retired policeman did not answer the door, the transwoman let herself in with the spare key. He was absent, not dead. Maybe he'd stormed back to Melba, who in late middle age retained the petrified grace of a flying horse on a tarnished Iberian coin. Actually he had met me by accident at Xenia's occasional workplace, the Pink Apple, where we had both gone in order to stop thinking about

Neva.—You don't get a lot of honesty out of people most of the time, he told me. So let's say you get a shooting and you have six witnesses. So that's six different stories that you're gonna get. You may find one of the witnesses is a girlfriend of the shooter. That's gonna give you a slightly different story. Our job is to read people and to wade through the crap. A lot of the times when we're doing interviews, we already know the answers to the questions that we're asking.

All right, I said, so what's the answer?

He laughed and slapped my shoulder.—I'll tell you if and only if you state the question.

Who or what is Neva? I said.

Correct. Richard, you've got no get-up-and-go, but you almost could have had the mind of a cop.

Coming from him, that was superlative. Like Judy, I felt so happy that a tear almost came. Clinking glasses with him, I said: The thing is, J. D., you don't know the answer to that one.

He flicked away air and said: I will. Meanwhile my job is to figure out if you are being honest or not.

Who, me?

All of you. You, Francine, Shantelle, Xenia, Samantha, Selene, Catalina, Al, Erin, Sandra and whoever else, Judy included. My job is to take bits of stories and fit them together to get the correct picture. Unfortunately, people don't have a lot of problems stepping on each other. And a lot of people (I'm talking about *you*) don't wanna be involved. You can have sixteen people who saw something, and only two will say, I saw it happen. And, Richard, you're not one of those two.

Sorry, I said.

No, I get it, he said (I loved him even more when he was magnanimous). They worry about their safety. They have to live there. They're worried about the shooter's friends coming back for retaliation against them.

Neva's not a shooter, I said.

Says you, he said. Maybe she is, or worse, and she's scoped out the back window, and they've owned that house for twenty-five years and they're just stuck.

I rent by the week, I said.

Stop interrupting me, he said. Renters or owners, you're all fuckin' *stuck.* You can't get away from *shit.* I try not to think that everybody's a liar. Unfortunately that's not the way it tends to come out.

Unaware how safe and happy he was, Judy scanned first Jojo's Liquors, then the Cinnabar. She checked the Y Bar again. Almost panicking, she even clipclopped all the way up to the Buddha Bar—the boundary of his most heroic voyaging.

A trim woman, wholesomely elegant, with short reddish hair—a sort of Julie Andrews type—was sitting at the counter. When she turned her head, the transwoman saw her face: young from a distance, maybe thirtyish; actually, fortyish. She was pretty.

In a low voice the bartender asked her something, to which she replied: No, no, no, I auditioned in L.A.; but there was a New York show and I went on the road; I was in Detroit and Phoenix and Nashville . . .

And that was the one with Sandrine Summers?

Yeah, it's the same show; they just took it outside.

Mesmerized (even Neva vanished from her head), Judy sat down four stools away, wondering how to creep closer. Nothing terrible happened, so she inched over, leaving a stool between them. Then, blushing and sweating, she said: Could I, um, buy you a drink? I couldn't help hearing . . .

For once, her victim was kind.—Thank you, said the woman. What's your name?

Judy.

I'm Helen. Are you at loose ends, Judy?

Well, not exactly. I heard you mention Sandrine Summers, and I thought . . . Well, I need advice. You see, I want to perform in musicals, or maybe just dance.

How old are you?

Forty-nine.

Well, you see, Judy, that's a bit late to . . .

But don't you think I look young for my age?

For your age, you look . . . I'll need to go soon. I'm sorry.

Helen, how did you get to be confident?

Well, I was pretty shy, I think, as a kid. I certainly was not part of the popular crowd; you know, they have different crowds, and I just kind of got along with everyone. I didn't have any really negative self-image. But when I started college, when I was a dancer they told me to lose weight. I think I was like nineteen. There were certainly girls in my year that had eating disorders. I was fairly, it was the first time I had to realize, I have to stop eating the way I did. Now, Judy—

I know I need to lose thirty pounds, maybe forty.

Well, then—

Can I please please ask you one more thing?

Of course, Judy, but then I really have to—

Did you always know you were beautiful?

Helen, wide-eyed, gently gesturing with long fingers, thin and graceful almost to frailty, perfect in her teeth, constantly making shapes with her hands, replied: I don't think I saw it like that. In Vegas I didn't really fit the mold; most of the girls had long hair; I had short hair; I had long legs; they like midriff.

But when you were a little girl—oh, you must have been so *cute*!

I danced as a kid and I had my social group really and my best friends used to do it, and I just continued. My teacher had gone to a performing arts college. I never saw it as being a beautiful woman. Being on the stage, Judy, well there's a little bit of a mask. I was fairly confident in my ability to dance. I also did musicals. Judy, my advice is work on your confidence. And now I'd better go.

Thank you for being so nice to me!

Don't mention it, said the retired dancer. Thanks for the drink. See you again, maybe.

Gulping her own drink and paying cash, the transwoman hurried out, hoping to follow Helen home, but the retired dancer, perhaps sensing some such scheme, had vanished, so there was nothing to do but buy at least one more drink (a much cheaper one) at the Y Bar, daydreaming of becoming a green-and-blue serpent-peacock, which is to say a Las Vegas dancerette; her name would be up in lights, two longhaired nubile assistants would dress and undress her, and every night there would be clapping like the static on her dead grandmother's radio.

Then in a sudden sorrowing nauseating dread (she was too worthless to get angry), she realized that *Helen had withheld the secret.* So Judy slid down and down from her dreams.

Next she remembered that the retired policeman had gone missing, about which she was supposed to be worried. Feeling *guilty* and *terrible* and all the rest of it, she prayed: Please, God, let J. D. be alive. If he is, I swear I'll spy on Neva, whatever he wants, just to . . . I'll do anything.

Running back to his place, she rang the buzzer. This time he answered.

I was frantic, she whispered. I mean, I wondered if you were okay.

He glared at her.

J. D., did I do something wrong?

Three fuckin' guesses. And that's why I dated Melba, who at least has a genuine working *pussy.* Do you hear me, bitch? Bitch, are you pissed off?

How could I be? she whispered.

Right *answer.* Good *girl.* Come in, then. Shut the door. You know where I want you. All right, bitch, now bend over and do your best Judy Garland.

I guess I—ow, not so hard!

Chuckling, he whipped her again.

I guess I—I just like nice people—ow!

So does Melba. Take it from the top, slut.

I guess I just like nice people and when someone has a lot of nice friends I'm sure to get along with them.

That's right. Now suck my dick again, bitch. Out of *principle.* Like that. Actually I didn't see Melba. Keep it up. By the way, I got a tax refund. *I said keep going.* Almost three hundred dollars. So if you want to . . . That's enough. Oh, what's the fucking difference? Turn on the history channel.

After the program was over (should we have H-bombed North Korea in 1953?), he pinched her cheek until her purring snores ended in one loud snort, and she opened her eyes. He laughed at her.

Sorry, she whispered. It was really interesting; I only . . .

Ready for the quiz?

Where's Korea anyway? Somewhere in Asia. Oh, I'm so stupid; I know I'm gonna flunk—

First question. If it's not for personal advantage, why's she doing it?

Who are you talking about?

He punched her in the stomach, not hard enough to hurt; it was merely a surprise. At the same time he clapped his hand over her mouth. Then he started pulling her hair. Her muffled cries saturated his hand with hot breath and saliva. He felt curious: Since he was pressuring her so hard about Neva, would she bite his hand? But no hint of that—good old Judy!

Now, he said, if I take my hand away, will you be calm and quiet?

Wide-eyed, she nodded three times.—You're almost pretty right now, he informed her. All right. Up goes my hand. Keep your word! That's my bitch. So. She doesn't pay you, and you're not paying her, so why's she doing it?

I *would* pay if she—

Why's she doing it, Frank?

That's not for me to know.

The Goddess moves in mysterious ways, huh? *Really*, Frank? You don't even go to church.

Maybe there's something dark that she—

At least you're trying. If you're correct, she's not a fraud, just a freak.

This isn't *right*, to backstab Neva!

What the fuck are you talking about? I've seen how you steal her panties and hoard her snotty nosewipes! You're *doing* it, Frank. So stop the hypocrisy and try for results. Work with me on this. Listen: If she's in pain she needs help. Don't you want to help her?

Help Neva? Sure. But I don't—

Hundred-dollar bills.

That's right; she always—

Why?

I tried to look inside her wallet, but she—

You'd give your crummy life for her, *right*?

But, J. D., do you really think she needs help?

Could be. And that's why we snoop. Do you read me, Sherlock?

Chain of Command

What is known as "G" or "government heat," is in reality a smoking-out process.

COURTNEY RYLEY COOPER, 1935

How then ought ye to guard yourselves?—By regarding her tears and her smiles as enemies, her stooping form, her hanging arms, and her disentangled hair as toils designed to entrap man's heart.

BUDDHA, date unknown

1

Melba had drummed her tattooed fingers on the restaurant table, her withered hair hanging over her face as she bestowed on him an exact repor about her rent, until her dear little cell phone (less magenta than Hunter's) tinkled and she spoke an address, most likely to some buyer or seller of coal tar heroin, after which the phone tinkled again and she ducked her head, muttering into it that she was on her way. Finally she said: Sure I knew her, but that was before she was Neva. She used to be Karen. Karen Strand. And she . . . Yeah. I guess we were friends. But she turned out to be just another heartless bitch. Actually I never met her; I . . . Maybe I wanted to pull your chain. Ha, ha, what a broken little chain you have, J. D.! And it don't even flush no more! Not for me, it don't. Actually I asked Baby, because she keeps up with all the bars, and she . . . Hey, do you wanna see another picture of me in the blue wig? See, this was before I evicted that sonofabitch Dino who kept stealing from me. The first time I caught him, I said, we won't say no more about it. Just don't fucking do it again. The fifth time, he had to go bye-bye. And what really hurts me is that I did so much for Dino. I fucking supported him for three years, and he ripped me off! But he did use to do my makeup. He kept me company after you left me. We had fun together.

I used to dress him up as a little girl. And we used to come back from thrift stores together with all kinds of cool shit. So in this picture, no, that's not the right picture, but it's, oh, yeah, that was the last time my ex ever let my son stay overnight, and I painted his face gold and he painted my face silver and that's . . .

What's Baby's number?

Here it is. See, it may not look like it but I'm organized.

The retired policeman gave her forty dollars for old times' sake and she fed it to her little red purse with barely a thank you.—And then that lady wanted to tell me about my paintings, she said, because they were so dark, she kept saying I'd been molested or something . . .

On the money, doll!

So fucking *what.*

Melba, you and I go way back. Remember when my dick used to get hard?

You're talking early Cretaceous, when the first dinosaurs . . . Anyway, you never put it in.

Judy doesn't know that.

Yeah. When you talk about Judy your voice gets different. I'm not stupid. I get it that you—

That I *what*?

Melba kept shrugging her shoulders and playing with her purse. She wore a thin black buckled collar around her wrinkled throat. When she tilted her head, squinting down at her laptop, she looked young and beautiful; then she decomposed again.

Once upon a time he used to date them both, a fact of which he continually reminded the transwoman, in order to keep her on the queer and narrow, although, no matter what he told her, pussy had never been his flavor of the month.

Once upon a Cretaceous time, right when Nancy Kerrigan was on track to win the Olympic gold medal in Norway, should have won it and even *would* have but for one-tenth of a point's difference between her and the Ukrainian dazzler Oksana Baiul, our Judy, whose career sometimes as we know paralleled Nancy Kerrigan's and who looked awfully well put together on that night, drew asymptotically close to taking first place in the retired policeman's blow job competition until Melba did something unexpected with her tongue. The two contestants were aware neither of the contest nor of the outcome. *He* felt entertained. Nowadays he was so far gone that squeezing his own dick made him tired.

He said: I know you had it rough when you were a kid. So did Judy.

Judy? Well, some kids are so cruel, like you're a pansy and not a man. They ought to teach kids that instead of covering things up, you, I mean, you could know that things are fluid . . .

And Melba's head began to sink, like a stripper slowly descending the dark stage-steps after she has gathered her clothes. Oh, yes; he could almost see her, silver-blonde and tawny, wriggling off her shawl and pretending to play with the straps of her panties. Once upon a Precambrian or Mesozoic time his favorite stripper had been Melba, sitting on the stage with her long legs spread, grinning and leaning forward to flirt with the businessmen who stared up her thighs, longing for a little bit of slit, then clitterclattering over to *him*, with that hot hurt hungry look in her eyes.

2

And you're sure that the lez used to be called Karen Strand?

No doubt, replied Baby, whose affect inspired the retired policeman into spectacular indifference.

He said: Why are you sure?

For one thing, I went to the Y Bar and asked her. So pay me my twenty bucks.

Groaning, he got out his wallet and counted out four fives, to make it more impressive. She counted them all over again. The poor old bitch must've had bad experiences, he thought. And look at her touch up her lipstick, as if that could possibly . . . Life is fuckin' sad.—Having thought that, he liked her better.

And she answered straight up, said Baby.

Then she must be lying.

See, here's a picture of her on my phone. I took it to show you, and she didn't care. She didn't even ask me why the fuck did I want to know. So then I reached out to a girl I went to school with, and she confirmed it.

What do you mean confirmed?

I mean she trotted out the name Karen Strand all by her lonesome. Recognized her straight off. And she and I go way back—

What's her name?

Latoya. She's like my big sister. She's—

Fuck that.

What do you mean?

I don't care what sisters do to each other. Just stay on track, because—

You have a migraine, right? That's what makes you mean.

Heartburn. Jesus Christ, it hurts—

Well, she's sitting right there behind the pool rack in case you want to give her something. The one in red.

Bring her over here.

For another twenty.

Fuck you, he said, limping over to Latoya's table.

Hi, said that individual. She looked fifty at the least.

Do you know Neva, or are you just another rusty link in Baby's chain of command?

I kind of resent that, mister.

Well, here's ten.

That's all I get? I just spent six dollars on this Bloody Mary and it's no damn good.

There's your life lesson. What they pour, they *adulterate.* Got that? They water down the fucking vodka. Then they extend the tomato juice. They cut spice mix with *whatever.* So as you go through life, my girl—

You gonna give?

Another ten after. So who's Neva?

Karen Strand.

How do you know?

See, we're the same age, but maybe we're not because in that picture Baby e-mailed me she still looks like some high school glamor chick, which I don't understand, because her mother's *ancient*, and Karen's gotta be up there with me and Baby. It's definitely her in the picture, except she looks hella pretty *now.* A lot better than I remember. But they say nine-tenths of that is confidence. I just heard somebody say that. Some retired dancer bitch. Well, back then Karen was skanky. A sick, nasty, skinny little thing that just to look at made me mad. She shoulda been drowned at birth. At Vallejo High I still went by Janet, and me and Marcie was like sisters. See, Marcie hated Karen, because Karen was a lez. I'm not prejudiced; I did what I could, but she . . .

Then what?

Nothing. Some older bitch turned her out. Karen was a bull dyke slut even in sophomore year, and by the time we graduated she was *experienced.*

Go on.

That's all. I saw her on the street with that hard old dyke; once Marcie and me, we ran into 'em in a bar, I'm gonna say Jingle's, but we just looked at them and they looked at us. No love lost. And until Baby showed me this picture, I never did see her since.

Where's Marcie?

We fell out.

What's your e-mail?

Lemme just write it for you on this napkin. I'm darkbitch64 at—

When did you graduate?

Class of 1983 and *proud* of it. *Go, Apaches! Go, go, Valley Joe!*

What about Karen?

Oh, she was a year ahead of me, but small and kind of immature for her age. Me and Marcie, well, it wasn't too nice, but we used to kind of tease her. Not that I'm prejudiced or nothing.

How did you tease her?

Oh, spit on her, stuff like that. We was just foolin' around. One time Marcie stuck a bloody tampon in her hair. That Karen was like a cockroach almost. Something about her . . . We *all* wanted to . . .

How did she react?

She never did nothing. I said to her, go on, Karen, you like to eat pussy, so put Marcie's tampon in your mouth and . . . And she fuckin' *did.* Just looked at me, didn't say a word. We got so grossed out—

Yep, you did everything for her. How were her grades?

Outstanding at first. Mousy little kiss-ass! Acted like she was going places. But after she started eating fur taco, she got Cs and Ds like us. So that was . . .

Here's ten.

Thank you. Am I done?

Keep talking.

For ten more, right? I'm starting to like you. Well, that older dyke I was telling you about, actually, for what she was she was sort of hot: silver crewcut and black nail polish, with almost a vampire look, and she was mean as fuck, so we gave her respect. Call her a lesbo and she'd right away start throwing rocks! I do remember that she drove a red Pontiac Conspiracy, which impressed us, and she called herself, well, some made up nickname, and once they started messing around, Karen would cut classes and—

And what?

They was even going into hotels. Back then, see, they never checked I.D.—

Which hotels?

I have no idea. But Marcie said—

You're on the outs with her.

That's no lie.

Can you find her?

Well, said Latoya, I think she goes on that bigdoughnut.com site, you know, the one where middle-aged ladies show off their titties; you have to be at least a thirty-eight double D—

Ask her the girlfriend's name.

No fuckin' way. I'm not reaching out to that doublecrossing—

If she doesn't have the name, get the names of the hotels. If she remembers something there'll be twenty for each of you.

That's not much.

On the bright side, thanks to me your beautiful friendship with Marcie will come screaming back to life. Besides, you hate Karen and I'm trying to get her in trouble.

For real?

Yeah. I hate her same as you. You graduated in 1983?

Sure.

That would make her class of 1982.

Whatever. Buy me a drink?

Here's ten, he said, and trudged away without another word to her or Baby because he despised both of them.

3

The dietician was a bespectacled young woman with an oval face—and slender, of course; he had to give her that. He enrolled her in the type that rarely winds up in court (especially nowadays, thanks to no-fault divorce) but likes to drop a dime on that scofflaw parked in a red zone, or the renters whose music gets too loud on Friday night, or the half-senile retiree who waters his lawn on a forbidden day. Well, he could live with that. All the time he was thinking about Judy, feeling sick because they had quarrelled again and she might not come back.

And you brought your meal calendar? the dietician began.

Yeah, here it is, he said. I gave up pastries in the morning—

That's *excellent*!

And I try to walk at least fifteen minutes a day. You see, my feet hurt when I—

Did your primary care doc refer you to a podiatrist?

That's not covered by my insurance.

I understand . . .—and he almost laughed, to watch her swivel away from that ugly subject, as if the limitations of his insurance were the result of his own free choice.—Well, you do know, Mr. Slager, that a minimum of thirty to sixty minutes a day would be a better starting point. Has anyone gone over your labs with you?

No.

All right. Can you see the screen, or shall I make the font larger? No? All right. Well, here's your blood glucose, and it's through the roof. And your triglycerides, your blood pressure—

The retired policeman, who knew exactly what it means when the suspect announces that she will now begin to lie, cut in as follows: Just tell me what the hell I'm supposed to do about it.

For starters, you need to lose at least ten percent of your body weight. How much did you weigh when you got your labs?

Two hundred and forty.

So twenty-four, even twenty-six pounds should be your initial weight loss goal. And have you made any other changes to your diet?

I've cut way back on the alcohol. I try to have no more than two shots at lunch time, and five or six shots at dinner. Is it true that beer is worse than whiskey?

A straight shot of hundred-proof whiskey is certainly less caloric than a twelve-ounce beer.

All right, I'll cut out the beer, he replied—an easy bargain to make, since he never drank it except with Xenia and the straight man. *Now* they were going places!

But this dietician bitch wasn't satisfied.—Mr. Slager, she patronized him, we generally recommend an absolute maximum of two shots a day. And you need to start eating more vegetables.

Yeah, well, I live in the goddamn ghetto. I go to the store, and the only vegetable I see's a bag of potato chips.

Do you have a freezer at home?

I used to have a refrigerator, you know, to chill the beer, but it quit working. Anyway, you heard me say I'm giving up beer.

We're just about at the end of our time, Mr. Slager. Any other questions you care to ask me?

How about dried fruit? I could keep a big bag of that around, and then when I got hungry—

The trouble is, it takes awhile to eat one apricot, but no time to eat six dried apricots, which means six times the sugar. But I think you're off to a good start, cutting out the pastries and walking a little.

Yeah, I feel slightly better than I used to . . .

Then let's check your weight on the way out. You were at two hundred and forty before, and that was how long ago?

Oh, three or four months . . .

Then you might have lost a couple of pounds already. Right this way. Do you want to take off your shoes?

Sure. Anything to get my weight down, he said, trying to make a joke of it. But that did not seem funny to her.

He stepped on the scale, and the red digits reported that he now weighed two hundred and fifty-six pounds.

The dietician inspected him in sadness and disappointment. He wanted to say: Don't look at me like I'm a motherfuckin' liar. Then he wondered how on earth he could possibly be heavier after his multitude of sacrifices.

He said: Well, I guess the best weight loss program for me's a bullet.

She tightened her mouth. He glared at the floor, humiliated.—But as soon as he limped into the elevator and out of the lobby his spirits reascended, and he practically sang to himself: Fuck that disapproving twat anyhow. And fuck that fuckin' fuckin' American General Hospital and every whitecoat who looks down on me. And fuck my swollen ankles; Jesus God, why don't I saw them off?

He caught a 38 Geary bus downtown, and hobbled the six blocks to the Y Bar. Now his best years marched back ahead of him.

The usual? said Francine.

Double it up!

You mean four shots?

Good gal; you actually know how to multiply.

Make it ten dollars. What's new?

Keep the change.

He wished that Judy would breeze here right now. Tonight, if she forgave him, he would tell her all about that snotty dietician and how he should have put her down.

4

Of course Judy did, so he did, until four in the morning, when his swollen ankles impelled him to send her clipclopping away—straight home, she claimed, but he supposed aloud that she might hustle along the way since her very first shift at the Pack and Ship (mazeltov, bitch!) would not be until two in the afternoon. She grinned in embarassment. What did he care? With her out of the picture, he booted up his screechy old desktop and prepared to punish his bleary eyes.—He told himself: You know what? I hate almost everything.—Well, not everything: He was already logged in on the good old SpiderWeb! Among other eternally glowing black-and-white ghosts pertaining to the Vallejo High website shone Karen Strand's senior portrait, a forlorn thumbnail on a graveyard page of the 1982 yearbook. His screen froze twice; he had to deploy a control-option-backslash-escape to get back to the homepage and start over; to hell with your so-called user interface. Click by goddamned click, he zoomed in, until her much reticulated likeness filled the screen: young, pale and troubled—Neva, but nonmagnetic, barren, defective (we in the business describe that as a leave-me-alone look). Regressing through the previous three years, he found her appearing progressively worse. As for Latoya, which is to say Janet Smith, she had certainly been prettier in her youth. But Karen and Neva, well, he could not figure that out. Was it impersonation or what? She had to be fifty-one years old.

Logic, he liked to remind Judy, can best be described as the orderly and sensible review of facts, conditions and events in a consistent and regular fashion. All fuckin' right! So we go back in time and Neva turns into something hardly worth spitting on. What occurred between then and now? Who did it?

He texted darkbitch64: *Will pay $20 for contact to Karen S's HS gf.* Then he took a drink and three sleeping pills.

Judy at School

Without love, the outward work is of no value; but whatever is done out of love, be it never so little, is wholly fruitful.

Thomas à Kempis, 1413

Those whom nature has sacrificed to her ends—her mysterious ends that often lie hidden—are sometimes endowed with a vast will to loving, with an endless capacity for suffering also, which must go hand in hand with their love.

Radclyffe Hall, 1928

1

And while I was dreaming of a giant angel who wore ten thousand eyes on her greenish-grey wings, Judy mouthwashed away a new friend's semen and lay down to think about Neva. To facilitate her thought processes, she masturbated: *Oh*, Neva, I'm sucking you inside *out*! (Nothing was as perfect as the taste of the lesbian's tongue, which was so long she could practically tickle her partners' throats; one time she and Shantelle were having a contest to see who could slam whose tongue in whose mouth the farthest, and the lesbian won when Shantelle started choking.—Stick yours out, the loser commanded, and was surprised that Neva's tongue did not *appear* exceptional; compared to it, however, hers was nothing but a broad little paddle.) And Judy climaxed roaringly. Then she fell asleep as thoroughly as if Shantelle had knocked her out cold.

She dreamed that she was front page news in a style magazine: Coming down the stairs in a goldensilver dress with her knees shinily perfect and a smile that would make even Sandra so jealous, she would be singing "Somewhere Over the Rainbow."

She awoke at noon, leaping happily out of bed, rushing to shower and moisturize, first shaving her chin (where electrolysis treatments had prematurely ceased for financial reasons), then razoring away every last hair on arm and leg and crotch, because tonight she had a date with Neva! She concealed, blushed, eyeshadowed, eyelined, lipsticked and glossed herself. Pouffing out her hair, which she generally pampered with five-dollar conditioner and which even Shantelle agreed was her best feature, she then chose exactly the right earrings, the bloodstone pair which the retired policeman had given her two birthdays ago. Going out to the hallway, she raised the window shade. Today it was drizzling again; each square stone of the sidewalk had become its own silver-grey, and a woman hurried by almost hidden in her lavender umbrella; then a blonde passed slowly with her sodden hair clinging to her shoulders and an unlit cigarette in her mouth; reflections of shoplights shone in soft yellow parallel diagonals as people walked over and through them. The transwoman's joy increased by the minute, like a steadily building euphoria of methamphetamine, until she grew almost fearful of it, so she approached the mirror and told her needy face: Buck up, girl! You're having a pretty good time *right now.* Right, girl? Right, girl? So snap out of it!—And she laughed at herself (turning away, however, from the reflection of her stained teeth).

At 1:55 in the afternoon she arrived at the Pack'N'Grin. Sweating, Bertha the manager said: Judy, see if you can help this man.

This man said: So I fail to see why you insist on my using Form 71-Z when even Cloud Express accepts a Form 3232, as this clip from their website *absolutely proves.*

Oh, said Judy. Oh, I'm really sorry.

Well, you may be *sorry,* but what the fuck does that do for me?

At that, the devil flew into our sweet, submissive Judy, who said: I'll do *anything* to make it right, absolutely *anything.*—She flickered her tongue and wriggled her hips. Then she pulled down her pants.

Bertha fired her right then. Judy told her: I sure did dodge a bullet.

Since she now had six hours to fill, she visited the Y Bar, where Sandra happened to be whispering something to Francine. Left out, Judy ran both hands through Sandra's long red hair.

Do you mind? said Sandra.

Insulted, she rushed out to the Cinnabar, where Erin sat texting somebody a secret. Judy sat down next to her, trying to read that communication.—What's up? inquired her *special friend.*

Will you tell me a story, *pretty please*?

Why that little girl voice?

Because I wanna be *cute.*

Well, you actually sound kind of fake. Why not just be yourself?

Because you got to be a little girl and I didn't.

Okay, sighed Erin. Desisting from her text, she turned the cell phone discreetly over, stroked back her hair and waited.

Carmen the barmaid marched bustily over, and Judy ordered a bourbon and ginger ale. Erin chose a fizzy water. Judy paid for both drinks: here's to unemployment!

All right, said Erin. I wasn't happy getting breasts. I got breasts when I was around nine, and it felt really odd. I thought other girls were excited about getting their breasts, and I thought, you can keep 'em; I don't want mine! I started wearing a lot of layers, trying to hide them. And I got acne; that's really not fun. I like big breasted women, but I always thought smaller breasts were more sexy. I wanted to be more androgynous. I liked boys that were more androgynous, boys that liked wearing makeup . . .

But how did you *feel*? How does a pubescent girl feel?

I don't remember, said Erin.

I mean, did you want to get penetrated? I feel so female when they—

I thought about just the simple science of it, you have the penis and the vagina and one is being penetrated and one is the penetrator, and if you talk about control issues, I don't know, it feels so complicated to think about. I love men who like getting it in the ass. Some guys like it rough, and that's easy for me since I'm not the most practiced person, but I don't like to hurt people; I don't like to hurt my lover.

I like to be hurt, gushed Judy.

We all know that! Well, there's different personalities, and a woman could maybe take on more of a role by playing that she does have a penis, or . . . Don't you have one? Anyway, I've gone down on a woman; I've made a few women come; I don't feel the need to have ass play with women, because I don't feel that they're out to penetrate me, whereas I feel psychologically penetrated by men all the time.

Judy said: You can do anything you want to me.

No thanks, said Erin.

But why? I mean, I'd really do anything.

Because there's only been a few women that I've been comfortable with. I think they were bisexual and open to exploring.

What about Neva?

Well, I've had flirtations with lesbians. I don't know any lesbian who hasn't fooled around with a guy once or twice. But I've never been in love with a woman, even though Neva's hella goodlooking. One of my ladies was kind of chunky; she had a nice body, nice big breasts, a big ass, short, bleached blonde hair . . . They each had their own strong personality. This girl, she really annoyed me at first; she had a septum piercing and tattoos and she chewed gum a lot—with her mouth open!—so I thought she was a really trashy person but I ended up having a really big crush on her, and I guess she liked me, because I ended up getting her off. She had a boyfriend. So we weren't a couple but we were a triple. It only lasted a little while, just a few months. Well, seems like most people are looking to couple up. He was separated from his fiancée but went back to her. She was interested in him but it didn't happen. I wanted to pair off with her since it didn't happen. I think what ended it was he was alone with me one day and we tried having sex just the two of us, just for fun, and it *wasn't* really fun. There wasn't a charge. It didn't feel gross; he was a friend and we knew each other's bodies, but there was something missing. I think *she* was missing. I think I only got hot when she was around. I think for her I was just something that happened once or twice. Now she's married with two kids. And I recently got in touch with him; he's separated from his wife, and I don't think he ever brought up what he and I used to do . . .

But then her phone buzzed, so Judy waved and then went browsing at Moosey's department store. After that she tried to turn a trick, but nobody was renting. Just as Karen Strand's cat Princess used to hide in the closet for fun (which was why she finally died from thirst), so Judy went home to be alone. She longed for goof-balls but proudly told herself: I'll economize. So she took a nap and then another shower. At eight p.m. she set off for the Hotel Reddy.

Neva, am I beautiful?

Of course, whispered her hostess, and kissed her ear.

And Judy even believed it, although by the time she descended those carpeted stairs to the street, once more she would already be feeling *nakedly ugly.*

She could not get enough of stroking the lesbian's upper arm in ever more rapid circles. Then her hand was on the lesbian's buttock, and her tongue was in the lesbian's mouth. They twirled tongue-tips for a long time, breathing heavily.

Neva, she said, he hits me.

Don't you want to value yourself?

But it feels *good.*

That's fine then. You enjoy being worthless, don't you, pretty girl? I can see your nipples getting hard . . . !

Let's please please *please* not talk about it.

Okay, honey, said the lesbian, who had been there before.

She stepped into the waistband of her strap-on, pulled it up, cinched it tight, lubricated it and penetrated the transwoman fast, hard and deep the way she liked it, so that she trembled and began groaning in a deep voice, then climaxed, baa-ing like a sheep. The lesbian felt good to have pleased her.

Gently running her hand through the lesbian's hair, Judy thanked her, then said: Neva, why do you love me?

Smiling and kissing her cheek, the lesbian said: For so many reasons—

But you love everybody! Are we all the same to you?

I swear there's nobody else like you, Judy. I love you for yourself.

What about everyone else?

It's just you and me right now.

But in two hours it won't be.

And then it will be again.

But it won't be forever!

Nothing is, except for things we don't understand.

Oh, well. Now will you slap my face?

They played that game for a good long while, until Judy's time was nearly up. How could she cling to the lesbian for a little longer and then maybe *longer*? Casting around for topics, she said: You're in pain, aren't you?

Oh, Judy, I know you want to help . . . !

Did somebody hurt you?

We all get hurt.

Who are you holding a torch for?

Everyone.

Including Francine?

Judy, those questions are not good for you.

Please, Neva, I want to know.

I see that.

Just tell me this: How often have you lied to me?

Never.

Why are you doing this?

I have to and I want to.

2

The retired policeman, even now not unwilling to grant his approval, opened a can of beer and said: Well, well. Looks like you had fun.

Oh, yes!

What about Erin?

What about her?

I saw you two in the Cinnabar.

No, that was just . . . It's just—

Just Neva.

Yeah.

Give me a suck.

She did. All the while she remembered how it had been to suck the lesbian's nipples, which were as tiny and round as the incised dots on a pair of dice.

3

It is true that whenever she had sex with anyone else she now felt sad, but when she had sex with Neva she was ecstatic; and this ecstasy endured, so that when she came back from being with her, she felt happy and ready to make the retired policeman happy, which is why (just like Neva) she fulfilled all her lover's scenarios and still had energy left over; thus their relationship became a shining machine.

Sometimes she started weeping because, frowning like a pitiless cost-cutter, he declined to commit to her; he might (which seemed unlikely) go back to Melba or his ex-wife or maybe stay single, but just when she had resigned herself to such possibilities, he would bend her over and call her his number one bitch.

What do you most hope for? asked the lesbian.

Can I really tell you? I mean, if I tell you, will you be upset?

Of course you can tell me.

I want to move in with him.

Hasn't he offered?

But I'm afraid we'll get into some big fight and then he'll throw me out—

Then use your female power, Judy! He wants you to. Or at least he's testing you to see if you will. It's not unethical to do that; look at the rules he plays by . . . ! Will you consider what I've said?

Okay, said the transwoman in a very small voice.

The lesbian, she who spoke to our bodies, was very busy just then; she had to fluff up her hair for the straight man, because he loved to run his hands through it. But the transwoman was saying: And you promise that if I do that you won't be mad?

I promise.

Can I ask you something else? said the transwoman.

Sure, said the lesbian.

I know this sounds kind of silly or crazy under the circumstances, but, but, am I still your primary relationship?

Of course, said the lesbian.

4

Seeking out the marvelous one, the lesbian, who unlike her sad mother could still climax all the way up to her pulsating cervix; appealing to her, hating our lives, we more often than not found ourselves babbling, even begging, as when Shantelle tearfully demanded: Neva, Neva, can't you please help me? I wanna be less angry.

How can I do that?

I don't know. And less proud. I . . . Because everything's empty, so what's the use?

Come closer, said the lesbian. Lay down your head, right here by my heart, and close your eyes.

In those days Shantelle considered the lesbian to be the most perfect being ever. She seemed delighted to do anything in bed; moreover, she was so good that Shantelle screamed herself hoarse. In other words, she was experienced, although so was Shantelle herself, who could top any girl, anytime, but there remained something fresh about Neva, who never appeared to be faking anything; although Shantelle, had she been more reflective, might have wondered why she knew so little about her idol's life—not that she would ordinarily have felt interested, although in this case, since the lesbian was so lovely and so kind, so unexcelled at giving and receiving satisfaction, Shantelle might not have minded at least learning how often she had tried men and crime; almost certainly she had never made children, her tummy being so smooth and her pussy so very very tight.

Without words the lesbian did something to her, so that I may as well call it magic. Then Shantelle, flickering her tongue between the lesbian's lips, seized hold of her head with easy triumphant domination.

5

As for Francine, whenever she unhooked her bra and stepped out of her panties in that room of the Reddy Hotel, she not only believed but felt that she and Neva were going to be a couple forever. What did the lesbian's other alliances, all initiated right across the counter from her even as she poured out the drinks, mean to her? For my part, whenever I sat down on my side of the lesbian's bed, bent over and began to unlace my shoes, I anticipated, if you like, manna, communion, maybe even some kind of Pentecost, but I never would have called her my girlfriend. She had her way, and very tactfully managed it, as I do declare, of checking the alarm clock, which never went off in my hearing, thank goodness. My well-off friends who can afford to go to therapists (even the transwoman sometimes went to one; I called him *the rapist*) inform me that in most every session comes the disagreeable moment when, while happily elucidating the most complex, interesting and worthwhile topic on earth, which is to say themselves, they find themselves unaccountably *checked*, perhaps by a sad smile, or a glance to the side; after which *the rapist*, who for fifty minutes has listened almost as would a true friend, gently but unashamedly says: We'll have to stop now—reminding my friends that this was never anything more than *paid listening over a pre-fixed block of time.* In the case of a prostitute the time may well be less inhumanly measured—by the orgasm, for instance (assuming that the client doesn't take too long). A wife offers up more fungible moments: the looked for bedtime intimacy, prospective duration undefined, may unexpectedly be converted into a mortgage conference, a live-streamed movie on Mammazoid, or a quarrel. By contrast, a sweet-eyed snuggly girlfriend gives eternity as long as it lasts; in other words, her sessions terminate not because she is rejecting her lover, but only on account of constraints imposed by this unfeeling world. What does it feel like for a Catholic at confession? Does the priest rush her along, or does she get the pleasure of fully disclosing her every sin? This I cannot know. But it does seem that if I went down on my knees, exposing my full vileness to the Goddess, I could go on day and night if that suited me. I have told you that my times with the lesbian felt much longer than they actually were; but even when it seemed that the end lay as impossibly far away as my own death, I never forgot it would come. I would dress and go out; then somebody else would come in. But the way that Francine experienced true love was that even the inevitable end counted for nothing. I knew that the lesbian loved me, but that made our twosome no more exclusive than as if I were a bride of Jesus in a whole convent of equally devout nuns (among whom Shantelle, happily overcome by sweetly desperate desire, now gripped the lesbian by her lovely buttocks, parted them, kneaded them and for the thousandth time began to lick her anus, which tasted like smoked leather, not long after which the lesbian, going down on Judy's atrophied little penis, took it in her mouth even as her victim spread the wings of Neva's vulva and licked it round and round until Neva began to sing in orgasm, not quite as E-beth used to do.) For Francine the rest of us were mere visitors; she loved Neva better than anyone, and Neva loved her the most. Well, how can I prove it wasn't so? Even when they were nailing down the lid of the lesbian's coffin, Francine was crooning (it gave me the creeps): *I promise you, Neva, oh, Neva, baby, I promise you it won't be long . . .*—And she lacked any suicidal ideation! I point this out only because I cannot understand it. How can each of us know and feel how others love? In a field of sunflowers, why doesn't each plant convert its solar nourishment into identical leaves and petals? And that is all I can tell you about Francine.

6

At each interval between loving us, the lesbian, checking her image in the mirror, felt at the sight of that reflected excellence the remotely pounding heart-rush of a methamphetamine addict who gets meaninglessly high, without any joy; for she took neither pride nor pleasure in herself; because her allure was impersonally objective: even she, its ostensible subject, could not avoid feeling it, as indeed she was called upon to do by expertise's practicalities; it would have been slovenly not to verify and reverify her power, for exactly the same reason that a wise butcher tests the edge of his knife before advancing on the pig. It was in this spirit that Judy Garland reminded us: *In the movies, your face is magnified, every little defect shows up multiplied a thousand times.* What was a girl to do, but police her defects?

But in action she couldn't be excellent—at least not to herself. To the rest of us she remained perfect; she killed us just right even without seeing the knife that trembled in her hands.

She lay in her rumpled bed, sweating and feverish, with infected tonsils that made her breath stink, and the transwoman was happier than she had ever been in her life, because she got to take care of her whom she loved.

Baby? Neva, baby, oh, God, what should I do?

Can you . . . hot water? Or tea?

In the cupboard, the transwoman found a box of chamomile tea. She considered that incredibly classy; she decided to start drinking it at home even if she didn't like it. She filled the electric kettle and plugged it in. Oh, how she wanted to be good to Neva! Taking out two mugs, she placed a teabag in each. Then she took a fifth of bourbon out of her handbag, because whiskey was so helpful for a sore throat! She filled Neva's mug a quarter of the way up with that amber-colored affection. Just to be social, she filled her own mug up halfway. Now what else could she do for her adorable lover? Remembering the bottle of codeines she had stolen from Erin weeks ago, more because she could than because she had desired them, she crushed six between two spoons, and divided the powder quite fairly between the mugs: two for Neva, who might not be used to them, and four for her. Now the kettle was shrilling, in that unearthly rising note that ever since she had overheard it from this very room reminded her of Sandra climaxing.

Drink your tea, honey. Oh, you poor, poor thing . . . Neva, you're the most wonderful person in the whole world! Let me help you sit up. Careful; it's really really hot . . . I added just a touch of booze to yours, to . . . Nothing else. Oh, Neva . . . !

Now they had finished their tea. The lesbian was already getting drowsy. Time to make sure the door was locked, and turn off the lesbian's cell phone! It would have been informative to scroll through the numbers of whoever had most recently called her, but the lesbian was staring at her vaguely through half-closed eyes.

Neva, Neva, girlfriend, girlfriend! Judy sang so happily—because Neva was all hers!

Sliding her big male hand into the lesbian's underpants, she parted the labia with forefinger and ring finger, then with the middle one began massaging the wet and silken clit while the lesbian moaned, half out of her mind with fever.

Neva? Neva, do you really love me?

Caressing the lesbian's sweaty hair, she lay beside her until nightfall, whispering to her, rocking her as if she were a doll.

7

What I've been hearing about you, said Francine, well, I'm telling you, this bunch would do anything for you.

That's so sweet, said the lesbian.

If they were smarter they'd be licking your shoes. They'd be saying: Neva, whatever the hell you want . . . !

But I don't want anything.

Then why are you here? Why not get out of here, or get a steady lover or slit your fuckin' throat? Come on, girl. Everybody wants something.

What do you want?

Why make it about me? I'm trying to help you, because I love you.

And I love you.

Then you wanna marry me?

I can't marry everybody.

Neva, you're the one for me.

I love you.

So you don't love me the way I love you.

Francine, you *are* special to me. I don't love anybody else the way I love you. But I have to love everyone an equal amount.

Why?

Because that's who I am. I can't disappoint them.

Then you'll disappoint all of us, sooner or later. Be careful.

I know how it has to end.

Yeah. Who doesn't? Now listen, baby. I don't just love you; I'm also your friend.

Thank you.

And I'm telling you: The others love you, but they're not your friends. They need you, so they'll turn against you.

I don't think so, said the lesbian.

And watch out for Shantelle.

It won't be the way you think. Could I have another?

Eight dollars, said Francine.

8

That was when Francine began to confide in me. She joined the retired policeman's camp, whose motto was: *Neva doesn't add up.*

I asked her: Do you think somebody can love more than one person at a time?

Sure.

Can you?

Never. Can you?

I don't know.

We were drinking happy hour tonics at the Cinnabar so that none of our friends could listen in. I was paying. She swirled her ice around and said: She pretends and even maybe tries to convince herself that we're all the same to her, but that can't be true unless we're all nothing to her.

I said: She loves me.

Well, she loves me, too, said Francine. She loves us both, all right, and she loves Judy, I know; *I* love Judy—but then what? That beats me. Sandra, sure; Xenia and Hunter, they're only semi-toxic; Al's harmless; Victoria's a maybe, but no goddamn way Shantelle . . .

Well, I said, what if she doesn't love anyone? Isn't that the same as loving everyone? I mean, that's what you said—

No, said Francine.

Carmen the barmaid filled Francine's glass and said: Professional courtesy.

Thanks, hon, said Francine.

What about you, mister? Last call for happy hour.

I'll pass, thanks.

You know you want it. Have one on me.

Okay, I said to be nice. Then I said: Francine, you add up.

So do you.

Thanks, honey. Then let's be friends.

Lesbi friends, she giggled, and kissed the air in my direction.

Some Names Are True

Self is an error . . . See things as they are and ye will be comforted.

BUDDHA, date unknown

Crime is intimately associated with female sexual inversion.

FRANK S. CAPRIO, M.D., date unknown

1

The transwoman said: The thing about being a policeman—

Yeah, bitch, what would you know about that?

You're not the only cop I've given blow jobs to.

He suddenly laughed.—All right, Judy. I believe you do know something. Now tell me about cops.

Well, you think you know people, and in a way you do, but only the bad parts and the hurt parts. That's all you see.

What else is there?

Nothing much, with most of us. But Neva's different.

Oh, *is* she!

I swear she is!

So she's perfect. She's got that *women's mark.* Her shit don't stink.

That's right.

Then she's lying to you.

Why would she?

Certain people, women mainly but also pedophiles and politicians, try to pretend to be perfect. A few of them even get away with it until they get in trouble. Where they get in trouble is believing their own lies. Now, Judy, am I perfect?

No.

Then pull down those panties, bend over and take it. Now you know what you have to say. What do you have to say, *bitch*?

The transwoman was grunting with pain. He kissed the back of her neck, then slapped her cheek so hard she fell down, and he was falling right on top of and inside her, continuing what he had started to do. But his heart started acting up and he lost his erection. Wheezing, he crabwalked to the bed and attempted to get into it. She got up, wide-eyed with worry, with her cheek still red from his slap, and helped him get safely under the blanket. He lay there gasping.

Honey, should I call the doctor?

Just get my pills . . . my pills . . .

The blue ones or the green ones?

Two greens and—a glass of water. Now I'm fine; I don't need a pill. Fuck those pills. Well, maybe one.

Here it is; it's good for you—

That's what *she* said, he jeered, choking down the tablet to please her.

Please, honey, just rest now. Do you want to be alone?

C'mere. Sit on the bed and look at me. Gimme one more. Maybe a blue. Now, I want you to wonder something. Take a pretty little wonder and . . .

I—

Why's Karen lying to you?

Why do you call her Karen?

Bcause she is. Now, what's she want? Is she lying to you because she's lying to herself, which is normal and harmless, or because she plans to get something out of you?

J. D., she's not like that—

What the *fuck* do you know, living in your shitty little dream world where girls have dicks and ugly homos like you can be beautiful and someday someone's actually going to *like* you? You know you're sick, right?

I know. And—

Then say it, Frank. Say: *I'm a sick homosexual.*

I'm a sick . . . But, J. D., the weird thing is, all Neva wants is to make us happy.

Well, then she's in some kind of business. She's selling something.

What are you selling?

Whatever it is, you're buying it, *bitch.* You keep coming back for more.

And you're lying to me?

I tell you what you want to hear, which is that you *stink.* And you want to hear it because it's true. You want to admit the truth so you can feel bad about yourself, and I like making you feel bad.

Because it makes me happy.

Sure, Judy. We do make each other happy, don't we?

I love you.

But you love her, too, *don't you*?

Yes.

Who do you love more, her or me?

Her. I'm sorry.

Good dog. Maybe she'll take you off my hands. And she's never asked you for money?

Not even for a loan, whereas Shantelle—

Now you've spoiled the mood. What the *fuck*, mentioning that skanky whore! Get the fuck out of here, and don't come back till I call you. Get. Now. Go on, Frank. Out, *out*!

Weeping, the transwoman hurried out, slamming the door. At the Y Bar her potential *special friend* Sandra hugged her, stroked her hair and even bought her a bourbon and ginger ale! She bought Sandra what passed for a daiquiri, which Sandra took three delighted sips of, growing flushed and dizzy. Then Judy bought two goofballs from Shantelle, which sure as hell brightened life up! At three in the morning she was tapping out catchy syncopations on the retired policeman's door.

What the fuck! Oh, who else would it be. Well, come in and come to bed.

Will you let me suck your cock?

Not tonight. It's my period.

Oh, you're so *funny.* Here goes.

And the retired policeman had to admit that just now his Judy was exceptionally industrious.

Ten minutes later she sat on the edge of the bed marveling: That was the most fun I've ever had from sucking dick!

Because you're hopped up. Your eyeballs look like jeepers creepers.

But it was *fun.*

All right, you had fun. *But Neva's different*, he bitterly quoted.

I still love you.

Then turn out the light, and no snoring.

2

She lay beside him thinking.

The lesbian served her breakfast in bed and was perfect to her in ever so many ways, but Judy had to admit that she still knew almost nothing of where this person came from, who her people were or even what she liked and hoped to get out of life, because even direct questions would be answered with such kisses and loving words that one quickly felt as ecstatic as being high on MDMA, which is to say not caring how the pills had been manufactured.

In the morning he began to interrogate her again. He said: Tell me one goddamned thing that you know about her.

About her past, well, she told me she had some kind of a crisis, a love crisis, and then—

And then she went home to Mommy, *right*?

No, there was this older woman who—

And now *she's* the older woman. Except she's not old yet. So that's a lie. The name Neva's another lie. Have you ever heard the name Karen Strand?

No, except when you—

Anyway, *she's* a fuckin' fake. Judy. Hey, Judy. You wanna have *fun*?

What do you mean?

Let's keep playing detective, and find out who your Neva really is. You got off to a good start. Now you're gonna snoop deeper.

No!

I thought you *loved* going deep into your little bitch.

Oh, J. D. . . . !

You *said* you would.

Well, I changed my mind.

Oh, you'll do it, because I told you so, and because you're a fucking lying kleptomaniac by nature as you know perfectly well, *Frank*; don't think I haven't noticed how you steal from me all the goddamned time—

I'm sorry! I'm really sorry—

Say, *I'm a no good thief.*

I'm a . . .

And you steal from Neva, *don't you*? Whatever you can get. All her dirty undies and crusty old tampons and whatever else you can *worship* with your hairy hands . . . ! Admit it.

I'm a no good thief.

And do you filch her cash? How many fucking times have you gone through *my* wallet?

I'm . . . Oh, no, I can't!

Can't *what*? Can't tell me, hey? Does she work?

No. I don't think so, said Judy, whose face indicated that she found this interrogation as unpleasant as extracting tight-pressed corpses one at a time from a World War II memory hole.—I really don't think so.

Does she use a credit card?

Cash . . . She's all cash.

Hundred-dollar bills. From a so-called sealskin pouch.

How did you know?

And she gives you money.

Well, sometimes.

Does *that* add up?

She loves me.

Exactly. You know why I see through both of you? Because I'm *honest.* And you've been pecking at her nest egg, haven't you? All cash, fucking *right*? Where does she keep it?

You said it. In a sealskin pouch.

Great. Well, where did she get it? You see what I'm driving at?

I've never taken a dime from Neva, except when she—

Do you fucking *ask* her? *Does she give you money? Do you take her money?* Confession time! Say it: *I steal from Neva.* Say it. Oh, you won't? That means you're a *thief.* Now look, Judy. Will you work with me on this or not? You can have Neva, but you need to keep me in the loop, or else! I've seen you taking your stupid selfies on that crappy little phone that you never answer anymore when I call. Next time she goes to the john, you open up her purse and take pictures of whatever you can. You run away when the toilet flushes, and she'll never know. It's called *roving surveillance.* Now I see that squirrelly look in your eyes; well, I don't care. Just tell me yes or no.

I'm scared.

Not of me! Listen. Think of all the fun you have jerking off to all your trashy actress magazines. This'll be like getting *secret background* on your favorite star. Don't you want the dirt on Neva? I'll coach you not to get caught. And I promise you something: We're doing this together, and we're having *fun.*

3

Before noon, darkbitch64 texted him that she had what he wanted, so he met her at four-o'-clock at the Blue Lamp. She had even brought Marcie.

Well, well, he said. Pay me fifty bucks for bringing you two lovebirds together.

She's not *that* good in bed, said Latoya, and Marcie screeched in delight.

He bought them each a Bullpizz Beer, at which they looked disgusted. He ordered himself a shot of Old Crow. Then he waited.

Karen's girlfriend was called E-beth, said Marcie. Kind of an unusual name. Must have been short for—

I get it, he said. What did she look like?

It's been a long time.

But you saw them come out of hotels?

Not actually, but one time at the bus stop I overheard them planning to meet at the motel just down the street, which I think was the Lazy Dog, and I'm sure that's demolished now. Anyhow, E-beth had a car, so they could have gone wherever.

Not good enough, said the retired policeman.

The ladies turned mean, demanding what he would do for them. He gave each a twenty.—And twenty more for E-beth's last name, or the name of a hotel they definitely checked into, or any photo of them together. I thought you saw them in some bar . . . No? Then *sayonara.*

As he walked out, he heard them bitchtalking him.

4

Fuck this, he said to himself. I need a drink.

Having nearly run out of Old Crow, he providently crept over to Jojo's Liquors, where Old Crow cost four dollars more than last week while Black Vulture was on special for twenty-nine ninety-nine, so he manned up and bought the Black Vulture. Fifteen minutes afterward his swollen feet were elevated, along with the rest of him, back home at Empire Residences. A water glass filled with Black Vulture lay literally at hand. Four swallows later, he was on the SpiderWeb, verifying that the Vallejo Police Department's call-for-assistance log contained no records before 1997. Well, what else would wisdom expect? All those expungements by the liberals in the Clinton administration, and then fucking liability shields and don't get me fucking started. The way he saw it, flag burning wasn't protected speech; it was *arson*, and he blamed Clinton for that. If some pinko lit a flag on fire and the flames burned down a building, then what the fuck was *that*, my fellow Americans? Sooner or later he'd need to shake down whomever Karen had lived with, her parents for certain, but they might be dead. First he wanted a positive visual identification; then he'd watch their faces when he . . .

The marvelous HonorShield police database remained tight-puckered against three deployments of his old password, which used to get him right in. *There* was another liberal improvement: running anybody's name for so-called "private" reasons now triggered major felony charges. What a world.

Whistling (his Black Vulture had somehow finished itself), he logged on alumni .connect.edu, which after seven dialogue boxes greeted him with: **Hey, ho, Valley Joe! Looking up your classmate Karen Strand (1982). Processing your request. Looking up Karen . . . Looking up Karen . . . Please wait. Please supply your credit card number now. Looking up Karen . . . For a list of 250 Karens in Vallejo at $10.00 please wait . . . Processing your Karen . . . System error. Please supply your credit card number now. Looking up Karen . . . Current address for Karen Strand: 73664 Triumph Drive, Vallejo, California. Last updated June 23, 1982. To send Karen a message please . . . For a list of 250 Karens in Vallejo at $10.00 please . . . Thank you for using Alumni Connect! Thank you for—**

Well, well. Karen Strand had fallen out of touch with her loving fans. He was not surprised.

5

I had to take the bus to Vegas in order to plead out to a misdemeanor charge before it worsened, but of course it was already worse. They let me out in ten days, since the public defender liked me. He said I'd *made an impression* on the judge, for which reason he advised me to stay clear of Vegas, and I cheerfully promised to do my best—because didn't I expect a date or two with Neva? The reddish stone of the courthouse above its double row of palms had done nothing for me anyhow. Of course steering clear hardly required my instant departure, so I entered the crowded smokiness of the Lucky Trouble Lounge at midnight, in order to be patted down by the sternly beautiful black security guard who was shaped like a bowling ball. I asked her to slap me but she refused. Approaching the counter (where an electronic slot machine had been built into every spot), I ordered two beers for six dollars. An ageing overweight blonde squeezed my arm, which made me happy. Then I spied two white girls in leather jackets. By the look of them they were barely old enough to drink milk. Their faces were delicate and perfect, their hair cut in mohawks, their ears multiply studded; their many-ringed hands continually caressed each other. A third girl, plainer, heavier and older, followed them like a satellite. I, who could tell you their stories even without being there, being already expert in not being present for my own life, could hardly stop spying on the lesbian couple. For a moment I even forgot Neva in my joy of looking.

As soon as I got back, I went to the Y Bar—where else? It was two in the afternoon. Xenia was arguing with Francine over a glass of sodawater. The only sincere drinker just then was Judy. Although I could not tell whether she had lost any of her paunch, her face had definitely thinned, paled and slightly aged; her nose was sharper, but what counted was how joyful she looked. She moved less heavily, and smiled more. She would never be beautiful, except to whomever loved her, but she looked alive. In other words, I barely recognized her.

Behind the bar, a synthesized voice was singing robo-tunefully like the auto-announcer at a train station. It squeaked and scraped into a more frantic key until Francine, seeing the transwoman rise up and approach the jukebox, shut off the robo-song so that Judy could play "Somewhere Over the Rainbow" with her blissed-out smile.

What are you doing for pleasure? I asked.

She laughed. Aside from fucktime? It's all fucktime.

I'm happy for you.

It's like an adventure, she said. And I just feel it's not too late, and I can do *anything*!

I slipped my arm around her. Her pupils were huge. Her back and shoulders felt so good to me under her rayon blouse that I didn't want to stop. And I wanted so much to stroke her long, long, hair, which excelled the cheap fishing-line stuff of so many strippers' and trannies' wigs (we pretended those were real); I didn't care that she had a penis; I would have been almost as happy, at least in that moment, burying my face in her warm fragrant hair as in Neva's, and I craved to slip my hand up her skirt and grip her buttock in my hand, but then it occurred to me that it might be hairy like a man's, and although that didn't impel me to repulsion, it did dim down my desire, although I still felt so happy and steady and good; even if she were a man maybe it would have been sweet to cradle her in my arms. I said nothing of this to Judy, who could not have suspected my thoughts anyhow. And I continued stroking her back, up and down and up and down, until she presently, trustingly laid her head against my shoulder.

6

I do have a few bullet points for Judy, Kendra announced.

Oh, said the transwoman.

First point: personal hygiene. If you want to be a part of our team, you absolutely have to . . .

Judy nodded and nodded, knowing that she would lose this job also.

All right, said Kendra, do you fully understand that?

Yes, said Judy, red and sweating.

Then enough said. Now, Judy, I do have one opportunity to run by you now. I'm sorry to say that a certain member of our sales force is no longer with us. We don't normally throw so big a challenge at our new hires, but, Judy, I'm prepared to let you work a double shift tonight. Of course you won't expect us to pay you additional, since you're on probation; it's more of a favor the company is granting you, to, you know, let you prove yourself. And, Judy, I can promise you that *we will be watching.* Are you ready?

Okay, her victim whispered.

I'll be listening in on your first three phoners. And then I'll e-mail a full report to Marketing. You're being timed as of *now.* You'd better get your headset on. Come on, Judy—*chop, chop!*

The auto dialler had already rung up the first prospect. Judy's screen read HAGGERTY SAM / BRIANNA.

Hello? said a woman's voice.

Um, is this Brianna Haggerty? said Judy. My name is Judy, and I'm calling on behalf of Kaiser Financial Services. I'm very excited to tell you about our new Schlieffen Plan—

The woman hung up. Miserable and embarrassed, Judy stared at the screen, which now read MARQUEZ IÑEZ / EVA.

Hello? said a woman.

Hi, said Judy. Um, I'm trying to contact Ms. Marquez on behalf of Kaiser—

Who's this?

My name is Judy, and I'm calling on behalf of Kaiser Financial Services. I'm very—

What are you trying to sell me?

You see, Ms. Marquez, I'm very excited to tell you about our new Schlieffen Plan—

What? What the fuck are you talking about?

Well, my name is Judy, and I—

The woman hung up. Judy was close to tears, and already the screen was reading WONG TIFFANY.

This is Tiffany, said a no-nonsense voice.

Oh, *hi*, Tiffany; my name is Judy, and I'm calling on behalf of Kaiser Financial Services. I'm very excited to—

Are you a broker? asked Tiffany. Because I already have two brokers. I fire them all the time.

Not exactly, Judy admitted. I'm—

So you *are* a broker. As I said, I keep two of you around. Not just one, but two. So what can you possibly do for me?

Ms. Wong, I'm just here to inform you about our new opportunity.

So you're not a broker. You're just some peon cold calling me on behalf of this Kaiser Financial whatever. Are you even in America? You sound like you're calling from the Philippines or something. Were you born in this country?

Yes, I was, said Judy. And, Tiffany—

Do *not* call me Tiffany. Do *not* ever call me again. Enter me on your do-not-call list right away; do you hear me?

Okay, said Judy. And I'm really really sorry—

Kendra pressed a button to disconnect the call. She appeared angry; Judy could not imagine why. Flinging both hands imperiously away from her head, she made herself comprehended: the transwoman pulled off her headphones and waited for punishment.

Judy, her tormentor began, what did you do wrong?

I . . . Well, on the first one maybe I didn't put enough sincerity into my voice—

What else?

I thought I did a really good job on the second one, but—

But you *failed.* She hung up on you, Judy! That's called *failure.* You had three failures in a row, and I'm going to have to write you up. Your last one was by far the worst. Judy, do you realize that you *apologized* for calling that woman, as if you were ashamed?

But what should I have said? She—

What should you have said? Did you or did you not waste all three sales prospects?

Well, I actually think they just weren't interested. Because the first one said—

Judy, are you talking back to me? Clueless I can work with, but not insubordinate.

I'm sorry. I mean, I'm really—

In the world of sales, *sorry* doesn't cut it, Kendra explained. Now get your headphones back on and work up your *conviction.* We're going to jump right back up on that horse that threw us and—

No, said Judy, standing up.

Excuse me?

I quit. I'm sorry for all the . . . Goodbye!

Judy, you're terminated, said Kendra into the collective silence of that call center whose every other pawn longed to do what Judy had just done. Nobody dared to look at her, but she knew herself to be the heroine of the minute. Perhaps it felt like this to be Shantelle and smash a bottle over somebody's head. It felt, as Shantelle might have said, *fuckin' GOOD.* And as soon as she was in the street, Judy raised her clenched fist and screeched with happiness.

Of course she proceeded straight to the Y Bar, where Sandra was informing Francine: He's just somebody I met, so I haven't seen him all that much, so, no, he's not a teacher or a student or anything like that. I don't want it to progress but I'm afraid that if I don't see someone I'll just get lonely again.

Running her hand through Sandra's hair, the new arrival inquired: You're talking about Louis, aren't you?

Judy, would you mind? You're messing up my hair. And I was having a private talk with Francine—

Guess what? I'm gonna buy you both a bigass drink, because I just quit and got fired at the same time from that stinking job—

Thank you, Judy. That's very generous. Now could you please . . . ?

Where's Neva?

I don't *know* where Neva is. (Judy had never heard Sandra so annoyed.)

Hey, Francine! cried Shantelle, rising up out of the darkness. Turn up the TV. I wanna—

Now for Golden State news, said the television. *A lesbian woman was assaulted by five people at a Krisp-O Chicken restaurant in Fresno.*

Lesbian woman? said Shantelle. What the fuck's wrong with *lesbian*?

If it doesn't progress or deepen or something like that, I don't know, said Sandra, and I am so terrified that Louis will just get frustrated.

Twenty-eight-year-old Melody Richards said she and her girlfriend had just ordered a double Fun Fryer when they were accosted by five other customers who began taunting her girlfriend Jordan, who—

I *know* that bitch! Shantelle boasted.

—prefers not to share her last name with us.—They said, you know, I had to keep my dyke ho bitch in check and like that, Richards told reporters. When she began defending Jordan . . .

Oh, my God, said Francine.

Oh, this is awful, said Sandra.

What? said Judy. What happened?

The group began pushing, shoving and punching Richards, knocking out several teeth and permanently injuring her right eye. Jordan said she struggles to keep her composure when she looks at her partner. It makes me want to cry every single time I look at her, Jordan said.

Maybe I actually *don't* know her, said Shantelle. Francine, would you top me off?

Seven dollars.

This is so terrible, said Sandra. I feel like we should do something.

The two women told reporters that the lack of help from bystanders made the situation worse. It makes me fear just to walk down the street, Richards said. Fresno police have classified the attack as a hate crime.

Judy burst into tears and said: It should have happened to me instead, because I'm *worthless.* Sandra, honey, don't you think I'm worthless?

7

Did you have fun with your bitch?

Hell, yeah!

What did you talk about? Or were you too busy chewing her oyster to . . . ?—and she saw in the set of his lips and the shining of his eyes his jealous anguish.

She said she's an only child—

And when you do things to her, and she does things to you . . . , he began, almost crazed with grief, then sat down, massaging his chest. She knew better than to say anything. (Sometimes she wondered whether it would be more sensible just to stay home and masturbate than to keep seeing Neva. Like me, she was already foreseeing the end.)—But now she brought him back into control: Out of her purse came a fifth of Old Crow.

Well, he said, leaning painfully toward her; she closed the gap, so that he could kiss her.

Rising, she washed two glasses. He was already fumbling under the cushion for that baggie of bright green Narcodan pills.

She poured out the shots, while he gave them each two tablets to chew on.

All right, Judy, my sexy little eyes and ears; what do you have for me?

Her driver's license—

Oh.—With a licked forefinger and a scrap of napkin he cleaned the screen of her cell phone. Then he got that fat black heavy ballpoint pen of his, with the nearly effaced silver lettering from Dreamsavers Credit Union.

Nice picture, he said. Neva's got glam even on a fuckin' ID card. Karen Strand. No Neva. Well, that checks out. Date of birth, 1986. Do you believe that? She don't look like twenty-nine. Maybe twenty-five. And the thing about her age is . . .

Is what?

How old do you imagine she really is?

Twenty-nine? Twenty-five?

Well, why does *that* stink? If you only knew what I knew! . . . Let me write down this shit—

And look *here*! she proudly crooned. *Surprise!*

Where was it?

Behind the first one.

Her old driver's license, so fuckin' what? Same picture, which is . . . Date of birth, 1964. Judy, you're a good dog. Let's hear you bow-wow.

Bow-wow! she chirped delightedly.

Want a treat?

Woof-woof!

My favorite degraded bitch! Did you know she actually *was* born in 1964?

But, J. D., how could she—

Exactly. So imagine her hooked up to a polygraph, maybe with a big dildo up her ass for local color, and you on the other end . . . What about cash?

What?

I said, what about her fucking cash? Where is it? Don't tell me it's all in that crappy little sealskin pouch. Next time she's bending you across her bed, feel under the mattress!

I don't know if it's there. And if she catches me—

All right. She gives everybody pills, right? Every night's fuckin' Christmas at Karen Strand's—

Maybe she doesn't like that name.

A name's just a name, *Frank.* But some names are true.

Humiliated in Skirts

I don't associate Frances Gumm with me—she's a girl I can read about the way other people do. I, Judy Garland, was born when I was twelve years old.

Judy Garland, 1951

This thing that you are is a sin against creation . . . I shall never be able to look at you now without thinking of the deadly insult of your face and your body to the memory of the father who bred you . . . In that letter you say things that may only be said between man and woman, and coming from you they are vile and filthy words of corruption—against nature, against God who created nature. My gorge rises; you have made me feel physically sick . . .

Radclyffe Hall, 1928

1

Of course even Judy, who pretended to remember the first moon landing and sometimes liked to tell stories about her flitterdancing years when Tenderloin Tessie, none of whose pubic hairs had yet turned from gold to silver, was the hostess at the 222 Club, had herself been almost young, once upon a time, and before that she had even been pretty just as a young woman is; before that, which is to say before Steve became Stephanie and Karen turned into Neva, there lived in Cleveland a certain Air Force lieutenant's son named Frank Masters who dated girls to get his parents off his back but made sure that the dates went nowhere: I can still see sad, wholesome Christine, tall, thin, boring and bespectacled; she compromised and more, but never achieved carnality. Born in 1966, the year when Judy Garland said: *I think I'm interesting; I have a perspective about me; I'd like to expose a lot of people who deserve it,* he tried to be as demure as Judy Garland smoothing out her dark blue sailor suit, but never got good enough.

When he was eleven he began playing doctor with Christine and Roxanne and the other Stephanie who had been born female; at sixteen he got initiated by nineteen-year-old Don, who was sometimes secretly Denise and dreamed of visiting Dr. Morrow, who six weeks after Don's twenty-first birthday would sell Denise the best lady parts she could ever own; it was Denise who gave Frank a special copy of Dr. Morrow's circular:

> To the typical female, whether
> genetic or transsexual, the most
> important sexual organ is the
> clitoris.

Frank was not certain what a clitoris was. He felt too ashamed to ask Denise. Meanwhile Dr. Morrow continued:

> Don't be satisfied simply to have a
> hole which can serve as a vagina for
> sexual intercourse.

Just as the twelve-year-old Judy Garland could already sing as if she were *a woman whose heart had been hurt*, so Judy's half-born namesake knew how to live hurt-hearted, longing to be so sweet and vanilla and smooth in her spanglebra, spanglepanties and long black wristguards, and if possible darkhaired with a black choker buckled tight around her throat, but above all slender, tall and *young.* (He assured Christine: Sleeping Beauty is my favorite princess of all time.) Born too early in too hulking a body to ever emulate the half-boyish look of kd lang, Frank clutched at the rich femininity of Dolly Parton, which could practically be eaten like ice cream. Yes, he clutched, but that grand tree upraised its branches; such fruit was not, or at least not yet, for him. And so young Judy felt lost in her youth, outspreading her big pale fingers against the wall. She kept whispering out of Frank's lips: *If I could only be somebody . . .*

Who can say why this withdrawn, dishonest little boy was not hostile, in which case his lies, then his threats, might have matured into rape and murder? Fortunately for society, he was self-hating like Karen Strand.

Frank saved up his allowance to buy *Family in Skirts, She Humiliated Me in Skirts* and *Panty Discipline*, which arrived in beige envelopes whose return address was Specialty Productions, Los Angeles; he masturbated to a grainy photo of a stern tall T-girl in a black corset who was whipping a man's hairy bottom; meanwhile he kept worshipping Judy Garland, whom *Time* magazine called *one of the more reliable song-pluggers in the business*; he wanted a girlfriend who looked like her. His father, whose ignorance had until now been a blessing, punished him for wearing lace panties which he had stolen from the neighbor's clothesline; as a veteran of degradation (which was usually inflicted either in the garage or the basement, because the father himself felt sickened while doing it, by the cowering boy, his sobs, his naked bottom and then his hideous screams), Frank anticipated the pain, his throat tightening with fear as they went downstairs; the worst part, even more unpleasant than pulling down his pants before his father and the avid listening silence of his mother upstairs, was the hard cruel revulsion etched on his father's face; then his father commenced beating him deeper and deeper down into a furry sack of darkness until Frank had thankfully lost sight of himself; and nearly half a century later, long after his parents had retired to Oxnard, California, and the lesbian had died, with the Y Bar sold into smithereens and Shantelle in another bad place (remembering that night in the multileveled parking garage in Los Angeles where her second virginity had been taken from her by four teenaged black boys who afterward at least did her the favor of calling her a red-hot niggah), on a certain foggy Thursday afternoon when Judy, *as* Judy, was helping her widowed mother clean the house for the real estate agent, she found the device her father had required for what the mother called a "prostate massage"; there came an instant when she nearly ran ravening to punch her big fists through windows and then throw the dildo in her mother's face; instead, because Judy was raised to meekly please, she sighed and dropped it into the garbage bag. Speaking of garbage, when *Tales from the Pink Mirror* entered the mailbox, Frank (who now preferred to be called Frankie) was still at band practice, and unfortunately the envelope was torn.—*What is this shit?* his father roared. *What the hell is wrong with you, you goddamned little pervert? This time I'm really going to beat it out of you,* at which Frankie looked up into his mother's face, not in hopes of help, which was hardly likely to come his way, but simply because he had been wondering what she felt on these occasions; her composed yet vaguely excited face was the most literally sickening thing that he had ever seen. That was when he graduated from being stripped and whipped to being punched in the face and chest. Both parents could hardly contain their loathing for him then, on account of his high-pitched effeminate screams. Fortunately, in place of creepy Christine he now had a girlfriend named Marjorie who loved him so much that she agreed to receive future packets from Specialty Productions. In the mimeographed catalogue accompanying *Schoolgirl in the Secret Service* he discovered an advertisement for a **Hip Helper. Watch him marvel at your great new shape.** Thinking it peculiar that no *her* would marvel, Frankie swore the delighted Marjorie to secrecy, then asked her opinion on a strictly hypothetical experiment. She very sweetly replied that if he were to model for her in his Hip Helper, she would utter nothing but compliments. Just as they were completing the mail order form (again Marjorie agreed to take delivery), her little brother Marvin came in without knocking, hoping that Frankie would join a three-part game of Chinese checkers. The boy was incurious; he didn't even notice the brochure about female mimics: *These lusty ladies will have you throbbing with desire. Order today!* Longing to take Marvin's penis in his mouth, then blushing and feeling sick, Frankie played one hasty game, then returned to Marjorie's bedroom where she sat giggling over his catalogue. **Now: Padded Bikini panties in stretch lace and stretch tricot. Available with Derriere Pads.**

The next time Marjorie presented him with a beige envelope, he knew that she hoped for him to open it in front of her, in order to continue being included in his joyful secret, but he apologized, invoked schoolwork, rushed home, leaped into bed (his father was at work and his mother at the grocery store), then masturbated to *Fated for Femininity.* Afterward he thought: I love Marjorie. I really do. She's the only one doesn't call me a freak. Someday I'll marry her. But I sure would like to meet a girl who favors Judy Garland; I wouldn't care even if she had a male organ or . . .

His parents happily, even gratefully gave him permission to stay out late with Marjorie. He overheard his mother saying: Thank God he's growing out of it—

He took Marjorie to a vampire movie in which the leading lady somehow resembled Judy Garland. Marjorie fell sweetly asleep on his shoulder. That was when he realized that she bored him.

He now kept his femme clothes hidden in a violin case at the back of Marjorie's closet. From the catalogue concerned with **LEATHER SHOES IN ALL SIZES (10–12 medium black only)**, he dreamed over high heeled pumps called Carmen, Faith and Tricia, but they were too expensive. His self-conception resembled the tremblings of a woman's umbrella in the wind.

By now his father had forgotten everything about Frankie's girly side; that was how his father loved him, by forgetting. And Frankie could only love his father by hating truth. He became Judy, then rushed home to masturbate. Afterward Judy's memories of this period took on the grey-green and reddish glitters of tiny stones swirling in a funerary mosaic.

Sweating and blushing, he told his parents that he had a date with Marjorie. His father gave him money. Then, almost choking with anxiety lest he be caught, he walked the sixteen blocks to Mabel's Club, drank a semilegal vodka and ginger ale and danced with a hairy-bellied drag queen named Princess who wore nothing but false breasts and a big black figleaf. He held her tight, and she was very kind. She was the one who knew that death is called *Little Wisdom.* In between kisses he told her that he wanted to be Judy.—Then do it, she said. He confessed that he just couldn't, at which Princess purred: What if I *command* you to? and his seventeen-year-old penis sprang up like an Apollo moon rocket.

Princess lost interest in him, but the next time he went to Mabel's, after drinking alone until he felt sorry for himself, his neediness lighted on a hard-built woman of fifty or so, whose square face, cropped hair and wise old eyes were comforting to him. He began weeping silently. (In those days he had not yet learned how to do it on purpose.) The woman watched him. He watched her. Finally he decided to look at the floor until he died.

Failing to die, he looked up, and the woman said: Hi, pervert.

Hello, said Frankie.

2

She lit a cigarette and said: It's funny that people only identify us based on our sex lives, and they call *us* the perverts. They're constantly applying their categories to us based on what we occasionally do, not based on who we are. My name's Sylvia, by the way.

Thanks for talking to me and I'm really really sorry, said the boy.

You're sorry, and do you have a name?

Frankie.

Are you in trouble or just sad?

I don't know.

I can see that. Did you run away?

No.

You mean, *not yet*! Show some spunk! Or do you plan to stop being a pervert?

I can't.

I grew up gay, obviously. I would never recommend it. It was hard, for sure, having to hide who you are. My stepfather beat me for falling in love with my straight girlfriends. Oh, you know about that, hey? And I'll bet you know about *can't have a gay person in a locker room!* In reality, my locker room experiences were, *don't look.* You were trained as a young person at least in my era to not look at people whom you can't have. That still sticks with me as an older woman. I don't look at straight women sexually. I don't do anything to disrespect their space. When you fall in love with your friends and you can't do anything about it, it can hurt. It's funny when they use that against us.

Frankie listened. It was then that he commenced his lifelong habit of asking women to tell him stories.

Well, boy, she concluded, go and be a pervert.

3

And just as Nancy Kerrigan's family took out loans in order to pay for her skating lessons, so Frankie borrowed money to finance Judy's little surgeries. By now he worked in a shoestore, but his wages defrayed almost nothing; the lender was poor Marjorie, who still hoped for the best.

Much later, Judy remembered her with the kind of love which derives from gratitude: Marjorie never ever outed her. If only she could have given that girl what she wanted! And in those later years, when Judy swung both ways, it would have been easy and fun to please Marjorie—assuming she could desire a flabby-breasted, hairy, male-bodied old bitch with a penchant for humiliation . . .

On that subject, it may be too reductive to claim that the corporal punishments she received at home made her into a submissive, but consider the following: MGM aborted Judy Garland's first baby against her wishes. (Joseph Mankiewicz once remarked that everybody from the MGM executives to her own mother treated her *like a thing.*) She had her second abortion by choice after the father, the bisexual Tyrone Power, read her love letters aloud to the Marines. Thus the detestable became the consensual.

Judy's Godfearing mother frequently guaranteed her a fiery afterlife on account of her failure to use the penis as our Lord had intended; there was another truth worth hating. Hating her body, Judy decided to rise in the flesh, because outside the flesh exists nothing.

Once at Mabel's she saw her lesbian angel again. So she asked her about God.

Sylvia replied: I was raised Catholic and I don't want any part of it. I would never hurt someone even if I didn't like you. And I'm not that wonderful of a human being. And then this amazing entity called God will throw you in the firepit just because you did something shitty. Do you believe in God?

I want to, said Judy.

Well, we went to church every fucking holiday: Spanish Mass, English Mass; it was just horrible. I remember one Sunday, I don't remember why we couldn't go to church that Sunday but I was happy about it; my godfather was praying to one of the Jesuses up on the wall and was praying and crying and screaming for forgiveness; I was thinking, this guy Jesus is kind of a dick because we go all the time and yet we're in trouble now. This entity that's supposed to be the most kind person of anyone is the one that punishes us.

Judy was convinced—because she had not yet met the Goddess.

Still hoping to find or become something as strong and competent as Martina Navratilova's hands, she lived out the years when closeted gay men called themselves *friends of Dorothy*, meaning of Judy Garland's most famous role.—Sylvia had said: I think that someone's coming out or making themselves public is their own choice. If they feel threatened or uncomfortable or fearful coming out, I would never, never push them out. I would talk about my own experiences and be their friend. I would only guide them through what was best for them.—And Judy most definitely felt fearful.—She hitchhiked all the way from the animal-bearing to the human-bearing trees of Paradise. Because covetousness was a sin and she coveted womanhood, which everyone assured her she would never attain, she felt as guilty as possible, all the while believing that from Frank's once upon a time could somehow be born Judy's happily ever after (just follow the Yellow Brick Road). Passing through New York City too late to see Chris Moore performing as Marlene Dietrich at Lee Brewster's club, in that most famous spell when Chris's face was still milk-smooth and she shook her head no to all her sweethearts, making tiny jingling sounds with her long earring-bells while plumping out her lips into something even better than a cunt, Judy was transported equally well by that same floor show's wide-smiling drag queen whose bowling-ball breasts commanded a wide field of fire indeed. She who first thought to know herself from what others said about her, who used to go to church to get cursed for being what she could not help but be, who would later pretend to know herself by eavesdropping on what was said about the lesbian, still hoped not to be sacrificed—as if she got to act like a man whenever she felt like it, and could then go back to being a woman simply to gratify her own lewdness. She looked into the mirror and said: *I'm disgusting.*

As her finances allowed, she visited the cosmetic surgeon in Oakland who took Travelers Insurance (electrolysis limited to one-hour sessions), and dropped in and out of Paulette's charm school in San Francisco. In those days trannies who wished to insult each other would use the word *homosexual.* Latin trannies were called *cha-chas.* Judy was *that ugly faggot.*

4

She threw herself at a bright-eyed T-girl named Kimara, who looked well put together with her puffy hair and that frill-line down the buttons of her dark blouse; by then Kimara's wife feared going out with her when they were both *en femme*, ever since a drunk had attacked them at a Halloween party. Judy felt the same fear. But it certainly did help to be a masochist.

You're not mature enough for a relationship, her new friend explained.

Tell me what to do, said Judy; please please tell me!

Come out of the closet.

Well, how did that go for you?

Kimara replied: I think for the most part I was really defensive and I said it was none of their business, and I do have this strong face in front of other people but it made me question myself. Then one of my really good friends—there were four of us, we would hang out all the time, she was almost like a sister, and I would sleep over—she was fine with it, but she told everybody in school and she made it seem like it was no big deal and she did not do it with any malicious intent. Well, Judy, I was really angry with her; I wasn't ready to come out because I didn't know what it meant, because you hear about bullying; you don't wanna carry that with you, and having people ask you all of these things makes it harder to deal with it . . .

Judy decided to live a little longer as Frank.

5

By 1988 she was almost ready to make a down payment on the big operation, but her hooker friend Danielle who later achieved true fame by getting raped and murdered scared her by describing what it had been like to wake up among cruelly contemptuous nurses who declined to give her enough Demerol; oh, Jesus, said Danielle, and then the stench when your vaginal dilator comes out, and *then* one of them damn nurses pounds it back in with her everlovin' fist, and you're *screaming* . . .

A year later Judy found herself confessionally drunk in the Ocean Club beside a quiet middle-aged lesbian named Reba who listened, patted her hand and consoled her: Women, we don't come out. We don't *go* out. It's harder as you get older. When I was coming out, that's where you met somebody, in a bar. But I tell you, women complain. They just don't come out.

I want to come out, Judy sobbed, and sometimes I *am* out, but I . . .

You've got a long row to hoe, dearie. Someday you'll be ready to be who you are. You still believe in God, don't you?

How did you know?

Reba laughed a little and said: Even though I can sit here and say I don't believe in God, I still want to hold on to that golden ticket. You have those fanatical straight people telling you you won't get into heaven, and there's a little part of you from childhood that makes you believe it. I did everything I could do to get kicked out of church. I did the worst thing: I got pregnant. I already had a father at home, so what I need one in the sky for? I think that was the first and only time I stood up to my Dad, because I said, they don't practice what they preach. And what could he say? Because he only showed up there for weddings and funerals.

And then what happened? whispered Judy, fascinated.

I came out. They disowned me. I told 'em it's your loss not mine; come back when you're ready. I didn't talk to 'em for a year. Then they called me.

You must have felt so humiliated . . .

I mean, I can see they had their own inner struggle, but I threw it in their faces every time I could. I always brought my girlfriends home until the day both my parents were dead. Then I went to an island—

What do you mean?

Judy, you're not ready to understand this, but there's a place for you. It's a place of women, and if you come out there, I promise you'll be loved. But you have to come out and—

Well, said Judy, it must have been easier for you. Because you look like a woman, a really really *pretty* woman, and I just don't.

Let's look at what's inside of Judy, not at what's outside of Judy. Women are not judgmental as far as a woman's body goes. I think we find the inner beauty more than the outer beauty. Because we've been judged all our lives.

Judy could not have said why that made her cry, but it did. She got up and ran away. Six months later she went back to the Ocean Club, but there was no Reba.

Ingesting a tab of lysergic acid, she grew very proud to win supernatural proof of the way that every other Earthling had single names while hers was doubled everywhere right through clouds and steel although no one knew of its doubling; once she came down she still felt that proof but could never explain it.

6

At Jingle's Bar in Vallejo she made a hot connection with a Cheyenne girl, kissing her and *kissing her* while fondling the girl's cunt, but the girl's ignorance caused Judy misery and terror which thickened about her mind until she could hardly see outward and downward to the truth: Judy was no longer a boy. And Judy kept dressing up more and more until the Cheyenne girl called her sick and crazy and returned to her parents.

Then she was living in Hollywood with a certain Norma Jean, who was crazy about her; their roommate was a young woman named Bunnie, who started fucking Norma Jean, just for a joke, after which they became a couple and left her. She cried herself to sleep, then dreamed that she was even more beautiful than the real Judy Garland.

In San Francisco the Black Rose Bar was still open in those days. There Judy met an old man who invited her to come see his autograph collection, the prize item being a communication from the most famous American transsexual ever, Christine Jorgensen. The envelope was printed MISS C. JORGENSEN, 31752 GRAND CANYON DRIVE, LAGUNA NIGUEL, CALIF. 92677, and the note, dated 1975, read: *I thank you for your interest.* Judy thought she had never read anything so classy.—The old man unzipped his pants. He said: Know why I picked you, honey? 'Cause you're as plug-ugly as I am.

7

Never as lucky as the famous tranny Angela Douglas (born Douglas Carl Czinki), who got arrested in Olympia, Washington, for hitchhiking on the freeway, after which, because she already passed so beautifully, they placed her in the women's section of Thurston County Jail, where she spent the whole night fucking a sex-starved young girl, Judy kept seeking love and pleasure, achieving mostly humiliation in skirts. Those were the years when ultrafeminists reserved the divine right of *definition.* They got to insist and argue over who was truly female. And so Judy was rejected by the Daughters of Bilitis for her *male-identified behavior.* In the *East Bay Express* she read an ad from a lesbian organization called SLUTS: Sisters Loving Unlimited TortureSex. Hoping to be torture-sexed, Judy attended a meeting, but was expelled on account of her penis. When she started blubbering, they jeered at her. On the way downstairs she realized that she had expected this to happen.

Money being the best medicine, she answered another more transactional advertisement, and soon a laughing Goddess was punishing Judy's testicles with electric wire and she had to thank the Goddess after each scream. Six weeks later she got raped by a cop and loved it.

You gotta flipflop, advised her hooker friend Danielle. I'd be bored if I was top all the time, or bottom all the time. I'm not into pain, but I don't mind a little injury.

I can't be a top, explained Judy, because I don't deserve it.

Whatever gets you off, yawned Danielle.

Bunnie had told her about a lesbian retreat up in Mendocino County. Judy bought a Green Tortoise bus ticket and rolled straight there. To increase her desirability, or as we more often used to say, her marketability, she was wearing a "black widow" waist cincher. Approaching the check-in tent, she passed a handpainted wooden sign which read:

> "I would like to see women realize
> that the punishment we feel has
> been created by men."
> -Arden Eversmeyer

Bracing for the worst, Judy now received her own male-created punishment. Calling her rapist, appropriator and agent of the patriarchy, they ran her off. The next bus for Los Angeles would leave in ten hours, so she, desperate to lurk out of sight, checked into a highwayside motel; and here her luck changed because a little blonde runaway with no place to go knocked on her door in hopes of using the shower, and within twenty minutes she was teaching Judy how to be a better girl: Don't you know that lesbians make love using their hands? Look, Judy. Here's what you do . . .—and Judy's spirits rocketed up to Cloud Nine!

The blonde was named Kara. Judy loved her more than anyone *ever.* So she proposed that they become a couple. Wide-eyed, Kara nodded. So they did it again, the young prostitute's pupils expanding deliciously into semi-precious marbles and all sounds dimming into silence. Phrases flittered behind Judy's eyes and she could not decide if they were trite or remarkable; then they began to ring like music. Kara lay passed out and breathing heavily. Judy ducked into the bathroom to, among other business, perfect her imitation of that dreamy and somehow grainy smile of the young T-girl in Vallejo who stood so still in her prom dress on the night before she was beaten to death. When she came out, Kara was gone, along with twenty dollars. Judy sat down, sobbing and slapping herself in the face. Then she cheered up, thinking: At least I've learned how to make love using my hands . . . !

8

So lonely that no one would hide her from her death, she practiced saying things to the mirror, such as: *The results have been so amazing,* or, *I wouldn't change a thing.* Then she memorized the proverbs of Judy Garland.

Yes, Judy was a masochist—but only because she would do anything to feel like a woman! (Trying to look alert and in the mood, she made herself as bulging-eyed as a certain Etruscan Sphinx.) The alternative was to live out the tale of the thirty-four-year-old, delicately pretty black T-girl who was serving eight years at Stillwater Correctional Institution in Illinois for inscribing graceful signatures on other women's checks.

So there she was, lifting up her blouse to proudly sadly lasciviously show off her big new estrogenized breasts, as she shyly peeked through eyelashes whose length rivaled that of her high heels. Still hoping to connect with anyone at all, woman to woman, she ran out of luck at a certain illegal after hours club. Her second arrest educated her with a glimpse of transsexuals covered with blood in the holding cell. Next time, because she had been caught in the act of fellatio while wearing men's clothes, they placed her among the male prisoners in the police bus; they were shouting obscenities at the drag queens in the women's cage at the back, as were the women. An accused murderess pulled off a drag queen's glasses and stomped on them; everybody cheered. Judy felt sick with excitement.

Pitying the taxpayers of Illinois, the prison doctor disallowed the estrogen pills that she had been swallowing since her nineteenth birthday, with the result that the aforesaid Judy Garland, whose legal name remained Frank Masters, watched her breasts melting away, her skin roughening and her face breaking out with stubble. To help her readjust to inborn biology, they housed her with men, who raped her day and night. By the time of her second suicide attempt the Department of Rehabilitation could well have congratulated itself on upholding reality; as for her lovers, one of them said: I guess you're learning to like it, bitch.—He was right, as was the retired policeman when he for his part eventually convinced himself that he had made the transwoman who she was (why, she even glowed at his success!), because by then she felt most like a woman when things were done to her.

9

I was on my fourth rum and sodapop when she first encountered Shantelle, who instantly reminded her of the old **ALL COLOR HARDCORE** catalogue (stored in Marjorie's closet) of **AGGRESSIVE WOMEN WHO DEMAND TO MEET YOU!** In payment for the occasional opportunity to be called, however sneeringly, and at the additional cost of degradation, abuse and violence, a female, or even just a stinking he-she with no right to flourish, Judy had long since given over every other valuable thing she owned: her childhood, her parents and much older sister who now all denied her, her name, such friends as she once used to have, and the list goes on like Francine's inventory of cheap liquor now watered down and drunk so that replacements could be ordered—and it was only now, with this goddess called Shantelle, that Judy saw the possibility, like a nickel shining on a sidewalk, of being able to be her new self, without further cost, and *with* maybe even a gain, by snatching back broken rotten bones of what no longer belonged to her, while Shantelle conveniently ignored all that, having more worthwhile projects locked and loaded in her high-capacity cranium.

Jittering somewhere between tipsy and shitfaced, the transwoman now announced to all of us: Well, my dream was always to be on television. I used to study so hard, hoping I could make the cut and be on a quiz show. But the truth is that I'd like to be Judy Garland. If I could look and act like her, I wouldn't mind dying like her. I want everyone to see me and think of happy endings.

Shantelle grinned and said: I'll bet it pays pretty fuckin' well, bein' a star, even some shitty little TV star.

I don't care about the money. I just want the experience, said Judy, her desire as vertical and easily read as the Odd Fellows sign on Market Street.

What experience? You ever been on television? You ever starred in a movie? You ever done a single fuckin' thing?

That's not so nice, said the transwoman. I'd thought maybe you want to play. Well, you know what? I—I'm not going to play with you.

Hey, Francine! Hey!

Hey what? Why on earth is everyone in such a goddamn hurry?

Pour Judy more poison, and I want a Cola and rye.

That's not your usual.

Fuck you. Then gimme a Peachy Keen over ice.

Seven dollars.

It should be six.

Well, it isn't. Do you want to order or not?

Whatever.

Whatever don't signify zippo to me.

Here's your stinkin' seven dollars. Now, Judy, since I just bought you a drink we're friends again.

All right.

And I'm gonna call you *honey.*

Thank you. I mean, that's really really nice—

Honey, don't every girl in this joint put on her own look?

Sure. Every girl's got her own face—

But you don't. You got Judy Garland's face.

Do you really think so? Oh, thank you, thank you!

So you put on the Judy Garland, and Xenia does the Xenia, and Francine gets steamed up over Martina Navratilova. Now what about me?

What about you? I mean, who do you want to be?

I could care less. What I'm askin' you, Judy, is what kind of face should I put on?

For what?

For money.

You don't need to think like that. You're beautiful. I'd give anything to be as beautiful as you. Oh, Jesus, I'd give anything.

What are you fuckin' cryin' for now?

I don't understand why you should come to me for advice. There's lots of smarter prettier women you could talk to. I'm just nothing, and you're someone who's going places. You and Xenia both perform at the Pink Apple! Honestly, I . . . Do you really not know who you want to be?

Oh, forget it. I'll get me some black, black lipstick and vamp up my eyes until they scream.

Did I hurt your feelings? I'm sorry. I never meant to—

My feelings, *honey*? That's rich.

There's a ninety-nine-cent store that sells black lipstick—

I think I'll put on my own Judy Garland. What do you say?

Go ahead. There's enough Judy for everyone.

Well, *you're* different. I thought I'd get a rise out of you.

I have a book of pictures you could see. They're all her. So when you're thinking about dresses and doing your makeup—

How long have you been into that shit?

Since I was a kid. I mean . . . And it's not shit. And I . . . What about you?

What about me *what*?

I mean, will you please please tell me a story about when you were a little girl?

Honey, are you a retard or just bone *dumb*?

Please, will you tell me? Pretty please, Shantelle; I swear I'll be so grateful . . .

All right, *honey*. Well, I remember feelin' different. When I was really really young in a sandbox I remember knowin' that I was different from them. Then a little girl thought I was a boy and I told her I was so I would get what I wanted. So we ended up in a closet kissin'. At age five! And at five I seduced a little four-year-old into bed and we was rollin' around and they caught us and separated us, even though we were in the same house.

Oh, I wish I could have rolled around with you . . . !

And I remember standin' in line with my aunt at a burrito place when I was really little and there was men standin' around just doing what I was doing, and I remember relatin' to them and feelin' weird about them and knowin' I was not supposed to feel that way. And I thought that because of the media or whatever stereotypes, women gotta dress more male to get women. When I was older and became a woman, hittin' my nineteen, twenty-one, twenty-two, it became, no, I wanna wear makeup, sexy bras, play with my femininity. But I'm very in tune with both sides of me, and I . . .—Where do you live?

At Post and Jones. We can go right now if you want.

You'd bring me right into your home?

Cross my heart I would. You're being so nice to me.

Francine, baby, would you pour Judy another and top me off?

What do you mean, top you off? A shot is a shot regardless.

All I want's a couple more drops of rye in my drink, because you put too much ice in it. I didn't even ask for ice and now it's fuckin' watery. Just a finger's worth of rye, right here in the same glass, and I'll even pay you two dollars.

Wait until I rinse out Al's glass.

No, right now, bitch. Here's your stinkin' five dollars.

You call me a bitch and I'll throw your drink in your face.

I didn't mean it. It's just that time of the month.

I'll bet you haven't had a period since your great-granddaughter quit pooping out monkeys. Now look at me, Shantelle. You see this baseball bat? You *ever* disrespect me again and I'll knock your teeth out, *bitch.* What do you say now? I'll tell you what to say! Say: *I'm sorry.*

I'm sorry. And you know what? Now I kind of like you.

Fine. Let's make nice. Here's two straight shots of rye, on the house. So we're friends, right?

Right, *bitch*! laughed Shantelle, throwing her glass at the barmaid's head.

Francine ducked and leveled her bat. The culprit doubled her fists. Judy was thrilled. And the retired policeman, who'd been sitting in the corner glowering at her for disrespecting him yesterday, stood up wearily to protect and serve: All right, Shantelle. You'd better go before she calls the law on you. That's right. Just go.

Shantelle spat on the floor, picked up her purse and walked out. In the doorway she turned around and stuck out her tongue. How she ever patched it up with Francine I never learned. (When I asked her, she explained: I'm that bad penny they talk about that just keeps coming back and back!)—Just now we supposed that she would be eighty-sixed forever. The transwoman, worried that it might somehow be her fault, burst into tears. At the same time she felt very, very excited.

Hey, J. D., she said. Let's kick back at your place.

The retired policeman shook his head.

Are you telling me it's over? Oh, God! And I've been so *kind* to you . . . !

Melba gives better blow jobs, he said, and we all laughed; even Francine couldn't help but chuckle at our favorite self-hating transgender clown.

Having scored her social triumph, Judy decided to go home for a good cry. She stopped at the corner market to pick up a family-sized bag of potato chips, a carton of cigarettes, a shrink-packed hot dog whose expiration date fell sometime during the still unimagined administration of President Trump, a fifth of Old Sailor, a pint of Old Crow for the retired policeman (whose memories were as dark and cold as the breasts of a bronze woman) and a two-liter bottle of SugarAid. Possessing all those treasures improved her mood. And at the corner of Post and Jones, Shantelle was waiting.

That was how they became *special friends*. Being Shantelle's *special friend* was special, all right, like thrusting one's hand into a crocodile's mouth. It worked out as in a fairytale.

10

Whenever the transwoman got teary-eyed over Judy Garland, this excited other women into their own tears; they valued her for this. And Shantelle did teach herself to declaim those famous words of Judy Garland's: *That's what I'm supposed to be, a legend.* In the end she decided to model her own look after Michelle Obama's. The next step was to turn against Judy, who practically pissed herself for humiliation; it was almost as good as show night.

After the departure of her next *special friend* Letitia, Judy grew literally half paralyzed with grief and dread. But then there came that certain wide old drag queen named Selene, who could have been a cement statue of herself, the way she raised one gloved arm in a wave like a cigar store Indian's; behind her sat the lesbian.

11

Loving truth, Judy hoped that Neva would without being asked know to put her tongue as far into her mouth as it would go. Meanwhile she worried that Neva might despise her once she really knew her.

And Neva said: Listen, Judy, you're never going to feel good about yourself until you decide that certain things need to happen to you.

I mean, certain things do happen, thank you very much! And they haven't been good—

What about when you decided to become a woman?

It wasn't something I decided; I always *was* and *am* a woman, and, frankly, Neva—

Laughing a little, the lesbian said: And frankly, you're pushing to get punished. But I'll never lose my temper with you. Do you know why?

Because you love me, said the transwoman obediently.

Correct. Now bend over and I'll spank you the way you like it. Tell me if it's not hard enough . . .

The lesbian asked more about her clients, so she told about the retired policeman, and the lesbian began rubbing her back and asked whether she still loved him, to which she replied that she did.—That's very good, said the lesbian, rubbing lubricant between Judy's buttocks.

Thrilled and enthusiastic (not to mention fortified with Shantelle's unhappiness pills), the transwoman worked so diligently, and accordingly collected such extraordinary tips, that in a mere four nights of sucking and swallowing on Jones Street she was able to deck herself out in the black skirt, black sequined top and high heels of the so-called "Garland" ensemble.

The Reptile Sheds Her Skin

Therefore, you must be in want while it is possible to fill you, and be full while it is possible for you to be in want, so that you may be able to fill yourselves the more.

"The Apocryphon of James," bef. 314

Only the most important things should be clothed in the honor of the symbol.

Friedrich Creuzer, bef. 1912

1

Meanwhile her master collated his information, as we say in the business. And just as an FBI agent who before his notes on the entrapped defendant reach the jury may "rewrite" certain passages in order to render his prey more convictable, so the retired policeman now patterned the data so as to give our precious Neva a certain slant. Either her driver's licenses were false, or else Karen Strand's high school yearbooks represented some other person. She had no juvenile record, but after thirty years her case files would have been destroyed, although her deviations might still inhabit a microfiche index in Vallejo, which he could probably trick his way into if he got off his ass and . . . Actually he felt very cheerful these days. Whenever the transwoman hit him up for money, he chuckled about *disbursing undercover funds.*

On one exceptionally undiabetic afternoon he even dropped in at the Y Bar, hoping to quiz the lesbian—who was absent. He overheard Francine telling Sandra: My dad told me in high school, when this gay friend who was clearly gay said hi, my dad said to me, don't talk to her; she's clearly bad. I was gay and he didn't want to believe it.

I'm sorry, said Sandra.

At that time, if you were gay, you must've been a man hater. The thing was . . . What's up, J. D.? Your usual?

A double.

These days your usual *is* a double.

Then make it a fuckin' triple.

Nine dollars. Happy hour price.

That makes me so happy I could just shit.

Two men in hunting clothes sat watching female mud wrestling on the wide television. Francine poured his Old Crow. One hunter said: I've never shot an AK. I'd like to. They've got *history.*—The other stared up at a grinning and very muddy girl, so the first one accordingly continued: And they have a beautiful, you know, that four-one-six that the military uses, but I'll bet they're payin' twenty-five hundred dollars apiece for 'em.—Said the retired policeman to himself: What*ever.*

Selene's *special friend* Samantha remembered him, so what the hell; he did his duty, buying her that famous wine cooler with the maraschino cherry and the two ice cubes (six dollars), then kissing that wrinkled, white-powdered, man-smelling cheek beneath which a flat silver earring as big around as a boxer's fist tepidly shimmered.

Is Neva one or two percent as sexy as you? he inquired.

Oh, you're so full of *shit,* Samantha said, stalking away pretend-angry. Then she came right back, like a skittish cat who prefers to be petted, but only on its own terms.—Thus Samantha, the old star, testy, generous and sometimes vicious, whom everyone would idolize after her death. He knew not even Judy would remember *him.*

Hey, Francine! Another wine and cherry for Sam, and whatever our sexy little Sandra wants.

Thirteen dollars.

Thank you! cried Sandra.

Don't mention it, jailbait.

Thanks, J. D., said Samantha. You in a cheating kind of mood?

Oh, all the time, Sam. Now listen. You say I'm full of shit. What about Neva?

Nothing wrong with *her.*

Nothing at all? Not even her tight little . . . ?

I'm sorry to disappoint you.

She's never lied to you, or been—

Lay off, J. D.

Just then the transwoman came in, and the retired policeman, feeling inexplicably discomfited, stood up.

2

Now came another of their hatefully meaningless scenes. It started there and continued all the way down the street to her apartment; he had not intended to pursue her; but the instant she, in grief and dread from his imprecations, turned unthinkingly right toward her place instead of left toward his, and he as unthinkingly followed her, she determined to flee him, which naturally turned into his clutching her arm as she helped him wheeze upstairs to the elevator.

She unlocked her door, and he threw himself down on a chair heaped with dirty laundry. Gazing around until he had caught his breath, he said: Once a pig, always a pig. Right, Frank?

She flushed, and for once the flush was angry.

I know what you're thinking, he said. You want to be rid of me. *Right?*

Stop it, she whispered, gazing out the window at a white-shrouded corpse-sleeper beside which a dark hooded figure maniacally flashed a glowing blue cell phone, shaking it like salt while Shantelle and a man in a white cap strolled behind him hand in hand; then came an unknown girl, and then possibly Xenia, who last year had been minding her own goddamned business, playing tranny rap at the volume appropriate for proper appreciation, when her downstairs neighbor called the police, who directed her to step out and speak to them, which she did, asserting her rights with sufficient enthusiasm that they decided to handcuff her. Due to shoulder surgery from 2011 she could not bend her shoulders back but they forced her arms anyway, put her in a squad car, then released her to chase after the Richmond Rapist. Her right shoulder and wrist were never the same, so she wanted to sue, but we all talked her out of it because we knew that people like us (myself excepted) will never win.—Even after the putative Xenia's vanishing, Judy kept looking out the window.

Aha, that proves it! You're raring to get away from me, but you don't have the courage. Ain't that right, Frankie boy? Why, I know you so well! You were born to crawl, Frank, but now you'd rather crawl to your Earth Mother and kiss her ass.

She stood staring at him, gripping her temples.

You know what? You're a user. You're a goddamned leech, he said. Remember when I paid full restitution for your gift card fraud at that stinking wig store? I should have let you go down.

Clenching her fists, she continued to say nothing, and the quarrel might have fizzed out like an old man's erection, were it not for the scrap of green he saw beneath her pillow. Before she could stop him, he pulled it violently out. With a nasty smile he wadded it up and inhaled with sarcastic soulfulness.—So that's what your Karen piglet smells like, he said. Or is that you I'm smelling, Frank? *Something* stinks . . . !

3

The story of the green scrap typifies all three of its principals.

Just as she used to sense her mother's midnight approaches well before the doorknob turned, so now the lesbian could smell the transwoman coming into the room—cheap deodorant, dimestore perfume and male sweat. For her part, of course, the transwoman adored the odor of Neva's body, and sometimes when she lay awake with the retired policeman snoring beside her she liked to scheme out ways of stealing her goddess's socks or panties—relics to be kept forever. She could have asked for a present, because when did the lesbian say no to anyone? But any such overt gift would have lacked the spice of secret transgression. Closing her eyes, Judy had nearly succeeded in imagining that she was inhaling Neva's breath when the retired policeman belched in his sleep. She rolled toward the wall. The most practical plan (originating in his instructions on *roving surveillance*) was to wait until Neva had to use the toilet, and then quickly, quietly open a dresser drawer. But as it happened, her quotidian female persecutor smoothed the way. One afternoon while helping to clean her hostess's apartment (hoping to pay herself in stray hairs, used tissues or whichever other souvenirs could be obtained), she felt under the sofa and found the first moon-green blouse that the lesbian used to wear so often to the Y Bar; it had been ripped down the front. Oh yes, Shantelle played rough!—From the dirty darkness the transwoman grabbled out all but two of the scattered buttons.—It's beyond saving, said the lesbian.

Neva, how did you feel when it happened?

All right.

You weren't angry?

She couldn't help it.

Has she ever raped you?

Judy, it's not good for you to ask what I do with others. It makes you unhappy, and it's also not fair to them.

I know, but . . . Will you buy another green blouse?

If you want me to.

Oh, I do! When can you?

The lesbian laughed sadly. The transwoman dropped the ruined blouse into the garbage bag, and then, when the lesbian went down the hall to get the vacuum cleaner, the blouse flew out of the bag and into a certain someone's purse. That wonderful feeling, almost as good as a climax, whenever she stole something and got it safely into her concealed possession, had abandoned her for ages; she didn't dare to shoplift anymore. *This* was failsafe. Her primary aim accomplished, she could now afford to be magnanimously honest, so when the other woman came back she asked: Neva, could I please have these buttons?

Sure, said the lesbian, knowing everything.

Did you have that blouse a long time?

Oh, not so long . . .

They vacuumed, mopped the kitchen, cleaned the refrigerator, dusted both closets, scrubbed the shower, disinfected the toilet, changed the sheets, then carried two loads to the laundromat. The transwoman was the happiest girl in the world!—because none of this counted against her apportioned time.

When she got home, just before dawn, waving at a silent someone in a miniskirt who stood in the half-dark (the woman's face shadowed nearly into skullishness as she offered herself bravely and sincerely to the darkness), Judy counted the buttons into an empty coffee can—counted and counted and *counted* them, because she'd already lost one!—and then, sitting down, pouring herself a double shot of bourbon, she took out the lesbian's blouse. Tenderly she smoothed it out. She brushed away lint and crumbs. Then she held it to her face, and took possession of what she had won: Neva's scent.

How could I describe her rapture? She felt as powerful as Wonder Woman! Giggling and giggling, so thrilled was she, she felt as if she were sitting so high in the opera house that if she only possessed a ladder on top of a ladder she might almost have touched the ceiling-disk, which was meant to mimic tropical sea-sky around the spearheaded golden crystals of the chandelier; of course that would have been too grand for her, so let me instead imagine looking from a dark balcony, way past you and me, down into the illuminated twiddlers in the orchestra pit.—Neatly folding her treasure, she enclosed it in a plastic bag, in order to preserve the fragrance as long as she could. Then she hid it in her lingerie drawer, meaning never to tell anybody. But it soon flew out of the bag and under her pillow, where the retired policeman so triumphantly discovered it.

4

When he implied that Neva stank, he knew that he transgressed, but, as so often happens when two people pass years in a "relationship," they had both grown careless of each other's feelings.

She said: Take that back. Please.

He laughed at her, so she snatched up a glass with her toothbrush in it and threw it at him. It struck him just below the eye, then fell unbroken to the carpet.

He laughed again.

5

While the lesbian was invariably sickened by self-loathing and the defeatist taint of failure whenever she had to leave someone, no matter how superficial or even abusive that person had been, Judy could not help but feel satisfaction in witnessing the distress of the very few lovers from whom she had actually separated of her own accord. Like many of us, she longed to feel "valuable." So when she proposed to leave the retired policeman and he got teary-eyed, she instantly took notice. Not being so high and mighty as to think (as would Shantelle) that this was right and reassuring, she felt overwhelmed. It nearly seemed as if she meant something! . . . —which alone sufficed to rescind their divorce.

Of course you love her, said he. You're two peas in a pod. Your parents rejected you, so you'll do anything for attention. And Karen's got her own reasons for fucking anything that moves. Just don't think you mean anything to her.

She says I do.

A pet reptile will crawl up your skirt to get warm, not because it loves you.

But Neva says—

People say all kinds of things, he explained. You say you're a woman. You even pretend to be Judy Garland. *Frank*, you're the phoniest little faggot that ever lived.

What does that make you?

I don't lie to myself. I know I'm a pervert, and misery loves company, period. Do you get that, bitch? You'd better memorize it, because there's going to be a quiz, *right now.* So pull up your dress and bend over.

Don't call me Frank.

Why not?

I said please don't call me Frank.

Whatever you say, bitch. You can call *me* Frank for all I care.

6

What she only half realized was that after such moments of estrangement, and sometimes even immediately after, his tenderness for her reblossomed; so that while she continued in the despairing certainty that he no longer loved her, he had already returned to the past when all was perfect between them; and although it may be correct to insist, as several of her predecessors stubbornly have, that we cannot cross the same river twice, or even once, he looked back and saw the water flowing over the place where they had crossed, so that whatever wound they had made in the water no longer mattered, whereas Judy stood wet and muddy on the far bank and asked herself why she should forget this. Hence he, forgiving by forgetting, quickly found her sorrow still occluding the inch of sunshine between them, and then, less offended than simply wearied, stood sadly aside, hardening her conviction of abandonment. Thus they went on alone together. Whenever she lost her desire for him, he used to go out to the hall in the middle of the night and masturbate. A few months later, when she began to experience increasing difficulty in sleeping, she would shake his shoulder to make him stop snoring, and after this began to happen several times each night, he started sleeping on the bathroom floor. As a matter of fact they both snored, as ageing people tend to do, and sometimes he would lie awake by the toilet, feeling her snores vibrating through the wall. From her point of view, he snored *like a monster* as she put it.

By now more infidelities were inevitable, and although one might have expected him to move first, the unfaithful party turned out to be her, not that she was actively to blame, since the game commenced when Melba, who had never given up insisting that the retired policeman remained the love of her life and that they were in actuality still together, decided to undermine Judy's inconvenient romance, which she could very easily do by seducing Judy, who after all was more susceptible than almost anyone who had ever lived. The first step was to flatter her, which took five minutes. The next was to slide her hand up her skirt, and as Melba accomplished this maneuver, right there at the Y Bar, she whispered in Judy's ear that she had with her two doses of a certain exotic love drug, and she also had a place. Although the transwoman had been warned never to accept Melba's various offers, the possibility that someone might desire her (in other words, no matter how *withholding* the retired policeman might become, Judy still *had options*), clinched the transaction; and Melba even paid for both their drinks.

7

These pink pills were supposed to be something snuggly-speedy combined with a synthetic version of the Peruvian hallucinogen ayahuasca, through which, the story went, one could literally see another's emotions; however, it spared its patients the vomiting that was a hallmark of true ayahuasca; anyhow, before either one of them had even climaxed once, the transwoman, who had barely begun to adore Melba's mons veneris, grew confused and fell rapidly asleep, snoring so loudly that first the lampshade and then the bedroom door itself began to vibrate, unless of course (the Goddess being unavailable for consultations) these vibrations might be simply a false perception caused by the drug, which presently carried Melba out of her own cold corpse and into the transwoman's mouth, behind her teeth, across her tongue and beyond her glottis until everything began to appear vaguely impossible, just as when one pays to descend beneath the street of some European city, finding interminable Roman structures in that narrow slice of upraised darkness; so it was when Melba went inside Judy's consciousness, or at least hallucinated that she had—and isn't belief nearly indistinguishable from fact?

To enter into this other woman's skull was to find herself within a grand stone basilica whose eyes were high narrow windows, colored by the stained glass of Judy's thoughts, across which sun and cloud chased each other in eternal insignificance, thereby muting and brightening their fixed figures; and nowhere in this grand space whose stone floor had been inscribed with dates and crude robed men in three-pointed hats was there either blood nor brainy miasma, because she, the penetrator, had herself become blood and brain, invisible to herself, happily hypnotized by the jeweled mosaics of thought-light: the saints were the ones whom she loved and could not stop praying to: the retired policeman, her father who had punished her, God as she conceived of Him (a kinder, fairer yet sterner version of the other two); and there beneath three-petaled red and lavender blossoms of illuminated glass stood everyone's true love, the lesbian, in a night-dress of ultramarine, outstretching her hand toward her unknown (at least to Judy) mother, weeping ruby tears; while in an adjacent window, although the skull's original inhabitant had pretended to forget her, darling, dangerous Shantelle, who longed for her love to swallow up all the others, smiled sleekly, with sunshine entering the nave most dazzlingly through her white, white teeth. Truth to tell, the presence of this latter intercessor did not trouble Melba nearly as much as the lesbian's, which was sufficiently prominent and beautiful as to be unforgivable—so much so, indeed, that the many mean, stained, wrecked, corrupted and broken aspects of Judy (for instance, the crypt of her childhood's skeletons, which had terrified their involuntary keeper all her life, or the broken statue from her late boyhood or girlhood, canted and armless, staring up as in agony) could not soften Melba into pity any more than the transwoman's continued insistence that the lesbian did not love her could do anything but, were that person at all human, drive the lesbian away. Naturally, Neva did and would love her. Therefore, Melba hated Judy. Had she pried up any mosaics from that stone skull-floor she would have realized how rotten her intended victim's attachments truly were: Judy would have loved *her* for nothing!—But Melba left her alone, and so by an error Judy's love for the retired policeman was saved.

8

Whistling, he unbuckled his belt and permitted Judy to kiss it for half a minute.—Oh, baby, she sighed, it smells so good, just like you . . .

Turn over, he said, and began carefully (gently at first) flogging her buttocks just the way that she liked it. She started weeping. He kissed the back of her neck. Then, to him most embarrassingly, he found himself weeping also. Judy was delighted. Saying nothing, he breathed hard, then suddenly whipped her once with considerable force so that she screamed.

That was a good one, babe! he chuckled. Oh, Jesus . . .

9

Judy's life, in short, proceeded on its quotidian way. She got high on goofballs, and when the straight man smirked at her, she giggled to me: Cool, I'm being recognized, but he's not gonna hound me for an autograph . . . !—Just as when some café opens on a rainy morning and a man hastens out into the rain, in his arms a neat stack of empty crates to be filled, while behind him the graffiti'd grating half rises, catching silver rain-light and greenish-yellow streetlight, and through the window one now sees the waitress pulling chairs off the tables and setting them right, so from the transwoman's open heart someone or something set out into the world as usual to forage for somebody or really anybody, while something else within her began dusting away cobwebs and mopping up last night's tears. But into the café people are already coming, lowering their umbrellas, greeting the waitress, choosing tables, setting down their purses, chatting or darting their fingers over their darling mobile phones, making dates, contentedly paying to be served, while into Judy nobody but the retired policeman and Neva went, not even the shivering woman whose umbrella now blew inside out.

Show Nights

I'm terribly critical, but sometimes I have liked myself.

JUDY GARLAND, 1948

Today's women who have sex with other women encounter intolerance wherever they live.

KAT HARDING, 2004

1

Now once more it was show night. Although a drunk had broken the catty pole, Francine was lining up glasses just the same, deploying ice and squirty fizzy water from the siphon, planting black plastic cocktail straws in each assemblage, and finally, just to be honest, swishing in a pinch of watered-down alcohol.

Xenia, whose silver dress had long since been just so, was informing Sandra: You see, my early experiences were with really femme girls. We were always really high, and there was a lot of whipping. I cheated on my butch speed dealer girlfriend and if even Neva wanted me to be faithful I would cheat on her too. Praise the Goddess she doesn't care!

Three dollars, said Francine. Sandra, you need another?

No, replied that girl, I'm good.

(Actually she was not so good, because last night she had been dreaming of the smoke-blackened windows of a ruined castle, whose tiles and glass had long broken and fallen. Cirrus clouds scudding through the doorways. She was inside, or maybe outside, waiting for Neva: the one who was so magical that she could for all Sandra knew sleep with a dead woman and still conceive a child! And somewhere, maybe behind the castle or else in the courtyard, rose a young beech tree whose waist was bent and whose green-fingered arms rose high up as it swayed to wind-music. Sandra was a young blonde girl in a red tartan skirt; she wore her hair in a knot, and her slender arms and legs were ever so white. She sat down on one of two facing stone seats at the edge of the roofless hall, hoping for Neva, looking out the broken sill of a window down at the shaking maples and oaks and beeches, while the wind hissed up and down. Neva would never come again! And Sandra awoke in tears.)

Shantelle had made herself over as a red-glowing girl with a red scarf tied turban-fashion around her forehead; her extra-long lashes flexed like dancing tarantulas. Casting down her glittering eyes into the glow of her phone, she texted some admirer or financial connection, while Xenia was explaining to Francine: When my girlfriend was doing business, Christobel would come and collect me from the strip club. Actually she had a friend who would pick me up without speaking, and she would take me to her house and it was very rough play . . . —while in the dark corner where the retired policeman so often sat, Al and I were compressing Judy's love handles so that she could zip herself into a thirteen-dollar fuck-me skirt. She was giggling with excitement; she loved to be operated on.

By now the Y Bar was becoming someone's dream of a canted orchestra, with everyone clapping to the tuba and the stage lighting up, Xenia teasing Shantelle, really asking for it, until Francine saved her from what she deserved. While I waited for the retired policeman, a naked-chested boy in a skirt and collar was already hugging everybody with a sparkly-eyelidded smile.—This might be one of our best show nights ever!—I remember a troop of show-hungry lesbians and G-girls, their young voices getting shriller as they caressed each other's naked shoulders while Francine pounded ice most crashingly, and I remember the backs and slumped shoulders of the line of European men leaning forward at the bar with their coats hanging on the chairs behind them and a line of blue light glowing behind Francine. By then we had finally gotten Judy packed into her outfit.

An immense lady with a pink plastic orchid and coarse plastic sparkles on her muttony pink shoulders kept photographing Shantelle with her cell phone, while sweating in her Hawaiian dress.—Do you want a selfie with her? asked the transwoman, trying to be helpful.—Just give her five dollars.

That's right, honey, said Shantelle. Five dollars fresh cash money. Even four; what the fuck.

The lady began sweating all the more for embarrassment, so Judy, knowing that emotion all too well, took her by the hand and led her up to Shantelle. The lady clenched her phone, not knowing what to do. Shantelle, growling lovingly, reeled her in with a long and lovely black arm, so that they snuggled side by side. Coaxing the phone away from her, Judy pressed the button three times; the lady beamed like a little child.

Clearing her throat, Francine boomed out: So let's not take the phones out of your pockets when the performers are onstage.

Now the retired policeman trudged in, fat and pale and sweating. I wondered how soon he would croak.

First up went Xenia. Her wide lips were almost black in the purple light, and although instead of dancing she was merely fiddling with her yellow boa and waddling in her sparkly silver dress, with a hat like a plastic fringe on her head, she looked beautiful to all of us, even to the retired policeman, who held out two dollars as she passed by. She did a stupendous job of lip-synching *oh, my love is like a seed, baby!* along with dead and gorgeously hoarse Janis Joplin. Meanwhile our well-travelled Xenia flirted, grinned—and appropriately froze at the song's end.—She scored; she must have made almost twenty dollars.

Second went Shantelle, as brazen as a yellow taxi turning a corner in disobedience of a red light, and some big spender folded a dollar bill into a paper airplane and shot it at her, shouting: *Come and get it!* at which Shantelle kicked it off the stage, and afterward, when he came up to complain she said: I'm already working for almost nothing. It ain't worth my while to pick up your stinking money.—We all laughed at the man.

(Xenia muttered to me: He's too tight to let into my panties. I don't trust his face.)

Lashing the crowd with her long red scarf, Shantelle whirled, pounded her heels to pounding music, kissed the lady in the Hawaiian dress, mutated into Michelle Obama, then became something more frightening, and again Shantelle, Shantelle, dazzling us and sucking up money—maybe as much as thirty real dollars! Now over her head flew that red skirt, which she flung onto the stage; she was down to her bra, garters and G-string, rippling her smooth wide buttocks in hypnotic waves as if she were a perfect transmitter or conductor of ecstasy. She sang *money money money money,* and to her it came; even I felt called upon to give her three ones.

By now it was standing room only, the crowd all magenta in the light, Francine beaming like a den mother to Girl Scouts; and a certain fat Judy Garland wannabe sort of kind of lookalike stepped into stardom, flicking her faux fur boa up off her smooth shoulders, raising her naked arms, then caressing herself all over! I don't deny I felt titillated. As she stripped off more and more, she began to look thinner and maybe somewhat glamorous. The retired policeman clapped like thunder, grinning like the proudest corpse you ever did see. This was what Judy lived for, to be the *real* Judy however deficiently; and right now she kept her mind on the advice that that Julie Andrews woman had given her at the Buddha Bar: Be confident, or, confidence is beauty, or something, something about confidence, whatever. Al blew her a kiss; Sandra was clapping and smiling and calling out her name; the retired policeman and I clinked glasses as she flashed her big titties just for a second, then shimmied out of her wrap, with a big warm smile, riding the music as if it were a dildo! I think she might have even made five or six dollars by now. Then the policeman held out a ten; she blew him a kiss. A girl with blood-red-henna'd hands, shoulders and arms was grinning up at her and then a lesbian couple began shouting in unison: Take your clothes off, yeah! *Yeah, Judy; yeah, Judy! . . .*—at which the transwoman—triumphant girl!—flickered her tongue at them and showed a long groove of pink prosthetic pussy between her perfectly shaved spread legs, and Francine cried out: *Give it up for Judy Garland!*

Then the man who had sent Shantelle a paper airplane reached out and groped Judy's breast. Since she kept smiling and laughing, everybody kept clapping and shouting, the moment masquerading as a triumph for Judy until he viciously pinched her nipple, harder and harder, as if he meant to pull it off. Judy was screaming.—*Sir!* said Francine. You let go of her *right now* and get *out.*—The man stared around him with beautiful green animal eyes. Then he pulled away his hand and punched Judy's breast, shouting: *Fucking queer!* Judy was screaming, then sobbing with pain.

The retired policeman wheezed to his feet, while Francine ducked for her baseball bat, at which the man whirled around with strange grace, sprang through the doorway and before we could decide what to do became a skinny silhouette spidering across a midnight street, while a bicycle twinkled like a star, losing itself within the unwinking lion-eyes of speedy black autos.

Judy's face was crumpled with pain and slimy with tears. It was the ugliest face I have ever seen—the waste product of hatred. I imagine that she felt more isolated than if she had been buried alive. In Francine's face, which was grim with readiness in case that man should come back, I thought I read something equally painful to perceive—the trembling of her lower lip, and a tendency to blink, which she had to hide to do her job.—Well, fuck it, said the retired policeman, who was all too calm. Judy, I'll take you home.

No! I don't want to go home! I was having such fun—

Honey, you let J. D. take you home now, said Francine. Get your things.

Weeping, Judy shambled toward the door. Two delighted Europeans kept filming everything. While the retired policeman was gathering up her coat and handbag, Francine hugged her, whispered in her ear, sat her down on a stool, then went out to reconnoiter the street, with her baseball bat ahead of her.

Honey, he's gone, she said. Don't worry. J. D. will go home with you.

I'll come along, I said, but Judy said: *No no no*, all the while shaking and trembling.

The retired policeman said: Thanks, Francine.—Judy gripped his arm, and they went out. I was surprised how long I could hear her crying.

Xenia said: I don't know why nobody didn't *do* anything.

Like what? said Shantelle in her best purring, snarling voice.

Well, I'd probably punch him, talk some shit, make some phone calls—

Why the fuck *didn't* you?

I'll call the police right now. I think the police are pretty cool people.

Get a life, said Francine. I told you he's *gone.* All right, everybody, show's over! Let's decompress—

Samantha lectured us all: It's a really bad idea to mix money, drinking men and drinking women . . . !

Oh, yeah? said Shantelle. Then why the fuck are *you* drinking?

Stop it, said Francine. Let's either close up or say a prayer for Judy or try to have fun or *something*—

Or *something*! cried Shantelle, and she danced so dazzlingly that we almost forgot about Judy. I who never did anything kept hoping that the lesbian would come in and make things right.

2

So I went home and felt guilty. My feeling resembled the headache that comes on at night, twenty-four hours after a so-called ecstasy pill is supposed to have worn off, the pain steady, cold and sharp behind one's eyes. I reminded myself that nobody could fix Judy and somebody closer to the door should have stopped that man. That was how my wife used to plan: *would have, could have* and *should have.* Then I poured myself a shot of Binco Jack and refined it with sodapop.

3

Just before dawn, when Judy, in tears, sought to pay Neva an unscheduled emergency visit, the latter unfortunately happened to be receiving the worship of Selene (I remember that bride in her egg-yellow wig, complaining about the light, swishing her crossed fingers at another toast to the bride and groom); but Catalina fortuitously peeked out through the quarter-open door of Room 545. She disliked the retired policeman not for himself but as a member of the oppressor class, because four summers ago, when a black-and-white stopped her in Fruitvale for not wearing a seatbelt and the officers demanded her license and registration, she failed to respond at the correct tempo, so the nearest cop grabbed her wrist, breaking her pinky finger and causing a hairline fracture in her arm, then marched her into the back seat of the black-and-white, after which they let her go; the medical bill was seventeen hundred dollars. Therefore, she also looked down on Judy.—Always in trouble, she said.

A man punched me tonight, Judy said. I don't know if my rib is cracked or just bruised; it hurts to breathe—

If you don't know, said Catalina, it's just bruised. Believe me: a cracked rib, you'll know.

Why's your door open all the time?

So I can see what's going on.

Who are you talking to? called a familiar voice, and peering around Catalina's neck came Carmen, the barmaid at the Cinnabar.

Oh, hi, the transwoman whispered.

Who punched you? asked Carmen. If it was J. D., the next Old Crow I serve him will be garnished with broken glass—

No, it was some strange man who . . . I was performing at the Y Bar. J. D. stood up for me, and so did Francine—

Honey, let her come in, said Carmen.

Catalina said: She always stays and stays. This is our private time together.

But she got hurt.

Squeezing shut her teary dog's eyes, Judy turned away.—Oh, come in, said Catalina.

I won't stay long, I promise, said Judy. I just . . .

Why did he punch you?

I . . . for being what I am.

Did you punch back?

No—

If I saw that, I would grab a chair or a glass and stop it. If I have to hit that person, I would hit that person. Why didn't you defend yourself?

He hated me, and I, I . . .

Hate, said Carmen slowly. I think it comes from men, and it comes back again from the ownership and the history of men owning women, and women are supposed to be obedient. I think sometimes there is the intimidation. A lesbian is male-hating and out to get men. I have a dad and a brother and I love them dearly, and I have friends who are straight males. Yet it can be perceived that we hate men. And you—

But I don't hate men; I really don't! I *date* men—

They walk all over you. I've seen you and J. D. together, so I know how he treats you.

Oh, she said.

Why do you let him?

I like it, she said steadily.

Catalina, proprietary and jealous, took Carmen's face in her hands and kissed her.—I'd better go, said Judy.

Listen, said Catalina. You seek out abuse and then you seek out sympathy. It gets boring for the rest of us. Why don't you pick one or the other?

I didn't ask that man to punch me, said Judy sullenly.

Catalina softened.—All right. Sit down. I can see my crazy girlfriend would rather play Neva Do-Gooder than let me eat her pussy *just the way she likes it.* Well, that's gonna be her loss. Judy, there's coffee on the stove; mugs are over there. Now what can we do for you? You won't get any sympathy fuck!

Judy made her best little-girl face and said: Tell me a story.

I knew it! cried Catalina in disgust. She comes leeching around—

Don't be so premenstrual, said Carmen. I'll tell Judy a story and in ten minutes we'll send her on her way and there will still be time for you to eat my pussy exactly the way *you like it.*

Judy flushed.

All right, continued Carmen. I'll tell you about hate. Hate can happen because a lot of the time men think they can join in or have that ability of changing a lesbian's mind. It's almost like, males think they can have a piece of that lesbian relationship, that ownership. The worst experience for me has been at my other job where I had this person who used to tell me I should kill myself for being gay, and what's the point of being a woman if you're like that; it's the waste of a woman. It was really hurtful because it treated me as worthless. I didn't have value because of who I am. You already grow up with this thing that being gay is a bad thing, especially as a Latina. It almost validates those cultural norms. But he was a white male, not Latino. We didn't get along anyway, so I try not to take it too personal. It was hard to just shut it off. After a long time I got to understand that my value was not attached to who I date.

If I were you, Judy, I would pull from my own experience, and, well, I think what helped me with anxiety and rejection is to get involved in my community—because it's my community that has made me. *There is a community out there for everybody.* When you find those people that love you and accept you regardless of your flaws, and just truly love you for who you are, that's very fulfilling.

But I've got no way to find that community, said Judy.

Catalina got cross and said: What are we to you then?

Carmen shushed her and continued: I would say to find one person that you trust, whether it's a best friend or a teacher or whatever that you can confide in.

Lighting up, Judy said: I have Neva!

They looked at her.—Well, said Carmen, you do, but here you are with us. And you still have resources, like a library. I think finding something there that makes you happy and where you can find other characters and other alternatives, maybe that would help you. I used to sit in a corner and look through books, and it was kind of an escape; I would read a lot of psychology books. I can see you don't like that. Well, your ten minutes is up.

Bye-bye, said Catalina.

Goodbye, Judy whispered, feeling disappointed—although she shouldn't have, seeing that every religion even of love has to be unloving and cruel to unbelievers.

4

At four in the afternoon the retired policeman was watching out the window of the Rainbow Laundry (NO TINTING, NO DYEING, NO PILLOW WASHING OR DRYING), sighting over the parking meter which temporarily legalized a teal-grey 2014 Ford Jimbo XR with that signature "handlebar" fender, then diagonally across the street to the green-headed doorway of the Mayfair Beauty Salon (My Hoa Uon Toc), waiting for her to come out; he could see a tall black tranny through the window, and then a cigarette-smoking hooker fell onto her face on the sidewalk outside; a pigeon descended; a man in the livery of the Department of Public Works wheeled a trash can. Finally he worked himself into a rage and entered the Mayfair Beauty Salon: No Judy.

He went home and waited. When she came in he said: Well, where the fuck were you?

J. D., you know this is when I get my hair done—

At Mayfair.

Sensing trouble, she said: Well, they didn't do such a good job last time, so I went back to Adriana and she—

He slapped her face. She sobbed loudly and apologized. Then they both felt better.

She was standing as he sat wheezily down on the edge of the bed. She bit her lip.

Why are you here? he asked coolly.

To please you.

That's right. And why do you go to Neva?

I . . . To, to worship her and—

He slapped her again, quite kindly and carefully, between her cheekbone and her lower jaw. She gasped.

He demanded: Who do you belong to, Neva or me?

You—

That's right, Frank. Now why do you go to Neva?

Please, J. D.—

She gets you off, *right*?

Judy nodded, sobbing ingratiatingly.

Well, you'd better think who the real submissive is.

5

She had been with Neva, of course: emergency comfort. Neva had kissed the bruise on her breast.

For Aphrodite it must be no strain to gratify (or punish) any number of lovers without mixing them up. As for the lesbian, the more she did, the more she was called upon to do, and you have perceived how well she managed it, even with a feeling of exhilaration; moreover, because she had been fitted for selfless loving, the stress never inhabited the acts themselves; nor did she tire of Francine's wrinkled buttocks or Xenia's self-hatred; what abortion of a goddess would Venus be, to be bored by us who were by definition her inferiors?

All the while she was gratifying Judy, she kept worrying that Xenia might be about to harm herself—although Hunter could be more volatile. While kissing Selene she suddenly remembered the scent of E-beth's hair.

Then it was my turn, but as she and I stood on the landing, there again appeared Xenia below us, weaving and screaming her heart out.

Oh, no; oh, no, wept the lesbian, who after all could not do everything.

6

No, said Xenia, it's not because you can't do it. It's because you set yourself up for failure. You and I, Judy, we can't be young. We can't be Neva. When we try, we fall flat.

Three dollars, said Francine.

But why the hell should he *punch* me?

Listen, girl, and those sad sad eyes and crusted mascara became temporarily infinitely dear to the transwoman as her big sister said: Get over it or get out of the game. You want inspiration? Back in the day I used to know this really ugly T-girl named Dolores when we were all hanging out at Prima Donna's, you know, before that stabbing. Well, Dolores never worked on herself enough, so she was *not* put together. She and I and this T-girl Renee used to go in on crystal together; it's a miracle how much more you can get in a bulk buy. And Dolores was always bitching about how she could never pass anyway and she didn't feel safe going downtown in a dress—all that other infantile cross-dresser shit. Well, guess what? She made the big time. She pulled herself together and moved to Mexico and went female twenty-four seven.

She got the operation?

Damned right! Had to sell a lot of ass to pay for it, but so what? And even though she's old and fat, well, Latinos just worship fat ladies! My point is, if Dolores can do it, so can you. Just stop whining and *do the work.* I'll help you.

That made Judy so happy that she ran home to masturbate, while Xenia remarked to Francine: That's one rude bitch! I try to give her advice and she takes off on me . . .

Three dollars, replied her oracle, who then reached behind the cash register, straightening that framed and glassed four-by-six-inch snapshot of two brunettes in bluejeans anchoring their arms on a beaming blonde in a broadbrimmed hat; and as her body occluded her hand she withdrew from behind the picture a twist of sticky plastic wrap which contained four pre-ordered goofballs of maximum strength. I met her at the dark side of the bar to slip her the money. When she pushed the pills down into my pocket, I kissed her shoulder.—Love you, too, she said.

7

Apprehensive that various lies might be sinking her deeper into the retired policeman's bad graces, Judy now committed her second theft on Neva's premises. She undertook it by claiming to reek of her previous worshipper (me). She said: And I, I feel a little nauseous right now, so how about if you go first?—Gazing lovingly at her with those huge brown eyes which we all suspected perceived every falsehood, the lesbian said: Okay, I'll shower now . . .—and after waiting for exactly one minute after water began to hiss down in the bathroom, Judy opened the lesbian's overnight bag and within the top flap's zippered inside pocket discovered right away a silly photo of some old lady and Neva as bellydancers in purple bras and sequined pants, with jingling mesh belts on their breasts, their arms outspread, big grins on their faces; and beneath that a faded, color-mutated snapshot of a braided young woman on a bed, reaching out to some lover; on the reverse an old-time feminine hand had written: *Waiting for E., Stanford '74.*

Forty years ago! Judy had been a six-year-old boy in Cleveland and Neva would have been unborn, or barely born. Maybe this *E.* was her mother.

The shower stopped. She heard Neva shampooing her hair. Then the water hissed again.

More photos: first the old bellydancer lady looking younger, in a moderately feminine sun-blouse, leaning up against the wooden wall of some outdoor beer garden, her grey bangs low over her eyes, smiling gently, as if at a lover; then in a second snapshot were lesbians at what must have been a Berkeley back yard party, given the San Francisco skyline in the background; the yard was lushly overgrown; several women wore rainbow shirts; the old lady was flipping patties on the barbeque, and the caption said *Soy Fest 1968 (Jen & Judith's engagement).*

Like the forethinking addict who harvests only a pill or two at a time from each medicine cabinet she invades, Judy, insisting to herself that she had to go easy on Neva, extracted nothing but those first two bits of evidence—the bellydancers and *Stanford '74.* Then she cleared the crime scene. She was sweating so heavily with fear that her shower was actually warranted, so she took it.

In Neva's bed she had a wonderful time, of course, but felt distracted. The lesbian smiled at her searchingly. The buzzer announced Francine. Then off went Judy to her master, who received the photographs, patted her on the head and said: Good dog, Frank.

What do they mean?

That's above your pay grade, puppydoll.

8

The tiny phone was burning against the lesbian's ear as Hunter continued: I feel like I did live a lie in that I slept through my first lesbian relationship and was in it for eight years. I had committed to it and I had to stick it out. She was my second girlfriend ever and at sixteen we lived together and then we were engaged. Are you listening? Neva, are you there?

Right here.

Well, it was a very emotionally abusive relationship. I had built this relationship with another woman and felt that I had to stick to it because I didn't want to prove other people right, because I wasn't able to deal with my coming out with hetero people. She would always tell me that I was not really gay, that I would end up with a man. So when we broke up I thought, maybe you do need to be with a man, and trying *that* was awful and that was how I learned who I was. And then, flash forward to Xenia, the love of my life! And you know, Neva, I've committed to her and will do whatever it takes to keep her, but she . . .

The lesbian waited.

She . . . Oh, Neva, I—

The lesbian said: She's promiscuous. Like me.

Thank you for saying it, because, you see, I don't come from that kind of background. I dislike it. It brings me down. Sometimes I just . . .

Okay, said the gentle lesbian. So you want to stop seeing me, and you want her to stop seeing me and return to you in a monogamous relationship.

That's right. When she turns tricks, I don't count that, because we all gotta survive.

If you and Xenia both stop coming to me, you know I'll understand. I'll still love you—

So you'll tell her . . . ?

I'm sorry, Hunter, but that's up to her, said the lesbian.

Cursing her, the other woman ended the call. The lesbian felt sick to her stomach. She closed her phone. Softly she began to sing the song of names that Reba had taught her: *E-beth, Reba, Belle and Lucia, Judy and Shantelle, Francine and Richard and Victoria and Sandra, Holly and Hunter . . .* Then she lay down, waiting for Sandra.

9

They had been in bed together, not thinking about the lesbian, and in the hilarious confiding ecstasy of the moment, Xenia, feeling something bubbling so happily up inside her, not sure whether to share it but wanting to because she had *no* secrets from Hunter, said: And you know, five months ago Sandra kissed me on the lips.

What? When was this? said Hunter in a sudden massive voice as if some concrete slab had automatically slid aside so that an anti-aircraft gun could come out.

We were at your house, and—

I know. I remember very well. When I went into the kitchen for a minute, and when I came out, you two were . . . Why, that bitch. My own best friend. I'm going to text her right now and let her have it.

No, she was drunk! It wasn't anything!

Did she put her tongue in your mouth?

Oh, no, Xenia lied.

When you kissed her, did you feel desire?

No, it was nothing like that; she was redfaced and tipsy . . . What are you doing?

I'm texting Sandra.

No, don't, said Xenia.

If I don't, will you promise to be faithful from now on?

Fine. I promise.

Including Neva.

Neva doesn't count. We all go to her, even you. We all *have* to go; you know that.

10

Another week went down the toilet. Samantha with her towering beehive and gravelly voice sat getting drunk for show night. Xenia, enthusiastically lucid on amphetamines, was holding forth to Selene: It's not to say that women are not orgasm focused. But lesbian sex has the possibility of being more emotional. There's an intuition that women have, a witchiness, and I tend to date artists and musicians and filmmakers, not to mention Neva, because they have their own psychic landscape, although Hunter, well, let's not get into that, but with women there's definitely a dance that goes on with a heart-pussy connection . . .

Selene opened a new box of false eyelashes. We had two hours to kill.

How's your health, Samantha? said eager Al.

Okay—so far.

That's all we can say. (What a genius he was!)

Others indeed found more than that to say:

No, Shantelle, they drew some fluid from her belly and it tested positive for ovarian cancer.

I believe it. My Mama got it even after they cut both her ovaries right out. First she felt tender on her right side . . .

In the dark corner where the retired policeman, as granite-hard and blank as the facade of the Federal Office Building, sometimes posted himself in order to spy on Judy, Sandra now began helping to arrange Shantelle's hair. The latter's new look, special for tonight, was intended to duplicate or maybe surpass the style-mask of the ultrafamous Paris Hilton.

I wish I knew what the stars really did on Christmas, said Sandra.

Shantelle yawned.—Probably they fight. Just like us.

A white man and a black man were snuggling at the bar, giggling, and Francine overheard the black man saying: No wig, no makeup, no tits, no—and the white man cut in: Just my . . .—That's right, honey. That's all I need, and you know where I need it.

The transwoman, whose earrings were the size of coasters, leaned over them for a quick meet-and-greet, which on show nights she bestowed on all comers, in order to support Francine, accomplish good in the world, and maybe do business—not to mention that she was curious to see what the black man was showing the white man on his phone's cracked screen: hunky Joes and Johns, of course, whose male organs each appeared to be thicker than the lesbian's wrist:—*Ooh,* said the transwoman. *Ooh*, they're cute.

The white man said: Get away from us, you stinking old queen.

The transwoman burst into tears. Since nobody looked her way, she began to sob at a higher volume.

What's the problem? said Francine.

That fat queen was spying on us. Tell her to leave us *alone.*

Listen, dude. Judy's part of the family and you're not. And she's a performer. You wanna treat my performers that way, you can leave.

Oh, she is? We didn't know. Sorry. We thought she was nosing into our business.

Judy, did you hear? They apologized, so stop your boo-hooing and give 'em space. And just so you know, if that man who hurt you comes in, I've got my baseball bat and Shantelle's gonna clock him. Selene, your skirt's unzipped just a teensy bit. C'mere. Turn around. All right; now you're good. No, sir; that's fourteen dollars, not eleven, and I *don't* know where the fuck Neva is . . .—while over by the toilets, blondes of all genders smiled palely in the darkness, waiting to perform. The catty pole remained out of order. A bald old man scuttled to refill his plastic bucket of popcorn. His hands shook, and the pouches beneath his eyes were as big as testicles.

Finally it was time. The familiar circle of light burst out on the shabby carpet by the ladies' room door, while a long dead chanteuse oozed synthetic wonder, crooning: *The luckiest people in the . . . WORLLLLLLLLLLD.*

The transwoman, satisfied to have been humiliated and then consoled, stepped into the light (which turned her blonde wig green) and began to dream herself into the proper mood. Reaching under the bar, Francine turned a knob. Blue lights whirled out of the disco ball like a swarm of flies. Judy smiled, put her hand on her hip, ran her tongue over her teeth and found a rough spot. She blushed. Ducking through the curtain, she pulled on the ladies' room door, which was unlocked, praise the Lord, and smiled into the mirror. What was stuck to her tooth? She couldn't see it. Well, if she couldn't, neither would they. Although she hardly needed to pee, she availed herself, then washed hands, maintained lipstick, winked at her reflection and unlocked the door, utterly prepared to gladden *the luckiest people in the . . . WORLLLLLLLLLD.* Our Europeans were waiting.

While one man informed a second: The merger feels very risky; all we get is sweat equity, and in the corner, Al kept opening and unclosing his fist beside his untouched drink as above his head the disco ball's stardust crawled on the black wall like smoke, Judy performed her act, and the Germans gave her so many one-dollar bills she nearly felt good about herself (although cruel Shantelle cried out: Is that a baby bump there, girl?—Shut up, said Francine.)—The second man replied to the first: We're dumping every dollar back into the company. Super lean. That wasn't our plan this year. Our plan was to grow. We've lost a lot of opportunities to be selling to our customers. But generally speaking the mergers are a little more difficult to put together.—Then came a new girl, one we had never seen before, decked out as a greenhaired Hawaiian princess, each of whose buttocks would have made a luau for half a dozen hungry lovers of sweet and sour pork; she was doing the hula dance without any hula, and Judy craved to steal the secret of her eyeshadow; her deliciously hairless armpits glittered with powder, and to the happy-happy music she whirled her hair round and round so that it took turns caressing the chests of the patrons in the bar and the knees of the more reclusive types who inhabited those two-seater niches against the wall. Even Francine was allured by this whirl and swirl of hair, of green hair flashing, and imagined lying down with the princess in a bed of palm leaves.

After the greenhaired girl, one of the blondes who appeared sexy from a distance came into the light, and her blotchy face powder, pouchy eyes and wrinkles were complemented by a crooked mouth that made her look as if she had suffered a stroke. God, thought the transwoman, I may be ugly but I'm not like *that,* which gave her great satisfaction. After that, she remembered to feel sad that the retired policeman was not here.

Then came the lesbian.

With Shantelle

Things are the other way round in the city of love. Blood-filled eyes become happy. It is you who trap yourself in the net, then laugh as you have yourself slaughtered.

BULLHE SHAH, bef. 1759

Interest is seldom pursued but at some hazard. He that hopes to gain much, has commonly something to lose . . . But envy may act without expence, or danger . . . its effects therefore are . . . always to be dreaded.

DR. SAMUEL JOHNSON, 1751

1

We were enjoying a faraway pink-lit girl.—She's so dramatic, said Shantelle, who before meeting Neva had sometimes wondered why she was so indifferent to everyone.—Makes such a big deal out of takin' off her damn panties.

Not as cute as you, said I, drinking in the girl's pinkness in the purple light.

It was the first time I had ever gone out with Shantelle. She said: My philosophy is, if someone's gonna hate me for nothing, I'll make him hate me for something. Now what about you?

I want to love you, I said.

Somebody wanna love me, I can live with that. You know who I love?

Neva.

That's right, and I watched her yearning, licking her lips, nerving herself up like the adolescent girl who stands at the makeup counter holding the bronze compact so long that she knows she is becoming a person of interest to the store's undercover detectives; if she is going to shoplift she needs to *move*, and in precisely that spirit she now said: So let's do a little business, honey. Gimme all your turns with her, and I'll give you everything.

If I say no, will you punch me?

She laughed. At the next table, the man in the baseball cap was stroking his girlfriend's hair while the onstage girl in the white tunic which now glowed blue whirled round and round from the pole, legs high in the air, then leaped down, gripping her breasts, laughing triumphantly, offering herself.—Next up came Xenia, who waved at us.

I have to give it up to that old bitch, Shantelle said. Look at her—half her teeth gone, and mascara like one of them washed out roads, but she keeps right on hustlin'. Hey, baby! Hey! Come on, Richard; give her five dollars.

I stood up and tucked a dollar bill into Xenia's G-string. The law said no touching, but at the Pink Apple everything went easy.

So how about it? said Xenia.

I need to kill myself first, I said. Give me time.

So that's a no, right? You're fuckin' tellin' me no.

Actually I pitied her. To the retired policeman (who felt fond of her) she was as weak, predictable and ultimately unimportant as the sobbing girl who laughs only upon getting arrested, but to me she was someone Judylike, who never stopped screaming or sobbing with need, causing me to think about her more than I wished.

My next turn's tomorrow at three, I told her. I already traded last month with Sandra, but—

But *what*?

I'll give you that one.

And what do I got to do?

Unable to think of anything that would be worth my sacrifice I said: Oh, just say you love me.

I love you, Richard. Ha, ha, you're too fuckin' much! Lemme run and tell Xenia . . .

2

On the following afternoon, Shantelle was spending my turn with Neva, and she promptly began to know that the sorrows of loving follow ever at one's shoulders, nattering and chittering all the way up the darkness for which we were made.

No, said Shantelle. You're gonna hear me out. You're *mine*, and that's all there is to it. *Mine*, and no one else's. Because I love you so much I'll fuckin' stab you if you—

The lesbian, well accustomed to this species of compliment, raised the other woman's hand to her lips.

Stroking Neva's belly, Shantelle gloried in cherishing her—this perfect lover who was always ready. And she forgot what she had been thinking the night before—about kidnapping her, or . . . Right now she felt extremely high. She said: The thing is, you and me . . . We gotta . . . Do you know why, honey?—at which the lesbian, wearily half-smiling, lowered her face, and then, anxious to please, looked Shantelle full on, so that the other woman unconsciously widened her nostrils, in order all the better to drink in the perfume of her gaze.

The lesbian had honeymoon bladder. She went to the bathroom and peed; maybe she was getting an infection. Shantelle tried to wait patiently on the sofa, but, unable to keep away any longer, she rushed in, gripped Neva's head for salvation and thrust her tongue into her mouth, rocking hard and quickly against her; and the charm of her (or whatever it was) rushed into Shantelle's brain like the night's first hit of crack cocaine.

What the Cat Caught

In the face of another's great excellence the only possible salvation is love.

GOETHE, 1809

The conscious prayer of the inferior may be that his choice may light on a greater than himself; but the subconscious intention of his self-preserving individuality must be to find a trustworthy servant for his own purposes.

GEORGE BERNARD SHAW, 1924

1

The lesbian was nearly always on time for our appointments. That made it easier for us to pretend that she was faithful to each of us alone.

Of course we all (except for self-secure Francine) longed to know exactly what she was doing, and with whom, whenever each of us was not with her. That was why the transwoman listened at the door. The highlight was hearing Sandra climaxing like a singing teakettle. In those days Holly liked fingering Neva and kissing her, so all the moans were muffled, but that just made it all the more exciting to listen in.

I remember that during that period my usual time was three p.m. on Thursdays, although like Shantelle and Judy I soon learned how to beg for extra meetings. When I came on foot, I made sure to walk sedately, in order to avoid being sweaty for the woman I loved.

Sometimes when I emerged from the elevator the transwoman would be sitting on the landing, weeping softly, her face flushed with humiliation; on happier occasions she was kneeling there, practice-pouting into her makeup mirror, doing her best Sophia Loren. Since the carpet was so grubby I would remind her that she might be soiling her dress. She liked it when I brushed the cigarette ash from her bottom, using the palms of both hands.

The two of us might hear Shantelle inside, cursing the lesbian for sending her away. (The transwoman courageously rolled her eyes.) Sometimes we heard the eternally invisible domestic abuse in Room 541, or else Catalina opened the door of Room 545 to wave. (Victoria was almost never home.) I knocked, and my predecessor stormed out—a cue for the transwoman to scurry downstairs. Shantelle and I kept getting along; we never stopped liking each other. (Whenever I can, she once chuckled into my ear, I find somebody willing to listen, and I tell 'em the worst thing that's happened to me. I shoot it in 'em just like poison! Hoo, is that *fun*!) So the lesbian would stand half inside, blowing her a farewell kiss, at which point Shantelle would ruefully rather than bitterly say: *whatever*!, stride past me, then either keep going in hopes of bullying the transwoman, who half-enjoyed that game, or else whirl around and ask me to lend her five dollars. I always had it ready, just in case. Then she'd say something like: Pull a good scream out of the bitch! at which I'd flatter her, one for-instance running: If you didn't do it, nobody can . . . —at which she and Neva laughed together. Just as immediately after crossing Bush Street, Taylor Street steepens into bejasmined affluence, so Shantelle's mood enriched itself then! She might even repeat that she loved me.—On the Saturday night after Thanksgiving I caught her listening all alone to the drizzle-drums from beneath an old awning in Chinatown, while fish-perfumed gratings drank in loneliness and rain, but please don't judge Shantelle by any such lapse; sneak peeks don't count!—She would punch the elevator call button and maybe slap my ass; once the steel doors closed on her the transwoman might sometimes be heard supercautiously shuffle-creeping back to listen at the door; and *then*, not until then, would I allow myself to raise my eyes, taking in the lesbian, who awaited me in the doorway.

The rest of the time I tried not to dwell on the interval now upon me, because here was my true life, for which I would gladly have thrown away all the rest; and any fool would be sad to admit that most of his life did not go for living. If what I truly was existed only now, then I preferred not to face the falseness of other hours. And should I ultimately manage to accomplish some other form of life (for instance, as when a shadow of illness descends into a woman's breastbone), I preferred not to know of what it might be made.

In other words, I couldn't stop thinking about Neva, she who sent forth airy light from her arms.

One night I was riding the bus on Mission Street, and a black woman was doing her best to provoke the black man across the aisle, crying: Go ahead and hit me, you bitch niggah! Suck my dick! I'll beat you down so bad no fag'll ever fuck yo ass again! Suck my dick, suck my dick!

He replied: You don't have no dick, you dyke niggah—

That's right; I'm a dyke, but you ain't no man; you nothin' but a bitch niggah. Hit me, niggah! Go ahead. Or you gonna just talk about it on your phone like some little girl?

Shut up, bitch—

Don't tell me to shut up. Go ahead. Hit me, hit me! Ain't you enough of a man to shut a woman up? I dare you! You ain't no niggah, you coal-black thick-lipped nig-*ger.* I'll kick yoah bitch ass—

He said: My grandma raised me right. I don't hit no woman who ain't hit me fust. You hit me fust, and you'll see.

She said: You coal-black bitch! Here's a woman that needs to be slapped down, and you ain't enough of a niggah to do the job—

It went on and on. I kept quiet. Finally the woman got off. The man was shaking to retain his self-control in the face of the immense volume and humiliation of her words. Another man told him: You did right, brothah. Police wouldn't've heard a word she said. They would only have heard you hit a woman.

I did and said nothing. Had Judy been there, she might have tried to act like the lesbian, putting out her love until they beat her unconscious. Had I tried to act like Neva, what would I have done? Neva of course would have only needed to be there for all parties to be happily drooling; she always had an unfair advantage, so what was I supposed to do? I did nothing, closing my eyes and dreaming about Neva's cunt, in which my ecstasies were eternally varying yet never unheavenly, like a single great hoard composed of the tiny lovely irregularities of golden Visigoth coins.

On that latter subject, if you were to ask me how I knew that she was the Goddess, or at least *my* Goddess, I would say that whenever I was inside her I would find myself reminding my penis: Pay attention to the cunt! . . . Do exactly what the cunt says! Right now the cunt is getting juicier; it's throbbing; it's giving you permission to thrust deeper and faster, so go ahead, but never fail to be guided by the cunt! The cunt will tell you what to do. You don't have permission to climax yet. Just obey the cunt in everything, and you'll achieve goodness. All right, now you can get ready; the cunt is on the verge of granting you full permission . . .

Because Neva understood me so perfectly (so I assume), she never asked me to talk about my life or any other matters.

There was no reason why she or anybody should have loved me. As for me, I had no one else to love.

I considered the possibility that my hopes and pleasures might soon be over. (I might have been the first who began to wonder whether we were actually better off for these séances.) Like the retired policeman, I knew everything on earth.

2

When I approached that doorway, she never took me into her arms. She stepped back, then once I had come in she closed the door behind me, quietly setting the deadbolt. Only then did she kiss me.

For the first few times I used to ejaculate the instant her tongue came into my mouth.

3

For almost any human beloved the eminence she had now reached would have been lifeless—not for her, because she truly felt that obligation to love.

I said that we "pretended" to ourselves that she was "faithful." But that is only a way of explaining it to whoever cannot understand. The real truth is that she belonged to each of us only, just as God does. And if you cannot believe this, then tell yourself that she misled us who demanded to be misled. She spoke easily but said little—she who for our sake hid her burning thoughts from us.

In compensation I have condemned myself to tell you the thoughts of us others.

4

Al's turn arrived. He was the curlyhaired boy watching her sadly from the corner; as she came closer she saw that his face was withered and blotched, just like the hands in his soft white sleeves.

Since he was called *gay*, and we called her *the lesbian*, what sort of intimacy would one expect them to reach? That made no difference, because as the ancient Spartan poet Alcman once sang: *Let no mortal fly to the sky, nor flee from wedding Aphrodite.* In other words, Al was not permitted to abstain.

Once upon a time, before the lesbian and before even Letitia, Al and Ed were drinking together, and on the bar between them lay a nineteen-year-old snapshot of Ed doing drag as Judy Garland, while on the overhead sports television came a noise like the shrieking and foot-stamping of some spoiled girl who wanted to be an actress; Francine was chuckling: Ed, you sure were a hot chick!—That was when the transwoman decided on a fling with Ed, who said: Sweetie, I'm *no way* going there.—But once he got distracted by his bone cancer, Judy, in a move that would have delighted Shantelle, moved in on Al; long before Ed even reached hospice, the transwoman was presenting herself on knees and elbows like a horse for Al to sweetly ride, which he did, caressing her back and whispering how sweet she was. Our Judy, in short, was a junior Neva: there for everyone! And she kept it up.—But was she really Al's kind?

Neva now took him away. Time for what those stapled mimeographed 1970s circulars used to refer to as *Double Domination: Petticoat Punishment!* To Al she seemed as coldly yet sensuously self-possessed as the goddess Isis, whose robe was tied between her marble breasts in a marble clasp or knot the undoing of which would leave one easy motion between her and nakedness. Their time lasted forever. He knelt on the floor while she stood over him, staring. Finally she touched his forehead. He could hardly bear it—for it is a terrible thing, as they say, to fall into the hands of the living Goddess.

In the end he practically crept away backward, while Catalina waved bye-bye from her open door. (But don't for a moment imagine that Al did not cherish this thing with the lesbian, this connection which could apparently be prolonged forever.) Then the lesbian, hearing on the stairs the footfalls of a bigbodied someone who was trying to walk lightly, knew that the transwoman would soon be ringing.

In the Y Bar we sat waiting for the lesbian. Finally an Italian inquired: How many dollars was the original cost of this bar?—A German lady looked up the answer on her phone.

5

Next came more rough sex with Shantelle, who, while not being the most empathetic of us, still could scarcely avoid perceiving that in the bright course of her pleasure-taking, an expression of discomfort, not yet anguish, slowly began to disturb the lesbian's masklike face; indeed, she gazed upon her tormentor with the same sorrowful steadiness which we find in depictions of the Virgin of Sorrows, whose breast has been pierced by a snakelike golden sword, while cherubim buzz around her like flies and vultures. Well, so what? Shantelle knew that pain is power.

Every night Shantelle would come into the bar, grinning and sometimes talking loudly to herself; Judy was afraid of her, and Xenia disliked her for picking fights, while Francine stayed calm and distant behind the counter.

Xenia said: But the thing about Shantelle is, she's always going to assume the worst about everyone she knows, and worse than worst about anyone she loves.

I think you're right, said the lesbian, smiling a little. But it doesn't matter.

One day Neva was making love at Shantelle's place, and in the next room of the transient hotel she heard a woman shouting obscenities at a little girl; the little girl screeched back and there came a slap. The woman ranted and scolded on and on; there was a pleasure in it, a sunny release; the woman was loving herself. The door slammed, and rapid footsteps shook the hall. Then the little girl sobbed for a long time; the lesbian could hear it through the wall; it infected her like somebody else's long ago pain. Shantelle paid it no attention since it was in her ears all the time. (Well, said Francine, I would say that Shantelle's a very cruel and dangerous person.) The lesbian brought her to satisfaction as quickly as she could, kissed her and hurried away. After that she most often received her in her own apartment, although of course when Shantelle preferred otherwise she had to go along.

Afterward she made time for Sandra, whom I overheard saying: You see, Neva, I've been very lonely. Being with Louis is better than being alone.

Okay.

Don't you have an opinion?

My opinion is that I love you; that's all.

And Sandra went away sad.

After her, I took my turn; and one day, believing that Neva might have the power to lift him back up, came the straight man himself, clutching at her with his skinny rigid fingers.

She called him honey and he said he adored her and could hardly wait to be in her arms again, at which she said: Yes, honey, I want that, too.

When do you want me to call you? I'm free tomorrow night.

Well, I don't know, because I might be seeing Judy, Richard, Samantha and Catalina.

Maybe Sunday, then.

Yeah, Sunday might be better, said the lesbian, in his opinion a little vaguely; and eventually they made a date for Sunday at noon. He did not want her to perceive how strangely terrible he felt, to know that tomorrow night she would be with Judy—although Sandra would have been worse. Why should it distress him? They both had other lovers, and, if anything, the fact that she had others helped him to hold up his head high in front of her when he did the same.

He played a round of liars' dice with Shantelle. She cheated, and he let her win. Then he rushed home and coiled up tightly in bed, neither crying nor wishing to cry, not exactly jealous as the word was usually meant, but deeply hurt, as though his stomach were bleeding. And he lay still for a long time being sad.

6

No, baby, I know what you actually need, I heard him say on occasion to both Sandra and Neva. In fact he only knew one thing:

When he was four years old he saw something dark yet bright with blood moving in the mouth of his grandmother's Siamese cat.—*Bad, bad!* his grandmother scolded. You killed another bird!

There was a smell of innards. His grandmother took the bird away. Maybe she buried it after it stopped moving.

The first time he saw a woman's slit, he remembered that scarlet brightness winding and twirling across feathers and then returning inward where the trembling bird had been eviscerated, the cat watching the boy wide-eyed, then streaking away to avoid his grandmother's anger and hopefully catch another bird.

Until he was grown he had wondered whether he belonged somewhere else—a typical reaction of any sentient life-form still immature and hence out of tune with this universe of cruelty. Not finding an answer, he did as we, and cheapened himself.

Sometimes he imagined walking on a beach, and somehow washing away his unknown trouble, although he was never sufficiently enlightened to dream of islands. He could almost envision the white-laced blue sea rising up in endless green shoulders.

Like the confirmed lawbreaker who always has and always will be framed by unimaginable powers disguised as police officers, he went on denying the awesome character of our universe. Finally he denied the Goddess.

In his early childhood there had been a girl named Naomi whose hand he held when they went walking through the grass. That was all he could later remember of her. He passed through other sweethearts, married, strayed and became Sandra's faraway boyfriend. By then his affections were nearly as pallid as the retired policeman's swollen belly. Sandra began to withdraw from him. She had her men and he his women; that was how it needed to be. But when she fell into Neva's orbit—and when he realized that she loved Neva more than him—he *felt* the gruesome pain of that scarlet gash, which this time was not the perfectly healthy groove below Sandra's belly but the bleeding explosion in his heart.

At the Cinnabar he informed me that on the first occasion when Sandra came to him after having been with the lesbian, he could not help but be distant; but having already understood and expected this, Sandra set herself very sincerely, patiently and lovingly to reassure him until he was melted, and when he sought his jealousy, it was gone! Presently came *his* first turn, followed by the next epoch. They had made a rule, which he had intended to enforce: Neither of them would bring Neva home to make love with her in their bed. But then he came to see that it was so inconvenient sometimes not to invite Neva over, and that restriction seemed silly. The first time after he had lain down beside Neva in their bed, when Sandra touched him he burst into tears. Their bed was changed now. It would never be the same. But she was as patient and affectionate as ever, so that what he had done came to feel like something he had offered up to all three of them. When Sandra brought Neva back, he expected the bed to feel soiled, but it didn't. Maybe it would have had there been some other lover, some smelly man; after all, this fellow was straight like me.

In a scripture called "The Song of the Pearl," the narrator, who must be a soul thrown down among us, and may also be a divine messenger to the rest of us, receives a letter that speaks to him in a woman's voice: *Remember that you are a son of kings and see the slavery of your life.* Did the straight man now become a prince reminded of his kingdom, or merely a slave distracted from his servitude?

Ordinarily his back hurt if he sat in one position for too long, but now he felt that he could watch over Neva forever, joyfully and without pain. On the sofa, she slept mostly on her side, wearing everything but her shoes, apparently smiling. The white evening light was as soft as silver between her and the doorway. Sparrows were cheeping and a coolness blew gently in. Sandra's two pug dogs scuttered happily across the floor, sometimes slipping and skating helplessly, much to their own astonishment; then they leaped up onto the sofa. One of them nestled behind Neva's head, while the other, outstretching its forelegs, made a curving descent through space, rushed to the door, wagged its tail, then slept. At five-o'-clock sharp he awoke her as promised, so that she could meet Francine at the Y Bar. At six-o'-clock Sandra came in.

7

He told me: Then I realized, if I love Neva I have to love who Neva is.

But *then* he thought about her opening her legs to Judy, Sandra, Shantelle, Xenia, Holly, Francine, Samantha, Al, Catalina, Erin, Selene, Victoria and me, and he felt *sick*! He felt *hot*, and began to breathe quickly and shallowly, clenching his fists. He was not angry, but could hardly endure the pain.

8

Whenever the lesbian pulled off her blouse, his nipples would harden. Her touch was like a cool wet sea-wind.

9

He went so crazy for her that he wanted her to drink a dozen plastic cups of water and then piss it out onto his face, but there were interruptions, and by the time her bladder was full the pills had worn off.

10

Once the lesbian got home, at a quarter past seven, in came Xenia. Once upon a time, not long after she had sodomized me for money (she'd advised me: with women I'm more of a bottom and with men I'm more toppy), I watched her looking through the diamonds of a grating in a Chinese grocery, watching all the pears, lemons and durians shine as gently as improved marzipan effigies of themselves, each one of which bore a crescent of light. She appeared unfulfilled. The retired policeman followed her up to the lesbian's apartment. He informed me that when she came out she appeared sadder than before, but why *wouldn't* he have said that, be it true or not? What I myself believe is that Neva charged her with ecstatic love and pleasure: In short, Xenia was moaning like a bumblebee.—Sweet Xenia! The earliest thing she could remember was climbing up in her crib and looking out at something so lovely that she had to reach it, so she clambered over the railing, fell down and hurt her eye. She told me this herself.—And if she did come downstairs looking sadder than before, maybe that was because she made herself be sad for the sake of humility and respect.

11

Francine would never let the lesbian go down on her because she didn't consider herself good enough for our Neva, who gladly went down on anybody. As for me, I always kissed Neva's feet, even when they were dirty. What if Xenia for the same reason denied herself some sort of after-completion? Worshipping Neva, we found it good manners to diminish ourselves. That was what the transwoman intended to convey when she texted the lesbian over and over.

12

Just as when one goes down Kearny toward Market Street, the most lusciously promising lights devolve into bank facades, chain pharmacies and luridly lit package stores, so our expectations of the lesbian necessarily imploded—likewise our self-expectations. But that was only what we pretended afterward. While it lasted, the more she gave us, the more we needed. And each of us received exactly the pleasure for which that person was fitted. For instance, over time she trained Victoria into a doublebarreled ecstasy by sliding her cunt-lubricated finger into the other woman's anus just when and never before her moans had reached a certain volume of sincerity, so that when she came she screamed herself hoarse for pleasure; while in Xenia's case the anal penetration extended rather than increased the delight, much as if a rapidly licking tongue slowed down near the end in order through frustrating the desperately slavering clitoris to build urgency and thereby amplify the final release; although Xenia would moan and tremble while the lesbian's finger was inside her bottom, she could never finish until the lesbian wiggled her finger back out, at which point her response resembled a nuclear reactor's when the control rods had fully withdrawn, so that fission could occur unhampered; at once Xenia began shaking and sobbing and corkscrewing her pelvis around the lesbian's tongue, which flickered ever faster while the lesbian stroked her smooth and panting belly; then and only then did Xenia laughingly sob in a long sweet orgasm.—But the retired policeman, who had long since grown cold to individual cases, set out to compare conflicting perceptions of Neva, and ultimately to arrange them into something whose truth would be demonstrated by its likeness to many other examples of the same type. *What was the lesbian*, not *who was she*, was the quantity, or character, or crime he determined to uncover. But not one of us had yet uncovered the slightest questionable aspect of her behavior.

13

Determined to get his darling out from under the lesbian, even if only for one night, he dragged the transwoman way down South of Market to the Tiger Zone, where at midnight the green light and the yellow light began flashing, the cylindrical cage pulsing in colors, and the electronic-ish discoish music welled up like wonderful nausea while barechested boys circulated, selling shots of ultrasweet low-proof green drinks in test tubes each of which in turn were tucked into a boy's waistband; the customer had to pull it out with his teeth.

Go ahead, bitch, suck it out of him, wheezed the retired policeman, patting her shoulder like an indulgent father; but the transwoman flushed and shook her head.

What? What's your goddamned problem?

The boy stood waiting.

She needs to get drunk first, the retired policeman explained, but the boy only grimaced. He hated stingy customers.

The truth was that Judy was afraid of doing something wrong, such as breaking her test tube before it left the boy's briefs.

A slender ultra-tall tranny began gliding round and round through the blackness, greeting fans. A stocky T-girl announced: *We also have Cherry the Vagina behind the bar. We've got Davy, Sean and Peaches walking around semi-hard.* Making short work of his quadruple shot of Old Crow, the retired policeman glanced into the adjacent booth, where a familiar redhead (he must have seen her at the Pink Apple or the Cinnabar) drew up her naked leg and sipped beer, yawning. The transwoman was already texting the lesbian.

He began to feel sadder than he supposed he had ever been before, but if he could have seen his whole life he would have admitted that this wasn't bad. Judy had plain forgotten him, but only for now. He thought of her leaving high and dry in favor of Cherry the Vagina, who hopefully didn't have one, but he wasn't going to do that, no more than a good father would abandon his little girl for acting out at nursery school. He was God's gift, he was. Back when he still cared about her, Melba once got cross at him because when she showed up two hours late and he bought her dinner and gave her a hundred dollars, then said he had to go (which, strange to say, was true), she thought he was trying to get rid of her. He didn't even punch her. What a pushover he was! And what did poor Judy know? So many mistakes for her to make, and before she knew it, he'd be dead! Delighted to envision how much she'd miss him then, he held out his glass, which Peaches, somewhat less than semi-hard, filled to the top with Old Crow. He took a happy swig, and his esophagus burned. Now his heartburn started acting up. Fortunately he'd charged his shirt pocket with a roll of magnesium carbonate tablets. Moronic Judy was still texting; he ought to punch her in the mouth. He willed himself back into the good old days, when that "all units" call sped him to the scene of the Sanchez murder—sirens and lights! There was no topping the thrill of being the first one to walk into the bedroom whose door had accrued seventeen bullet holes, never mind find old Sanchez lying face down, shot four times through the back and bludgeoned, with the naked wife leaning rigidly inside the shower, shot between the eyes, and *then*, best of all, down in the cellar, that pretty baby girl . . . ! He still got excited thinking about that. And finally he took Judy home.

14

I should have booked you for possession, Frank. You know how I got you off?

But I didn't—

Don't interrupt me. I told the sergeant you were mentally disabled. Then he said to me, he said: *Oh, let that he-she bitch walk.*

Oh, J. D. . . . !

Sure had fun patting you down.

Thank you, honey.

Do me a favor and rub some of that red tiger balm on my ankles; they're fuckin' killing me. Sometimes I crave a bullet, Frank.

My name is Judy.

All right. Do a good job and I'll call you Judy. What the hell do I care? How long has it been?

Nine years now, she said, just then comprehending that this apartment had become part of her simply because she had wept and climaxed here, been beaten by him willingly and unwillingly on these premises, cleaned his toilet (not well), vacuumed his floor no worse than he, crushed the cockroaches that annoyed him, until the place became as old to her as her own grey hair which she clumsily dyed and pretended to forget; all this was or had become her pride.

Vallejo, he was saying. I never forget an arrest. And you were so . . . Hey, whatever happened to those scumbags you were with? Don't tell me. Prison time! That Reggie Peters was a crappy little . . . And didn't Rivas kick the bucket?

You knew that anyway.

I did but I forgot, so it doesn't count. Overdosed in fuckin' *jail*! Hey, I got this Nazi video; let's watch it; pour me a drink . . .

15

She said that she's seen too many people suffer in love, so she . . .

Wants to fix it.

How did you know?

Mommy will make it all better, right, *bitch*?

But that's how Neva thinks!

That's the sickest thing I ever—

But she *can*. We all go away happy.

Get out, he said in wrathful pain.

16

When he first heard about the lesbian, whom he categorized as a *sophisticated deviant*, his alert possessiveness had instantly reared up into the bitter uneasiness which used to be his working state, but Judy had never appeared stabler (which is to say duller, plainer and more beaten down); and it had now been more than a year since with her originally intimidated and soon delighted connivance he had promulgated their game: she brought back from the Y Bar whichever real names she could score, together with their ages, addresses and dependents; then he deduced their social security numbers, after which he amused himself and her by discovering who they actually were, which meant unpacking their smelly lies and betrayals. Francine, for instance, was actually Cora Justice from Kentucky. (Judy cried: *oh, my God!* He laughed and tickled her.) She had served four years for possession of a controlled substance with intent to sell. To impress Judy he logged on to the website PoliceTracker, locating a bench warrant against Francine in Stockton, where she always claimed to be from. He had to give her credit, the way she'd rubbed away her Appalachian accent.

To him they were all the same, from the transwoman pretending to be Judy Garland to the murderess from San Leandro whom he had once brought to justice and who sat bright-eyed at her death penalty hearing, smiling and waving to anyone who might be a reporter.—And he flattered himself that all his jealousies were likewise the same.

In his first month on the force they had taught him the acronym JDLR: *Just don't look right.* That was why one stopped a car, prowling around for probable cause. That was why one hunted for bugs in the lesbian's goddamn woodwork.

A so-called *women's mark*, an impossible birthdate of 1964, no visible means of support, a sealskin billfold that never ran out of hundred-dollar bills, intercourse with any and every soul of us, *for nothing*; eternal patience with Judy, whom not even he could stand: JDLR, wouldn't you say?

For the other two members of that triangle, life grew inconvenient although not actually alarming; as when the lesbian, preferring not to be up all night and believing that Judy would only, as promised, keep on the phone with the retired policeman for five minutes, persuaded her that each of them should take her fourth blue dolphin right now, so that it would build on the declining high of the earlier three, as indeed it should have since the huge-eyed transwoman, now giggling, capering and weaving, intended immediately after lying to her loving law enforcer to drink the lesbian's pee, while the lesbian to please her had agreed to drink at least a few drops of the transwoman's—a perfectly practical plan which came unstuck because the retired policeman happened to be in such a suspicious and bullying mood that the terrified transwoman could not hang up for more than an hour, by which time the lesbian, less divine than human, had long since let out her hoarded-up bladderfull drop by discreet drop in order to preserve the retired policeman, suspect what he might, from *knowing* that Neva was with his darling; by now the transwoman was losing control of herself and rocking back and forth on the lesbian's lap while holding the phone out with a silly grin; and the lesbian, who pitied the retired policeman as much as she did the rest of us, rose up and paced barefoot, silently but ever faster, from one wall to the other of the carpeted room, and just for pleasure began to stroke the cold grimy wall, suddenly kissing it, which the transwoman later confessed swelled her full of extreme jealousy; and as the telephone interrogation dragged on, both women grew more nervous, for the energy within the blue dolphins had to go somewhere, and since it could not express itself in the lovely lovely joy for which it had been manufactured, it bubbled out in vain sad jitteriness. To be sure, the lesbian, concentrating on what the old woman on the island had taught her, managed to love the policeman, Judy *and* the wall. Silently she sang: *E-beth, Reba, Belle and Lucia, Judy and Shantelle, Francine and Richard and Victoria and Sandra . . .* She never sang her mother's name. As for the old lady on the island, that one had laid down her name, so the lesbian never knew it. She thought about Hunter and faintly wished to hurt herself. Then she sang: *Holly and Hunter, Samantha, Xenia and Selene . . .* Judy had a worse time of it. But just like the cuckolded TV star who tried neurofeedback in hopes of getting over the humiliation, she did her homework, buying from Francine extra-strength downers which when washed down with vodka pressed her lovingly down in her bed like big hot furry tabby cats purring against her breastbone, after which she slid slowly backward into the dark waters of dreams, becoming like Sandra a mermaid at last. When she awoke, dehydrated and nauseous, with half the day gone and memories of Neva already alienated from her like the scenes on a Greek water jug painted ever so long ago, she recited to the mirror what Judy Garland had told *Silver Screen* in 1948: *I don't enjoy my troubles that much to dwell on them.* Often, alas, she still felt blue—just like Judy Garland. Then she uttered her idol's declamation to *Motion Picture* from 1950: *I'm unscathed, unscarred, unembittered . . .*—following which she ate half a dozen darling white doughnuts.

She managed, putting her best face on and feeling really, really wonderful about herself even when she got outclassed halfway up the block by the nylon glitter of a lavender raincoat drinking in every car's headlights which swayed across her triumphant rival's bust like heliotropic sunflowers—the transwoman had never seen her before; she must be a G-girl streetwalker, and the waxy shining of her naked knees, which were even more young and perfect than marzipan pears, awed our Judy; her tall shiny black boots whose zippers had begun to fail made Judy long to lick them, even if only for an instant! . . .—but once she hastened up to make her acquaintance, the G-girl said: Hey, tranny, get out of my light.—So that was a trifle excruciating, but Judy hurried to the Y Bar, where Shantelle blew her an unexpected kiss; then she was back in the groove, so to speak, because Tuesday was her date night with the lesbian!

17

But then Francine's mother died. She cancelled her shift; grumbling Bubbles (AKA Alicia) had to fill in for her, not that she couldn't use the extra tips. And Francine dialled up the lesbian, saying: Neva, I know you're watching over me. For twelve years I haven't talked to her, and now it's too late. What am I going to do? God, I don't know; I . . . Help me, Neva!

So the lesbian cancelled her dates with all of us for that day. I was sad, but after all, I never pretended that I deserved her. Victoria sulked; Shantelle went on the war path. And now Neva was all alone with Francine, with their cell phones off and the shades down, and Francine was smiling at her, so happy to love and be loved; but the lesbian felt sick with lonely guilt at the thought of the transwoman waiting for her so sadly and patiently.

Let's each take a shower, said the lesbian brightly, and she took the first one, emerging from the bathroom pink and damp, naked but for the towel around her hips, which she smilingly wriggled so that Francine gasped with excitement.—I'll be waiting for you in bed, cooed the lesbian, to which Francine inquired: With your legs wide open?—Hurry and come to me, darling; then you'll see.

As soon as she heard the shower going, the lesbian, making sure that the bathroom door was shut, rushed into the kitchen, which was in all the apartment farthest away, turned on her cell phone and dialled up the transwoman, who answered right away: Neva! Neva, I need you so bad! Can I come over now?

I'm sorry, Judy, but I have something to do tonight. I'll call you tomorrow—

Who is it? What's wrong? Is something wrong?

The lesbian, staring at the wall with shadowed eyes, turned up her mouth in a weary half-smile to say: Judy, I have to go—

The shower stopped. Then it started again. Francine must have been shampooing her hair.

You *promised* me!

No, I didn't. I said I'd try.

Say you love me.

I love you.

How much do you love me?

Enough to hold you very very tightly . . .

Say something else.

Where are you, Neva? called Francine.

I love you, but I have to go now, and the lesbian turned off her phone, knowing that the transwoman would be in tears.

For a fact, Judy considered herself betrayed; it would have been even worse had she known (she soon found out) that Francine had stolen her turn. Almost at once she began to feel physically sick from the rejection.

In her underwear drawer she kept from her young male days a magazine tear sheet of a tall T-girl in a fluffy wig, a corset, panties and garters, straddling a passive man who lay on his side; and just as in most hunting magazines one will find a portrait of some successful fellow sitting on his just-killed lion, moose or buffalo, twisting the dead head upright to face the camera, so the T-girl had taken her prey's neck in one hand and his head in the other, bending it up into the light of this world. Judy used to find comfort in masturbating to this image. Now she pulled it out and tried to desire it, in order to reject Neva, but since it now did nothing for her, she tore it up in a rage.

Lying on her back, naked, spread-eagled and disheartened, she sought to tune in to the fashion channel, but there was only news. The television said: *Police are offering a ten-thousand-dollar reward for information leading to the arrest and conviction of four men who allegedly kidnapped and gang-raped for forty-five minutes a twenty-six-year-old Alameda woman, who was left naked when they stole her car.*

Judy wondered if she would enjoy being gang-raped and then maybe beaten to death.

The attack, which occurred yesterday night, is being treated as a hate crime because of comments the suspects made about the victim's sexual orientation. The woman is openly lesbian and had a rainbow sticker on her license plate, a symbol of gay pride.

Judy giggled. Who didn't know what a rainbow meant? Not that Neva . . .

The ordeal began around eight-o'-clock p.m. in the seven hundred block of Crawford Street, the police said. The woman was sexually assaulted in that location upon exiting her car.

She almost wished—well, not really—that this had happened to Neva. Now she began to masturbate.

Forced back into her vehicle . . . driven nine blocks away to the eleven hundred block of Garland Avenue, where she was repeatedly . . .

No, I still love Neva. It would be better if it happened to me.

Police described the first suspect, believed to be the leader, as a Latino man in his thirties, who stands about five feet eight inches tall.

And when she came to my funeral, she'd be really really sorry! Oh, I *like* that! And she'd bend down to kiss me, and I'd . . .

An African American man of undetermined aged who weighs a hundred ninety pounds, and . . .

And she climaxed.

She thought about getting someone to buzz her into the Hotel Reddy so that she could listen at Neva's keyhole, or else maybe invite herself into Catalina's room to be spoonfed Neva stories. Instead she sat somewhat dully at her makeup mirror, watching a tear tremble loose from her left eye. It had been months since she had looked so ugly to herself. There were times when girl power fables bucked her up, but just now no consolation came even from reminding herself that after Nancy Kerrigan fell down during her skating routine at the Seattle Goodwill Games, she wept, longing for someone to lift her up and dress her in thunderclouds, then trained harder for next time; when she wavered again during a combination jump in Prague she moaned *I just want to die,* then, having *skated smoothly and confidently* in Detroit, was assaulted by that man with a metal rod, so that she could not compete in the Nationals—but went on to win the silver Olympic medal in Lillehammer. Well, maybe two or three goofballs would make her feel like Nancy. Where could she get some? It would be too humiliating to go to the Y Bar, where even the Europeans knew she was supposed to be at Neva's. The retired policeman might have pills. She'd better hide from him how upset she felt. Her mascara was smeared; she fixed it, then went on crying. Oh, well.

It was a rainy night, and as she turned up Taylor Street from Market Street she smelled ganja where a black man in a wool cap stood without apparent reference to the accumulation of droplets on his transparent yellow poncho. Families and happy young techie couples rushed past her, into the Golden Gate Theatre to take in *The King and I,* a hilarious musical which the transwoman would certainly have loved to pay, had she possessed so much, her own $116 to watch, because it had won the Palladium Palm Award just last year or possibly the year before that; although one old lady had come for another reason; as she explained to an acquaintance: No, it's part of the season; I had to buy the whole season in order to get *Hamilton* tickets!—at which the acquaintance reassured her: You know, it was a great production; I read about it on buzzywuzzy.com. Do you ever go on buzzywuzzy.com? Well, you really should!— . . . the sidewalk gleaming greenish-grey beneath the streetlights while the transwoman, slightly fucked up on goofballs, sincerely tried and honestly failed to count the lights on the marquee, then swished away tight-hipped beneath her polka-dotted umbrella. Now she was looking for somewhere to dial up the lesbian. The location had to be a tiny bit private, because right now everybody in the world was looking her up and down, judging her and secretly laughing at her, or maybe simply despising her for looking so ugly and goddamned *fake.* And now, just as Apollo gazes across the horizon, gripping his lyre, so stood a lordly young policeman with his hand on his rhythm stick. Terrified that he would search her and find pills, she almost stumbled but inhaled sharply, then crept past him with her eyes directed in full submission to the sidewalk.—The first doorway stank of excrement. She powered on her phone; Neva's voicemail was full. Meanwhile, a block farther up Taylor, Shantelle bowed her head against the drizzle, likewise walking away from the Golden Gate; now she was passing the orange and blue neon of the Hotel Warfield, and lusting after a blonde's rubber boots that flashed and glared with glamor while her own high heels clicked over the lovely bright grating of a manhole.

It took Judy three hours to turn a trick, and her customer wasn't very nice. She staggered away spitting and feeling sorry for herself; after awhile she made tears come. Despite her anger, the lesbian remained as bright to her as the Christmas tree in front of the Warwick Hotel, as seen from across the street on a rainy, windy November night.

Ducking into the Y Bar, just in case, she found Xenia holding forth: So last night I caught a guy aiming his phone at me when I was onstage at the Pink Apple, and he said, oh, I'm texting my fiancée. Those smart phones, they have a flash, so I know what he was really doing. I grabbed the phone and I put it in my underwear. The guy wasn't tipping me, and he was blaming it all on his lady, so I wouldn't give it back . . .—and for almost the first time the Y Bar felt like prison to Judy, in part because Francine was absent, so after only two drinks (twelve dollars), she fled again. Five blocks up the hill at Hobo's Piano Bar, where the wine was still watered down, although at least the water wasn't, the balding pianist bowed studiously over the ivories, playing them glittery-jazzy, and Judy ordered a glass of the house white, hoping to feel high-class, but the bartender struck her as contemptuous, and she wasn't going to stand for that, so she tipped him a single dollar, clippety-clopped over to the Mermaid, hesitated at the ten-dollar cover, paid it and dove in. That strip club's golden twitchings as of a vast school of sardines, and all those girly-fingers like the urgently wriggling pseudopods of anemones, lost Judy in the aqueous element. Bewildered in that spectacularly almost loving golden sunniness of kelp, she swam from drink to drink, fixing on a fortyish brunette at one of the high round tables, while the handsome shaveheaded bartender dried the glasses. Now Judy was getting drunk, so she ate half a goofball just to smooth out her perceptions, but the half was so much more than fifty percent that it seemed pointless to leave the remainder to crumble away in her pocket; hence frugal Judy dispatched that, too. The rising and falling of the golden crown of kelp made the waves appear to be breathing. She felt, oh, so happy, or maybe just nauseous. The fortyish brunette was saying: Yeah, he's mad at me now, 'cause I said horribly dirty things to him at the Doughnut Hole.—Then Judy started sweating. Why did they keep the Mermaid so goddamn hot? Wisely eschewing elevated temperatures, she ran outside, and when a yellow taxi swam past like a tuna with shiny light on its sides, she told herself: Dorothy, you're not in Kansas anymore. Click your heels together three times and say: *There's no place like home. There's no place like . . .*

So in the end she did buzz into the Hotel Reddy to eavesdrop on Neva. Through the door of Room 543 she could hear Hunter's gasping voice: I . . . want to stop—

Now? came Neva's voice. (Judy was touching herself again.)

Not yet, just a—a little more . . .

Now?

Oh—

Unless you tell me to stop, I'm going to hurt you again. Because you want it, Hunter. Now.

Oh—

Now.

Oh. Oh, I'm coming—

But Judy wasn't! She gnashed her teeth, because Neva wasn't doing it to *her.*

What the fuck's wrong with you now, bitch? demanded the retired policeman. First you didn't have time for me; now you're moping around here as if your plastic tits fell off. Oh, *I* get it. Your rancid little piece of lesbo ass oozed away from you, so I'm second best, and that don't rate with you no more. I'm sick of you. I mean it, Frank. Get out of here and leave me alone. Get out; *get out*; oh, this goddamned pain in my chest . . . ! Go suck off little boys or whatever the fuck . . . Out, out—

When he had medicated away his rage, he sat there deciding what to do. Like our last good President, George W. Bush, he sometimes referred to himself as *the decider.*

First of all, he said to himself, I won't live without Judy. But I can't ever let her know how much leverage she's got. Secondly, she's not responsible for her actions. Brains between her goddamned legs! A true female in that respect. So I've got to make the decisions for us two. Now, what about Karen Strand? I don't give a shit if she cornholes Judy every night, but she's not going to pry her away from me *or* break her tranny heart. No fuckin' more. Time to do something. Maybe some time-server who started teaching at Vallejo High in 1980 is still doddering around, and if Karen ever acted out, maybe he or she would remember, if I . . . Lemme think. That would be thirty-five years, but somebody who got hired at let's say age twenty-five . . .

First he dropped by the Y Bar to ingest some liquid courage. Most of us were out on business, but Al sat alone, pasty-faced and sleepless, so the retired policeman kindly explained to him why he supported the procedure called *stop-and-frisk*: Most of the criminals that get apprehended are on proactive—you know, stopping people jaywalking, stopping people with a taillight out. Over my last five years alone I did several thousand car stops, and gave maybe fifty tickets tops. All right, Al, my point is, why is this person nervous? Who does this car belong to? Driver says: I dunno. Oh, okay, now I got probable cause!

Al said: What about *driving while black*? 'Cause African Americans say—

Fuck them. What about *driving while Neva*?

That shut him up. Al too longed to apprehend her.

Now feeling like a million bucks, the retired policeman went home. Once more he inspected, which is to say gloated over, that Judy-extracted ancient snapshot of Neva's: the braided girl on the bed stretching out her arms to nobody, not to mention its reverse caption: *Waiting for E., Stanford '74.* Latoya and Marcie had never returned his text about E-beth, so he got back to Baby, who turned him on to Raven, who was wearing a short emerald skirt with the waist drawn well in.

All right, he said. Tell me where you know her from.

My real name's Mariah Chambers. I went to high school with Karen, in Vallejo.

You were friends?

No, I kept clear of her, said Raven. She had troubles, and I sure as heck didn't need more of those.

Do you remember what her troubles were?

You're a cop, right?

Yeah, but you're not the suspect. We're trying to solve a cold case crime, and off the record, Mariah, there may be a reward.

What kind of reward?

Let's get back to Karen's troubles.

Sure, she said cheerfully. For one thing, she came out lesbian. I never cared much about that, but a lot of people in our crowd didn't accept it. So I thought, why get involved?

That was wise. Now, what were *your* troubles?

Not your business, and here she stood and turned away, raising her arms above her head like a ballerina.

Family troubles?

You could say that, said Raven, sitting down again.

What about Karen's family?

I do remember that her mother came to graduation. She acted very proud of Karen. But, well, that girl was always weird. Lost, pale and out of place. Jumpy, you know, like she was hiding something or maybe afraid of something.

You think all she was hiding was her being a lesbian?

She didn't hide it. She couldn't. She was often seen with this older girl, whose name I don't remember; that girl didn't go to our school.

Can you describe this other girl's appearance?

After all these years, no. For one thing, I'm not attracted to women.

And how did Karen seem?

With her? Ecstatic.

What about the rest of the time?

Dull. Sad. Unattractive . . .

Did she go to bed with any teacher? Sometimes a young girl gets a crush on an older woman who—

No. The teachers kept away from her. I told you she was a mess. And she had that bull dyke girlfriend—

When was the last time you saw her?

At graduation.

And the other girl?

She didn't come to graduation. I never saw her afterward.

Look at this snapshot. Do you recognize her?

No.

Now read what it says on the back.

Waiting for E., Stanford '74. Well, that was four years before we graduated. I wish you coulda seen me as a freshman! Actually, I may be on retrochicks.com. You wanna see me, cop? No? Then I don't wanna see you, either. And Karen's girlfriend was, well, but I'd be amazed if she went to Stanford. I mean, neither she or Karen were brainy types. None of us were. That was one thing I'll say for Karen: She wasn't stuck up. But that braided gal doesn't ring a bell. Why should she? I'm no stinking dyke, and besides, it's been forty fuckin' years.

Forty, huh? I bet you didn't get an "A" in math.

Laying down the other photo, of the lesbian and some old lady pretending to be bellydancers, he said: What about this?

Well, that's Karen all right. Pretty well put together, actually. How does she look now?

Not bad for her age, he said.

I look better, right?

Sure, he said. Who's the other woman?

No, I never saw that granny in my life. She's a piece of work.

18

On a Mormon genealogical website he learned that Karen Strand's mother was Rosemary, née Symonds, and born in 1939; hence she must now be seventy-six. She gave birth to Karen in 1964 and in 1976 divorced Kevin Strand, who suicided in 1991, so visiting him would scarcely further the investigation. Effortlessly the retired policeman entered Rosemary Strand's medical records. She was a cervical cancer survivor. Her gynecologist had been Dr. Clark Nisbet. According to her social security file she had lost sixteen years as a secretary for a small downtown business called Smile Associates, and fourteen performing part time labor for a Mrs. Lily McKay of 2287 Delta Drive. Following her divorce she had claimed Karen as a dependent on her tax return through 1982, the year of the girl's high school graduation. From the county assessor he learned that she owned real property at 73664 Triumph Drive in Vallejo.

As for Karen Strand, she had apparently filed no income tax before 1982 or after 1986, when her medical history likewise ended. She might have been murdered then, and very likely, given Neva's pseudo-nubile appearance, her identity had been stolen by some younger relative. No criminal records rose up. She had worked for low wages at a luggage shop, a library and a soda parlor, the last in 1985. Well, what did he care?

19

Judy came in shining.

Francine said: Did you win the lottery or what?

No, I just . . . This guy in a pickup truck took me around the block, and he, well, he did everything.

Then you did win the fucking lottery, said Xenia. The *fucking* lottery—ha, ha! Buy me a beer.

Me, too, rich bitch, said Francine.

Judy said: Well, okay, but I . . . I mean, I actually didn't make anything.

Xenia looked, for the first time ever, shocked. She said: Why the hell not?

He kind of overpowered me, said Judy.

You mean he raped you?

Not exactly. We mutually agreed that it would be more exciting if—

You know what you are? said Xenia. You're a goddamned scab. You make it worse for the rest of us.

That's not fair.

Xenia came up so close she was breathing in Judy's face. She said: I'm a sex worker, so I feel that I should be paid. If I'm going to go through the trouble to get cast in the role of the domme, if I'm gonna beat somebody up, whether or not it's fun for me—

Easy does it, said Francine.

I'm sorry, said Judy. Now I feel so worthless—

See what you've done? said Francine. You know, Xenia, you're a smart and beautiful lady. You've got all the advantages. Let Judy do what she wants; I mean, it's her frickin' body—

Aw, you're so nice to me, said Judy. Can I buy Xenia a beer?

Three dollars.

And for you—

Come on, Judy, it's not like you're some big shot banker or—

Or Neva, said Xenia with an angry smirk.

But I want to, said Judy.

Your funeral, babe. Nine dollars, so that makes twelve. And your usual?

Yes, please.

That's eighteen total.

The transwoman laid down a twenty, and then Xenia, not ashamed of herself but possibly sorry for Judy, raised her glass and said: Cheers.

They all toasted each other.

Then Selene came in. For some time now she had left off her wedding ring. She proceeded to the dark side of the counter, by the retired policeman's corner. When

Francine went to serve her, she leaned forward to commence some private business, leaving Xenia and Judy to themselves while the straight man, who like so many ordinary people simply could not conceive that someone else (never mind oneself) could honestly love several people at the same time, sat forgotten by the toilet, wondering: Is Neva tricking us and do we want to be tricked? Finally he clapped on his headphones, which injected into his skull a kind of dream of lazy or frenetic girls' pumping buttocks that turned from pink to blue as the music boomed *ass ass ass ass.*

After awhile Xenia said: Did I really make you feel worthless or do you just like saying that? I mean, you're a happy goddamned masochist. You're a fuckin' hoot—

Judy replied steadily: So you do those things for money. I mean, I thought—

Look, said Xenia. In my personal life I definitely play dirty and I date rough. I date prostitutes. I feel so supportive of them that I think, why shouldn't I?

Flushing and hesitating, Judy finally said: Would you possibly wanna play dirty with me?

With *you*? You stinking fat slut . . . !

Judy's lower lip trembled.

See? You *like* that! Sure I'll play with you. Let's go make up in bed. I'm gonna beat you to death and bite off your earlobe for a souvenir.

Smiling, Judy burst into tears. She kissed Xenia's hands, staring into her face like a young girl who masturbates in front of a mirror.

Come on, called Francine. You two play nice.

What the fuck does *she* know? cried Xenia with a beautiful laugh. She and Judy disposed of their drinks in two swallows apiece, then went round the corner. After fifteen minutes Hunter stuck in her head; she was searching for Xenia, so none of us said anything. Then the lesbian came in. The straight man upraised his cell phone and, tapping it, leaned smilingly forward, so that Neva did likewise, bending compliantly over her own cell phone to receive what he was sending her: a photograph of him with his hand in his underpants. So they departed together, and two old men craned their heads, watching the back of the lesbian's head as she went out. On our television a superhero trembled through space like a dragonfly that has been sprayed with insecticide, then in a final spasm punched through the wall of a spacecraft in order to rescue the blonde. Two hours later the cheating lovebirds returned; Judy was limping but wore that same shit-eating smile as when she played "Somewhere Over the Rainbow" on the jukebox; and Xenia slapped her on the ass. Francine shook her head, but that could hardly mar their bright new friendship. And more might have come of it right then, but the lesbian glided wearily in.

20

It was Judy's turn. That day the retired policeman had said: Now here's what you're gonna do. Are you listening, bitch?

The transwoman nodded eagerly.

I want you to get hold of her phone. Can you bring it here?

Oh, no! *No*, no, no! How could I?

Well, then can your phone take pictures?

Well, I'm not smart, so I don't need a smart phone. That's what I always say—

First you're gonna practice. Next time Karen goes to piss, you're into her purse like a fly on shit, and you're opening her phone and then closing it; do you hear me?

Yes, honey.

Fine. You're gonna do that until you gain confidence. How many times have you stolen a john's pills? There's nothing to it.

All right, I'll try.

Then you'll take my phone, and if you lose it I'll fucking kill you. Do you wanna know what I'll do to you? Do you, bitch?

I swear I won't lose your phone. But what if somebody takes it?

No one will take it if you don't show it. The whole world knows there's nothing in that ratty handbag of yours but condoms and snotty toilet paper, so *don't get caught.* That's all there is to it. Do you understand?

Judy should have photographed whatever she could, but sometimes her phone uttered incriminating musical moans and she was too nervous to remember how to turn those off. She settled for non-virtual theft. In the top inside flap of that famous overnight bag there remained more photoportraits to steal, so while Neva was in the bathroom her nasty guest withdrew two more: a very dark black-and-white snapshot of a beautiful young woman in some poolhall or bar, her right arm nearly as luminous as the cue ball, her perfect face concentrated on the table, and behind her the backside of a plainer woman in a skimpy dress which tied up behind the neck; then came a color photo of the beautiful girl on what appeared to be an airport tarmac, her slightly wavy hair down around her shoulders, the top button of her white blouse undone; she was smiling.

This time Judy felt less scared. She even had fun.

21

But what are you looking for? she begged. Just tell me so I can—

She has a secret. That's obvious. What do most people want to hide? Money, sex, love, drugs or murder. What else is there?

What else? I—What is it for me?

You lie, you cheat and you steal. You'd do anything for a climax, a nickel or a pat on the head. I doubt you have the guts to murder. Everything else, probably . . .

What about you?

Oh, me? My secret is I never had a fucking life. I risked my ass on the street for nothing and then I got old and now I'm waiting to die, so just to take my mind off—

I know. *I'm* your secret. Baby, tell me I'm your secret!

Sure. That's exactly it. You're my secret bitch. Getting excited now, are you? I s'pose that means you need another spanking. What a world.

What a world, what a world! And then she *melted*, and Judy Garland—

Took it up the ass, just like you. And the Wicked Witch of the West rode my ever-lovin' broomstick.

So did Judy, then and there—because wasn't she his dear little secret? And perhaps *she* was the reason that the lesbian's secret, real or supposed, had fastened its teeth upon the retired policeman, so that he could not get away from its pinching. When Judy licked her forefinger and then slowly traced it around his nipple, the nipple sprang up and even his tired old penis began to straighten.

22

And Sandra, with her ovoid breasts floating above the soapsuds, played mermaid in their bathtub, all the while trying to reassure the straight man. When he asked why she stayed with Neva, she answered: I suppose it's a form of escape but also a connection. I feel so rootless, unattached, floating right now; I want to connect with someone whom I love . . . , and she added as an afterthought, *and with you whom I love,* but the straight man didn't buy it.

23

Well, we could spend longer periods together, said the lesbian.

But what good would that do? cried Sandra. Then I'd only have to lie more to Louis, or come and go and lie and never be in the moment . . .

24

Ever more often came that feeling when Sandra would agonize for half an hour about whether to *text* the straight man back or *call* him back, and then she decided that if she called him he probably wouldn't be there, so she called him, and of course he was there, so she sat naked on top of the lesbian talking to him with a big smile and with her big black spectacles on; as silently as she could, the lesbian got out from under her, and went into the bathroom to sit on the toilet and wait, listening to Sandra slam her wine glass down and chitterchat, thinking: This is hell, sitting cold and sad on the toilet minute after minute with her knees trembling. Then she remembered what her purpose was, and softly sang Reba's song of names.—Oh! said Sandra. What do they say, honey? Isn't that kind of an international chain?

25

Admit it, Neva. You play it cool, but you're the same as me: a whore for attention.

Maybe I shouldn't talk about it.

Why not? cried Judy, glorying in that warmish-hot feeling that she could invite into her chest at any time by thinking about the lesbian.

Because it sounds weird.

Tell me, girlfriend! Please tell me!

Well, the thing is, I do feel happy to be loved but I . . .

But you what?

I do it for you.

What? So you're just doing me a favor, is that it?

No, because I kind of *have* to do it.

What do you mean?

C'mere, Judy. You want to suck my breast—

Neva, I'm trying to be a good friend but I'm afraid I may be too selfish . . .

26

Sending Judy on her way, the lesbian received my worship, and her anus tightened around me in much the same way that Shantelle's hand was guaranteed to slam around any little packet of crystal or powder even when she didn't know which drug it was. Then she went next door to service Catalina, who said: We need to talk, because I keep thinking about you and I'm trying not to get irritated. Can't you understand how this is for me?

I think so.

For me, it's not that it mentally matters. But physically, if I do get an orgasm, even with Carmen, it's just more healing than if I don't. It feels like a circle, like complete. Is that how it is for you?

Sure, honey, said the lesbian.

And when you're doing it to me, Neva, oh, God! Do you want me to leave Carmen for you?

No, honey.

Because I would, you know. I swear by all the saints! Do you believe me?

Of course I do, said the lesbian.

Then why don't you want me?

You know I do.

Neva, whenever I'm in your arms I do feel desired and loved, but then you go away. And most of the time you're not with me, and I watch all those others go in and out; then I start doubting what we have. And I *can't stand it—*

What about Carmen?

To hell with her. I only want you.

But before we met—

That was different. Everything changes . . .

Will you do something for me, Catalina?

Anything!

Keep making Carmen happy. Do it for me.

So you're leaving me.

No, honey. Do you want to get closer to me?

You know I do.

I already love you unconditionally, and our love is only going to grow. You feel desperate because you want more, right?

Catalina nodded, staring at her like a child.

That means you love me more. And I love you more, but you don't know how to feel it. Now what I ask you to do is take even better care of Carmen, try to make her happier and more fulfilled, and see if my love comes through to you better. I want you to try it, for me, and then we'll talk again.

When?

In two months.

No. I won't wait that long.

Okay, said the lesbian. Let's give it a month. And then we'll sit down together, you and Carmen and me . . .

27

Tell me a story, said Judy.

No, said Shantelle, thrusting her middle finger at the television. That ain't Jennifer Lopez's real face. Just look at her. She's definitely had botox, and fuck knows about the nasolabial folds.

Tell me a story about Neva.

Get lost. Hey, Sandra, where's your boyfriend?

Right now we're not actually seeing each other.

I don't give a shit about that. I want somebody to play liars' dice with. He's a good one 'cause he always loses.

Giving up on Shantelle, Judy eavesdropped on Francine, who had poured herself a Hell's Balls and was telling Sandra: When I was like sixteen, the quarterback of the football team wanted me to suck his cock and I was like, okay. He really actually liked me and it was the first experience that I had with someone liking me. Until then I never got to experience what it was like to have someone interested in me. My girlfriends would cry to me when their boyfriends broke up with them. I broke one boy's heart but not that quarterback's. But I also got married to a woman when I was seventeen. But I would also never have said I'm a lesbian—

Selene, who had just gotten a butterfly tattooed right below her navel, was standing by the door complaining into her phone: So then Ricardo started saying he was too busy selling furniture to see me at night. And I was like, *really*? I thought we were married. Then he Blurfed me and Xenia to justify himself. And Xenia got so mad she even deleted her Blurf account. Is *that* so? That's because you're not Xenia. And besides, Neva's on a completely different level from you.

You mean, Ricardo *dumped* you? said Judy.

No one had taken her bait about Jennifer Lopez, so Shantelle, who was wearing huge sunglasses to better resemble a badass, set the hook anew: Francine, did you pick up those rumors about Angelina Jolie?

No.

That bitch won't even have the guts to kill herself when the time comes.

Why pretend to know what you don't know? You want a refill?

Pretty please? Judy interjected.

Pretty please what? Shantelle and I were having a conversation, and besides, your glass is half full.

Wishing that she could lock herself away from everyone, the transwoman dragged her fingers back and forth across the sticky counter. Indifference felt as bitter to her as contempt. Fortunately, just then little Erin came in. Judy hugged her; Judy kissed her over and over; Judy bought her a drink.—Um, *thank* you! said Erin.

Will you tell me a story?

About what? said Erin. I don't really—

About anything. No. I mean, about you. Because you're so goddamn *interesting.*

I am? Oh, okay, said Erin. But I really have to—

I'll buy you another drink, I promise!

No, I'm good. Let me think . . . Judy, sometimes you act kind of weird. I don't mean to hurt your feelings, but . . . About when I was little, right? 'Cause that's what gets you off. Oh, my . . . Well, I remember kind of waking up outside of my bed when I started sleeping in my room, and I started to have dreams that were sexual.

If only I'd been right next to you! cried Judy, but Erin continued: The thing that makes me unhappy in my life is that I was taken advantage of when I was nine. He was forty. I was curious and he went along with it. He asked me a few years ago if I would have sex with him again and I said no, that's not acceptable. There was a family intervention. Well, so we had sex. Maybe that's why I was not happy later about getting breasts. I remember him showing me a picture of his daughter who was a few years older than me, and I asked him, do you have sex with her? and he got mad and said, no, she's my daughter, and I'd thought I was like his daughter, too, so I felt disrespected.

Well, asked Judy, what if he'd had sex with her too?

Then it would have been okay.

A refill for Erin! cried Judy, delighted to be running this show.

Two dollars, said Francine (it was only fizzy water).

Erin raised her drink almost to her lips, then put it down and said: I feel awkward when young men in high school notice me. I feel an attraction, but if you're under eighteen I don't wanna play. Even under twenty-one I don't wanna play. I just want to know that someone's been in the world a bit longer, so he'll . . . See you, Judy; I've gotta go. Now I feel upset, I don't know why—

Why the hell did she rush off like that? said Shantelle.

Chase her down and ask her, said Francine. Judy, hon, you need a refill.

Oh, I do? Okay—

Six dollars.

Then Selene, who was either high or else just practicing for show night, began slowly spreading her thighs on the empty stage.

28

It was four in the morning. The lesbian might be sleeping now, assuming that she ever did. How many hours did she need? Unlike the retired policeman, I had realized that such considerations did not matter. Whenever we humans desired one another, understanding our object of desire concerned us only insofar as the knowledge facilitated our purpose: How does she like to do it, and how can I persuade her to lower her guard?

Then it was five, and Melba visited the lesbian, in hopes of learning how to make the retired policeman love her again.

29

Six hours later his dry tongue awoke him, so he treated himself to a stiff shot of Old Crow. His ankles swelled up right away. He made a date with his informant Mariah Chambers. Then he lay down. In the afternoon he rolled into Ladykiller's with that black-and-white snapshot of the beautiful young woman playing pool.

No, said Mariah Chambers, I don't recognize her, but that place must be Jingle's. Oh, how we used to get shitfaced there! No problem with underaged drinking; they were the *best.* I spent some of the best nights of my youth puking in the weeds behind Jingle's. And that's where I learned how to give blow jobs. I actually give a really good blow job. It's one thing I pride myself on. And see the wallpaper? Dude, that is classic *ugly.* I used to rack pool there with the dick who became my first husband. He wrecked my life, because—

Because you spoiled him with Class A-1 blow jobs.

Fuck you!

Can you tell when that photo was taken?

Could have been any time. Jingle's never changes. That wallpaper's really . . . Why not ask the geezers in there?

All right. Where is it?

Oh, you can walk there from Vallejo High. It's . . . Let me see that again. You know what? That's got to be Karen's girlfriend. Elaine or Eloise or something like that; *E* something . . . What a memory I have! Are you really gonna go to Jingle's?

Sure.

Will you do something for me? Order a Hot Bitch in my honor. You don't have to drink it. Just . . . You know, that place was the *best.* And that was *the* drink.

Was it Karen's drink?

Who gives a fuck about that twisted little queer? I hope she died from AIDS, *screaming.* Buy me another drink. Now I like you. You're on my wavelength, even if you are a cop. Don't queers make you sick?

Uh huh, he said. So you're telling me that was *the* drink.

All the cool girls drank it. That was the in thing, you know, to be a hot bitch. And you know what? I'm still trying. Did I tell you I give A plus blow jobs? My secret is that I really like to swallow.

Let's keep it a secret, he said.

30

Judy was in his bad graces again, so he declined to take her to Vallejo, especially since that sloppy bitch would only fuck up his business. But she was willing to do anything, I mean *anything,* to make him love her again, so he said: You steal from Karen, *right?*

Well, I wouldn't exactly call it—

When you take money from my wallet without asking, is that stealing or not?

I, I, yes it is, but I don't do that anymore.

You mean since yesterday. So she gives you money?

Sometimes.

More than I do?

I'm sorry, J. D.

Oh, that's all right. I fuckin' forgive her. Well, get me some money. Steal me or beg me one of her world-renowned hundred-dollar bills, because I'm going to Vallejo to drink a Hot Bitch. Ask Karen if she knows what a Hot Bitch is. Pay attention and tell me exactly what she says. When are you dating her next?

Well, I . . .

From your guilty look, it must be soon. Is it today? Aha, it *is.* Then I want a hundred dollars tomorrow. Do that, and I won't call you Frank all week.

J. D., I'm a little scared.

Of *what*?

The way she looks at me, I believe she knows everything.

Grimacing like an over-eater surprised by acid reflux, he said: Well then, let her know. What the hell do I care?

So the next day she brought him a crisp hundred-dollar note, series 1987, apparently uncirculated, so he patted her on the head and said: Good dog, Frank. Now, did you ask her what I told you to?

Yes, honey, and as soon as I said Hot Bitch she looked really sad.

And then what?

She asked me if that question came from you.

And?

And I said yes. And she said to tell you that she used to order that drink with her girlfriend.

What else?

And that you can come and see her whenever—

Whenever I take a fuckin' number, he said. Does she wash her pussy in between, or do y'all just swap bodily fluids? You know what a petri dish is?

No, I'm sorry—

Of course you don't. Well, I didn't marry you for your education. All right, Frank, run along. Go sniff assholes like the sad old coonhound you are, and—

That's not nice.

It isn't? *Whoops!* he shouted in delight. Now out you go.

After locating the establishment's coordinates on sleazebardiver@lushies.ru, our emperor of Empire Residences rode the Amtrak to Martinez, decided not to invite his ex-sister-in-law to lunch, ordered up a ride from that underdog of a smart phone application called Hitch, and seven minutes later was easing his throbbing ankles out of the car, whose operator, a Mr. Abdul Buruma, he tipped two dollars.

Jingle's delighted him even from the outside. Two matches, and he could burn the place down.

The automated teller machine must have come in during the 1990s, but the cigarette machine looked vintage. There were three televisions; back in 1982 there wouldn't have been more than one. As for that plastic dragonfly dangling on wires from the ceiling, well, quien sabe, Lone Ranger? This place was even better than the Y Bar.

No, I never knew her name, said the old barmaid. Is she in trouble?

Not at all, replied the retired policeman. Her great-aunt in Wisconsin died last year, and it turns out there's a legacy involved, so they hired me to bring her the good news. I shouldn't say this, but we're talking significant money, more than you or I will probably see.

Well, I play the lottery, said the barmaid, so never say never.

Never, said the retired policeman.

Are you mocking me?

Never, said the retired policeman. Anyhow, it sure would be a shame if we couldn't drop a little joy into this lucky lady's hand. Very pretty from the look of her.

Oh, she was. We always used to call her *killer*, because she'd bring in one girl after the other, and they went goo-goo for her like she was the bee's knees. In those days we minded our own business. It wasn't like today, where you can't hardly get away from being spied on. I guess we all knew she was gay, but the thing about Jingle's is, we have each other's backs. You do your business, and nobody's going to snitch on you.

I can relate to that, he said. I'm a capitalist myself.

What does that mean?

I mean how long did your pretty little *killer* girl keep coming in here?

Well, gosh, I should say, for at least twenty years. She kept getting older, and the other girls didn't, and then she started coming with a gal that couldn't have been that much younger, and they were an item for, oh, I would say a good two or three years, and then they just stopped.

Have you seen this person? he inquired, sliding Karen Strand's photograph across that wraparound Formica bar.

No, mister. Her I don't recognize. Before my time, maybe. Anyway, what do you want with her? Are you telling me she got some kind of legacy, too?

Never say never, he advised her.

You're full of it, she said.

In that case I'll take a Hot Bitch, straight up, so I can send it straight down.

Now *there's* a cruise down memory lane. We hardly ever get an order for those anymore. Now everybody wants to drink a Hell's Balls, although they're actually not that different, in flavor at least. But I should warn you that a Hot Bitch is kind of a girly drink. Are you sure that's what you want?

Well, I've never tried one. You see, this friend of mine . . .

Say no more. I don't get between a man and his friends.

Maybe you and I will be friends. And if *killer* wants to get in between us, if you see what I mean—

Now that I think about it, the lady you're looking for, that was definitely *her* drink. I wish I could tell her name, but I never knew it. One Hot Bitch, coming up!

All the other old lizards in the bar upraised their scaly necks and flexed their claws in delight, telling each other: Did you hear that? That fucker just ordered a Hot Bitch! Did you ever? The first man who ever—

And so the retired policeman had finally accomplished some good in the world. He'd brought the twentieth century back.

His Hot Bitch was pink and oh, so sweet, just like Sandra's idea of a mermaid's pussy. He choked it down with a double Old Crow.

31

On the following day nearly all of us were at the Y Bar, waiting for darkness in case a naked tattooed woman might come laughing and gliding across the stage, or else maybe the lesbian would arrive. (The next turn would be Erin's; her upside-down face reminded the retired policeman of a doll's head.) Sandra dropped in to ask whether anyone had found her hairbrush in the vicinity of all those bottles of ours, which resembled radioactive jewels. Meanwhile Xenia stopped by to use the toilet. Just then she appeared as frail as a certain tiny treasure looted from an Egyptian sarcophagus: a wide-eyed bird-woman, whose pubic hair was painted on.—I've only been out fourteen years, she told me. I told my son, what I do in my bedroom is none of your business and when you're in your bedroom it's not my business. He's not real impolite, because if he was I'd kill him.—I should have asked her how much worse were tomb-robbers than death itself. But when the retired policeman breezed in, I forgot.—Shantelle, in her camisole and nothing else, sat at the bar with her long hair falling down her spine, and her back and shoulders glowing reddish-orange while the bottles glowed blue and green like ocean jewels. Meanwhile Alicia, also known as Bubbles, kept bitching about covering Francine's shifts, when she actually felt delighted. (Francine, of course, was at the Hotel Reddy getting that old time religion from Neva.)

What's your pleasure? said Alicia.

Offended by her ignorance, the retired policeman said: Old Crow. Two shots, straight up.

Well, that goddamned *cunt* dribbled out his poison adequately, but then, get *this*: She plumped a fat ice cube in it!—Here you go, she proudly said.

I told you straight up.

Irritably, Alicia fished out the ice cube with two fingers and flipped it into the sink. He was just fixing to cut her a new asshole when the lesbian walked in.

She looked more tired than he remembered. Most of all she resembled a woman who lives off men, or women, or admiration, or something. Even he could not help but experience her promise of the new, much as when an airplane passenger overgazes the dawning earth whose misty purple-silver, neither darkness nor ocean, sometimes hints at rivers and roads, and whose upper edge is bordered red beneath a wider stripe of orange shading into yellow. But he rejected these sensations, recategorizing her as equivalent to an entry-level television actress, or maybe one of those young lingerie models whom department stores use once or twice in the Sunday advertising sections of dying newspapers because each one can smile innocently, with her pubis sweetly rounded but eternally coincidentally slitless as she cocks her head, pretending (cheating *bitch*!) not to notice that she is in her undies, while above her they show off kitchen appliances and below her the supermarket has peddled cheap ham with the pinkness, unlike hers, enhanced.

Shantelle gazed at her with jealous adoration, whispering some obscenity into her ear. Neva smiled back. He longed to punch them both in the teeth.

Then Al walked in, at which point the investigation's subject kissed Shantelle's cheek, waved to Alicia and took Al's hand. They walked out.

She's not even a lez, he realized. Well, he had known that before, but for some reason it enraged him all the more.

Upraising his drink, he approached Shantelle, determined to rake through her mind about Neva, but she misconstrued his end goal and had long since re-decided never to date this fat old white freak who missed the good old Ohio days when a murderess would be fried in the electric chair.

Eight dollars, said Alicia.

Seven, he said.

Excuse me, sir?

It's *seven dollars.* That's your goddamned *price.* Do you get it?

It's eight dollars, sir. Now, are you gonna pay me or is there gonna be trouble?

I'm not drinkin' it, he said.

Drink it or not, you're paying for it.

You don't know the law. The law is that you don't have to pay until you consume whatever food or drink is being sold to you, and I didn't consume it because I didn't order an ice cube *or* your dirty fingers in my drink, *bitch.* And did you ever hear of California Health and Safety Code Number Sixty-Nine? It particularly pertains to the unclean actions of women. Now pay attention: When a female inserts her grubby fingers in the so-called orifice of a previously used shotglass, thereby endangering her customer in his prospective performance of a no-salt rim job . . .

Alicia was yelling and swearing; Shantelle was hurraying—good girl!—and he Sieg Heil'd us all, mission *accomplished*! But Al and this Karen Strand were already out of sight. He knew where Karen lived, of course, but in the absence of a warrant he could wait. You see, he was retired.

I'm calling the police, said Alicia. And she actually picked up the phone.

I'll save you the trouble, he replied cheerfully. Here's a police tip: If it's a legitimate license plate they can trace it, but if it's an undercover license plate it'll come back blank. That's free of charge. So long, cunt.

When the transwoman heard about this adventure, she consoled him that he had had another sneak peek at the lesbian—a chance to weigh in, vote and even feel significant. And then, strange to say, when this darling Judy of his slowly, slowly lowered her head toward his crotch, and her hair began to brush against his thigh, he felt a tingling of the same stream of pleasure-electrons that *she* felt whenever she was with the lesbian, and his penis sprang erect the way it used to do when he was a young and healthy man.

32

Now what was it about Karen Strand, he asked himself. Why didn't I step in? Oh. I see. I'm getting soft.

The fact was that he had been dazzled, which he would not admit to himself.

All night long he sat drinking in bed, wondering how it would be to fuck a woman like that, a woman so perfect, at least as met the eye, that he could only half believe in her, which sweetened the fantasy much as was the case when the transwoman was doing certain things to him and he to her if he was tipsy or high on pain pills while she was high on something else, in order to pretend to be real and he could pretend that real was what he wanted.

But he never did touch Neva, preventing any exception from vandalizing the astonishing general truth that no one ever made love with her while pretending *she* was someone else.

The next day, determined to get back up on that metaphorical bucking horse (a principle equally well observed by Judy, who despite having overscheduled herself with Neva kept tricking, doing her job better than before), he returned to the Y Bar, whose inhabitants now turned toward him, on account of the streetshine that he brought by standing in the opened door, just within which leaned Shantelle, observing him in much the same way as Karen Strand's cat Princess used to watch the world through half-closed eyes, basking on the sofa, while some well-wisher deposited meaty tidbits into her dish; whenever the admirer looked back Princess pretended to be asleep, but once she felt alone she would gobble it up; and in this spirit Shantelle said: Hey, come in or go the fuck away; you're hurting our eyes, at which he came in, and the door fell shut behind him.

Well, Francine, he said.

Double Old Crow straight up? was her reply.

Yeah. No. I want ice, he said, just to throw her off.

Xenia winked at him and said: How about it?

How about *what*?

You know. I can feel a boner from two miles away. I'm like a mosquito sensing cholesterol.

Oh, yeah? Well, keep sucking Judy's blood. I'm not interested.

In her bitchiest voice she replied: I don't charge Judy. The only reason I'd *ever* go to bed with you is to make some fresh money. And if you think you're so god-damned hot—

Enough, said Francine.

Turning his back on that jilted houri, he stood looking the lesbian up and down. Then he sized her up as follows: Guilty as hell.

As coolly neutral as the marble likeness of a Roman maiden—thoughtful, lovely, smooth and pale—she nodded at him, then turned patiently back to Shantelle. It now began to seem that he had in fact seen her on television, but if her career had gone anywhere good, why the *fuck* was she here? Besides, no Karen Strand appeared in the "RealNames" window of StarHunter.com. Faithfully hating her, he made up his mind that since she had not already gotten what she deserved, she soon enough would, *amen*!

Eight dollars, said Francine.

I thought it was happy hour, he said.

That just goes for well drinks. You didn't specify, so it's four and four. If you want me to dump it out and pour you a fucking well drink, just say so.

Pour me a fucking well drink.

Seven dollars, said Francine, flicking the unwanted double down the sink. She looked very angry.

He slid ten singles across the bar and said: Sorry about your mother.

Her face froze down. The death was her private business, evidently. Well, he could respect that even though she was a goddamned bulldogging bitch.—Finally she said: Thanks, J. D.

But why did Karen Strand remind him of someone familiar? He remembered admiring on his television screen the sultry mug shot of the twenty-seven-year-old mother whom the assistant district attorney called *a calculating child killer.* Melba, who adored the true crime channel, informed him that when they brought in this defendant, who was as pretty as a Christmas package in her handcuffs, for the opening day of her trial, she began to sob and her lawyer hugged her (seeing which, Melba had to masturbate); after which Judy, anxious to outdo Melba, advised him that this murderess frequently vomited in the prison van on her morning commute to the courthouse; the thought of that darkhaired defendant in distress certainly got him going; he liked it when he came in Judy's mouth and she gagged, which she rarely did, more's the pity; sometime he should order her to . . . During the trial, the *child killer* kept sweetly tissuing away her tears. Her name was Kimberly Kenniston.

She could weep for her brain-dead son, and then calmly, cheerfully answer questions. She had poisoned his feeding tube with salt in order to get sympathy. They nailed her after she phoned up her friend and asked her to throw away the feeding bag in secret. It was a very entertaining case which included a sexy district attorney named Chrissy Borealis and some sweet autopsy photos.

Another? inquired Francine.

Triple it up, and no ice.

Nine dollars.

Staring at Karen Strand (the silently singing woman who offered strong drink to her lovers) until he could project her image within his closed eyelids, he now decided that she resembled a bored college girl who would slum it here for a month or two, then disappear to law school or some all-American corporate job, something wonderful, like monetizing things that used to be free. But Karen Strand was thirty-six now, or fifty-one, or *whatever.* According to his research she had never gone to college. Here she was, our perpetual social worker, playing Lady Bountiful to welfare queens. He'd checked the SpiderWeb: no marriage reported for that individual, no arrest, no Vallejo teacher sex scandal during her high school years, no girl-on-girl statutory rape then, either, although even if some motel called the police the officer might have just instructed Karen and her girlfriend to get lost, after which—human nature!—any busy cop would have dropped it. We were too fuckin' innocent back then, he realized. An opposite sex encounter with that age difference would have been charged as a sex crime, but lesbos always did get away with murder.

He found himself hoping for another blast of Karen's famous charm, but maybe it was just as well that he didn't feel anything. To hell with her anyhow.

Shantelle's cell phone buzzed. Removing it from her purse, she offered its glowing screen to the lesbian, and then they both giggled. That infuriated him.

A grinning German blonde, built like a refrigerator, stood waiting by the toilets. Shantelle, queen of the world, stood up, kissed the back of Neva's head and went to negotiate. Taking the German woman by the hand she said: No, I got my policy. I only put out when you get me high. High or loaded, either one.

Good, said the Deutscher.

Okay, let's get this over with, said Shantelle, and out they went. He liked that; he liked anyone who did business straight up—unlike, say, Judy, the lesbian and me, who kept compliantly trying to swallow down whatever had been predicted for us.

But now once more he had to fight off Neva's glamor, allure, or whatever the hell it was; she almost offered the sad young eyes and smooth young skin of Judy Garland. His Judy was right; there was something about her, some cheap magic or power that he wished he could smash. Once he knew for sure that she would never come on to him, and he could forget all about everything except what he had been put on earth to do, he got over his disappointment and almost liked her; she was attractive enough, except that he hated vaginas.

He stood up on his squishy aching feet and marched into her light.

Hi, she said.

You don't fool me, *Karen Strand.*

I'm sorry, said the lesbian.

Why did you change your name?

Whether it is true that beauty brings sadness, that look in the retired policeman's face, that pitiless cruelty glaring out through his weakly watering eyes, was nothing if not sad. It was as simple and gruesome as a promontory of black bones.

The lesbian said: I never liked the name Karen.

He grunted, staring at her.

I think you're J. D., she said.

That makes you a regular private detective.

I have a favor to ask you, she said. Will you step outside with me?

He reveled in their faces. Francine's had gone waxlike, and Victoria's was openly envious.

Sure.

Finishing his drink in one go, he held the door for her ironically. As soon as they reached the corner she asked: Could we please talk about Judy?

Said the retired policeman: You read my mind.

33

He had expected some confession whose purpose would be to weaken his possession of Judy, but she now said, with the air less of a guilty defendant than of a witness trying to remember whether or not a light happened to be shining through a certain bathroom window on a certain night: I'm wondering if she needs help.

Yeah, *baby*! What she needs is for you to leave her the fuck alone.

Not yet, said the lesbian.

Rage blossomed happily in his heart.—Then I won't leave you alone, he said. Karen, or Neva, or whatever your name is . . .

She said nothing. Why did her expression refuse to change?

And I wanna see this *women's mark* of yours.

The lesbian pulled up her blouse.—It's here but you can't see it.

But Judy could. What bullshit.

She could.

I said what fuckin' *bullshit*!

She let her blouse back down, trying to smile at him.

Pulling out the snapshot of the braided woman at Stanford, he asked: Who's this?

Oh! said the lesbian. I guess Judy—

I told her to. Trying to get dirt on you. You want it back?

Would you like to have it?

How about this one? Who's this old bag? I'll bet she was more than your bellydancing teacher.

She smiled.—That person was dear to me. Keep it if you like.

So she's dead?

Yes, some time ago.

You were bellydancing professionally?

Just for fun.

Where was this?

On an island.

Are you lying to me, Karen?

Do you want me to? I will if you—

Will you shoot Judy in the head?

No.

Will you leave her the fuck alone?

If she asks me to.

Here; take your goddamn pictures.

Thank you, said the lesbian.

Last but not least, he snarled, thrusting in her face the black-and-white photo of the beautiful woman playing pool.

The lesbian kept smiling, but he thought he saw her twitch.

Well?

She was someone else I loved.

Is she dead?

I don't know.

Well, cut my dick off. Anyway, what's your opinion of Judy now?

That I love her.

She stole from you and—

Because she loves you, and you told her to.

How does that make you feel?

I want people to love each other, said the lesbian.

I'll just bet you do. Fuckin' *freak*!

Now could I ask *you* something?

Let me guess. Do I hit Judy? Better yet, *why* do I hit Judy? I'll tell you something, bitch. The stupidest call I ever took was when the husband was beating the wife and she was screaming; soon as they came out we had 'em drunk in public and then I said, asshole, you like to beat up women; try a man! . . .—and then the wife started shouting, don't bother my husband! They deserved each other, they were in paradise. Well, that's my fuckin' paradise. Do you get it? I said, do you fuckin' get it, cunt?

Yes, said the lesbian.

Was that what you wanted to know?

The lesbian nodded.

No, I won't punch you out, he said. You're not my type. I don't hit women until they beg me. And I'm pretty sure you're not Karen Strand. Or let's say you're like Shakespeare: Someone else wrote those plays, but he happened to have the same name.

Or not, said the lesbian, trying to smile at him.

You'd better not say you love me.

Okay.

Look, he said, rolling his tongue inside his cheeks. What happened to Karen once you assumed her identity? Did you kill her?

She smiled at him.—Is that what you want me to say?

No. I want the truth. But I don't expect to get it from you, since you're a liar. Who are you?

Karen Strand and Neva.

You're telling me that you're the same person who graduated from Vallejo High in 1982?

The same, she said calmly.

You look almost the same. But you can't. How old are you?

I lost those years . . .

You're fifty-one and you look to be under twenty-five. How do you explain that?

You won't believe it. Witch magic—

Oh, *please.*

And you won't believe this: I love Judy, and I—

What do you mean, you fuckin' *love* her? I can hardly wait to watch her get dumped! By *you*, Karen. Stop holding your nose and take a whiff of Judy. Then you'll fuckin' . . . It's gonna be the laugh of the season.

I love her.

You love everyone, I hear.

Oh yes, she replied.

As I said, you're a freak. You make me sick. You're like a crapper that anyone can use. I'd rather use my own goddamn toilet. It's more private, with less risk of disease.

I understand.

Don't you ever get angry?

When you need me to I will.

What the fuck! he shouted.

J. D., Judy's in trouble—

Because you're feeding her false hopes, and you won't put a stop to it. Now listen. I don't care who you are and what you've done. All I want is for you to lay off her. Do that, and I'll leave you alone.

That's up to Judy, said the lesbian.

Then he did crave to punch that beautiful face of hers into bleeding ruins. He said: I don't know what you are, but once I find out, I'm going to get you.

I love you, she repeated. He didn't buy it.

He was already striding away when she called his name, at which he turned back toward her with doubled fists. She said: The place where they made me Neva is an island. You could go there, and if you took Judy—

I don't get it, he said.

I can show you on a map. And if Judy—

Shut the fuck up about Judy, he told her, at which she looked very sad.

34

The transwoman actually *was* in trouble. Huge-eyed and open-mouthed, she attended to another of Sandra's on-request stories of her childhood: I remember reading this book, *The Plains of Passage*, the fourth book in the *Clan of the Cave Bear* series . . .

Involuntarily Judy was licking her lips. She had a shiner on her left eye, and there were bruise marks on her throat. She imagined her tongue crawling up and down between Sandra's legs, drinking in Sandra's mermaid womanliness so that she, Judy, could become more female.

And by the time that book came out, said Sandra, I was physically mature, and I—

Oh, please don't stop telling me! You started doing *something* . . . !

You see, Judy, there was a lot of sex in it, but I didn't understand all that. But by the time that book came out I was a little older, and I remember reading these incredibly graphic descriptions of sex, and that was the first time I had heard of oral sex at all. I actually thought it was a really bad book; all they did for seven hundred pages was travel across these plains and stop to have sex. But I remember getting a physical feeling from reading them.

So you touched yourself! I knew it! How were you feeling? Right now I want to . . . Francine, you should really listen in, because, *oh, my God.*

No thanks, said Francine while serving me a rum and sodapop. I crooked my finger at her, and when she bent toward me I whispered an interrogative about Judy's love marks. In answer she touched my shoulder. Then she started washing glasses.

I think it was two feelings, said Sandra. One was curiosity and another was horror that it would happen, being repulsed by it, but all these descriptions, yes, I also did feel a sort of tingling between my legs, so I kept reading. But I still didn't know how to intensify that feeling. I didn't understand the idea of masturbation; I didn't realize that if I touched myself, that feeling would intensify—

Well, *I* figured that out when I was little. But my Daddy would come in to beat me. If they'd walked in on you—

But they didn't, said Sandra. They didn't care about me.

If you were my mother and I was snuggling you and then I started touching myself, would you hold me tight?

Would you be a boy or a girl?

A girl! No, a boy, I guess. And I'd turn into a girl when you slid your hand—

Not if I were your mother. I remember when my friend Harriet, when her son Lincoln was masturbating when he was only four years old, and he had no real reason to stop. She was talking to him and she was trying to explain that this is something you do by yourself, and it's not bad, but you should do it in your bed and not mine.

Judy interrupted: Well, Neva was willing!

Willing to do what?

Last week I asked her if we could play the incest game. You know, mother and daughter. And she was like, whatever.

Was it nice?

You know Neva's the best!

Was she smiling?

Well, for a minute she looked kind of sad, but, you know, Neva has to do whatever we want, because—

Judy, how can you say that? That's not nice!

Well, you know I'm just nasty. I'm no good, because—

Blushing, maybe because the peach schnapps was going to her head, Sandra patted the transwoman's hand. Then she said: Honey, are you all right? What happened to your eye?

35

In the bar called Ladykiller's, grimacing over a tallish watered-down beer and (because they were out of Old Crow) a watered-down shot of Black Vulture, the retired policeman waited for a person of interest to tire of trolling the burlesque clubs of Broadway—not that any of them, even Foxy's, whose chorus of whispering singing girls was currently assisted by synthesizer and drums to underscore their fake urgencies, could begin to imitate the crystalline flashing of a school of anchovies, which was why the retired policeman preferred to save his money for drinking alone, baiting Neva, jawboning with Francine, giving me life lessons or else dating the transwoman, so why the fuck did Johnny keep spending his money there and not here? Eleven-o'-clock, and finally a motorized wheelchair groaned slowly in, with a backpack hanging behind it, accompanied by a trailing brightcolored fetish: a chain of bras and panties. Sitting back on the long worn black naugahyde couch that wrapped around the back wall, the retired policeman watched Johnny roll up to the bar. On one television screen was news; on another, an assassination thriller, and on the third, a glowing advertisement for Mardi Gras.

I'll have a draft, said Johnny.

Evenly smiling, pouring watered-down drinks, the young bartender asked where Johnny was from.

Right here.

I don't remember seeing you before. Six dollars.

The retired policeman stood up, which hurt. Checking his pocket for his wallet, he waved to the man in the wheelchair.

All right, said Johnny. You pay.

The retired policeman dragged his two drinks over. His ankles ached even though the compression socks were so tight that his feet were going numb and cold. Each step he took made him feel as if razorblades were slicing into his arches and cigarette lighters were burning his heels. When he stood still, it felt as if a long scalpel had sliced sideways into each foot from just above the arch. Grunting with pain, he counted out eight one-dollar bills on the counter. Then he sat down next to Johnny.

Thanks, said the bartender.

Well, said Johnny, how you been?

Great.

You don't look it.

Neither do you.

At least I don't lie about it. Actually, maybe you are doing great. I heard *great* news about you. Heard you're actually *dating* Judy.

That's right.

And that's why you asked me—

You hit the bull's eye, Sherlock.

Where did you meet her?

At the Doughnut Hole.

You're shittin' me! They closed that place down ten years ago!

Four.

What do you mean, four? Couldn't have been under six. I'll bet you busted her and she did whatever in your stinkin' squad car—

Four years, Johnny. Vice closed it down.

Who else? Was it you that dropped that dime?

Off duty I never called in on anybody except for violence, and you know it. Now what are you pissy about? I didn't take her away from you.

You said it. I fired the bitch. And now you're dating her. That stinking he-she bitch. Judy don't deserve to live. Got into my wallet and . . . And you're getting it from *him*. Guess what that says about you?

Johnny, my friend, if you weren't a cripple I'd pour that beer over your head and kick your teeth right out your ass.

You truly met her at the Doughnut Hole? I would have sworn, not even Judy—

So do you have what I asked you for or would you rather fuckin' goad me until I do kick you in the teeth?

I heard her door open at about two in the morning, I should say.

At the Rosebud Motel?

Oh, no. This was Judy's place.

And you just happened to be there.

Well, you know how I like to listen, for old times' sake. So my check came in, and I said to the clerk, I said, gimme the room next to hers, just for tonight. And there was some fellow—

This was Tuesday or Wednesday?

Wednesday. It wasn't Al or any of her regulars. He was talking loudly to her right outside, but I couldn't catch what she was answering, because she kept her voice down. And then the man went in, and the door closed real soft but firm, you know what I'm sayin'? She keeps her bed right up against my wall, so, well, sound travels. That's my meat. And it couldn't have been more than five minutes before that bed was creaking and creaking against my wall, about as fast and hard as I've ever heard it go. Then it just *stopped.* I counted three. And then I heard the scream, definitely a female scream, at least as female as Judy gets, and it kept going on until something heavy hit the wall, and then it stopped.

How long did this go on?

They started doing their business right past two, I would say. He must have conked her ten minutes later; it was for sure less than fifteen. So then I heard the door open. I waited till it had closed, and I could hear him pass my room; I should say he was moving pretty quick, like he didn't want to be found after what he'd just done. Here's a memory stick showing him on the lobby video; you'll see he's—

How much?

Oh, whatever, J. D. For old times' sake. I mean, you and I were fuckin' the same goddamn—

36

So what happened to you? he said.

I was having fun.

You look like hell. Are you sure it was all fun?

I promise, she said.

Well, Johnny was next door wanking off. He said you got hurt—

He was *listening*? How *embarrassing*, she said with a happy smile.

He's one of us, said her lover. He don't care how fake the pussy is.

37

This is what he looks like, he said, laying down a pixelated printout, then looking discreetly away from it, across the next table at the glazed look in a young man's eyes as he stared across the top of another man's head at the naked girl who kicked playfully back at him, rapidly opening and closing her buttocks. Then her next song began, and she somehow hooked her buttocks over her ear.

Why ask me? said Shantelle, so thirsty to be loved. I'm not a killer; I'm just a hardass niggah bitch. You wanna killer, you better get a big strong man.

You can do it, brown sugar. You're hard and fast and mean. Just fuck him up a little.

For what?

For Judy. He choked her and punched her, so I want revenge.

I don't care shit about her.

Sometimes you do.

What do I get?

Twenty years in Folsom Prison.

That's a good one, J. D. I said, that's a motherfuckin' good one!

I'll let you in on my business, he said, well aware that hardly anything was sweeter to her than minding the business of others. Now look. I hate Neva—

You do? I'm gonna tell her—ha, ha, *ha*!

Go right ahead, bitch. Now, do you want to do business or not?

Buy me a drink.

They were at the Pink Apple, where fewer nosy Parkers would know them. The mistress of ceremonies was instructing the world: *That's how you make noise when people show you body parts.*

He got her a Peachy Keen. She made a face and said it wasn't sweet enough; Francine made it better. He told her that her breath stank and she would soon lose her teeth like Xenia, so why didn't she fuckin' get healthy?—Like *you,* she said, laughing in his face.

Now this is to your benefit, he said. I want Neva to leave my bitch alone. No Neva for Judy means more Neva for you, if you can swoop in.

Swoop swoop, she laughed, baring her teeth and showing her claws.

That's beautiful, babe. Oh, you get me going, you *sweet* pterodactyl.

Put it to me, she said.

I love it when you talk dirty. Just break his nose or something. Then I'll send one of my dudes by, to enlighten him that it was for Judy and he'd better fuckin'—

Wow, Shantelle said. You do love your bitch! I'd give anything to be the bitch of somebody who loved me like that, but that ain't gonna happen, 'cause—

What about Neva? Don't she take care of you?

Oh, fuck you, said Shantelle.

Well, do you want more of her or not?

I'll take what I can get, she said—subscribing to our collective belief that if we could simply boil up around Neva, we could carry her off (or, clinging, be carried by her) to wherever it was that we had once expected to go, and just because none of us had gotten there yet did not mean that there was no such place. (The mistress of ceremonies said: *And that amazing performer who . . .*)

Perfect. So mess him up a bit and I'll give you two hundred dollars cash money. He's in Room 213 of the Ganesha Motel, paid up until Friday. It's that dump on Mission and—

I know.

And he's crazy about black pussy. Just knock on his door and he'll let you right in. Here's a hundred up front.

In a dream, Shantelle turned the bill over and over. Then she started.—That's Neva's money, she said. I know by the date on it.

So what if it is?

Laughing a little, she said: I guess we're all hangin' on Neva's sugar tit. But does she know about this?

What the fuck do you think?

Are you gonna tell her?

No, he said. I promise.

Watching her, he discovered that she must be less accomplished in violence than she pretended: he had never seen her so anxious!—But then she smiled, calming herself by remembering all the times she had shoplifted and burgled without getting caught. He folded up the printout into a three-by-three-inch square. Then he slid it into her hand, and it went to wherever the hundred-dollar bill had gone.

38

His best friend the security guard did not answer his call, which as usual went straight to voicemail, so he called Shantelle, but her voicemail was full. High and dry was how he felt, like an ice cube all alone in a shotglass. He crept and wobbled all the way to the Buddha Bar, where the lady who resembled Julie Andrews was coaching some young girl: Women make a lot of money out in Vegas cocktailing. I cocktailed one year. You'd cocktail and then you would dance or sing. I hated it. You were glorified cocktailing and then you would dance. But you could make good money. I only worked three days a week and I pulled in a pretty good wage. Most dancers know that the longevity of their careers is not going to be great . . . —What did the retired policeman care? So he made a date with Melba at Neon Mary's. Until now she'd kept shyly calling him, convinced that he hated her, because on half the infrequent occasions he tried to check in, her phone was cut off for nonpayment, so that she never knew or believed that he had indeed tried to reach her. So they sat facing each other at a sticky wobbly table, while to his left a naked girl was bending over, wiggling her pale buttocks at the world in general, then seizing the catty pole, corkscrewing herself round and round, and Melba kept stumbling and stuttering over her words, sounding weary and old: where the fuck had her glory gone? The naked girl was hanging by an arm and a leg, upside down, whirling slowly down the pole, flexing her long tattooed legs with the same meaningless grace as a lobster wriggling its feelers; he showed Melba an old joke image he had on his phone, of her sucking his cock; but he had forgotten that she hated every photo of herself unless she had taken it. Once upon a time there had even been bright young Melba with blue light on her face, twirling round this very pole, with her hair brushing the floor. Well, fuck it. Another girl now climbed the pole, clamping herself around it, beginning to spin down, never looking at either of her three prospective clients in the front row, while he now deployed the black-and-white photo of the beautiful woman playing pool.

That's actually one good thing about getting old, said Melba, cramming a wrinkled cigarette between her wrinkled lips; at least your memories may pick up cash value.

He gave her a ten.

Big spender, she pouted.

He gave her a nickel, and she laughed. He grinned and pounded the table, thinking: Wait till I tell Judy! Well, well; but Judy must be putting out for the lesbian this very minute; how did they even do it? Tongues, thumbs and you know what; maybe even *lowdown treatment.*

He snapped his finger. Sistina the barmaid refilled his triple Old Crow.

What about me? asked Melba.

All right, Sisty; bring her another vodka and cranberry.

Once Sistina was out of earshot he said: Give.

Who is she?

You'd better fuckin' tell me. That Strand bitch woman said, and I quote: *She was someone I loved.*

Romantic, said Melba. Well, that might be Elizabeth Jackson. I never knew she was such a hottie, back in the day.

You fucked her.

Oh, no. She's picky. For one thing, she's a cougar. Goes after younger meat. I think at that time she did live in Vallejo or Martinez or someplace like that. There was this place called Jingle's where . . . Never mind; you don't know shit about Jingle's. If she was doing Karen, she would have been at least four or five years older. These days the age difference is wider, from what I hear, but as you so clearly indicate, I'm old and out of touch.

A new girl was whirling upside down so easily down the pole, her nipples the color of her hair, wiggling her buttocks for the silent young businessman in the front row, then loudly slapping her ass, slamming her high heels together. Melba said sadly: I used to do that for you.

Back in the day, he said. Thanks, Mel.

You're never going to leave Judy, are you?

He gulped the rest of his Old Crow and said: I never leave them. They always leave me.

I tried and tried to come back to you.

Yeah, he said.

It was just past six-o'-clock in late May, when the streaks of light on the floor might still be mistaken for late afternoon sun—and indeed if any quitter were to descend the grubby black stairs just now, he would come into painfully bright sunshine. That was what happened to the retired policeman.

39

Put your leg on me, darling, the lesbian said, and began to masturbate so urgently that she climaxed within a minute, pretending that she was wearing a strap-on and had gone deep inside Victoria, or perhaps imagining she had become Judy, and Victoria was deep inside *her* and (speaking of Judy) beating her until she bled—how should I know? I'm making this up as best I can. Even in orgasm she was far away.

What are you thinking? said Victoria. Are you sleepy? Why don't you talk to me?

Reminded that Victoria needed time and gentleness, the lesbian made herself kiss her—back to business!—and right away could feel Victoria's heart pound against hers.

Victoria said: These are the words that come to me now: *encouragement, power, gentle restraint.*

Yes, honey, said the lesbian.

Victoria was getting high. Her eyeballs were larger than dimes. Neva's breast became the horizon. Fuzzily she murmured: You can fuck me; we need to discuss . . .

Okay, said the lesbian, holding her tight.

My hands, my mouth on you, yes, let's discuss. Let's take a shower together. Because . . . I like it when you please yourself, and . . .

Thank you, darling.

I said you can please yourself and I can watch. Neva, the day you first touched my neck was *oh,* so erotic; that's the energy I like.

I love you, said the lesbian.

Yours is the specific love through which I'm going to represent myself. It's like someone saying I will follow Aphrodite, not Athena. But, Neva, who can Aphrodite follow? I don't know because I'm so . . .

The lesbian kissed her again and again. Then she brought them each a glass of water. Her cell phone began vibrating: Judy, no doubt.

And I love hearing your echoes, Neva. Do you hear anything right now?

Your heart—

I guess I hear the words as you must have spoken them. They're all the colors. I need to go down on you, because . . . because I'm so in love with you, journeying back through my mind to . . . Substitute *you* for *me* and *me* for *you* and all human problems vanish. *So* in *love*, Neva!

Knowing what the other woman now wanted, the lesbian strapped on her harness and opened Victoria's legs. Victoria said: Neva, I was born to love you.

And they loved each other, but several nights later Victoria remembered another of those questions which she'd never asked Neva.

40

. . . And this time I could not get enough of gently kneading the lesbian's breasts hour after hour while she lay with her head on my shoulder, dreamily moaning. When I tried to specify any *quality* of the pleasure she was giving me, the investigation did not so much as fail (since failure never got a foothold in these séances our crew had with the lesbian) as carry me into rosy hazy caverns of dream; but it seems to me now that when I was playing with her sweet soft breasts, stroking and squeezing them as carefully as a trained retriever dog fits his mouth around the fresh-killed game bird to bring it intact to the hunter, the pleasure most definitely did not originate in my fingers themselves, although I certainly felt it there; rather, it came out of her, passing into me like a tingling warmth; my hands merely completed the circuit; I could almost see it rising up out of my darling, the loving light of life itself, faithfully and effortlessly emitted for me by the woman whom I loved more than anyone. As to what this pleasure consisted of, I can hardly tell you. It was simultaneously warm and cool, drowsy yet rich in movement-impulsions; to repeat, I could not get enough of rubbing my hands over Neva! Sometimes she would murmur to me, it never mattered what, or she might stroke my hair while I fulfilled my sudden craving to lick her pussy, or I'd find her white teeth coming closer and closer because without even knowing it I had been lured toward her smiling mouth; we would kiss with a long sweet flickering of tongues even as my hands slid up and down her back while she held me trustfully. And this pleasure was complete in itself, obviating any need of narrow labor toward some climax; it was perfect, utterly fulfilling and therefore subjectively eternal. Having spent many nights with prostitutes, I was long since accustomed to watching the clock, to see how my joys were draining away; but ten minutes of clasping Neva in my arms passed as slowly as forty with another woman, so that after four or five hours with her I felt as if I had received half a week's worth; and leaving the Hotel Reddy, a calm happy alertness kept me company for a long while. To be sure, each time I came down from *that* got a little worse, until I began to see why my heroin addict friends referred to what they did as *getting well.*

41

Wow, I'm standing next to fucking *Neva*! said Anna, who was gorgeous despite being a thirty-five-year-old addict; she kept calling her friends the most beautifully perfect individuals on earth, then quarrelling with them.

She told the lesbian that what she wanted was to be squeezed into a piece of meat, then fucked and *fucked*, violently, because she was a masochist; she used to seek out fat old men to be her lovers because they desired her so much, but then she met a beautiful thin young sadist with green eyes who used to sit on her face with his testicles covering her nose so that she was choking for breath as he climaxed into her mouth, but he left her because she was *evil*, he said.—The only person she loved was her little brother, who had said that if she ever killed herself it would destroy him; that was when she realized that the definition of loving someone was overcoming one's longing to kill oneself, and living drearily on for that person's sake.

It's like that for you, Neva, isn't it? I see it in your face.

Well, I love everyone—

That's 'cause you're lying to yourself. You're so sad, you're worse off than me!

The lesbian embraced her.

Say it! Say you're the worst off.

I'm the worst off.

No. You don't mean it; it's just a goddamn echo . . .—and Neva could not help remembering how Victoria had also murmured about echoes. To calm herself she commenced that voicelesss song: *E-beth, Reba, Belle and Lucia, Judy and*

Shantelle . . . Meanwhile, to make her laugh (everything seemed to be happening too quickly), Anna told her about the time she was in Berlin and really *really* needed heroin, so she rushed off to the K-damm in her nightgown and pretended to be French to sound more sexy. And to make her happy, the lesbian laughed.

She promised to meet Anna at the Cinnabar upon completing her obligation of drinking with Erin and Sandra, who as it happened both arrived on time despite Sandra's extra-long mermaid dream; but because Francine had a headache and chills, I won't say from what cause, the drinks took a long time to come, after which the lesbian had to reassure Shantelle, who snarled: Neva, don't pretend you give a fuck about me . . . !—while Anna kept storming in, ever more angry and unbelieving. On her third appearance, the faded postcard of the breast with pink spectacles balanced on it tumbled off the topmost shelf of bottles, and Shantelle informed Anna: You're *outed*, bitch. That makes you a motherfuckin' *jinx.*—You be nice, said Francine.—Since Anna would not trust and believe, the lesbian walked home alone, for a novelty and a relief. She sat at the kitchen table and listened to a voicemail from Samantha, who sounded lonely and junked out: I'm sorry but I'm starting to understand . . . I . . . I'm just worried about things that I've mentioned, and it's hard seeing you and leaving you; it messes with my heart. I wish we were deeper in each other's lives. It's hard for me to admit to myself that this is how it is.

Staring into the mirror, she thought: I cannot believe how and who I am.

Then her phone rang; it was Shantelle.

42

By then the transwoman began to feel very old and ugly and wrinkled, so she did what her mother always used to do on sad days, which was first to get some money—accomplished in the daughter's case by dropping by the Y Bar, bringing home a German and turning an easy trick (otherwise she would have stolen from Neva's wallet)—and then to spend that money on a facial, which Judy found to be best accomplished at the beauty parlor on Larkin Street where Vietnamese Suzette always treated her lovingly and gave her a good hard scalp massage, scratching away with long magenta fingernails, after which it came time for the anti-ageing treatment and the concealer, which almost hid the black eye and bruises.—Oh, what a lady! cried Suzette, clapping her hands. Beautiful lady!—That was what our Judy needed to hear! It was what Egyptian embalmers and that crowd referred to as *the formula for coming forth by day.* So Judy came forth. She felt less beautiful than in Neva's arms, but pretty enough, maybe.

Longing to present herself, she ran to the Hotel Reddy and rang the buzzer, but the lesbian did not answer.

So she rang Room 545. Catalina buzzed her in. Judy ran upstairs getting her tear glands in working order. By the time she reached the third floor she was weeping exuberantly. In a little girl voice she said: I'm super lonesome for Neva!

Catalina laughed at her. She said: You know she's busy fucking! That's what she does.

And you're not jealous?

Not jealous, no more. Anyway, what's it to you? Aren't you a goddamn prostitute?

Neva's my number one, sobbed Judy. And now I know she's your number one, and—

Everybody else's. I'll bet you even J. D.'s doing her. So get over it. My first girlfriend, when I was maybe twenty, twenty-one, me and her weren't doing so good because she started talking to her ex again and I was not okay with that. They just wanted to be friends, but I was not okay with it. So at that time we were done for awhile and I moved up here and then she wanted to come visit me, so we were together, and then she found someone and I found Carmen and Neva, so who cares, Judy? You hear me? Who cares? Now go downstairs and fuck somebody else. That'll cheer you up. Why does Neva have to rescue the whole world? Make it easy on her. I'm trying to be nice, because Carmen told me to, but you get on my nerves. Bye-bye now.

So the transwoman went to the Y Bar, trolling for sympathy. Erin sat alone, drinking a fizzy water. Judy said: Will you please please *please* be nice to me?

Erin thought about it. She was a thorough young lady who sincerely considered our propositions.—Okay, she said.

How do I look?

Well, your bruises are almost gone . . .

Tell me I'm pretty.

You're pretty.

Do you mean it? Tell me a story about—

I knew it!

Will you will you *will* you? About when you were little? Oh, please, Erin!

All right. Well, I think when I was really young I first started, but it didn't become a habit until I was between twelve or fifteen and I masturbated a lot. This girl and I had sex pretty often. Then I had a lover that liked to be choked and done in the ass. I liked being with him. He was very skinny and feminine. He was one of the ones I wanted to marry and have kids with. I have too much feeling for him to see him anymore. It would just make me sad. That's it, Judy. The end.

That *can't* be the end!

Well, it is.

Please, Erin! Just one more—

Well, I had a fascination with porno magazines since I was twelve. So I started looking at other women's vulvas. And I became a stripper when I was nineteen. That was when I started checking myself out. I had a big mirror. I was just being selfish and entertaining myself. I got more comfortable with my body. And I liked the physicality of dancing. I always was a very physical little girl who never got to play soccer or ballet. Pole dancing was my first time . . .

And when the lesbian appeared in the doorway of the Y Bar, Francine held in a breath, not knowing that what fixated her was trying to decide what made the lesbian appear so unreal and unaware of herself, or simply un-self-consciously poised without arrogance, perfectly put together as if she had been born that way—and then the lesbian saw her and smiled.

43

As for Xenia, first drinking Old German Lager and then licking her lips as she watched the lesbian through half-closed eyelids, floating down into the perfect darkness, she said: Neva, I don't have sex anymore. Of course I had a lot of sex; I'm a pretty girl; but just because I got better and better at it doesn't mean I ever liked it. I like that I'm pleasing other people . . .

What about Hunter?

Oh, Jesus, that clingy little . . .

Does she please you?

Not anymore.

I can, said the lesbian.

No! I *do not* want you to! Let me just please you and I . . . Neva, I'm really *really* good at it.

Okay, said the lesbian. And, Xenia, I want you to do something else for me.

Anything!

I know you look down on Judy because she's needy and not well put together. She needs help. Will you give her some confidence lessons?

But she's so—

I know. The thing is, she's sincerely trying to improve. She's not like Shantelle—I'm telling you this in confidence!—who is more beautiful than Judy will ever be, but so broken that all I can do for her is numb the pain—

What about me?

Well, honey, you're more self-reliant than they are. Judy needs someone to keep telling her she's not worthless, and Shantelle needs, well, to delay the time when she gets into bad trouble. You and I, Xenia, well, where should I begin? You're so special to me—

Are you going to give me instructions about Hunter?

No, said the lesbian.

Because Catalina told me that you wouldn't let her dump Carmen, even though all she wants is you. And I think she's very very frustrated—

That's between Catalina and me.

And what's between Hunter and you? Does she talk shit about me?

No. She cries a lot. She loves you, and she knows she might lose you . . .

And then what do *you* say?

That she might lose you.

I don't want to hear any more.

Good, said the lesbian. Now show me how you please me, and Xenia began working on her, forgetting all about inconvenient Hunter, hence worshipping or as I should say *controlling* Neva in her expertly mindful way, lifting up her head from time to time to verify the progress of this operation, so she drank in and gloried in the lesbian's ascent: her nostrils flaring and her eyes closing as she dreamed her way to the first spasm when her lips suddenly parted—her white teeth ground loudly together and her forehead tightly wrinkled—

44

Of course Xenia told Francine what Neva had said about Shantelle. Francine shushed her. When she got drunk she told me, and I warned that if she failed to keep it quiet, Shantelle would break her nose at the very least. So she told Judy, who told the retired policeman, but in the end nobody, not even Al, told Shantelle.

Meanwhile Xenia, accompanied by her Old German Lager, sat down with the transwoman, who made goo-goo eyes and said: *Oh!*

Her benefactress regarded her sternly.

Do you want to . . . Why are you here? Will you tell me a story?

No. Neva asked me to coach you.

She did? Ooh, how sweet of her! I know you look down on me, so this must be, um, an unpleasant assignment—

Shut up, Judy. I like you fine. Do you aspire to anything?

To pass as a woman.

Fine. Get to work. You're obese and hairy, and you stink.

I know, but even though I try and try—

No you don't. Get off your ass and stop being a fat slug. Prove yourself. Once you look better I'll try to help you, although Hunter'll be like *raging jealous*—

Xenia, do you think they'd like me at the Pink Apple?

No.

What if I lost weight?

I'll believe it when I see it.

And then they'd like me?

How the fuck would I know?

If you were onstage and someone started to—I mean, what would you do about unwanted attention?

I would do nothing. I would roll around on stage and finger myself . . . Fuck 'em all.

But, Xenia, I'm afraid—

Get over it. The worst is already happening to you *every day*. So what the hell do you care?

Can you tell me something?

What?

What did Neva say about me?

She said fuck off. Hey, Francine, I've got to run so keep the change . . .

And Judy left Francine to babysit her bourbon and ginger ale. She went to the ladies' room and came back pale and hollow-eyed, wondering how to stop caring.

Just Kiss Me

My only desire is to make love and not have love made to me. I don't feel the need for it or the desire for it . . . I like the power of being able to satisfy her.

LESBIAN PRISON INMATE, *ca.* 1960

1

Are you busy? asked Sandra. You sound as if I shouldn't keep you on the phone too long . . .

I'm busy doing nothing, said the straight man, but I can talk for five minutes. How's your bleeding?

Much *much* better, and the advice nurse said . . . But I have something important to tell you.

All right, he said, getting ready for anything.

It's unpleasant, actually.

He waited.

I had sex with someone else.

Of course you did.

No, Louis, that's not . . . I mean, there was this boy, and we . . . I don't love him, you don't have to worry, and I didn't get an orgasm, but . . .

Who was it?

From her silence he could tell that she would tell him as little as possible, at which he thought: Oh, to hell with it.

The truth was that he never would have cared except that she was making it into a drama. She reminded him of the heavy, pretty woman who had looked so lost in the mug shot that the retired policeman once showed around the Y Bar, just for jollies; she and her boyfriend had performed what the newspaper called *numerous sex acts* upon a fourteen-year-old girl. As the woman explained to the arresting officers: *She was willing to do it. I don't regret it, because she was willing to do it.*

He was a boy from—from out of town, she said into his ear, and he invited me for a drink, so I . . . And it was really nice.

Good for you, he said.

Louis, are you—are you angry at me?

Not at all.

How do you feel about it?

Fine.

No, really, how does it make you feel?

Well, he said patiently, it doesn't make me feel good, but it's okay.

I hurt you, didn't I? Oh, I'm so sorry!

No, don't worry about it.

And I thought you'd be proud of me for having an adventure! And instead you . . .

You know I gave you permission. I always do.

I *betrayed* you. I thought you wouldn't mind. And you . . .

She was sobbing her heart out. He thought it a bit much that she needed him to comfort her. At least this new lover wasn't Neva.

You'd better get tested, he reminded her.

No, I used a condom and that virus-killing gel. But if you want me to . . .

Why don't you lie down and rest some more? The doctor said you need to take extra good care of yourself for the next few days.

See, I knew you were mad at me! You won't talk to me anymore! Oh, honey, I'm so, so sorry! I'll never do it again . . .

Sure. Well, you rest up and we'll talk soon.

Will you call me later and tell me you love me?

All right.

Tell me you still love me.

I still love you.

And I'm still you're favorite girl.

That's right. I've got to go.

'Bye, she wept.

He closed his phone, which rang back almost immediately. She called him half a dozen times while he sat very still at Bolero's Dance Bar, massaging his headache. They didn't stock Patriot Dry Lager so he had to drink Bomber Brown at twice the price.

2

Sandra, who was usually either happily or nervously chatty, meanwhile informed the lesbian: I can say though that never once in my entire life have I ever wished to be a man. Everything that I like about myself or about this world is always the antithesis of traditional masculinity. I've always had this horror of that. The men who are aggressive and really love football and sports and are abrupt and loud, I've always kind of . . .

Holding her, the lesbian said: You know who you are. That's really good . . .

But what about *you*? Were you always so confident and, um, I mean, so *perfect*? And so, so loving to everyone . . .

Oh, I *do* love you, said the lesbian.

Soon Sandra was screaming, straining her sweaty throat, saliva streaming silvery from her dark mouth; and they then lay at peace together, with the lesbian's hand lolling between Sandra's wide-spread thighs.

Am I being too personal? Sandra resumed. Because I kind of thought that since you and I are so intimate, you wouldn't mind if I asked. I tell you everything, and if you had any troubles, Neva, I mean, I'd like to . . .

Just kiss me, said the lesbian.

3

Sandra went home to cry and remember Neva. For the second time the straight man had moved out (and Hunter, who now in order to avenge another Xenian infidelity violated her lesbian principles in order to take ecstasy with him, cried out: *I've never had so much fun sucking dick!*—almost exactly as Judy had done). Sandra was feeling chilly, so she wriggled under the covers with her two pug dogs. Soon she was dreaming of playing hide and seek with other mermaids in a kelp forest whose long nipple-studded fronds gestured like the fluttering garments and desires of Sappho's bygone maidens; then, gazing upon the lesbian, she lost her power of speech; when the seaweed finally parted before her it was almost as good as when the lesbian's green blouse slipped slightly down her left shoulder, because here was the secret sacred glowing green place in the darkness where she would be breast to pale breast with Neva, oh, with Neva, our lesbian forever.

4

It must have been right around then that Francine informed me: Something's going on with Judy.

It always is, I said.

No, she's less simple. It's like she's growing up.

I don't know. Maybe she's more aware, but . . .

But what?

Nothing.

Six dollars.

I paid and said: It's sweet that you care about her—

Don't you? She's stretched awfully thin.

Francine, that's part of growing up. You learn to lie and compartmentalize, and then you stop being simple. You stretch yourself thin, and then you die. By the way, can I buy a couple of pills?

What kind?

Oh, any opioid.

You want two? Eighteen dollars, and I'm not clearing any profit.

Thanks, Francine. You're one in a million. And you know what? Come to think of it, our little Judy's finally losing weight.

5

So was the lesbian, who now sat with her chin in her hand, listening to another message from Selene: Hey, babe, I'm out with my friend Brittney from New York and we're drinking gin and catching up, but I'm thinking about you and missing you because you feel so far away. Ricardo's avoiding me. But I went to Mass with my father and ate the Sacrament and lit a candle, and we all sang; it was really beautiful. I do wanna talk to you, because it's been a long time, honey . . .—Her sleepy-sad heroin voice always made the lesbian think of tabby cats basking in a secret room. Just then the lesbian longed to die in her arms.

Victoria called to remind her that they were supposed to meet at Dimestore Do-nuts in half an hour. Francine texted: U R MY # 1. Then I called to invite her to my birthday.

6

That day Selene had just begun her period, so her vulva was dry on the outside and slippery with blood within. (I who never saw it remember the spectacular rawness of her gash, bright pink, bounded by the wavering ovoid of her ultra-thin labia, with screaming blonde pubic hair sprouting away from it in all directions.) The lesbian kissed her for a long time. Selene was timid at first, kissing lightly and then pulling back, until the lesbian, suddenly and surprisingly desiring her (a feeling which almost never visited her anymore) pulled her by the back of the head and stuck her tongue deeper in her mouth, then felt ashamed, because she was not Selene's mother. Selene's heart was pounding like a rabbit's.

Selene had tiny little pinprick nipples. Soon the lesbian was lapping and sucking them, until Selene, who had never asked Neva what she used to be before she turned perfect, slowly learned to trust in her.

After half a dozen meetings the lesbian could bring her fairly easily to orgasm, knowing that what she needed was penetration in the superior position. She was one of the lesbian's quietest lovers. At first she climaxed as if in secret. Whether that were truly so, which would imply an innate distrustfulness, or whether her body or personality was simply not demonstrative, could be set aside; the telltale sign was deeper breathing; whereas Holly, who achieved her release within five minutes given competent oral stimulation, would laugh and gasp.

Holly's and Selene's periods came at the same time. Neva loved Holly—you know she had to!—but she cherished that sweet fresh taste when Selene was newly bleeding.

If she had had to admit to herself why she felt more drawn to Selene than to Holly, the truth might have come out: In appearance the former favored E-beth. But how did that *affect* anything? Why did God prefer Abel's sacrifice of a slaughtered lamb to Cain's first fruits? Why was one hero favored by Venus, and another passed over? Love is luck—hence we were all the luckier to be loved equally. Meanwhile Francine, wide-faced, gazed woodenly down at the bar, feeling warm and at rest, which is to say happily sad to be longing for the lesbian.

Holly and Selene, Judy and Shantelle, Al, Xenia and me! What was she supposed to do with the fact that Judy was dependent, and Shantelle vindictive and probably dangerous? (Those who dilate upon the mysteries of Venus should not forget that her worshippers' heterogeneity is just as mysterious.) Neva knew that she must toil extra carefully, in order to love Shantelle equally with the others. (More and more often Shantelle wept in her arms, crying out: *Why the hell do you love me?*) Anyhow, all Neva needed to do was love and love, until she was finished.

Sometimes she still liked to think about the island, but rarely about her sisters who had loved her; she remembered the trees, the moss and the dark house where she had lain down in the old woman's arms.

7

Shantelle was angry with her again; she left a dozen obscenely furious messages. The lesbian listened carefully to every one.

She was the enlightened one called Never Despise, who even when they beat and mocked her told the masses *I dare not slight you, because you are all to become Buddhas.*

8

Now let me tell you about the transwoman's weight loss program.

It happened one night at the Y Bar that she saw Xenia and the lesbian enter the women's restroom hand in hand. She heard the lock click, and then the water came on. What were they doing? While the water ran, the toilet flushed twice. The water ran for a half-minute more, then stopped. They came out giggling.

Feeling rejected, she blocked their way and said: Neva, how about a kiss?

Just a second, honey. I'll be right there—

Hey, Neva, said Xenia, you're with *me* right now. You're not with Judy.

Stroking Xenia's hair, the lesbian said: I'm with both of you.

Francine watched sadly from behind the bar.

Francine, make Neva and Xenia a drink! I'm with *both* of 'em, goddamn it . . . !

Judy, you can't afford to keep buying everybody drinks.

Well, fuck it! *Somewhere over the rainbow* I can!

Shantelle burst out laughing. Francine said nothing.

The lesbian and Xenia sat down beside each other, whispering. A green banknote came out of the sealskin pouch. Francine stood drying glasses.

Hey! I said make Neva a fuckin' drink! But Xenia can buy her *own* stinkin' drink because she's just a . . . I don't know. Oh, what the *hell*! Xenia's my friend! Hey, Xenia, aren't you my friend? I'd do anything for you, even share Neva. I mean it, 'cause you're my . . .

Francine leaned over the bar, stared down Shantelle's laugh and said: What did you sell her?

Three blue dolphins. She was gonna take 'em home and party with J. D., but she—

Francine approached the transwoman, who was bouncing up and down on her stool laughing. Gently she said: Judy, you're shitfaced. Why don't you go home?

You kickin' me out? I said, you kickin' me out?

Yes I am. Just for tonight.

Are you mad at me?

No, sweetie. Now please go home and lie down.

Francine?

What?

Neva wouldn't kiss me.

Well, you just give her some space. Honey, I want you to go now.

Do you know why?

Because you're shitfaced.

I know I'm . . . I'm . . . But Neva wouldn't kiss me, because . . .

Go home. Right now.

Her breath smelled like *puke.* That's why. And Xenia's, too. Go smell 'em both if you don't believe me. They . . .

Al, will you please take Judy home?

All right.

Hey, Neva, why are you and your little bitch having puke parties? I'm telling on you!

Judy, said Francine, you need to get out of their business and go home. If you don't leave in one minute I'm gonna eighty-six you.

For how long?

Twenty-four hours.

All right, I'm going. I'm gonna make myself throw up and pretend I'm Neva. Actually I all the sudden feel kind of . . .

Since Al had not lifted his fat ass from the barstool (he was busy laughing, as if the memorial snapshot of his deceased boyfriend Ed no longer touched him), I took her by the hand. She punched me, not hard; her half-closed fist was flaccid. I slapped her cheek, and she burst into tears, then came along with me like a lamb.

But as soon as we had gone around the corner she dug in her heels. Stroking her hair, I told her to please, please let me get her home before something bad happened, but she shook off my hand. I stood watching her, and it was just like old times with my wife when I could see what was coming but froze until it happened. And then Judy, imitating her betters, bent over and stuck her finger down her throat.

9

The lesbian lay down alone for once. Closing her eyes, feeling chilly and achey, she seemed to see that old Mission style house with the green, green lawn, and someone looking out from behind the curtain. It seemed as if she did not exist. She looked into the mirror and failed to believe in herself. She went on existing, swallowing, breathing and secreting until late that night when Catalina called to say: I have a pomegranate, and I'm about to cut it open and eat the seeds. If you were here I'd feed you one seed at a time—

Oh, baby, that's so sweet—

Neva, I'm so frustrated right now! Because I want to do intimate things with you.

It won't be long, honey. Five days.

Is there anything I can have ready for you?

Yes, said the lesbian, and whispered something into the phone.

Catalina promised, laughing.

And then once again the transwoman slept with her head on the lesbian's shoulder, snoring gently, while the lesbian stroked her lovely hair.

After an hour, she gently lifted up the other woman's head and got up to pee.

I love you, Neva, said her groggy, sleepy lover.

I love you, too.

I love you so much! You're so wonderful . . .

I adore you, Judy.

When do we have to leave?

Oh, probably in half an hour, said the lesbian gently.

No!

The lesbian bent and kissed her lips. Softly closing the door, she went to the bathroom. She sat down on the toilet. When the urine gushed out, her clitoris tingled, thanks to the bittersweet new drug they had both swallowed. She licked a finger and rubbed it round and round her hard nipple, yawning. Everything felt good; the headache had not yet come on. She wiped herself and inspected the toilet paper: no blood. Then she flushed the toilet. Her bare feet felt very hot against the cold floor. Yawning again, she went back to the transwoman, who grabbed her, greedily pulled up her nightdress and began to suck. The lesbian caressed her. Oh, it felt so good to run her hand through Judy's hair! And now she was climaxing quickly and easily, after which it was Judy's turn. If she could only give Judy a screaming orgasm, everything would be all right.

We'd better go now, the lesbian said.

I won't let you go, said the transwoman in a throaty, almost growling voice; the lesbian kissed her lips, feeling dizzy for no reason. The transwoman kissed her back, and so another quarter-hour went by. Gently the lesbian pushed back the covers and began to sit up. The transwoman looked sad. Very slowly she fastened her bra.

10

Two hours later Judy was kissing Al goodnight beneath the glowing blue cross of Cumberland Church on Stone and Jackson, gazing through him and down night-wet pavement painted with streetlights and taillights all the way to the crystal-white loveliness of the Bay Bridge.

He said: I'll still tip you, but this time you didn't put your heart into it.

Sorry! I thought I—

Your boyfriend's right. I've heard him call you *Frank.* You're a man who pretends to be a woman. I'm a man who—

No, I'm a *woman!*—but it came out in a whisper.

And I paid you to be with me, but all the time you were thinking about *her!*

How did you know?

And *she's* a polyamorous *slut* whom you call a lesbian just because you're too lazy to throw down words of more than three syllables . . .

The transwoman fled. She texted Sandra over and over until Sandra finally answered. They met at the Y Bar. Her redhaired friend looked very tired. She said: Judy, what's wrong? It sounded like some kind of emergency—

I'm sorry; I'm sorry!

I only have a minute, but tell me . . .

I was already jonesing for Neva, jonesing *bad*, and then Al told me . . .—she burst into tears. Sandra sighed.

He said I was just a . . .

Usual? said Francine.

I'm buying, said selfless Sandra.

Six times two makes twelve dollars.

Here's thirteen.

Thanks, hon.

He said I'm not—

Judy, I consider you a woman, one hundred percent. A beautiful woman who—

How Judy loved Sandra just then! (Her heart was as transparent as the lesbian's skin and flesh, which showed the flickering flame of her beneath.) If they became *special friends*, she'd go to bed with Sandra every night, even if someday Sandra stopped being in the mood. No, Judy would never mind that!—Tell me a story, she entreated. *Please!*

I'm sorry, Judy, but in just a second I need to go.

Just tell one thing, so I can learn. What's your relationship to your pussy?

I don't know, honestly. I mean, how can I answer that?

You were born with a vagina. What's that like? To always have that feminine . . . —I know, I know, you need to run out, but just for one minute; I feel so upset—

All right, said Sandra. I went on a few dates but I never let anybody kiss me or touch me; I don't think I had any relationship to it. My first gynecological exam was very traumatic; she was nice but it hurt so much and it felt so wrong.

What do you mean?

It felt physically wrong when she put the speculum in. It's uncomfortable to the point where it feels that it must be hurting your body. I was hyperventilating to the point where I almost passed out. I was maybe thirteen or fourteen. I was having problems with period pain like a lot of people do at that age. I think it was just a bad memory. I don't think she did anything wrong.

And that's all you remember?

I remember being in ninth grade and I remember being in a play, and being so conscious that my vagina smelled so badly that everybody could smell it and I was so horrified. I would get my period and I would really want to take a shower and my Mom wouldn't let me. I remember being so conscious that I had this dirty secret that no one else had.

A *dirty secret*, the transwoman slowly repeated. Because I—

Judy, I really have to go now. We all have dirty secrets when we're young. Then we get older and we realize everybody else has had them. I'll see you. 'Bye, Xenia! 'Bye, Francine!

11

Just where did Sandra really have to go?—Three guesses!

Francine knew. But Francine's new resolution was to mind fewer people's business. When the lesbian first introduced Judy to bulimia, the latter, not knowing that if she kept it up she would rot her teeth and endanger her health, believed that she had found the perfect way to eat whatever she wanted and not pay for it. Taking her aside, Francine, who when she was young had practiced the same trick, informed her that once she had begun *having to do it* more and more (so she put it), she began to feel a *darkness*, which she subdivided into first worry and then anguish—at which Judy tried to deflect her, asking: Do you think Erin does it? Because she's a frail little thing, with tiny little boobs.—Francine said: Let's talk about *you*. Then Judy for once showed her claws: You sell us booze and goofballs all the time, so why the *fuck* should you care? *I* know: it's because you can't *make money* off my little puke parties . . .—Francine actually turned pale. She clutched at her chest and sat down. Realizing how badly she had hurt her, Judy started sobbing: I'm sorry; I didn't mean it; it's just that I'm ashamed, and, besides, Neva does it and you don't get in her face. Francine, I'm really really sorry . . .—Fine, the barmaid grated. We won't talk about it anymore.

So. Sandra was cheating and worrying about it. Judy was bulimic. Not my business, thought Francine.

A headache descended on me. I took a goofball. Xenia, wearing a thick parka, from which I inferred that she too had a case of the coming-down chills, sat rubbing her head and either sobbing or shivering, while on television the last of the old-time cowboys twirled a lariat the better to snag something alien.—Hey, Francine, she finally said. I'm sick of beer. Could I get a shot of Cockteaser, please?—Just then the lesbian came in.

12

How are your mood swings? asked the straight man. (He was trying to pay attention—how sweet!)

Well, really good except for one thing. There's something that's been making me really really nervous.

What's that?

It's about you and me. It's not terrible, but it's, well . . .

What is it? he said wearily.

Someone invited me to fly to Los Angeles with him this weekend. I said I'd go.

Okay.

He just called yesterday and I couldn't reach you. So I said yes. Was that okay?

I have to support you.

How do you really feel about it? Tell me honestly, because if you don't want me to do it I can call him back and say I'm not coming. You know that you're my best friend and my boyfriend and the one my heart is devoted to, although I do feel called to . . .

Yes, it does seem that part of your heart is devoted to him, he agreed, trying to ignore the pain.

What do you really truly think?

If he penetrates you and you have a great climax and you don't think of me, that's all right. If you think of me, don't feel bad. Don't get pregnant unless you want to.

But I don't want to! Of course I don't!

Then don't.

But I feel like a terrible person, wept Sandra. You know that if you told me not to, I would call him up and tell him I'd changed my mind.

Of course I know that.

And don't you remember that I offered to come to Boston with you? If you tell me to run away with you to Boston that's exactly what I'd do, because you're the one I want to spend the rest of my life with.

Sure, honey.

Don't you still think it could work out? I mean, not this year or next year, but maybe someday . . .

Why not?

Are you angry with me? Am I hurting you?

Feeling that to reveal his pain to her would be the equivalent of violating her sarcophagus, he asked: What do you want me to say?

Sandra began sobbing. She said: I feel like I'm hurting you! And you know I'd do anything not to hurt you . . .

I give you permission. I'd be a hypocrite if I didn't.

But am I ruining our relationship? Do you promise to tell me if I am?

Sure.

You say *sure*, but what does that really mean?

I support you.

And you'll never leave me no matter what?

That's right.

I feel like we're drifting apart. You only have twenty minutes on the phone. And he calls me every day; he wants to talk an hour or even four hours, and now even his sister is texting me . . .

The straight man gave her permission again and again. So of course she cancelled her date with the man from Los Angeles and went to the lesbian, secretly.

Neva, what do you want to do with me tonight?

Let's play mermaids, said the lesbian.

13

Later that night Neva was gripping Selene's head between her soft fair thighs; then, her mind wandered so that for a moment she was dreaming that this was E-beth, her mother or herself whom she was pleasuring, as if she might be alone and high on ecstasy, touching her own cunt which only appeared to be someone else's. Then she came back to who and what she was, remembering that she had been placed on this earth in order to love, and therefore took Selene into her mind, much as she would have taken some strange man's penis into her mouth, concentrating on doing what she was supposed to do.

She dreamed that somebody dead was saying to her: *Tonight one more time and then tomorrow the truth.* The next day she went to visit her mother.

Her mother took her hand. Her mother gripped her wrist very tightly, sinking her fingernails in.

But you never do look on the bright side, said her mother. It gets pretty depressing to hear your views.

Wishing at odd intervals to open her heart to the woman who had borne her, and was so often pleasant to children (although when their company persisted her smile might go weary or even ironical), the lesbian watched her, hoping for a way in to intimacy, but her mother liked to talk about dead neighbors and the humiliations they had suffered while dying; also about comical embarrassments in the lesbian's own childhood—sometimes the mother pretended to sympathize with those old small sadnesses: see how much she loved her daughter!—but to the lesbian, at least (who might have been wrong), it seemed that her mother too obviously *enjoyed* these memories! The time that Karen had wet her panties when she slept over at Aunt Kate's, not to mention the time that Marina's mother had caught Karen and Marina playing doctor and Karen's mother had to take her home—oh, how uncomfortable we'd all felt! . . . What about little Karen? Didn't she remember that disgrace with Marina? We'd all been quite shocked. And did she know that Marina's parents were divorced, and Marina's mother, who had kept in touch, was now *very, very* unhappy? Marina had not turned out well. Here was a Christmas card from Marina's mother. Didn't she want to see it? *Why* didn't she? Well, then here was a letter from Aunt Kate. In her widowhood she had become *very, very* lonely.

Screwing up her courage, the lesbian said: Mother, it's getting to be the time of year when I have nightmares.

Don't think I don't have nightmares, too, the mother immediately retorted with immense bitterness.

Since there was nothing else to say, her mother turned on the television so that they could watch the old uncolorized rerun about an ingenuous young bride who grows ever more traumatized in her husband's forest-girded seaside domain because she cannot compete with the first wife's beautiful, accomplished and as it turns out evil ghost; the husband finally admits to having shot her because *she was vicious, damnable, rotten through and through . . . She was not even normal.*

Imagine! said the mother. Karen, what did he mean when he said the woman was *not even normal*?

Maybe she was a lesbian, said her daughter.

I suppose, said her mother. How terrible! Yes, maybe that was it.

14

On the way back she stopped in Martinez to service an old lover.

When Terra met her at the station, the lesbian, realizing that once somebody saw her first wrinkle everybody else would, too, was already feeling run down, most likely from days of insufficient sleep, although the train had been stuffy and stinking of urine, the food foul; so no wonder she was hot and nauseated even in the cold rain. Terra kissed her adoringly. The lesbian's head was hurting. They went out for dinner to a Chinese place that Terra chose; maybe it was because each dish had been heavily salted that the headache worsened, until presently the lesbian, even though trying her best, perceived the beginnings of uneasy puzzlement on her lover's face; on their plates and in the serving dishes most of the meal was cooling down. Laying her hand on Terra's, she said: Are you full? That's what I thought. Let's take the rest back to our place and lie down . . .

Twenty minutes later, commencing to lick Terra's slit, she was shivering with chills, and the increasingly urgent motions of her sweetheart's pelvis made her dizzy. But Terra was laughing and roaring with joy; then her climax danced her deeper and deeper into another world, until she finally stopped, laughed as if she were being tickled, and gasped: Okay, Neva, I've got to . . . got to recharge—

Laying her head on the lover's breast, the lesbian kissed the nipple, but Terra started away; she was happily burned out; so the lesbian felt fulfilled.

Her headache worsened. Terra fell happily asleep beside her. It got colder and colder. Finally the lesbian, unable to feel her toes and fingers, sat up and by feel located the bottle of analgesic tablets. She washed down two with the quarter-glass of stale water that lay beside the bed. She longed for one of Francine's goofballs. The chills moderated, but the headache grew no better, and her belly began to ache. All night she lay still, so as not to wake up Terra. Dully she tried to work out how she would satisfy her in the morning.

Fortunately, Terra slept until late. Then they cuddled and snuggled. The lesbian felt so lightheaded that she feared sitting up. But when it came time to go out for coffee, they went; she had two extra shots, which made her slightly warmer and more alert; then she said: Girlfriend, I'm not feeling well; I need to lie down . . .

So they went back to lie down. The lesbian pleasured her partner, then lay up against her, drinking in her warmth weakly and needily.

Terra was getting bored. They went out for a walk. The lesbian could not help but ask: How far will it be?—But she went the distance, a good two or three miles; then it was back to bed.

Terra texted her friends, then made a date for brunch with another woman. Of course Neva was welcome to come, Terra said.

When those two went out, the lesbian lay in bed, barely able to move. Even her fingers felt weak and strange. Knowing that this would not do, she took a little black heart-shaped pill that Francine had presented for a love-offering, and right away she felt like a happy horny virgin!

Terra drove her to Richmond, where there was fog on pines and oleanders, while sparrow-songs echoed through the concrete of the rapid transit station; then came the high musical tone as the doors closed, the almost musical whine of motion, tracks washed out in the fog, white-streaked grey clouds low above crammed little houses, the Berkeley hills purple ahead, like the tall towers of San Francisco's financial district to the right, and at the El Cerrito Plaza stop a young blonde in a leopard-print baseball cap sat down, looked away, stared at her and slowly said: I need someone to talk to.—Okay, the lesbian replied; and for the next twenty minutes San Francisco enlarged itself as she listened to the tale of the cruel father who appropriately replaced himself with the cruel husband, after which the blonde gave her a teary hug (an open-handed slap from Shantelle might have gone down better), with the mallscapes of the East Bay now behind them; so many times I have watched her embrace us in her wordless love; shall it ever be told of her that she would speak?

15

As you see, even Neva, shining among all the women and transwomen in that dark place, could not help but tire sometimes. Even the most long-enduring radioluminescence must diminish according to the law of half-life, and as for fleshly glowing, well, poor Judy Garland proved *that* rule. Full faithfully we tended Neva's altars, raising our glasses all at once, gazing upward at nothing. Then she came in.

I remember from one occasion her smile slowly widening as she swung her head from side to side between two suitors, with her black-painted fingernails spread across the gin and tonic which she very slowly sipped even though it could not have incapacitated her since it was mostly ice cubes; she was careful just the same. What made her so seductive? We couldn't stop speculating. Had we figured it out, we would hardly have loved her half as much.

Around her, *we* at least never got tired! She pushed all Francine's anxieties away; all our sad and exhausted days got swept by the lesbian into a magical garbage bag! Victoria had no anxiety about anything now, because lying in the lesbian's arms made life so charming. As for me, just watching the lesbian's top slip off her shoulders to go sliding down, and then seeing her bra unhooking, that was as good as the gentleness which followed. And now everyone wanted to be Shantelle's friend, because she got to fuck the magic lesbian—and oh, that rush

Shantelle got, whenever she could steal the transwoman's turn! Splendid Neva, empress of vaginal flowers, was anything sweet for you? I cannot imagine how it must have been to be the one who tried never to tell anybody no. Worst of all, I would guess, was that falling tone in the transwoman's voice when the lesbian had been chatting on the phone with her and then said: Well, I have to go, at which the transwoman would whisper: Yeah, I know, and the lesbian felt like an old married man hanging up on his shining young mistress . . .—because she was now depriving desperate Judy of love! Soon enough their next appointment would come due; then she would be cradling the transwoman's head against her heart and murmuring sweet words few of which their recipient could later quite remember, their import being how sorry she was to have made the transwoman sad—but she truly said *sorry!* and who else ever told Judy that?—And the lesbian went on to say that she was *looking* at Judy right now, *seeing* her for who she was; and who she was (continued the lesbian, but maybe not in so many words because when I lay them out this way, they sound stupid) was the lesbian's precious girl, whom she would always, always be; the lesbian further guaranteed (so I have been apprised) that her tenderness for the transwoman would die only when both of them did.

We were all unique to ourselves, and so we knew that our love stories had never been told before. To *her* with her infinite experience, I suppose we must each have been as typical as the father whose baby will not stop crying, an offense which can only be ended by beating the baby to death. And the lesbian gamely whispered: Darling, I know you're sad because you believe that part of my heart is closed to you now, but don't worry, honey; please . . .

But it *is* closed! You're not going to stop doing things with Victoria and not telling me about them—

Judy, if I fed a stray cat that was starving, would that take away any of my love for you?

A lover is not an animal, except maybe to you!

No one could ever replace you, and I don't *want* anyone to! *Judy!*—and Neva sounded so very nearly desperate that how could we not believe her?—*Judy, listen to me!* Judy, over and over I've shown how much pleasure you give me . . . ! My body will always be open to you; you know my soul is . . . !

To me these assurances rang phony; of course I heard them secondhand. Meanwhile the avid transwoman begged: Tell me more!

Judy, when we lie side by side with your hand between my legs . . .

Oh, Neva!

Judy, when you kiss me into infinity . . .

Do I really? I know you have to go soon. Will you stay with me for five more minutes?

Of course. Now listen. Maybe things are changing, but, Judy, does that have to be a bad thing? If I find fulfillment with someone else—

Don't say that.

Darling, don't cry. Please, honey, don't feel sad. Oh, do you want to cry? Okay, go ahead and cry in my arms . . .

Can I ask you something?

Laughing a little, the lesbian said: Well, you always do!

Does that mean no?

It means go ahead.

Neva, do we really fulfill you? Sometimes I think you're just going through the motions—

Why would I do that?

Because . . . I can't understand it, actually. And that's why I . . . But how can you love so many people? Anyway, you have to go now. You have to go. I get it.

16

Leaning across the bar (and just for practice borrowing so well as she could the semblance of some glistening-faced, glassy-eyed actress in trouble), the trans-woman said in a low voice: Francine, can I tell you something?

Shoot.

Promise you won't tell?

I promise.

Just now I heard Neva in the bathroom. She was making herself vomit again—

How do you know she isn't sick?

When she comes out she'll act all normal. You watch her.

I don't need to. It's her business, so butt out.

But I'm telling you—

You've told me before, don't you remember? We all know about it. Leave her be.

So the transwoman rushed off to tattle to the retired policeman. From the way he acted, she was pretty sure he'd just dated Melba again. So she ran into the bathroom crying, turned on the water and had herself a private little puke party. When she came out she was smiling.

You put one over on me, did you? sneered her lover. Go brush your teeth again. Fuck, how you stink . . . !

The transwoman turned red. This was even more degrading than getting caught shoplifting. Defiantly, trying for once to fight off the shame, she told him: *Neva taught me how—*

How to stink? You taught yourself, you shitty little whore. And you know what? You think your trick is so special? When Melba blows me, she's under orders to swallow. So she does: good *girl.* Then she runs straight to the sink and sicks it up. For *hygiene*, bitch. But she carries a bottle of mouthwash with her, so she's way ahead of you. But I will say it's interesting that Karen Strand is bulimic.

Please, J. D.! Don't run her down—

Bulimic is not an insult. It's a diagnosis.

Oh.

And *now* he remembered how eagerly Judy had reported that that child murderess Kimberly Kenniston had vomited in the prison van on her way to trial; count on his puking bitch to raise *that* subject!

As *serenely* tough as J. Edgar Hoover posing for a portrait, he continued: Don't you worry, Frank. I'm closing in on her.

Thirst

Therefore, if I may not draw from the fullness of the Fountain, nor fully quench my thirst, I will yet place my lips to this heavenly spring, and receive some drops to allay my thirst.

THOMAS À KEMPIS, *ca.* 1413

Jesus said, "He who will drink from my mouth will become like me."

"THE GOSPEL OF THOMAS," *ca.* 2nd cent.

1

And so they disembarked from the island ferry; he had chewed or choked down all his medications but was in a bad way, leaning on her and biting his lip to keep from groaning while she wheeled their one suitcase down the gangplank. It was high tide. The transwoman had begged him to bring her here. Neva's sealskin pouch had supplied the money, so actually Judy was bringing him. She still believed in happily ever afters.

They walked three blocks and checked in at the Grey Goose Lodge, an establishment recommended by Neva: ninety-six dollars a night; he cursed and shook his wobbling head. Now he needed to lie down. She had already unpacked the "value"-sized bottle of Old Crow and was hanging up her skirts and blouses in the closet when someone tapped briskly on the door. It was the chambermaid, proffering a complimentary naturopathic incense candle.—What crap, said the retired policeman. The chambermaid looked sad, so the transwoman said: Please, J. D., let her come in and . . .—Her lover lay wheezing angrily.

Shall I? said the chambermaid.

I guess so, said Judy. I mean, it sounds really nice. I don't know anything about pressure points and chakras and all that . . .

The chambermaid, who was tall, slender and old, with long white hair loose on her shoulders, came very quietly in. She said: I can set it up by the bed, or over there by the window—

Keep it the fuck away from me, gasped the retired policeman.

Then is right here by the window okay? What do you think, ma'am?

Thrilled to have been addressed so kindly, the transwoman nodded. The chambermaid flitted out to her hall cart and returned with a brass candle holder whose base was an ovoid dish studded all around with nipples. From the center of this peculiarity rose an anatomically detailed vertebral column supporting three horizontal rings engraved with yohni symbols. Down through the rings the woman now slid a dark candle, unevenly brown, with long pale fibers showing through the wax. She lit it.

That smells really high-class, said Judy. There's something familiar and something . . .

Local herbs, said the chambermaid.

The strange perfume filled the room.

J. D., is it bothering you? asked the transwoman, but he did not answer.

Oh, she said. He's asleep.

He'll stay asleep as long as he needs to, said the chambermaid. That's witch's mallow. No male thing can resist it.

What is this? What are you doing?

Neva told us about you. Reba's waiting.

I can't! I won't leave my boyfriend. What are you doing to him? I'm calling the police—

Judy, asked the woman, do you love Neva?

I—yes.

Does she love you?

Yes.

Do you believe in her?

I—

Then believe in yourself! You're awake, aren't you? That proves you're female. Come with us. I promise he'll be taken care of. We're going to be very very good to you, Judy. We're going to love you. And just to make you happy, we'll give you a long hard beating.

The woman took Judy's hands in hers. Then she kissed her. Judy blushed. She felt warm, relaxed and confused, as if she had eaten too many marijuana brownies.

Perhaps enough of Frank Masters remained in her blood and bones to be affected by the witch's mallow. She could hardly decline a beating—and how could she go against Neva, who after all had sent her here?—and if something happened to J. D., that would be really, really horrible, but . . . Gripping Judy's face in both hands, the woman breathed into her open mouth and sucked her lower lip. Judy moaned.

2

They were outside, at the edge of town, in some lichen-bearded place of fernlike peelings and fingerclaws, cedar foliage, jagged tree-silhouettes in mist. They were on a trail. Judy was lost. Her eye ached with the brightness of that silver-white fog.

Is this place where Neva was made?

Yes.

I want to be just like her.

You can't, said a woman. You'll have to be you.

But Neva—

There's only one of her and one of you. Who are you, Judy?

I don't know.

Are you Frank?

Never!

You don't want to keep any part of Frank?

How can I answer that? I mean, I—

Do you need us to beat you now?

Whatever Neva wants me to do; whatever she wants to do to me . . .

They stripped her and stretched her over a stump, whipping her with cedar wands as red as salmonflesh and stroking her hair while she wept.

Who are you? they kept asking. The world went round and round.

They said: Tell us you're Frank.

No!

Tell us you're Judy.

In her ecstasy of failure she only wept.

They stopped. They said: Judy, let's talk.

Placing sandals on her feet, they led her to a wide grey beach-shelf of sandstone which was overhung by grizzled tree-beards, and as she stood bleeding and wavering they took her knee-deep into the inlet. Then they began pouring dippers of seawater over her head. At first she screamed because it was so cold. They scrubbed her up and down. The salt water stung her wounds and she howled. They washed her hair. She was trembling and her teeth were chattering. They led her up the trail to the fire and rubbed her dry. She never stopped sobbing. They oiled, massaged and spanked her, kissed her and wrapped her in a warm blanket. They made her drink something bitter. Then they laid her down on a pallet by the fire.—Don't sit up, they said.

A bluehaired girl named Colleen sat down by her and asked: Are you named after Judy Garland?

The transwoman nodded three times.

She's a huge part of my culture. Sometimes I want to be in that culture, although right now I'm here. My ex-girlfriend used to beat me in time with Judy Garland records.

The transwoman smiled for the first time.

I understand why she represents queerness, Colleen went on. She was highly maternal. Have you ever seen the TV special with her and Liza Minnelli, and the way that Judy *is* with Liza? She was just so vulnerable and maternal and free and tragic! Maybe you can be like that.

God, I'm . . . I'm not free—

Are you maternal?

No. I . . . I'm vulnerable, because . . . But not tragic, because they laugh at me—

Do you like that?

No . . .

Be honest. You're like me. Doesn't humiliation get you off?

Sullenly she replied: I don't know. I wanna go home; let me go!

Laughing at her, Colleen said: Click your magic shoes together three times and say: *There's no place like home. There's no place like home.*

Judy started blubbering.—What a *production*, laughed Colleen. Do you want me to slap you? It might be fun.

There came no answer.

Judy, do you want to be happy?

Sure—

You have to have experiences with someone that really cares about you. You might have had a lot of bad experiences, submissive experiences with people who didn't care about you. But now you've been with Neva. That might be your turning point. Now stop crying, or I'll refuse to beat you when you need it. Are you warm enough? I'll lie down beside you. Give me some blanket, girl! All right. What pretty hair you have. Can you feel me holding you? Now, why do you hate yourself?

Because I'm fat and old and stupid and *disgusting.*

What that represents is just fucking misogyny. Being trans feminine means being valueless if you don't watch out. To be a woman you think you have to be fuckin' *pretty.* But that's not the way that reality works at all. Are you sleepy? Good. Now give me a kiss.

3

She woke up in another woman's arms. The woman's face was freckled and dark, and her thighs the color of unripe tropical fruits. Judy was very hungry. They made her drink something to do away with that urge, and while she was vomiting into the cesspit the freckled woman kept stroking her hair while two others held her hands. They had her wash out her mouth with something like spearmint. Then they led her back to her pallet by the campfire. She found herself suckling the freckled woman, whose areolae were pricked out with lovely irregularities as of handsmithed golden coins. No milk came out. When she opened her eyes again, the freckled woman was sitting beside her carding a skein of wool. Judy raised her head. She saw trees and pale evening sky.

They asked again if she wished to be happy, to which she replied: Doesn't everybody?

Not our Neva, they proudly answered.

4

It was a cold morning, severe and wet. The moss-clothed leafless trees stood still and yet alive, so different from her, and the sun was a white stain in the grey sky.

They asked if she was hungry. She nodded, so they gave her more of that bitter drink. They led her to the cesspit and she began to vomit, believing that the more she could suffer for the lesbian's sake, the more pleasing would she become to her. There came a long and gentle flogging, building in just the way she liked; until, thinking of Neva, she climaxed and briefly lost her power of speech.

Then the freckled woman came and said: We're still trying to understand you. Do you remember what Colleen said to you?

I told her I was disgusting, and—

Then what?

Then nothing. Where's J. D.? What have you done to him?

Do you love him more than Neva?

Where's my boyfriend? You fucking . . .—Then she wept again, while they watched her.

5

Let's talk, said Colleen.

I don't want to, said Judy.

What *do* you want to do?

I don't know.

Exactly. So let's talk about you.

Judy closed her eyes.

Colleen said: I don't know anything about being male, but I know that presenting femininity in the world, if you have the world *seeing* you, then you know what it's about.

Then you know what exactly? said Judy, feeling dizzy.

It's about how you're read.

I want to be read as . . . as a lady.

Oh, really? said Colleen. What kind of lady are you?

I, I, I'm a whore.

That's a good true answer, said Colleen. I'm aware that the life of a trans prostitute is extremely scary. So that's who you are?

Sure, said Judy sullenly.

Around her neck Colleen placed a greenish pendant with wings outspread like an eagle's. Judy flushed for confusion.

I have trans femme friends who have had to experience it from cis women too, getting told both that you're not a woman and definitely not a man. Yeah, that's a very dangerous and vulnerable place to be. And I have so much respect for them, Judy. So much respect for you.

For *me*?

Oh, yes.

Then I, I respect *you*, for being a beautiful out lesbian who—

When I was in high school I had shame around it. I quickly realized that being shameless is my thing. Not allowing shame.

But how is that possible? the transwoman demanded. Because all the time I—

Shame is kind of the same category as jealousy. *I don't accept it.* I don't accept it but I also know that people are programmed to feel it. It's not a real natural healthy human experience.

Judy said nothing. She didn't believe it.

6

Behind a tree of white flowers like a stately candelabrum stood a little yellow house with lacework curtains. Colleen took her by the hand and led her there. An old woman was waiting in the doorway.

I'm Reba, she said.

Where's J. D.? What's happened to him?

Come in, said Reba.

Open-mouthed, Judy crept forward like some newly adolescent girl who so greatly fears a shameful menstrual accident that all month long she worries that a bellyache might be a cramp, or that any feeling at all down there might be blood dripping between her legs. She thought: Whatever Neva wants me to do; whatever she wants to do to me . . .—Yet then she stopped.

Colleen said: Go on, Judy. Follow that fuckin' Yellow Brick Road.—So she had to go inside with the old lady.

Now, Judy, whom do you love more, J. D. or Neva?

Neva.

Will you leave him for her?

I don't know.

So I thought. We're keeping him asleep. Come sit down.

And Judy sat at the kitchen table, letting Reba take her hand and smile at her while she smiled back politely. She felt terrified, as anyone would have in the old Jewish tales when the demon princess kisses someone with the kiss of death.

Reba seated herself in a rocking chair, and began carding wool with a bronze comb. The only comfort Judy felt came from her greenish pendant.

Over the counter hung Lynda Koolish's classic photograph of Margie Adam, snow-faced and young, with the sleeves rolled up her muscular, hairy arms as she leaned over the piano, closing her eyes, parting her lips in a music-seeking smile. Judy had never before seen it.

Reba said: Have you ever heard the tale of the teacher who gave her student everything, then was abandoned?

No, said Judy.

Well, that's what Neva did. And that's what the teacher wanted.

Why?

Well, it was the best thing.

And you were the teacher?

Oh, no. Neva's had a hard life, loving all of *you*. Who else has the stomach for it? Wife or goddess to everyone and soul mate to none, oh, my . . .

Reba's hair was as delicate as the white and beige of linen plainweave. She came and stood over Judy. Slowly she drew Judy's face in between her breasts. Then she stepped away, looking. After awhile she kissed her, and the ecstasy of the spirit flittered down. Judy felt turned inside out. How was she supposed to know the difference between a mother and a lover anyhow?

She seemed to be looking down upon herself as she worshipped Reba's pussy, her head moving up and down like a seal's black head among dark kelp.

7

There came a knock. The old lady said nothing. After another knock the freckled woman came in. On the kitchen table she placed a vial. Then she bent down, kissed Reba on the forehead and departed.

Look, said Reba.

In the vial was a tiny shard of something coral-pink.

Reba said: This is a transuranium element called ladium. Our island holds the only known deposit. From its position in the periodic table it should be radioactive with a very brief half-life, but that's actually not the case. Do you understand what I'm saying?

No, Judy whispered.

Do you want to be a lady once and for all?

I am one.

Then why do you let your boyfriend call you Frank?

Neva told you!

No, *he* did, in his sleep. Listen, Judy. Ladium reacts violently with anything male. If I place it in contact with your body, you may suffer serious burns or worse. The reaction will be instantaneous. You may be maimed or even killed, but whatever remains of you will be entirely female. Do you want to try?

Do you, I mean, do you think I'll be killed?

I doubt it, but I can't say. You know I'm not trying to murder you, Judy.

God, I feel afraid . . . !

If it does kill you, you won't suffer. If it burns you, we'll nurse you.

What about J. D.?

We'll keep him asleep as long as you want us to.

Judy craved to escape herself through this old woman who cared for her without perhaps desiring her. But no; she didn't want to get burned away!

What if I want to go away just the way I am, with J. D., and . . . ?

You mean, would we allow you?

Judy nodded.

Of course. But we wouldn't let you remember much.

Then Judy, bewildered as usual, said what she always used to say: *If I could only be somebody . . .*

You can, said Reba. Now shall I?

Judy hesitated, then finally nodded, believing that the old lady had spoken all.

Reba opened the vial. A pink vapor began swirling out. Reba sucked some of it into her mouth, blew it out and grinned. Then she waited. Leaning gingerly forward, Judy smelled something like the sweaty fragrance of healthy topless young women driving nails and chopping firewood. She heard not a voice but the faraway mother of a voice. Then her nose began stinging and bleeding as if she had inhaled sulfuric acid. Terrified, she bolted into the kitchen. With a sorrowful smile Reba closed the vial.

8

I myself would not have liked to be wearing Judy's panties just then! Perhaps she should have been pining outright for the retired policeman, or hoping somehow not merely to die in Neva's arms, but to ensure that the two of them died together. But she didn't care to live or die at all. She merely felt ashamed. Had I been there I would have told her: *Click your heels together three times and say . . .*

They took her up a hill to a place where she could oversee threads of mist stretched midway across the mountains, and then a maze of islets, severed fingers furry with trees, clouds like the disarticulated bones of a hand, lying miraculously unscattered, with trees and channels beneath them. Going ahead, Reba knelt and kissed a certain stone. They said: Our teacher is buried here.

On the other side of the grave was a blackberry hollow, and down there the retired policeman was sitting bound and gagged on a chair like some Pharaoh's stone effigy which vandals have been chipping at. He was snoring over a brazier of witch's mallow.

A muscular young lesbian with a shaved head, a dragon tattoo on her forearm and a leather collar squatted over the brazier, pissed, and its smoke sizzled out. Then she went away. After awhile the retired policeman opened his eyes.

What he saw beneath the crow's claw spread of cedar leaves was a lesbian. With her shining eyes, pale high forehead and dark butch haircut she reminded him of the mug shot of Alvin Karpis, who was Public Enemy Number One back in January 1935.

She said nothing to him.

Where's Judy? he said.

They brought her forward. As usual, she was reeling and crying like one who comes to implore forgiveness when it is too late for the wrong to be righted but not too late for the sinner to be comforted. She felt ashamed. Suddenly she turned to them and said, as if this knowledge could help her: Neva has the women's mark.

Oh, you saw it?

She showed it to me! I want it; I want it!

At this they withdrew and murmured angrily. Presently someone pulled off her greenish pendant. But Reba looked on; she appeared to pity her.

9

How long was I asleep? he said.

Oh, the whole three days. They wanted to change the sheets, and then they were going to call a doctor, but you—

It still stinks of that fucking aromatherapy bullshit. When I see that bitch who made me sick—

No, J. D., she was really really nice! She took your temperature and everything. When you were sleeping I had a chat with her. Oh, I'm so sleepy. And she said: *Judy, just learn to be shameless.* And—

What's that supposed to mean?

I don't remember, she said, trying and already failing to remember the touch of Neva and the smell of her hair.

J. D., she said then, I really, really want to be pretty.

That'll be the day, he said.

I don't know, but I feel somehow glad we came here even if we didn't do much.—Actually she was feeling tentative and out of sorts.

He said nothing, so she tried his patience another inch: It was relaxing, I guess.

It was a fucking waste. Pour me a drink, he said.

I guess you're right, she said. I don't know why I made us come here. Oh, God, I hate myself.

Shut up, he said.

I feel so worthless—

If you don't enjoy what you're doing, he said to her, why the hell are you doing it? Find what you like and go do it instead of bitching about it.

The whiskey hurt his stomach, so he staggered to the toilet.

10

It was checkout time. Once the retired policeman was in the corridor calling the elevator, Judy left a tip for the kind chambermaid; *he* would have yelled to see her waste money like that. Trudging to the harbor, they reembarked. He said: For once you don't stink . . .—at which she finally believed with all her heart that she was sometimes very pleasing to him. There are many who can love without concern for the beloved's sensations, but Judy, like her namesake, aimed to captivate! She might love Neva infinitely more than her retired policeman—she *did*!—and Neva certainly loved her, but how could she ever please Neva? Expectation of the likely answer made her throat seize up.

On deck they saw a happy old lesbian couple caressing each other with wrinkled hands; Judy thought: I want this. Click your heels together three times and say . . . *There's no one like Neva. There's no one like Neva. There's no* . . .—Then the ferry began to hum across the cold and milky strait whose low isles were uninterrupted by anything. It is just as well that neither of them were acquainted with Judy Garland's recurrent nightmare about standing on the deck of a ship that had just been christened and was about to disembark on her maiden voyage when it began to sink, and everyone stood at attention as if nothing were the matter while the water rose up to their necks, and then the young star woke up.

They went home to the Y Bar, where Xenia was saying: I dated this Ph.D., this woman who's a sexologist, and she told me what makes a predator . . .—But Neva was absent, so Judy bought pills from Francine, kissed the retired policeman goodnight, locked herself into her room and got high. Strutting and striding in her garters, she, confident again, rolled her tongue in her mouth and longed to fuck all of us just as Neva did.

11

Scurrying over to the Hotel Reddy, she decided not to announce herself. Within five minutes a man came out. Judy rushed to catch the door before it shut. The man frowned, but Judy was already *in*!

Creeping upstairs, Judy, passing by Catalina's partially open door, heard that person say, evidently on the phone and probably to Neva: It was really hard. It really impacted our sexual life. Because of her dishonesty, because of her cheating, it really damaged that emotional connection that we had.

Neva's door was closed and silent. As she approached, Catalina's door began to creak wider. Judy fled.

12

She went to the Y Bar, but found only Hunter blubbering drunkenly to Francine: I had a dream that Xenia left me, and when I told her I felt anguish she just *laughed* at me . . .

So she went to the Cinnabar to see Carmen, who smiled at her.

She ordered a bourbon and ginger ale for a dollar more than at the Y Bar. When Carmen brought it, Judy said: I need to ask you something.

Carmen looked tired and patient.

I don't know who I am.

So?

How do I decide if I'm a man or a woman?

What do you want from me?

I mean, did you always know who you are?

I feel like I always knew, said Carmen. I didn't have the concept of what that meant, but I knew that I was different, thinking that girls were really pretty and I just wanted to be their friend. As a kid it was just like that innocent love-and-wanna-play kind of thing. It wasn't until I got older that I started to understand what that meant. It was probably around eighth grade when I realized, oh, this is a thing. I was very feminine with my hair and my makeup and so forth. There's this box that they lock us into, of lesbian hair and being mannish; but it's not a cookie cutter kind of thing. We're all people like everybody else. I still wasn't sure that *lesbian* was a title that I wanted to take on, not wanting to disappoint my parents, or label myself and end up changing my mind. I felt that I had to commit to that term for all my life. So I came out as bisexual at first, and that was easier. And it wasn't until I was an adult that I dropped that and . . .

And Carmen lifted up Judy's drink, wiped obsessively beneath it with her napkin and daydreamed about her lost love at the Silver Fox bar in Bakersfield: styrofoam snowballs and plastic snowflakes in the mirror above the shining army of glasses, Steely Dan on the speaker, Christmas stockings in the names of Britt and Marisa, three muted televisions, one showing a commercial for cars, another set to sports, the last to news; and there sat the lost love, Glenda, who, longhaired, friendly and cheerful, munched on olives and maraschino cherries all day and sometimes used to hold Carmen's hand right there at the curved old wooden counter; the first time they kissed, Carmen got so tingly and swoony that the bottles of gin and whiskey glowed an even deeper red in the glamor-hell beneath the bar.

What about Neva? asked Judy.

What about her? said Carmen wearily.

I think she hides who she is.

Well, what if she did have a secret and let's say a certain Judy wanted to tell people and ran her mouth? Have you ever been outed?

Well, I . . .

Maybe you don't understand what it means to out people! For me it was someone randomly saying like, oh, I hear you're gay now, or, oh, you think it's cool but you haven't been with a real man. And for Neva, who knows what her secret is?

But she has one?

Honey, we all do.

Because she was locked out of Neva's secret, Judy felt more lonely than ever. Closing her eyes, she seemed to see a fog as subtle as if bleached and broken clamshells had been thinly silvered.

13

She went home, locked the door, opened her lingerie drawer, opened the plastic bag and withdrew the torn blouse that she had stolen from the lesbian. She kissed it. She said: Neva, tell me what to do.

Of course there came no answer.

Closing her eyes, she seemed to see for a moment a tall, strong broadshouldered woman with a lovely neck and long dark hair, glossy black lips and sad, sad eyes. Could that be her? She so much wanted it to be. Where had she seen that person? She would never remember that the source was one of those illicit catalogues from her boyhood days; her girlfriend Marjorie used to keep it hidden for her; it had consisted of photocopied sheets stapled together: **TRANSVESTITES IN BONDAGE**, page thirteen, **Queen of Hearts**. Shaking away that image, she pressed the lesbian's blouse to her face and began to masturbate.

Neva and the Baby-killers

He shall come forth by day after he [has died], and he shall perform all the transformations which his heart shall dictate, and he shall escape from the fire.

The Egyptian Book of the Dead

Then the female spiritual presence came in the form of the snake, the instructor, and it taught them . . . "It is not the case that you will surely die, for from jealousy he said this to you. Rather, your eyes will open and you will be like gods, recognizing evil and good."

The Gnostic Scriptures

1

Had I spent any time living as opposed to dreaming my life, this story would run as brief and easy as a fairytale, in which case I should have plastered over ambiguities, repeating the simple claim that from the instant we saw her, we had to have her—even Shantelle seized the faith that the medicine between Neva's legs would be good for her!—but since I feel chilly, nauseous and dizzy, let me lie in bed longer, the better to proffer exceptions.

I am not as good at doing nothing as I used to be. This remembering exercise, which purports to explain the lesbian, is one of my methods for avoiding my diminishing opportunities to, as Judy would say, *make something of myself.* I love the past. It reminds me of that room I used to have, a carpeted place where I did nothing.

2

When I remember my room I feel happy, not that the lesbian ever visited me there, but indeed it was my home when I knew her. I only moved to the Amity Hotel after Neva's death, when the Y Bar began to fail me and certain petty authorities invited me to relocate my social triumphs.

The first hotel I tried on that strangely warm foggy January afternoon after my eviction from the illegal basement apartment in Daly City was a multistorey old brick establishment; someone buzzed me in, and I pulled in the gratinged metal door behind me until it clicked shut. Up the stinking carpeted stairs I went, looking away from the wide-angled mirror in the landing. The old Indian lady at the desk merely said: No vacancy.—So I walked half a block west to the next hotel, whose doorbell had been shucked from its socket, then to three old hotels of varying griminess which were all residential only, no cash allowed. Finally I reached the Saint Brendan. It looked slightly less shabby than the others, and the front door swung in with a push, not an electric buzz, daunting me with regard to the potential price. The lobby did not stink, although every chair held an unshaven old man doing nothing—a reassuring touch. The price was $109, plus tax, which made $127, if only around six hundred per week (by the time they threw me out in 2016 it was nearly eight), and the clerk required a credit card.—I'll pay a cash deposit, I said, but the clerk, whose business suit and lordliness proclaimed him in fact an assistant manager or better, explained: We have to have a credit card. We're going to run the card and put a seven-day hold on the money even if you reverse the charges and pay cash when you check out.—Oh, I said (and here I sounded exactly like Judy). Okay.—The manager appeared very occupied with his wealth of unparalleled concerns, so I dragged out everything, insisting on a corner room and asking where was a good place to get coffee and breakfast, until he, practically biting his lip, beckoned another man, Latino, middle-aged, more simply dressed, and commanded: Miguel, take care of this. A *walk-in*, he added disgustedly.

In my wallet I kept somebody's silver plastic frequent flyer card from Aphrodite Airlines, which had somehow come into my possession in the course of three nights with a lady who had called herself Ukrainian; I now presented this to Miguel as my credit card. He slid it through the groove on the magnetic reader, but nothing happened.—Maybe damaged, he said.

Well, do you want to go ahead and call them? I don't mind, and—again just like Judy!—I even cocked my head and smiled.

It's for the customer to call.

Then will you not rent me a room? Or can I pay a deposit?

Miguel looked right and left. Just give me a deposit.

Here's a hundred dollars.

Looking me gently up and down, he said: We can make it fifty. Here. I take your hundred, and now half for you, half for me.

Thanks for your kindness, I said, knowing that he knew what I had done and excused it.

I lived my life like that. Unmentioned deals were my meat.—Consider the bad husband who, meaning to make amends, asks his wife whether she would like to celebrate their twentieth anniversary, at which she reminds him that it is their twenty-second, not that he ever cared, so he points out that she has never cared, either, or at least has never brought it up, while he is the one bringing it up now, to which she bitterly repeats that he has never *ever* cared, so he corrects her: Aren't I caring now?—No, he doesn't care.—So he wants to know why she won't listen, at which she gratingly informs him that he's *never cared*; hence in rational self-defense he raises his voice; by the end of that dinner they agree not to celebrate their anniversary—all her fault!—I was accomplished at all that.—Among the saddest sensations is to be sad without knowing why. Praise the Goddess, I was unfailingly sad for good reason; I was an efficient blame machine.

Miguel lasted for only eight months; he was always good to me. And I felt, if this makes sense to you, somehow taken care of in that room.

3

What if there were something worthwhile outside and beyond me? Judy's ordeal on the island demonstrates how frightening that would be. We all thought we wanted to become greater and better, and maybe Neva could have made us that way instead of being our masturbatory echo; or maybe she *was* that way and we simply failed, as mortals will, to make wise and thankful use of what she gave us.—The one who truly aimed high, and got what he aimed at, was the straight man.

4

I have told you how as a boy he was haunted by what the cat caught, but he would never have told his autobiography that way. He might have once been longing for some other world, but by now his childish past had taken on the bleak vacuity of ancient ruins beneath the dirt. Nowadays when he drank even just half a bottle of Patriot Dry Lager his ears began ringing; sometimes the ringing woke him up at night. But Neva helped him forget what he had done to himself.

By definition of the great suicide Dr. Wilhelm Stekel, he was a parapathic, having germinated so multibranched a fetishistic system that his pain howled safely lost within it, while he drank Patriot Dry Lager at his ease and solved universal questions; Stekel would have insisted that these fetishes allowed him to avoid the so-called responsibilities of life, including sexual intercourse, but I who control this tale categorically forbid the introduction of gloomy notions. (Were I anyone but me I would call for help—get me out of this ocean whose only two genders are drowners and mermaids!)—The straight man's parapathy sometimes, but only sometimes, made him believe that Neva, who had given him everything by causing him to love her, never had nor would give him anything, let alone her unknown slit which he so miserably and gloriously desired, and lost whenever she got dressed.

5

Here is how *he* would have told it:

Certain natures are more fitted for the pursuits of Mars than the adoration of Venus; never mind the atheists who would have been burned alive in the old times; in my century those latter sorts improved Russian Orthodox cathedrals by means of explosives. In other words, while I admittedly fell for the lesbian, to the retired policeman she never became anything more than the fraudster Karen Strand. (Around that time he—strange for him—actually dreamed and *remembered* his dream of how the real Karen Strand might, must or at least *should* be: a haunted old lesbian sitting alone and nearly broken at her tiny kitchen table, which was covered with a simple white cloth, as all the colors around her withdrew into plum and mauve.) As for the straight man, well, like any true drinker, he was a scientist. Retesting and extending his hypotheses about what might be best for him, he ordered his Patriot Dry Lager, verified its consistency, evaluated its effects and through daily experiments worked out whether arithmetical increases in his blood alcohol concentration amplified his inner man according to a linear or a nonlinear curve. I did the same with my poison, but I was an outright devotee; I sought specifically to maximize my happiness and minimize my cirrhosis, while the straight man appears to have been after understanding. Like the rationalist who finds himself bemused by the rapturous séances of Pentecostals, or the diligent old husband who takes his Erectalis pill at dawn, solely in order to satisfy the wife after breakfast, he observed what Neva was doing to us, and, wishing to sum up rather than experience that phenomenon, set out to elucidate it. Here I could quote the old saw that *Venus is not mocked*; but isn't she, daily and nightly, without repercussions? Besides, since one cannot love too much—as the transwoman's case proves—why should over-inquisitiveness be dangerous? My provisional answer is that true love, being intimate, may terminate tidily in carnage or marriage; whereas curiosity, being more neutrally active, propels the seeker toward increasingly inhuman situations, which might prove poisonous, airless or worse.

I admit that like many Martians he had once been Venusian, thanks first to a long involvement with his wife, in whose cruel, fairskinned ovoid face he once almost perceived divinity, or at least otherness. She had dark hair, and her hands glittered with rings. He first saw her when she was almost twenty-one, running barefoot along the dark grey arcs of wet sand which fronted each inlet, waves swerving and whitening in the arch-holes of jagged red rocks, then bursting into blasts of foam. When he kissed her, her small eyes partly closed; then she flickered her surprisingly green gaze at him to see if he might be watching. Concurrently and subsequently came Sandra, who finally told me: I was so naive. I kept dreaming and hoping that we would be together someday; I used to plan out which songs we would dance to at our wedding, and now I know that it will never happen, at least not until I'm fifty or even older and then what's the use? Oh, I'm sorry I'm so emotional! I broke up with Louis, and he sent me a long e-mail about how maybe we'll still end up happily ever after.

I'm sorry, said I, while Francine mixed me another rum and sodapop.

But I am getting ahead of myself. To break up with the straight man (who impressed the retired policeman nearly as much as had the Navy deserter who kicked a five-year-old boy in the eye with intent to maim), Sandra first needed to *be* with him, so let me now report about that part, when his wife snarled out something about *when you went to San Francisco.*

Knowing that he could not let that pass, he said: What are you talking about?

I know what you're up to. It must be difficult living a double life, said his wife wearily.

But I went to see the new client.

Yeah, right. If you're going to San Francisco, you should just say you're going to San Francisco, she said, forgetting that she had threatened to divorce him if he ever went back there to visit his mistress.

So a week later, off he went to San Francisco, where Sandra waited at the Y Bar. Topic Number One was his wife, about whom she said: The way she treated you is so wrong! I really despise her. I feel such tenderness for you, and also jealousy of how devoted you've been to her.

And did you have a nice time with your other boyfriend? he asked.

Oh, yes, well, we went to a very beautiful beach, although it was quite windy, and we watched people fishing, and the weather was really really beautiful . . .—as if she and this other man had simply met for an afternoon and not even held hands, and there had been no motel with a double bed for her to lie in with her legs open while he ejaculated inside her and smeared himself all over her lips, hair and breasts; that was what most hurt the straight man; had she calmly, cheerfully related all their sex acts, reporting all the promises the other man had whispered, and describing what she felt while he was breathing his breath on her and gluing himself to her with sweat, then the straight man would have felt better, so he convinced himself; it was the fact of his being closed out that tortured him.

She tried to be kind; without acting guilty or defensive (for what was there to be guilty about?). In short, she pivoted around that topic, asking how he was, then describing what she needed to accomplish today and what her pets were just then doing.

And have you been with Neva?

Oh, you know, she said.

(He did.)

She asked: Do you feel close to me right now or distant?

He felt very distant. He said: Oh, everything's good . . . We'll see what happens when we're together . . .

He could hardly bear to remain next to her. He felt sick. He did not hate her, but those unspoken other things that she had done and would go on doing made him feel as if she were gently smiling and lovingly murmuring while razoring off random pieces of his flesh. Closing his eyes, he tried to imagine the sea, and on the kelp-strands a dense black beadwork of tiny mussel shells. He saw nothing; he heard something like static. As soon as he could, he returned home and lied to his wife.

6

The next time he saw Sandra she said: I have to tell you. That girl I kissed last time, I slept beside her two or three times, and we kissed some more. Do I have to tell you everything? Yes, I had one orgasm. But we didn't do the things that you and I do. Well, we did some of them. She's called Neva. But I still love you; don't think I don't. Are you angry at me? I wish you were angry. You're not like other men . . .

It was the ordinary tragedy of an old man and a young woman. She used to promise him that she would be faithful and he could keep having other women. He always said: I won't hold you to that because it's not fair.—And she would say: But I *want* to.

He had never wished to have a baby with her, until she finally gave up; she told him that she had lost hope; she spoke of all the things she used to want for them, and instead of feeling relieved he was sad. He had told her: I'll do it for you, but we have to keep it secret, and I need to know how you'll feel when the baby's sick and crying and you've gotten no sleep and I'm not there.—She had said: I think I'd hate you.—So it was all for the best that there would be no baby. After he bought his airplane ticket to California, in order to come and see her, he dialled her up and said that they could talk about the baby again if she wanted to; maybe there was some way to please all parties, including the unborn child, and he sincerely longed to explain how exciting the idea of their baby sometimes was; he also asked if she would buy some contraceptive jelly for the first night, so that they could be spontaneous and passionate without having to decide that question when they would be tired—for of course she had gone off the pill; the fertility clinic was tracking her cycle, and anytime she wished she could drive up there for her progesterone shot and then open her legs there in the clean white room while someone wearing rubber gloves slid a long tube up her and then inseminated her with the sperm of either the Mexican-German boy with the blue-green eyes or else the blond Russian boy who wrote poetry; for five hundred dollars additional they had allowed her to read their writing samples. She had said: Does it make you feel sad when I talk about this? Would you rather not know?—No, he said bravely; I'm happy for you.—When he arrived she was waiting to drive him to the motel, where it turned out that she had not bought the contraceptive jelly, because she was tired and not in the mood, so he held her and they fell asleep. The next day they went to the pharmacy and bought the jelly. He felt sad and frustrated when they used it; he licked her pussy until she climaxed, after which instead of rushing inside her as he always used to do, he had to help her prepare the jelly, which came with a different kind of applicator than the one he used to know; so the business took awhile, and they both worried that maybe she had not squirted enough of it up herself, but they completed the act and then lay there. The next day they did it again. Then she told him about the other boy whom she had kissed. She said that not long ago she and this other boy (whose name she would not say, so to move the conversation along he began to call him Manfred) had slept in the same bed for two nights, but they had not done any of the things that she and the straight man did together; he had not touched her in that way, although she had had one climax, whose story she preferred not to describe; in fact, although the straight man was not to worry or ever believe that she did not love him best, and although she and Manfred were not serious at all (they were actually about to end things, in part because Manfred was also married), it made her feel *anxious* to discuss Manfred, who would therefore now be a closed topic between her and the straight man. Moreover, for some reason she did not seem to be feeling very sensual right now. Maybe it would be better if they stopped making love. So the straight man tried to live with that. Since she used to ask his advice on things, he would now as they drove around (once even as far as Half Moon Bay) sometimes inquire into how her boss was treating her or whether she had decided to keep her apartment; but for some reason she seemed to resent whatever he asked. So he was feeling pretty sad by then. It got so that he could barely force himself to say anything. He stared straight ahead, and she cried out: You look as if you hate me!

The next morning she asked what he wanted to do that day, and he said: Let's separate for a few hours.

That was fine with her; she missed her pets anyway.

He wrote her a letter to explain how he felt.

And on Ninth by Harrison, almost across from the Civic Center Motor Inn, he stared into an empty plate glass window at a blue carpet whose dust bore a double line of bootprints; these merged into the reflection of the alley behind him, then entered barren garagelike darknesses. When she came back they sat in a park while she read the letter. He said: I'm not angry at you, which he thought was true. He said: These are my feelings.

What made him feel worst was the new rule that now and forever Manfred would not be his business. He told her that from now on his other women would not be her business, either. She looked a little sad. She used to ask him about them all the time. Sometimes what she asked made him sad or uncomfortable, but he had always answered. She looked at him steadily. She said: I didn't expect this, but, all right.

He said: I believe in symmetry. If you close off part of your heart to me, then I need to do the same to you or I'll feel rejected.

I know that's how you are, she said.

So they agreed on that. Now he was on track to become as completely what he was as the deacon who stole everything of value from the Baptist church.

She said that if it were so important to him she would try to be as she called it *open and sexual* with him, and he would be her only boy while the trip lasted. After that, things might possibly change. Since she was trying, he agreed, although he somehow felt sadder than ever.

So they started fucking again. She was very sexy and enthusiastic. (From her point of view it was all about him gripping her round the waist and breathing redfaced into her ear.) He felt very needy and grateful because he had thought that it was all over.

He had felt sad in many other ways before. He had never before felt sad in this way. The smell of her skin and the taste of her pussy now made a kind of sunset in his skull.

7

When they first began making love four years before she had been very tight and dry; she said it was how she was made; they would always need to use lubricant. He was tender, considerate and experienced; soon she was taking it up the ass. He had sex drugs galore, and one of the happiest moments of his life was when they were both drunk and wasted on empathy pills and he lay on his back with his cock sticking straight up, and without any lubricant she slammed herself down on him with a joyous roar. In the morning she was a little sore, of course, but they kept loving in that direction. And now with her off the birth control her pussy was juicier and thirstier than ever; it had always tasted sweet, but now it had even fresher and more exciting notes; she must be throwing off make-my-baby hormones. He had always desired her, but never so much as this. He couldn't stop touching her. He sucked and *sucked* her, holding her, kissing her lips and sucking her tongue while his fingers carefully brought her forward, desperate for her rabbitlike cry of fulfillment which was thin, high, frail, and ever so sweet to him.

And then they had to get the applicator. They had learned to fill it full of jelly first. Even so there was that pause while they reached for it and then he or she squeezed it in.

He tried to joke about it; he wanted it to be funny. Tipsy and laughing, dying to penetrate her, he rolled the empty applicator aside and said: All right, you pretty baby-killer, you!

He'd reach down below the Bible drawer for the applicator and say: All right, let's kill our baby now!

And she would smile ever more palely, and after the third or fourth time she said: That makes me sad . . .

He never told her how sad *he* was. It was monstrous to him, that she was going to make a baby in a clinic with some stranger's sperm, when she kept killing his!—He was my brother in selfishness; we all operated so far below our Neva!

Sometimes he'd eat Sandra's pussy until she screamed out her third or fourth climax, and then he'd put his penis inside her, just for a minute; she'd look worried but allow it, because she trusted him. And he'd start thrusting carefully in and out; it felt so good; he'd say: Do you want me to stop?

She always nodded, until one night when she said: Oh, oh, I don't know!

And he was so close; he wanted so much to come inside her and give her the baby, but he knew that if he did they'd both feel even sadder later, so he got off her and they killed another baby.

Then Manfred returned to his wife, the straight man dreamed of dead birds and Sandra started worshipping Neva in earnest.

8

Just as a fraternity man first snorts coke because the brothers offer it, then snorts coke because that way he can drink all night and never get drunk, then snorts coke and skips the booze, so Sandra first accepted the offer of Neva to be social, then found out that loving Neva helped her to love the straight man, then realized that she did not need the straight man at all. But she loved him; he was her boy; she had promised to never ever leave him even if she sometimes might close this or that heart-ventricle to him.

Spying on Sandra and the lesbian, he saw their pallid heads approach each other in the lurid doorway; then those two were staring sightlessly into each other's skulls.

9

Again she gave her word that whenever they were alone together her body and soul would be utterly open to him, not just to keep that old commitment but also because she sincerely wanted it so; indeed, she was longing to open herself to him all the way, until he could see right up her, all the way to her fluttering bloody heart.

Meanwhile, strictly to further his scientific curiosity, he began visiting Neva.

And so he and Sandra moved back in together.

10

I can't help but feel that you are punishing me for what I did and said, Sandra told him. I do feel chastised. And it is especially hard when you say that we can't talk about it for an unknown length of time.

Something about the straight man had always been difficult and dark. Granting that his fundamental unavailability (as Sandra explained to Neva) was part of who he was, which is why she respected it, by that very token *he* ought to respect how lonely it made her.

Neva nodded, held her and kissed her. (Last night she had dreamed that the only place to make love with Judy was her mother's unmade bed, which smelled. She further dreamed that her mother stood in the doorway giving her such advices as: Don't forget her pussy. Remember her pussy.—Then her mother waited outside the closed door, listening.)

But how do you *feel* about it? her adorer demanded.

The lesbian replied: How I feel is that I love you.

But you're not jealous when Louis and I . . .—I don't understand. And what do you suppose it's like for *me* when Louis comes over here, or you see him while I'm waiting outside?

Neva said nothing.

Thus the first instance when Sandra began to tell her: I don't understand why you won't open up to me when I am so willing to open up to you.

Or, as another crucified soul once cried out: *My Goddess, my Goddess, why have you forsaken me?*

11

Naturally she did close herself off from *him.* She hoped to live exclusively in the gold chamber of the lesbian's womb.

Although for a fairytale eternity she swam along beside Neva like a champion mermaid heroine, she was now getting weighed down by the secret, or, as she described it, the pressure of the secret, which pushed her deeper underwater; she was getting tired.

12

You know that I love you, don't you? asked Sandra. This matter of Geoffrey is a little odd, but I know you understand, and I'm so grateful for your support and advice. I never could have gone through with it if you hadn't helped me.

Well, and did he propose? asked the straight man.

Oh, no! But we had a very, very nice time.

Just remember, honey: Every day that he doesn't return to his wife is another victory for you.

I guess so . . . Darling, are you sad about something?

I'm happy for you.

That isn't what I asked.

Of course I support you. I'm proud that you're making yourself happy.

But you know that I love you, *too*!

Of course I know . . .

And that I desire you . . .

Sure, he said. Not long before, she would have said: Don't you know that I love you the most?—She used to say: Louis, I worry that you're slipping away . . .

13

It might have been less frightening for her to propel herself down deeper as if she were a Neva-imitating intercessor for still more feeble and troubled mermaids such as Judy; indeed, the cunning pretense of acting so might facilitate her own escape; for *The Gnostic Scriptures* most truly proclaim that between us and the light above there is a veil, and upon the veil has grown a shadow, so that to ascend now means to enter into confusion and terror; hence it is best to go down first, and grow accustomed to the true darkness before venturing into the false kind. But Sandra had trouble being false; the most she could be was secretive. When she stretched her hand down to Judy she sincerely meant to help her, even if the latter drowning mermaid pulled her farther into death. So she was preparing herself to see through Neva's shadow without realizing she did so. Meanwhile the straight man most scientifically plunged himself into the opacity which clothed Neva's naked luminescence, because having blinded himself to all prior mysteries, he craved this one. But it was false darkness which he inhaled, without understanding the true one. And so he and Sandra were equally and separately lost.

14

And what do you do? the straight man inquired on their first so-called date.

What do you mean? returned the lesbian.

I mean, what do you do for *money*? Jesus, what else could I mean?

Nothing.

That's pretty weird.

She was silent.

But that's you, isn't it, Neva? Pretty and weird. You don't charge for it?

I would never do that.

Then how do you live?

Like this . . .

Drinking in her face, he tasted that calm wide-eyed gaze of a woman waiting to make love without desire.

15

He had money. He took her to the opera: an opportunity for Spanish damsels to click their castanets and show some leg (the conductor's wrist waving like seaweed); in came swishing girls in red corsets, necklace-gleam and cheek-shine of a smiling lady in the darkness; and then two young women with brilliants in their ears, leaning against the railing of the orchestra pit, staring back up at the boxes together through the same cell phone screen. Beside him, the lesbian's white hand stroked her white leg up and down; something was itching her. On his other side was a pink skirt and shining knees slightly parted; their owner had sat down without acknowledging his nod. He looked: a pretty woman held a faux-jeweled clutch most tightly under her shaven armpit. The lesbian, knowing what he was up to and in fact quite relieved to be ignored for once, watched the ballerinas spreading their thighs and crabwalking sideways.

As the world expanded, its silences got louder, and gold shone brighter and brighter, as if it were gold and silver together, while the hair of blondes turned almost green. He had bought a glass bangle for the lesbian, who presently slipped it off and began to run her forefinger around its inside. He longed to smell her face. The ring sparkled on her finger; he longed to lick it.

Now the ballet had something to do with a certain magenta empress with a face of crystalline fungus. Her flabby old labia were hanging like the formerly silver curtains in a long dead noble's private box at the opera. Now here was the lesbian with her white skirt slipping up her thighs as she hovered over him, grasshoppering her legs as she struggled not to be borne away.

Wake up, wake up, said Sandra. Honey, you're tossing and turning—

16

Unable, so she claimed, to understand the straight man's talk of bargains and agreements, meanwhile sinking into dark water, while the lesbian shone, with respites, farther and farther above her, Sandra felt even more alone than before.

As I have said, this woman was the loveliest-hearted of Neva's worshippers. When we others victimized her, her reaction almost always was the innocent grief of a child, unmixed with anger. She performed at least as many patient kindnesses for Judy as Francine, and far more than Xenia. Nurturing to stray cats and dogs, glowing with affection and infinitely deserving of it, Sandra sank quite slowly into desperation. A constant lover, companionable and present, would so far as she could see have saved her.—I remember when I used to think like that.

Tell me how much you love me, she begged.

I love you . . . began the lesbian, but Sandra said: Tell me something you've never told me before.

I love you enough to snuggle you and . . .

And what? asked Sandra anxiously.

Enough to hold you tight . . .

The lesbian was feeling very tired.

I adore you. Do you adore me?

Of course I do—

Are you as passionate about me as in the very beginning?

Yes, I am—

Are you *more* passionate? Because I'm more passionate about you every day.

Me, too, said the lesbian.

17

And the straight man continued his researches. Experiments were all they were; he swore he felt no attachment to Neva. (Often he'd just as soon play liars' dice with Shantelle!) As Sandra withdrew ever farther from him, he considered our universe from the objective side, his penis not yet throbbing with need but certainly beginning to call attention to itself, in a way that as yet remained less desperate than pleasurably anticipatory, like the way one's mouth waters when a succulent dessert arrives at the dinner table; he lay awake at night imagining thrusting into this girl or that woman, not necessarily Neva—who received him well, of course. She made him feel something that he used to feel which pills sometimes persuaded him had revisited him however temporarily and half-heartedly; this thing was his life itself which once used to stir in his heart and penis and had now deserted him as coolly as our first love leaves us, for he was used up now, flabby and tired, greyfaced and complaining, worrying all the time about money and the future, as if worry could somehow save him from his predestined hole in the ground. Smiling, his life departed him, casting around for someone less boring. Fortunately, there remained several diverting questions to dig into, such as: (I) Could someone *improve* Neva? (Let's not forget that the Grand Inquisitor improved Jesus's work, and the Prophet Muhammed later did much the same.) (II) When we had no choice but to love her, on account of how perfect she was, then *did we* truly, purely love her?

There came a sad Monday night of two flabby dancers in alternation who for a long time puzzled over which song to dial up on the jukebox and then halfway through it kept slowly disinfecting the catty pole. Why did he even visit the Pink Apple, anyhow? One girl looked better from the front than the back; she lured him into a twenty-dollar private dance during which he never forgot Sandra. The other dancer, the redhead, kept making a show of her ass, so that quiet men in ball caps placed money for her on the edge of the stage; she didn't help him away from Sandra, either. (Discovering Neva, a girl in leather bent her wrists across her breasts, then turned up the corners of her mouth in a smile so impossibly wide and deep as to encompass the entire lower hemisphere of a perfect circle.) The barmaid owed him two dollars in change but pretended to know nothing about it and kept nagging him to tip the dancers. Worn out, he made another date with the lesbian, longing for her pity if for nothing better.

He inquired: You're not actually a lesbian, are you?

No, people just call me that.

So what are you?

Whatever you make me.

By then his outspread fingers could not desist from the oscillating caresses through which they drank in pleasure from her milky-white breast—indeed, this pleasure *tasted* like rich sweet milk—and from her soft smooth shoulder, which tasted like sweat, meat, sexual excitement; and from her perfect upper arm, whose flavor the fingertips never identified before they simply had to rush back to gently kneading pleasure out of her breast, drinking it greedily through every ridge and whorl, while she smiled at him and sweetly kneaded his penis, a procedure which felt so good that he took one hand away from her and began to play with himself, one hand for him and one for her and both of them (he insisted) equally happy, their fingers drinking in the joy which propelled them into something that pretended to be eternity.

But the lesbian sat up. She threw on her green blouse, and right away, the straight man began to feel cold from right under his heart all the way down to his icy feet. Our Neva was about to go away!

He could have visited her as often as the rest of us; but, preferring not to lose himself, contented himself with one encounter every other week. The closer he got to her, the more he longed to smell her. He meditated on the delightful sight of her clitoral hood. Given the way he wished to be portrayed it would be inappropriate of me to mention her searing kisses and her body seething against his; I'm told that he once burned his mouth on her red-hot pussy, but who can believe such sentimental lies? His sensations in her bed and after were curious, to say the least; everything grew new and brightly colored at the moment of climax; then, in direct proportion to the duration and physical distance of their separation, rather grey. Furthermore, each time he departed from her, the greyness thickened. Had he been capable of rapture, his erotic intervals with Neva might have gotten correspondingly richer, but he was not someone of that sort. Having heard how it was with Francine, Judy, Shantelle, Sandra and me, he found this no stranger than he had expected. But his solitary bed did get colder, and his ceiling lower.

He found a Mexican girl in a summer dress who was flying around a catty pole, then spreading her legs to show that she had somehow lost her underwear; doing pullups, flashing her bottom in the red night, she somersaulted naked up the pole and descended upside-down, her arms outstretched and her breasts hard and fake. She was gripping the pole between her thighs solely, inching down until her long hair swept the floor and the men shrieked hosannahs. Next came a Chinese girl who was just as beautiful but who forgot to put on her smile until she was onstage; the strobe made him nauseous. So he went back to Sandra and the lesbian.

The truth is that he could not really make his way. Peering into the lesbian's persona, he thought to see a cramped dark chamber in which something glittered. And what that something was he longed to see.

He asked the retired policeman, of course. From that source he received all the sinister interpretations that anyone could have wanted. Next he asked me; I promised him that Neva would irradiate him with the stream of pleasure.

All right, Francine. Tell me what *you* know.

The barmaid answered: Well, she's wonderful.

Pulling open the Y Bar's swinging door, he felt nearly as he had when in his boyhood he stood on the rocky rim of a carp pond, spying out what might be beneath the water's brown-green mirror: fingernails of fire flicking by in a slow rainstorm (surely goldfish); and then the edge of a waterlily-island twitched as two glistening black claws pulled it down, and a face, half black, half blue, with crimson eye-beads, peered alertly up, hoping to catch some prey. Or, in the magnificent words of Frank S. Caprio, M.D.: *In almost every large city, one can find a particular tavern or café where male and female inverts congregate. These places frequently change, for when the establishment becomes notorious as a hangout for "queers" some civic or religious group tries to have them closed.* Amidst the beautiful things dwelled some other kind of thing. Perhaps it was not a monster but a mermaid. As yet he still loved Sandra more than Neva.—What a stupid tautology to say that this story could have ended differently!

Almost *Flagrante Delicto*

Wanting-to-know is an offspring of the desire for power, the striving for expansion, existence, sexuality, pleasure . . . Whatever presents itself as theoretical enlightenment . . . can never reach its alleged goals . . .

PETER SLOTERDIJK, 1987

Here, a barbed wire entanglement of various factors confronts the man who would hunt down a criminal.

J. EDGAR HOOVER, *ca.* 1935

1

And the retired policeman turned over a photograph from what must have been the 1970s or early eighties: six young women in bluejeans sitting on the carpeted floor of an office, a row of potted plants on a window shelf. Farthest away was a certain longhaired girl by the French doors, one knee raised, the other folded on the floor with her fist clenched on it, her firm round breasts outlined beneath her flimsy shirt; she wore a gentle, neutral expression. Another darker-haired woman was on a beanbag cushion with her thighs comfortably spread, raising a single lens reflex camera and tenderly half-smiling out at us while a black Labrador retriever nuzzled her shoulder; she must have been taking this picture; she and all the others were reflected in the mirror. Third was the face of a curlyhaired roundfaced girl, very low, resting against the upper arm of the fourth, who was another longhaired young woman with lovely teeth who smiled most widely and sincerely, her eyes shining. Beside this latter and a trifle apart from her was most definitely Karen Strand, who remained so hauntingly unchanged in 2015; and then, most distinct from these others, sat a chunky, shorthaired butch in an embroidered shirt, smiling, but only at the dog, which she was stroking. He looked again and again at the photo. Most conspicuous was that lovely smile of the darker-haired woman, although he felt more attracted to the blonde by the French doors, who gazed so palely and watchfully from far away. On the reverse side a feminine hand had pencilled: *Jen, Anne, Sunwomon, E-beth, Karen & Diane.*

The longhaired smiling woman near Karen was surely the beautiful woman who was playing pool in that photograph from Jingle's: E-beth. So Elizabeth Jackson was definitely a *person of interest.*

He looked back at the photo of *Soy Fest 1968 (Jen & Judith's engagement).* Yup. Same Jen. Where was Judith here? Literally out of the picture. Good old Jen got around—the bitch.

Laying down *Soy Fest 1968*, he picked up a color snapshot (dated 1995) of three chubby goddamn middle-aged dykes, the same *Diane, Jen & Anne*, sitting in a row of kitchen chairs while an unknown butch, apparently *Rainbow*, stood behind a tiny table with a blue-checked cloth; the table was set with apples, pastries, tea and paper plates. Fuck them all.

He redeployed the snapshot of *Waiting for E., Stanford '74.* Blind alley. Time to make Judy steal some more.

At the Y Bar he now made nice with Neva, pretending to be under her so-called spell, regaling her with what was called *important chickenshit in the cop shop.*—I was the youngest to make sergeant, he informed her, and Judy, who had never heard this, glowed like a goddamn radioactive dildo, while even Francine looked impressed.

Back then we had our own way of enforcing things, he explained, and Shantelle (who had been wishing she could afford to buy the lesbian long black leather pants like the celebrity Olivia Culpa wore) stopped doing her nails to listen. The deal was to be a cowboy and use your own imagination and keep the bad guys moving. We had a whole book of mug shots and cars, so we knew who the bad guys were. We knew what the rules were and they knew what the rules were. The idea was to keep them off their guard. If they were driving slowly in a shopping mall lot we would enforce the vagrancy laws against them; this was prevention more than apprehension.

Seven dollars, said Francine. Actually, you know fuckin' what, J. D.? This one's on the house. Your stories are amazing.

Thanks, baby, he said, watching the lesbian's lip form in another of what he called her *camouflage smiles.*

So, he continued, I saw these two guys in a red Chevy Viper 6, you know, the yuppie car of the day, and it didn't look like they belonged in it. Back in the day, we used to say JDLR—

Just don't look right, the transwoman proudly interpreted.

Good job, Judy. But don't interrupt Daddy, or I'll spank you. Well, and then I got a call on fraudulent use of a credit card, but what happened was the bellhop from the Sleepytime Motel in Daly City remembered someone leaving in a red Chevy Viper, so I went in and got security; we keyed it open, and it's *up against the wall, asshole!*

Shantelle's mouth opened. She said: J. D., how could you not be scared when you busted in there?

I was nuts. I'm *still* nuts. So I liked it. You really act; you don't have time to think. You know, there's real fear, too, but action overcomes any real sense of fear.

This one's on you, said Francine. Seven dollars.

Actually, said the lesbian, let me buy him a drink.—Out came a hundred-dollar bill.

Looking her up and down, he said: And then of course I've got to have an air-tight case.

2

A twentyish man with hair pomaded just so sat down at the bar and waited.

What can I get you? asked Francine.

Actually, he replied, I do think I would be willing to try a margarita with one and a half limes muddled in and, let's see, exactly two fingers of Porfirio Díaz *añejo* tequila.

We don't carry that brand.

Well, what do you carry?

Sir, our tequila's all on this shelf right in front of you, so you figure out what you want while I help my other customers. Xenia, you ready for a refill?

Yeah. And I'm buying for Hunter.

Where is she? She complains when her ice melts.

She just texted me; she's right around the corner. I want to be a good girl-friend and—

Fine. I'll put her ice in a cup and she can add it herself. Ten dollars.

Excuse me, said the pomaded man.

All right, sir, do you know what you want?

I do want to reach out to you, said the man, just to let you know that your customer service is not what I expect, you know, when I go out.

So sorry, said Francine, gritting her teeth.

And I'm going to send out a negative review of you and your establishment on metrodrinky.com. Are you familiar with metrodrinky.com? Because it's a very, very—

Fuck you, said Francine, and all the rest of us cheered.

Stunned and pale, the young man got to his feet and ran out, looking over his shoulder as if he expected us to assault him. Francine said: Hey everybody, thanks for having my back. How about a round on the house?

And then Hunter came in, surprised and delighted to find her fresh-made double Slambang awaiting her, while Judy came out of the bathroom grinning and stinking like vomit.

3

Behind the cash register at the Y Bar leaned that seldom remarked glassed and framed four-by-six-inch color snapshot of two darkhaired women in bluejeans leaning in against each other and resting their arms on a blonde in a broad-brimmed hat who was smiling, holding each one's hand. After the blonde, the brunette on the right looked happiest, and then the brunette on the left, with hard Appalachian features, holding tight to the other two, but not really smiling, almost desperate.

Although she had altered her appearance since then, the retired policeman recognized the brunette as Francine—who at Shantelle's request now increased the volume of the television, because it was declaiming: *Police say they are investigating an assault on two transgender women by four men who had been harassing them because of their gender identity. The video went viral on www.hatecrimesxxx.com and shows the women being threatened and insulted for about three minutes, until a man kicked at one of the women. When her friend tried to defend her, she was attacked by other men, beaten and stripped naked.*

Turning to Judy, Shantelle (trying to smile in the mirror so that she would look like the celebrity Lupita Nyong'o, although no matter what she did, Shantelle's smile didn't look *nice*) raised her glass and said: Hey, bitch, ain't that your fantasy?

Show some respect, said Francine.

People on the bus made no effort to stop the assault. Instead, many cheered and took videos on their phones. The women told reporters that the incident had led them to move out of state.

Shantelle said: I can't help but feel like one of them T-girls was instigating the fight. I ain't saying those dudes had any right to fuckin' touch her, but I for one wouldn't never be screaming in the faces of a group of males who outnumber me on a bus at night—

Sure you would, said Francine, and she was so right that we all laughed. That was how we put that latest hate crime behind us.

Groaning, the retired policeman got up. Judy hastened to take his hand. They went slowly home to Empire Residences, where he lay down and said: Judy, I told you you're going to be my eyes and ears. And you've done a damn good job with those photos. Do you know what *flagrante delicto* means?

No, J. D., I never took Latin.

It means something like *busted in the middle of the act.* You know that story Shantelle likes to drop about the time she saw a pair of earrings at the jewelry counter at Gracey's Emporium and couldn't help but take 'em?

The transwoman nodded, fascinated.

Well, she either took 'em or she didn't. We don't know. But if we'd seen her take 'em, that would be *flagrante delicto.* You get it now?

She nodded again.

So the plan is, we want to catch your little Karen in *flagrante delicto.* And I think she's got something to do with credit card fraud, he explained.

Oh, J. D., you're so *smart*!

. . . Then his penis exploded again and again into her mouth like a machine gun.

The Lucky Star

But I've always said that I was born under a Lucky Star, somewhere Over the Rainbow.

JUDY GARLAND, 1940

A woman's natural quality is to attract, and having attracted, to enchain.

MRS. H. R. HAWEIS, 1878

1

Next Xenia got to have the lesbian again; and if Xenia's story could be as joyful as she longed it to be, it would be safely enclosed within the rarely fortunate case of a woman who is instructed by Truth Herself . . . and through the agency of another woman!—since like best follows like.

The rich complexity of the lesbian's wonderfully sweaty hair expanded beneath Xenia's fingertips, until it almost seemed that she was recognizing and loving each dark brown strand for its own self. Stroking the lesbian's creamy biceps was like sliding over an endless perfect surface, roaming frictionlessly over an impossible smoothness. With sudden greedy anxiety she wondered what part of this body she might be missing. She needed to adore all of her. The best place therefore would be her anus. Whispering to the other woman to please roll over, she first laid down her head on those soft buttocks, then began gripping and kneading them in a fury of pleasure. Now she pulled them apart, and there was the little round hole with its halo of pink. Hungrily she plumped her mouth against it and began to lick, round and round and round. It tasted sweet, bitter and very clean. After awhile the lesbian began moaning softly. This stimulated the worshipper all the more, and before she knew it she was breathing fast and begging the lesbian: Pee in my mouth, oh, please . . .

Are you sure?

Oh, yes, Neva, because that's what you did for Judy.

She told you that?

No, Shantelle did. Please, honey, that's what I need right now from you . . .

And so the lesbian found herself squatting an inch above Xenia's mouth, slowly, lovingly giving her first a few almost tasteless droplets and then the entire warm stream that tasted faintly like tea and somehow conveyed to Xenia (her eyes were closed, to keep them from getting wet) a *silvery* impression; it actually tasted like silver, which is to say quiet, lovely, glowingly metallic, not luminous in and of itself but reflective of the light of her who was giving it.

Neva, do you love me the most?

I love everyone the most.

What about Judy?

The same.

But I'm smarter, and I don't whine and I do *not* stink.

Why talk about Judy behind her back?

But what is it about her? The way you're being, it's hurtful to me. Neva, I'm a human being, and I deserve to be loved right.

The thing is—

You are so insensitive! Don't you get it? I'm offering you everything, and you—oh, fuck you . . . Neva, don't forget how fucked up I am. I'm *lonely*! Please *help me all the time.*

I'll think of you all the time, but I won't be there all the time. Honey, try your best . . .

2

When Xenia was home, trying to force herself to spend the whole goddamn night with whiny Hunter, all the time thinking back on the things that she and Neva had done, it began to seem that if she had not been in that condition of magic rapture, the lesbian's pussy would have tasted stronger than it did, for there had been much sweating and pissing without showering; moreover its various grooves, platforms, ridges, cavities and zones would have been more distinct; another woman might have demanded: *focus on my clit!,* and it was not that there was no clit, but somehow the pussy had become greater and more mysterious and at the same time more one entity, a kind of sweet-tasting fiery jelly whose awareness was far greater than Xenia's and whose ability to receive Xenia's love was both endless and perceptible;

it waxed hot and liquid, trembled internally and coerced them both into uttering stroboscopic moans. Remembering how I always told my penis: *pay attention to the cunt!*, Xenia wondered whether the lesbian could somehow become nothing less than pure cunt, loving and excited and receptive without individuality, and yet utterly conscious; that was what Xenia wanted to be, in order to escape her future of loss.

Hunter was staring at her sadly, so Xenia fed them each two opioids.

3

Having patched up their latest contretemps, they set Neva aside and decided on a Saturday outing in Tiburon. (Judy, who was looking distinctly more slender, gave them plastic-wrapped flowers, and Hunter said: *Awww!*) Xenia was in the back seat of Hunter's car, with Hunter's brother's big white dog drooling on her wrist and breathing moist foul breath in her face. The smell became less tolerable. Meanwhile, Hunter was in the front passenger seat, chatting with her brother and sucking on a hot-cinnamon-flavored gumball, whose sickening artificial sweetness rose out on Hunter's breath and diffused through the entire car. Xenia rolled down her window.—Would you mind? said Hunter's brother. We can't hear a thing.—Xenia rolled the window back up. The nauseating odors made her stomach ache sharply. She pushed the dog's head away from her. Regarding her mildly, the dog strained against her hand. She was sweating with nausea. Cool drops sprang out on her forehead and ran into her eyes. A migraine's rhythmic assaults inside her head increased her misery, but not as much as the hot flash or whatever it was that drenched her hair and neck and glued her blouse to her back, her pants to her thighs—so that she suddenly understood that she must be in withdrawal, but for what?

She was jonesing for the lesbian.

Oh, she loved so much to lie there drinking in the lesbian's caresses; wherever she was touched, that part of her began to sing! She could hardly wait to get away from Hunter—

4

Once upon a time she had temporarily inhabited the tall narrow golden glow of the Best Hotel. Once she had had a wife, and twice a husband. She'd once cohabited with a lady who'd purchased tits in Mexicali and whose cock retained its original powers; the lady then seduced a rich jet pilot, elevating Xenia into free loneliness. Now she had Neva.—She washed her face, then lay down awhile in her darling's arms. But what if their date were to come to an end? Was she wasting her eternity? Sitting up and groping round for her strap-on so that she could penetrate the lesbian, she suddenly felt dizzy and almost nauseous. The pleasure was nearly too much. The light seemed to be flickering, which made the shadows pulse. The stripes on the sheets began flashing so overwhelmingly that vomit rose into her mouth, and she swallowed it down, not wishing to disgrace herself there in the lesbian's bed. She closed her eyes.—The lesbian said: What's wrong, honey?—Oozing back down beside her where everything was so soft and perfect and only good things could happen, Xenia said: I don't want to; it's too cold up there so far away from you . . .—and burst into tears. Comfortingly the lesbian held and began deeply kissing her so that their tongues whirled round and round in each other's mouths. Xenia was screaming with pleasure, but the lesbian's tongue kept the sound from coming out, and the pleasure was heightened for being thus restrained, controlled by her. Now the lesbian, knowing what she wanted, lay down on top of her with all her weight and gripped her wrists. She said: Xenia, you're my prisoner and I can do to you whatever I want to. And what I want to do is *kiss you and kiss you*, oh, yes, honey, to *kiss you* . . . and gripped Xenia's tongue between her teeth, all the while rubbing their nipples together, and almost at once Xenia began convulsing in an orgasm so unbearably perfect that she wished to die from it.

And later, possibly because she was still coming down from the experience, the scent of Neva's concentrated urine in the unflushed toilet was wildly exciting to her, as if she were a stag and Neva a pissing doe in estrus.

But afterward (because only gods and goddesses need not pay for their pleasures) the food tasted sickeningly greasy and salty, although it was only stir-fried vegetables with no salt in it.

Her cell phone chimed. Hunter was calling and calling. Xenia turned it off.

5

. . . Although everything was already determined by the irresistible immensity of her loving force, from each of our individual points of view we made unique choices to love her, choices which the retired policeman's example proved that we did not have to make; and because she loved each of us differently, seeing who we were and responding to our natures just as a talented equestrienne conforms herself to the horse she rides, neck-reining, whispering or spurring according to the animal's nature, we did not uniformly feel betrayed by the fact of her riding others before and after each of us—which is not to say that some worshippers were not more patient than others. In Judy's case, for instance, there were always emergencies.

Whenever we came to Neva our hearts were pounding; and when we left we found ourselves bedazzled, dizzy, exhausted, with headaches, sore throats and various photosensitivities. The better Neva made us feel, the more depleted we were afterward. How could it be any other way?

6

Kissing the lesbian goodbye, Xenia turned resolutely toward the stairs, but not resolutely enough to prevent her looking once more over her shoulder at her who stood in the doorway, blowing an extra kiss. She began to descend the carpeted stairs. With each new step between her and Neva she felt sadder. She tried to understand what the sadness was about, but it did not seem to be about any specific thing. Sorrow became grief, and her eyes vomited effortless tears. The overhead lights appeared to flicker; they hurt her eyes. Her head began to hurt. She longed to be alone in the dark somewhere, curled up and sobbing.

7

Shantelle, smilingly playing with her clitoris, pretending that she was slowly feeding the lesbian sleeping pills adulterated with fentanyl, playing with her, only playing, which is to say systematically and discreetly following a deliberately murderous procedure, sat up in the double bed and listened to the lesbian being sick in the bathroom. The door was closed, and cold water ran loudly in the sink, but Shantelle could hear almost as well as a feral kitten. She was not charmed, remembering when her girlfriend Charisse got shot in the back of the head and started vomiting on her.

Finally the lesbian staggered palely out. Shantelle explained: Neva, you don't need nobody but me. Gimme a chance; I'll love you so good you'll be screamin'.

You're already such a good lover, said the lesbian.

Come over here, said Shantelle.

The lesbian stood before her.

Neva, I fucked up some guy who never did me wrong.

Oh, said the lesbian.

Ask me why.

Why?

I did it for money. J. D. paid me two hundred dollars, and it looked like money that Judy stole from your wallet. An' I . . . an' I took it and did it. I feel bad.

Honey, you wanna tell me more?

He choked Judy and hit her upside the head, so from J. D.'s point of view, he was just protectin' his bitch.

He loves her, said the lesbian.

He wants to get her away from you. He said if I help him, maybe there'll be more of you for me to get into, you see what I'm saying?

Sure, said the lesbian.

How does that make you feel? Goddamn it, girl, don't you ever get mad?

I have something for you, said the lesbian. Let me get it from the closet. I bought you this white blouse; I was thinking it would look nice on you.

8

And sitting in the Y Bar to the right of the black man in the yellow city vest who sat enchanted by the dark screen of his little phone, I tried to understand Neva. It felt like trying to remember exactly where stood the Diana Hotel, where I once stayed; was it on Ninth and Harrison or maybe Ninth and Folsom? Beside me sat the retired policeman, who was thinking: Maybe Karen's like the shoplifter who can't even explain why she loves to steal.—Beneath the dormant disco ball, the straight man played liars' dice with Shantelle.

On our muted television the beautiful Chinese anchorwoman pulled her best somber look while the crawling caption said ***BREAKING NEWS: NEW INFO ON WHITE ON BLACK POLICE SHOOTING IN SAN MATEO: BLACK TEEN SHOT 16 TIMES IN BACK WHILE FLEEING IN STOLEN CAR: BREAKING NEWS: BREAKING NEWS.***

We all watched the ***BREAKING NEWS***, hoping for anything exciting to happen. The retired policeman came to life. As Sir Walter Scott wrote about his wholesome romantic hero Waverley, *the conversation gradually assumed the tone best qualified for the display of his talents and acquisitions.*

He said: I knew right away that this was a clean arrest. The kid had already tried to take the gun, and that was proved forensically, and the cop still had the guts to go out to arrest him. Then he gets on the freeway and recklessly—

But in the fuckin' *back*! said Shantelle. What the goddamn fuck *for*?

They hang you out to dry, he explained. Here's a brave cop just trying to protect the public, and then the department, well, they bend to the pressure of the community in many ways. What they were trying to do by not giving out the information on the shooting, well, they thought it would fuel even more violence. That kind of community, you can understand it—

What do you mean, *that kind of community*? What's that code for?

Let me finish, Shantelle. Often the choices they make make no fuckin' difference at all. I'm not excusing the bad shoots. But this courageous officer who put his life on the line and now finds himself suspended, well, let's just say I've lost all respect for that chief of police.

One of you goddam pigs just *executed* a man on account of his color. And you sit there on your fat white ass and tell me—

Returning from the bathroom (I won't say she didn't smell a trifle like puke), the lesbian approached Shantelle, who whirled on her to say: You shut the fuck up, white bitch! Get away from me!

You be nice to Neva, said Francine.

Oh, *fuck* you all! Nobody cares . . . !

I see you looking at that glass, said Francine. You so much as wrap your hand around it right now and you're eighty-sixed *forever.* I won't have no racial violence. You start to lift it up and I'm ready with the baseball bat.

I love you, Shantelle, said the lesbian.

Shantelle (otherwise known as the black Judy Garland) cocked her fist, so Francine whipped the bat down onto her knuckles and she screamed. For a moment everything else stopped while Shantelle stared at her bleeding hand as if it were an offering from the Three Wise Men; then, even as she opened her mouth to really truly screech, the lesbian said: Come on, honey. I'll take you to the doctor.—They began to leave; then Neva came back to collect Shantelle's purse.

Well, said the retired policeman, there's a lawsuit about to happen.

Francine grinned an ugly grin.—I know how to hit, she said.

I suppose she was anxious on the inside. But as it turned out, she was right. Shantelle came back in two hours, making a big show with an icepack on her hand, but before she could say a word, Francine told her: Now you listen. I saved you from assaulting Neva or J. D. and maybe going to jail. You shut up and make nice and I won't eighty-six you. Now do you want to shake hands and make up or do you want to be banned for life? Well? All right then. One Peachy Keen over ice coming up, on the house. And, J. D., do me a favor. Just dial down your political commentary a little. Some people may be sensitive.

Oh, fuck you, said the retired policeman, but then she poured him his own consolation.

9

And they never leave me alone, said Francine. Sometimes I get so stressed out I can't sleep. I'm so sick of this I wanna just . . .

C'mere, honey, said the lesbian. Give me a kiss.

Oh, Neva, the world's in such sad shape and we're all such losers and *I can't fucking stand it*! God knows, even Shantelle had a point . . . !

So did you, said the lesbian.

What are you, anyway? You only tell us what we wanna hear . . .

I'm trying to love you.

Oh, Neva, I'm sorry; I didn't mean it. Hold me. Hold me tight; I can't stand it—

10

Although she had now lost eleven pounds, the transwoman had momentarily given up on passing or even improving herself. She was my brother and I her sister because neither one of us could be troubled to stop being drowning mermaids even though two or three flips of our scaly tails would have kept us from sinking deeper. I entertained myself with the idea of overdosing on goofballs, while she lay awake at night fantasizing about licking the lesbian's anus, to indulge her appetite for degradation.

You know what I keep imagining about you and me?

The lesbian caressed the back of her neck, saying: Tell me, Judy.

We're in a fancy restaurant. And suddenly I stand up, so that everybody stops talking and looks at me. And then I piss myself. And you shout at me and call me all kinds of names, and walk out, so I have to pay the check. And everybody's disgusted with me. And finally they let me go, and you're waiting for me across the street, and you tell me that I'm your good little girl.

Is that really what you want?

I think so. Would you do that with me?

I'd never shout at you in public. If you want to pee on yourself, I'll hug you, and we'll pay and go home.

But then you'd get piss all over you.

That's okay, said the lesbian.

Would you still love me?

Sure.

Neva?

We need to get dressed now.

Whose turn is it?

Someone's.

You mean you won't tell me?

It never makes you happy.

Tell me.

Richard's.

Oh. I don't mind him so much, because he's just a nothing. I hope he has fun. You think he's gonna off himself with goofballs?

Not yet, said the lesbian.

I know you'll be nice to him.

Sit up, honey, and I'll hook your bra.

Neva, I want to love you better and *better.* What should I do?

Sweetie, you already love me very well.

That's what you told Shantelle and Xenia and everybody. I want to be the best.

Can you be better with J. D.?

What do you mean?

Love him. That's the way to love me.

Neva, don't throw me away! I'll do anything—

Okay, said the lesbian.

What will you make me do?

Keep losing weight. Brush your teeth. Work on your look. Xenia and I will help you practice.

And Sandra . . . !

Sandra loves you, too.

And if I don't make the grade you'll fire me, right?

Well, I'll just keep loving you, said the lesbian.

11

Judy got the message, or at least some of it. She tried to be more independent, to as we Californians said *work on herself.* She stuck a feather down her throat.

She went to the Pink Apple, and, penetrating the long line of fishnetted buttocks and bare backs with black straps, bought drinks for a dancer named Starfire with whom she wanted to fall in love, maybe just to show Neva. Just as they sat down, a woman in nothing but a jockstrap, black leather fringes and a black bra announced in a deep bass voice: *You will not reveal your choice. We have gotten out the most talented, bootylicious female talent for you . . .*

Frankly, I don't know how people can live in the spotlight like that, said her new friend.

The transwoman said: I wanna be more like Judy Garland, or at least like you—

Sorry, Judy, but you're—

Oh, I know, I know! Especially since I'm so *disgusting . . .*

You're not disgusting, Starfire assured her, perhaps a trifle mechanically. But right now I gotta—

Oh, really? I always heard I was disgusting. But I've lost *almost* forty pounds. You think I could be a showgirl?

Well, in Vegas the minimum height is five foot eight, so you'd qualify there, and maybe you could do the naked-chested part, but frankly, Judy, even in a dump like this—

You mean you've worked in Vegas? Wow, I'm so lucky to meet you!

Nice to meet you, too. And good for you for aspiring to something. Hopefully you'll get . . . But you know what? Vegas stinks. It's a good old boys' town. The Strip looks shiny to outsiders. But we don't party on Friday because we can't afford it. Of course all the money is in stripping. And San Francisco is the worst. And you know what else? I'm tired and the tips are bad tonight, so I think I'll go home.

Can you tell I'm a T-girl?

Never would have guessed, said Starfire sarcastically.

So what would your manager in Vegas have said if . . . if some really beautiful tranny who *passed* wanted to join the chorus line?

I don't know. I think if a guy could pass for a girl, well, our manager Angie hated boob jobs, but if they were beautiful she would let them out onstage. Actually we had a famous tranny named Heavy John Twinkle; I think she got her hip injections way back in the sixties, and that so damaged her body . . . But here you can look like *whatever*, so . . . See ya, Judy.

And Judy went home dreaming! By now she'd lost thirteen pounds, which is not quite forty, but still respectable. She could go her own way—without Neva or the retired policeman—and dominate the line, flaunting her big fat tits, flinging them around and singing "Somewhere Over the Rainbow"!

But no! Neva was her brightest star of all . . . !

12

Indeed, Neva continued to seem perfect in every way—a situation which, whether or not it is possible, becomes fundamentally intolerable, which is why every divinity must sooner or later be overthrown—but by no means too soon, and not without a replacement. Anyhow, we were still far away from *that.*

Oh, thank you, Neva, thank you! we all cried out.

And the lesbian bent over all of us, apparently thousand-armed, so many of us did she hold in her gentle hands.

Onscreen

In those days, I thought you achieved a state of loving by acting out those airy gestures.

NATALIE WOOD, 1966

We *have been* that mind, but we have never *known* it.

CARL JUNG, 1961

There may only be perhaps one or two moments that you feel proud of, and these can be easily missed if someone gets up to buy a bag of popcorn.

NATALIE WOOD, 1966

On the television an airbrushed actress mother and daughter were carefully cuddling, with their long-lashed eyes pretending to see each other but actually alluring us . . .—and not a hair mussed, no smear on the lipstick, oh, no; for a second Xenia could not look away; then she was confiding to Francine: I can sense it on my radar as a sex worker because I am there to be desired and enjoyed, but in the real world I am so clueless. In the real world no one approaches each other anymore.

Three dollars, said Francine.

Here. Honestly, I'm pretty clueless in my real life. I mean, don't you think so? Somebody has to hit me over the head, or I think they're just being friendly.

Come on, said Francine. You're a real smart lady.

I'm used to just rejection after rejection, said Xenia. I'm in my forties, so it's definitely different. I'm a woman, and we get hornier and culturally less desirable.

I desire you! said Judy.

Well, slut, you don't count—but she smiled and laid her hand on Judy's arm.

And Judy, who when she was very high could sometimes see in herself the charming chubby alertness of Natalie Wood's baby photographs, now laughed along with the rest of us as soon as she remembered that no matter what Starfire had said, she and Starfire were both *disgusting.*

Neva was not quite so new to us anymore, but it remained so exciting to just walk past the apartment where she lived and watch people go in and out as we wondered which of them might be close to her through affection, knowledge or proximity. The retired policeman told her: I'll do what it takes to get you out of town.—She replied: It won't be much longer.

Divings of a Mermaid

Two women very much in love do not shun the ecstasy of the senses, nor do they shun a sensuality less concentrated than the orgasm, and more warming. It is this unresolved and undemanding sensuality that finds happiness in an exchange of glances, an arm laid on a shoulder, and is thrilled by the odor of sun-warmed wheat caught in a head of hair.

COLETTE, 1941

We lose our identities quickly in what we're doing, we women. And you give it back to us when you show us that we're basically your sweetheart . . .

JUDY GARLAND, 1955

1

Sandra had been wanting to come and see the straight man, who in despair temporarily removed to Boston. It was going to be in March for sure. She was going to let him know exactly what dates worked for her.

Then at the beginning of February, she kept putting it off, so he finally asked her to please let him know by Saturday.

On Saturday she called but she only had ten minutes because she was very busy.—Well, I keep looking at my schedule and I'm perplexed, she explained. I might be able to get away from Friday night to Sunday night; maybe I could cancel one Friday shift . . .

That's not much time considering the long flight all the way out here, he said, wanting to make it easier for her.

That she accepted gratefully. She was going to call him soon.

He would maybe try and come and see her in March, he said; he knew it was his turn . . .

She did not sound excited.

He said: And by the way, sweetheart, you know that I accept your having another boyfriend. Since it looks now as if you're not going to see me for awhile, I know you need sex and companionship.

She had said she had to break up with that boyfriend in January, before coming to see the straight man. So she had lied. And to this little hint she now made no reply at all.

She did say: You know you're my darling boy . . .—But formerly she would have said something like: You know that I love you more than anyone else.

So he came uninvited. They parted sweetly enough; that was harmless; he went to play liars' dice with Shantelle.

He felt a lonely sorrowful pain around his heart, amorphous, roughly egg-shaped. It went on and on. Finally he decided to consider it pleasant. At once he felt a green thrill of pain; so he was a masochist . . . but the pleasure only went so far.

2

Not knowing what else to do, he made a date with the lesbian.

Like a Suspect Who Loves Only to Please

You don't want a child bride with a flower-mind cluttering up the landscape. Well, that's all right, too. We will be what you want us to be . . . *We will be anything you want* . . . As long as you want it, and make it clear that you do.

JUDY GARLAND, 1955

Thou knowest how like to flame our nature is . . .

THE GODDESS RUMOR, inciting the women of Lemnos to murder their husbands

1

As the transwoman lay beside the retired policeman in his sagging queen-sized bed, languidly high on little pills which were as pink as bloodshot eyes, the shadow of the Erskine Towers rotated faster and faster around the ceiling, like the minute hand of the doomsday clock. She grabbed his penis for support, but everything kept going round and round. She tried to suck him off, but started retching, so with almost intolerable effort, as if her head weighed more than a hundred cannonballs, she dragged her face inch by inch up his sallow belly, gasping, choking down puke until finally she could lay her cheek against his exploding heart. She lay there for a long time. When she could open her eyes without any risk of vomiting, she upraised her head to look down on him. Red and swollen from the pills, he rattled out breaths like links of anchor-chain. She felt happy. Her head crashed down upon his breastbone, and she fell asleep.

A week later they were chugging cans of beer; then she ducked into the bathroom and closed the door so that he wouldn't catch her gobbling those expired mint chocolates she could get for two dollars a handful at Bizzmart; their agreement was that if she ate junk food without his permission he could slap her face ten times *hard*, not that she didn't like that, nor would he have withheld permission to snack had she only groveled in the fashion that they both adored, but nowadays it made her feel more truly herself to hold out on him, keeping secrets, stealing privileges in harmless little ways. Still, she did hate to get fat! Whenever she looked down at her hairy paunch she felt sick. Then she remembered the interesting trick that the lesbian had taught her. Running the water so that he wouldn't hear, she tickled her tonsils with a pipe cleaner and instantly, almost painlessly extruded hot brown vomit into the toilet. Afterward her throat burned and she felt a trifle weak but not the slightest bit nauseated, so why not declare victory? (She'd regressed a little; her weight loss was now only nine pounds.)—*Hey!* he called.—In a moment he would come in, she being forbidden to lock the door.—Almost ready! she cried back. Gargling with his mouthwash, then burying the candy wrappers under the hairy, moldy toilet paper tubes in his wastebasket, she washed her hands, zipped up her purse, splashed perfume on both cheeks, brushed her hair and hastened out in titillated dread of his all-seeing glare. Fortunately or unfortunately, he had turned his face to the television, where *The Wizard of Oz* shimmered in blue and white.

If she could have seen the thoughts shining inside his skull, she would surely have recognized the soft lavender-grey radiance of the lesbian.—Well, was she clueless? By now we all had rights to her, having made her who she was, levered her right into stardom, goddesshood or whatever was called that position over our heads into which all our hands had raised her, so that she floated upon our love, which was our will; it would have been much the same had we borne her merrily out to hang from a streetlamp.

Jocularly slapping his sweetheart's cheeks, he teased her: I know what you're thinking!

Then, to better entertain them both, he bent her over his knee, pulled up her skirt and down her panties, swished the rubber whip, and before landing the first stroke recited: *No star has been the subject of so many rumors as Judy Garland, so to get the truth about this wonderfully clever little star, I subjected her to our low-down treatment.*

They both burst out laughing. They knew how to live!

Then she went out to make money; and on Monday afternoon, while she was folding her fresh-dried laundry at the Kleen-O-Mat and singing a little song whose words consisted of *Neva, Neva, Neva*, he yawned, waddled out of bed, booted up his groaning old desktop computer, which was slow but perfect, not unlike him, swallowed a pain pill and deepened his fieldwork, just for kicks.—The fact that the lesbian kept encouraging Judy to be everything to him left him the opposite of grateful.

His best friend, the tall black security guard in the huge sunglasses, who mourned for the days before Judy had become the sweet and desired one, agreed with him about stop-and-frisk. That was the only way to stop Islamic militants.

Powering down, he put on his pants and slippers, limped out into the hall, verifying that his door was fastened, called the elevator, listened with moderate wonderment to himself wheezing, and down he went, down Jones Street past the good old Hotel Krupa and the restaurant "Chutney," which like him stayed on the far side of trendy, past the parking garage that the neighbors pissed in, down to Ellis and around a homeless couple's tent that should have been ticketed for occluding the sidewalk, down to Turk and then left on Venus Alley. The Box Club wasn't open yet, but the Y Bar sure as shit *was*, with Shantelle, metal-eyed like the goddess Nike in her marble wreath, smoking a guaranteed medicinal reefer in front. Seeing him, she got the giggles: Whazzup, J. D., you wanna handcuff me or something? Oh. You reportin' for booty call? Well, guess what? Your hairy bitch got *caught*, so you're *ridiculous*. Stuck in Neva's flypaper. You feel me, J. D.? You feel what I'm sayin' or *what*?

Want a drink? he groaned.

Oh, sure. I mean, if you're buyin.' Or payin' me to fuck up some dude's face, or *whatever*. But then do I have to buy *you* anything?

Breathing heavily, he made his way into the darkness, with her dancing on sunbeams behind him. Neva was absent; I believe she was currently entertaining Al, who liked to bow down without ever touching her.* There sat Sandra texting her gentleman friend in Los Angeles, *discreetly*, for it was not so much that she sought to keep secrets from the straight man or the lesbian (although that was, to be sure, the practical result) as that these other relationships were unsure; hence describing

---

* Thoreau, 1852: *In this relation we deal with one whom we respect more religiously even than we respect our better selves, and we shall necessarily conduct ourselves as in the presence of God. What presence can be more awful to the lover than that of his beloved?*

them engendered anxiety and suffering in her, because to name meant to fix on and grasp, and grasping at dreamy cobwebs couldn't ever work out, as the lesbian must understand, being herself a mermaid whose translucent fish-flesh might not be all there . . .—not to mention the fact that the straight man must never find out.—But all these things must change, she insisted to herself, and I was the only one who overheard her thoughts. Her phone played the first four notes of "Snow White." Bending over it and rushing toward the ladies' room, she murmured: I don't know; I don't know. He has *not* told his wife that he is doing this.

Two workers in waterproof orange coveralls commenced their liquid afternoon breakfast, tucking their yellow helmets between their feet as they sat at the counter, grinning over at Victoria, who always courted our Neva very sweetly, as had always been her habit, especially when she was at her most predatory; farther into the darkness, Xenia exchanged something for something with Francine, then skittered out. Victoria picked up Xenia's half-empty beer, sniffed it and made a face. The construction workers fell silent.

Meanwhile the retired policeman marched up to the bar. He felt dizzy, and his legs tingled all the way up to his knees. For an instant he thought he saw a pair of almost naked legs shining in the darkness.

Usual? said Francine, who was old enough to remember watching television reruns of the occasion when Martina Navratilova played tennis against the heterosexual blonde Chris Evert. Oh, did Francine look it! Maybe that was why he almost liked her.

No, make it a triple. Or two doubles, I mean, what the fuck. Shantelle, what do you want?

You'll never know.

Sighing, Francine poured out three jiggers of Old Crow into a family-sized shotglass, then made a Peachy Keen over ice for Shantelle. She said: Sixteen dollars.

The retired policeman laid down a twenty.—Keep it, he said.

J. D., have you forgotten? You owed me ten dollars anyhow. And if you need more—

My bad, he said. He gave her another twenty. She returned him fourteen. He left the four singles on the counter and stuffed the ten down Shantelle's cleavage.

Gettin' fresh with me? she said. You want some company?

Misery loves company. Neva makes us miserable. Therefore . . .

Watch it, said Francine.

Focusing on business, Shantelle now said: J. D., lemme introduce myself. The first thing you need to know is that I love cocaine.

Look, Shantelle, let's you and I do something about that Neva bitch.

He was playing and testing more than anything else. But he was not unready when Shantelle rose up purple-faced and breathing hard, meaning to punch him in the face, at which he reached across the bar, wrapped his hand around a heavy bottle of bourbon and sat waiting and watching her delightedly. The construction workers applauded.—Break it up, you two! said Francine, who obviously considered Shantelle to be the threat because instead of challenging the retired policeman's hold on his weapon, she bent behind the bar and rose up with her baseball bat, facing Shantelle—who thought better of her impulse.

All right, she said. I'm over it. But, mister, don't go hatin' on Neva.

That's not her name, he explained. He had taken it upon his shoulders to guide us through the maze that was the lesbian.

Sit back down, Shantelle, said Francine. Here's a refill for each of you, on the house. Next topic.

As uncouth as the man who would part two lesbians, the retired policeman slugged down his free drink. Then he inquired: Does *anybody* hate Neva?

Don't *be* like that, warned Francine . . .—because if only the lesbian turned out to be real, then we who were lucky enough to love and be loved by her might become real by reflection, in just the same way that moonlight can actually deserve to be called sunlight.

The retired policeman suddenly felt dreary. He whom it now seemed that no one ever desired sat bent over the bar, drinking watered-down whiskey as his envies went flittering like those two departing construction workers. What did he even wish for? Being retired, he wasn't supposed to care about anything. Shantelle, whose heart was likewise armored like Saint Michael, sat smoothing her nails with an emery board, wondering if he and she would do business; meanwhile he imagined sucking the hollow pimpled ruby breast of the light fixture en route to the toilets; he glanced at that television screen on which a huge blue-and-green keyboard played itself while a tiny human figure toiled back and forth in front of it; while at the bar, where by late afternoon men would be leaning on their elbows shouting for wine, three middle-aged G-girls, evidently employees of some dreary bank or insurance company, sat slumming it on their lunch hour.

This is the line of our interpretation, explained the bossiest. So I said, you just tell your accountant . . .

Well, but the schedules . . .

It's so *amazing.*

They're fielding the referrals, but they don't actually hear back.

Oh, that's just silly. It really is. And then that impacts our releases.

No that's no problem at all. If you could send me the information . . .

The retired policeman raised his glass to them. The bossiest said: Eww, did you see that old perv?

Excuse me, said Francine. He's a regular, and a friend of mine, so you be nice.

The G-girls laughed at her. For a moment he watched their images beside the pink neon sign of the Y Bar shining backward in the long mirror. There came the bluish flickering of a cell phone in the darkness. Xenia came back in; she was telling Francine: No, that was the first time I ever saw her sick, and he wondered if she might be referring to Karen Strand.

He saw Shantelle's reflection spying on his, so he crooked his finger and she came.

He said: Know why I like you? Because your shit don't stink. You don't hate on Neva or any fuckin' soul. If some gangbangers raped your mother you'd scurry to church and pray for them, *wouldn't you*? Oh, no, he continued as her face began to snarl, I'm just foolin' around. You want to do business?

Francine, gimme another.

Seven dollars.

Don't look at me. J. D.'s paying; he *promised.*

Sure. Now answer the fuckin' question. What bitch do you like to hate on?

You. I bet you're some kinda Republican.

Who else? Come on; you must have a shit list.

Well, Francine's always bitching at me about one thing or another. And I go here and I go there, and just when I'm about comfortable, Neva informs me it's time to go, so she can fuck somebody else. Makes me want to slap her. And then you . . .

Drink some water, said Francine.

I get so tired of Neva kicking me out. I mean, what the *fuck*?

Poor baby, he muttered.

She never just lets me *be* with her, Shantelle continued. If I wanna stay all night, she starts bitching at me.

Uh huh, he said. So let's do a deal—

He had long since begun to conceive of the lesbian as some kind of spider-goddess who squatted high in the darkness, weaving tricks and trouble, electrifying the transwoman's wasted face.

When she came in, he stood up. She approached him, and Francine silently mixed her gin and tonic. By now those two had an understanding: Neva's drinks were on the house, and this fact was not to be mentioned.

Just at that moment I who like the retired policeman kept abreast of everything overheard Xenia asking Judy if maybe she deserved to be lonely; Judy snuffled, somewhere between hurt and cross; then Xenia said: Well, I know I do.—And right then those two might have gotten closer, but Judy insisted on complaining of unwellness, and for once Francine declined to give or sell her a pill! Then Sandra came in, evidently suffering from the chills, at which Xenia decided that it was her turn to vent about something left hurtfully unsaid at Sandra's birthday, which had been last week and to which I was not invited; poor Sandra of course reassured and apologized. Then, with the heliotropism of sunflowers, they too turned their heads toward the lesbian.

Like any true blue hero, the retired policeman had locked his eyes on her from the get-go. As silently as a ballerina falling to earth, she sat down beside him. Shantelle stood close, hoping to invade their private business.

The lesbian said: J. D., are you okay? You don't look well.

He triumphantly replied: Guess what, Karen? I tracked down E-beth, and she *does not* like you.

A quicksilver flash of anguish blighted her face; this delighted him.

2

Elizabeth Jackson was a widowed lesbian, aged fifty-nine. Hence she was eight years older than Karen Strand, whose seduction by her most definitely constituted statutory rape. He'd known it all along. Now she called herself Eliza. That was what those perverts did (and Karen Strand was a case in point). They changed their names, so they could keep on offending against the tenderest little cunts in our great society. Oh, yes: Elizabeth used to be E-beth, before which she was Betty Ann, who for all he knew used to invite the neighbor girls over to play doctor with her little sister, because wouldn't that be the hallmark of a stinking lez?

He rang the bell, and she opened the door, waiting: a slender, attractive old woman with silver bangs.

Are you Ms. Jackson? he said.

What are you selling?

He showed his badge.—Officer Slager, S.F.P.D., he said. Ms. Jackson, I'd like to talk to you about a person in your past.

Who is it?

May I come in, ma'am?

If you have to.

She stood aside, and he entered. There were three well-kept cats side by side on the sofa. Rainbow crystals hung in the window. Through the back window he could see a hot tub with steam rising out of it.

Since she did not invite him to sit down, he picked the most comfortable-appearing armchair, and she frowned a little, watching him with her hands on her hips. Before she could grow angrier he stared into her eyes and inquired: Do you know the name Karen Strand?

No, she said instantly.

Now that's interesting, he said. People tell me different.

Which people? she alertly demanded.

Well, Karen Strand, for one. Why would she lie about knowing you?

What's this about?

There's been some trouble, he said happily.

What trouble?

Now it's your turn to answer questions. Are you going to keep on denying that you know Karen Strand?

I don't know her, not anymore.

But you know who she is. Why'd you tell me different?

So I made a mistake, she said, and it was all he could do not to laugh because she reminded him of the defendant who in his first interrogation confessed only to digging secret burial pits. So what? I haven't seen her in years.

How many?

At least thirty.

And why did you part ways?

Lack of common interest.

What was your prior common interest?

The woman looked on the verge of being incensed. She had an authority problem. But he had to hand it to her, the way she instantly mastered herself, in order to conceal from him their long gone *common interest*, which of course had been bearded clam.—Officer, she said, you're not being forthcoming.

Neither are you. Now, Ms. Jackson, this is a serious situation—

She's missing?

You said it, not me. How much do you care?

What line of questioning is this?

Oho, so you've been questioned before! Practice makes perfect, I hope. Now, Ms. Jackson—

How long has she been missing?

First maybe you can tell me about your association.

Well, Karen was my, I mean, I was a sort of mentor to her when she was in high school. A very troubled girl. When she started stalking me, I had to end it.

How long did your association continue?

Oh, I would say maybe two years.

And she threatened you?

Nothing like that. She wouldn't leave me alone.

What do you mean by that?

Just what I said.

So you were her mentor. What did you teach her?

Oh, social skills, life skills. Karen had no friends. She was very needy, and I—

Took an *interest.*

Officer, I don't like your tone.

Can you describe your last contact with her?

It was such a long time ago, said E-beth. I don't know if I can . . .

How old was she?

Well, she was in high school, as I said. Sixteen, seventeen . . .

And then it ended?

Well, not right away. Karen became, well, insufferable.

And you knew her in Vallejo?

That's right.

When were you last back there?

Ages ago, said the old woman.

Do you know Karen's mother?

Oh, is she still alive? I almost never saw her. There was some tension between her and Karen, so I, well, I tried to take Karen's side. I was never inside that house. And after I told Karen not to contact me I certainly had no reason to see her mother.

So the mother didn't like you.

It was mutual.

Aha. And how would you describe Karen?

Very self-absorbed. She couldn't acknowledge anyone other than herself. It was very wearing to be around her, actually.

What made her that way?

Officer Slager, why not tell me what all this is about?

Karen has been missing for a long time—

How long?

Maybe not long, and maybe for thirty years, in which case someone has taken her identity. Do you recognize this person?

He showed her a photograph of Neva. E-beth looked at it and said: Well, it looks like Karen. But I don't really know. I hope nothing has happened to her. But as I said it's been many years and we never had much in common.

Ms. Jackson, what aren't you telling me?

Glaring at him, she said: Please get out of my house.

Chuckling, then wheezing, he rose and said: At Jingle's Bar they still remember you as *killer.* Apparently you lured quite a few young girls in there.

She started trembling.—Get out. I know my rights.

He said: The statute of limitations never runs out for predators like you. So I just may see you around.

She sat down suddenly.

He limped to the door. Then he said: Karen may be dead. If you help me find out what happened to her, I'll forget about this other old history. Sure has been a pleasure.

3

So he now taunted the lesbian, whose glassy demeanor was as potentially damning as an accused murderer's public indifference to a missing child's whereabouts.

She said she never had much in common with you, Karen. She said you were just a self-absorbed little cunt. You couldn't acknowledge anyone other than yourself, she said. It was very wearing to be around you, she said. Any response?

She was silent.

I know what you're going to say. You'll say *I love her.* Right, Karen? Don't you just *love* to turn the other cheek?

That's right, said the lesbian.

I called her a pedophile, he explained. Because she *is.* Right?

I do still love her, said the lesbian. I always will.

But she got her hooks into you when you were underage. I said to her, I said: *The statute of limitations never runs out for perverts like you.* That shut her up. Because *she turned you out.* And from what I learned at Jingle's, she sounds like a serial molester. Maybe even concurrent for all I fuckin' know. I'll bet when she was doing you she had other pussy on the side. And then she fired you, right? She got tired of self-absorbed little Karen. Well, guess who's the self-absorbed one? Well, Karen? Or are you Karen? You gonna answer me or will I have to escalate this?

The lesbian answered: You don't care about her except to get to me. And I won't discuss the lives of other people.

So commendable! A gangbanger refuses to snitch on his confederates, and instantly he becomes a man of honor. In your case it's Stockholm Syndrome. Are you familiar with that cultural reference?

Sure, said the lesbian.

All right. Maybe you *are* older than you look. So lemme ask you something. How do your lovey-dovey values square with the case of a woman who preys on young girls?

Maybe she loves them.

In other words, you take the Fifth. You refuse the polygraph. Have it your way, Karen. I'll keep digging up dirt. How does that suit you?

Okay, said the lesbian.

Becoming professorial, he instructed her: There's a certain kind of suspect who loves only to please. Usually it's a female thing. That type, she'll confess to anything, just to put a smile on the arresting officer's face. Have I nailed you, Karen? Have I?

Sure. Tell me how to please you, she said.

4

By then his ladylove, whose weight loss presently totalled seventeen pounds, had returned several times to the Buddha Bar in search of that retired dancer Helen who was once so gracious, but she never found her. So after doing business with one of those two construction workers in waterproof orange coveralls who sometimes patronized the Y Bar (while she was sucking him off he said: There's nothin' worse than *cold, wet, windy*, except bein' in a tall metal structure when there's lightning. Yeah, babe. I'm sayin' to myself, I'm gonna get fried! Yeah, babe; go faster. Well, it was rainin' so hard that we couldn't see shit and I had to tell the guy who was runnin' the crane what to do. Yeah, babe! Oh, *yeah*, babe! Now *beat* it, tranny bitch!), she clipclopped to the Pink Apple to re-parasitize Starfire—who, strange to say, appeared less than delighted, but Judy, who'd learned a few tricks from Shantelle, not to mention her own worst customers, slipped her two goofballs and promised to (a) pay for all the drinks and (b) get out before the busy time started. Once the first goofball kicked in, Starfire chewed up the second. Then her pupils enlarged and she began stroking Judy's hair quite tenderly, saying: The world of trannies must be so different. I think that they're really suffering. But you . . . Show business . . . I think that my mind is so divorced from show business . . .

I wanna be a showgirl so bad, Judy whined, sucking on Starfire's earlobe.

Hey, that feels . . . Cut it out! I tend to be a person that's really in the moment. I tend to get really annoyed with showgirls because they live in a fantasy. This is not the real world. They're so obsessed. I was in New York, I was in Broadway; they're so in love with that whole thing.

Wow! You were on Broadway! I mean, tell me about *that*!

The girls I looked at, I was training with, I looked to them, not to Baryshnikov. There's no crime in reaching for something . . .

Who's Baryshnikov?

You know, it's just a job. I hate it very much as a job where you punch a time clock and you have to park in the employee lot. Many years ago in Vegas, before the gangsters got out, showgirls were treated like royalty: Park where you want; just had to come in dressed to the nines. I could never get my head around punching a time clock and then taking your clothes off.

Well, I bet you were the favorite!

No, I was not the favorite. Judy, you know what you need? Botox. I think you should just take it, and be realistic. Well, it looks weird, puffy lips and . . . Oh, my, I lost my train of thought. What the fuck did you give me? But it feels so good . . .

Starfire, could I please please kiss you, just once?

Judy, I'm not a dyke.

Oh, sorry, sorry! I mean . . . You could just spit into my mouth or something.

Okay, I'll kiss you on the cheek, but . . . man, I feel goddamned *good*!

Can I buy you another drink?

What the hell . . . I wanna . . . gimme another Patriot Dry and then I'll go and piss it out. You know, you're kind of . . .

Feeling topnotch, Judy went to the bar, ordered, paid and provided. Right away she began stroking Starfire's hair. She giggled and laid her head on Judy's shoulder. The barman shot them a grim look, but what the fuck did those lovebirds care?

Now, Starfire, Judy whispered, tell me about your body. I just *love* your body.

I actually have very bad body self-image. I was the object of everyone's harassment. Very flatchested, while my other girlfriends had just such great boobs. So I had to get a personality. It makes you dig deeper. You don't have to like the things you go through. I always have a little bit of anger inside me. I was like the ugly girl on the bench. So I wanted to get out. I don't need this shit. I can get out there and do whatever I want to do. Like right now I can . . . But some girls don't know anything else. But right now . . . Right now I feel sick . . .

Then she threw up all over Judy.

5

I admit that there is far too much vomiting in this book, and I keep telling Judy to stop making it happen. But as you know, it was fundamentally Neva's fault.

Judy tried to lead her date home, and take *extra special* care of her, but Starfire preferred to stagger out cursing, so Judy, terrified of the angry bartender, fled in her own fashion and direction. She got home, showered in her clothes, showered naked, went to bed and happily masturbated, imagining that she was in a costume bristling with faux diamonds, emeralds, sapphires and rubies—in fact, she was the queen of the showgirl lineup and Neva kept begging her to come back but Judy just *wouldn't*! Neva was weeping, and then Judy said . . .

6

Two afternoons later, the lesbian, postponing her other commitments, visited the Pink Apple to apologize on Judy's behalf. Starfire was still furious, but money, sympathy and charm worked their own effect.—I mean, said the dancer, what are you, her mother or something?

Something like that, said the lesbian.

But you fuck her.

The lesbian nodded.

Well, that's *just* like a mother! All right, Neva, what do you want?

Someday she's going to be on her own. And she's not realistic—

She's a *creep*! She *drugged* me and got *all over me*—

Starfire, she—

My real name's Amy.

Hi.

Hi.

Amy, the thing is that Judy actually had a success once or twice at the Y Bar, before a man assaulted her. Now she's not confident. And just a little applause made her so happy . . . !

Because she was a tranny on amateur night! In this town people are good sports; they give it up for trannies when they show some heart, but that's . . .

So you're saying Judy has heart.

Yeah. Now I think about it, one time I did see her act, but it must not have been at the Y Bar because I never enter that stinking joint. And, sure, she was so *out there* that it was a hoot! An easygoing, tipsy audience on a Friday night in a trans-friendly town, and a T-girl stoned out of her mind who'd do anything to please, well, that can be a winning formula sometimes, but does she understand her limitations? And by the way, Neva, *do not* encourage her to bother me again *ever*, because if she does I'll punch her right in her fat hairy chin. Do you get that?

Okay, said the lesbian.

And, Neva, I'm trying not to be mean, but aren't you kind of an enabler? Because Judy basically took advantage of me. She has the M.O. of a molester.

I love Judy.

Well, where does that leave *me*?

I love you, too, said the lesbian.

Bullshit! Although I will admit that you're pretty hot. Not that I go for women really.

You wanna come over and see me?

Sure, Neva. Text me your phone number and we'll . . . Now look. I remember one night when we were all up there in the line in Vegas and there was a woman, obviously a newlywed, sitting in King's Row, and her husband was sitting there big-eyed, admiring all these naked tits, and I'm looking at this woman, truly bent out of shape, and she didn't realize what we looked like at home; it was all illusion. Now, to create illusion you have to be a little cold. You have to see yourself for who you are. And your Judy wants to sit in King's Row looking at *herself* in the line, and that's not possible. She can only be in one place at a time. Which one is it?

King's Row, said the lesbian. Or even the back row would—

Exactly. I mean, she's not like you and me. Admit it, Neva: You and I are stars together. And I, I find it very strange to be saying this, because I'm not a dyke, but I find you very attractive. Do you think you could like me?

I love you, said the lesbian.

Starfire kissed her. Then she *really* kissed her. She said: Well, I wanna know, the way I am set up right now, am I guaranteed a job in your bed *forever*?

Sure, said the lesbian. Everything's forever.

Wow! You even have a sense of humor! Oh, well. What the fuck. It's all illusion . . .

7

By now Shantelle often came over drunk or high. Sometimes she would slap the lesbian around. Mostly she hit her open-handed on the cheek, although sometimes she walloped her on the buttocks. As Xenia used to tell me: We do eroticize violence. What else are we gonna do with it? We absorb it. We have to deal with it. I enjoy getting slapped by the right girl; Judy's into it, Sandra wants it without realizing it . . .—so why shouldn't Neva?

A hard slap in the mouth, a little blood . . .—Oh, I'm sorry, Neva, so sorry . . . I didn't mean it; it's just that I got fuckin' jealous—

Hit me some more if you want to.

No. If I do, I might kill you.

That's okay.

But then you'd get away from me. *Are you trying to run away, bitch?*

Shantelle, I'm right here. Now let me get on top of you . . .

What would have happened if Thomas or Peter, craving to be closer to Jesus than anyone, had tried to gain His exclusive attention, and threatened to kill Him had He bestowed love on any other disciple? Would He have offered Himself to such a murder, thereby saving Judas from guilt? Would this sacrifice have been as acceptable to God as the judicial execution He suffered on the cross, which symmetrically cancelled out Adam and Eve's violation of the law about eating certain apples?—It was these questions that I solved for all time in my room at the Saint Brendan, with my feet up and a rum and sodapop in my hand.

8

And we almost never have sex anymore, said Hunter. Lately I feel like I'm nothing more than one of your peripheral friends.

Seven dollars, said Francine, and just as Sandra, urgently pulling the lips of her vulva apart, prepared for Neva's touch, the barmaid shucked the cap of another Old German Lager for Xenia. She turned it over because sometimes there was a contest involving lucky numbers, but this inside was merely wet, cold and blank.

An ancient Vietnamese hooker came in and said: I'll take a Diablo Lite, I said a Diablo Lite, and I'll be right back from the restroom. Hi, Xenia. Hi, Shantelle.

Unsmiling, Francine said: Pay first, Mai.

Fuck you! said the old lady, storming out.

Actually, said Xenia, you're the one who turns me down for sex over and over. In the nighttime you're too tired; in the morning you're not in the mood. So I'd say you're deceiving yourself.

All you want is to eat my pussy, said Hunter. And there are many many times when I can't come and you could just penetrate me with my Pink Lizzie or—

But I don't want to penetrate you if you're not in the mood. You make it seem as if you're just lying there being a hole for me, and that's like rape.

It just strikes you that way because of your history, said Hunter. I *refuse* to let you call it rape. *That's* bad faith—

Hey, you two, said Francine. Keep it cool.

Besides, said Hunter, you're not interested in me. All you care about is Neva.

You know I love you—

And all you ever do is complain. You know what I mean. Why don't you go to the doctor and do something about it?

Yes, Hunter.

Yes, Hunter means that you're not going to do anything. And you've been dishonest with me. I'm not willing to be your number two paramour. Or number six, or—

Xenia kept quiet.

Neva can do it, said Hunter. We all agree she's one of a kind. But you're actually a—

Watch it, said Francine.

You pretend this and that, and I won't do it anymore, said Hunter. I'm finished.

Fine, said Xenia, losing patience. Francine, how much do I owe?

For you or both?

For both.

Fourteen dollars.

Xenia threw down a five and ten and began to walk out, while Hunter wept into her drink. In came the lesbian.

9

And of course when Hunter told me about her times with you, said Sandra, she—

She's basically a lesbian, the straight man interrupted. She only fucked me to get back at Xenia, and I fucked her because I was lonely and you were—

Well, darling, but what she said confirmed what I already felt, that I want you to make love to me so I can lose myself in those beautiful moments. When you and I are together, when you hold me and touch me, there's nobody else.

Except Neva, he said. What's wrong with *that* picture?

10

Neva, not herself, which is to say mildly affected by marijuana, looked over the muted glitterings of the bottles behind the bar, as if she might be counting them, and then, as if the transwoman had just now asserted this particular issue, told her almost coldly: To say that I'm a *lesbian* is true, but how much is it *really* true? I love Richard and Al and J. D. and—

Are you okay? asked Francine.

And it makes me feel as if I'm nobody . . .

These words reminded Judy of the black girl Letitia for whom she used to be so crazy, the one with the sleek voice and shining black hair and, oh, that stunning white smile . . . !

I don't know that it's a lesbian attribute, the lesbian continued bitterly, but I guess if it were it would help people like you to simplify me.

And Judy woke up shocked; she'd been dreaming of Letitia all along! Our collective sweetheart would never say anything so unpleasant!

Dreaming again, she woke up in the lesbian's arms, with a thrilling tingly feeling unlike her craving to be held and praised by the retired policeman immediately after he had beaten her.

Coming Down

The point is that it is impossible to retain equanimity in the midst of pleasures which are not only intense, but also abnormal and harmful, unless one has often disdained permissible pleasure . . .

PLUTARCH, bef. *ca.* 120 A.D.

United soules are not satisfied with embraces, but desire each to be truely the other, which being impossible, their desires are infinite, and must proceed without a possibility of satisfaction.

SIR THOMAS BROWNE, *ca.* 1643

1

Xenia took another turn with the lesbian. Soon she was in heaven—and not alone, Neva being both companion and cause . . . !—They climaxed. They kissed. They rested. And slowly, like an almost buoyant object descending into the ocean, that peaceful post-amorous fulfillment began to withdraw, leaving Xenia suddenly chilly.

Again her turn was over. She went home, trudging through the clammy darkness. Lying down in her unmade bed and playing with herself in order to milk out just a trifle more pleasure from that fulfillingness which still inhabited her (come to me now; come to me now), she began to feel cold. Rolling herself up in her blanket, she lay on her back, warm again, happy just to *be*, which was one lesson that loving the lesbian had taught her. For nearly an hour that feeling nourished her, although the air in the room kept getting chillier. She wrapped the blanket around her head, and that helped, but whenever she inhaled, the chill came inside her. Then her forehead began to ache. How lonely she was! Should she make up with Hunter? She was shivering; her teeth were chattering; was she coming down with the flu? The wise thing would be, as always, self-medication—for instance, two of those analgesic tablets which were marketed in a little pink bottle as Happy Mense—for today's working women who won't let *any* time of the month get them down! But they were in the bathroom, a good thirty steps away. So she put off going, just as she sometimes did when her bladder woke her up in the middle of the night and she told herself: Just another half-hour, since I'm so sleepy . . . And the same denouement announced itself; she couldn't delay any longer. This headache was a nasty one; she never got migraines, but maybe they felt like this. Unwinding the covers and sitting up, she trembled in the dire cold. She placed the soles of her bare feet on the ice-cold floor. Her toes went numb. As soon as she stood up she felt nauseous, but she hardly suspected that she was going to throw up; without any warning contraction of her stomach, the vomit rose up effortlessly into her mouth, thick and coarse; at first she tried to swallow it back down but then she choked on it, so it spewed down her nightgown and onto the carpet. Lifting up the hem to retain as much of it as she could, she waddled to the bathroom, and just before she reached the toilet a much stronger spasm overtook her, spraying vomit onto the mirror. She took off her nightgown and dropped it into the laundry basket. Then she scrubbed up what she could with both towels. Tomorrow, when she felt better, she would do it right. The chattering of her teeth hurt her ears. Maybe a hot shower would help her; she needed to wash herself anyhow. Stepping into the comforting warm stream, she gained an instant of ease before she began exploding with diarrhea.

2

Right away came Hunter, complaining to her heart's content about Xenia, then getting raptured in the lesbian's arms, as if this long high climax comprised, if this will not sound too strange, her best chance of freedom.—Lacing up her black shitkicker boots, she said: Neva, I feel so good and tough right now, I wish I could grow a moustache! I want hair on my arms! I want to fuck you with a six-foot cock! Oh, Neva, you're the friggin' *best.*

I love you, too, said Neva.

Humming and singing (she happened to be very very high), Hunter walked all the way down to the bus stop catty-corner from the Diana Market on Folsom, where she'd first met Xenia; she was half-hoping to see her right there—as likely as a sudden rising of the Decker Electric Company's two articulated security doors. A motorcycle screamed past her ear, then after three breaths came a black car and a white car, and she began to realize that unless she could be in Neva's arms forever she was *lost.*

3

It's really too cold . . . , said Sandra.

Ignoring this, the straight man crawled to the foot of the bed and began to lick her vulva, an act which up until now had infallibly aroused her, but after a good ten minutes she had not responded in any way except to lay her hand on the top of his head, so he stopped, presently returning to her side, after which some moments passed, and then she said: Don't you like making love with me anymore?

You weren't in the mood, he explained.

You still could have gone inside me.

When you're not aroused it's not arousing for me, either.

Mmm, she said; then *nothing* was said until he told her: I had better do some work.—He had given away his white dog and moved back in with Sandra, so he felt unappreciated. In the bathroom he imagined the lesbian squatting over him, slowly impaling herself on his penis, supporting herself one-handed on the headboard so that to him she felt weightless.

4

Whenever he called nowadays, Sandra was all business—friendly and intellectual and social and helpful, just not intimate—although she always said *I love you.*

He called and Sandra did not call back; she *always* called back.

He called and Sandra picked up the phone and said she had only ten minutes; she *never* said that.

She talked about politics, not her longing to lose herself in holding him and making love.

Scratching his baldness, he said: How are you feeling?

Oh, everything's fine . . .

Has your life changed somehow?

It's all the same. Well, I'd better go now—

Could I ask one more question? I won't take long—

Of course.

Are you in another relationship now?

What do you mean? she said.

Well, are you having sex with someone else?

Well, that boy, I've seen him again.

You've seen him? You mean you've had sex with him?

Yes.

He felt a very strange complex emotion, not quite jealousy or masochistic pleasure, but sadness and sickness that he could not help but further stimulate, as if scratching a scab to make it bleed. He felt very very hollow.

Then Sandra's phone rang. Her face shone; it was Neva.

5

Meanwhile the lesbian's breasts were inexplicably aching, and she too felt nauseous. Don't dare claim that *she* was poisoning us!—It came to be the transwoman's turn, and the next day both partners felt nauseous. But hadn't Neva *always* been queasy, or was the retired policeman lying to me about that part?—With the mother now finally schooled by the daughter's physical repulsion, it had become the lesbian's duty to unschool her, loving her unconditionally. But couldn't she put it off a tiny bit longer? She could well remember her with her mouth wide open and her eyes screwed shut, her tongue loosely floating and her fingers whirring like a weaver's, warping and wefting the joy she needed; now Neva knew exactly how to give it to her. Once upon a time her mother had been a darkhaired young woman with a wedding ring on her hand, standing nude, gripping her crotch with both hands, staring down at the place from whence her pleasure came. Now she was yellowish and wrinkled, still putting on lipstick as if that could make her young. Her pitilessness had decayed into mere loneliness. Meanwhile the transwoman was slowly licking round and round the lesbian's clitoris, then gliding her tongue up and down the vestibule of her slit while her middle finger twirled deep inside and her forefinger went right to the hilt up the lesbian's anus; while the lesbian, flushed and burning hot, sweating deliciously, rolling and moaning, reached down to stroke Judy's hand, moaning and coming, but not at the peak yet, climaxing on and on in slow plenitude with no need ever to finish while the transwoman, her heart pounding and her head hammering from love, lost understanding of who she was and what she was doing but continued to be carried along so happily by the incomprehensible doing of it, sinking deeper into the lesbian's cunt which was now the world to her; the lesbian's sweaty moans might as well have been her own; and when the lesbian finally shouted in orgasm the transwoman rushed on top of her, entering her with her anachronistically huge penis while she slammed her dripping mouth against the lesbian's, sucking her tongue and lips, riding her faster and faster until they both screamed. The lesbian was bright red and sweating crazily into the sodden sheets. Giggling, the transwoman approached her ear and whispered: My judgment might be, as they say, drug impaired, but how would you like another pill?—You have more? said the lesbian, thrilled. I think can handle more.—Are you sure? This stuff's from Selene, so it's gonna be good . . .—Yes yes *yes*! cried the lesbian, kissing her with innumerable loud lip-smacks, so the transwoman, thrilled to feel loved, got the other two doses from her purse, and they both laughed over the words **NOT FOR HUMAN CONSUMPTION**.

While the lesbian snored loudly beside her, Judy was slowly, slowly coming down off the drug; she began to prickle with icy chills, so she held the lesbian tight, gripping her by the breasts, and the lesbian snorted in her sleep, stopped breathing for an instant, then began panting slowly. When her eyes finally opened, they were darker and greener than usual.

Judy had a haunted feeling, as if something were lamenting far away. She crept home to sniff the lesbian's blouse and masturbate, but once she got into bed all she could do was shiver. The good news was that she'd lost eighteen pounds.

At two in the afternoon the lesbian dropped in to the Y Bar for a pick-me-up, but after Francine poured out her gin and tonic and she picked up the glass, the first tiny swallow stung her stomach. Well, but isn't gin supposed to be hard on digestion? The dark and narrow room felt very hot. Lifting the glass to her lips, she swished around no more than a teaspoonful on her tongue, just to distract herself from the stomach ache, but her head began to throb, her saliva thickened; then suddenly she became certain that she would vomit. Rushing to the ladies' restroom, she bent over the stinking toilet and retched. For a long time the badness refused to come up; finally she tickled her throat and won. Then she returned to us.

Are you okay, hon? said Francine.

Then Hunter came in weeping. Wrapping both arms around her, the lesbian took her home, where her guest railed against Xenia, who had introduced her to meth of all kinds, including one very high-class kind which made her very nauseous, so that next day Xenia, whose lovingkindness even I consider limited, dropped her off at a Dayglo Diner to use the ladies' room to vomit in, after which while she was waiting for Xenia she sat in the grass literally foaming at the mouth. A man asked if she were all right. She said that she was. Then Xenia took her to the hospital and dropped her off. The nurse asked what was wrong. Hunter, naively believing that she had to be honest, confessed to the meth, after which the nurse grew disapproving and even cruel, insisting on catheterizing her for the urine test even though she was perfectly capable of peeing into a cup without any help; fearing this procedure, Hunter argued and eventually wept, after which the nurse rewarded her with a nice tranquilizer before the catheter went in. And now Xenia had friggin' *left* her!—C'mere, honey, said the lesbian . . .

Half an hour later, a suit-and-tie man who sometimes came on show nights was sitting on Hunter's stool, explaining to his cell phone about business books, strong free cash flow, servicing existing customers and getting the key players to buy in; while the retired policeman was telling the straight man about the last time he requalified, on a recent windy day when rain blew in all the shooters' faces; he broke leather faster than the best of them, outshooting that stuck-up range officer twat who was just beginning her second clip when he had exhausted his third, so that all the other shooters froze into awe, after which they wanted him to go up against the asshole from Fish and Game, but *that* dude had a cutaway holster, which wasn't sporting, so the retired policeman said fuck it.—That's great, said the straight man, you sure showed them something.—But how was the straight man truly feeling? What did he care about guns? He remembered how his former lover, the one before Sandra, had once after their breakup permitted him to stay in her guest room, but acted very dry and almost grim with him, not asking him about his life or family even though he politely served her such questions, and in the morning through the bedroom door he heard her warmly laughing with her other guest, a young woman whom she barely knew. That was how he felt among all of us at the Y Bar, except sometimes with Sandra and very occasionally with Francine (almost never with the retired policeman, whose scrupulous inflictions of logic wore him out). As for Neva, he believed her to be the one who always went in search of whoever was lost.

On the brighter side of the bar, Sandra, whose friendship with the straight man both he and she now called *amicable*, was meanwhile informing all of us *special friends*: There's a really beautiful video of *The Judy Garland Show* when she and Barbra Streisand sing this medley together and it's so beautiful the way their voices are blending together, but it's so tragic, because Judy Garland had this great talent and couldn't keep it together, whereas Barbra Streisand *could* get it together . . . And, and I can't keep it together—I can't! Suddenly I feel *so sad* . . . !

Never mind, hon, said Francine. You getting the chills?

How did you know?

We all go through *whatever* once she sends us home. Here, baby. Chew this up quick so nobody sees; it's five hundred milligrams . . .

The straight man watched Sandra palm something into her mouth, and instinctively the retired policeman watched the straight man, who was remembering Neva's hair still swirling across his shoulder when she began to turn away, at which he, hunching down his head, unable to get enough of her, realized that her fragrance was light; it was the light itself. But he could often smell Sandra on her, and sometimes he could taste her on Sandra; how could he take to himself, to himself only, our lesbian, the lovely one, straining her against him, sucking her lips into his mouth, pulling her ever more tightly into his soul, until Sandra and the rest of us could no longer bar him from his peace? He loved Sandra, but she had sawn into his heart, which is why the enthusiastic, almost mirthful hatred in his smiling gaze reminded the retired policeman of the time he had arrested a wife-beater in the act, and presently appeared to testify against him, at which the monster, who had been foolish enough to submit to cross-examination, stood at the witness stand stuttering and giggling, then blurted out: If she had fallen downstairs and died you'd still convict me with some other circumstantial evidence! . . .—and in due time pled insanity.

Meanwhile the transwoman sat home with diarrhea. When she saw the mirror image of her collapsing face, she told it: Bad news, Judy. Not even your old fans will tune in.—And that night we all waited for the golden-crowned lesbian, she whom we all believed to know the truth and now lay in bed, feeling hot and tired, with chilly prickles in her scalp.

But what about *her* emotions? Well, she had a sense of ready calm as she never used to when she had been a little girl named Karen, knowing that her mother would presently arrive in her bed. At least she no longer had to anticipate the touch of that hand; and at the Y Bar she never needed to believe the promises of her own lovers (this was one reason why we loved her).—Aside from an embrace and a cheek-kiss apiece, the mother now never tried . . . well, it is true that often when they promenaded down the block, she would clutch Neva's arm for support;

the poor lady was getting very old.—When she first received her power on the island, the lesbian had worried about practicing love without feeling it, but of course with her antennae perceiving the vibrations of Xenia's faraway silent anguish and of Sandra's longing probing thoughts, that apprehension most certainly solved itself. Had I been Catholic I would have called her Our Lady of Sorrows. But how could she truly be sorry for anything? Shouldn't the Goddess be sufficient unto herself? Besides, what was she supposed to look for but troubles and crosses?

Again she let herself imagine returning to the island, not so much to be mended by the love of those other women as to converse with them about the old lesbian who had completed her mother's achievement of making her who she was, although one of them (Reba, evidently) must now have become the old woman, who would necessarily love her differently and therefore make her sad. In short, she knew enough not to go back there. As for E-beth, she might have gained weight, and wrinkles, and unless she dyed it, her hair would be white or grey. Would the retired policeman have a current picture? E-beth, formerly her favorite stranger, was travelling toward death without her!—The lesbian sat up and combed her hair, because right then Sandra was waking up joyful and getting happier and happier: Tonight she would be eating the lesbian's pussy and not simply pleasing her but pleasing her *greatly.* And she was going to whisper: I want to be in a sea-green bed in a crumbling underwater castle with fish swimming in and out the windows as I kiss you and use my hand to make you climax, Neva, and we lock our fish-tails together . . .—And she would confess: Louis is hurt, and I do feel bad that a lot of our conversation concerning you and me was about, you know, other things, but when I ask the other girls, Neva, they just tell me to do what I would want to do, which is to say, lie. So I lie. Darling, do you ever lie?—Oh, but the lesbian felt tired! Fortunately, Francine, whose hands were utterly satisfied but never satiated with Neva's body, allowed me to run the Y Bar for half an hour so that she could bring her darling a gift: eight doses of yellow serum! because of all of us (aside from me) it was only she, who had seen angels come and go, who wondered how long the lesbian could possibly stay at altitude, and when she would stop being what she was; she knew that Neva needed help! And the lesbian, leaning back and bracing her elbow on the arm of the sofa, raised one slender leg as high as her heart and held it, gripping it fast and gazing far away while Francine squatted greedily to worship her. Then came intermission.—Knowing that the yellow serum was available made Neva's time with Sandra glide easily by; and the very next morning Francine came rushing over so that she and Neva could sample the first two doses. Neva of course was up for anything—because as her mother had so often told her, to be a woman is to care for others.

Here's to you, honey, said the lesbian.

They drank down their medicine, which seized hold of them within twenty minutes, so that after half an hour our moonstruck Francine found herself rubbing her hand round and round the lesbian's buttock, whirling her tongue ever more rapidly in the lesbian's mouth until she had forgotten how to stop, gasping with astonished joy whenever the lesbian thrust her tongue into *her* mouth, which dominated her so pleasingly and perfectly; now the flats of their two tongues were sliding back and forth against each other, and Francine climaxed with a muffled scream. The climax went on and on. She was kneading the lesbian's breast; she could hardly bear to let go, but her caresses were informed by some wordless conviction that it was incumbent on her to maintain the coherence and perhaps even the existence of the lesbian's body: unless she kept fondling every part of Neva, she would lose her, piece by piece!—And touching her all over was anyhow such a pleasure, worshipping her belly with both hands, stroking it like a swimmer, then dipping her forefingers down into the hot wet groove whose labia were still swollen with excitement—because, you see, the lesbian loved her! the lesbian desired her!—and spreading her fingertips wide to part the folds around her lover's clitoris, lightly, rapidly whirling it round and round and round while her tongue danced in the lesbian's mouth, she licked the back of her teeth, longing to get bitten off and swallowed—and as she panted inside the lesbian's mouth, her arms rushed up and down that adorable back, to preserve, remember and glorify its smooth firmness; desperate with joy she gripped the lesbian's perfect buttocks and pulled them apart . . .

Then it was Sandra's turn, followed (indiscreetly) by the straight man's, Erin's, Starfire's (and, yes, it was so good that whenever she began to kiss the lesbian she tasted something indescribable at the back of her throat!), Victoria's, mine and, most importantly, Judy's; and *then*, lying on her back with her knees up and fluid coldly trickling from her vagina, the transwoman's head heavy and loudly snoring on her shoulder, the lesbian felt herself beginning to come down from the yellow serum, only a little at first, as if she had been lying effortlessly underwater and now the water had drained away from her forehead, which began to feel cool even as her mind began to chill; the transwoman snored sweetly on, and very lightly, the lesbian, still determined to do the best by comforting us, stroked her hair.

Now a bit of the warm underwater sensation had departed Neva's heart. She was sorry to feel it go.

Her naked shoulders were cold; she wished to pull up the covers, but that would have woken the transwoman. Goosepimples beset her upper arms.

Finally the transwoman's eyelids trembled. The lesbian kissed her lustily on the mouth.—I love so you much . . . said her friend, to which the lesbian replied: And *I* love *you*!—They were both in the mood again. Rolling over, the lesbian got into her strap-on and penetrated her friend, who groaned and grunted with pleasure while the lesbian moaned sincerely or maybe just politely; how could Judy tell?—Never forget your feelings, the old woman on the island had warned, and Neva tried to live up to this, but when Aphrodite bestows herself upon us defectives, why should she *reveal* whatever it is that she feels? Better that we don't know! (If I had to guess, I'd suppose that Neva—not Aphrodite!—felt, as ever, guilty toward all these people who adored her.)

Judy lay snoring and drooling. Remembering what she used to do on the island, the lesbian licked up her drool. Then she rose and began to make dinner.

I'll keep you company, said the sleepy transwoman.

Honey, you just relax. I'll come and get you when it's ready, okay?

I feel so lazy . . . Neva, you *spoil* me!

The lesbian kissed her forehead. Before the sausages were done, the transwoman wandered into the kitchen, naked but for a pair of socks.—She said: My heart feels all fluttery!

I'm sorry. Did I give you too much of a dose?

No, I like this feeling . . . I really *like* it—

Do you want to do it again next time?

Whatever we do is good. I love you.

I love you, too.

I love you so much!

Thank you, Judy. Would you like a beer?

What the hell . . . Why not? Oh, my heart feels . . . feels fuckin' *good.* Neva?

Yes, honey?

Neva, I, I'm so happy, I want to scowl and stamp my feet like Martina Navratilova! And then *kiss you all over*!

And take advice from Xenia?

Why the fuck not? And be your bitch while you're my bitch, and then . . . What was I saying? I feel strange; I need to lie down.

Her hostess tucked her into bed, knowing that sooner or later Judy's abandonment fixation, like Shantelle's, must crystallize out as resentment, which would express itself in grudge-statements drearily repeated with escalating anger, which Neva's most submissive apologies could only temporarily appease, and that at the price of a sick bruised feeling around her heart which could not but retain in itself any aggression or even abuse; her heart bled for us because it had to bleed anyhow.

An hour later the lesbian, alone, lay in bed and began to shiver. She opened the closet and found the old grey chamois shirt she used to wear on the island. As soon as she finished buttoning it over her heart, she felt better. Reentering the sweaty sheets, she stared up at the ceiling. Her buttocks were sore. What had she and the transwoman been doing down there? She pulled the bedspread up around her neck to sing the song of names: *E-beth, Reba, Belle and Lucia . . .*—By the window the radiator whispered.

Her cell phone chimed, then sent the call to voicemail. It was the transwoman saying: I just bought some new high heels and I'm walking around the room to see if they're too tight. Please, Neva, can I come over and model them for you?

6

Her mother mostly knew not to touch her, but after the fourth or fifth glass of wine, when everyone else had left the table, and the lesbian sat patiently across from her while she slowly chewed her salad, she might suddenly grasp her wrist with a cold and bony hand.

Because she had appeared without notice, the neighbor Mrs. Immler was also there.

The lesbian rose to help Mrs. Immler with the dishes.

Can't you sit until I'm finished? her mother said angrily. I've barely begun my salad.

I've been sitting and sitting, replied the lesbian—the most she ever talked back to her mother, and as soon as she said it she felt guilty. All the same, she rose, leaving her mother sitting all alone at the big table, and went into the kitchen where Mrs. Immler was putting away the food.

The lesbian began to tear off a sheet of aluminum foil in which to wrap the fingerling potatoes.

No, Karen, said Mrs. Immler. You'll just mess it up. When will you ever grow up? After all these years you still look like a child. Why can't you go back and keep your mother company?

This last she seemed to say extra loudly, for the mother's benefit.

Then why don't you sit with us, and then we'll all clean up together?

No, said Mrs. Immler, and who am I to say that Neva was or was not then illuminated by the miracle of shame, which reveals us to ourselves so that we may look within our flesh and see the sad skeletons of our origins?

And then after a long time she and her mother were sitting alone by the fire.

Her mother poured herself another glass of wine. She said: I just feel so cozy here.

The lesbian stared into the flames.

Isn't it cozy here?

It sure is.

Karen, why are you annoyed with Mrs. Immler?

Who told you I was?

Oh, I don't know. But I gather you're very annoyed with her.

No. I'm not upset at her at all.

Well, I've been told that you were. *I* don't know.

They sat in silence.

I just love this fire, said her mother, pouring herself more wine. Don't you just love it?

It's very nice.

They were sitting side by side. Her mother reached out and gripped the lesbian's hand. The lesbian kept breathing as evenly as she could.

The lesbian presently said: Mom, I have a lot of friends in San Francisco, and some of them are needy, but they all love me and I try to love them back. But sometimes I feel tired. Do you have any advice for me?

No, said her mother.

I've been thinking about going away . . .

I'm not surprised, Karen, because that's what you do.

Mom, I don't feel well. What should I do?

Her mother closed her eyes. The lesbian waited for her to say something. Finally the lesbian said: Well, Mom, you must be getting tired.

Oh, no. I'm not tired at all. Are you?

Not very.

It's really really nice by this fire, said her mother. But why are you annoyed at Mrs. Immler?

Can I get you anything, Mom?

Not a thing, said the mother, tightening her grip on the lesbian's wrist.

The lesbian sat still for as long as she could. Then she said: I think I'll go upstairs for awhile.

Oh, so soon?

I think I'll go lie down.

I didn't realize you were so tired.

I'll see you in awhile, Mom.

It's so lovely by this fire.

7

We were all wasting our lives at the Y Bar; just then Samantha (in red, with waves of flowers in her red hair) surprised herself by experiencing sexual feelings for Judy, who now looked almost svelte, but easily set them aside in consideration that Judy would want too much; meanwhile Shantelle was instructing Sandra: Bitch, you may be drop dead gorgeous, but, bitch, I'm tellin' you; you need to eat some niggah food, get you some hips, 'cause a man likes a bitch with parts he can grab onto, while Xenia held forth over her Old German Lager: The thing about young people today is that nobody is willing to commit to gender anymore, I feel like it's war on femininity. The world of the longhaired butch is a dying breed. When did it become illegal to be a high femme? I feel so old school with my fucking tits and my long hair . . .—Judy stopped listening. She felt sad and dirty, as if she had recently gone away from Neva or were coming down from ecstasy or both, and began thinking back on last time, when Neva had called a ride for her, which was probably intended in love but might have been a sign that Neva was tired of her; her understanding was that she could stay until seven p.m., but Neva had called the ride service at 6:20 or maybe 6:40; and then, since Judy felt too blue to go straight home, she took herself out to Fatty's Pizza, and when she asked the counter girl: May I sit over here? the reply was: No, sit over there, and Judy felt insulted. Admitting the possibility that her jangled state had a straightforwardly biochemical cause, she still could not help but feel sad. Had Neva grown tired of her, *she* must have been a bad guest—*disgusting* as usual. Perhaps she should phone Neva to apologize, and explain again how much she loved her, but what if that worsened the situation? Or she could thank her one more time, just in case . . .

The counter girl kept bringing out everybody else's pizza. The man who had ordered after Judy was already eating his. She listened to her belly gurgle. After half an hour, she began to feel quite wretched. Well, she was expert at that.

The place was dark. Why had she been forbidden from sitting by the window, where she could at least have watched the happy hurryings of others? The customers ate in silence. Judy stared down at her cell phone as if she were expecting a call—from Neva, for instance. At last the counter girl slammed down a lukewarm pizza before her. Well, thought Judy, it's what I deserve.

8

And the lesbian, who knew by heart exactly what we wanted, now began to alter the menu, to keep us (so the retired policeman theorized) in that state of ecstatic dependent spontaneity. This meant that our schedules changed.

I came in to the Y Bar fresh from Neva's mouth, enriched by that steady, strong and wide-awake sense of beautifully passing time, of a present moment that I truly felt and lived in as it and I moved endlessly forward together, so that I was not spending and certainly not losing time, but travelling with it, rightly and appropriately, through the noon-bright eternity that someday, but not this moment, would change from infinite to finite. Turning neither back nor forward, I lived as it seemed that I always should have done, without anxiety or grief, quietly, joyfully resolute to keep journeying. Needing no food or water, although my tongue licked at my dry lips, free in my painless being, seeking nothing, I sat down while Francine silently poured out my poison.

Judy and Sandra sat side by side sweating and shivering; for Sandra it felt like the bad old days when the straight man used to ejaculate inside her when she was ovulating, after which he would make her take the morning after pill, whose hormones induced desperate weepiness; of course barren Judy lacked that memory-baseline. Economical Francine sold them a single pill for their headaches, so they had to split it; fortunately, we were accomplished at that. I perceived or more likely hallucinated the swelling sweet affectionate chattiness of these two women whom only now was I coming to know; even as the transwoman imagined herself made famous by a headline that said **JUDY'S HEARTBREAK**, accompanied by a photograph of her looking heroic and sad and wearing metallic eye shadow—but then her head hurt. She said: Sandra, I'm so stupid, I mean, really *really* stupid!

Don't say that, honey, and the other woman patted her hand.

But I really don't know *anything*! Neva said . . .

She said what?

Oh, who the fuck cares? I'd kill myself to please her, but there's no fuckin' way, and it makes me feel . . . Tell me a story, Sandra. *Please!* Another story about how it is to be a woman.

But you are one.

I wish . . .

Excuse me; I need to call Neva. Oh, my mother's texting but I won't answer in case Neva might be calling.

What do you need to call Neva for? I want to call her, too!

Actually someone's calling me. I don't know who it is. I was hoping it was Neva. No, it's still not ringing. Sorry, Judy, but I'm really not—

Please. Because I hurt inside. I'm no good. I'm *disgusting.*

What's with you today? Gosh, it's chilly in here!

Just take my mind off . . . I mean, tell me how it is—

Are you sick?

Oh, no no *no*! Are you?

I . . . What were you asking? Oh. How it is to be a woman? First you tell *me* something.

I'm disgusting. That's all.

Judy—

Now what about you?

Well, I just think about the way that men describe sex and the way women describe sex. For men it's a hardening and for women it's a softening.

The transwoman brightly interrupted: And when a man goes down on you . . .

I don't know what the physical desire is for a man to do it! They tell me, but I don't understand it. But as far as going down on a man, I do it and I don't really mind it. Whether it's a boyfriend or whether it's Neva, I feel like, well, I love you and I want to like explore your body. Excuse me, Judy, but I don't feel well.

You look terrible. I feel terrible. Why don't you come back to my place and, you know, get warm?

That's a nice offer, but—

Don't you like me?

I need to pull the covers over me and . . . I've really got to go right now. Sorry. I love you, Judy—

I love you, too. Please don't go . . .

Feeling desolate, the transwoman went to see the retired policeman, who showed her forensic microphotographs to teach her about the greater acidity, more numerous bacteria and increased frequency of microscopic scales in menstrual blood; while Sandra went home and called Neva, who actually answered. She sounded tired.

I'm sorry! said Sandra. I didn't mean to bother you—

Honey, what's wrong?

Of course I still want in my heart for you to be the mother of our baby, but I understand all the inherent difficulty and sadness that might create . . .

You know I love you, said the lesbian.

Please can I come over? Just for five minutes to kiss you?

Okay, said the lesbian.

And Sandra came running. Neva was in her nightgown. Sandra said: Tell me another thing you've never told me before. Then I'll go, I promise.

I'll tell you something. Will you memorize it and teach it to Judy?

It's for her?

For both of you. I heard this from an old lady I used to know. She lived on an island in a place where there were mermaids. And she used to say all the time: *If you bring forth what is within you, what you have will save you. If you have nothing within you, what you do not have within you will kill you.*

That's strange. She really said that to you?

No, honey. Well, she said it to me but it was *for* you and Judy and everybody else but me. I'm in a worse case.

Oh, baby! That makes me worried.

No, I shouldn't have said that. Now can you repeat what I told you?

If you bring forth what is within you . . .

And they practiced it until Sandra had it by heart.

Now it's yours, said the lesbian. Will you please teach it to Judy? I've got to rest . . .

Okay. Oh, Neva, I wish you'd let me take care of you . . . !

And she buried her face between the lesbian's legs.

But the lesbian was already softly snoring. Unlike Judy, Sandra did not belong to the category of people called *invasives.* She even refrained from kissing the other woman.

9

Much later that night it was my turn. When I rang the buzzer, the transwoman let me in, looked at me with her big blue cow eyes, blushed, then quickly ran down the stairs. I closed the door behind her. The lesbian was in the bedroom, face down on the bed, with her nightgown pulled up above her waist, weeping almost silently. I saw a shiny stain underneath her. That wouldn't stop *me*! I touched the back of her neck, a contact she always liked, or at least pretended to; and with her, what was the difference?

She began sobbing.

Was Judy mean to you? I asked.

No, never! How could she be? She's so . . . I'm just tired.

After that she was as silent as a moonrise. For all I know she was seeing her mother's face smiling meaninglessly. How important could I have been to her? I repeat: She was lying on the unmade bed, with her eyes closed and her legs wide open, waiting to give me the sacrament before the next of us rang the bell. So I took; I received; I remarried the lovely rush which was happiness refined into a habit of energy.

10

Perplexed by my sensations, I went to chat with Natalie, named after a certain tragically drowned movie actress, who lived half-time on or in a sleeping bag behind the two garbage bins which serviced the three Pakistani restaurants on Jones Street; sometimes she used to invite herself upstairs, in order to move her bowels, shower and shoot up heroin, mumbling and spreading wide her thighs on my toilet seat with her bluejeans round her ankles while seeking the least compromised vein for her happiness. Once the needle went in I would hear her murmuring furry prayers of gratitude as her head sank like the evening sun and the ends of her long hair swept the water in the toilet bowl like sensitive crayfish-whiskers; then I'd hoist her into bed with me, and in the morning she would smile and fuck me. Once I joined the lesbian's roster of lovers I lost my desire for Natalie, who anyway had opened her legs for me merely, so I had assumed, to repay her obligation; but on the first morning that I stroked Natalie's hair and rolled away she burst into tears. So I fucked her out of loving pity, just as Neva did for me; if what they used to say in church held good, whatever I did for Natalie I was doing for Neva. After that, my relationship with Natalie became even sweeter, and sometimes I actually sought her out, even when she had shut herself up in her sleeping bag and disguised herself as a corpse. Like a feral cat who learns to associate a certain person with food instead of violence, Natalie gave me the gift of her trust without hoping for more than interruptions in her pain. I could tell her everything because she never remembered anything. That afternoon I found her defecating onto a pile of cocktail napkins. Caching her sleeping bag in the lefthand garbage bin, the other one being padlocked, we went to my place. She was jonesing, of course, and had no junk, so I fixed her up with two of Francine's fattest white pills; then she took a shower, trampling her soaped-up clothes in the tub while she shampooed her beautiful hair. Since her sweatpants still stank, we left them soaking. No matter how many times I changed the water it went grey. I offered to shake in a good slug of dishwashing detergent, but Natalie muttered: *useless . . . ,* wobbling on her skinny abscessed legs. Then Francine's pills started to kick in.—Oh, God, she said. I can think again. But I . . . Then she passed out.

I unzipped her purse, and a cockroach ran out. I almost killed it, but would Neva have been so cruel? Condoms and lubricant, license to drive and summons to appear, a rancid hot dog and a cracked cell phone, such made up Natalie's wealth, but where was her money? I would have fixed her better, but my rent was due. Remembering that Judy owed me, I dialled her up, but she admitted what of course I knew, that she could not now and might never pay me back. Enduring first her excuses and then her self-loathing, I could almost see her gazing up at me like a skinny, open-mouthed boy, effeminate and frail, longing to be hurt. Next I called Shantelle. I said I needed something for a sick friend. If she would only help me, I'd give her my turn with Neva, which was today, in fact. Shantelle, who struck me as one of those women who make their own misery, and hate others because that is psychically less expensive than despising themselves, was up for it; indeed, Shantelle was down for it, hungry to illuminate the already shining lesbian with her own desire (as she used to tell us: I love my Neva! I'd kill anybody over her!); she came flying up Geary Street with the cold hard minimum of magic white powder and even kissed my lips for gratitude; I saw her off; then, parting my striped blue curtains, I looked out the window at the pillars and cornices of the old Pierce-Arrow showroom, while a police cruiser shrilled faintly far away, like someone's abandoned baby. Cars went hissing through puddles. I felt chilly and chillier even though the central heating hummed faithfully on and off. Just overhead someone kept dragging something heavy. Oh, how blue I felt! I tried to cheer up by imagining myself dead and in heaven, where the sun will surely be a round stage red as fire, with a pallid stripper wiggling her pale thighs upon it, and her arms high above her head, forever and ever, amen. Finally Natalie woke up retching. I gave her the medicine. For a long time I could hear her on the toilet, groaning and swearing; for vein-hunting she ranked with the best of them. Once she had triumphed enough to thank me, she staggered in to fuck me, thinking that that was what I wanted. I was solid cold by then, jonesing for Neva. So I mixed myself a rum and sodapop.—That's disgusting, said Natalie. I drained the bathtub. She trampled her clothes as dry as she could and I helped her hang them from the curtain rod.—Do you want a hot dog? said Natalie.—In half an hour it would have been my turn with Neva. I turned on my phone, just in case she should call.—Won't you fuck me? said Natalie. I need you inside me. And excuse me for asking, but do you have any more H? I'm feeling better but not quite well. Would you mind looking at my phone? A drunken client tried to take advantage, so I banged him in the teeth, and now I . . . Why won't you fuck me?

I undressed and we lay down under the blankets. I kept shivering; it felt so good to squeeze my sweet warm Natalie who now smelled clean; behind her hair I hid from the world.

The phone rang; it was the lesbian. Her voice made me desperate, not only because I needed her but also because her guilt was contagious: She must have been aware that what she did to each of us in bed was *to us* more important than why she did it. Somehow she endured and even accepted our fundamental lovelessness, like a candle that burns on and on without oxygen.

(It was true enough that she could not love another without knowing her, but for her own part she aspired to be loved without being known, because her love was willed and measured according to the case, that being easy for her, while her case was not easy for us. *Her love was better than ours.*)

I assured her that Shantelle was not lying; I had truly given up my turn. Neva said she loved me and was proud of me. I said I loved her and quickly turned off the phone so that I would not burst into tears.

Let me guess, said Natalie sleepily. That's your wife.—She began to squeeze my penis.—No, your girlfriend. I mean, your significant other, your main bitch, whatever. Could I borrow ten dollars?

My main bitch, I said.

Ha! Right now *I'm* your main bitch!—And she played with me, sucked me and straddled me, but I went soft and nearly started crying.

Huh, said Natalie. Guess it's serious. Or else there's codeine or something in your system. Hey, you got any codeine? Never mind, lover.

I felt colder and colder. I squeezed her against me.

You wanna tell me your troubles? she said. What did you dose on? You know you're ice cold! Hey. Hey, honey. Sweetie. What's your name again?

Richard.

That's right. But you can't get hard, so I'm gonna call you Tricky Dick. Now lemme massage you, and then we'll . . . Do you have any condoms?

I'm in love, I said.

No wonder you're so sad.

Talk to me, I said. Just hold me and talk to me.

About what? You want me to talk dirty to you? I've got condoms if you don't.

Right now Shantelle would be screaming her way into the first or second climax of the afternoon. Grinding my teeth, I asked Natalie whether she loved anybody, and she laughed. Then she said: You've been good to me. You're a good one. What's your name?

Richard.

Richard, lemme tell you about love. First it starts as herpes. Oh, sometimes love is all you need, just like the song says. I was being sarcastic. The thing about love is . . . What was I . . . ? Honey, if you don't stand for something, you fall for everything . . .—and then Natalie was the one who burst into tears! I held her; she sobbed herself out against me, and I felt better to have comforted her. Then she said: If you don't love something like even a rock . . . Love is a funny thing. Makes people jealous and do crazy things. I know I love my country, amen, and I'm sick and tired of those people using our Constitution against us. But this town is very, they're making it very socioeconomic. Nothing's PC anymore. You can't even use the N-word. So why can people go and use the school system, using Obama T-shirts on the campus? Why can't they say *love God*? Because when my boyfriend died, I should have . . . But I do love God. I love Jesus.

If you were Jesus, could you love everybody all the time?

Well, seeing as how . . . A female Jesus, it would probably be very effective, actually. People are used to being spread thin. Baby, I can spread myself so thin for you right now. You want some pussy? Excuse me; I forgot you can't . . . If I was Jesus I'd stand by you; I'm all for *stand by your man*, but how do you feel about being Secretary of fuckin' State and letting Benghazi go down? There was twelve of 'em, right. And if God was one of us, and a bitch, a nice-looking bitch who just loved like one of us . . . ! I'm not sure most people would handle that.

I asked her: Does Jesus stand by you?

Of course He does.

Then why do you and I feel like this?

He wants us to—

I think Neva is Jesus. But not exactly. Do you have a partner who will watch your back?

I keep thinking I do and then they *stab* me in the back. There's one bitch, who when I track her down for stealing my good luck charm I'm gonna . . . Who's Neva?

She's like Jesus.

There's some heavy hittin' Cherokees out there. Does she have Native American blood?

I don't know.

Exactly, said Natalie. And my personal opinion, I don't know; I'm not sure, actually. They have some . . . They wanna . . . That's why I don't watch movies. Is Neva real? I guess so, 'cause I heard her talk to you. Well, she's probably surveyed some men, to see if . . . And we could question how many men—we'd start with a hundred: *What would you think if God was a woman?* I'm not sure I could handle that, actually. Honey, you're not so cold anymore. Are you feeling better?

I kissed her and thought: If you don't stand for something, you fall for everything.

11

I can always tell, said the straight man.

Tell what?

When you're having sex with your girlfriend.

Don't call her that. You're my *boy*friend.

Your other lover, then.

My—my, yes. Neva's my other lover.

There was a silence, and she asked: Are you there?

Yes.

Hi!

Hello, Sandra . . .

How can you tell?

He was going to say: *You get more evasive*, but did not mean to hurt her, so he pulled the punch and said: You talk more briefly; you're less open and loving; you want to get off the phone.

I'm sorry; I'm sorry! It seems all I ever do is disappoint you!

No; I'm not disappointed. It is what it is.

She sobbed: I just want to make everybody happy!

He laughed, then said: That's working out so well for Neva.

12

As soon as it came my turn again, I was spreading Neva's buttocks with both hands while she rode me in the way that she claimed always to like; who knew what she actually liked? (Don't say I didn't care to please her; we all longed not just to delight but even to protect the one we worshipped, in the kindly spirit of the photographer who would jolly Natalie Wood into doing nude shots, and then, once the cameras were loaded would first administer a glass of wine in order to numb her, after which the makeup girl would hold a towel around her while she sat down; then of course the towel went away, because it was time to use her.) Judy once told me that she never fantasized about a man until he grew familiar in her mind. I remarked that I had fantasized about Neva from the very first, at which Judy then laughingly confessed that she had done the same even at Selene's wedding when Neva came into the Y Bar wearing that moon-green blouse and Sandra had been so understanding. And Neva smiled at me; when I closed my eyes I went on seeing that smile, which I could thus compare to Natalie's, one upper tooth of which resembled a blackened coin minted in the reign of Nero.

When I marched into the Y Bar for my postcoital rum and sodapop, my fellow worshippers were denouncing international terrorism, supporting the troops and debating whether Lacey was a sexy lesbian name. Samantha was sad; and seeing her weeping, the transwoman also burst into tears without knowing why. This irritated the retired policeman, who had been hectoring her as follows: All right, Judy. That's what you would do. But what would Neva do? And what's her number one hot button? If we press it, she goes apeshit, or whatever.—I laid out a five and a one for Francine, who mixed my poison. The straight man, glowering at me so that the whites of his eyes burned like torture-lamps, crooked his slender forefinger and said: *Cheers!* We clinked our poisons; then Francine opened another beer for Xenia.

Wow, cried Samantha, I was just thinking that Neva really sizzles today! What is it about her?

You know what's puzzling me? said Xenia. It's Neva's *look.* I can't figure out how she does it. I don't even know what her look is. There's nothing that special about any part of her, and yet somehow . . .

Three dollars, said Francine.

Don't you get sick of that beer? asked Samantha.

Oh, I'll bet Neva knows a thing or two about makeup, said Sandra.

No, Shantelle, said Xenia, you need a more balanced look. Now I think you should darken your roots by at least three shades.

You gotta be crazy.

So you'll try it?

Sure.

Overflowing with kindness toward Neva, our untier of knots, longing to serve her as she would never serve herself, Judy sat in the retired policeman's dark corner, rocking and gripping her head. Francine murmured to Shantelle, who shook her head until Francine gave her a five-dollar bill, which she snatched with the suddenness of a frog whose tongue flashes out to catch a fly, after which she grudgingly rose, went to Judy and said: Open, bitch.—Judy did. Shantelle lobbed a pill in.

Judy sat alone for a long time, breathing heavily. Finally the medicine took effect, and she looked up. We were all ignoring her, the better to aggravate our own troubles.

Xenia, she said.

Xenia kept flirting with Samantha—who had just come out of the lesbian's bedroom feeling taller than anyone else.

Slowly the transwoman rose. I was watching; in her condition it was quite heroic of her. Swaying, she sat down next to Xenia.

Usual? said Francine.

Can you please please gimme a glass of water? I feel like shit.

Guess what? said Shantelle. That's what you are.

Be nice, said Francine.

I don't care, said Judy. Xenia, did you hear me? I *don't fuckin' care.*

Congratulations, said Xenia.

Can I buy you a . . . ?

Whatever.

Three dollars, said Francine. And here's your water, hon.

Thanks, said Xenia, staring wearily down at her latest Old German Lager (I always hated that stuff).

I said, don't you get sick of that beer? asked Samantha.

Will you come back here with me? said Judy.

Samantha and Shantelle started hooting together: *Pop her cherry, pop her cherry!*

Shut up, said Francine.

Xenia picked up her beer and trudged back into the darkness with Judy. They sat down.—What? said Xenia.

You said to come back to you when I—

You're a stinking cow, said Xenia.

Judy began to cry silently.

Oh, cut it out. I was just kidding you. See, you do care.

Not so much—

All right.

Do you?

Do I *what*?

Do you get hurt?

Judy, I think a lot of what I experience is that backstabbing kind of thing. You may not get the apartment, but nobody tells you why you didn't. It might be because you're too butch. It's the same kind of prejudice black folks get. I've had people yell at me on the street. I can say, I'm a dyke, but I don't want people yelling it on the street. It still hurts, but I can ignore it. I just think they're immature. Now *what do you want*?

Help me audition at the Pink Apple. I've lost eighteen pounds—

What put you up to that?

There was this dancer named Starfire who used to work the chorus line in Vegas, and she said she could see me in King's Row. She said I have potential. She—

Oh, come on. Why don't you audition to be a Slimways Sexmate? We'll call you the cover model cow.

You promised Neva you'd help me.

Oh, she told you that?

No, you did.

Did I? Well, what the hell; I'll give you another friggin' lesson. You want to succeed as a dancer?

You know I do.

Well, you're losing weight. Your legs aren't quite so ugly, and your belly's showing twins instead of triplets. That's good. Lose a lot more. And your boobs are okay but your face is horrendous. Go get some work done.

Okay, but—

And *don't* ask me what and where. Now. What's success?

Applause. Everyone wanting to date me—

Wrong. Success equals money. That's all there is. Now do you fucking get it?

Yes, Xenia.

What a good submissive. You never know how much money you're gonna make. Sometimes you don't make your rent. A lot of people don't wanna pay. Just now at the Y Bar I don't see anyone who's gonna pull out the big money. And when my radar tells me the same thing at the Pink Apple, you know what I do?

You go home.

Good girl.

But you're a performer; you're a, I mean, a sexy woman—

I don't see myself as sexual. I don't care what they think. If they call out something insulting it can't ruin my night, whereas you get one insult and you go home boo-hooing. Do you think a real woman would act like that?

How would you know if you're the most beautiful?

Judy, you'll never have to worry about that.

But how *would* you know?

The only way I'd know is if I was making the most money. Or if I . . . Look. I mean, I just do my job. I just come and get naked and then go home. You go home when you're done. Isn't that how it is for you when you're sucking dick behind some garbage can?

Not exactly. Sometimes I feel really happy to do that, because—

Oh, shut up, freak. Now what mistake are you making right now?

Caring—

Right. So enough with that fuckin' *caring.* On Tuesdays at the Pink Apple it's just me and Eva and sometimes Starfire, who as I happen to know quite well *never* said you have *potential*, because she fuckin' *hates* you, but usually she takes Tuesdays off to be with her son. So me and Eva, we do three songs on and three songs off. When I'm on I don't care and when I'm off I don't care. Because I don't really sell a lot of dates. I get turned down; they don't want 'em. My energy's not super inviting. That's how it works for me in the real world, so that nobody can get to me, ever. That's why Hunter thinks I'm frigid. Well, that's just old Xenia! I know I'm lucky. Sure, I'd be better off if I could sell myself at the Apple or even here, but the way I am, I can't just turn that off. So maybe I'm not getting rich, but they can all kiss my ass.

I'll kiss your ass—

Neva's is more to my liking. All I ever gave you was a pity fuck. Anyway, I mostly don't do sex anymore, but I used to. There was this four-foot-and-something black gentleman named Miles and he'd meet me anywhere, and he made up a rule that after three a.m. he'd only snort cocaine off a stripper's titties. So he'd snort and snort; it went on and on. Yeah, I used to work in a much more fast-paced club, so I used to have a lot more fun, but . . .

So you did care.

So what if I did? You work some more on your *not* caring! When they can't hurt you, you can stay onstage as long as possible. It's hard to pull yourself away from money talking. You want to show dance? Getting money is putting on a show. So. Lose another fifteen pounds. Fix your ugly mug. Then come to me, and we'll try it—only so I can get Brownie points with Neva . . .

13

Staring me up and down in that all-seeing way of his (in his way he knew us all even better than did Neva), the retired policeman inquired: Have you ever heard the term *the shitting burglar*? There's the thrill of the burglary itself. They lose their bowel control. They could become dangerous, because they want the thrill to continue. Psychologically, Neva's slaves are like that. Do you get it, Richard? *I'm talking about you.*

I want the thrill to continue, I confessed.

Good man! The guy who admits guilt right off the bat, that's the guy I can work with. I've always liked you, buddy.

Thanks, I said. I know I'm not worth much—

That's right. No one is. *And you know it!* You're one of us—way ahead of the rest. Now tell me: What in fuck's name's gonna happen to you?

I almost explained that what the lesbian offered was emancipation from anything quotidian such as washing dishes, going to work or buying toilet paper, all of which went far to wreck nearly any partnership-for-life. Must any equal marriage wind up use-stained like a yellowed tooth? None of us, even the marriageable few, wished to believe so. I for my part once washed our dishes happily, because it was for the one I loved, but there came the night when she yawned at me, and the morning when she snapped at me, and the week when she made it clear that I was to leave her alone; had she been telling this story she would have rolled out my own failures to tell, but to me it truly seemed that I had done everything to respect the glamor of our coupled lives—which she had broken. Although I must have done my part to break it, I would have sworn even to the lesbian that I had never been spiteful or even impatient, although perhaps I had been lazy without knowing it; whatever Michelle and I had done, the romance drained away, leaving a stain around the bathtub drain; let's say I was the one to scrub it. Times with the lesbian were never long enough, but that was because they never got boring.—But instead of explaining, I finished my drink. Carmen topped us off, after which I said: Well, it's got to end badly, because everything does. I mean, there's that hole in the ground waiting . . .

Neva's preying on you, he said.

But what's she getting out of it?

I agree she's a pretty weird case.

You must have seen a lot of villains, I said, because I loved to hear him talk.

Licking the rim of his glass, he began: Most of the sociopaths that I've encountered I've not encountered as a cop. Passive-aggressive people like Neva, they're the worst. But it's all about categories: those who commit crime for profit, those who do it because it's a lifestyle, and those who have sociopathic tendencies. There are thieves who would murder child molesters. There are people who see nothing wrong with being a child molester who would never steal anything.

But why's Neva the worst? I asked.

I'm working on it, he said.

I was coming down from her, and the headache tortured me. He could see that I needed to go. Returning home, I locked myself in and lay down to think about the lesbian, the one who cared with love and pain for all of our wounds; the recentness of our separation kept her so real that I could almost taste her, smell her and feel her as if her face were still against mine and my hands were worshipping her hot smooth buttocks, over and over forever; the warm happy sexy certainty remained in my heart but my legs were already starting to get cold; oh, God, I was coming down and *down* off my Neva . . . !

14

. . . And Neva wanted to desire the transwoman but could not even though she loved her, so she swallowed a dropperful of green extract from the herbal shop on Haight Street and in half an hour began to get what she called *that feeling*, oh, that wonderful feeling of wanting and even craving whomever would soon be in her arms.

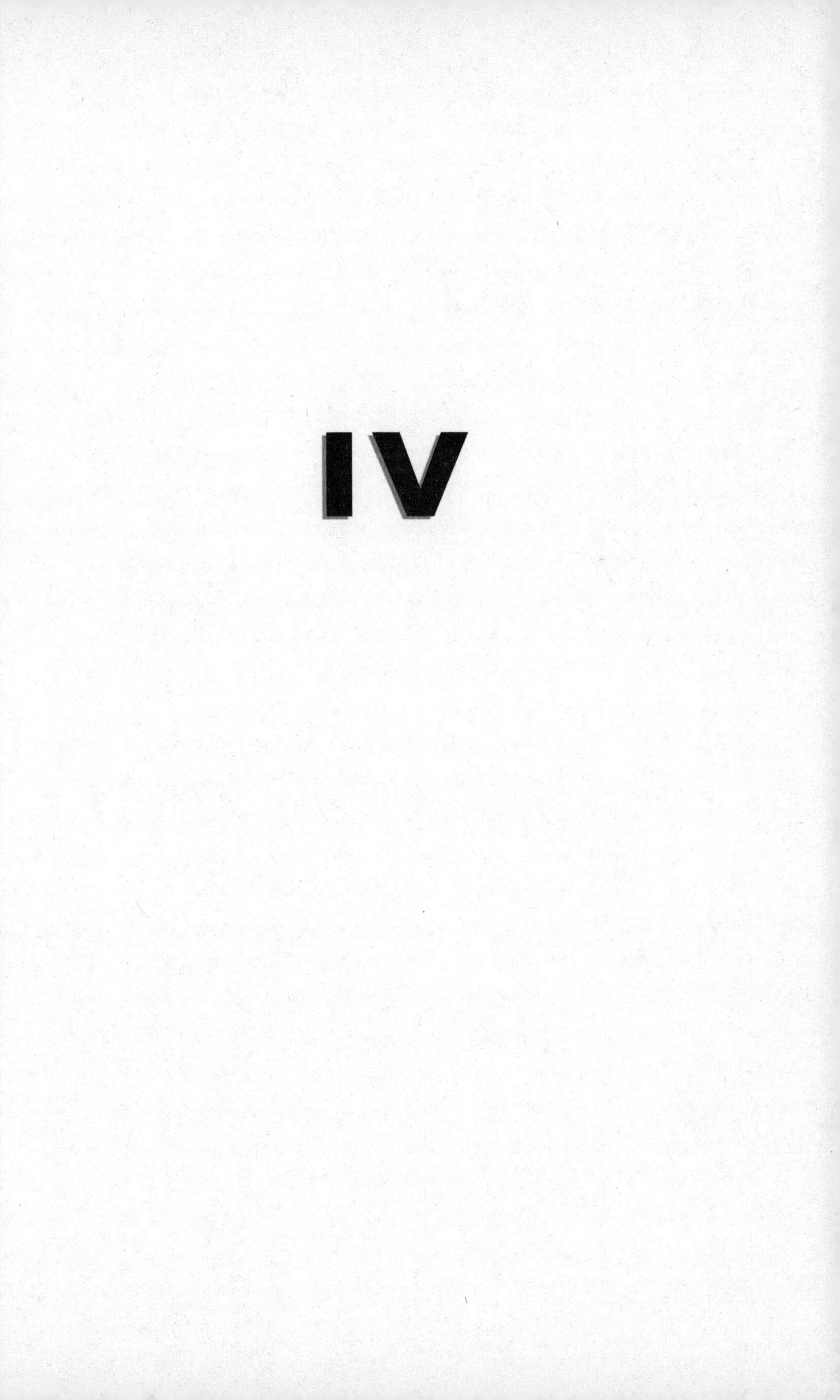

IV

Without Shame or Limit

All my life I have tried to do whatever was expected of me . . .

JUDY GARLAND, 1951

Not many of us have the names and identities we were born with . . . You think, can this be me they're talking about? . . . It's as if people were confusing you with some role you played on the screen.

JUDY GARLAND, 1951

1

But still we tried to believe that it could go on like this forever, each of us drinking honey from between the lesbian's thighs—honey like milk and fire, honey like moonlight; and no matter what happened there would always be more. Why not? Xenia imagined that she would someday amass *enough* pills, MGM planned to keep Judy Garland docile and prepubescent, I thought to live off my savings, the policeman dreamed of running Neva out of town, while the transwoman kept right on hoping to become as wholesomely pretty as the Olympic skating champion Nancy Kerrigan: Maybe a memory foam bra with the perfect measurements would make Neva not merely love her, but actually *fall* for her . . . !—Among the glittering glassware of the Y Bar went our darkhaired girl, carrying all our most precious desires. We watched as if we were far away—because we were—but our hearts opened wider than Shantelle's legs. Starfire was somewhere in that picture; so was the woman who resembled Julie Andrews. Even the straight man, halfway determined as he was to become independent of the lesbian who had tormented him so much, watched his resentment altering back into fascination exactly as swiftly as she appeared, passing in and out of us, while we waited in ambush. Meanwhile Neva made herself vomit. (Judy kept doing that for beauty's sake; even I tried it once, just to be like Neva.) Washing the glasses,

Francine smiled without knowing it. The lesbian's approach was moonrise. My emerald heart vibrated like the last drop hesitating on the lip of an upturned bottle of gin (I actually felt corroded with anxiety). Taking leave of her, but first following the reflection of a streetlamp across a dark puddle, I rushed off to have my loneliness sucked away by the transwoman. This felt very pure. (She tattled to the retired policeman, who grinned and clapped me on the back.) Meanwhile the lesbian made her bed and touched up her lipstick. She went next door to comfort Catalina, then down to Room 547 to take care of Victoria—but only in the absence of the latter's sister Helga. Then she returned to the nest. Holding her phone close, she listened to a new voicemail from Shantelle: Hi, baby, it's me. I know that even though this ain't good for me I'm gonna think all about you tonight and I'm gonna say your name and touch myself when I think about you. I love you so much and wish everything was different because then half my problems would be solved.—Thus another typical communication from Neva's fan club. And Neva ministered to each of us with the quiet kindness of the victim's advocate who sits in the room while the police are taking evidence and then, when they warn her that she will get billed for the rape kit unless she agrees *right now* to press charges, gently, calmly informs the woman that she will never get billed and does not have to decide anything right now.—The knowledge that we could never believe her biography fatigued her, but that burden every goddess must bear. I suspect that when she looked in the mirror the emiserating beauty of her face occasionally aroused self-hatred (come to me, E-beth, come to me; Xenia, Richard, Shantelle and Victoria, come to me); more often, it relieved her, proving her still qualified to love us. She knew us all by heart: Sandra felt hornier when she was ovulating while Hunter got in the mood just before her period came on. Judy wanted to *be done to*; I wanted to *do with*; Victoria most needed caresses and slow romantic words.

Now it was Samantha's turn.

You look tired, Neva.

No, honey, I'm just . . .

Look at that! A grey hair! Shall I pull it out?

Sure.

Poor Neva! Pretty soon you'll be like the rest of us.

I love you and I'm sorry for—for being different . . .

Have you tried Etruscan Formula? It'll cover you all the way to the roots. Don't feel sad; I'll never tell.

Of course she rushed into the Y Bar waving the evidence and shouting: Look what I pulled out of Neva! The bitch is going grey. Now she can't lord it over us anymore.

Don't be mean, said Xenia, who was strangely delighted at the news.

As for me, I rejected Saint Augustine's weird certainty that *what suffers no change, is better than what can be changed.* Now that I knew she could get old, the lesbian grew all the more loveable to me.* I still wonder how much power she had ever owned to light her way ahead, and whether in our times with her she withheld herself out of fidelity or selfishness.

Francine took the grey hair out of Samantha's hand and pretended to throw it out, but actually kept it among her secret treasures.

2

Meanwhile the retired policeman did unremitting justice to the investigation. (His most glorious time had been finding the night club owner hidden under garbage bags in the garage, shot over and over in the face; and in the den the night club owner's mother beside the live-in stripper girlfriend, the former simply bludgeoned to death and the latter with her panties pulled down and her long hair glued to the carpet by coagulated blood.) To him the lesbian might as well have been lovely, merciless Athena, with her deep dark eyepits (whose inlaid pupils had long since washed away), her unfriendly lips and her ravishingly smooth skin, the Gorgon grinning blankly at her breast. His questions found her staring poutingly down, her concerns inhuman to ours.

I arrested a few sex offenders, he told Francine. Wand wavers. I think it can accelerate into rape and worse.

Well, J. D., what the fuck do you think about us?

I always saw prostitution and any kind of consensual sex as human behavior and that's what you do and it's none of my business. I remember I was in the

---

* I imagined that as she aged she might manage temporarily to recompense her losses; experience and retrospection would enhance her brilliance at recognizing when a woman was about to leave her. The love-words might be the same, but their fervor was lacking; and when she ever so slightly withheld herself in bed, there came no answering increase in the ardor of the defecting partner. The girl who had loved every dish that Neva cooked now fussed and picked at her food and asked that her eggs be cooked separately without onions. The one who woke and slept when Neva did now slept till noon, then stayed up until three in the morning. Slowly and naturally the lesbian would lose all her satellites, leaving me as her only one, forever and ever, amen.

military and this guy started buying me a beer, and he says, how would you like a blow job? I had nothing against him.

No, you wouldn't!

Fuck you.

Seven dollars.

That's all it costs to fuck you, honey? Then Judy's ripping me off. Sometimes the bitch even demands a hot shower.

You're too much, said Francine.

Look. The good guys would rather arrest rustlers than the barmaid that's working. I think that's right on. I got nothing against you, baby. If you had a dick I might even date you. Oh, God, but I did relish when I made a good bust, especially as a patrolman: high speed, well over a hundred miles an hour on Christmas Day; the road was slick, and I ran two of 'em down on foot and the third one ended up knocking on the door of a cop's house, and I had to count the money and *all* the evidence! I was *high.* High on adrenaline! When I put the cuffs on them, I . . .

The lesbian came in. His plans for her were not quite perfected, so he got up and went home.

3

Right away his Judy came clipclopping inopportunely upstairs like an ugly old horse. He started slapping her around because she loved Neva more than him. She screamed, sobbed and begged for forgiveness; that part was still perfect. Then she unzipped his pants, and he sighed. Afterward they got wasted on Old Crow and she said: I mean, don't you feel like we have a connection, you and I?

Judy, if *I* did, then *you* wouldn't, because it's all about my being cruel to you. *Right, bitch?*

Please don't send me away. I'll do anything; I'll mop the floor with my tongue—

Run along now, he said, literally shoving her out the door while the neighbors watched delightedly.

(Have you ever loved more than one person at a time? I feel so guilty, she sobbed, and the lesbian, who should have accepted all other loves, felt momentary horror and dread—because as the Scriptures ran: *I am a jealous Goddess.*)

4

He meanwhile tourniqueted off another of his attachments: Melba, who kept visiting the ladies' room for a very long time with her bulky purse, after which she said that she had forgotten to pee. She had also forgotten to bring the lowdown on E-beth's other little jailbait bitches. She then proposed to come into his room to smoke her heroin, which was in a vaporizer, and she promised that a vaporizer would not set off the smoke detector although she admitted that she felt unfamiliar with vaporizers. He said that he would keep her company anywhere while she smoked her heroin, only not in his room, that not being his most prized setting for a high-class felony; so then Melba became sullen and hateful and opened her cell phone to call a bearded boy in a rattletrap van filled with cigarette smoke; he was one of the several drivers whom Melba had on call for this or that undisclosed reason, and when the retired policeman got into the front seat to discuss their next meeting, the bearded boy at once began to drive toward some unknown place, at which the policeman explained that he would be getting out at the next corner. He who used to be unwillingly impelled toward her smile decided not to see Melba again. Waiting for Judy to come home, he settled back in bed and poured himself a shot, devouring old true stories of crimes against young girls.

The buzzer rang. He struggled into his slippers and pressed the button on the wall. When Judy arrived, he said: Hey, babe, you're looking thin and beautiful.

5

But Judy now glimpsed the lesbian with Victoria. That night she dreamed of spying on them. She dreamed of whispering lovingly to the retired policeman, and he became the woman he should always have been.

The Paratrooper

> By oneself evil is done; by oneself one suffers; by oneself evil is left undone; by oneself one is purified. Purity and impurity belong to oneself; no one can purify another.
>
> BUDDHA, date unknown

A bluehaired girl sat down and said: Do you remember me?

I'm sorry, but—

Good. My name's Colleen.

Oh, said the transwoman; then, just in case her forgetting this person was yet another failure to be compensated for, smiled widely and said: Where do you come from?

I kind of parachuted in.

Francine stood stonily behind the bar, with the football game so white and bustling upon the ultragreen field of our television. Shantelle was boasting, drunk and proud: Neva's a grown-ass woman, and I know what she's gonna do. And I told her, if you wanna cheat, just tell me and I'm *down* for it! How many other bitches gonna give their ho so much rope?

A single vodka, straight up, said Colleen.

Four dollars.

Let me get that, said Judy.

That's appropriate, said her neighbor, because do you know who I am?

Judy thought for a long time. Francine slammed down Colleen's shotglass, and Shantelle, whose head kept alertly swaying upon that long sensitive neck of hers, succeeded in shoplifting two dollars which a departing Norwegian tourist had left for a tip.

I know, said Judy. You're my . . . my pretty little angel, and I love you.

Oh, hell, said Francine. What are you high on now?

Judy giggled.

Colleen slipped an arm around her and said: Tell me one thing you know.

I'm . . . I'm disgusting.

That's right. You remember that. So embrace your disgustingness!

But Starfire said—

Who cares? Be disgusting.

Are you making fun of me?

Only if you want me to. Now what does Neva say?

If you bring forth what is within you—

What you have will save you. You're good.

But what the fuck does it mean?

Francine was staring at them.

Don't stop, Judy. *If you have nothing within you . . .*

What you do not have within you will kill you. That's for *you*, Shantelle!

Judy, be nice, said Francine.

Okay, I'll . . . Shantelle, I wanna buy my friend a goofball. Make her happy, and . . .

And so half an hour later Colleen, lolling her head on Judy's shoulder, was slurring out: I think you're part of the same soul cluster as me. I mean, you're in the family. Like, Marilyn Monroe is queer. Have you seen the video of her smoking pot with two lesbians? Before that I never knew that she was queer, but I have seen her in this video, and yes, Judy, she's one of *us*, acting totally dominant to this little femme. Because we're actually a really small family, with our queer ancestors mostly killed. So many of our ancestors were murdered by men. Just to know where we would be now if we had elders . . . ! Oh, Judy, I feel bad . . .

The transwoman was nodding off, almost snoring. Francine asked me to help them back to Judy's place to sleep it off. They were so far gone that it was (as Al would have said) like herding cats. But I finally got Judy's key ring out of her purse and propelled them to the bed. Just before I closed the door I heard the blue-haired woman say: You've been with Neva and you've been with me. We both care about you . . .

The next day Judy came into the Y Bar smiling. She said: Francine, how do I look?

Oh, honey, you look fine. You're losing weight, and—

I look *disgusting*! she shouted. And I'm proud of it!

Whatever, said Francine.

Auditions

> You see, I'm so tired of reading articles in the newspapers and magazines in which I'm described as neurotic, psychotic, idiotic, or any "otic" the writer can think of—and also that I am, as I've read too often, a desperately sick woman.
>
> JUDY GARLAND, 1951

> First of all, I had grown up in the belief that my only worth was in connection with my ability to get parts.
>
> NATALIE WOOD, 1966

1

And a couple months ago I met this lady named Helen, who . . . Neva, she was almost *famous*! She performed in Nashville with Sandrine Summers—a dancer—I should have told you that before, but I got too excited . . . !

The lesbian smiled, fondly or patiently.

It was at the Buddha Bar. And she even let me buy her a drink! And she was beautiful just like Julie Andrews, but she said being beautiful's not the point; the main thing is for me to *work on my confidence*; that's how she—oh, what the fuck's the use? I'm *fat and old and ugly and stupid*; even J. D. says I smell bad—

Well, do you?

I don't know. Starfire said no. Actually, I don't care. But I've lost *twenty-three pounds*!

Judy, take a shower every day. Brush your teeth more. Lose another ten pounds. Will you try?

No, I'm too *worthless* . . . ! she sobbed.

Then don't do it for you. Do it for me. You'll please me if you do it; I'll love you even more—

Really?

I promise.

What if I don't do it?

Then I'll—love you even more! Come take a shower with me.

And Neva, pitying the way the sadness went on for her and the retired policeman year after year, promised to love her and *love her* no matter what.

And I will help you in any other way you ask me to.

Will you help me kill myself?

Yes, said the lesbian.

Tell me something nice. That's how Sandra talks—

You're beautiful.

No, I'm not. I'm disgusting. But you know what, Neva? I just realized that *I don't care.* Did you like those glamor shots I did on my phone?

The ones you texted me? Yes, honey. Meet me in the shower.

2

In the lesbian's dream, Sandra truly had become a mermaid; they were both slowly swimming at least fifteen feet beneath the surface of a warm and fetid green sea, and she needed very urgently to hood Sandra with a length of heavy seaweed cloth, or perhaps she needed Sandra to help her mantle herself, but either way, they both had to breathe, Sandra still more than she, but the other woman did not complain; she would have done anything for Neva, *anything*! and so they stayed beneath the dazzling white skin of their world. Now she grew more certain that she was the one being mantled; Sandra was sacrificing herself for Neva's fulfillment; her doe-like eyes grew wide, intoxicated and desperate; algae stuck ickily to her long neck, and her reddish hair rose up and wrapped itself around Neva's naked body; yes, they were both naked, and they both really, really needed to breathe . . . !—The lesbian woke up, gasping oxygen in.

Almost at once her buzzer rang. It was Sandra's turn.

3

Sandra staggered downstairs, shivering. She had learned that curling up alone in bed on such occasions worsened her comedown symptoms, so she proceeded to the Y Bar, where Francine, unasked, slipped her half a goofball—the first purple kind that Sandra had ever tried—and pretty soon her chills flew away and her headache descended into her spine, although the nausea remained wrapped tightly around her liver, sometimes flexing its spider arms around other portions of her insides, at which moments she felt extremely close to soiling herself with a dark brown gush of cold vomit. Laying a hand on her hand, Francine slipped her three bright blue tummy mints.

And all the while, Sandra sought to outline her latest memories of Neva in the golden ink of gratitude. Francine mixed her a drink: wine and orange juice, the glass so impossibly cold that her fingers went numb touching it. Oh, when the lesbian lay down on top of her, breast to breast, mouth to mouth, slit to slit—the lovely-haired lesbian . . . !—But Sandra's spine was freezing again. Cherishing all the things that she and Neva had just accomplished together, those secret things that lovers do, she sat wishing to complete herself in death now that she had been possessed by such bliss.

Erin was right under the television screen, drinking her customary fizzy water. (Back in her drinking days, Erin held a party at her house, and among the guests was a man whom she found attractive. She got drunk. After the party was over, the man came back into her house, entered her room and raped her. Erin was so out of it that she just lay there letting it happen, but just as he finished she began to cry. He left, and she told no one for years.)

In came Judy, who was longing all the more to imitate the lesbian's grace. Sandra, stretched too thin, felt annoyance at the pathetic creature, who could not help using and draining her. Sandra was achey; if Judy sat down next to her she'd slap her! And Judy sat down next to her, of *course*, turning her big blue eyes so hopefully and dependently on Sandra's face.

Sandra had always loved animals. She now had two cats and a dog at home. Whenever she found a stray pet she would take it in and doctor it so that it could better sell itself at the pound. Sandra had a catlike face while Judy was of a doggish sort. Of all of us I would call Sandra the most open-hearted. In short, she could not abandon Judy.

Judy's breath stank. Judy raked her unclean fingernails through Sandra's hair—because Sandra now took the place of Neva as *she who could open our hearts' locks.*

Sandra said: Darling, I've got the flu or something. Right now it doesn't feel good, being touched . . .

So you hate me.

No, no, I love you—

You promise?

I promise, and Sandra smiled in spite of herself.

Are you my *special friend*?

Of course I am. Francine, how about a drink for Judy?

Six dollars.

Oh, Sandra, I love you so much! Will you tell me about breasts?

What about them?

Well, about growing up and . . .

Well, let me see. It's been a long time—

But you look so young! I'd do anything to look like you. Sandra, could I hug you, just for a minute? Then I swear I won't touch you . . . Just like *this*! Oh, thank you. Now please tell me—

I guess my breasts were a different thing from what I expected. My breasts confounded me. I was probably conscious of them when I was eleven or twelve. My mother tried to get me to wear a bra and I didn't want to, because I wanted to be a kid, not a teenager. She would tell me I couldn't go somewhere unless I put on a bra and I would refuse.

Sandra, continued Judy in the language of secret eagerness, is a woman's personality different from a man's?

You tell me. You've been both.

Well, based on my experience I would say it is. But maybe I was never male at all, just a little . . .—But I asked *you*.

No, I don't think so. I think it's more about individuals—

Then Sandra's phone buzzed. Neva invited her to come straight back over! It was as if she knew of Sandra's kindness to Judy, and wanted to reward her. The rest of us got jealous, I can tell you!

And so Sandra rushed happily back to her beloved; and that something, that strange luminescence possessed by, or inflicted upon, not even one in millions of men and women, that charismatic quantity which departs as inexplicably as it comes—for often, though not always, it pertains to youth, and not merely to the so-called "false flower" of physical grace, but also at least as much to that kindred sunny openness of which we are gradually robbed by life's stings—tricked Sandra into reading into her beloved a godlike coherence of body, heart and purpose which might have been biology's accident: Why are some people most drawn to a certain color, and how can a stag be lured toward the hunter by means of a few drops of urine from a doe in heat? The answers to such questions may be comic or pathetic. Perhaps Neva gave off a hormonal fragrance irresistible to most of us—she was everyone's favorite color! . . . —Another possible solution: Just as in fairytales a prince may fall in love with a faraway princess as a simple result of hearing her praised, so might a celebrity-worshipper surrender to attractions purveyed even by a black-and-white television screen over whose actresses' faces static swarms like a horde of killer bees. The feeling that Sandra had for Neva—we called it love—projected Neva's face most hauntingly and beautifully upon the ceiling of her skull, so that Neva smiled down upon the nutlike lobes of Sandra's brain . . . and the first time that Neva allowed her to hold her smooth little hand, Sandra felt as if they were kissing each other's brains.

4

Xenia's voice said: I keep falling asleep because someone gave me a Tranquilex and two mellow reds and I washed 'em down with beer, but I'm feeling sad, because I'm all alone down here in the basement and *you're not here.*

I'm sorry, said the lesbian.

Neva, I'm feeling really frustrated.

I understand.

I feel like things are different since last time we were together.

Oh, said the lesbian.

I was sexually intimate with Louis—you know, that straight man.

Well, I hope he gave you a nice orgasm.

But, Neva, you're the one who put me in this box. I was just your lover and you had other people, so maybe I was malicious when I did it with Louis . . .

Were you? I hope you didn't do it for that reason.

I can tell that you want to get me off the phone soon. And I've been avoiding Hunter, because she—

Pretty soon.

Who's coming over?

Francine.

Neva, I feel so sad. And I'm very wet right now.

I wish I could be there with you.

But then you'd disappoint Francine.

That's right.

I'm touching myself. When I'm with Louis or Hunter I actually want to be with you but you're not there, and I love you so much. Do you believe me?

Of course I do. And I love *you* so much.

I feel really guilty, but I don't know whether to be guilty toward you or toward them, because I . . . Can you call me back later tonight?

I can call you tomorrow, said the lesbian.

Okay, said Xenia. Oh, God. Maybe I'll go see Hunter and get her to . . .

She hung up.

The lesbian answered the next call on the first ring.—Well, sweetie Sandra!

There was a long silence, and then Sandra said: Hello . . .

Where are you?

I'm sitting under the same tree where I was yesterday, but it's not raining anymore and there are people all around me and I feel so nervous . . .

Then the lesbian knew. She said: Is it over?

Sandra started to cry. I love you so much, and I tried to be fearless; I thought we could do anything together, and I was willing to be everything to you, but since you weren't the same I started feeling like a fool . . .

I understand, said the lesbian.

Are you going to be okay?

Of course, honey, and I'll always love you. Do you want me to say goodbye now?

Sandra sobbed and sobbed.—Goodbye, she finally whispered. Then she hung up.

The buzzer rang. Shantelle had arrived. Joyfully high on a handful of blue pills, she began gripping the lesbian's head while the lesbian sucked, sucked and *sucked* her purple-brown nipple, which would be very sore the next morning, and Shantelle, for whom thinking about touching Neva was almost like planning out a shoplifting mission at Gracey's department store, was saying: I love you so damn much and I hate you so much that what I can see right now is . . . Go ahead, shoot me, ho! I see me slappin' your face until it gets to bleedin' and me with my foot on your face and I'm grindin' your face into the sidewalk and you're just *lookin'* at me when I give you two black eyes to teach you to be only with *me*, *forever*, and under the ground is the skull of your dead grandfather and when I give you two black eyes his eyes come back into his skull so he can . . . so he . . .—to which the lesbian, saddened and frightened, if only a trifle, at the implication of these words, kept sucking Shantelle's nipple and gliding her hand up and down her body from shoulder to buttock, so happy and giving in her touching, while Shantelle went on crooning her violent visions, remembering the cool white glowing evenings of late spring in Los Angeles, the clean and shining traffic on Western, a fat white girl on a bus bench, and Shantelle's little boy (whom she had signed over to her grandmother forever because he was no fucking good) playing with her braids for the last time; a cool breeze; yellow price numbers on a gas station's pumps, steady silent airplanes in the cloudless sky; then the tall glass cliffs of skyscrapers, boom boxes vibrating out of car windows as she rushed down Wilshire past rows of Korean restaurants, and the feeling of openness when she accelerated on the freeway onramp late at night and found herself almost alone on that winding concrete ribbon, speeding into the stars!—even as her flesh went on swelling, flushing, sweating and blossoming under the lesbian's touch.

Then came Francine, after which the phone rang. It was Xenia saying: I didn't bring it up because I was kind of lying to myself. But I do have somebody else who's attracted to me. She didn't show up at work for a week, and then a cop called me to ask if I knew where she was, and I didn't even exactly know her apartment number, but she has a crush on me, and that kind of moved my heart. She was really pale, in really bad shape. She'd been doing a lot of drugs, because she's so attracted to me . . .

And you're sure she loves you? asked the lesbian.

Well, it's funny, because that's kind of trusting my intuition. But I think that's a strength of mine. You're thinking about Hunter, aren't you?

That's right, said the lesbian, who was feeling sad and tired. Xenia was saying: I wasn't fluid about it; I probably compartmentalized. Lesbians can't say that word. We . . . I'm really really high right now. So it turned into that sort of messy pyramid spiderweb and the top was your name with a heart around it, and that's why I feel calm talking about it, because you're the best thing in my heart, but I'm lonely . . .

Me too, said the lesbian.

When we were intimate, it was so clear to me. And still I would die for you, and I have these fearless love feelings for you.

Since Xenia was waiting for her to say something loving and comforting and healing as usual, the lesbian slowly said: I had a fantasy. If I couldn't solve the problem any other way, I could maybe overdose in your arms.

That would be nice. But I'd want to die, too. I wouldn't like to be left all alone with your corpse getting cold . . .

If you want to, we both can, said the lesbian. Or if you want just me to die . . .

Neva, are you okay?

Yes, honey, and I love you so much. If it's all right with you I'm going to lie down now.

5

I want to make you happy the way I did before, Judy pleaded, and how could the lesbian not make *her* happy then?

Aren't you curious? moaned Judy. Don't you want to know what I taste like tonight?

Tell me you desire me, said Judy.

The lesbian lifted her mouth from the other woman's penis and murmured: I desire you.

Then she went back to sucking.

Tell me you adore me.

I adore you, said the lesbian.

Tell me you love me more than anyone else.

But by now the lesbian was tired, so she just kept sucking. No goddess answers all our prayers.

6

Hey, babe, it's your Xenia calling. I wanted to call you earlier but I was in a bad mood. But now I took more goofballs, so I'm feeling . . . *whee!* Neva, Neva, I wanted to say goodnight and let you know that I had another teenaged dream about you. You were in a coffin-sized refrigerator that was down here, and then you came out to surprise me. It was a good dream, very sexual and suspenseful toward the end because we were deciding who was going to climax first and who was going to die first in our special game, and I think the one to go first was me, but I'm not sure because your being in the dream kind of blurred all the other details, and I . . . Well, I should probably sleep now because I have to wake up at five a.m. to get to work, but I just wanna say goodnight, and I'm thinking of you and hope to hear from you soon . . .

7

Judy, I have news, said the lesbian. Remember those glamor shots? I kept the best five on my phone. This morning I went down to the Tiger Zone, and Xenia's friend Duane scrolled through them. He wants to give you a lip-synch audition on Friday.

Oh, my God! Neva, that's . . . But I *can't.*

Would you do it for me?

To please you?

That's right.

Because—because you'll love me?

Yes, said the lesbian.

Then I'll do it. But I've got to get some pills—maybe two blue dolphins or just one.

Take three, and bring one with you for security. But Xenia's about to ring the doorbell, so help me strip the bed. Thanks. Do you have everything?

I'll fit the clean sheets on.

Are those your condoms on the sofa?

Oh, I forgot. Neva, I can't find my house keys.

Here they are.

Where were they?

You put them under the bed. Did you do that on purpose?

Yes, Neva.

I love you. Give me a kiss.

. . . And the doorbell buzzed.

8

A woman unlocked two heavy wooden doors which were graffiti'd, paint-splashed and crookedly overlain with consumerist decals; from across the street the transwoman saw beyond that woman a long pallid flight of stairs rising invitingly to some unknown place—but then the door closed.

Two young women hurried wet and laughing down the sidewalk, stopping suddenly to share a kiss. The transwoman strained her eyes to see, hoping they would do something else. Already they were around the corner.

Like the ever disoriented Natalie, lately blissed out, who hastened back to the mound of feces and trash behind which she customarily bought her chemical happiness, Judy went home to imagine the lesbian. Just now it seemed that to have her was like owning some golden jewel—beautiful yellow-gold!—cold, yes, but ready like a reptile to lie against someone and absorb her warmth . . .—then it got put away again, and went cold again.

9

And did you feel any pleasure when your mother touched you?

It was only about what she wanted. That's all.

Because when my uncle molested me, he used to eat my pussy, and I . . .

You enjoyed it, said the lesbian.

Yes, Xenia replied.

And that's why you like me to give you pleasure now, and I like to give you pleasure now.

No, it can't be that simplistic!

Why not?

Neva, I want to ask you something.

All right.

Do you think that you or I could have wanted it, or somehow done something to—

I want it now, whispered the lesbian, leaning forward and kissing her buttock.

Please, Neva, tell me . . . !

Now close your eyes and don't think anymore.

10

So it came time to audition. In Judy's fantasies a rise to stardom was generally as slow and reliable as the escalators in the Regional Justice Center of Las Vegas: first dim corner entertainment, next spokeswoman for a new deodorant brand that was *inspiring, sexy and bold*, then maybe even a chorus line flower in a remake of some black-and-white Hollywood "classic," oh, *yeah* . . . !—but the nearer she came to her moment of being "discovered," the more loudly her stomach fizzed and gurgled. Longing to overcome her body odor, she rushed down to the RiteDrug and took an "explorer"-sized bottle from the shelf, then realized that with the family size she could truly SAVE, so that was what she bought. Half an hour later, she was in the shower, rubbing it all over herself. And just as the advertisement promised, she could feel it enhancing, healing, smoothing, cleansing and *improving* her right through her skin! She felt younger and prettier. For good measure, she launched another secret puke party, which made her feel shaky but racked her total weight loss up to nineteen pounds. Pouting because the retired policeman refused to buy her the lime-green cross-body bag with the columns of sequins on it, haunting discount stores in hope of the unprecedented blouse that would help her change her style, listening with all her soul when the little television advised: *Deep, penetrating moisture for that smooth, youthful look*, throwing three shades of lipstick into her darling party clutch, she covered every feminine base.

Neva, am I beautiful?

Tickling her, the lesbian said: You're *beautifully disgusting*! and they both laughed.

11

Behind the Tiger Zone's golden tinsel curtain, up the green-and-purple-illuminated steps, lay a narrow chamber carpeted with crimson and walled with endometrial lining, and behind that the next incarnation of talent waited. Judy emerged; she was born and quickly died, after which the Tiger Zone decided that she would be *maybe not a good fit*, but the Pink Apple said (according to Neva-nudged Xenia) *like, sure, whatever.*

Xenia laid it out: I don't have much of a routine. I get up and I look at my computer to see if I'm gonna work. The manager at Pink Apple decides that. We don't choreograph our dances. It's just like moving around. You don't have to be skilled at all. Some of the best strippers don't have any training at all. If there's nothing doing there, I see what I can score down here. It's all easy money. I was homeless. I just walked into the Pink Apple and got a job. I'll keep stripping for maybe another year . . .

Richard says you're quitting in July.

Well, what does that bitch know about *me*? The hell with him.

I'll bet you feel like a real woman when you—

No, I just kind of do my thing and don't pay attention to people very much. If they give me money I'm gonna get naked. That's what I'm here for. I don't care either way. And you know what your problem is? You still fuckin' care. As long as they can see you care, they're gonna shit on you. They'll shit on you regardless, but when you care it's more sad. All right; there's your lesson for today. Look me up when you make more progress on your not caring.

I promise I don't care about anything.

Your funeral, *Frank*.

Don't call me that.

See? You care.

Okay, I'm sorry; you can call me Frank.

Then you're ready, so I'll call you Judy. Let's go, girl! And you know something funny? When they ask me what's between my legs I always say: No, I'm not a tranny. I'm just an ugly old lady. That floors 'em, because then they realize that *I don't care.* How much weight did you lose?

Thirty pounds.

Don't lie to me, bitch.

Twenty pounds.

Whatever.

There was a stage with a red curtain, an atmosphere like a very large and crowded living room, half-nude G-girls loitering, lip-synching T-girls strutting around, taking sides in the eternal debate as to who was the best actress ever. (Neva, the one about whom our sensations turned, was already in the audience, encircled by admirers, smiling graciously all the way to the end of this thing that was being done to her.) Judy thought the G-girls looked down on the T-girls, but let's say that was only her neurosis.—This was the big time: plump, pretty girls whose cheek-blush glowed in the red light and whose long crucifix-earrings and double crescent-earrings and various whatchamacallits glitter-jiggled whenever they hugged, *oh, my GOD.* Xenia outshone them; she wore a gold crescent across her throat, and her canyon of cleavage went halfway down to her navel. A big man with a moustached smile was demanding: Don't I get some change for my dollar? to which she replied: If you're the last in line, then what you get is what you get.—When she saw Judy her black-outlined eyes narrowed into teardrop-slits.

So why are you here, actually? said she. Because with your so-called outfit you won't make any money!

Maybe I'll please someone—

I'd bet my last fuckin' nickel you won't. That tight dress makes you look like a sausage wrapped in razor wire.

Two fat Goth girls rubbed hips, giggling together.

I'm sorry, said Judy. But you said . . . I mean, I should have—

Too late now.

Just as Marlene Dietrich so often had to vomit once or twice on the way to a morning shoot at Paramount, so Judy now felt queasy, but she replied: Even so, it just feels like the right thing for me to do.

Please yourself, said Xenia.

Can I buy you a beer? I mean, it would be my honor to—

And you know, honey, white looks shitty on you, because your skin is so red and coarse. I myself will always wear red—didn't I tell you?—because I believe red makes men hungry. Men do have a type they glom onto, but they're hungry for something and—

But, Xenia, you're not wearing red.

That's because I . . .—oh, fuck you anyway.

Here came battling cones of light green and yellow, white and pink, pulsing circles on the floor, planetoids orbiting through rays, the disco balls slowly turning, the dance floor still empty, with the canned music pounding in Judy's breastbone. Where had Neva gone? She felt sicker than ever.

Never expecting to be as graceful as the blonde stripper on the round stage who, almost ignored on account of the six other strippers each on her own respective round stage, reminded me of a figure skater because her high heels glided across the ice-blue stage in between each naked twirl, Judy nonetheless hoped to earn a handful of dollars or maybe some applause. Xenia was pep-talking a dithering old man: Sweetie, with your money you're the king of the world.—From the bar, Starfire uncrossed her ankles and fired off a hellishly nasty look at Judy.

The manager came to oversee and dominate Judy. (Yes, reader, he picked the right girl!) His goal was to stand a hundred and one percent behind the company. To him all these dancers were scum. Just as our greatest pharmaceutical companies saw clear to advertise their poisons on television once those previously significant middlemen called *doctors* had been sufficiently weakened, so he wished to go straight to the almighty *customer base*—this gay couple, that wide-eyed crossdresser in a striped skirt, those two women sitting with their legs open, gazing unsmilingly straight ahead—cutting out human performers in favor of cheap, consistent video porn. Whenever he fired someone he'd say something like: She couldn't even make up her mind about paying her bills, so come *on.*

He now said: What's your name?

Judy. You know, like Judy Garland.

I was never a fan. You're Number Six.

Okay, she said, feeling hot and nauseated. Xenia would be Number Thirteen.

So I had my crown on, and this big purple *gown* on, a T-girl was droning. Judy wondered what she was talking about. A sexy G-girl kept pushing drinks on everyone. There was already a twenty-dollar cover (which even Judy and Xenia had to pay), then a two-drink minimum, not to mention five dollars to take a photo with the drag queen emcee on Tranny Bingo nights. Neva had not yet returned. A young man in horn rim spectacles changed a hundred-dollar bill into ones which he kept giving out by the handful. A tall broad drag queen in a loose silver and blue robe, pasty-fleshed, flattered her public by asking about their job and birthdays while the other performers got ready. Two boys dreamed their way out onto the shimmering empty floor, dancing in each other's arms. Judy bit her nails.

Then Number One was already flashing and swaying her milk-white flesh, outspreading her long blonde hair, while her buttocks pulsed back and forth. This tall one could lip-synch so well with her wide mouth and dark dark lips that Judy felt seriously outclassed. Now for applause, which Judy Garland called *the* most *beautiful music in the whole world*! The worshipping little boys were laughing and bowing down as they rushed forward to plant dollar bills in Number One's crotch.

Number Two, almost as glamorous as Shantelle, was a tall black T-girl in a long silver dress with the ultrablue light on her so that she was all different kinds of blue, her skin a chocolate-blue, her massive wig silver-blue, her rhinestone earrings and choker silver rainbows of blue; when men sprinted forward to give her a dollar or two she would winkingly kiss her O of thumb and forefinger.

The retired policeman, knowing that Judy would never do anything of value without first consulting him, sat beaming in the audience right next to (finally!) the lesbian—who of course was perfect, while Judy was trash. But with each shot of watered-down bourbon, the music hurt Judy's ears less and grew more exciting. Besides, Neva was here! Bachelorettes kept darting up, giggling happily to stuff dollar bills between each T-girl's boobs. Telling herself, *Soon this will happen to me!*, Judy felt almost thrilled.

Number Four was a wide tall-wigged drag queen with huge eyelashes and a deep bass voice. Thick-belted like a roll of carpet lashed to a pickup truck, with her rhinestone earrings down to her shoulders and her rhinestone necklace halfway down her belly, she sang "Follow the Yellow Brick Road," leaving Judy envious and despondent.

Number Five was three black ladies in starry glitterskirts with silverpearly lavender lipstick shining on their parted lips, swishing their arms, moving a trifle more heavily, perhaps, than certain G-girls, but still convincing. They were so glamorous that Judy's heart sank further.

Number Six, said the manager. *Go, go, go!*

She emerged from the curtain and the spotlight stuck to her like a leech, and then, instead of lip-synching or dancing or even merely swaying, she stood helpless and humiliated, for all the world like a painted skeleton in a cage. Then she started sobbing.

A drunk shouted: Shake your ass, you big fat cow!

The retired policeman clapped as loudly as he could, but it didn't help. She dared not gaze at Neva. Starfire was laughing at her. Or maybe she . . .

Number Seven, said the manager.

Lowering her eyes, the lesbian turned sadly away.—Judy would have done anything to be dead.

From behind the red curtain came someone with the black-banged wig and pale face and loose black dress, very glamorous, with glittering eyes in a Liza Minnelli face, who said: Out of my way, fatty!—Everyone laughed at Judy.

She ran to the ladies' room and tried to lock herself in, but there was no lock. She could hear Number Seven singing *What makes a man a man?*

After a long time the lesbian came in. When she laid her hand on Judy's neck, Judy shrugged it off, saying: I'm fine.

No, honey, you're not, said the lesbian. Come here and let me hold you. Please?

No.

Just for me—

All right, said Judy, sobbing with relief. Tears and snot soaked Neva's hair.

Now come on out and sit with us.

It was almost stupendous the way that Number Eleven orbited so rapidly around the catty pole, holding on with one hand above the other, with her body five feet up and parallel to the stage, and her thighs always spread, crablike; her legs made a questing claw whose pincers were sharpened by her long high heels; she rushed around on her side, with her dark wig nearly touching our workaday Earth and funneling outward into a wide display of aggression or invitation outshining her faraway breasts and head.

The retired policeman held Judy's hand.

Approaching Neva, the dreamy androgyne of a certain marble Dionysus murmured something to her; then a lesbian in coveralls and a butch haircut said to Judy: Do you remember me?

No.

Good. I'll tell you something humiliating that happened to me. Wouldn't you like that?

I don't know, Judy whispered.

Well, one time I was holding hands with another girl in Wenatchee, Washington, and people were honking and shouting: *Make out!* It all depends on where you are. There's an island where I live; you might have been there, too. Over there they treat normies as freaks.

Irritably the retired policeman cut in: I'm a freak, you're a freak. Judy sure is a fuckin' stinkin' freak—

The butch woman laughed in his face. Judy leaped up and ran outside, while the retired policeman sat drinking, sullenly afflicted by a vision of the lovely high-breasted lesbian squatting nude and offering her shining pink seashell to his impotence.

12

So she had failed the audition—oh, what a disgrace! (Once again she had thought to escape from going down the way that we all must go.) Trembling, blubbering and snivelling, she incarnated her namesake: yes, she almost could have been Judy Garland crying to see how ugly she appeared in the film *Pigskin Parade*—or if you're tired of that comparison, how about Natalie Wood when she lost the Oscars competition to Sophia Loren in 1962? If only she'd worn red according to Xenia's advice . . . !

When she got to the Y Bar, it was twenty minutes before last call. The blue-haired paratrooper Colleen was drinking by herself.

Oh, hi, Judy whispered.

C'mere, said Colleen. Give me a kiss.

Oh, I feel so blue, like I'm maybe not even a woman. But then men . . . At the Pink Apple it was all about attracting men, even though I saw plenty of chicks with money, so I don't . . .

You don't what?

I mean, tell me: what's the best thing about loving another woman?

The emotional deepness, replied her friend. You know we get socialized to be so self-conscious, so when we're with somebody else we're so self-conscious as well. But there's this other language, this understanding.

I don't get it. I'm not even female, so how would I?

Sure you do. Think about how men are. They are not allowed to show their pain; they don't let themselves feel. The men that I see in my life, they are sometimes afraid to hug another man, except in soccer games which I love watching because my brother can hug another guy; otherwise they're like *sticks.* And you know what? We women know when we're being shitty. Men, well, generally, they all think they're the best ever. Judy, do you think you're the best?

Not hardly.

Same here. Now what are we, you and I? One, two, three—

Disgusting! cried Judy gleefully.

That's why you need a woman. Guess what? I'm a friend of Neva's, and she just texted me she's waiting for you—

Oh! How do you know her?

Honey, she's lying there wearing nothing but a big fat strap-on!

Judy practically clapped her hands. Off she ran, straight to Neva's. Catalina's door was closed, but Neva's was open: Time for a hug and a kiss and—

I want to watch you, the transwoman said. You know, with others, while I sit in the corner and touch myself, and I wouldn't be allowed to come near you—

Judy, haven't you had enough degradation tonight?

Please, oh, pretty please! So I can learn . . . ! I'll do anything! I want to watch you with a man—

Why?

I'm not sure. Maybe I'm not a lesbian. I mean, I do have a boyfriend and I . . . Neva, should I give up on women?

Are you done with me?

No! But please, please let me watch you with somebody, with . . .

Okay, said the lesbian.

So she called me up, and I rushed straight over, overjoyed at my extra turn. I felt embarrassed at first, that Judy was watching. But she *begged* me. Besides, the instant Neva spat in my mouth, I got over my shame. In utter silence, fascinated, ashamed, miserably jealous and very, very excited, Judy kept us company. When I told Neva: I'm willing for my love to be eaten up by you until there's none left for anybody else, and I *want* that; I'm begging you!, Judy started masturbating, of course. Then she and Neva went to sleep in the bedroom while I sacked out on the couch.

13

Xenia arrived in the morning. She said: Neva, I swear I did my best, but she—

What was up with her?

You mean, where did her self-sabotage come from? My sense is that these are things happened early on. So, once upon a time Judy was a little boy, and, well, he's starting to cross-dress, and he's very submissive sexually and maybe he's already a street kid, and I'll bet you his father once tied him to a radiator and abused him . . .

We all come from dirt, said the lesbian. Honey, will you please keep helping her?

She's got *issues*. I mean, until she helps herself . . .

Please, Xenia, said the lesbian. Do it for me.

14

I told you, said Xenia.

Maybe I should just give up . . .

What's your mantra?

Follow the Yellow Brick Road.

That's dumb. Try this one: *I'm a big fat cow.*

That's mean.

Well, that's what that asshole called you when you froze up. Why couldn't you go on with your act?

I'm sorry.

Sorry doesn't cut it. You need to own it, so say it.

I'm a big fat cow. I'm a big fat cow. I'm a big fat cow who—takes it up the ass!

Good girl. What a *good little* big fat masochist. Now, why did you freeze that night? What was in your ugly head?

I was afraid they'd laugh at me. And they did—

They did not. They were sorry for you, which is worse. Another reason why sorry doesn't cut it. Judy, I stuck out my neck for you, and you put me in a bad position.

So what should I do?

You said it: Give up.

I don't want to.

Then don't. Go get some meth to help you with your confidence. Then I'll watch you practice.

I'm afraid.

Haven't you put me out enough? And think how Neva feels—

Okay, I'll do it for you.

15

Well, what do you want *me* to do about it? Starfire demanded. I told you, she groped me and got me so stoned I was violently ill, and then she just left me there to . . .

Please do it for me, said the lesbian.

Xenia's trying to help her by making her think she can do it. I'd try to help her by telling her how shitty the job is. Is that what you want?

But she's afraid—

Maybe she'll work harder then. Where is she?

You can talk to her right here.

What, and then as soon as I leave you'll fuck her?

That's right, said the lesbian.

No.

Okay.

When I say no, I mean no.

So as soon as Judy rang the buzzer, there was Neva making coffee while Judy sat wide-eyed on the sofa beside Starfire, who said: You know, it really sucks, getting disgusting guys laughing at you. You saw how it was the other night. It's kind of rough. Getting those guys to buy those super pricey drinks, it's a misery. You have to compartmentalize, just pack it up. Don't you at least partly identify as a guy?

That's so mean, said Judy.

No it isn't. Men have the ability to compartmentalize. They can go on two different dates in the same day. We women usually can't do it, but I had one stripper friend who had stars taped up in her van, a real hippie child; she had her black book: *I call all these guys.* She decided to be an escort to do a study. She ended up being killed. Well, maybe that's not the most encouraging example, but the fact is, if you wanna perform you can't keep it real. Judy Garland was not real; she was something that her mother and the industry cobbled together, to make money. So shut yourself down and—

Now that's interesting, said the transwoman, because Xenia told me something like that. She said I have to stop caring. But you care, don't you, Neva? You're not just faking it when you say you love us?

Honey, I care. Starfire, do you want cream or sugar? We've never had coffee together . . .

Black is fine, said Starfire. Judy, do you see these tattoos? That first one was in 1993, which was the year I got married. Then I got so sick of doing the same show every night. Finally I said I'm getting the hell out of there, so I ended up working another contract. She said okay, honey, you can go, and if you want to come back in six months you can. So I went out to get tattoos right away, so I would never again be in show business. They want to see unblemished and beautiful women. Last year I was gonna get them removed, and my daughter said, Mom, they're a part of your life. The reason I was so intent on getting out was because my first contract, my friend Camellia, had given fourteen years of her life to Jaybird's, and they treated her like yesterday's trash. I think that they felt they would get rid of the weak ones, the ones that would . . . She tried to go with the flow. But even though she's on a billboard, when she tried to go back they wouldn't hire her. There you go, Judy. That's why I wash windows and moonlight at the Pink Apple for peanuts.

Judy said: I don't care if they treat me like trash. I wanna be looked at and . . . I mean, Neva, wherever *you* go they start drooling. I'd give anything to have that. What does it feel like?

It's what I'm here for, said the lesbian.

And it's what Judy Garland was here for! She had her ups and downs, but she . . . Well, she's *immortal.*

Starfire said: Well, you and I are not.

But you—

My mother grew up very poor and always wanted to dance. She put me in dance class because I was so shy I would hide under the bed. She put me in dance to get me out of my shell. I just happened to be good at it. They were grooming me to be a ballerina and I got into that dance class in New York, and they all looked like me and could dance better, but the difference was they wanted it and I didn't. But I was in goddamn Mobile, Alabama. Followed in my sister's footsteps, being a secretary, and it was horrible, so I got my Actor's Equity card. And all the time I'm thinking, I can't even get a job at a Disney audition. Actually I worked for a number of years as an exotic dancer. Men would say to me, you need to get out of here. You're not like these other girls. You're a *nice* girl. So I went to Jaybird's, and I got hired as a Palmleaf Girl. Oh, my God, what a cattle call! I had a friend who auditioned five times or six times. If Angie didn't like your nose, or your eyes . . . So it was an honor to be chosen. The headpiece was only a headpiece but it seemed like a lot of weight to me. I was swaying. Angie had favorites. They would get all the paying gigs, modeling and so on. I went into the audience and I bitched. The next week I got a gig with New York Glammies. I got a good seventy-five bucks. Donald Trump came once. He didn't even look at the stage. He was too busy looking around, either to check out his protection from the boys in the suits with the earpieces, or to make sure people would see him. So there's your fame for you, Judy. I remember Victor Vidalis, you know, the TV actor, following me all around and I almost knocked him over. I had this hat for the Army-Navy portion of the show, with these two pieces of foam, and I remember thinking, what the fuck, dude? I'm walking around with no clothes on. When I quit, my mother was angry because now she couldn't tell her friends her daughter was a showgirl. After I quit I tried out for one other show at the Berghof and I didn't get hired for that and I decided I would just be a waitress. I always felt that the dancing thing was just limited. I'm not educated, not beyond high school.

Well, I'm not educated, either, said Judy. And I'd do anything to . . .

Anything? said Starfire. First of all, you're lazy. Second, you have no discipline. If you can't lose your flab, what does that say about you? Third, you don't have any pride. You're like the ones who just hang on until they get fired. When they don't get the hint, don't be looking in the magic mirror; look in the real one. I think people of your kind, well, Judy, I think they're not very realistic about what they look like. They had to tell Susie, you need to retire. In fact she was a beautiful woman, great woman, but she was fifty-three. It was common to have yourself a boob job. Angie would not let you go out there with one, unless you had a really good one. Susie had about six sets of implants, and after that the doctor said, there's not really anything else I can do for you.

At this Judy went into the bathroom to make herself vomit, so that she would be more beautiful for Neva. Starfire looked wound up. The lesbian held her hand. Starfire said slowly: But I think that a lot of us, we knew that Angie loved us, regardless of entertainment director changes. I'm sure I could have worked into my mid-forties. I knew that was an open door for me. But I would rather clean houses and shine shoes. Well, I do miss the old days, because dancing's so . . . You get off work at one in the morning and you go to the Four Daisies and you get yourself a big fat slice of Sicilian pizza and never gain a pound.

16

Judy went walking, in order to clear her head. She went all the way to Bryant Street.

On the wide battleship-grey topmost concrete step of the portico whose *raison d'être* was six locked steel doors all in a row, she sat down, smoked a strictly medicinal joint, tried to decipher the graffiti on the parked trailer truck, watched grey nothingness go by on that grey Saturday morning, until finally something actually happened: a young man in shorts, with a messenger bag over his shoulder, came up the sidewalk, ogling his cell phone until he tripped.

She asked herself what, if anything, Neva and Starfire would *both* advise her to do. The answer appeared to be: Stop feeling sorry for myself.

But I like to be humiliated.

That's different, because I've sworn to embrace my disgustingness.

All right, Judy, she agreed.

She went home to wash her clothes, thoughtfully inhaling the pseudo-fresh smell, ultimately nauseating, of the soap and bleach and fabric softener at the laundromat. Starfire was a blessing and an abettor, while Neva was the one in whom our hearts rested.

She spied the old Asian in the baseball cap who also came here every Saturday; he had lined his cart with a heavy duty garbage bag; while her laundry went around she saw him tenderly fix another man's spectacles, rejoining the temple to the lens frame with a screwdriver no longer than his thumbnail; and she thought: What have *I* done for anybody?

Well, I make J. D. happy.

Only because he—

And Neva loves me!

Because she'd love anyone.

17

But the retired policeman bought me a double rum and sodapop at the Cinnabar, where two women were just then coming out from the restroom arm in arm. He was sore at Neva for encouraging Judy beyond her capabilities. He said: Soliciting, engaging, loitering is a misdemeanor. Now, all of you are claiming that Karen won't take a dime for turning a trick. But how many men and women has she flat-backed? It's got to be hundreds at least. Now, engaging in prostitution is only a felony if they're HIV positive and they know they're HIV positive. Well, what's the likelihood that Karen *doesn't* have something? Come on, man. That should be an attempted homicide charge.

She never gave me anything, I said.

Have you gotten tested?

I confessed that I never had and never would, at which he said: I mean, you are knowingly . . . That's like my taking out my revolver and shooting in your direction.

18

Listen, said Shantelle, who was slouching sexily against the wall like Natalie Wood in *West Side Story.* Neva's settin' us up against each other.

No, because Neva loves us.

Bitch, how could Neva ever love *you*? Think about it. Anybody claims to love you, she gotta be *lyin'* to you. *Now* do you feel it?

Blinking rapidly, the transwoman insisted: Neva loves me. And she loves you.

Xenia now said in such a slow slurred voice (staring into the mirror) that she could have been speaking to herself, in which case her interjection would have been a coincidence: I would want for the criticizing to stop, because there's so much hatred for women *among themselves*; you're not supposed to be like this kind or that kind of woman. That hatred, we feel it, so we vomit it out. We have to stop spreading it. I've caught myself doing it. What's the right way to be? I'm more comfortable around people who . . . who are more, I mean, more attentive to . . .

Richard, would you take her home? said Francine.

Which one of them? I said.

Xenia wandered away.

Forget it, said Francine.

Samantha, filled with fresh knowledge thanks to a new European friend, was asking Selene: Have you ever been to *Denmark* or *Germany* or wherever, where they pay more taxes, but . . . ?

Beginning to emote with all the conviction of some avaricious enlarger of the

Roman Empire, Shantelle led Judy outside and continued: Maybe you got the advantage, bein' stupid. But you gotta prove it.

Prove what?

I don't know. Maybe I'm high. Fine. But . . . Forget that. Now what about sharin' Neva fifty-fifty, just you and me? Instead of seein' her for an hour every two or three days, you could have her all day, and I'd have her all night! All fuckin' *night* . . . ! What would you say to that?

That's impossible.

Not if you and I go fifty-fifty. Judy, if you turn me down I'm gonna be your enemy for life. I'll never stop poundin' on you. But if you do like I say, I mean *exactly now*, we're gonna have Neva together, just you and me, forever—

What do I have to do?

We're gonna learn everything about her. When the time comes, I'll tell you what to do. Yes or no?

Unable to say no, of course she said yes. Then Shantelle took her home and fucked her just the way she liked it, until she was weeping and screaming. It was almost as good as being with the lesbian.

19

I who had overheard everything asked Francine: Does Shantelle have any kind of point? I'm not saying Neva's actively pitting us against each other—

Then what *are* you saying?

I've never had as much love in my life as I do now.

Same here.

Well, are you happier?

What a question! Sure—

I am, too, when I'm with her. The rest of the time . . .

But isn't that human nature? she said. We always want more.

By the way, is *she* human? What does *she* want?

Rattling glassware in the sink, Francine said: Let's drop it.

20

Neva was out, so Judy rang Catalina's buzzer and said: I told you I want to be a lesbian—

Then be one, said her hostess, standing unwelcomingly in the doorway.

How do I do it?

Well, I didn't become one; I was born one. But what are you anyway? Don't you still fuck that retired cop?

It used to be for money, but—

Lighting a cigarette, Catalina said: So you love him, or you love the abuse?

I, I don't know.

What's the use of asking you anything? But here you are, nosing into my business again.

I'm sorry, and I sure do appreciate it. You know how Hillary Clinton keeps saying, *it takes a village to raise a child*? Well, it's taking all of you to raise Judy, and I—

You're too much, said Catalina.

I'm just saying hello. Okay? Just wanted to say hi. Um, *hi*! Am I being inappropriate? I don't want anything. Are you bored with me yet?

Yes, said Catalina.

I'm sorry.

Oh, God, I give up. Come in. Sit down. I've got a late shift at the grocery market pretty soon, but whatever. And I'm already tired, and you annoy me, and how is learning who I am going to help you figure out who you are?

I don't know, said Judy miserably.

Fine. I was already attracted to women when I was little. I remember one time when we lived in some apartments and that hallway where, that outside hallway, the alley, and I found a porn magazine and it had women, and I had weird feelings, and nice feelings, and those women, they were looking like my teacher. She was a very pretty white woman.

And did she . . . ?

Be quiet. I used to play family with a lot of the girls that were my neighbors. I always liked boys that were more like feminine looking and I did have boyfriends. But I didn't know that that could be like my life until I started realizing that I had real crush feelings for a woman when I was eighteen. I was afraid because I knew that my mom was not gonna be okay with it. She makes the rules; she's the boss. My mom, she caught us one time in my room, and my mom she said that she was gonna tell my dad, but she had never brought up my dad as a power figure and she said: what do you think your dad will say? At first I told her that I would stop seeing this girl, that I would fix it. I had had boyfriends before. In the room that we were in there was a door to the back yard, so that girl just ran out. And after I was done talking to mom I went looking for her, and she was in the neighborhood, and I had her stop, and she was so sad. My mom told me that it was her fault, because she had wanted a boy. I stopped for about a week. And then I was playing soccer at the time and my coach told me he had a gay aunt and she was dying of cancer because she couldn't accept who she really was, and I thought that was so scary, so that same night, I hooked up with my girlfriend, and she was so happy. But my girlfriend's family had her do conversion therapy. Then her mom brought me a picture of her son and said, isn't he attractive, don't you wanna be with him? Very traumatizing, being pushed into being a normie. It lasted four or five weeks. Then our relationship was open and people just had to deal with it. Within just three or four months it was out in the air. Her mom and dad called me, and they said that if I didn't stop calling her they were going to call my mom, and they said if I wanted to be with her I would have to get surgery; so I had to show my mom the e-mails that were harassing. And my mom told them that I was nineteen and Tenicia was nineteen, so we would both do what we were gonna do. My dad told me to keep it private and not post anything on Babble or those other sites. I said nothing, but I was so hurt. I felt mad but I didn't tell him. My brother, my sister, they were super cool with it immediately. The rest of my family, they never told me anything. My grandpa, my grandma, nobody. But back in Mexico, I had a cousin that was also coming out, and my mom had my sister, what's wrong, so they could both vent about their lesbian daughters. But maybe you're not a woman, Judy. You might be something else.

21

What was she, then? For that matter, what was Neva?

Victoria could not bear to take her hands off the lesbian's body; even touching her all the time with one hand was not enough; while the straight man stayed home, unable to stop dwelling on the many lovely things that the lesbian had done to him while he lay so ecstatically open and helpless, driven beyond mindlessness by pleasure's bloody assaults; and Shantelle kept happily choking her in little pulses (the victim, purple-faced and wheezing, smiled up at her) . . .—after which she demanded that Neva keep rubbing her cunt all night, up and down, up and down, which Neva did, until she finally whispered that she was getting tired.—Then fire Judy and Francine and all them other bitches, replied Shantelle. It's your fuckin' problem for being a slut.—So the lesbian resumed rubbing, all the while wondering whether she had shut off the front left burner of the gas stove.—Oh, you motherfuckin' *slut,* groaned Shantelle, ho bitch; you're *nobody's* bitch but mine. Neva, Neva sweetheart, ain't you my precious little bitch?—Neva nodded gamely.—Vermilion neon and vermilion traffic lights from Taylor and O'Farrell kept sweetly staining their faces and hands. In the morning that couple flew downstairs and up the street like newlyweds, drinking coffee and eating pastry at the Fat Girl Bakery. But the transwoman, ever more inflamed at being no more loved than us others, longed to sink her teeth into her dear Neva's white throat; because just as Nancy Kerrigan once said about her Olympic rival Kristi Yamaguchi, *competing never gets in the way of our friendship.*—Shantelle, of course, seeing how the lesbian smiled at Judy, felt a sharp pain in the center of her breastbone.

Up came my lucky number. Ascending the carpeted stairs, I found the lairs of other residents no more distracting than the relief carvings on the lintels of false doors. Although she usually preferred not to sit on top of me (but upon request, of course, she would and did) because it went in too deep and hurt her ovaries, this time without my even asking her (not I but my penis required it) she immediately leaped on top of me, roaring with apparent pleasure as she slid down my hard, hard erection, doing this thing for which she had been born; and with her shoulders thrown back and her beautiful breasts bouncing, the nipples hard and fat as berries, she rode me like the wind (I forget where to, maybe the lost city of Ai Khoum), climaxing like nobody's business, laughing and growling with her hair swaying back and forth as I reached up to squeeze her breasts, and then (following Shantelle's example) gently squeezed her throat with both hands. She had toys; just for me she was wearing the black leather collar of consensual victimhood. The next time my wish was for her to beat me black and blue, which she sweetly did, sitting on my back; then she turned me over and began slapping my face into ever warmer happiness, my head rocking back and forth on the pillow, kept in motion by her palms, while she who comforted the lonely smiled down at me until I found myself lost in some adorable place of having given her everything, upon which I was sacrificed, used and slapped deeper and deeper down into my grave where I longed and deserved to be—killed lovingly and intimately by the lesbian! Finally her wrists were tired. As soon as she stopped, that cold forlorn feeling settled on me, and my burning face, craving endorphins, caving into loneliness, almost seemed to be dissolving away. Massaging her wrists with some of Francine's yellow serum, she lay down on top of me for awhile. Then she checked the messages on her cell phone—what a good soldier! Here I might as well quote from a three-page editorial letter from this publisher remarking that *to be honest, I do wonder whether some readers will simply tire of, for example, all the climaxing in the book. Of all the descriptions of sex acts . . . Does that end up having a bit of a deadening/boring effect?* Well, I do suspect that Neva was getting somewhat deadened—but Al was on his way over, followed by the straight man; and no matter how much we drank from Neva, repletion would have been as impossible as ceasing to run our fingers over the gentle tapering of that fluted golden cup which we found close by the remains of Queen Puabi, when we dug up the city of Ur. She was buried in the company of nine hundred angels, each of whom had wings of lapis and a tail of gold. When we scraped away the hardpacked dirt, they opened their jeweled eyes and flew away; but she who had exceeded them could not reenter her bones. Across her skull lay solid gold ribbons, leaves and flowers, and a row of lapis-centered golden disks to shade her complexion from the devouring sun of Ur. Turning away from her, we quarreled over her golden cup.

Rehearsals and Performances

I must add that I washed my neck and the top of my bosom with calf leather soaked in water and sheep's foot lotion, and it was from this type of care that my skin remained sweet and white.

THE ABBÉ DE CHOISY (who dressed as a woman), date unknown

It is beauty which gives birth to love, and beauty is ordinarily the share of women.

THE ABBÉ DE CHOISY

I see only a beautiful woman and why forbid myself to love her?

THE ABBÉ DE CHOISY

In fact the mothers would not mistrust me in a thousand years, and I believe—God forgive me—that they would have put me to bed with their daughters without any scruple.

THE ABBÉ DE CHOISY

1

Trying to tell out to myself whatever it was I knew of her, the lesbian who was teaching me how to love, I went looking for Natalie again and behind those two garbage bins where she should have been I saw Judy kneeling before a man's crotch; her profile could have been an acolyte's carved out on a votive frieze. She rose and spat while the man turned away to zip up his pants. I stepped aside. When Judy came out she said: God, do I need a drink.

Of course you do, I said, so we went to the Y Bar, where Victoria sat showing off her brand new look.

Hi, said Judy, wide-eyed like a starstruck fan.

Hi, said Victoria.

Gimme a triple, said Judy. You know why? Because it's *payday.*

What do you mean? You want three times as much bourbon in your ginger ale?

No, I want . . . Gimme a triple shot of Old Crow straight up.

Just like your old man, said Francine. How's he doing?

I don't know.

Nine dollars.

Victoria, is that olive oil on your face?

It most certainly isn't.

Well, my face is not as high-quality as yours anyhow. Do you think olive oil would be right for me? Because I can't—

Oh, no, Judy, shea butter is a must have, said Victoria. Or would you rather completely give up on your skin? You see, your complexion needs *help.*

Observing her reinvigorated earnestness, I deduced that through teaching, persuasion, desperation or other inducements the transwoman had been led into another effort at reincarnating her namesake. She promised me that she had now lost a total of twenty-two pounds, and for all I know she was even telling the truth. Trying to assist, I repeated Natalie's motivational mantra: *If you don't stand for something, you fall for everything.*

What the fuck's *that* about? demanded Shantelle.

It means, good for Judy, because she's trying to—

I don't care.

Well, keep your not caring to yourself, said Francine, snappishly I thought. Shantelle, imagining that she was about to do something awful which glowed right out of her head so that everyone could see it and was therefore excitedly watching her, fired off her best evil smile, but by then we had more to entertain us, because Xenia had just marched in, wearing her trademark red, and Judy immediately commenced pumping her: Please, big sister, can you tell when people like your act?

Actually, no.

Your usual? asked Francine.

I guess so.

Three dollars.

Keep the change. Now, Judy, what did Shantelle just say?

That she doesn't care.

Do you care?

No.

About anything?

No, I swear.

What if somebody started beating you to death?

I—

Come on, Frank! Just say it!

I wouldn't care.

All right then. If you keep saying it, someday you'll mean it, and then nobody can hurt you. Now what did you want? Oh, yeah: If I was really good . . . When you're really good at performing, you're really confident, and then you'll draw a bigger crowd, and that includes assholes. Girls are mean, especially in wedding showers. Bachelorettes, they are always drunker than the men, and they feel very entitled just because they have vaginas. So. There are two kinds of girls who come to my shows. There are hardcore lesbians, and there are girls who come to hate. When the boyfriends start getting excited, the girlfriends get unhappy, and they take it out on me. And when that happens, what do I say?

I . . . *I don't care.*

Gold star for Judy. How much weight have you lost?

Twenty-eight pounds.

Bullshit.

I don't care!

Good for you. Are you practicing your routine?

Sure, I—

Don't lie to me.

But I *am.*

We'll see next Thursday. You'd better not fuck up.

2

We all knew that among the greatest pleasures of Judy's life was the anticipatory fantasy of feminine success, which she would have defined as *lustful attention.* For her no distinction existed between worship and objectification. Perhaps that was also true for the first Judy Garland. It certainly applied to everyone I knew, possibly excluding Neva. To the heroes, heroines, accomplishers, etcetera goes the joy of doing. But to the rest of the human race, who can hardly aspire to anything better than sitting at the Y Bar, dreaming is all there is. And thank the Goddess that is so! For where would all those doers be, without, say, Victoria and me to applaud once the doers were already down to the pasties, their mouths wriggling into femmie-femmie smiles, their buttocks all a-wriggle-jiggle while the mistress of ceremonies expounded upon *a group of lovely ladies that came in today to break all kinds of records*?

3

One of the best parts of my own life continued to be anticipating my turn with the lesbian: forty minutes to go, then twenty, and at five I would be at the top of those carpeted stairs, waiting for Francine, Ed or Shantelle to come floating out on a wave of diminishing happiness. Once Neva opened the door for me and I started kissing her, even if I could taste Francine or Ed or Shantelle in her mouth I didn't care, because everything became pure. What still astonished me was the sudden *luxuriance of time.* Between foreplay, afterplay and orgasm no longer existed any difference. I could stroke her upper arm or lick her lips for half an hour straight, never tiring or growing urgent to do some other thing, which reminded her of her mother's fiddlings in her underpants, and the way her mother would play perfectly tenderly with Karen's vulva so long as she was not crossed; she could have been any considerate lover, even me; but the instant that the child began to back away, the fingers would pinch, the long nails would dig, poke and stab, worrying at the girl's labia, scratching her clitoris, bruising her and sometimes making her bleed. My penis might be stiff and throbbing for that entire while, and maybe Neva would touch it or suck it but that felt neither better nor worse than rubbing her arm! Everything was perfect. If I penetrated her I never knew when I would climax, and when I did, the unceasing flickering of our tongues pleased me no less than before. Could this have been how it was for her? I remember licking and sucking her pussy; she would utter long soft moans, and sometimes begin to move, but never as if she were approaching release. When I later asked her how she had felt, she would always assure me that she had been climaxing steadily for the entire while. My conclusion is that she, the one whom we desperately magnified, was either *always* climaxing, day and night, alone or in company, like an efflorescing spring—or else that she lied for all of our sakes. (I, who sometimes write as if I know what others felt and did, love to make up stories.)

4

Next Thursday was only four days away. Having now lost twenty-three pounds, the transwoman bought a box of gratitude chocolates for her idol. Now she was wondering whether she could control herself enough not to eat them. Of course the lesbian would graciously unwrap it in her presence, thank her, select the smallest bonbon, praise it, then pass the box to her, at which point she could get away with eating up to four without seeming gluttonous—and it would be so generous to wait until then! Not that Neva would mind if she did open the box right now, just to verify that no chocolate was missing . . .

What's in your purse? said the retired policeman.

Oh, some . . . some chocolates.

For *me*? he laughed.

She flushed.

Well?

That's right—

You're the most hilarious liar ever, he informed her. You would've gone straight to the electric chair . . . ! Now listen, Frank. You cheat on me left and right. Just for a change, step out on your crappy little Karen Strand. Come on, bitch! Open 'em up!

So she did. After all, just now her darling lesbian was walled in by Shantelle's legs.

That's my girl. Come snuggle up beside me. One for me and two for you; one for me and three for you . . .

Chuckling, they stuffed their faces until they had gobbled up all three dozen. It was the most fun they'd had in ages.

Then he turned on the crime channel and fell asleep in her arms. She lay licking her lips. That chocolate had had the perfect texture: somewhere between grainy and pasty; the taste had been sweet and floury, like a Japanese chestnut candy, or Neva's pussy, or . . . If only there were more!

Truth to tell, nowadays, and why this was she could not say, holding the lesbian in her arms gave her less pleasure than sadness, although this sadness was more precious to her than anything else.

That was when she began considering, as she later told me, that if she truly loved Neva she ought to kill herself on the landing of the carpeted stairs where all of us passed to and fro in accomplishing our trysts; she had not the courage to slit her throat, nor the knowledge to unlock the retired policeman's gun safe, so it would have to be pills—any opioids, really, or even cheap and nauseating barbiturates, so long as fentanyl could help her along; and for that her go-to bitch would be Shantelle. But could she actually go through with this, or would she chicken out? Better to lock herself into Neva's affections. And that is why I kept observing the transwoman whispering and winking, digging her fingers into the lesbian's arm, desperately trying to look cute.

Sorry I'm Bleeding

The love of pleasure begets grief and the dread of pain causes fear.

BUDDHA, date unknown

1

Sandra said: Sorry I'm bleeding.

That's okay, said the lesbian.

She sent Sandra away happy; then came Holly, who was also bleeding.

Come to think of it, Holly was always bleeding. And one night Holly called her, weeping.

What's wrong? asked the lesbian.

Don't worry, honey; the doctor said I'll probably be all right, but I'll have to get a hysterectomy; I'm a little scared . . .

I'll come with you, said the lesbian.

She had to cancel on Francine, who resented it graciously.

The waiting room was bright and fake, with a yawning receptionist reigning over sad women reading celebrity magazines. Shining like an October moon over an altar of women, the lesbian held Holly's left hand while Holly's right hand paged through a tabloid. The lesbian looked down into Holly's lap and read: *She told me that she sleeps in a silk nightgown, that she must have eight hours of sleep or she's a wreck, and that she often gathers her friends in her room and holds a back-scratching party. Everyone sits in a circle and scratches everyone else's back. "If you haven't had your back scratched, you haven't lived!" Judy said.*

Holly Liebling, said the receptionist.

Holly and the lesbian approached the end of the counter, where a nurse stood with a clipboard. Smiling into the lesbian's face, the nurse said warmly: You must be Holly.

I am, said Holly.

The nurse regarded her with disappointment. She said: And who's this?

My partner Neva. I want her to come in.

The nurse peeped at Neva, who smiled at her. That settled it; who could resist the lesbian?

She led them to the consultation room, took Holly's temperature and pulse, and left them. The lesbian helped her sweetheart change into a gown. Then the gynecologist came in. Holly lay down with her feet in the stirrups while the lesbian stood at the side of the table, holding her hand. After a quick and gentle examination, the gynecologist went out, returned almost at once and said: I think we'd better schedule the procedure as soon as possible.

Swallowing hard, Holly said: Do I have cancer?

It's still in the very early stage, and I'm confident we can entirely remove the problem, said the gynecologist.

Oh, my God, said Holly. Oh, my God.

I love you, said the lesbian, squeezing her hand.

Oh, God, I love you, too! Neva, I'm afraid—

The gynecologist said: Ms. Liebling, you're a lucky lady to have such a beautiful partner. How long have you been together?

A year, said the lesbian.

Off and on, inserted Holly, bursting into tears.

I see, said the gynecologist. Well, I think we've caught this in time. I'll leave you now, and if you would, on your way out just talk with Cindy and she can help you schedule your surgery. Nice to meet you, Neva.

On the day of Holly's hysterectomy the lesbian kept her company on the streetcar. She sat next to her in the waiting room. She held her hand when the anesthetic went into her arm. When Holly was dead asleep and snoring, she went to the waiting room and closed her eyes. She felt so tired, nauseous and cold! After two hours they brought Holly out in a wheelchair.—No, explained Cindy, her insurance doesn't cover any overnights.

With great effort, Holly slurred out: Please, Neva, can I stay at your place?

Of course, said the lesbian.

And all night she held the other woman, who snored trustfully in her arms. Through the next day Holly rested, tended by the adorable lesbian; until by nightfall she had far enough recovered to drink in the utterly fulfilling sensation of caressing Neva's shoulder, buttock, belly or breast, round and round, over and over.

But on the day after that, well, as you can well imagine, she had to go, because the rest of us needed our turns.

2

Girlfriend, girlfriend, girlfriend! sang the transwoman.

What is it, honey?

No, I was just singing your name. By the way, you *are* going grey. But, Neva, if I ask you something, will you promise not to get mad?

I promise.

Who's the love of your life?

You are.

And Shantelle?

Sure.

Who was the one before all of us?

Well, there was an old woman on an island. And she—

Is that true? I know! And you were both mermaids, right? So you loved her more than you love me.

No, Judy.

And before her? Why do you look so sad? That means I'm getting warm, aren't I? What was her name?

The lesbian closed her eyes. She was getting cramps.

Neva, you've never held out on me before!

Of course I have. Some things are private.

You mean, you really won't tell me?

She called herself E-beth but we—

And you loved her the most?

Well, at the time I did.

Where is she?

I don't know.

You'll never marry me and live with me, will you?

No, honey, said the lesbian. Just a minute; I need to—

What about *her*? If she came and said, Neva, please take me back; I'll do anything . . . ?

She wouldn't.

But if she did . . .

Judy, that was long ago. She couldn't understand me now.

Well, *I* can. You know how much I love you! Don't I understand you? Tell the truth, Neva!

I'll be right back, said the lesbian, rushing to the bathroom to have diarrhea. She hurried, because Judy was waiting; Judy was demanding: Don't I? I need to know!

You understand the part of me that—

Excuse me, but that's evasive *bullshit.* Are you going to make me cry?

I was saying, the part of me that loves you in the way you love me. There's a different part for everybody.

You're saying that nobody gets the whole you. Right?

You can put it that way . . .

Well, I don't believe it. I just don't.

I'm sorry, said the lesbian.

It's not very nice, the transwoman sobbed. I feel so . . .

Please forgive me, said the lesbian. And she bought her a stick of fancy lip-plumping gel for an early Christmas present.

3

When Shantelle raised the same topic, the argument played out differently. To be specific, she hit the lesbian again.

For an instant her rage exhilarated her; she resembled Athena scream-grinning, with golden feathers blossoming from her shoulder-wings. She longed to crush Neva into red and brown stains.

Then she worried about what Neva would do. Other women she'd punched around had stopped fucking her, stopped loving her, attacked her or called the police. But Neva only smiled at her.

Neva had a black eye. Neva kept smiling and silently weeping. Shantelle felt so sad she could hardly stand it!

She craved to drink from her mouth, and thus be her, but most of all she needed to destroy that smile.

She said: Maybe you're tryin' to act like Buddha or Jesus or something. Well, Neva, guess what? By pretendin' not to care you're just a goddamn coward. Come to think of it, you're a *motherfuckin'* coward.

Motherfucking, that's me, said the lesbian.

Sorry, babe, said Shantelle. I don't know why I said that. But anyway, so what? Just because I cursed you out, you gotta make a grudge against me?

No, I love you the same.

Clenching her fists, Shantelle demanded: Why won't you let me in? Bitch, *what are you doin' to me*?

Coolly and steadily (that being the way to reach this woman) the lesbian said: I'm pretty simple, actually—just legs and tits and three holes for people to use. Mostly I don't feel or plan anything—

When I punched you, you sure as shit felt something then!

Neva smiled at her.

Didn't you, bitch?

No, it happened to someone else.

That's a lie! Look at them tears! And you're *always* schemin' things out, callin' us here, sendin' us away—

I'm only reactive.

What does that mean?

It means you lead and I follow.

Shantelle's face locked down. She ran out, slamming the door. The lesbian got up to ice her black eyes. A quarter-hour later Shantelle came knocking and pounding. The lesbian did not answer. Shantelle began kicking the door until the manager and his cousin expelled her.

An hour after that it was Francine's turn. At the first knock, the door opened.

Neva, my God, what happened to you?

Come lie down with me, sweetheart.

Why won't you tell me?

The lesbian, smiling at the other woman so lovingly or at least compliantly, thought: You can't even begin to know me.—She said: Everything's okay.—Her eyes rolled up and she began snoring.

And until one in the morning Francine watched the lesbian huddled on the dark bed, so slender and hollowed out that the bed might as well have been empty.

4

That was the point when she finally asked me what we should do for Neva.

There perched Samantha with her wine cooler and Xenia with her Old German Lager, who was confessing to Sandra: You know, I just didn't think about it then, because I had kids; I never had an orgasm until I was with a woman . . .—and then, proceeding rightward, Holly, Selene and Victoria, like those pairs of sad girls who sit side by side in the dark back booths of strip clubs, waiting for enough men to enter that the bright blonde whirling and squatting girls in the blue light will accept reinforcements; now Francine and I had become the bright deciders; our names went up in secret lights.—Just then the Europeans were absent, leaving our contingent of slummers perfectly well represented by the pretty intern who loved to talk about babies and who now explained to Francine that her mother had phoned her aunt, who was absolutely forcing her to pick out a graduation dress for which her mother would pay. Francine said: Tell your mother to buy *me* a dress, at which the intern awoke from her dream of sisterhood to realize that she was in the wrong place and maybe even in trouble. She fled quickly, leaving no tip, and that was all we ever saw of her.

I, who nearly always advocated doing nothing, reminded Francine that to our knowledge the retired policeman had blacked the transwoman's eye on at least two occasions, and we had stayed out of it. Anyhow, wasn't Neva a grownup?

That's because Judy's different. Their relationship, you know—

She thrives on it.

I know, I know. But when Shantelle hits Neva, that's *not* consensual.

How can you tell, Francine? Who knows what Neva lets others do to her? Listen. Are you ready to swear that she *ever* gets off?

Yes.

You bring her to orgasm, every time?

Don't you?

That's the point. Are we all such red-hot lovers, or does she—

Neva does not fake it. Not *ever.* And if you are so fucked up—

So what gets her off? *Everything*, right?

But, Richard, how do you feel, seeing that bruise?

I hate Shantelle for hurting her. But Neva—

Did you ask her?

About this? No.

Well, I did.

I can guess what she told you: Don't worry, and it's okay . . .

You nailed it.

So let's not go against Neva. But if you want to warn Shantelle—

Then she'll starting raging.

So you'll eighty-six her—

And she'll go charging off and maybe . . .

Exactly. What if she really does hurt her?

Just as when one sees a hooded mound of clothes in a wheelchair on Taylor Street, and cannot tell whether a person is inside, so I now stared into Francine, who might as well have been a robot; then I went out, somewhere, anywhere, which is to say into the lovely jet-blackness of Taylor Street on this rainy night when headlights shone like precious and semiprecious beads; I decided to hook up with the retired policeman.

5

Her high school girlfriend was Elizabeth Jackson, he said.

You mean Jane Doe, I said.

Fuck off, smartass. In her junior and senior years Karen Strand checked into at least four hotel rooms with an Elizabeth Jackson, who was then either twenty-three or twenty-six. This may be the same Elizabeth Jackson who was charged with statutory rape in 1996. And that's significant, because when a *woman* does it, he informed me in a well-nursed rage, they usually let her off, as in this case. You or I wouldn't have a chance.

Yeah, I said.

Our background was the lovely body of a stripper squatting in the rosy light, writhing on the floor, working her buttocks into a sort of pout, slowly pulling down her G-string, then touching her hair with both hands, doubtless in order to give her breasts a lift, while an old couple quietly watched her, hand in hand; two chairs away from them was the rugged old man who kept quietly respectfully stepping up to the stage to lay down another dollar-offering; behind him sat the two of us, addressing the matter of Neva.

Since the retired policeman was getting distracted, I asked: Who was raped?

Another high school girl, Virgilie Ferraro from Martinez, who insisted it was consensual: Elizabeth Jackson was the love of her goddamn life. Well, the D.A. didn't give a shit about the love part.

What happened to Virgilie?

Became an elementary school teacher. Maybe she's passing on whatever Elizabeth taught her. You know, physical education.

What about Elizabeth?

Never even had to register as a sex offender. Clerks in a medical marijuana dispensary in El Cerrito. Apparently keeps clear of Vallejo, where the crime took place; that's also where Karen went to high school.

I said nothing, so he continued: Used to be a dog groomer, but she fuckin' loves *cats.* I've been to her place. Wide-eyed furballs everywhere. The kennel or whatever it is just changed owners, but she's still . . .

I told him: *If you don't stand for something, you fall for everything.*

Suddenly as out of sorts as a stripper who gets suddenly called upon to be awake before noon, he looked me up and down, saying: What the hell does *that* mean?

Oh, I said. It's motivational.

Well, keep me away from that positive bullshit. I only do negativity.

Is Elizabeth positive or negative?

I depolarized her. Made it clear I was on to her about our Karen. Gave her some fear. Now, Richard, don't babble about this, not to Judy by a long shot and not even to Francine. I'm almost where I want to be, and you're not gonna muck it up. Okay?

Okay.

Neva really *is* Karen Strand, or someone who looks like her. The Jackson bitch gave a positive I.D. I told her I'd come back, but I may not need to. Well, Sherlock? What's my next move?

Finishing my bourbon and sodapop, I proposed: DNA test?

He laughed at me. He said: You wanna take away the interactive element. Without that, how can a cop get his jollies? And the lab in Hayward charges up to fifteen hundred to run an envelope that may or may not have saliva or little pieces of skin. The accuracy is still quite controversial, apparently. They've isolated sixteen segments of the DNA string, and at each of those sites, they lock on a link, and then, you know, they can't quite do homo- *versus* heterozygous . . .—but that's above your goddamn pay grade.

Then send in the cavalry. Call in an air strike. No, wait! I said. Why not interview Karen's relatives?

Frowning, he said: If this were a novel, you'd have spoiled my suspense.

6

Holly called weeping, because her labs had come back neither dirty nor clean; she didn't know how to get through the next four days until her second biopsy. She said: Neva, I can't even think; I can't sleep; I'm so nervous, and now they're docking my pay at work and if I miss another day this week I'll get a letter of reprimand—

Honey, come and see me, said the lesbian.

But isn't it Francine's turn?

I'll explain it to her. Don't worry.

She came to cry and be held. The lesbian embraced her tightly, stroking her back in that way which for Holly was magic. Finally the sad woman fell asleep.

When she awoke it was three in the morning. The lesbian, thirsty, hungry and exhausted, was still holding her, staring at the wall, subsumed in unceasing guilty dread about failing her and all of us. Holly said: Oh, my God, Neva, you look worn out . . . !

I didn't want to let go of you. Because I love you.

I wish I could do something for you. It's not fair, the way you take care of all of us.

But it makes me happy to be loved. Holly, I . . .

Oh, you look so tired! Are you hungry? I could order up some pizza, or we could go out; that halal place on the corner is really fast—

Are you hungry?

No, just . . . just shaken up—

Let's go to bed, said the lesbian. Just sleep in my arms.

Neva, if I could do one thing for you, what would it be?

The lesbian said: Well, it would make me very happy if you'd kind of take Judy in hand and—

I don't care shit about fucking Judy! I want to show my love for *you*! What's *wrong* with you, Neva, that you . . .—Fine. I'm sorry. If that's what you want, I'll go to her and . . . What am I supposed to do?

Teach her about being a woman. She's always picking everyone's brains. She maybe or maybe not wants to be a lesbian—

But she's with that prick who beats her and—

I know, said the lesbian. But we can't do anything about that. Let me just pee and brush my teeth. And when you're ready we can turn out the light.

7

At seven-forty-five that morning, when Holly crept wearily off to work, Neva was finally alone between appointments. She who had become the garment around us, the living robe which loved and sorrowed for what she covered, sat staring ahead, counting the various ways in which she had failed us. Instead of lifting us all up according to our deepest desires, she had betrayed and blighted us, evidently because she had not loved us enough. Now I wish I could have led her down Market Street to the curb across from Golden State Mall where in the smell of marijuana emitted by three young men with their glowing cell phones at the ready the amplified prophet announced: *If I look at the moral law thou shalt not steal, I've stolen; that's on my record; I've looked at my neighbor's wife with lust, so I've committed adultery, so we've all failed.* But she continued sinking down her checklist: How could she better exert her suffering heart so as to save us? How strange to realize that understanding was not helping! She knew us so well: the way that Al could best relieve his loneliness by praying to her at arm's length in the darkened room; Xenia's desperate desire to be considered wise; the concentrated taste of Sandra's redhaired pussy, which stayed on sheets and fingers, and the strangely milder taste when she was menstruating, and . . . She declined to sing Reba's song of names, and now someone was ringing the buzzer.

8

In came a long message from Xenia: I really did want to get a few things across to you, Neva. First of all, I was only forty-five minutes late. You had no idea how it impacted me. I sent a message to you and I walked miles and miles to get to you and I was really really upset. I had Energol and Hormonex and all kinds of drugs for you and I . . .

9

When I dropped by the Y Bar that day, Francine was clocking out early—very early.

Are you okay? I asked.

Not well, she grated.

At first I supposed that she was merely coming down from too much crystal. Her sweaty face kept going red and white like an old time neon sign. Then something made me ask: Is it from Neva?

And that hard, wary bitch burst into tears!

I said: Let me walk with you a bit.

She nodded rapidly. I knew that she was ashamed to break down in front of us. Alicia had just clocked in. She stood behind the bar gloating.

Francine lived somewhere on Turk Street. As soon as we had gone around the corner I said: Come home with me.

What the fuck do you mean? said my coy companion.

I love you, I said. And I never realized it until I saw you in pain. You love Neva and Judy, and so do I. Please, Francine, I can't stand to see you sad.

I'm fine, she said.

Let me hold you and be good to you, I said.

Forget it, she said.

Francine, I whispered, sweet little Francine of mine, I've got medicine.

You do? What kind?

The best you've ever had.

What color is it?

Brown.

Powder? All right.

So I took her up to my place, bringing her by the more inviting way, past the late night pizza place where they spoke Arabic to each other and police cars sped ruby-like behind the white-graffiti'd window. And I showed her respect by not holding her hand. We passed the new cannabis shop by Penthe's Bar and the Hotel Garland, where a tall glamorous T-girl came out and gloated: Now I've got *drugs*!, at which Francine and I smiled at each other. When we came up out of the Tenderloin at Geary and Van Ness with the rebar shining at the construction site across the street and the windows of the old auto showroom gleaming, I heard her inhale suddenly as if she were surprised or worse, so I carefully did not look at her. Then we were going upstairs. She suddenly stopped as if she feared me, so I told her: You don't have to stay. I'll give you medicine and then if you want to go home I'll be sad but it'll be fine.

She smiled.

As it happened, that day I had made my bed and even changed the sheets. She stood by the door, holding her purse. I poured out two glasses of equal portions cherry soda and All-American Rum. Then she came slowly closer, so that I could finally close the door. Handing her a cocktail, I said: Seven dollars! and she giggled. She raised it to her pretty lips and I said: Bottoms up!—We clinked glasses. When that round was gone, she pulled out a pint bottle of Binco Jack. We sat down on the edge of the bed. The afternoon was already looking up.

When's your turn? I asked her.

Not for two more days. She's so wonderful but sometimes I can't stand it.

I get the chills afterward.

Well, I get hot flashes, as you can see. But don't tell anyone.

I promise.

Each time it gets worse and worse—

Come on, baby, I said. What part of life doesn't?

She laughed a little. Then she said: Richard, I've got to go.

Listen, I told her. I've got two doses of pure brown molly, and Shantelle *does not* know. We can't have Neva all the time, so we've got to figure out how to get by. Francine, I do love you. And what I want to do with you right now is take ecstasy and lie down with you and hold you and stroke your hair and make you feel *cherished.*

Oh, stop it, she said. But she was already untying her shoes.

I went into the bathroom and closed the door, because it wasn't her business how much molly I actually had, nor where I kept it. I poured out all my Fat Save brand headache pills, and then from the bottom of the bottle my hooked forefinger extracted that wrinkled baggie of crumbly, bitter brown rocks. Breaking off two doses (cheapskates got by with point one five grams but for this romantic date I eyeballed point three grams each), I packed away the evidence, and then, just in case Francine might be a thief, dropped the pill bottle into my pants pocket. Then I flushed the toilet for verisimilitude. When I came out, she was staring at the wall.

Ready to take your medicine? I asked.

All right, she said in a trembling voice.

With the aid of her Binco Jack we gagged down that foul-tasting stuff.

You wanna lie down with me?

Sure.

I had already stripped to my underwear while she was still wearily unhooking her bra. I didn't even know whether she had a cock or a slit. Jonesing for sugar, I drank another slug of cherry soda, which by the way tasted just like cough drops. Francine didn't want any more. I got under the blanket and closed my eyes. After awhile she crawled in next to me. Her hands and feet felt very cold.

Honey, I said, do you want to come lie in my arms?

Not yet. I . . . I might have made a mistake, coming here.

Just stay a few minutes, until the molly kicks in. Then decide. And right now we can talk about Neva—

No. Please don't.

You want to talk about anything?

No. All right, just hold me.

She rolled into my arms, and I clasped her as gently as I could, so that she would not feel trapped.

I was already starting to get that hot rising dizzy nauseous feeling. I closed my eyes, waiting for the good part.

I'm feeling it, said Francine.

How does it feel?

Wonderful.

I began caressing her sweaty grey hair, and it felt almost as good as touching Neva. She started getting giggly and chatty. I began rubbing her back. Her skin felt impossibly delightfully smooth. Touching her buttock for the very first time, I could hardly believe how perfectly exactly right it was. She upturned her face, and we began kissing, licking each other's tongues. She was moaning and I was breathing hard, and Francine was saying: Oh, Richard, I love you so much.

Thank you for loving me, because I'm so happy with you, so happy with my sweet, adorable Francine . . .

I caressed her all over, faster and faster. The more I touched her, the more infinite her skin and flesh became, until she was an entire universe and more, far more than I could ever adore, so that I went crazy with gratitude for her. She was babbling thanks and love and sweet silly things which she sometimes forgot before she had finished saying them. All I wanted to do just then was to kiss her—kiss her and *kiss her*! I needed her lovely face close to mine forever. We kissed and licked each other's mouths until our tongues were raw, thereby surpassing that famous time when Judy Garland first collapsed on the set and the MGM doctor gave her some pills to make her feel *on top of the world* in ten minutes. I got up to bring us some water and swayed, wondering if I would vomit. Then slowly, very very carefully, I filled two glasses and brought them back to bed. Wise Francine drank all hers down. Although my mouth felt very dry, it was all I could do to get down two swallows. Then I crashed back down on my back, and Francine began playing sweetly with my limp penis. It felt so good I could hardly move. Then I took her breasts in my hands and started kneading them. They were so ethereally and mysteriously hot and semiliquid that I couldn't get enough of them. Forgetting to play with me, Francine lay there moaning her sweetest little *oh-oh-ohs.* When she stroked her hair down and widened her eyes at me I realized that she was even more beautiful than the lovely dead actress Natalie Wood. After seven hours we started coming down, so I broke off for each of us another half dose, and we reentered our happy eternity. At two in the morning we descended again. I got my customary chills, and Francine got her hot flashes. My stomach cramped, and a headache was coming on. Francine said she was hungry, so I made her a peanut butter sandwich. After two bites she couldn't eat any more. I put the plate in the fridge to keep the cockroaches away. She had some medical marijuana that was calibrated for pain, and I had sleeping pills. We swallowed some of each before the withdrawal got worse.

Francine was getting sleepy—lucky girl! Stroking my arm, she yawned: Oh, baby, I love you so much . . .

I plunged my happy hand into the deep tight valley between her sweaty breasts, after which she fell asleep. I lay beside her for a long time, in awe of how precious she was.

In the morning we both felt tired and jangled, but she kissed me goodbye quite sweetly. Later that day I remembered how delicious it had been when she was sucking one of my nipples and I was rubbing the other one. So I lay down and began fondling myself. Although the drug had left me, my body had learned something, or possibly relearned the almost undifferentiated pleasure of which an infant must be capable. I tried to feel what Francine might have felt had I been touching her there. And after a few seconds, not nearly as swiftly as the lesbian could sometimes appear within my heart, some of our bliss returned to me. Lacking urgency or direction, it was nothing like the rising, need-laced pleasure on the road to orgasm. When I took a walk to buy toilet paper and sodapop, the euphoria almost seemed to be growing back, like the miracle of a second erection, but in this section of my life, with the skyscrapers of the Financial District blocky grey against the gunmetal blue of the sky, I was shivering and my head was hurting. So I went home and lay down. It occurred to me that if I took molly often enough, I might acquire a readier habit of self-fulfillment, which, like the possession of arithmetic, could serve me whenever I pleased. Arithmetic, of course, had long since taught me that there is no something for nothing, so I wondered what the price would be. But if I could somehow feel this pleasure by and for myself, then I could get out of craving Neva all the time. Just then, how I hated her for my loneliness! I tried to call her, but she did not answer and her voicemail was full.

10

That afternoon I made a point of going down to the Y Bar right at four-thirty when Francine's shift began and the place was peaceful. She poured me a rum and sodapop on the house. When I drank it, my teeth ached.

Leaning forward so that Xenia could not hear, I murmured that I remembered exactly what she did to me, how I penetrated her with two fingers and what her sweat smelled like just before she climaxed, at which she shyly yet trustingly smiled.—What about you? I asked, and she said: I remember lying in your arms and feeling so safe and so loved and . . . No, Victoria, hold your horses; Richard and I have some personal business.—And I also remember . . . All right, Xenia, I'm coming.

But just then Shantelle swished in, along with Neva and Judy and everyone; we all stared up at the television, which had been self-importantly glowing the turquoise hue of Egyptian faience, and saw the outcome of the Supreme Court decision on Friday, June 26, 2015 (the vote went 5 to 4): a whitehaired woman who looked like a man sticking her tongue in a plump middle-aged woman's mouth, a young black woman gently holding a bespectacled blonde white woman's face as she began to kiss her, a black woman with reddish-blonde braids kissing a black man in a baseball cap (he turned out to be a black woman), two bespectacled butches in army outfits kissing each other hard, two plump, stubbly young men in baseball caps deeply kissing each other: Traci Bliss Panzner and Julie Ann Lake, Marge Eide and Ann Sorrell, Lena Williams and Crystal Zimmer, Stephanie Ward and Lori Hazelton, Thomas Kirdahy and Terence McNally, Tom Fennell and Christopher Brown.

Well, I said, at least they stand for something.

While you fall for *everything*! cried Shantelle, running up and kissing my ear.

We were all happy; just then I felt as fresh as rainy nights in wet blank glowing alleys, with cable cars humming around the corner—and the transwoman likewise wanted to celebrate. High on Francine's discounted goofballs, she cried out: Hey, all of you! Let's . . . let's play a kissing game with Neva! We'll each get one kiss out of her, and then we kiss each other, and then she has to kiss us again, and she will, because . . .

Sandra, said Francine, take her home. Do you mind?

As soon as Sandra helped her up, the transwoman fell up against her. Moaning with desire, she began kissing Sandra's face.—Oh, oh, oh, she muttered; you're my sweet little mermaid! Let's play the kissing game . . . !

Sandra laughed, kissed her back three times and said: Okay, honey, let's get you home—. . . at which Judy crashed down to the floor and started snoring.

Francine, Sandra and I took her by the arms and legs. She weighed less than I expected. We tucked her behind the bar, on the shelf where boxes of sodapop were stored. Then we kept right on playing the kissing game. Neva was up for it; she was laughing and we were screaming!

When Judy woke up, we stretched her out on the naugahyde sofa below the mirror, with her head in the lap of Holly, whom she barely knew.

Holly said: Do you want me to teach you?

Teach me what? Oh, tell me a story.

You don't need that. Neva said you—

You mean Neva's making you do this?

No, she asked me and I said I would. She said you're trying to figure out who you are—

Well, I'm a woman. I may not look like it, but I don't care; I accept the fact that I'm *disgusting.* I'm a woman who loves women, and I wanna be around women all the time.

But that fat cop you hang around with—

Takes care of me, and I love him.

I give up, said Holly.

Wait! You mean you'd really answer questions?

Do I have to? said Holly, sick and tired of Judy.

I mean, you're a full on lesbian, right?

Why on earth would straight relationships exist except to make babies?

So you've never had sex with a man?

I've had experiences with men but not with any men I like. I have never dated men. I have hooked up with men for a funny time and for sex work. It's not interesting except that I can sort of feel my own effect on someone from my own sex worker standpoint. I've seen how men have affected women that I'm attracted to, and that's exciting for me. If the woman is interested in the man, just because of that I might be interested in fucking him.

If you had sex with me would you feel you were with a man?

It doesn't have to do with genitals. I've had sex with transwomen but I don't consider them as different from any other lesbian. Don't you know that a lot of femmes-for-femmes are transwomen?

Well, said Judy excitedly, does that mean you wanna fuck me?

I'm not interested.

Oh.

Look, Judy. There are some people that are more okay with bodies and vaginas and whatever. Mostly, penises are kind of weird but if I like the person I like everything about them. If I like the person I like everything about you. It's just that I don't know you.

Well, do you wanna get to know me?

Judy, I'm trying to be your friend, not your lover. I already love someone else.

Who?

None of your business.

Please, please, pretty please?

Fine. I'm in love with Neva, and that's enough for me.

The transwoman sat up. She said: Thanks for trying to help me. What you said is interesting, and maybe when I think it over I'll . . . I don't know, but the last thing you said made me really really sad. Although I knew it all along—

That's because you love being sad. Judy, I don't have the right to say what anyone else's experience is. I have felt feminine, and felt feminine things all my life. I have never been attracted to masculine things. I know there are people who are genuinely attracted to one type of person for awhile and then another type for awhile. I think you are attracted to females that have more masculine traits, that are in control. But you don't have to stay the same. Maybe if you stopped trying to define yourself you'd feel better. Anyway . . .

Kiss me, said Judy.

See you later, said Holly.

11

At the Y Bar we gloated over a new blonde with a fair slim hand, her legs shining like fruit, but compared to our idol she didn't even achieve a zero; then the retired policeman came in.

He took Neva to the back of the Cinnabar. She stood looking at him. On the arm of the booth he laid down a photograph of her mother.

Slowly the lesbian sat down. She said: Why are you showing me this?

The Old Fake

The Goddess who knew though I knew not hath caused darkness . . .

Akkadian Penitential Tablet, bef. 17th cent. B.C.

I believe you should be critical of yourself but not overcritical. The latter inhibits you too much.

Judy Garland, 1946

1

When the retired policeman disembarked from the Amtrak in Martinez, his swollen ankles were pulsing with pain until he longed for them to burst. If I live another couple of years I'll have to buy something to lean on, he thought. Maybe I can find a sword-cane at the Berkeley fleamarket, and modify it . . .—Ignoring the conductor's outstretched hand, he shifted his right foot down onto the plastic stepping stool, then heroically plunked down his left, and finally, holding his breath against the pain, achieved the platform itself. Crossing the track, he trudged through the tiny station and spied the blue 2007 V6 Pawnee Plus Desalb of his ex-sister-in-law Betty Connover, the only one of his former in-laws who had taken his side in the divorce. As J. Edgar Hoover put it so well: *No one can defy the laws of our civilization year upon year and atone for it mainly by refraining from criminality for a few months.* And that summed up Betty, who for the eleven years of his marriage had snubbed, insulted and humiliated him at every family holiday, then stood up for him, and finally forgotten him. All the same, he owed her one; and furthermore, when he had called to ask for the loan of her car she had been sweet to him, as if he were nearly back in the years when he was young and could have lived in three dimensions. Upon hearing that his destination was Vallejo she even offered to drive him, although that might have been because she distrusted his driving ability, not that he had ever been held responsible for the most negligible fender-bender.

He got into the passenger seat. Betty was chewing gum.

Hiya, he said, buckling his seatbelt.

Been a long time, J. D. How's your health?

Great, he answered savagely.

I saw you limping. What've you got—fallen arches?

Neuropathy, he said.

Betty giggled.—You always were a walking encyclopedia.

She started the ignition.

How's the family? he asked.

Well, Roger's diabetes is worse. He won't take care of himself, and Annabel doesn't know what to do. And then Mona's in trouble again—but Doris might not want you to know—

What about you? he said. You're the one I care about.

Oh, you know, said Betty. Just the same. After awhile, a gal just sort of gives up and . . .

73664 Triumph Drive, he said.

Was that 64 or 664?

73664 Triumph Drive.

Okay, it's in the GPS. You always were goal-oriented, said Betty. But frankly, J. D., I'm worried about you. You look like a mess. Are you taking care of yourself?

After awhile, he informed her, a guy just sort of gives up.

Oh, she said. So that's how it is.

Turning off the freeway, they now rounded two corners of the high school's long white shedlike buildings, whose accompanying wrought-iron fence he dated at two or three decades after Karen Strand's teenaged days—since our prosperity index now incorporated mass shootings—followed Nebraska Street past the stadium, and then turned left onto Broadway, presently passing the boarded-up Jingle's Bar, from which an old man now carefully crept; turned left again into a neighborhood of curtained Mission style houses going down Amador past the First Church of Religious Science, then left on Capitol, past the two grey bungalows; left and left again on Florida where acacia trees partially occluded the sky with their great yellow-green flower-clouds as Betty inquired, glancing at him in the mirror: Are you dating anyone?

Sort of kind of, he said.

Who is she?

His name's Frank, but he calls himself Judy. Worst of both worlds.

Oh, J. D.! Are you coming out after all these years? After your divorce Annabel said to me—

I'm not anything, he said. An old fake, just like Frank.

That's not so.

All right then. Just a pervert working on cirrhosis.

What's that supposed to mean? J. D., I love you. We all love you still. Why do we never hear from you? Oh, now I'm getting upset . . .

Look, he said. What do *you* want out of life?

She drove awhile, then said: I wish I knew.

Exactly, he said, wishing he could switch on the radio.

They parked at the curb in front of Mrs. Strand's house. He said: If you want to come in, don't say anything. Just say hello and then keep quiet, so I can—

Never mind, said Betty. I don't wanna rain on your parade. You take your time and don't worry about me.

What will you do?

Text my grandnieces.

Thanks, he said, managing not to groan while swinging his legs out of the car.

Betty said: J. D., you're so brave. Don't you ever get afraid?

He proudly said: Honey, this is my life. This is what I do. Let's say I'm on gang detail. Twenty dudes hang out in some asshole's front lawn every day, I'm the type of guy that's gonna walk up and smoke a cigarette with 'em and see what the fuck is goin' on.

You're my hero, she said.

He patted her thigh and she squeezed his hand. Then he stood up, closing the door behind him. An octagonal window watched him.

He climbed the brick steps to Mrs. Strand's house (ten of them and after a right turn seven more steps) onto the shaded porch and rang the bell. The woman opened the door almost at once. She was still more elegant than elderly. If I were into pussy maybe I could see my way into doing her, he decided. But not even Betty turns me on. I wish she did, because I love her. And incest would turn me on. And Judy's gonna fuckin' leave me.—Mrs. Strand, somewhat more decrepit on close inspection, had small but very alert eyes. Her mouth resembled her daughter's, never mind the sagging corners. But I still like her, thought the retired policeman. There's something about her I relate to. Go figure, Sherlock.

She had colored her hair brown and left it long and loose around her shoulders; it was grey at the roots.

I'm afraid my daughter was always terribly unhappy, said Mrs. Strand. There was a period where I hoped . . . Well, Karen's therapist called it *pseudoadjustment to life.* I'll always remember that.

Well, he inquired, and was she born that way?

Oh, I don't know. She seemed . . . Well, there was always something withdrawn about my Karen.

Uh huh, he said. I mean, do tell.

Well, I'd call it a talent for acting, said Mrs. Strand. You know, I used to take Karen to movies all the time, even though we really couldn't afford it. We did her hair and bought her pretty clothes. But she was such a needy child, and ultimately . . . Sorry, Mr. Slager, but when I get to thinking about Karen I just . . .

Did Karen have a favorite actress?

I think I'm going to say Natalie Wood. Have you ever seen *Miracle on 34th Street*, where that *cute, cute* little girl is sitting on John Payne's lap, whispering in his ear while he puts his hand on her darling little knee? Well, Karen would have done anything to be that girl. Oh, and do you remember Natalie's bubble bath scene in *Driftwood*? What innocent little eyes she has, and those bubbles cover just enough of her to . . . They say she was actually wearing bloomers, but you can't tell. Now what about you, Mr. Slager? Would you take a little bourbon?

I sure would. Thank you, ma'am; that hits the spot. Yes, that's perfect. Well, I won't lie to you. I've always been a Judy Garland fan.

Oh, yes! But did you ever see Natalie Wood playing Alice in Wonderland? What was that film? I'm drawing a blank—

Wasn't it that TV special? proposed the charmingly helpful retired policeman.

You know, it *was*! And you could just kind of see her little ankles peeping out of that ruffled pinafore with the checks on it; she was *almost* sitting on Norman Kraft's lap, and the way he was looking at her . . . ! Undressing her with his eyes, I should say. Rather comical . . .

Thank you, Mrs. Strand. You have fine taste in bourbon.

Oh, do you really think so? It's Atkins Number Seven Reserve. You're such a *nice* man. Well, and would you like to see some albums of my little Karen?

Sure would. You know, I just *love* little girls.

Now in this one I think she looks sort of like Natalie Wood, don't you? I once had her hair waved in the same style, not that she . . . Look what a sweet, sweet smile she had! Such a good little girl . . .

So where exactly *is* little Karen? he inquired.

I like to say, somewhere over the rainbow.

Well, well, he said to her. You old fake!

I beg your pardon! What did you just say to me?

I said you *take the cake* for best metaphor anywhere. You're a very intelligent woman, Mrs. Strand.

Oh. I thought you said something else.

You really do take the cake, ma'am. I mean it. I've never met a woman like you.

I'm the only one who's ever understood Karen. She always was a terribly lonely child; maybe something's wrong with her hormones. Then she ran away. Well, I've done all I can for her, and now I just don't know.

When did she run away?

Many years ago. It was actually on July 27, 1983, when my Karen left me. On the anniversary I always get so sad—

And where did Karen go?

She wouldn't say. She'd been in some kind of awful relationship with, with this person, and then she . . .

And have you seen her since?

Oh, yes. My little Karen comes home every now and then. But she's always been secretive. She tells me almost nothing about her life. And sometimes I feel so shut out, Mr. Slager; oh, you wouldn't believe . . .

When was the last time she visited you?

Well, let me see. It wasn't long ago. Maybe about three months.

And when's her birthday?

Well, that's another date I never forget. Little Karen came into this world on September the third, 1964. When I think back on that, it doesn't seem so long ago, but of course . . .

So your little Karen would be fifty-one years old.

Well, I guess she would be. Hard to accept that, somehow. It's not easy for a mother, watching her child get old.

Would you say that Karen looks her age?

What a question to ask a mother! Really, Mr. Slager—

May I pour you a little more bourbon?

Oh, such a gentleman! And please help yourself. What brand do you normally drink?

Mrs. Strand, I'm an Old Crow man, and not ashamed of it.

Old Crow! But isn't that what the—

It is. But on the force, that's what we drank. After a tough night on patrol, before a tough night on patrol, you get my drift. I remember one time when a young girl was shot in the head with a twenty-two, and I had to tell the mother.

How awful!

Yeah, it was quite a slaughterhouse. Not just one shot, you see. Pretty well unlocked the good old cranial vault. Well, I don't mind telling you that I ducked into the bathroom and took a nip of Old Crow.

I see, said Mrs. Strand.

Now, ma'am, I have to tell you that we have concerns about your dear little Karen.

What on earth do you mean?

I'll repeat my question. Karen is fifty-one years old. Does she look fifty-one?

Well, she . . . She'll always be my little girl.

He smirked at her. Then he reached past her and topped himself off with Atkins Number Seven Reserve.

Mr. Slager, what are you implying?

When a lady gets to fifty-one, she might look sixty and if she's lucky she might look forty, or with good genetics and a moderate diet maybe once in a lavender moon somewhere around thirty-five, but she's not going to look nineteen, is she?

I don't know, said Mrs. Strand, all in a flutter.

Well, he said, reopening the last album. Here's little Karen at her graduation. Very pretty girl, I have to say.

Well, *thank* you, but I don't see what you're—

Now here's a photo we took of Karen last week.

Oh, my God! What's that horrible place?

It's a bar which I'm sorry to tell you is notorious for perversions. We arrest somebody there almost every night. Now, is that Karen?

I'm afraid so. Oh, *oh*!

And when she comes to visit you, that's how she looks?

Well, I, yes, it is. Is Karen in any kind of trouble?

Now, Mrs. Strand, your dear little Karen of 1982 looks exactly like your postmenopausal Karen of 2015. How do you explain that?

But the woman, finally realizing him to be an enemy, glowered at him. Pouring himself another generous measure of Atkins Number Seven Reserve, he said: Mrs. Strand, we can do this the easy way or we can take it to the next level. It's all the same to me.

What do you *want*?

I hate to suggest this, but could Karen have been put out of the way?

Are you trying to tell me that she's *dead*?

Well, is she?

No, Mr. Slager; she most certainly is *not*, and I'm not sure I appreciate this turn in our conversation. As you can see for yourself, she's exactly the same Karen, and I do know my very own daughter.

Fabulous, he said. Exactly the same Karen. For the third time, how do you explain that?

She hesitated. She swigged her bourbon. She reminded him of the forty-eight-year-old mother who drugged, restrained and pillow-suffocated her four-year-old boy; when the story hit the newspapers the attention thrilled her. She said: You win, Mr. Slager. I confess I've noticed it. And I don't understand it. But there's a lot I don't understand about Karen. And, as I said to you, what mother wants to see her daughter get old? To me it's a *blessing.* Do you believe in God?

Oh, I'm right with the Lord.

Oh, you are? Well, I've never mentioned this to anybody but you. *Karen has not changed*—

And she doesn't visit anyone else in town?

Not to my knowledge. My poor Karen never made any real friends, and she doesn't like to go out. So we just stay in. We watch television, and I make her all her favorite dishes from when she was a child. And I don't question it, because—

You've never asked her why she looks so young?

No. I've already told you that my Karen is very secretive.

Have you ever quizzed her on something that only the real Karen could know?

But she *is* the real Karen. And we have lovely chats all the time about when she was a little girl, and—

And what?

Mrs. Strand said proudly: You wouldn't believe how affectionate she was.

2

Well? said Betty.

It's a complicated case, he said.

3

Perhaps not all of us have done something we remain ashamed of throughout our lives, and those of us who have prefer not to think of whatever bad thing we have done, so that for years it pretends not to exist, and we hold our heads high. But eternal secrecy is superhuman. It requires not only an obvious fortitude, but also a less obvious foresightedness. The one who has done the bad thing may not at first recognize how bad it was. He thinks himself still to be clean, and perhaps, because doing evil sometimes feels unpleasant, he unburdens himself to a friend, as any clean person might do. Yesterday his friend told him his troubles; today he pays back the favor. But just as he begins to feel eased, his friend looks at him in a strange new way and says: I wish you hadn't told me that.—Then it begins. He and his former friend never speak of it again. In time they are friends no more. Years go by; his former friend marries an unknown woman and divorces her. One day by chance one-time confider meets the ex-wife and greets her kindly, in memory of his old friend; she gazes on him in cold watchful disgust, and at once he knows: *his friend told her.* His friend told the woman this thing which for so many years now had not existed, and is now back in the world, never to be gotten rid of. And then five or ten years later he falls out with another woman who as she is leaving him says coolly: By the way, I heard that you did this thing.—It isn't true, he says, and she says nothing.

What was it for the retired policeman? Well, who even cares? He's hardly a character in this book. Actually, it was his honorable vocation to find out what it was for the rest of us—especially for Neva.

Once upon a time in the Y Bar, whose foreground was then dominated by the tourist girl whose stunning legs looked even more naked than naked in the stockings which decorated them right up to the fringe of her cut-off short-shorts, I overheard him say to Neva: One time I put the cuffs on a charmer named Summer Marie who'd been appointed as her grandmother's financial guardian. Dementia, about as bad as it gets before they chain you to your shit-stained mattress. Well,

Summer Marie started selling off the old goner's jewelry right away. Next she drilled into her safety deposit box. Karen, are you getting me?

I think so, said the lesbian.

She opened up eighteen charge accounts in the grandmother's name: National Dollar, Junie's Bridal, you know, all the big names. She was a real fuckin' entrepreneur. When I busted her there were bite marks, a black eye, two broken ribs and a bloodied mouth on old Granny! You see, Summer Marie wanted more, and Granny would have given it to her, but she was too senile to remember where she used to hide the cash. You'd never go that far, would you?

No, said the lesbian.

What if it was your mother?

I love her.

You love everyone, don't you?

That's right, said the lesbian.

Well, the real Karen Strand has got to be an old bag. I mean, she's older than Judy. So who got killed?

You like this, said the lesbian.

Smiling, he said: That's right.

Then you can do it as many times as you like. But right now it's Holly's turn. Do you want to come over tomorrow morning and do this some more?

When's Judy's turn?

Yesterday.

Would you lie to me?

If you told me to.

Are you lying now?

The lesbian smiled at him.

It's a date, he said.

I love you, said the lesbian.

He said: You crooked bitch.

4

He called Judy, whose phone went straight to voicemail. He called her again three more times.

Where the fuck did she go all day? he said to himself. Where, but to Neva?

Where the fuck were you?

Trying to get a job at Buzzmart, but they—

Bullshit.

Honey, I swear—

No way that would have taken you so long. Should I beat the truth out of you? No, you're not worth it.

5

So he got his hair cut at the Eddy Street Barber Shop, right across from the police station. Since he was a regular, the price for him was still fifteen dollars, but he gave the man a twenty. Then he limped over to the Reddy Hotel, Room 543. Neva had a bottle of Old Crow waiting for him. Pretty soon he was saying: The toughest one I ever had was, well, Karen, I had a call, a child neglect call. A neighbor from this apartment called and here's this woman and she's got two, one in diapers, dirty diapers at that, and the other was a little older, and there's feces on the wall, and I didn't have the most pleasant childhood in the world and I was the oldest child and I had to clean up my little brothers, and when you see that it's so disturbing . . . *Look at me.* Yeah. All right, Karen, what happened to you? Don't fuckin' lie to me. Abandonment? No, you look physically healthy, aside from your stupid little puke parties that don't fool anybody. If Judy dies from that bulimia, I'll fuckin' smash your head in. So. Abuse. What was it? Come on, Karen, tell Daddy. What did Daddy do? Oh, I just *love* this!

She answered: Tell me what happened to you.

You know, I don't give a fuck, because you're not drinking with me and I hate your goddamned . . . Oh, what's the point? And your mother's gonna keep the faith. Good for her—a champion old bag! I actually enjoy her, because she's just like me. But your days are numbered, Karen. Your story stinks, and I'm gonna drive you out of here. You wanna know why?

For Judy.

Good *girl.*

Now. Does your biography add up or not? I'd say it doesn't. Are you with me?

Okay, said the lesbian.

Then what do you propose to do about it?

You don't know your own secret, she said.

So what? You get the fuck out of here so I can have my Judy back.

I love you, said the lesbian.

You said that yesterday and the day before. And you know what?

But I really do.

If you love me, get the fuck out of this town. Did you hear me, bitch? *Get out!*

Excuse me, she said. The bathroom door closed behind her. He heard the toilet flush, but without any prior sounds, so he opened the unlocked door, catching her as she bent ever so gracefully, lifting the top of the toilet tank—and then whirled round to see him . . . at which she welcomingly, unquestioningly *smiled*—and he thought: I *have* to see what she's hidden there! Silently letting down the lid, she advanced to the doorway and said: Okay.

Okay *what*?

I want to do what you want. I just don't know how to—

In the long run they won't give a shit. They won't even remember you. How can they, when they don't even love themselves?

But Judy's almost ready to—

Stay away from her.

No, said the lesbian.

What do you mean? he asked. He was astonished, because how often did the hypocritically accommodating bitch ever utter that word?

Xenia's got her another slot at the Pink Apple in two weeks. Did you know that?

Sure, he lied.

Let's you and Xenia and me work on her confidence. And then—

She'll fuckin' crash and burn again. Anyway, the Pink Apple's just a crappy little . . . I mean, whether or not anyone claps for Judy in some dumb little tranny chorus line's not gonna make or break her.

Do it for me, said the lesbian.

He stared. He chuckled. Then he said: I love to negotiate.

Lifting the lid of the toilet tank, she asked him: Did you want to see?

He looked. He saw baggies of powder and baggies of pills all happily floating. He said: I'm gonna drop a dime on you.

Okay, said the lesbian. What else did my mother say?

She loves it that her itsy-bitsy Karen has never gotten old. Are you gonna kill yourself or not?

I'll do something. But Xenia thinks that this time Judy's got a better chance—

He turned his back on her and went out. To demonstrate his contempt, he left behind the bottle of Old Crow.

6

The transwoman grabbed at Neva's hand, and Neva smiled, secretly running her tongue over a mouth-sore. Then I made my requests, and when they failed of brisk fulfillment I dragged them right to the Y Bar at lunchtime, where those red Japanese lanterns glowed by the restroom, and within them the bulb glowing like a fat vermilion clitoris, while Xenia carefully swished one of her false eyelashes around in her cocktail, evidently in hopes of dissolving a clot of glue, and I for once took my drink and sat alone (which is to say catty-corner to trembly old Bradley who as of last week unspeakingly, unspeakably bartended the first shift) just beyond the bar, in order to see Xenia and all the empty stools backward in the long mirror, then waited for Neva, drank another bourbon and sodapop, waited, texted Neva and called her even as Sandra continually reached out with nervous needy tendrils, calling and calling the lesbian's little blue phone without leaving any message, probing to see if the line was busy . . .

7

I dreamed that I was spying on them, as indeed I was, and in my dream I could see an occasion when the lesbian was holding the transwoman's hand and they stepped off the curb in some jarring way which injured the transwoman's wrist so that she cried out in angry pain, and although the lesbian said she was sorry, the transwoman then bitterly responded: So am I.—This second apology, if that was what it was, struck the lesbian as ambiguous, as if Judy, instead of being sorry that she had scolded the lesbian, might in fact have meant to express sheer sorrow at having been hurt, so that after that the lesbian did not care to hold her hand, and a quarter-hour later when the lesbian stopped to check her lipstick in that tiny narrow mirror that Xenia had once given her, the transwoman proceeded to another bench; and when the lesbian looked over that way she saw her sitting with her head hanging down, with such an expression of woe and despair on her face as shocked the lesbian into grief and the tenderest pity, but on account of that incident on the curb, and ever so many others which had happened that spring (for instance, the transwoman, having been informed how much it offended the lesbian to be told over and over *you don't love me*, had now begun to almost offhandedly say: We have a bad relationship), the lesbian could not help but feel anger intermixed with her loving compassion, and when she considered the prospect of once again getting scolded for twisting the transwoman's wrist she pulled her hand away when the transwoman timidly reached out; then in silence they strode down the sidewalk, with the lesbian to the left of and slightly behind the transwoman; later the lesbian was cooking dinner while the transwoman, weary and aching, feeling old, sat on the sofa with her head in her hands; and once the potatoes were done and the asparagus was halfway tender so that it was time to add three spoonfuls of lentils from the can, the lesbian turned round smiling to say: I love you, but the transwoman wore a mask of misery, and she replied: I know how you *really* feel.

But that was nothing but a stupid dream. In fact we all got along in our various combinations, just as in the days when one used to play "Sardines" at Judy Garland's mansion, two people of any sex hiding in the dark until they cared to be found; I remember for instance the pleasing afternoon when the Y Bar had been booked for an engagement party by two old women in purple shirts and white slacks, one bespectacled, the other not, both with identical brown bangs; I saw them cutting some species of cake, then embracing and deeply kissing; meanwhile, in the dark corner by the toilet, Xenia was teasing the transwoman: Have you been to a place called Crunch down on Howard Street? Oh, they make just the most amazing doughnuts. Judy, you should go there. Weren't you trying to put on another fifty pounds?—at which the transwoman commenced weeping as usual, so that the lesbian, our light-giver for life, touched a middle finger to the back of her neck in that special way she had which always made the other woman feel electric. Massaging her shoulders, she said: Judy, what's wrong?

Are you always going to love me?

Of course I will, honey—I promise.

But nobody can be everything to another person. That's impossible, right? I want you to be everything to me, but I'm starting to realize . . .

Am I everything to you now?

Yes . . .

So don't worry. I'll always be, cross my heart . . .

I wish I could dress like a secretary for you. Or a cleaning lady. I'd like to clean your toilet while you slap me and tell me I'm no good—

Judy, are you listening?

Yes, Neva—

I'll never slap you unless you want me to. And I'll only slap you because you're such a good girl.

No, I'm a bad girl. A *bad girl*!

You're a very good bad girl, honey, so come home with me and I'll give you your reward.

So Judy followed her, of course. And the lesbian went into the bathroom, closed the door, sat down on the toilet, silently lifted the top of the tank and set it face down on her lap. There was a new baggie of greyish-white powder attached to it with black electrician's tape. She pinched out a double dose and licked her fingers clean.

Neva? Neva, are you okay? the transwoman called anxiously.

Almost ready! the lesbian called back cheerfully.

What are you doing, Neva?

Whatever she called out echoed in her own ears like old songs to one who has gone away, even here in the darkness where the shining copper suns of the lesbian's bracelets proved that no one had to be alone.

Neva returned smiling to her lover. Her hair was of some bright unknown color. She said: I want you to take care of Xenia, because she looks up to you.

How do you know? breathed the transwoman, fascinated.

I just do. Do you promise?

Okay. I—

You'll do it for me.

That's right.

And the transwoman, reveling in bowing before her, sobbing into her hands, felt, if not very happy, at least coherent, while the lesbian waited patiently to kiss her. They made up in bed. Nowadays the transwoman always licked the lesbian's toes almost desperately. Right now she longed for that trembly, shaken sensation she experienced whenever the retired policeman had whipped her for a long hard time.

8

So when Xenia's dog had to be put to sleep and Xenia asked Francine to come with her for moral support, Judy volunteered to keep them both company; she was the one who stroked the old dog's tumorous head all the way to the vet, because Francine was sitting in the front seat of the taxi and Xenia was weeping. Francine and Judy stood side by side, watching Xenia as the vet upraised the syringe.—Oh, God, just a minute, just a minute more, sobbed Xenia, and so the vet waited pleasantly. Francine took Xenia's hand.—He won't feel a thing, said the vet. Are you ready now?—Xenia nodded and blew her nose. The vet leaned forward while the transwoman stared at everything with her mouth open. The dog did not even twitch. The vet placed his stethoscope against the animal's chest. Everyone waited. The vet said: He's gone.—The transwoman gripped Xenia's other hand. Xenia touched the corpse very quickly and lightly. Then she stood up. When she turned around to face her friends, Judy, seeing how much Xenia grieved, burst into tears.

9

When the lesbian and the transwoman had each taken two blue dolphins, which roared through their nerve endings so excitingly that the lesbian gave them each another, the transwoman's cell phone rang. It was the retired policeman.

Oh, said the transwoman. Oh, no. I feel very nervous.

But he knows.

But today I was supposed to be applying for temp jobs . . .

Well, Judy, do you need to answer it?

I have to. I think I'm being paranoid, but it's also true that he has watched me unlock the screen of my cell phone so often that he can probably do it, and last night after I called you he brought it to me and said: Don't you need this? And it was *unlocked*, Neva! I know I'm in the wrong to be in a hotel room straddling you like this when I told him I was sick, but he always spies on me!

Smiling lovingly, the lesbian stroked her hair and asked: Do you know what you'll tell him?

I can't make up my mind, but I have to at least text him right now. If he doesn't answer I can turn my phone off, but . . . Neva, I don't know what to do!

The lesbian had never stopped stroking her hair. She said: Go ahead and text him now, sweetheart. Get it over with so you can find some peace.

Oh, Neva! I do love you! You know that, don't you?

Of course I do.

The transwoman sat still on top of the lesbian, who waited patiently. Whenever the transwoman got afraid, her body gave off a musk that was not unpleasant. The lesbian licked her armpit.

Neva, why can't we just be together, you and me? I'd marry you . . .

I know you would, honey. I love you very much. Now why torture yourself any longer? Go ahead and text him. Be brave.

The transwoman had scarcely cobbled together half a dozen characters when her cracked phone rang.—Oh, uh, hi, honey, she said. No, I mean I'm not so much sick as drowsy. No, I didn't mean it that way. I'm sorry. I'm really sorry. I know I'm a flawed person, but . . . What? No, it's really true, I swear. And when you're asking me when I last saw Neva, how am I supposed to know the date? You're right. I agree that I should know the date, but I'm not as smart as you are. You sure remember everything. No, that wasn't an accusation; I'm sorry you think so. I didn't mean to make you feel attacked. No, that's not true, honey! I swear I've never used with Neva. You're the only one I use with. Now I'm feeling really sad. I feel as if I'm no good to you. Yes, I agree that I'm no good. I agree that I'm just a trash bitch who doesn't deserve to live. I'm really really sorry. I—no, please don't go! I'll do anything! Hello? Hello?—Neva, he hung up and now he's not answering. What should I do?

Turn off your phone and put it back in your purse. Judy, listen to me. You know that I love you?

Oh, Neva! Neva, I love you so much! I'll always want to be with you—

Okay. Right now you're with me. I do love you and I want to make you happy. Are you feeling the medicine?

Well, I was, but now I feel all speedy and jangled. He's going to hit me when he sees me—

Then don't let him see you.

But I can't—

Judy, look into my eyes. Do you see my pupils?

They're really really big. You look like a beautiful space alien. Ha, ha!

So do you. That drug is trying to help you and I want to help you. In two days you'll be on at the Pink Apple and you'll be a *star.* Relax, Judy; I'm going to kiss your feet.

But how can you do that? I'm not good enough for you, and besides, I need to cut my toenails.

I'm going to lick your toes. How does that feel?

Ah! Ah! Ah! Oh, Neva, don't stop.

10

I cashed my check and went home to rest my swollen ankles. Since I was out of sodapop, I turned on another opiate of the masses, and a cat-eyed lady in a white lab coat tittered: *Brown spots on your face and hands? A prominent surgeon reveals your secret fix—for under twenty dollars!*—after which the beautifully pensive anchorwoman (about whom Selene and Holly both had fantasies) told us her latest bedtime story: *For the second time this year, the same transgender woman has apparently been the target of a hate crime on the streets of San Francisco. On February fourth, Lori Ann Lombardo and her girlfriend Carmela Sanchez were leaving a bus in the city's Tenderloin neighborhood. Lombardo was stabbed in the face and chest by an unknown Caucasian man, who had followed them off the bus, expressing homophobic slurs against both women. The next attack against Lombardo took place yesterday night when she was walking alone near the intersection of Seventeenth and Mission streets, police said. A man and a woman allegedly shouted obscenities at her, after which the woman threw hot coffee in her face and the man punched her at least three times. Police say that both suspects remain in custody at the San Francisco County Jail, and that the video surveillance content is being analyzed. Officers said that two witnesses corroborated . . .*

That news dragged me down, so I set out for the Y Bar to buy a quick cheer-up (six dollars). Selene was saying: It's like when Ellen Icicle had to perform at a mall just to cover the rent of her Malibu mansion—

That's *tragic,* said Victoria, while Judy and Shantelle kept leaning smilingly into each other's faces like the two post-menopausal ladies in that ad for the vaginal hormone ring. Behind the bar, Francine posed as grandly as if she alone could smooth our Neva's heart, caressing away all pain.

Last night I had tried once more to pin Neva down. I pointed out that I loved her; I had proved my love; all I needed was for her to get rid of everyone else and spend the rest of her life in my arms . . . Of course her answer, not curt but also not informative, filled me with dread and grief.

I admitted that it belonged to her to come to us and go from us as best suited her, and that her reasons were hers alone.

The lesbian came in with the retired policeman, and the way Xenia stared at them, it was as if her eyeballs were of blindly shining stone. As for the straight man, he could not stop watching the way that Neva's buttocks pivoted around her unseen cunt as she walked toward the cash register. How could she be so faultless in every way? Was it self-confidence? But she was never arrogant; she had that slightly self-effacing way about her that makes generosity most successful. (Part of deciding that she was now living her truest life was renouncing all hope of living any other way. Or as Natalie Wood, renamed so by her producer, once explained: *You try to find in yourself the essence of someone else's feelings.*) So he hunched his head, unable to get enough of the lesbian. And in that moment, which the rest of us would have spent wondering how we would be remembered, the lesbian hoped only that she would leave no trace and would vanish safely six feet under the illusion she had woven. But the transwoman's desperate desire kept growing ever stronger; she reveled in sobbing into her hands, feeling utterly coherent, while the lesbian waited patiently to kiss her; with Shantelle on her left and Judy on her right, Neva's concern was how to please them both, or, if that proved impossible, how to at least appease them to a minimal degree, so that they would go on loving her. At the Cinnabar the retired policeman insisted that she was prepared to kill herself rather than be understood, but he entertained the sophomoric idea that to understand someone is to understand just what she is afraid of. When I demanded to know what Neva feared, he answered with contemptuous slowness: *Everything.*—He might have been accurate when he said that she would do anything to avoid exposure . . .—but on the other hand, she never lied to him who was an honest liar; when Judy called him to report that according to Shantelle Neva had locked herself in the bathroom to take pills, he gloated, for hiding equaled dishonesty plus weakness. Well, what did *he* fear? Refusing to become fatalistic merely because thanks to the lesbian—who now haunted his speculations like some beautiful darkhaired murder defendant—his happy nights of beating and sodomizing Judy, then winning games of checkers against her (true to her nature, she played to lose) might be coming to an end, he persevered—stoic old fake! I kept saying to him that Neva feared nothing; she concealed only her superhumanness; he said: Oh, no. Her mother knows something, and I'm gonna hook it out of the old hag! *Hola*, Carmencita, fill us both up!

We were *all* free now; and the transwoman, having climaxed again and again, laid down her head between the lesbian's breasts and let everything go, her woeful hopes, resentful aspirations and everything good and bad, all bleeding pleasurably away—if she could only die like this!—she was hemorrhaging, lightening, hollowing out until nothing remained but sleep. For her part, Neva began dreaming of the straight man bowing over a row of graves.

11

Neva visited her mother and came home, after which something happened inside her skull; had she been older she might have wondered whether she had just experienced a minor stroke; the way it felt was that unknown things had squeezed her tight, then squeezed her out into some new place; to be more precise, the things that she had been trying to be and to avoid being, the things she kept doing to protect us from sadness, and the things we demanded of her, all of these forces and entities which had pressed upon her for so long now gripped her almost to death, crushing and strangling her, forcing her down and down through a series of hot dark merciless contractions, advancing her toward her own end, expelling her through rings of slimy muscle, until she *came out*, falling cold and free as if her brain were hemorrhaging—when all that had taken place was that she realized: *I cannot do this anymore*, and she felt so free and empty, falling into the easy abyss of powerlessness, fighting nothing, letting go of everything. Meanwhile the transwoman kept calling her over and over.

12

The next morning she woke up feeling anxious about some new unknown thing—the retired policeman was never wrong!—and when she went to the bathroom she saw in the mirror that she had definitely begun to get old. Her face looked tired, and some of the plump pinkness had gone out of it. A wrinkle across the bridge of her nose stood out like a scar.

Being complete and perfect, she never wondered whether she ought to begin giving less to others. She might have told herself (but not in words): I still believe that what I am doing is not wrong. But if something turns out otherwise, I can always square myself through suicide, or . . . Or what? Well, if I only find a good method I'll be all right. It's nothing that we don't all have to go through, one way or another.

And her heart lifted whenever she thought this. She could do what she had been placed on earth to do, and then when that got to be too much she could just go underground. People might blame her, but she would be safe; they could not do anything to her then!

But the foregoing remains a merest interpolation. Lost in the lazy delusions of my own desires, I impute to her whatever thought processes Judy or I might have possessed, had we been beautiful and loveable forever. More likely, Neva thought of nothing anymore. Isn't that what perfection decrees? (My own warped mentation no longer halts itself.)

13

Neva, look me in the eye. Are you telling me everything?

Of course I am, the lesbian wearily replied, sick with weary dread.

Then why won't you look me in the eye?

Smiling, the lesbian rose, brought her face close to the other woman's, and kissed her.

Sandra said: I'm feeling a lot of confusion, but this pain is another way of experiencing my love for you. Neva, I want you here . . .

The lesbian held her hand.

Sandra continued: I just tell myself this isn't real, Neva. I remember when what we felt was somehow just more innocent in a way, I can't say why . . . But seeing you with others, *I can't stand it*!

The lesbian waited. Gently withdrawing her hand, Sandra said: Maybe I'll go back to Louis and start a family with him, although maybe that would make me feel more alone, if I were still also seeing you secretly and . . . I just don't know how to face this. I don't blame you. I'm feeling a *hotness* about the sex; it's not quite a betrayal, Neva, but maybe it is, but the profound love that I have for you, I . . . I feel so stupid now! But I want your life to be happy, Neva. Are you happy?

Sweetheart, don't worry, said the lesbian.

We are kind of in our own world, and maybe I'm delusional, but if we stay in our own world when we're together then maybe that's all that matters. I mean, do you think so?

Of course I do.

I feel that you understand more about you and me than I do. Maybe what we're doing is the best for me; I don't know. Do you think it is? I mean, do you have anything to say to me? I can't stand it—

One word, said the lesbian. *Mermaids.*

But that's . . . Do you really believe it?

Close your eyes.

But *what do you want*? Who are you? Oh, Neva, you're hurting me so much . . . !

The lesbian came close. Shutting her eyes, Sandra kissed her desperately.

Some Warmth That Wasn't There

Most of them have never heard of the word Lesbian . . . But they knew something was wrong . . . Some warmth that wasn't there . . . I put it to him straight. Did he know she was a Lez when he was working with her? He said no, never suspected it for one minute. He knew there was something lacking, but he blamed himself.

JOHN O'HARA, 1966

Alas, he knew not how dire a monster was she for whose marriage couch he yearned . . .

VALERIUS FLACCUS, *ca.* 70–90 A.D.

It works for a while—but only for a while. Because, late at night, when the paying customers have all gone home, the applause becomes a booming, empty echo, and that's not pleasant.

JUDY GARLAND, 1969

1

I sincerely wanted what was best for Neva; I was as responsible a citizen as the husband who stabbed to death his runaway wife for the sake of the children. (As Shantelle so tenderly put it: Neva, I'm sick of this goddamn shit and someday I'm gonna have a gun in my hand.) I would do whatever it took to honor that happy feeling when we were rushing up her carpeted stairs to love Neva, whose beauty was challenging, burdensome and outright hateful to all the G-girls who were young, ready and naked-shouldered like the silent screen actress Mabel Normand . . . and Francine, peering semi-covertly across the bar, perceived the lesbian was upset for once, which was a good thing, because the bitch had it coming to her; while Sandra, taking a recess from being Judy's *special friend*, whispered to Neva another potentially true story about turning into mermaids . . . and the lesbian chewed some transparent powder, feeling better even before it made her better; she took deep breaths, trying to accelerate her metabolism so that the happy powder would help her sooner; now she was unexpectedly remembering that first time so long ago with E-beth, who was smiling and weeping at the same time, her eyes closed, her lips stretched as wide as they would go, with her teeth shining and shining; it was as if she had learned something terribly sad but accepted it and taken it into herself until it became happy; then came that crooked smile which Karen came to know so thoroughly . . .—As for Sandra, she always lost herself in herself, dripping wet, moaning ever more loudly, then squeaking like a sweet little mouse. Hunter for her part used to be silent for a long time but gradually began rotating her hips faster and faster; when she finally began to moan she was almost there; she screamed herself raw in a trembling voice; after her death the lesbian kept remembering her. Holly would say, oh, God, oh, *God*, and burst into laughter when she came. I can't tell you what I did, but the straight man came quickly, rigidly and repeatedly. (About him Holly said to Neva: There is something that I have noticed with guys that are supermale. I feel something for them, because they come on to me, because I've gotten a lot of attention all my life, and that is something very exciting to me, and they're so cocky and egotistical and into themselves and I'm so thrown off by it that it works in a sense, that I don't just say, fuck off. You almost have me interested!) Xenia began to moan almost at once, steadily but softly, wriggling her hips as she went; when she climaxed it was nearly imperceptible to any lover (she said that she often let her mind wander and then the orgasm would be a surprise). Erin writhed almost silently, then began to moan in a strange humming almost metallic way like a harmonica, finally coming silently. As for Shantelle, it now turned out that even she could be reduced to pleading, while E-beth, yes, E-beth . . .—and Sandra told that lonely woman: But then you must understand that when I don't hear from you for days or weeks, I may develop emotional relationships with others . . .—and just as a manta ray sometimes raises the tip of its wing above the water's surface, so the transwoman, uplifting one heavy eyelid, stared across the retired policeman's jowls and began to think. It was almost Pink Apple time!

Nowadays her sessions with the retired policeman resembled chewing ecstasy crystals with a lover whom due to the antidepressant in her bloodstream it does not affect, so that one's loving happy desire and intimacy are all the while rendered schizoid by the lover's bored talk of what happened at the office. As for him, he was long since used to some warmth that wasn't there.

But she wanted to be more of a woman—which is to say, more like Neva. Therefore, she aspired to send him away happy. Recollecting this, she instantly felt as motivated and determined to be perfect as Judy Garland had been once they discharged her from the hospital in 1960 and she promised herself *no more pills ever.* That same year Bennett Cerf called her *a good girl,* I mean a good guilty girl, and everything went on in Technicolor until they found her on the toilet seat, livid and perfect with rigor mortis.

Charged with the hot love which the lesbian had bestowed upon her, our Judy now loved with tenderness and desire both the frankness of his hairy testicles and the vastness of his yellow abdomen. So she knelt down and worshipped him until he was gratified. Happy that their appropriate power relations had been restored, he rolled her over and used her repeatedly; the way she kept biting her lips to keep in the screams of pain betokened consent; now she was sobbing steadily and groaning at every thrust; when he finally climaxed and pulled out there was blood on his penis, but not so much; that kind of pain went away almost at once; he gave her an affectionate spank on the nearest buttock and said: That was pretty good, babe.

Proud of her progress, she flew off to her goddess for further coaching and therapy.

Neva, how do you see me?

What does Xenia say?

I'm asking you.

Are you asking how I see who you are or how I see who you want to be?

I don't know. Maybe the second . . .

Well, I see a strong, tall woman with a beautiful neck and long dark hair, and sad, sad eyes. Such pretty eyes—

How can I be her?

Take better care of yourself. Keep losing weight. You've already slimmed down so well. Shave better. Wash your hair when it's greasy. You're almost there—

Tomorrow night. At the Pink Apple, Neva! Can you believe it? Oh, my *God*!

I'll be there.

But will you do please please something for me?

The lesbian smiled and waited.

Let's have a little puke party right now. That way I can lose more weight, and I, I actually get really excited to watch you do it. I don't know why, but it's really *hot.*

Okay, said the lesbian.

You first, her guest commanded, starting to play with herself.

So Judy kept looking better and better. Just as MGM's doctors prescribed Benzedrine, the miracle drug, to keep Judy Garland teensy-weensy at ninety-five pounds, with a nightly course of barbiturates for sleep, so *our* Judy faithfully obeyed her own regimen of uppers and downers—but no goddamn buttermilk on her face to take away the freckles! A quick bag of doughnuts, followed by a vomit-and-go; heavier concealer, eyelashes straight out of the box, even a couple of push-ups, squat thrusts and leg lifts, oh, *yeah*! So she dressed up and prepared to be *liked* at the Pink Apple. She hoped to do the same for the whole wide world!

2

For Xenia the worst time to work was Christmas, because that was when everybody had the saddest story, and sometimes she nearly broke down. She came to the Y Bar for light relief, and to Neva for, well, you know.

To the retired policeman she confided: I have the whole Christmas tree, and I'm goin' after her . . .

You're talking about Karen Strand, right? Suits me. She's a shitty piece of work. You get your hooks in her and drag her out of state; then I swear I'll give you a fuckin' medal.

Xenia laughed. She liked him all the better for not being competition.

The manager under whose cruel gaze Judy had previously disgraced herself was off tonight. Xenia had planned accordingly.

Judy sat wringing her hands, wishing for even just point one grams of ecstasy, or maybe a taste of yellow serum. This time she had listened to Xenia and Neva, and dressed in a long loose sky-blue "mother of the bride" dress. When she had first resisted their advice, they reminded her of the time at the Y Bar when she tried to copy the supermodel Tyra Banks and appeared in khaki-esque coveralls; even Francine rolled her eyes and said: Judy, don't you see how it clings to your tummy? That outfit is actually too tight for you. Now, if you don't want to lose weight . . .—by which time the transwoman was sobbing loudly, and everyone got entertained, especially the Scandinavians—a pretty torture from which she was released only when Al opened his cracked smart phone to say: No, that was before my divorce.—By now, of course, she actually *had* lost weight—twenty-six pounds and counting, thanks to her secret puke parties. And just for a change, why not avoid humiliation?

But where was Neva?

Xenia ordered two Old German Lagers and the retired policeman ordered a triple shot of Old Crow straight up, while Judy got a bourbon and ginger ale. Shaking his head, he demanded: What the hell are you nursing it for? If you're going to drink, then fuckin' *drink.*

I'm worried that I might have to pee during my act.

Then make your act a golden shower. What the fuck do you care?

Judy smiled and looked away. Then they all sat watching the current stripper, whose buttocks clenched and unclenched as tirelessly as the muscles of some filter-feeding mollusk, ingesting and straining money out of the darkness.

Now it was time for tranny bingo. Mistress Merkin, the announcer, was a lovely drag queen, big and blonde, with dark eyelashes almost long enough to hang our coats on. She began explaining: The long sheets have three boxes. Each sheet is one game. You've got your little dauber . . .

You wanna play? asked the retired policeman.

No, honey; I'm too nervous—

And there's a *punishment,* the fat blonde laughed, waving a paddle.

The two fat and well-sequined G-girls sitting side by side behind Xenia began shouting with laughter.

Neva said she'd come, but I don't see her, said Judy.

Well, did she promise?

Not exactly—

You are—a WINNER! boomed the drag queen, waving her white arms.

Then the tall emcee was kissing and pulling at the prettiest young bridesmaids and bachelorettes, dragging them up onto the stage, where, although they had shaken their heads desperately and literally dug in their heels, they now capered in delight. Poor Judy couldn't follow what was happening. She always got stupid when she was scared.

A hipster girl nattered on her cell phone, while her date or boyfriend earnestly marked both their bingo cards.

The *lowest* number leads you to a *bed of punishment.* And there's worse for cheaters. All together: *NO—FAKE—BINGO!*

The next winner was a lovely Latina wearing a paper crown. She toasted the Latina beside her.

The new manager came over and said: Xenia, you're Number One tonight. And what's your friend's name?

Judy, said Judy.

Do you have any experience?

Well, I've performed at the Y Bar—

Oh, *that* place, he said.

I vouch for her, said Xenia.

Well, said the manager, the stakes are low, so what do I care? Okay, Judy; you'll be Number Six. Don't let us down.

Thank you, sir, she whispered.

Just don't be lame, said the manager, striding off to number other girls.

Loudly slapping Judy's shoulder, the retired policeman said: Knock 'em dead, babe.

She nodded, too anxious even to speak.

And now, said the manager, *our all-star ambisexuals. First up, please welcome Miss Xenia Ruffles.*

Everyone clapped and whistled. Xenia began her new routine, wiggling and lip-synching to Nancy Sinatra: *These boots were made for walkin'* . . .

Not bad, said the retired policeman, upraising his shotglass, only to discover that it was empty. (Sometimes, to keep up his mind-conditioning, he'd memorize the clothes that the murdered daughter had been wearing, the blue woolen jersey with half-sleeves, the black cashmere stockings and all the rest, so that once the envelopes of evidence came to be introduced at the trial, he'd be right there and ready with identifications.—He rolled around in gore because that made him a better cop.)

More than half the patrons clapped for Xenia. Young women crammed dollar bills in her G-string, and her eyes darkened with excitement. As for Judy, she had a feeling she would fail again.

And Xenia raised her arms, burying her hands in her pretty hair, so that the straight man, re-jilted by Sandra, could truly appreciate this person's breasts; her act was over, so let the gleaning begin! He rubbed his chin, stared and bitched about his job. They sat talking like college students, she naked on the edge of the platform and he clothed. She descended to sit on his lap, there at the edge of the bar.

Hunter glowered. Suddenly she stood and went out.

And now, said the manager, *let's show some love for Mistress Fancy. She has the magic cape that goes all the way from* here *to* there*!*

Mistress Fancy emerged from the red curtain, waving both hands. Sick with fear, Judy whispered: I've gotta pee.

Then pee.

But Judy didn't dare move. She was afraid that someone might look at her. If only Neva would arrive!—But Neva, who had certainly intended to cheer her on, got waylaid by Catalina, who was gripping her by both wrists and saying in a rush: I think the expectations we're taught as a woman come down to: you have to get married and take care of a family and so on;—but when a woman of color doesn't do all that, you're judged a lot harsher. So you have to stand up with grace. I'm undocumented, Neva. Did you ever know that? In college I never got that financial aid; I had to pay out of pocket. I'm still paying back my loans. And you know, as the females in our culture, we're supposed to take care of our parents. That's the difference between a white woman and a brown. I am a brown person. I'll bet your parents don't expect anything from you. I'll bet your Mom wasn't one percent as strict as my Mom. You're a liberal white girl, so you got to do *whatever.* And that's why you think you can treat me any way you feel like. Well, Neva, it *hurts* me! But I'm brown and you're white, so what the fuck do you care? Excuse me, Neva, I know you have to go . . .

I love you, said the lesbian.

Don't talk down to me.

Please come here, said the lesbian, who then did whatever she had to so that Catalina went away fulfilled.

In those days Hunter was trying not to see the lesbian too often, just to maintain herself the way she was, but she did need to see her a little more and then a little more, sometimes on ecstasy or some other drug, and she had begun to notice changes in herself that made her disappointed. She was turning in her school papers late or never. She was less loving to her mother. She felt more numb to everything, and when the transwoman asked her if that was a good thing or a bad thing she said that it was mostly bad.

She was hoping to get through the semester. She called Neva and said: I'm feeling very rejected and sexually frustrated. And Xenia's bad to me.

Don't worry, honey, said the lesbian. When we're together we're going to invent sexual positions that no humans have ever tried.

You're so kind . . . she whispered. I love you so much . . .

Hunter now like so many of us went walking to and fro on this earth, just as Satan used to do; and before she knew it she was sitting in the Buddha Bar, where an elegant middle-aged woman whose "look" favored that of Julie Andrews was answering a starstruck younger femme: I never had anything really bad, like I would talk to the manager. You're handing out alcohol and people are drunk. At one point we had little tiny dresses with heels, fishnets. Black. They would put you in an area, and someone would go, *cocktails*! If you worked the high roller room that was always nice. Then the touching and grabbing wouldn't happen. No, sweetheart. Oh, no. I never touch anyone in the audience. Go-go girls? Sure, it's a living, but it's not really what I want to do. I would imagine that you're dealing with people you don't want to deal with.

Hunter eavesdropped—which was as pointless as suddenly bringing to mind the Hotel Western on Leavenworth; all the same, she imagined kneeling down before the Julie Andrews lady and giving herself utterly to this wise and stately person who would tell her how to live and then maybe . . . She was telling the starstruck girl: I mean, you work for good people and you get paid, but not always . . .

Meanwhile the lesbian sat wondering whether it would be better or worse for Hunter to break up with Xenia, who kept making her cry and apologize, but as it happened Hunter was the one who kept calling Xenia, not the other way around. She had told Neva: I'm the type of person that has to be pushed until I can't be pushed anymore, and then . . .

Just then at the Pink Apple, Mistress Fancy was wriggling up and down the aisle, soliciting for her pension fund. The retired policeman reared up chuckling. Mistress Fancy smacked her lips when he stuck another dollar bill on her bra, everything glitterglam and spangly. Then he sat down, saying: Get ahold of yourself, Judy bitch.

Number Three was a hulking old black T-girl who sang *You better lick it before you stick it*, chomping her lips for greedy joy every time some worshipper held out a dollar bill; she would seize hold of men's and women's hands and drag them up onstage; her grip made you think that your finger or wrist had been caught in a paper shredder; the retired policeman laughed until he choked. Xenia was still swishing around with her fans and glamorously air-kissing her enemies. Judy wished someone would shoot her in the head.

In the ladies' room her bluehaired friend Colleen was smoking a joint. She asked Judy: Do you remember me?

Sure. Did you parachute in?

I've got something for you.

Oh. I mean, you really do? Thank you. By the way, I've got to—

And now, said the manager, *let's give it up for Princess Tiger Girl.*

Open your mouth. What I've got for you is a kiss.

Judy did her best to swallow Colleen's tongue. She was adoring it because it opened her up like daylight. Then Colleen said: I love you, Judy. You know why? Because I love women, and you're trying so hard to be one of us.

How do I look to you?

I dated a couple of people who have looked very different, like you, but my partner now, she's pretty feminine. What it comes down to is, I don't care how you look. You're Judy and that's enough! I told you before and you forgot it, so I'm telling you now: When you feel disgusting, embrace your disgustingness. Now get out there and shine. But you'd better pee first. Hurry up now.

And now, let's rock the house for our longest-playing act ever, Miss Iris Quintana.

Judy rushed into the stall and peed while Colleen kissed her.—Good, said Colleen. Now here's a present from Neva . . .—depositing on her tongue a drop of yellow serum.

You know Neva!

I've told you that. Go out there and make us proud. Hurry, hurry!

Hitching herself up, she rushed to take her place behind the red curtain just in time to witness the final twirls of Iris Quintana, who reincarnated long dead, golden-eyelashed Natalie Wood with a golden butterfly in her hair, flaunting her thighs in a gold-mesh micro-minidress. Judy should have been terrified. Instead, she was roaringly eager.

And now, please welcome Miss Judy Garland, straight from the Land of Oz!

Lip-synching to "Somewhere Over the Rainbow," Judy marched out to strut her stuff. Although she strove as well as any movie actress not to be human, the applause was tepid, and she was already wishing to hide, but then the yellow serum began to flood her with confidence. Remembering a certain stripper from somewhere who had kept caressing her own buttock, then slid down her thong-strap in quest of hard cash money, Judy now yanked her dress up to her belly button, waggled her buttocks and shouted: *I wanna be disgusting!* Then they all roared, loving her. Even the retired policeman was beaming.

They egged her on. The raunchier she got, the better she did, feeling so lucid in the night, shrugging and laughing, the tops of her breasts shining like dreams as she strutted so immense and wonderful. Playing a symphony of garters and thighs, a breast or two and that clenching and unclenching bottom, Judy had herself a crazy crazy time flying around the catty pole! While Judy Garland kept singing *why, oh, why can't I,* the other Judy was mouthing: *Fuck me, fuck me! I wanna FUCK!* And it transpired that the audience could read lips.

Winking into the impossibly doll-like eyes of a glossyhaired G-girl, Judy shouted: Come on, baby!—The G-girl smiled and blushed. Judy felt *powerful*—much like the T-girl who confessed to murders she didn't commit in order to get more attention.

They leaped up and mobbed her with one-dollar bills. One fan even gave her a five. Xenia was laughing and yelling. When her song was over, horny drunks invited her to their tables. A boy wanted to lick her mouth. An elderly Japanese gentleman made arrangements to meet her at the restroom door in order to buy her used panties for fifty dollars. Licking a lesbian's cheek goodbye, goodbye, Judy departed for her next rendezvous, where she was soon pumping her buttocks in the lap of a young man in a business suit whose smile mixed embarrassment with astounded happiness.

3

And so she received full membership in this paradise of girls with perfect long blonde hair which felt to her stroking hand like fishing line. It was almost as marvelous as her avatar's doubly dreamy moment when Norma Shearer had given her a brand-new cream-colored makeup kit and, oh, God, Clark Gable was sitting at the very next table! (Judy had never made *that* comparison before.)

Knowing that loving the lesbian as profoundly as the lesbian loved her was impossible but that not attempting to do so would be evil, Judy still felt relief, to love only herself for awhile. At closing time she continued sorrowfully perfect, wriggling her receding buttocks in the darkness. By then Colleen had vanished but that didn't matter because at two a.m. Judy had a date with her ultra-favorite sweetheart!

You see, said Neva, you didn't need me. I'm so proud of you—

But where were you?

You know.

That's okay. Anyhow, tonight I got to feel what it's like to be you, or maybe just a little like you, and, oh, Neva, it was all stars and spangles!

I'm glad, said the lesbian.

It's like that for you, isn't it?

I love you, Judy.

In the dawn the lesbian awoke with the transwoman nestling against her shoulder, and the transwoman's face was almost beautiful when she opened her big blue eyes and murmured sleepily: I love you so much . . .

Shantelle's Medicine

The feminine faculty of anticipating or inventing what can and will happen is acute, and almost unknown to men. A woman knows all about a crime she may possibly commit . . . But what woman has not been disappointed in her crime, once she has committed it and the murdered lover lies there at her feet?

COLETTE, 1941

Perhaps in most people's careers it occurs that they are bitterly disappointed in the one thing that really counted.

NATALIE WOOD, 1966

1

Our deliciously perverted impositions on Neva—cheating to lengthen our turns, stealing the clothes she had worn (by now even Al possessed a modest collection of her underwear), became their own hilarious rewards—but don't get me wrong; I was better than the others—why, I even tried to celebrate her, knowing that there is no such thing as possession of another person (yet all the while determined to somehow keep her tight against me forever); and none of us had any idea as to whether she supposed she could love forever, although ever since we'd caught her with that lone grey hair (that cheatin' *bitch*! cried Shantelle), we anticipated ecstatic ringside views of inevitability: the entire complicated shimmering projection beginning to collapse like pancake makeup cracking on a woman's face, defeated by sweat and time. I'm not saying that Neva deserved what she was going to get. But if she'd only let us in on her secrets . . . ! Maybe that was how it had to be. We are told that the Goddess wishes us to know Her, but in fact She reveals to us only the least fold of Herself, like a masked woman who uncovers her face only in darkness, and then only for a single haunting kiss. So it was with the lesbian, whose love required her both to know us and to prevent us from knowing much about her.—You know, said Xenia, it's like there's some warmth that isn't there.

2

Speaking of Xenia, Hunter now called Neva to report, giggling and high: There's only one little cross. I marked it, and my dog marked it. Another girlfriend, *down*!

Are you going to be all right?

Oh, sure. You know what they say: *Make* you *a priority before you make your partner a priority.* And also, we're friends because our community is small. Xenia's probably gonna be in the parties this summer, so it's better to just smooth it over for everybody's sake. Maybe I'll avoid the Y Bar for awhile . . .

How's Xenia?

Why not ask the next time you fuck her? She's probably having the time of her life. Neva, I . . . Could I come see you? I need to be held—

Okay, honey, said the lesbian.

3

As for the warmth that Judy still imagined, of light on shoulders and breasts and spangled hips, of being the almost whole and perfect female who incarnated herself by whirling round and round, riding down the melting light on her buttocks and into her own delicious spine in order to console herself for and even usurp Neva's spine and the darkness between Neva's buttocks, as we all lusted, and the lights crawled more and more, she had won that, she hoped maybe forever (which meant, for whatever indefinite corridor of months she could see partway down)—but our Judy was, as you know, especially sensitive to upsets, and what now happened with Hunter knocked her into sobbing disequilibrium.

4

The lesbian sat on the edge of her bed, alone for another twenty minutes, held her phone to her ear and listened to another groggy message from Hunter: Hey, babe, I was so happy to hear your voice again; it really cheered me up; so I'm calling you from bed; I'm all wrapped up in blankets, and I wish you were here to take off these funny sweatpants I'm wearing. Last night I was feeling sad about Xenia so I took some morphine and it's not working too well but it's real nice to wake up at dawn. Baby, thank you so much for giving me your high school picture. It made me so happy. I just can't take my eyes off your tits. In different lights they seem to be different things, I think. They're breathing a little bit right through that T-shirt; I wish you weren't wearing it. I'm excited you're going to be with me soon but I'm nervous, too. I hope I don't feel too guilty. I'm okay; I'm trying to be healthy. Lonely for Xenia, but . . . Just had a little bit of heroin in my bathroom . . . I guess I've been thinking about you even more . . . I've been coming to bed, sick, sick, sick with two blankets under me and four blankets over me. I think about having you with me. I love you so much. Honey, please call me . . . Honey, what are you doing now? Where are you? I had this idea; maybe you're in someone's bed, and under someone's blanket. I admit I'm jealous of Judy right now. And Shantelle, and Richard, and that goddamn Xenia . . . Whatever you're doing, *stop, stop.* Come over here and embrace me . . .

5

Hunter had adored Xenia; all year she loved only her (aside from Neva, of course). Because she was crazy about holidays, or rather the idea of holidays, but in actuality felt sad to spend them with her parents and sister, she invited Xenia up to see National Women's Day with her, and by eleven p.m. her sweetheart, who was considerably older, had grown very tired, but Hunter really, really wanted to stay up until midnight, so they did, and kissed each other, proclaiming their undying love, after which Hunter begged to stay up for another couple of hours, but Xenia said that in that case she would go sleep in the other room, at which Hunter agreed to turn out the light, but tossed and turned in bed; truth to tell, Hunter was quite the night owl. The next day Xenia sucked one last long sweet orgasm out of her. But now Hunter acted worried about herpes; she insisted that even skin-to-skin contact might spread it, so when it came Xenia's turn she was permitted only to masturbate while her stern young lover held her. That day Hunter kept interrupting no matter what Xenia said. Xenia cooked breakfast, lunch and dinner; each time Hunter required that her own portion be made to unique specifications. The day after that, while they were waiting for Hunter's airport shuttle to come, Xenia, whom I have always celebrated for her expert experience, could perceive all too well that her companion had tired of her, so she felt relief right at the final weary embrace, when Hunter recited the stale lesson that she loved Xenia so very much. Her voicemail calmly ran: I have a feeling that you're going to leave me, and all night her phone was silent except for a five-second I love you from Neva; the next morning she woke up to find that Hunter had called her back, saying: That message made me very, very sad. Of course I still love you!—Xenia called Hunter, but Hunter didn't call her. So she called Hunter again; in other words, no one could blame her for anything.—After the fifth ring Hunter said: The reason I was so sad was that I loved only you last year but I'm not sure that I want to do that this year.—Maybe you need to leave me, said Xenia, but Hunter said: I can't ever leave anybody. I'm too weak.—It will never be easier than now, said Xenia. You want to do it; it's part of your New Year's resolution; make it clean . . .—and so Hunter left her. A little sorry for her, slightly amused, mildly relieved and mostly cold, Xenia said: You can call me whenever you like, but I'm not going to call you anymore.—Hunter tried to say something, but her cell phone suddenly had poor reception.—I'm going to say goodbye now, Xenia said.—Goodbye, said Hunter.—So long, said Xenia, hanging up, after which the loneliness began to nibble at her, so she dialled up Sandra, and then of course Neva, both of whom considerately unfolded several loving not to mention erotic ideations they had manufactured. As long as Xenia stayed on the phone she was happy. Then she hung up. It was dark outside. She began to feel drearier and drearier, even though she knew that nobody needed six girlfriends; she was freer now and more honest; it wasn't as if she missed that crybaby, who had craved to be seen, and to go out everywhere holding Xenia's hand, and maybe even with medical assistance make a baby that they would raise together, although who could blame her for such desires? Xenia sat listening to the dark, reminding herself that she had dodged a bullet. Finally, with a halfway bitter smile, she began to do the lunch dishes.

Meanwhile Hunter rushed triumphantly over to the lesbian's.

Neva, she said, I'm all yours. I broke up with Xenia and I'm feeling so free—

Honey, are you okay? asked the lesbian.

I feel fucking *great*! Should have done this months ago! Oh, Neva, Neva, Neva!

Come in, said the lesbian.

Hunter said: The reason I've been so sad was that I loved only you, but I had to pretend for Xenia. She's so goddamned fragile. But you know how I found the strength? I realized I could do this *for us.*

The lesbian held her hand.

Oh, Neva, I'm so crazy about you! I can't think of anything but . . . Fuck me now.

The lesbian obliged.

Then Hunter said: I'm moving in with you. And I want to marry you. Francine says we can celebrate at the bar. You remember Selene's wedding? That's where we met . . .

Inhaling her entreaties, the lesbian held her for a long time, until the buzzer rang: my turn.

6

And *then*, said the retired policeman, when I was putting the cuffs on he kept whining: *Officer, that's not rape; I'm only ripping off a little pussy!* The whole force was laughing all night.

Ha *ha*, said Judy, who was curling her eyelashes.

Do you have a date with Neva?

Oh, I'm just going out to make a little money.

With Al?

How did you know?

I always know. Well, brush your stinkin' teeth when you're done.

I promise.

And off she went to warm Neva's bed. She hugged me as I was leaving.

7

Hunter went out into six-o'-clock on a Friday evening, where foreign tourist families caught the breeze in Union Square, as the cable car, so packed with riders that some of them leaned outward through the open doorways, rang its friendly yet authoritative bell and, flying its flags, clanked down the metal grooves of Powell Street to a place where a corner branch of a national bank pretended to be glamorous, a police car sirened its dangerously rapid way through traffic, and a long-haired young Brazilian woman came running up to someone, beaming, with her cell phone angled outward. Just as a murder may be classified by whether or not the victim's pockets were turned out, so lives may as well be sorted based on the presence or absence of sadness. Hunter was a sad one, but on the curb a femme was hugging a chunky black-clad butch; they stood looking into each other's eyes, then simultaneously stared down at their white-glowing phones. Weren't they an inspiration? Hunter licked her lips, but Neva's taste had been swallowed away. As for Xenia, Hunter now subscribed to the retired policeman's line: That goddamned cunt couldn't pass her polygraph.—Three yellow taxi cabs, a grey one and a white one underscored the red awnings and plate glass windows of the lingerie shop, and the wind blew cooler. Storey after yellow-bricked storey of the Chancellor Hotel punched a salient high into the indifferent sky. The angled fire escape ladder between each two balconies combined with them to make a Z. And those Zs went up, over and over into the cloudlessness. A middle-aged chestnut blonde in a floral-patterned knee-length skirt stopped on the corner, aimed her cell phone, and took a photo of that towering brickscape. A man in a grey-blue suit stood on a traffic island, leaning over a little woman and shaking his fist in her face. Then they both boarded the cable car. The amplified street prophet cried: *No amount of good works that you can do can restore you to God. It says in First Corinthians . . .*

Fuck you, said Hunter.

Hearing her, the prophet insisted: *Oh, no, sister; we're all valuable to God. He had you on His drawing board. The claims that Jesus made . . . Because if you look at all of Jesus's teachings . . . because He said I am the Door. It was not Moses; it was My Father, and anyone who eats of his bread . . . I am the living bread . . . Eat of Me and you will live forever.*

But I don't want to, said Hunter.

8

As soon as Sandra and the transwoman came into the Y Bar, Francine crooked her finger at them, which she had never done before, and as they prepared to take their accustomed stools before the center of the counter, she beckoned them to the end, which people sat at only because they were ignoramuses or because the place was otherwise full, because the smell of the toilets reached here; when they were safely out of earshot of everyone but me, Francine leaned forward to say in the lowest voice she could (whispering had always been beyond her): Hunter hanged herself this morning. I just got a call from her mother. Nobody else knows yet; the police were really nice and said they'd keep it quiet as long as they could.

Sandra began weeping. She looked beautiful with her tearstained freckles and her big brown eyes and her long caramel-red hair. She kept choking: I'm sorry; I'm so, so sorry . . .

Judy said: We need to find Neva right away.

Find her? You know where she is, said Francine. *Seeing* somebody, as you would put it. They won't like being interrupted. Better to call—

I'm trying now, said Sandra. Oh. Her phone is off and her voicemail is full.

Maybe it's messages from Hunter—

Or else Xenia found out and—

Where *is* Xenia?

She must be at work—

What's Neva going to do?

You know how she takes on everything. We have to make sure she doesn't blame herself—

Francine had already poured each woman her usual. She wouldn't take any money. Suddenly she rushed into the powder room, coming out pale, with bloodshot eyes.

Sandra said: I really think we should go and be with Neva right now.

Okay, said the transwoman.

I stood up and said: I'll go, too.

Oh, you heard? said Sandra. Judy said nothing, but took my hand.

Just then Shantelle came in.—Don't tell her, Judy whispered in high excitement. Quick, let's just go . . .

So we did. When the elevator doors parted we saw the police, but they were merely handcuffing the wife-beater in Room 541. Catalina's door was closed; likewise Victoria's. The lesbian opened her door immediately. She too had been crying, but when Judy later reported that to the retired policeman, he opined, as would the straight man, that she had faked it. As soon as they came in, the two women embraced her, and she sagged between them, exploding with sobs. I stood wondering what to do. In the living room, sitting on the sofa, was Jayna the beautician, who by some coincidence also loved the lesbian, and had evidently offered up her service, for a white towel lay outspread beside her, bearing shears and a pile of the lesbian's adorable hair. When the transwoman saw that, she unconsciously and helplessly inhaled. All she could think of now was how she might steal a handful of those precious strands.

Jayna did not get up to greet us. On her face we visitors saw the look we knew so well from each other's faces—the look of coitus interruptus.

Neva, honey, how are you managing?

I'm trying to be happy, because it's what she wanted . . .

What about Xenia?

Not wishing to inflict myself on others, I sat down alone in the kitchenette with the light off. After awhile Neva came to me and touched my shoulder. I asked her to sit on my lap and she did. Jayna regarded me with jealous dislike. Meanwhile,

Judy broke out a fifth of Old Crow from her purse and poured us each a shot. She said: Neva, maybe I'm out of line to ask this, but is it true that you and Hunter were getting married?

That's what she wanted, the lesbian repeated.

But *were* you?

No. That's why she . . .

Neva, baby, said Sandra, I love you so so much! And this was *not your fault*! I'll be thinking about you all the time. If you need me to come over and—

Same here, said Judy quickly.

As it happens, said Jayna, I was already here.

Then Shantelle came rushing in. She said: Did you hear that Hunter offed herself? Her Mama had to break the bedroom door down but by then it was too late. And they said the bitch's face swelled up like a, I dunno, a goddamn *balloon*, all 'cause Neva wouldn't put out! Now that's what I call a fuckin' compliment. Neva, honey, we're all of us gonna be dyin' for you . . .

The lesbian stood up. That was the first time I ever saw her flinch.

Look at her! Shantelle gloated. Bitch can't take the heat—

Hoping to protect Neva, I approached the snakelike woman in that spirit of deferential, almost fawning discretion appropriate to our mutual business; impatiently she accompanied me to the bathroom, saying: Well, whadya want?

I still could not imagine what I would say, but a half-seen idea, like a long school bus suddenly emerging into view of my corner window, and then melting into the fog, leaving behind a bright yellow impression of softened butter, finally inspired me thus: Shantelle, I'm jonesing bad—

So fuckin' *what*? Am I your bitch?

I said the first thing that came into my head: Hey, I want to do what Hunter did, but I don't want to suffer. Can you fix me up?

With the cold-eyed caution of a middle manager who has never possessed a senior executive's power, and therefore escaped many self-delusions, she said: Don't bullshit me.

Help me out and I'll give you my turn.

With *her*? Again? Can't you get it up no more?

My business is my business, I said.

Then it sure ain't mine, so *fuck you.* Anyhow, you had your turn yesterday.

I traded with Al, so there's one coming to me tomorrow.

Fine. You always been straight with me. You want high-class China white or straight fentanyl?

Logic time, I said. If I paid you for heroin you'd just give me fentanyl because once I croak I can't complain, right?

Shantelle laughed, hugged me and said: Oh, I just *love* you!

Now look, I said. I want the good stuff. If it's fifty times stronger than heroin, half a gram should be way more than enough. But let me buy a whole gram, just to—

You're ridiculous. A hundred micrograms is gonna be, like, Richard, good fuckin' night. Ha, ha, ha! Good night, motherfucker!

Are you *sure*?

Yeah yeah *yeah.* Gimme the money.

How much?

Eighty dollars.

By now Neva had composed herself, but I had to go through with it for the sake of consistency. I gave Shantelle four twenties—enough to kill four of us if the stuff was pure enough. She promised delivery tomorrow when the Y Bar opened. We understood each other. Then she got back into her usual groove, calling Neva *that dumb little white girl, that skanky white bitch.*—I can't be her friend no more. She don't respect herself . . .—When I left, she was sucking Neva's earlobe and Jayna had smashed a coffee cup on the floor.

Now I had no money for dinner. I went home and brushed my teeth over and over, so that the stinging clean flavor of Minty-Hinty toothpaste would trick me out of being hungry. Unfortunately, my gums kept bleeding, so the taste was foul, just like my life. I might have dated Francine, but she was on shift, and besides, what if we brought each other down?

The next day Shantelle was only half an hour late. She had the stuff: a fingernail's worth of powder in a wrinkled plastic bag. She said: Remember me in your will!

I tried to think of a comeback; I wanted to delight her with some cleverly obscene bequest, but my comedy generator was burned out, probably because I had lost tonight's turn with Neva.

When are you gonna do it? she asked. Lemme be there; I wanna watch. And J. D.'s gonna love it; you know how *that* fucker is.

I said: It might just be insurance.

In fact the fentanyl went to a different purpose, because the next time I was with Neva I told her all about it, to remind her how much I loved her. We were sitting in her kitchenette. She knew I was hungry, so she had made us tomato soup with crackers crumbled on top. When I finished, she laid her hand on mine and said: Please give your stuff to me.

And right away I felt pleasure and relief. Of course it was Neva that I had bought the poison for!—Back in the days when I still read literature, and sometimes even by mistake great literature, the rule used to be that if a gun appears in Acts II or III, it had better go off in Act V. Hence I now promised myself never to be surprised if and when she did it.

9

She gave Xenia an extra turn, of course. That lady, grieving for Hunter, raging at her and of course blaming herself, followed the path of self-sufficiency; in other words, she tried to hide her feelings. Bearing patiently the smell of her old age, the lesbian serviced her until she was ready to weep and be held.

Next she called Francine to check on the latter's liver biopsy: clean. Then she fucked Shantelle for two hours (that would have been my turn); and because this woman was enjoying her so much, growing so elated that the lesbian refused to be cruel and explain who she was, it might have been the best ever: Shantelle's orgasmic cries resembled the screams of a mother who has just been presented with her daughter's corpse at the morgue.—Dutiful Neva!—She felt a light and peaceful emptiness, as if she had secretly purged her stomach of every meal she had eaten for many days; she felt dizzy and her ears were ringing, and she felt safely cut off from everything.

10

She attended Hunter's funeral. Again she became the transwoman's psychotherapist, first for forty-five minutes on the phone, then for a half-hour emergency hug-and-suck. After that it was time to service the straight man. Twisting Neva's breast as earnestly as Natalie Wood tuning both knobs of her squarish blue television set, Xenia penetrated her from behind with a double dildo. Bracing herself wearily on her hands and knees, she managed not to be overwhelmed by Xenia's panting. (How they loved each other!) Then she gave Sandra just what she needed; she even made time for Samantha, Selene and me, not to mention Victoria—who had no anxiety about anything now, because lying in the lesbian's arms took that away. By then Neva felt pretty tired, I can tell you! As soon as she had fulfilled these obligations, and gotten rid of us, she sat on the edge of her fresh-made bed, rocking back and forth.

Neva's Surprise

> I hope . . . that other girls who read Joan's bitter story will learn the folly of entering into a Lesbian relationship.
>
> *Life Romances* magazine, 1953

1

All right, said the retired policeman, scratching his belly. So start with what you do remember.

I was supposed to meet her at Ladykiller's—

Why not the Y Bar?

I don't know. Anyway, as you know, I usually came to her place—

So what did she say?

She texted, to say that—

Show me.

I can't. I was so upset when she stood me up that I wasn't paying attention, and my phone fell into the toilet.

Frank, you sure are a pathetic bitch. Well, when was the last time you saw her?

At her place.

And how did she act then? asked her lover, beginning to enjoy himself.

Wonderful. Same as ever.

And if she'd had something on her mind, would you have noticed?

Of course. Neva and I are soul mates.

Judy, you're a piece of work. Can you remember one goddamned thing she said?

She said she loved me.

So what else is new? I give up. I can't fuckin' help you. End of investigation. Neva's tired of you and everybody else. She's seducing new people. Bring me a beer. But first, watch this! I'm calling your fuckin' phone, and even though you tried to trick me and put it on vibrate, I can *see* your stupid purse move! Why'd you lie to me, Frank?

Because—because she—

Answer me right now, you faggot sonofabitch!

Please, please don't! Now I'm so afraid . . .

Good. Then give.

Neva promised to move in with me. She gave up her place yesterday. Her roller bag's in my—

And what about me?

I . . . I don't know.

So that's how it is. True love. You lied to me and now she lied to you. Ain't *that* poetic justice?

Oh, God, oh God! I'm so sorry but I just couldn't—

He slapped her lightly on the cheek. She dared not even cringe. He slapped her again. Then he said: Now, Frank, what's the main difference between you lying to me and Karen lying to you? Which is worse? How long've we been together? *Answer me.* Better yet, answer your stinkin' phone. Looks like you're in luck, boy! Must be Karen. Your shitty old purse is vibrating like mad. Go ahead, Frank. Answer it right here in front of me.

Flushing and trembling, the transwoman removed her flip phone and opened it. The retired policeman watched her, smiling grimly.

Oh, he said. Just a text. Is it a robo-text? Poor little Frank.

But the transwoman now paled; the retired policeman had never seen the like—except maybe in that newspaper photo of the blankly submissive face of Bruno Hauptmann with its turned-up eyes. (The attorney general had said: *We demand the penalty of murder in the first degree.* Hauptmann never admitted anything. His triple answer to the cross-examination: *To a certain extent.*)

The color seemed not merely to bleed but to sink out of Judy. First her forehead went white, then her cheeks and even her lips, her neck, her hands.

She sat down. Her mouth stayed open.

Well? said her master.

Judy took a deep breath. She said: Neva got married.

2

It had happened according to the usual chemical laws.—You're not going to be a virgin much longer, growled the straight man, and Sandra giggled; they were now both pulling off each other's clothes in happy desperation, and he went down on her until she was laughing in her orgasmic happiness; then she said: I need you inside me, and he reared up eagerly, only to feel his erection waste away. Again and again they tried; she did everything, touching, stroking, sucking, pleading, and the more she needed it, the more under pressure he felt; soon she was weeping: Oh, God, I need you in me so bad . . . Please, baby . . . Why can't you . . . ?

And he didn't even feel ashamed. A sad lassitude only slightly touched by nausea left him more dreamy than otherwise. Sandra forgave him, of course. It wasn't his fault that he was getting old! She still loved him exactly the same.—Off she rushed to the lesbian.

Now they were kissing. As soon as the lesbian's tongue entered her mouth, she lost control of herself, twitching and pissing like a fresh-shot cow. The bed seemed to swerve and capsize; Sandra no longer knew up from down. The lesbian was riding her or she was sitting on top of the lesbian, slamming their cunts together, grinding pelvis against pelvis as the bed flew through space. After a long fall through darkness they struck concrete, shattering into slime laced with skeleton-chips, drooling in agonizing orgasms. Sandra groaned in ecstasy. Sunlight jolted through her like semen.

Oh, girlfriend, I feel so much better now, she said.

The lesbian took her hand.

The time we had was *perfect*!

Smilingly, Neva kissed her cheek.

And I feel so much closer to you. Do you feel the same?

Oh, yes, said the lesbian.

I want to be with you for the rest of our lives, said Sandra. Again the lesbian kissed her, at which non-answer Sandra took on an expression not unlike that of the longhaired girl who threw back her head and slammed shut her eyes, sobbing and smiling in agony, while the defense lawyer sat with his arm around her shoulder, clenching his fist on a folder of documents and squinting up in outrage at the verdict of guilty regarding a perfectly altruistic occasion when the girl had texted a troubled boy until he agreed to gas himself in his truck; when he began to feel afraid and stepped out, she directed him back into the vehicle, which solved his problems.—Sandra was already getting the chills. The dawn-bright lesbian, so sensitive and quick, was already proffering a glass of water and two sky-blue analgesic tablets. Her clitoris was a medallion of Cybele and her nipples were pink jade, and there was nothing imperfect in her.

Sandra, shivering in Neva's bathrobe, said: I, you know, I am *your girl forever.*

Thank you, said the lesbian, whose previous lovers resembled a line of ballerinas frozen in darkness with their long narrow arms uprisen.

Sandra said: One thing I've learned: You're vulnerable. I need to remember that. Part of me has always worshipped you; I just never realized that I had the power to hurt you—

Don't worry, said the lesbian.

But I don't *want* to hurt you!

You're my pretty mermaid . . .

What about Judy? Isn't she your mermaid, too?

I just want to give everyone unconditional love.

But *why*? Why aren't I enough for you?

One of these days *I* won't be enough, said the lesbian.

But romantic Sandra denied that there would ever be new mermaids in the sea. Inhaling the entreaties which were made to her, Neva regarded her with the smile of the Apollonian woman whose carver had condemned her to be part of a marble column, staring pupillessly across void sunshine at a fat limestone owl for Athena.

3

When the straight man came to drink his own share of manna, for which he had been hungering ever since Sandra left him, it seemed the worst thing that could have happened, short of his own death, which he self-pityingly told himself that Neva might bring about.

It was before noon. His achievements reminded him of the acrid after-note in the fragrance of the tandoori ovens on Hyde Street.

When the lesbian, sitting on his lap so that he could enter her from behind, gazed down between his ankles, that somehow made him feel abandoned and therefore enraged.—She makes me *sick*, he thought. I want to run away from her, or kill her, or marry her forever.—In fact his sickness was the selfsame anxiety that he felt whenever she murmured something to Shantelle or Judy or me, something that he could not hear.—As for her, she found herself dreaming of a little wooden girl, naked but for a collar of beads, who stood with her head down. This was very different from the feeling she used to get in the pit of her stomach when she had to sit beside her mother for a long time.

Finally they completed their sexual acts to his satisfaction. She watched the reflection of his bald head in the long mirror, and the light so pink on his soft hairless shoulders. He was sobbing: Oh, Neva, I need you so bad; Neva, don't leave me. Don't you love me?

Oh, I do love you, said the lesbian.

He woke up feeling as if he had hardly slept enough. It seemed a little more difficult to get ready for work. As he walked down to the streetcar stop he began sweating and sweltering, although it was not very hot outside. It must be the humidity. When he got to the office, he sat down and broke out in a sweat. He wondered if he were getting ill. His stomach felt queasy, and he had a headache. Then he suddenly realized he was finally addicted to Neva. Of course that was her fault.

4

And if I don't see you tomorrow . . . said Sandra.

Why wouldn't you? he demanded.

If I can't—

Are you still my girlfriend?

I . . . I, yes, I guess I still am.

Dismayed and angered by the lukewarmness of her reply, the straight man longed to kill someone. But it seemed more practical to elevate the lesbian into a person caught by marriage and hence unavailable to others.

He told Sandra that he was going back to his wife. In fact he had divorced her, and was proposing to the lesbian.

5

Sandra was sobbing as soon as the lesbian answered the phone. She said: He told his wife, and then she gave him a choice, and at first he chose me; he moved into a hotel, and he was going to be with me, and I was so overjoyed; I never thought anyone would leave someone else for me, but this morning he called and said he's going back to her, and, Neva, I know that everything's changed between us and you don't love me as much because you hardly ever call me and when I call you I know you can hardly wait to get off the phone, and I'm sorry I'm crying but I just feel so empty with such a long long time of being lonely ahead of me . . .

All right, said the lesbian calmly. Tell me all about it.

No, wait; first tell me how you are—

We can get to that later. Now how are you feeling right now? Sad? Anxious? Desperate?

I, I, I . . .—She was gasping for breath.

You're a beautiful, intelligent, loving woman, and I will always love you. Did you want to marry him?

I'm so sorry—

When he left his wife, were you ready to go to him?

I was, I was overjoyed that he, I don't know, but probably . . . You're not angry?

Of course not, Sandra. You and I can't marry, so . . .

But *why* can't we?

What do you love the most about him?

I'm not criticizing you, Neva, but he always had time for me; he'd text me or call me for an hour or more every day, which made me feel so attached; he wanted to introduce me to his family; he was interested in everything about my life . . .

Was he good in bed?

Yes . . .

And kind and intelligent, I would think . . .

Yes, yes, he is . . .

And what's happening with him now?

He, he said he couldn't talk to me for a long time, maybe a month or two, but then he'd tell me how he was doing, and I . . .

Remember this, said the lesbian almost sternly. You were fifty percent of the relationship, so the breakup was fifty percent your responsibility. That means you have fifty percent of the power right now. He changed his mind about you several times. You can change your mind, too. You can call him and give him twenty-four hours to take you back, and if he doesn't then he's not to contact you ever. You can fly out there and drop in on him and his wife. You can wait one week or two months or six months. You can do whatever will bring you strength and peace. Just now it's as if he raped you; he took your power away. You may not get him back, but you can take back your power and make your own decision—

I can? I don't know why, but that makes me feel a little better.

Make a decision and follow it. And right now, when you're already feeling bad, if you want to leave me, it's all right. I'll never be everything you want. Make a list of how he and I and everyone else helped you and disappointed you in our various ways . . .

I thought our being in love was enough, but it isn't—

Don't worry about me, said the lesbian, and she gave the other woman all the advice she could.

You're very wise . . .

The lesbian closed up the phone, ashamed and sad that she had not married Sandra. Just then Xenia called. It was another emergency.

6

. . . And Shantelle, desperately biting her neck as they rubbed clitorises together, quickly climaxed and screamed in the distress of an overwhelming happiness.

Oh, Neva, I wanna have a face like you.

You're beautiful to me, I swear—

But you got a *look.* When I try an' copy it, it won't turn out. What's your secret?

Should we put on makeup together?

Yes! crowed Shantelle, laughing and clapping her hands. (I wish you could have seen that sweet slow smile whenever she felt that Neva truly loved her.) And pretty soon the lesbian was making up both their faces so they could pass for sisters. In the lesbian's lap, softly singing her favorite pop songs, Shantelle hoped for the best new songs for all women to sing, but when the lesbian had finished, and showed her their two faces side by side in the mirror, Shantelle shouted: *You still look better! You did that on purpose!*

The lesbian tried to kiss her, but Shantelle punched her again.

7

Her multiple involvements, which cured us with a touch, made it all the more crucial for the lesbian to keep every date, and although most of her lovers (the transwoman decidedly excepted) could be occasionally expected to call her with changes of plan, most of those the result of mere lateness—because who was so fulfilled, or self-loving, as to cancel out on hyper-scheduled Neva? (the ones who did that were the losers who stood up their probation officers and neglected to buy an impounded vehicle out of the towing garage before the fees exceeded the value of the car)—the lesbian herself tried never to keep anyone waiting for more than five minutes, which rule she was proud of. That was why the straight man had every reason to expect her in that upstairs Thai restaurant on Castro Street, a few doors down from the Q Bar, where he, the bus having brought him nearly half an hour too early, sat hoping for lesbians, but found only one female couple in a high-backed booth, each young woman leaning toward the other but only to stare into her cell phone, and that went on and on while the straight man watched one or another of the televisions in the flesh-pink wall whose ornamental lattice, which might have been an actual grating but in his opinion was only painted, resembled a black lace garter laid across a wide, wide flatness of glowing hairless thigh. There were television screens wherever he looked. There were single men gazing down into their cell phones, and because they were not women he began to hate them. At least the place didn't stink the way the Y Bar did. Paying for his beer, he went out into the rain. It was dinnertime. Climbing the stairs, he took a table for two. The smiling waiter soon learned to hang back. Looking out past two bearded men who were holding hands in a table at the bay window, the straight man watched the reddish stripe of a long bus swimming up Castro Street, and the marquee of the theater engaged him with neon like frozen fire. There were many rectangles of reddish darkness in the high arched window above the marquee; he counted them.—No, he told the waiter.—A small crowd lined up by the ticket booth. The marquee said:

NOIR FILM FESTIVAL 1/12–21

BERLIN 7 BEYOND 1/14–17

The crowd slid and slithered into the theater. Now the ticket-taker sat alone again in his illuminated booth, and gusts of rain struck the shining black asphalt. The male couple had finished now. He had been here an hour. Throwing down five dollars on the table, he brushed past the waiter and went downstairs, alert and nearly indomitable with anger.

8

Glowering at her so that the whites of his eyes burned like torture-lamps, he crooked his slender forefinger and said that it was *she* who had manipulated him for so long.

I don't give a fuck about Xenia, he said.

To underscore this point, the straight man slapped her. She tripped and bumped her knee, crying out; that sounded phony to him. Even then he kept wondering: Why have I never been raped? I'm the one who needs to be . . .—yearning for the lesbian to be against the dark velvet, spreading her long white legs to show the red gash.

9

I wish I could be the way I used to be, said Sandra. I wish I could be happy being faithful, but I just get lonely. I, you know, I guess I'd like to stop cheating, and I want you, and I wish . . . I still don't know when we're going to see each other next, but I get a little despairing since I . . . I mean (she was sobbing), if I could have everything the way I wanted it, it wouldn't have to be secret and I could have a baby or at least see you a lot more.

Yeah, said the straight man.

I've never regretted it and never stopped loving you. You've always been a complete marvel to me; it's true I was in love with Neva and wanted to make a life with her but I never stopped loving you. I think maybe calling her a girlfriend might be stretching it, but I do feel a sense of gratitude and tenderness and love and guilt all together. But I do think about you all the time . . .

Well, he asked bitterly, then do you imagine me when her dildo's inside you and you're climaxing?

I don't claim that absolutely in that moment I'm thinking about you, but when I'm alone and I close my eyes I want this to be our little world—

Are you getting more attached?

I don't want that. And I'm sure she'll get over it but I guess she'll . . .

He waited.

And when I get lonely I get anxious, she explained, and when I get anxious I seek other company.

10

Because it was Neva's task to tolerate anything, all the way to the end, he exhausted his rage in her. I myself sometimes saw her as some sandstone female figure whose arms have been broken off and whose knees and nose have been chipped away, while still she smiles with severe sadness, offering her single breast and simple hairless slit, tilting her head and crossing her ringed ankles forever.

Neva, he demanded, why don't you love me?

I do, she said.

Then you'll stop it with everyone else?

No, she said, waiting for him to hit her again.

He was breathing loudly. He said: What about Xenia? She took my turn. Won't you at least give that bitch up?

I'll make it up to you, said the lesbian.

Slamming his way out of there, stamping downstairs, he right away began to crave her; actually, it felt as if she were calling him to her—wasn't he now hearing her?—but summoning him without any promise, so that he could not help but wonder whether what he heard might be his heart calling to her, and thus echoing in his own chambers of living blood.

So he wooed our Neva; he flew her to Hawaii for a long weekend. They lived high-class on barbequed tuna steaks, sweet and sour roast pig and of course Patriot Dry Lager. Outside their hotel window, two trees breeze-danced like one tall woman bending against another, nuzzling her throat.

After fucking her until she could barely walk, he celebrated by body surfing, leaving her to sit alone on a tree-root and listen to the breeze blow her sweat away while the bright ocean exhaled hissingly and inhaled almost silently. All around her a wall of skinny tree-trunks and their spider-roots guarded her safely in, as if she had returned to that other island where the old lesbian first loved and healed her of what some might have called her humanity. A young family approached in a line, the girls and women all tiny-breasted in string bikinis; leaving the hot sun they came into her shade and began to ascend the mucky trail. The trees were squeaking around her, and she sat drinking in sea-oxygen.

She looked up. At once the people gathered around her.—I just want you all to be happy. I want to make everyone happy, said the lesbian, pale and bright-eyed like a sick child.

11

Their suite was candle-lit; he had paid extra for that. Impatiently he pulled her through the doorway.

Of course she would never forget the time when the door opened on the island and she first stood in front of that old lady, who looked her up and down, not as if (so the girl supposed) the girl were nothing, but only as if whatever the old lady's gaze took away was not the girl's business; meanwhile the girl continued to be certain that the old lady saw nothing in her; even counting those nighttime submissions to her mother; that gaze made her awfully sad; on the other hand, she had never felt so worthless as at the moment when she realized that E-beth had stopped loving her. Perhaps that was why she allowed the old lady to do what her mother had, in order to prove herself good for something, even if only that one thing; but being young, scared and for what she if definitely not I would have called the last time in her life the object rather than the subject of something that was about to happen, she lacked any notion much less articulation of whatever she was wanting or feeling; and then when the old lady opened the door again and went in, leaving it open so that the girl understood that she was supposed to enter, which she did, still not knowing anything, and numb to whatever might now be done to her since whatever that might be (such was the certitude of inexperience) weighed so light in comparison to the anguish which E-beth had inflicted, making her live each hour as though with her chest slit open, each breath an irritation of the unhealing wound which if it did not bleed and gurgle was no less intractable and quite possibly fatal (if she wanted anything it was death, if that could come without the terror of dying), she found darkness and the scent of drying herbs, but still had not yet beheld what was precious. Now it was time for the next thing.

12

Closing her eyes there in the hotel room, she seemed to see the transwoman's white, white face and white hands as she hurried down the dark street where steam arose from a sewer grating. Judy, little sister, how will you live and love now?—When the straight man came in, there she was: Neva the beguiler and the giver of sacred pain.

Had he forgiven her yet? Consider the tale of the faithful Jewish wife who was so lovely that a wizard lusted after her the instant he glimpsed the new dress that a tailor was sewing for her, and therefore bribed the tailor to secrete a certain magic charm within the seam. (He was far from the only one, but no matter how we all acted, we were always behaving precisely as she expected us to.) As soon as the wife pulled the dress down over her head, her womb hungered to be filled by this man whom she had never seen, so after promising to meet her husband in the synagogue she rushed to the wizard's house. They thrust their tongues into each other's mouths and he was gripping her breasts as she began to whimper with lust, and he lifted her up into his arms and carried her to the bed. As he pulled her dress up to her neck he was already throwing her down onto her back, burying his mouth between her legs, *oh, Neva, oh, Neva,* then jumping on top of her so that they both screamed with excitement; he was rutting in her now, and they were both groaning and worshipping each other; she couldn't stand to have anything between them, so she ripped the dress off over her head and then there was no charm. Horrified, she put on the dress to leave, at which she could not stand not to fuck him over and over, so she pulled it off again . . . and then burst into tears of rage and guilt . . . and ran away in her chemise, leaving the cursed dress behind! Since it happened to be Yom Kippur, no one except the retired policeman saw her running through the streets in her unmentionables. Keeping her shame a secret from her husband, she told him that illness had kept her from the synagogue. Meanwhile the wizard sold her dress in the market in order to get another victim. The husband recognized it and bought it a second time to test his wife. Hiding it, he asked her where it was. The woman lied, insisting that she had lost it, at which then he showed it to her and she confessed. He took the dress to the rabbinic court. They cut open its seams and found the charm, upon which they summoned the tailor, who confessed. The wizard was executed, while the poor tailor had to become a water carrier forever; the sixteenth-century German story does not report how well the woman and her husband afterward got on; but I like to hope that after a few beatings their marriage went on even better than before.

13

Marlene Dietrich boasted of being able to fake orgasms, and why not? Wouldn't that have been a credit to any actress? So what if Neva were also faking it, so long as she remained a good fake?

And so he bent over her, feeling an apparently insatiable excitement. She smiled patiently. Stroking her hair, he murmured: Neva, do you want to, or are you, you know, too sore down there?

Of course I want to, replied the lesbian.

That was when he took his resolution: Protecting her from us others who did not want her to love him, he would tell her story to her until she believed. In his pocket waited the engagement ring, which accompanied that prior communication from the retired policeman, whom she also needed to please.

14

Now, after lying in bed with Shantelle and gently rocking that tigerish woman into a peaceful drowse, Neva listened to her voicemails.—*And I feel a little worried,* whispered Xenia, *because I'm very sweaty and tingly in a bad way . . .* Then from dread Neva's mouth went as dry as if she were on meth, because what if Xenia had now fallen into terrible need? The Y Bar's reflected bottles and their glass shelves went higgledy-piggledy; I remember the shining whiskey in the glowing shotglasses and the lesbian's hands pink and flashing, her white blouse glowing purple, the retired policeman's head aching on this hot spring night, the fan blades still, pallid and silent like the dead light bulbs above them. Meanwhile the lesbian and Cora Justice, better known as Francine, were sitting in the lesbian's kitchenette, facing each other across the little table. A bottle of wine stood between them. The lesbian's glass was still nearly full. The other woman drained hers, set it down a trifle too hard, reached across the table and snatched at the lesbian's hand, kissing and kissing it.

For the last time Neva took her into her arms; and with that happy feeling literally in her heart (the lesbian snoring sweetly on her shoulder, liquidly, like the cooing of a pigeon), Francine decided that she might as well go on living. She gobbled up pleasure like Judy Garland stuffing her face with chocolate cake and candy bars! Neva's name remained last and first among us!

While the lesbian slept beside her, the barmaid threw off the blanket and began fingering herself, so gratefully joyful just to play without need or expectation of climax, which must have been something like how it was to be a little thing in her crib, giving herself pleasure and comfort until she fell asleep.

In her sleep, the lesbian muttered: *Don't.*

But Francine lay remembering how when she was five Jocelyn from across the street had come over to show how her toenail had fallen off, and Francine had never seen anything more astounding! Inhaling the perfume of Neva's armpit, she closed her eyes, and it seemed as if she remained awake, thinking about Neva and Jocelyn, but now she came awake for real because it was cold and the bed was in motion as Neva sat up to begin dressing. Francine could hardly bear it. Unlike Judy, she had never been a groveller, so she did bear it, dragging her street clothes back over her aching nerves, kissing Neva goodbye like a quick brave soldier; then she went home, shivering. She was now a white dead woman, kohl-painted with eyes, hair, lips, breasts and vulva. Her stomach echoed emptily, but she had no appetite. Dizzily she staggered back to the ice-cold toilet for more diarrhea.

15

How else could this story have ended? A Catholic hermeneuticist once warned that should any merely human model of thought or being seek to present the Spirit in its own right, *the model, by remaining tacit, supplants the source of Revelation with only human ignorance and pride and inflicts despair.* Neva's way was then the merest *model.* Offering perfection imperfectly, she inflicted despair.—I reject this because I still love her. (Even now I feel suddenly warm within when I recall my Neva—the one who gave every part of herself to others.—Then, of course, I get cold again.)

Did she truly know all too well that the rest of us could not regard love as a sacrament, but only as an instrument of satisfaction? (How did *she* regard it? When would her face get old and gruesome with suffering?—No, Judy, she said; you don't want to be like me.) So far as I can tell, she accepted that everything she did was for nothing, and that after she had finished doing her utmost, all of us would go on without her—in which case ignorance and pride might have burdened her very little.—But did she inflict despair? And what would that imply about her?

Meanwhile, *The Lucky Star* continues in this exclusive form, as performed by the original cast for up to twenty-three episodes.

16

Infuriated by the lesbian's essential emptiness—she might as well have been her own fiction—the retired policeman dug deeper: no California vehicle registration in the name of a Karen Strand with the birthdates of 1964 or 1986, but the car might be in someone else's name or she might not drive. He ran the driver's license with the fake birthdate of 1986. That had been faithfully renewed ever since 2009. The other license had never expired. He couldn't figure it out; he drank Black Vulture. Meanwhile the lesbian was woken up by her first nightmare about Hunter's suicide. Her breastbone ached with grief. She and Hunter had been lying in a large pullout bed, which was not actually Hunter's bed but was here the setting, pretending to be real as did this dream-Hunter who wished for them to lie down side by side on this wide soft bed with its Western-patterned blankets; the rules were that they remained fully clothed and not touch each other. The lesbian could not understand why. They lay there and she longed to touch the other woman but could not. She awoke with her breastbone aching. Tomorrow it would be worse, no doubt. It was seven in the morning; the air was already warm and sticky. She hunted for the magic which would put her right.

As for me, sometimes I even pretended to be a woman, asking Neva to do certain special things to me, but that didn't get me any closer to her. The ecstasy of being crushed down into speechless bleeding darkness relieved me from being myself, but swept me farther from the one I worshipped. I admit that sometimes when she beat me I could at least bear a portion of her otherwise undivided pain. (She often wore the calm face of Santa Eulàlia while they are piercing her breasts out, making twin fountains of cinnabar, while a cloud watches patiently.) And what should I expect? Since she, being all-loving, was so much greater than all of us, how could I even imagine "knowing" her? Almost immune to my phantasmal discontents, Judy meanwhile lay on her side, guzzling at the lesbian's vulva, while the lesbian braced the sole of her little foot against the inside of the transwoman's knee, moaning happily as if she were about to climax. And Judy's orgasm protracted itself into an endless scream! The lesbian held her, remembering the smell of the house where she had been a child, and the way the morning would take possession of her stuffed animals on the windowsill. Judy said: You'd never just stop loving me, would you? Neva shook her head, and the transwoman began breathing rapidly and loudly almost in the middle of a sentence. Now she was asleep in earnest, snoring happily, bubbling from mouth and nose, looking old. The lesbian pressed her lips against her lover's cheek and stayed there for a long time, sleepily holding her; she felt chilly, but the transwoman was still sweating even in her sleep, for which she'd blamed menopause . . . Next up was Holly, who, greedily drinking up more tequila and more rum, began to slur her speech.

I love you.

I love you, too, the lesbian brightly said.

I love you so much . . . More than you know . . . I can't let you leave me. If you go away I'll miss you too much; I'll—are you going to leave me?

No, said the lesbian, feeling anxious.

Never?

I'll never leave you, even if I sometimes—

Did I tell you about my biopsy? It came back negative. I'm gonna live, Neva! I'm gonna live!

I'm very happy for you—

Let's go away and live on a mountain somewhere . . .

Then the lesbian, who had worried that she might not feel desire for Holly, found herself happily lusting after all. She began to stroke Holly's inner thighs. Then she began to kiss her between her legs; and Holly, who usually climaxed rapidly and powerfully, this time ascended more gently toward orgasm, which upon reaching she inhabited for a long stretch of uncharacteristically honeyed moans.

Holly's last time consisted in part of her reporting to Neva: Well, I did what you wanted and had a talk with Judy. You know, that girl is so fucked up! She keeps going on and on about being disgusting. But being part of the queer community and finding freaks, that will help her a lot. Because if she can just embrace her freaky disgusting nature, then it doesn't matter so much if she's not attractive . . .

You're her community, said Neva. You and Richard and Xenia and Francine and even J. D. Do you promise to remember that?

I promise if you do something for me, said Holly. You *know* what I want you to do . . . !

Okay, said the lesbian.

Then came more appointments. Neva had us all down by heart! In the beginning getting to know us had felt like descending a flight of stone steps, shining her lantern down into a deep suite of cells. Now she could pass through walls. Her lantern's lush shadows retained the virtue of changing, however meaninglessly, that ashen, grooved, dead rockscape. Our rectangular tombs had been long since robbed. Around Shantelle the brick walls swelled outward as if concealing something, while my own being was comprised of roofless suites and incomplete arch-roofed tunnels. Penetrating ever deeper inside us all, Neva continued down a wide circular staircase in the white rock of hopelessness, and sweeping down into a dark archway doubly overlined with bricks, down into the kingdom of wells, graves, V-shaped pavements, meaningless walls, lost courtyards, grinning furnaces . . . and each of us in turn lay down with her to raise up cries of joy.

But even as the transwoman lay dreaming that she and Neva were dancing in outer space (they both had lovely white legs and red skirts; and could scissor-kick their way from one galaxy to another, twirling side by side to atonal piano music), the lesbian and the straight man now bought a marriage license—apparently as foolish a plan as if the retired policeman had set out to trim his own toenails, or, worse yet, walked all the way to Jojo's Liquors without wearing his compression socks.—But if you were to ask me why she would attach herself to so obviously unsatisfactory a mate, I would need to remind you for the thirteenth time that by definition a goddess dwells among a deficit of equals.

I do, they said.

Francine, who briefly felt bitter, opined to me that they had married to try to evade their destiny. But what else could have been the destiny of her adorable Neva, which is to say the one as hateful to Francine as any other lover who abandons and forgets? I myself interpreted the marriage as a logical endgame—because the persuasions of Judy's fingers, and her starry plastic jewels, were matched in too many elsewheres.

Incapable of seeing ahead to Act IV, the retired policeman sat down suddenly in that stinking armchair. Deal-breaking bitch! He felt dizzy and confused.

Well, Neva, said Judy, far away and trying to smile, *bon* fuckin' *voyage.*

The Bloodsucker

I could beleeve that Spirits use with man the act of carnality, and that in both sexes; I conceive they may assume, steale, or contrive a body, wherein they may be action enough to content decrepit lusts or passion to satisfy more active veneries . . .

SIR THOMAS BROWNE, *ca.* 1643

The vampire is prone to be fascinated with an engrossing vehemence, resembling the passion of love, by particular persons . . . It will never desist until it has satiated its passion, and drained the very life of its coveted victim. But it will, in these cases, husband and protract its murderous enjoyment with the refinement of an epicure, and heighten it by the gradual approaches of an artful courtship. In these cases it seems to yearn for something like sympathy and consent. In ordinary ones it goes direct to its object, overpowers with violence, and strangles and exhausts often in a single feast.

J. SHERIDAN LE FANU, 1872

If you don't stand for something, you fall for everything, Shantelle advised me. Have you heard that one before?

Her mouth kept twitching.

What do you stand for? I asked.

Will you help me kill Neva? She comes between me and every fuckin' body else! She already offed Hunter, and who the fuck's gonna be next?

Shantelle, I said, I love you—to which she replied: You an' Francine an' every other worthless bitch! That's just what Neva taught you to say—goddamn that motherfucker . . . ! Oh, I feel so cold; I feel so bad . . . But I fall for her every time she puts her little booty shorts on. But hey! What the fuck are *you* about? Why ain't you dead yet?

Fortunately, her phone rang. She said into it: Hey, baby; Xenia broke up with her girlfriend who offed herself and it's *fabulous* because she's texting me an' crying in my arms while I fuck her and that's like why we get together . . .

In those days Judy was also crying in my arms. We agreed that to love Neva was to be with her and in her. As for the retired policeman, he bought me a round at the Cinnabar and explained that he was trying to get Neva because she simply couldn't help but take the life out of other women.

I hate lies, he said. I'm proud of being proud. Judy Garland images are exploitative and dirty, all right; they're harmful like drugs. Not that you and I do drugs. Right, Sherlock? My good old Judy's fucked up. So am I and so are you. Let's stick to the goddamn truth.

I went down to the Y Bar all alone, and by the entrance sat a kindly-looking old lesbian whom I had never seen before. Her name was Reba. I asked her how to live my life. Patting my hand, she said: It's love, isn't it?

I nodded.

She said: For each person that I've been with, I've learned something about myself. The women I was with in my twenties I think helped shape the woman I am now. I've had more than fifty partners, and there's only a few of them I regret. That's one thing about lesbians: When we break up, we stay friends.

I said: I don't know what I've learned.

Then pay attention, dearie.—No thanks, Francine; I'm off to a hot date with some island mermaids . . .

I decided to pay better attention when my turn came up. Here is what came of it:

Neva was bleeding on the last occasion of our intimacy. As soon as I first kissed her, my nipples sprang up harder than hers! Seeing what I wanted and laughing a little, she sat on the edge of the bed, spreading her thighs so that I could kneel down to worship. I remember this whenever I see that diorite statue of the goddess Hathor with her great sundisk and cowhorns, staring pupillessly down before her, plump-cheeked, smooth-faced, full-lipped and gentle, with wheels around her nipples. My heart was pounding so rapidly with pleasure that I longed to vomit up all my own blood and die into peaceful darkness. When she had made me perfect, I might have cried out, but it is difficult now to project myself back into that lost place. My face was bloody from her. Lying down as if in death, I waited until she bent over me and breathed her breath into my mouth. Her breast was the horizon. My heart was at peace.

Just as the Egyptians sometimes painted eyes on their sarcophagi so that the corpses could see out of them, so I now daubed my areolae round and round with that fresh menstrual blood of Neva's, absorbing her divine female proteins into my need, so that I would be a little more like her, and maybe my nipples would even come alive like hers.

V

How Francine and I Coped

Nothing had ever happened to me that a good piece of apple pie couldn't cure!

JUDY GARLAND, 1942

1

The dealer, who was young and handsome, lived in an elegant apartment on the twenty-eighth floor of the Erskine Towers. Being accustomed to street transactions, I was surprised that the doorman made Xenia and me sign in. Well, what did I know about success?

I looked out his window. I told him he had a nice view. He did not care.

No, he advised us, the brown is more natural than the white. It comes from Indonesian sassafras. Of course that stuff has blood on it. When ten guys go out with machine guns to poach those trees, and eleven guys with guns meet them, the ten guys all get killed. So you buy from me, you have blood on your hands.

And you're saying point one five grams is the right dose?

He nodded.

Sometimes it takes me point three to get high, maybe because of my body weight. Do you think that can harm me?

Just experiment, he said, not very interested.

How often can I safely use it?

Do your own research, he said.

Xenia, who was our go-between (she kept getting high and wringing her hands over her daughter who must soon go out into the nightmare jungle of maleness), now said: I try not to use it more than once every ten days.

I mean, I said, you're the expert. Can you give me any advice? Does it cause brain damage?

He replied: Ask your friends if they see any change in you. I just sell the stuff. What it does to you, I don't care.

Is it addictive?

No.

If I take more than I need to get high, am I just wasting it?

It'll kill you, he said. I sold to one kid who thought, well, if point one five grams is good, a whole gram will be great. He went into convulsions. His party friends waited too long to call the ambulance. What it does is alter your thermoregulation. If you want to play with the dosage, check yourself with a thermometer. When your core temperature goes above one oh six, you're gone.

Xenia had given me a gram of cocaine, just to be kind. Now she said: Did you bring that with you? Anyone else feeling like doing a line?

I got out the little baggie. She did a line and he did a line. His professional assessment was that it was good stuff. Then I put the coke away.

Now for business. Xenia bought a gram of his brown molly, and I bought two grams. He offered to vacuum pack the stuff, but we were both going to use it soon. I thanked him for the happiness he had sold me.

After he had counted our money, he showed off ten thousand hits' worth of blotter acid with the old Beatles logos on it.—On the house, he joked. Although it was in a clear plastic bag I did not touch it, not caring for the surprise of hallucinogens absorbed through the skin. He was proud of his product, and maybe I should have praised it more, but, to tell you the truth, just then I was feeling pretty sad about Neva. I managed to smile and say something complimentary. Then he locked the LSD back into his safe.

He showed us a big bag of psilocybin mushrooms.

Thinking grandly, just in case some year I became a success, I asked: If I ever bought in a large quantity, would you give me a discount on your ecstasy?

Sure.

And how much can I safely carry before it's considered possession with intent to sell?

You're white and getting old, so what do you care? he said. You'll get some pricey defense lawyer, and he'll get you off. He'll go to the D.A., who'll say, no, I have to convict on this one, and then he'll sell five black guys down the river and you'll get probation.

Then he wanted to do another line, so I broke out the coke again. I asked how well coke went with ecstasy, and he said it went great. Then I hid the stuff away again, right next to my molly, and said goodbye to both of them. As soon as I got home, I made a date with Francine.

She showed up ready to party hard; her eyelids were red from weeping. She had called in sick at the Y Bar; Alicia AKA Bubbles swooped in to score those extra hours. I poured us each a rum and sodapop. Then we choked down point four grams apiece of that sickeningly bitter stuff. (Here's to blood on our hands, I said.) Half an hour later I vomited, but it wasn't so bad. Francine barely felt nauseated.

2

I worshipped her body all day. She moaned, sang and exclaimed. Whenever I held her tight, she whispered in the voice of a little girl at church that she had never been so happy. The longer I caressed the undersides of her sweaty little breasts and messed up her hair, the closer to her I felt. This time she had shaved her slit, supposedly for me but more likely for Neva. I couldn't get enough of going down on her and listening to her long soft moans. After awhile, she would pull me back up to her face so that we could resume kissing.

I had imagined doing it with Francine the way I liked it with Neva, which is to say, her lying on her side with one thigh clasped across mine and her pussy rubbing against my leg while I began to masturbate and she promised that she loved me. But with Francine in my arms it was all so good I didn't care which way was up.

After five hours, when we had just begun to come down, I broke out the cocaine. She wanted it up her ass, so I licked my finger, covered it with powder and slid it in.

Oh, she said. Oh, I'm getting high in my butt! Feels so good . . .

So I packed the rest of it into myself. Having given her most of it, I didn't feel much, but the light whitened and a pleasant alertness cut through the dreaminess of the ecstasy. I fingered a little more brown powder into each of our mouths. Soon I was massaging her darling buttocks, whispering to her while she sang to me, and everything felt right. Later on we played dress-up, and it was so sweet to be *en femme* with my arm around a real woman who desired me that for a moment I could almost imagine I was Neva.

It was all eternal so long as it lasted. Eight hours later, when we were coming down from the molly, afflicted by stomach cramps and vicious headaches, we went our separate ways. Through the window I heard the throbbing of a gravel truck, and the tuned sibilance of brakes. Of course we were sorry to part. But what was the use? After that respite we got right back to jonesing for Neva.

3

I ventured into the Cinnabar and told the retired policeman all about it.

He said: You should have dated Judy. She could use the money.

But Francine could use the love.

Well, Freud would ask, does Francine feel tender toward you? If not, she's not in love.

She says she needs me.

That's not love.

What is it then?

Ask your friggin' *Goddess.*

4

Looking out the window past the rusty strut which helped support the signboard, letting my gaze descend the windows of the Pierce-Arrow showroom, I saw a locked door three gratings away, and sitting up against it, stretching out their legs on the sidewalk, a white man and a black man, passing the time not unlike me, with a tall can of malt liquor beside each one. I mixed myself an extra tall rum and sodapop, even stronger and sweeter than what Francine prepared at the Y Bar. My head was pounding, so I chewed up three of Neva's Menstru-Bliss tablets. Then, because I had developed cavities in three teeth, I recovered the scrap of wax paper which Francine had incompletely licked, and scored seven more grains of brown molly to rub on my gums. The narrow, piercing pains in those teeth, which if they were sounds would have been shrill piccolo-notes, did not go away, but they began to annoy me less. My flulike aches, chills and hot flashes required more treatment. So I deployed the big guns: two five-hundred-milligram Narcodans—a departing gift from my loving Francine. Now I felt self-reliant; I had solved my own problems. In a mellower state of mind (barely even missing Neva), I returned to the corner window, watching a line of double-breasted cars sizzle toward me, shining their little yellow nipples, then passing beneath my notice. I wondered why it felt as if I were wasting these instants of my life. Couldn't I, as Californians say, *be in the moment*, as I had so successfully done with Francine in my arms?

On either side of the two men, but not close enough to rescue from an aggressive snatch, lay their piled blankets and duffels. I disapproved; I told myself: If I'm homeless, I'll travel more lightly, with my baggage right beside me.—But what did I know about how and why they lived?

Ten steps up the hill from the black man, on a long bier of cardboard, lay what appeared to be a blanket-wrapped corpse, its knees drawn up; hour after hour it never moved.

After a long time, two policemen marched up and rewarded the two homeless men with tickets. The men held the long strips of paper up into the light, trying sincerely to apprehend their mysteries. Then they discussed the universe's future heat-death with the officers, considering all phases and possibilities even while accepting the ultimate outcome, and so the discussion went for a good quarter-hour, gradually becoming emphatic, then impassioned, after which the authorities rode away on their motorcycles, and the two men leaned together, reading each other's citations.

The corpse-thing continued not to move. I watched it quietly, not minding my room's faint stink, which Francine claimed not to notice. Because this rented time drained away so slowly, I seemed to be getting more for the money. To enhance the moment, I poured myself another rum and sodapop, looking down at the walk signal, watching its orange numbers count back and back until the orange hand of forbiddenness overruled them. I closed my striped blue curtains, then opened them again.

It almost seemed as if one could see very far from that window, block after block up the line of glowing-nippled taxi cabs and yellow-starred black limousines, all the way to where the twin lines of butter-yellow streetlights folded into each other on the black horizon.

Then rapid heavy steps approached the room, and a key turned in the lock. A man strode in.—Oh, *sorry, sorry, sorry*! said the man mechanically, turning on his heel.

I had never seen him before. Why his key fit my lock I was better off not understanding. Congratulating myself that no molly lay in sight, I told him: That's all right, and because further words might have been appropriate I added: Oh, so this is how it is.—After that I solved my worry by means of deadbolt and chain.

At dusk I spied sweet black Shantelle in her black parka dancing across the crosswalk's white skeleton.

I was still looking down at the two dark men-figures at midnight, wishfully half-mistaking one of them for the lesbian.

I put my feet up, remembering my happiest time on meth, when I stood counting the yellow bricks on the facade of the grand apartment building on Sutter and Jones.

I wondered whether this story could ever have happened (of course not), and why on earth it had to be Neva, and why E-beth, and all the rest—as if the question of why any one of us exists at all was not sufficiently bemusing in and of itself to pass at least three songs' worth in the jukebox that once used to occupy the back corner of the Y Bar by the ladies' room, until they had pulled the jukebox out and junked it, then replaced it with that giant television which they kept always muted on the sports channel.

Unable to sleep, fighting off the molly headache with the last of my rum, I watched another yellow-windowed rainy dawn, as a man in a dark parka and a white cap began rolling up a long white tarp on the sidewalk while the same two men from yesterday sat miserably against the grating; now he was unrolling it again and fixing its corners to the frame of that doorway, enclosing the two men in a lean-to, but it kept coming down on them, so he got angry and began to jump on it and kick it. Who were they to him? I felt too tired to understand anything but the sparkle of traffic seen through headlights, like tears creeping out from mascara.

How Sandra Coped

You won't be a really happy person unless you also achieve success as a woman. And for most women, that includes a happy marriage.

JUDY GARLAND, 1946

At times I have been pretty much of a walking advertisement for sleeping pills.

JUDY GARLAND, 1950

And in Sandra's dream it was the middle of a summer morning whose temperature lay exactly between clammy and humid; kirkstones loomed like chimneys out of the daisy-starred grass. She was now a girl of about sixteen, wearing a red tartan skirt. Two grey wood pigeons and one white gull stood atop the grassy wall of the roofless old church. And Sandra went seeking Neva. She wandered into a garden of black and red roses. It became late morning, and the sun came glaring out, brightening the gilded weathercocks still on the pointed roofs as the tinny bill tolled eleven. Where was Neva? Despondent, the girl searched among boulders shagged with orange lichen. Just behind the cupola of an old stone tomb was a stone wall and then a thickly nettled forest with a squat volcanic peak rising above it like a castle. Now her sorrow wearied her, and she sat on the wall, wondering whether she would ever again see the lesbian. The breeze brought the smell of roses. Her loneliness was comforted by the stately strutting and lordly nodding of a wood pigeon who marched round and round her feet just in case there might be a breadcrumb. Sandra felt sorry that she had nothing for him. He cooed and gurgled up at her; he was plump and grey. Since she could do nothing else for him, she began to stroke his bluish-grey head and white collar. At once he grew and blossomed into Neva. Delighted, Sandra tried to kiss her, but Neva turned her mouth away. Sandra felt more hurt than she had ever been in her life. But Neva held her tight and carried her up into the air. Looking back, she glimpsed a vast maple, shaped like a rounded pyramid, towering over the church wall, and then they were already flashing oceanward, and in the dark sea appeared a familiar great grey rock that whitened with increasing nearness, then began to give off a urinous smell; now the whiteness was glaring; it was comprised of gannets by the thousands. The birds rose up screaming around them. The ones who remained nesting on the dark rock reminded her of pale rose-petals on green grass; and suddenly the smell of guano became the smell of flowers. Neva carried her gently down onto a hillock of moss. Smiling, she turned her face toward Sandra at last. They began kissing forever, with Neva's tongue in her mouth, but then Sandra woke up.

Narrower Than It Used to Be

My body is the beloved; my heart is the beloved. It is the beloved who is my life.

Bullhe Shah, bef. 1759

I am in the darke to all the world, and my nearest friends behold mee but in a cloud.

Sir Thomas Browne, *ca.* 1643

1

In *Dishonored*, when Marlene Dietrich sashays to her execution in a fur-trimmed suit, a certain tone was established; as for the lesbian, when it came time to fulfill her own obligation she did not even apply lipstick.

Before marrying, of course she had had to visit her mother.

By the time she picked up her car from the garage in Richmond she was already bearing that slightly rundown sensation as if from too much ecstasy, not enough sleep, maybe not enough water and then drinking vodka first thing in the morning (which was one in the afternoon), but why be a drama queen? Let's just say she had a headache.

A black-and-white pulled her over.—Your registration's expired, said the officer.

I'm sorry, said the lesbian.

I mean, *seriously* expired, said the officer. There must be a glitch in our system. Ma'am, let's see your license.

The lesbian gave it to him.

That's your actual date of birth? said the officer. I don't fuckin' believe this.

Well, said the lesbian, it is.

You sure don't look your age, said the officer.

The lesbian replied: I love you, officer.

He said: You've got a screw loose. Oh, fuck it, and he drove off.

First she rolled past E-beth's old apartment; why not? It was yellow-painted, gentrified, subdivided. Accordingly she drove to Jingle's. She decided that she'd drunk enough Hot Bitches in her life. So she rounded that corner: Go, go, Valley Joe!

Then she saw the old street, now much narrower than it used to be, and the sad toy neighborhood that was dying with it; then she was parking at the curb in front of the old Mission style house whose lawn was not quite so green and even as before; and the pain of that place had nothing to do with her; it was simply a place that was poisoned; anyone who came there would have felt the same sickness, or at least anyone would have who knew the place, or was at all sensitive—as was *she*, the lesbian, the one whom everyone loved so long as she stayed away from here.

It was late afternoon and the curtains were drawn. She sat in the car, watching the neighbors' house for no reason; their window had never been open and now it wore a big sloppy curtain inside it. They had painted their garage door lime green; bougainvillea had overgrown the side window; her mother must not like that. She got out, quietly closed the door (she thought she saw something flicker behind the dim-grey window over the garage), squeezed the auto-lock button on her key, ran a hand through her hair, and began to approach the front door, which now opened, with her mother standing inside, smiling and waiting.

The instant she came within reach, her mother's arms closed around her, and her mother's mouth was seeking her. This time the lesbian meant to do nothing that would make the old woman disappointed. So she stood there and allowed her mother to kiss her. Her mother's embrace tightened. The lesbian knew that she was supposed to kiss her mother back. Why couldn't she do it? Was her power finally departing? Turning her face toward her, she kissed her mother's cheek. Then she waited for her mother to let go.

Wearily, not without bitterness, but not surprised, either, the rejected mother made her arms fall away. She stepped backward so that the lesbian could enter the house. But she did not withdraw herself very far at all. The lesbian wondered whether her mother would grab at her again if she tried to go past, so she took two steps deeper beyond the doorway and then stood gazing down at her mother's shoes.

She decided: If she kisses my mouth again I'll let her tongue go in. If she still wants to use me I'll open my legs. After all . . .

Well, said her mother. It's so good to see you!

You too, said the lesbian.

Do come in, said her mother, leading her back in through the dark years.

She could scarcely believe that she had ever belonged to this place, or it to her. It had so little to do with her; she could barely even breathe here! Its familiarity made it all the more inimical. It was the sort of place where no one ever should have lived, and probably no one had ever actually survived there. Because she had been away for so long, it seemed that she must have come from somewhere else before she ever accidentally *was* here. She could see this house, but she could not understand it. Like her mother, the house had grown so old and little that the lesbian half expected to bump her head on the ceiling. To be sure, ceilings used to be built lower back in those days; walls were narrower and rugs were darker. It was strangely hard to breathe in here. Her mother was watching her with an expression of triumph.

She should have asked how her mother was, but for some reason just couldn't do it. Her mother did not ask her, either.

Nothing happened for a moment; then her mother began to weep, saying: My little Karen's finally getting old.

2

You must be tired, said her mother.

Oh, I'm okay, said the lesbian.

You promise?

I promise.

Would you like a glass of grape juice? I went out and bought grape juice, because you always used to love that so much when you were little.

Thanks, Mom, I'll have a glass . . .

Do you remember how you used to love it? You used to beg me for more. Well, of course you couldn't remember that; you were so very, very little . . .

No, I don't remember.

And you can have cheese and crackers. Would you like some of those?

Oh, no thank you, Mother. I just ate.

Are you sure? Because I made a special trip to the store to get cheese and crackers for you.

Maybe in awhile, said the lesbian, shivering the way she did whenever she was coming off the yellow serum.

Karen, do you know what kind of crackers I got for you?

No, I don't.

Won't you even guess?

Well, there are so many kinds . . .

But it's the brand you always adored! I got them just for you!

Unable at first to bear looking into her mother's eyes, in which she would surely find the despair of being unloved, the lesbian took a deep breath, then gazed at her, and even smiled.

Karen, what's wrong? You look so strange!

Mother, I love you.

What does *that* mean?

Nothing.

If you won't talk about it . . . Well, you've always been secretive. How do you think that makes me feel?

I'm sorry, Mother.

Well. I've been going through the hall closet, said her mother. Because I won't live forever.

Yes, Mother.

It's been very, very difficult.

I'm sorry . . .

Karen, I have to tell you. I wish you could have helped me.

You didn't ask me.

I didn't? I'm sure I asked you.

No, Mother. You didn't.

Well, you're so busy with your various—*friends.* You probably wouldn't have had time.

Maybe not, said the lesbian, miserably diminished, shrinking back into a little girl in the darkness.

Do you know what I found?

What was it? said the patient child.

I'd saved all your little dresses. Oh, you wouldn't believe how teeny-tiny you were! So adorable, your dresses. And I even saved your little panties. Would you like to see them?

No, thank you, Mother.

Oh, you wouldn't? Why wouldn't you?

Mother, would you like to go out for dinner? I can drive us.

Karen, won't you look at your sweet little things? Not even for one minute? Don't you even care?

All right, Mother. Show me.

Are you sure? Do you really want to?

Yes, I'm sure.

I'm only doing this because you want to. Because, honestly . . . Well, look at these dear little panties. I used to pull them off to change you, which you can't remember, of course. You were very slow, Karen. You used to wee-wee in your panties until you were, oh, four years old. Maybe even five. But how *adorable* you were when I pulled your panties down! You used to love it when I rubbed you with baby powder. Do you remember that at all?

Mother, I think I'll go lie down.

Lie down! But we haven't even had dinner! What about dinner?

Okay, let's go out. Where should we go?

The lesbian, fearing, wavering and smothering, tried to imagine what the old woman on the island would have done. The old woman would have lovingly choked her until she began swooning, all the while encouraging her to pretend that she was already dead, so that she need not be afraid. How would she wish to act, if she could be with her mother while she was dying? This was how she should act now. As a famous sufferer said, hell *is the suffering of being unable to love.*

3

After dinner they sat in the living room, doing nothing. Her mother turned on the television: Natalie Wood was modeling Movie Star Bread (fifty-five calories a slice). Judy Garland was showing off her three sets of false eyelashes, *for small, average and large audiences.* Finally the lesbian said goodnight and went to lie down on what she always called her *girl bed*, with her old dolls and stuffed animals still around her.

She felt dizzy, and the ceiling seemed lower here; the walls were tighter; any second now the doorhandle would quietly begin to turn, and then her mother would come in. Or was that over now?

The house was silent. Her mother must be sitting up in the living room.

The lesbian opened her bedroom door as quietly as she could. She crept down the hall to the bathroom, locked herself in and vomited. No sound came from the living room.

Returning to her *girl bed*, she turned out the light. Later she dreamed (although it might have truly happened) that her mother was with her; ever so lovingly she raised up the daughter's head and rested it on her breast.

That Certain Tone

But they that sometimes liked my company
Like lice away from dead bodies they crawl . . .

Sir Thomas Wyatt, *ca.* 1540

Lycóris, no woman used to be more darling to me than you.
Now Glýcera fills up my entire heart.

Martial, 1st cent. A.D.

You must learn to let go and accept what is happening now, rather than try to cling to outworn interests.

Judy Garland, 1946

1

On their honeymoon they went to Carmel, and the straight man texted the good news to all his relatives and business connections (I sometimes suspect that the retired policeman had talked him into this), while the lesbian experienced the feeling which habit had bleached down from raw red anxiety to the kind of long dead sadness one accrues from seeing a pinkish-white hunk of human tissue slowly shed particles into formaldehyde in which it hangs in exemplification of neutral buoyancy; thus her emotion once her efforts to reach Shantelle's phone without compromising herself had failed. (To wed is to become mortal.) She knew that Shantelle (now doubtless glowering, with her hand on her hip), had been hopefully expecting to hear her voice since mid-morning, and now it was almost six, with canned arias beginning to blare out of Italian restaurants, the straight man whistling while digging his fingers into her shoulder, and the last commuters waiting at the bus stop. Pine tree shadows grew across apartment buildings, and the seaside swelter chilled into clamminess. A little blonde girl in a denim skirt toddled up the sidewalk, with her parents gliding indulgently behind. The child stopped, looked into the lesbian's face, giggled and flew into her arms! The parents hurried up, alarmed and furious. But as soon as they looked into the lesbian's eyes, of course they were all smiles.

She *loves* you! laughed the mother. I've never seen her do that with anybody—

Except you, said the husband fondly, laying his hand on the wife's beefy shoulders.

What's your name, sweetie? asked the lesbian, and the child laughed so happily up at her.

Andrea? Andrea, come on back now, the mother said.

No! shrieked the little girl, gripping the lesbian's legs.

Andrea, said the father ineffectually, you come back right now.

Excuse us, the mother commanded the lesbian, snatching back her unfaithful offspring, who wept and kicked as they carried her off.

And the lesbian, watching that spoiled child be forced, felt as if her past were a cemetery whose graves now reared open, vomiting their contents all over her. Fortunately, Francine had given her a wedding present: brown powder. She went upstairs and ate some. It was bitter and foul.

I can almost see her looking very small and uncomfortable in her wide double bed, with her arms clasped over her tight-pressed knees, which were drawn up against her breasts, in what was captioned *a rare nude portrait of Natalie Wood in her French rococo-inspired bedroom, 1966.*

2

At least the straight man had what he wanted. As he entered her she gazed into his face with calm affection, knowing that at first this would hurt, and then, once she gave in to it, it would grow sweet. And he who had come to believe that there were no mysteries anywhere must now keep faith in the ordinariness of Neva. But I say again that *Venus is not mocked.* I once read in a certain of the retired policeman's crackly old paperbacks that when Alexander the Great's soldiers, having just conquered Miletua, and now seeking to secure all its edifices, dared to enter the temple of Ceres, someone *met them with a flame,* as the Roman compiler puts it, and then blinded them, *lest they should see secrets known only to women.* Why should the straight man's doom be any different, now that he had tempted the Goddess?

After troubled dreams and meditations of his home being burgled four different times came a vision of a young blonde girl with perfect skin, fresh- and sweet-smelling—oh, her young pink face and white teeth! She was so real and he was so sure of her. For a long time after awakening he could not believe that he had not just seen her. Then his wife came out of the bathroom. He looked at her, and realized that she was *old.*

3

But I would hardly mean you to believe that theirs was not a perfect honeymoon. For one thing, he indulged himself in Tiefflieger beer, whose label had taken both third and fourth place thanks to its downpointing silhouette of a dive-bomber within a crimson circle. Had any customer ever presumed to ask for such an item at the Y Bar, Francine would have shrugged, unless she felt sufficiently exuberant to laugh in his face. Tiefflieger is marketed for its mellow hops—amber clarity—noble flavor! As for the bride, she too was a quality item: the long hot echo of what she used to be.

4

When one begins to come down from low-grade ecstasy mixed with meth, the exhilaration, which previously seemed utterly fundamental, in other words a pure and radiantly translucent atmosphere, now as it falls away comes to resemble a soft blanket, not in any way stifling but most definitely interposing, because as the wonderful feeling continues to withdraw from one's entire body into one's fingertips, preparatory to fading further, a sensation of clarity manifests itself, pretending to be, as perhaps it actually is, something which was there all along, something alert, cool and even cold (this last perhaps a relic of ecstasy's quasi-synesthesia, because as the warmth of that intimacy drug departs, the feet get cold, and the lovely fever in breasts, groin, buttocks and forehead wisps away; so much for that blanket, after which the underlying skeleton of meth remains, less sentimental, more alert—moderated, to be sure, by the ecstasy's still measurable blood concentrations; one possesses just as much energy as before, and it remains perfectly pleasant to caress one's partner, or even to dance naked on the carpet; in some ways it is even better, for a penis can now spring up more easily, and ejaculate with an orgasm more direct and concentrated than on ecstasy, which had facilitated the creation of orgasm-like happinesses along one's entire skin, just as a cockroach can see with its entire body; that was over now, to be sure, but one speaks and listens better; one discusses, compares and even plans, because the end is perceptible—a false end, actually, because even after both parties are yawning and feeling pleasantly sleepy, such sensations are merely more thin blankets beneath which the obdurate meth skeleton lies on its back, glaring straight up, in obedience to whose example the formerly ecstatic couple lie very still in bed with the lights out, getting more and more tired and trying to sleep; perhaps one party will lie very still, thinking: If only she'll stop sighing and thrashing around I might be able to drift off, while the other one is thinking: I feel so desperate; I'm so jangled; I can't stand to lie next to him like this; I've got to go home even right now at five in the morning—and she even gets up, dresses, fumblingly tries to pack, and he wearily gets up to help her, at which she lies down on the carpet, weeping.

That was how Neva now began to feel. She reminded herself that to love and be loved was always beautiful.

5

Her husband got up to piss. On his return he found her sitting up in their bed, staring and shivering.

He went out; he felt like standing on the beach; she, as Californians express it, apparently "needed her space." His pessimistic tolerance was as rich as those kelp-festooned, barnacled, lichened sea-rocks. He felt as sweetly sad as the transwoman did when leaving the retired policeman's place after a night of abasement.

He scanned the shore for women. If his luck held he might behold some golden-skinned blonde on her back, drawing up her knees and luxuriously spreading her thighs. Wouldn't that be a fine palate-cleanser?—But he found no one except for himself.

He thought: One thing I will say for Neva. She's always dynamite in bed. I can't get enough of her. But evidently I'm not enough for her, or she wouldn't be such a slut. And that insults me. Neva's not as nice as she used to be.

Then he opened his cell phone, in order to reply to Sandra's congratulations.

6

The blonde little chambermaid came in. And after the third time she mentioned that she was a submissive, the lesbian picked up the hint and patiently inquired into her fantasies, at which the maid hiked up her skirt, pulled down her panties (which she had made herself on her sewing machine), and bent over the chair with her arms and breasts hanging down. Smiling a little, the lesbian dragged a cold length of nickel chain down her spine and between her buttocks. She said: Your bottom would look very pretty with marks on it, to which the chambermaid eagerly replied: I've been there.

(It would be easy to say, as so many later did, that the lesbian had no "moral center."—Or, if you like, she was never good enough.—But none of *us* were rooted in anything; therefore, we had to root ourselves in her, and she in us—a mutually temporary combination, hence no good for roots. And was it so unforgivable, to love and be loved?)

She offered the wide brown disk of her anus. So the lesbian had to pleasure her. Why not? She wasn't even here. When it was over, the blonde lay strewn across her bed like a golden chariot halted in mid-career.

7

The straight man burst in, ready to be serviced. Neva lay back, gripped her ankles and pulled them apart to receive him. Very excited, he remembered something he had heard some weeks ago at the Buddha Bar, where a middle-aged lady who vaguely resembled Julie Andrews was instructing two exotic dancers: There's something about watching someone who could hurt herself that . . . there's a kind of morbid appeal. When you're on the stage you're kind of vulnerable.

8

After he went out again, the lesbian answered her phone.

I won't blame you, Shantelle surprisingly said, but I'm feelin' fuckin' disappointed 'cause I had taken that day off from work and I was feeling well and . . .

I got married, said the lesbian.

What the fuck are you talking about? I'm your *girlfriend*!

The lesbian, she who alone could shine over the immensity of Shantelle's love, explained: I'm in Carmel right now, on my honeymoon.

There used to be something magnificent and highly erotic when Shantelle lost her temper; the lesbian liked it when Shantelle slapped her face and beat her. Just now she merely felt that familiar ache in the center of her chest, of grief and of dread that the impending growth of that grief might be desperately insupportable; yet all the while there was something clean and proud in her, that she was finally being true to herself alone.

I just don't understand, said Shantelle in a dull voice that Neva had never heard before. I feel frustrated. I feel so angry! Because some people I got absolutely no interest in and never want to hear about did something in Hawaii! You know what? Leave me the fuck alone! Don't you ever talk to me no more!

And she slammed down the phone. Neva had a feeling of relief.

She lay on her back watching the ceiling fan spin like the propeller of a lazy plane to nowhere, with the string for its power switch and the string for the light bulb that hung down from it like a robot angel's teat twitching both more moderately and more evenly than the hip-fringes that hung from a certain stripper's panties at the Pink Apple. She watched it until it made her sleepy. She had a headache.

She looked at her phone and saw that Shantelle had called but not left a message. Judy had called her eight times in the last hour.

She stood up. She brushed her hair and opened the door. The little girl Andrea came running toward her, shouting with glee.

9

Upon her husband's return, they strolled around the tide pools of Point Lobos. A woman in a red skirt was taking a man's photograph, the hem riding maniacally up her thighs. Young men clambered over the rocks. Couples showed each other cell phone photos. A Japanese couple took three selfies, in obedience to what Freud asserted about the individual in the group: *His emotions become extraordinarily intensified, while his intellectual ability becomes markedly reduced . . .* The straight man was clutching at her with his skinny rigid fingers, and the white white foam slithering in through the dark channel of barnacles.

The lesbian gazed down at those dark green kelp-fingers, strangely like palm-fronds, outspread rays of a green sky in the black sky of a tide pool, whose patchy galaxies crawled with crabs.

Excuse me, said a man. Would you please take our picture? We just got married!

The lesbian took his cell phone and aimed it.

That's great, said the man. I'll take your picture if you want—

No, said the straight man.

From a higher point they now overlooked the sea, which was overlain by a reflected cloud-mass that reminded her of cornstarch dissolving in water.

How would it feel to dive down in there? First there would be the coldness in her nose, then the sound of her pulse, the smell and choking taste of the sea, while above her the dark kelp-pods would ride the waves like the heads of a bird-horde.

Neva, he said, you look so far away.

She squeezed his hand.

He demanded: What are you thinking?

I love you, she said.

He fucked her raw; she never complained.

The Absolute Latest

"Honestly, I'm in no hurry to grow up," Judy continued, her large eyes serious and a plaintive note of sincerity in her face.

ROBERT McILWAINE, 1939

She doesn't want to grow up. She wears short skirts, no makeup off the set.

GLADYS HALL, 1938

But gosh, everyone who knows me at all says I'm *not* grown up!

JUDY GARLAND, 1939

The lesbian had promised to be back from her honeymoon by six, or six-thirty at the absolute latest. If anything happened she was supposed to call the room. Judy's phone was most definitely on. She unplugged it, just for an instant. She held it to her ear. That was how she listened to the passage of time, which on Saturdays was most often represented to her by the whirling stormclouds of clothes in the bank of dryers whose porthole vistas seemed at the same time to look out onto something grand and to repeat the same constricted circling almost without end—the end, of course, infallibly presenting itself once the money ran out.

At seven-fifty she began to feel sick to her stomach. She looked at the lesbian's roller suitcase on the floor, and the lesbian's bottles of pills on the dresser, and the photographs of her and the lesbian together that the lesbian had taken and laid out in two neat rows. (The famous overnight bag was gone, of course.) Like a good secret agent, she looked under the bed, finding nothing but dustballs, a live cockroach and a business card bearing two interlinked female symbols. She was wondering whether Neva might have been killed in a car accident, or if she could be trapped on the phone with Shantelle, or had the straight man waylaid her and dragged her back to his house? She knew that Neva was almost perfect; her sole flaw was her inability to say no.

Judy wondered what to do. She might or might not have just enough money to pay for the hotel, but what should she do with Neva's belongings? And since she had checked in under a false name, without showing identification, what if they refused to accept cash, or insisted on seeing a driver's license? Hungry and dispirited, she waited for the phone to ring, fearing that if she called the lesbian's phone and the lesbian happened to be with the straight man, whom she had often heard hectoring her, something bad might occur . . .—while Xenia was thinking, not without an IQ boost from her Old German Lager: What are all these others to her? She can't really love them all; that's impossible. I wonder if she'll ever explain it to me? And how can I put myself forward? I wish I were five years younger; maybe I can lose ten pounds if it'll do any good. If stinking old Judy can do it . . . Oh, I'd do anything if I could pull off wearing a super-tight pencil skirt! Anyhow, I'd better be very careful not to act like an idiot.

As for me, I was already fantasizing what I would do with her next Wednesday; I'd ask if she could come over and she would say she could; then I'd give her a generous pinch of sugar-brown MDMA crystals, after which I'd start playing with her nipples; I'd eat my MDMA a half hour after that, so that I could still function, if you know what I mean. That night I dreamed that she stood in her dark blue dress before a red curtain, with a golden halo around her head.

The retired policeman got out of bed before ten, although the toes of his left foot ached so fiercely with the icy hotness of peripheral neuropathy that he would rather have stayed in until late afternoon, when the transwoman would honor her appointment to massage his feet and swollen ankles; but he was on the greatest case of his career, so after checking his mailbox he limped down those seven grand steps, pushed open the glass door and emerged from Empire Residences into the nasty world of Karen Strand. By eleven-thirty he had walked all six of those Turk Street blocks, and now pretended to tan himself in the hemispherical glow of the Best Auto Repair parking garage, until the vermilion hand on the street sign changed to the emerald disk that meant *go*, permitting that law-abiding gentleman to trudge round the corner, creeping through a crowd of Latin types who stood shouting outside the grocery store, while the old hotel signs kept overhanging like pallid hooks. Shouldering open the righthand swinging door, he scanned the sticky tables in our stuffy dark bar which smelled of bad breath and toilets. Francine eyed him as if she had forgotten who he was. Just then that washed out old postcard of the giant breast with pink spectacles on it fell off the shelf. Francine failed to notice; he should have told her, but until that first shot of Old Crow went down he lacked the get-up-and-go, so she repeatedly stepped on it, marching back and forth on Drink Patrol; finally it was sticking to her shoe, and then she picked it up, sighed, reread it once and dropped it into the garbage can. Wearily she poured out his Old Crow.—Fuck that, he said, to remind her that the customer is always right. Then he ordered a glass of cherry soda with two shots of bourbon in it, in honor of his diabetes.—Six dollars, she said. He tipped her three so that she would love him.—An old man as fat and pale as a banana slug sat in one of the front row seats stretching out his pallid ectoplasmic arms in yearning to the sleek blonde T-girl who reached back toward him with a fake smile; she must have seen the color of his money.

Francine refilled his glass (and on the dark side of the bar, around her secret packet closed Shantelle's hand, as rapidly and violently as a snapping turtle biting off a child's finger).

Now see it our way, the retired policeman insisted. A robbery at the shoe repair place, where the business is ninety percent cash, so some guy had a gun, so the off duty officer was wrestling the guy and he was getting his ass kicked, so he shot the guy, lost his job. Now look. He fought the robber for three fuckin' minutes. Three minutes is, well, it's a long time to wrestle somebody when you're going at it. Full punches for three minutes straight! I'll bet after a minute and a half you're gonna be thinking, *fuck this*. And he was at a place that was being robbed at gunpoint, and he tried to stop the violence, got hung out to dry on the basis of blood alcohol. You just never know what the calculation's gonna be. Coulda been a liability issue. Well, he got his job back through arbitration. Now what's he gonna do? He's gonna sue the department. Now do you worry about everything you do on a daily basis, forever and ever?

He's a friend of yours, said Francine. And you care about him, so—

Suicide, he said brightly.

Oh, shit, said Francine. J. D., I'm so so sorry.

The retired policeman waited for Judy, longing to grab her by both cheeks and shake her head back and forth while she barked like a dog. Finally he opened his old flip phone. When he dialled her up, she did not answer, so he went home.

As soon as he was out of the picture, that cunning lady came in, the pleats of her skirt shining whiter than blue and bluer than white. (To be more specific, she wore a short white skirt and a lace top, just like Nancy Kerrigan's skating ensemble in Detroit just before she was assaulted.) She wasn't exactly worried, because we had not yet arrived at the absolute latest. Having scammed her way out of that hotel room, she felt almost exhilarated; maybe she would perform again this Friday at the Pink Apple! So she clicked her shotglass against Shantelle's, and they chanted in chorus: *That's what I'm supposed to be, a legend.*

Al crept in, looking even more pale and rubbery than at Ed's wake. He sat down beside me and said: I just can't understand why someone would do that. She was so sweet to me at first. I always treated her right. And then to ghost me like this, it's not fair. I texted her four times last Sunday. And we used to text each other like fifty times a day. When I left her place on Saturday, she was still calling me her husband.

Did you tell her to?

Well, yeah, but she didn't seem to mind. Now look. Do you think it's right, what Neva's doing? Can you see any excuse for her behavior?

I thought about it. Then I said: No.

Until we were in the Piggy Gobble this morning I still had some hope, but now I'm ninety-nine percent sure it's over, he said, checking his cell phone again, in case Neva might have texted. I think if she gets in touch with me today, I won't answer until tomorrow.

I almost had to laugh, watching Al trying over and over, never successfully, to understand the sudden mystery that was Neva. It distracted me from my own fear, grief and hatred.

In the niche above the bar I spied a snapshot of two chunky old women embracing in a fern-licked doorway.

Francine dropped a glass, which did not break. She fumbled with the remote control, and the television suddenly boomed: *Six months ago, I hadn't known my true love existed, but now I can't imagine a world without her—*

Sorry, said Francine, turning the volume down.

The television showed a commercial about the military keeping America safe, amen.—Look, said Xenia. My son flies helicopters for the U.S. Army. Up in Fairbanks, Alaska. He's a lieutenant-colonel. Can you top that?

Anytime I want to, said Shantelle—who now called the lesbian's little white phone to apologize for having been such a mess, but the voicemailbox was full.

Like a dog sitting on her hind legs with her nose straight forward, trying to become a perfect triangle of readiness, the transwoman prepared herself for the lesbian's arrival. The Y Bar was silent because our Neva was *late.* Francine finished washing the glasses, so she washed them all over again.

Anyway, said Xenia, the Army bitch in that commercial was really hot.

You mean sexy? said Selene.

Sure.

Sexiness is really alluring, said Selene, but lately I've been wondering: What exactly is charisma?

Finishing her Old German Lager in a single noble breath, Xenia set down the bottle, grinned and said: Charisma? Well, that's just like before life beats the shit out of you. What is alluring is the *sparkly bright energy.* Sexuality is very alluring. I'm thinking of my friend Mariah, who's covered in tattoos, you know, cat tattoos. Maybe it's because of her kindness and her intelligence, I don't know, but she truly catches your eye—

Then Francine said: What about Neva? What's *her* charisma?

I don't know, said Xenia, and then they all fell silent.

No, said Shantelle, smiling and making a partially folded-in improvement on the Fascist salute, her elbow locked tight against her red-bra'd right booby—a move stolen from a Mexican showgirl she'd once seen in Vegas.—There never *was* no such person as Queen of the Whores, although I did once know this crazy white bitch named Domino who went around with high pretensions. But that was nothin' like what Neva does—

Closing her eyes, Judy pretended that she was being kidnapped by Neva, who would beat her just right.

After a long time Sandra came in, looking for Neva. Judy sat wringing her hands, while Shantelle tried again to call the lesbian, whose phone went straight to voicemail. Accordingly Shantelle called two other fresh bitches she had lined up, both of whom proved available, so after that was arranged she called Neva again, but this time Neva's phone was off. Now Shantelle's mother was calling her; the bitch must be fresh out of prison. Shantelle decided not to answer, in case the lesbian should call. Triumphantly she announced: Someone's calling me. I don't know who it is. It may be Neva. I was hoping it was Neva even though it's an 866 area code. No, it's a telemarketer. And you know fucking what? Neva's phone's still not ringing.

The Y Bar felt as stifling as the inner chamber of a buried sandstone temple, where condemned ones prolong their doom by sucking oxygen from the grooved hieroglyphs in the walls. Slowly, slowly Judy moved her drink so that she could sit next to that patient friend, with whose long red hair she began to play. Shantelle began fidgeting, rubbing her naked knees together as if some perfume arose from between them, while Sandra smiled anxiously.

Judy said: Tell me a story.

Just right now I'm kind of tired . . .

Then will you answer a question?

Okay, sweetie.

Is lesbian love different from the heterosexual kind? I mean—

Well, said Sandra, I think a lesbian couple has to be different from a heterosexual couple. I feel that there's a certain amount of fear when you're being penetrated; there's a certain amount of fear about being overpowered; and I don't think you can escape that. With lesbians there's a different kind of fear but it can't be that.

What do you mean? said Judy. Every good girl wears a strap-on.

You know, said Sandra, I remember that when I was a senior in college, I lived in a house with three girls and a guy; and I remember them talking about it; I remember this girl getting ready to have sex with him and having her say how scary it was when you're face to face with a penis and my roommate Janie saying, yeah, when you're right there it's terrifying. The first time when I was naked with a guy, I only agreed to touch it with my foot. By the time I was with Louis, I was kind of over that. They start to look more similar. They're almost like mythical. I think one thing that surprises me about penises is that they all look sort of innocent and clean.

Judy said: Tell me a story about penises!—at which Xenia came to Sandra's rescue as follows: Did you see that picture of Madonna? They say she got filler in her cheeks, and now her face looks so fat!

Sandra replied: Well, what do you expect? She's fifty-eight!

Fifty-nine, said Francine.

And we all had great fun trashing poor Madonna, forgetting how old our very own Neva might be; until the transwoman finally stood up for the abused star: Well, you know, I'd give anything to look like her.

Judy, sweetheart, not even plastic surgery would do you any good. You know what you need the most? I'll bet it's something you've never thought of, but it would really, really help.

What is it? Oh, please tell me what it is!

A *bath.*

Then they all started laughing at her; Shantelle chortled so much that she choked on an ice cube, and then Francine got to show off her expertise at the Heimlich Maneuver. The transwoman missed that glorious moment; she crouched in the bathroom crying.

Pretty soon she was over it, of course; in her life she had heard worse—and what about poor Judy Garland weeping all night because *Three Smart Girls* had made Deanna Durbin into a star? *Our* Judy counted her motherfucking blessings. She went home without saying goodbye to anyone, and no one said goodbye to her; then she took off her clothes and sniffed her armpits. All she could smell was deodorant; maybe Shantelle had just been teasing her. Just in case, she drew herself a nice hot bath, with lavender suds that obscured the filthiness of the tub, then got in and lay there, thinking about those photos of the stars with their filler. The before and after pictures of Kimora Lee Simmons, who was now forty-one, showed a definite plumping out of her lips. And now everybody was running Kimora down! Could you believe it? The transwoman longed to take her in her arms and hug her. Actually, she wouldn't mind getting her own lip job. How much did Kimora's plastic surgeon charge? Ten thousand at least, probably. Oh, well.

Now it came time to fulfill her next obligation.

All right, said the retired policeman. I s'pose you want to watch something romantic. Some chick flick with bitches moaning about men and putting them down and all the time trying to *get* them.

Well, there's one I heard about from Francine. What's it called? It's a true-life story where this girl gets abducted—

So far I'm liking it. Let's act it out, *right now*!—and he drew out his Smith & Wesson from behind the pillow, cocked it and said: Down on your knees, *bitch*! Open your mouth, *bitch*! I'm gonna stick this gun in your mouth and pull the trigger so Shantelle can scurry over and scrub away your so-called brains!

In a French maid outfit?

That's right. Sure. We can watch your stupid chick flick. But unless you can remember what it is—

I know. Let me call the bar.

Don't call the fucking bar.

Why not?

Because you'll start blibbery-blabbing with those other bitches and I'll get jealous.

You *will*? That's so sweet. Anyway, I promised you we could watch *Shark Hunters.*

That's right. Here it is on my queue. Will you pass me my pills?

Sure, baby.

And she poured them each a double bourbon, so he could wash down his cholesterol medicine and she could help her estrogen pill go down glowing.

After the movie she tried and tried to suck him off, but nothing happened. Then he struggled to sit up and at least spank her, but felt too dizzy. She looked away.

Now you'll probably get some little bitch and leave me, he said.

She remained kneeling on the floor. Presently he began snoring.

Since Neva had not called her, she went back to the Y Bar, where Xenia was whispering into her sky-blue phone: Hey, baby; I was just calling to say I was thinking about you and missing you; I don't know if it's okay to love you or stop loving you and it's so hard; I just wanted to let you know I was thinking about you. For the next twelve hours I'm going to be in love with you again. Oh, Neva, I wish everything was different.

Now Judy was worried, so she needed to get drunk. Setting herself heavily down next to Sandra, she ran her man's hand lovingly through the other woman's long red hair with a force that almost anybody else (not Neva, of course) would have considered invasive. Sandra smiled brightly. She was a swan-necked, Celtic-looking lady with cat's-eye glasses and a heart-shaped mouth. If she had not been so infallibly kind, Judy might have been jealous of her. It also helped that Sandra's open smile and freckled young skin, not to mention the largeness of her beautiful brownish-green eyes, afforded her a vulnerable appearance; not even the retired policeman ever cared to insult her. She was a slender lovely girl, and her vulva was even more heart-shaped than her mouth.—Seven dollars, said Francine, after which Judy inquired: Are you . . . I mean, why do so many girls want to be mermaids?

Because mermaids are in fairytales and they're very free, replied Sandra right away.

What do you mean, free?

Well, Judy, unlike a lot of girls in fairytales, they're not trapped in a tower or a cottage or an ogre's dungeon, so they can go anywhere, and there's an inherent beauty about them with their swirling hair and their tails; don't you think so? I know you're worried; please don't worry; Neva will be walking in any minute! Anyway, I mean, by their very existence they're magical! A lot of children of both sexes want to have animal friends, and mermaids are friends with dolphins and fish and starfish, so they have all these animal friends in this, well, this whole world . . .

I don't have any animal friends, said Judy. I don't even have any human friends, except you and Neva—

And *me*, the barmaid interjected.

You're right, said the transwoman. Sorry, Francine; *sorry*!

And J. D. loves you—

Well, fuck him; I wanna be a mermaid! Gimme another.

Seven dollars.

And one for Sandra—

Six dollars.

Thanks, Judy. That's very sweet.

And one for you.

No thanks, hon. Save your money.

Whose turn is it?

Mine, said Sandra in a small happy voice.

Oh, said Judy. Oh, you're so lucky.

I know, said Sandra. Do you want to hear more about mermaids?

Yes yes *yes*!

So they go on fabulous adventures because that is what living underwater is. A mermaid is not dissimilar from a magical creature that lives among the stars, but we can't really see that. We can imagine a garden but it's a coral garden, and I . . .

And they're *girls*, said the transwoman lasciviously.

Actually, I think that most people don't think about the sex of the mermaid.

There's something very romantic about them, because they love pirates and sailors, but it's hard to see how a mermaid can be violated. A lot of little girls, that's not even a part of their imaginings.

I'll bet it was yours, said Judy, laying her hand on Sandra's, but the other woman insisted: I've never really thought that much about the sexual lives of mermaids; that's not something that comes to mind automatically. Does a prince marry this girl, and what happens? This doesn't seem to happen with mermaids, because they're so free.

And you're free, aren't you?

No, said Sandra. Not really. I tend to think about the swimming and the adventure, and when I imagine myself as a mermaid I'm still me and I still don't necessarily imagine myself as having the tail; I can go underwater and be friends with dolphins and still have sex if I want to . . .

In came the twentysomething lipstick lesbian whose very own cell phone application had now gone viral—as fulfilling an accomplishment as stealing the Lindbergh baby, never mind the semiliterate German English of the ransom note; she ordered a glass of red wine, which embarrassed Francine, who finally unearthed an expired gallon of Captain Mark's Rondalay from the closet; meanwhile the lipstick lesbian was twirtling and twortling ten-character messages to her followers on the SpiderWeb.

Eight dollars, said Francine.

The lipstick lesbian took a sip and spat it back into the glass. She said: I'm not drinking this shit.

You still owe me eight dollars.

No, she said.

Francine, who had been wringing her hands for uneasiness about Neva, came out from behind the bar with a smile and a baseball bat. We all wanted blood. But just then Al came in; he needed a date, so the transwoman hurried out with him, anxious to, as Shantelle would say, *get it over with,* in order to be there for Neva. When she came back, Francine was scrubbing the counter.

More to Tell

Q. Do you think if she had lived her status would have been elevated to living legend . . . ?

A. I don't think so . . . She was only a really good actress when she had a great director.

INTERVIEW WITH MICHAEL CHILDERS, about Natalie Wood

I used paint remover on her, took off her glamorous clothes and put her in front of the camera, naked and gasping.

ELIA KAZAN, describing how he directed Natalie Wood in *Splendor in the Grass*

1

Naturally the retired policeman knew it first. When my phone rang I was disappointed not to read the lesbian's number in that dingy grey-green plastic window below the brand name's screaming cursive (I had locked myself into a three-year contract with my Q-Spot Osiris Pocket Mini); but when he said: Meet me at the Cinnabar and no bullshit, I knew it was going to be good.

I got there before he did. Carmen changed the lesbian's hundred-dollar bill and even volunteered the wireless password in case there had been anyone anywhere else who could possibly have cared to hear from me. Sipping my rum and sodapop to make it last, I eavesdropped on her discussing religion with an old Latina who now said: So I know they talk about snakes and female goddesses as transformational and we all have one inside of us that both causes evil and cures evil. My spiritual beliefs are in the making forever.—Carmen said: Well, there's a lady named Neva who . . .—Then *he* minced painfully in. I already had deployed his usual double shot, facing mine, on that table in the back.

That Strand bitch offed herself, he said. I bet you didn't hear she married Louis on Monday.

I don't get it, I said. Sure I knew she—

You don't get *what*? he asked triumphantly, slamming down his empty glass.

You're telling me Neva's dead? For what?

If you were a lesbian married to Louis, how would you like it?

Well, I said, Neva's not exactly a—

But you call her that, *don't* you? Maybe she was. She sure brought out Judy's so-called feminine side.

Judy must be upset, I said, still not believing it.

I want you to tell her. Ain't you the genius at spreading bad news? Anyway, you . . . you're fond of her.

I love Judy.

That's nice. Is that why you bought my fucking drink?

Hey, said Carmen. Keep it smooth back there.

Still not believing what he had told me although I simultaneously believed *him*, I said: It's not adding up. First of all—

Mrs. Strand called me, he said. She was hoping I could sweep the details under the rug.

And did you?

Well, I went out there, had a chat with the coroner—

And you saw Neva.

Deadest bitch I've laid eyes on all week. Blue in the face. Toxicology'll be done tomorrow most likely; I'm betting on fentanyl, but they wouldn't show me the baggie. And you know what, Richard? That finally gives me one thing to like about Karen Strand. That's how I plan to go. Fentanyl's a sure thing, and painless.

Above and behind his head, the television now displayed a vertical shot down onto the angled patterns of a basketball court, the gaze next pivoting nauseatingly for the fifteenth rebound: *And he scored! Tazee McShaq has never yet missed a shot for Philadelphia! Wow, that was an extremely late whistle . . .*—while Carmen, yawning, emptied the trash.

Where's Louis?

Oh, they let him go. He was the one pounding on the door, which makes him a piss-poor suspect. They did trick him into a drug test—bright boys down there in Carmel. Well, amazingly enough he came up clean.

And he married her, I said.

Look at you! Wishing you'd been the bridegroom, hah? Whole world makes me fuckin' *sick.*

I went to the bar and bought him and me another drink while he sat there grinning.

All right, he said—and so help me, he even began to gesture, I think to further his own enjoyment. He reminded me of a lawyer-plaintiff whose performance I once (because his case preceded mine) had to watch in Vegas: Every time he mentioned that the defendant was seeking to wire seventy-five thousand dollars (to part of which he laid claim) into an account in Mexicali, the lawyer would jerk his thumb downward, as if south of the border meant *underground.* In the retired policeman's case, I would have needed to be a connoisseur of athletics to do justice to his antics. So let me simply report what he said:

All right, he married her, and what's stranger is that she married *him*; we'll never know why. They had themselves a honeymoon right there in Carmel, and she didn't even tell her mother; it was all secret, just a goddamn civil ceremony. And why they did it there, well, unless she was already planning to off herself and wanted to make it easier for Mrs. Strand . . .

You like the old lady, don't you?

Oh, she's a piece of work, like me. Takes one to know one. Well, so there was some family from Cleveland staying at the same hotel. Little girl was just crazy about our Karen; wouldn't leave her alone. You get it now?

No, I said.

That's because your mind ain't dirty enough. So this little girl, right before dinner time Louis's down at the beach desperately texting Sandra (good alibi!), and everyone's gone crazy hunting for little Andrea. Police come in. Surveillance footage shows no Andrea on the first floor all afternoon, so unless it's another Baby Lindbergh case, Andrea's still somewhere in the hotel. They go door to door; parents were in hysterics; I love that kind of energy. Well, finally they get to Louis and Karen's room. And they're hearing moans, but after all it's the fuckin' bridal suite. Door was unlocked. And there's Karen and Andrea. Can't ever start 'em too early, right? Now this will turn you on. They had to literally pry that kid off of Karen, not that Karen was resisting: the little girl was in heaven and wanted to stay there! Not a stitch on either of 'em. Don't that kinda turn your stomach? I'll tell you, Richard, in my childhood I've seen a few things, but . . . But Karen was not a problem, aside from *being* the problem. She told the girl to go back to Mommy, and the girl was not havin' it! Well, they ordered Karen to get up and dressed before they put the cuffs on. Andrea was screaming for Karen! While they were trying to figure out how to get her decent and quiet, Karen faded away. She did it just right—stone dead so fast she didn't vomit even once. And guess what? he said. You'll like this—no feces in the lower bowel. No fuckin' *women's mark* anywhere, of course. And Louis didn't show up for two full hours . . .

He had more to tell, and Carmen had more to sell on this foggy afternoon with two homeless-owned dogs yapping at each other outside and then there came a car crash; through the open door we could all hear the breaking glass and then the applause.

Finally he said: What's your opinion? Do some little girls need to be touched?

Finishing my drink, I replied: Did you?

2

Distrusting the retired policeman for the same reason that I disbelieved in the lesbian's death, I decided to meet her mother (whom I had never met), so I set off immediately to rid myself of that vile obligation.

From the retired policeman's many heroic autobiographies I remembered El Camino Real and Amador, and the silent Mission style houses across from Vallejo High, with their windows drawn; then Broadway and then those various lefts and lefts and rights until . . .

Before I could ring the bell, the front door opened as if by itself, and there was the old lady waiting.

Do I know you? she asked.

I'm a friend of your daughter's.

Oh! Another of Karen's *friends*! Well. How nice to meet you. Won't you sit down?

I would have preferred to give it to her right there, standing up, but the lesbian would never have treated anybody thus, so I followed her into the kitchen and seated myself at the table while she filled the teakettle. Setting it on the stove, she turned to me, and now I had to gaze into her eyes.

Something else has happened, said Mrs. Strand.

I replied only *yes*, but even that easy monosyllable fell cracked and twisted from my mouth.

Well?

I'm sorry; she's—

Then she stood watching me while I sat familiarizing myself with the synthetic wood-grain of the kitchen table, until the kettle began to whistle.

Wait a second, I said. You worked with J. D. on this.

J. D. who?

That cop.

Her face narrowed into nastiness and she said: I have no idea what you think I know, but get out.

I choked out: Mrs. Strand, I loved Neva—

Well, she said, what do you suppose this is like for *me*?

Raised Again

God raises Job again . . . Many years pass by, and he has other children and loves them. But how could he love those new ones when those first children are no more . . . ? . . . It's the great mystery of human life that old grief passes gradually into quiet tender joy.

DOSTOYEVSKY, 1880

All these patients cry miserably for cure . . . But they must not be believed. They only act as if they had really wanted freedom . . .

WILHELM STEKEL, bef. 1930

1

I would mislead you if you carried away the impression that she got to be admired by her public one last time, like Judy Garland in that glass-topped white casket. To be sure, it *was* as if we were all bearing her on our shoulders to the grave, in a file even longer than the mid-morning soup line at Saint Anthony's, but because she had been more than any of us, now she was longer than our multitude, so that her legs and feet continued stiffly far behind (the transwoman longing to be buried alive beside her), and no matter how we struggled to catch it, kiss it and touch it, her head went before us; we were determined to save it from hanging down in the dust; not one strand of her adorable hair would be soiled by dirt, not until the dirt smothered all of her!—but it was safe anyhow, on that long rigid neck. So it seemed; it also seemed as if we were fighting over her beautiful rigid corpse, which we had all exposed, bitten, penetrated, drunk from, slobbered on and used; but of course this parade, like so many of our fantasies, could never even have been organized, much less consummated; the last event for which we had showed up in concert had been Selene's wedding. We weren't there, and of course neither was E-beth. Francine talked about holding a wake, but even she was too demoralized to plan any such thing, so I feel grateful that someone competent took charge: Karen's funeral would be a strictly private function, arranged and attended solely by her mother; indeed, as Wally Beery had said on the airwaves way back in 1935: *Oh, I'm so proud of you, Judy. I bet your mother's proud of you, too. Isn't that your ma sitting right down there in the front row?*

The whispering horror, incredulity, and various gloatings (call them verbal headlines punctuated with booze) were infinite while they lasted. They lasted not long at all. Let me therefore move on to our closing summations:

Well, she always made me feel good, said Al, who died of cirrhosis soon after.

Actually, Francine reminded him, you were terrified of her.

Don't speak ill of the departed, he said. She might lay a curse on you.

I need help, said Xenia. I need help to get over her. I don't know what she had, but now she's gone.

You could see something real inside her and not just acting, said an Austrian tourist.

Well, but she was sure going downhill, said my favorite German.

What a caring girl, said a Dutchwoman whom our Neva had sent away happy.

An angel, I one-upped him.

Oh, she's *with* the angels now, said Francine.

Victoria grew silent, then went away, dry-eyed.

I told you, said the retired policeman. It's the old JDLR thing. *Just don't look right.* That's why stop-and-frisk is a real good idea, for the sake of the public. Cops kind of know.

Meanwhile the straight man's memories of her kept sinking into the earth. He wisely avoided the funeral.

Sandra, who kept in touch with him for almost three months, told me, as I would have expected, that he could not stop speaking of the lesbian, apparently hoping that even if she could not be restored to him, some fragrance or light of hers could touch him even from the grave.—Sandra mourned her more sincerely, or deeply, or something, than he, which offended him, so that he cut the connection. (For half a year her period wouldn't come.) The retired policeman, who as you know loved to gift me with his own interpretations, proposed that their quarrel was nothing more than a relitigation of history. The death itself more than satisfied him; it was that story's best ending. Consider the way James Dean crashed to death not even a month before *Rebel Without a Cause* hit the theaters . . . and in due time Dean's costar, smoldering little Natalie Wood, conveniently drowned herself! Now they were both immortal. So was Neva.—And here's another oddity from this case, he said. You remember that sealskin pouch she had? Well, of course the boys were hoping for a little assets forfeiture, and when they turned it out on the evidence table, more hundred-dollar bills came out than . . . Well, let's just say they couldn't fit them back inside again. Sergeant Corasaniti has a new Glock .45, and the department's going to get decent riot gear, and even the pathologist is a happy man.

With a "better" husband, would she have survived and even scored a crystal or two of reagent-grade contentment? After all, she and Judy were sisters: how they both needed to please! Had Neva somehow consummated her needs entirely through the straight man, how would the story have ended? I can almost see her and him embracing, mouth to mouth and tongue to tongue until they suffocated; that's what monogamy is.—From his point of view, all she did was turn her smile from one soul to another, never meaning anything close to love.—But I never cared about *him.*

I thought about the way that the love and the sex with Neva used to go on and on, and now would never come back again. Without her, my arms and legs began to ache. When the grief had swelled some time in my chest, it metastasized, ringing and pounding in my head, oozing slimily down my sore throat, exhausting my eyes and chilling the back of my neck. My back ached and I got swollen glands; sores bloomed in my mouth, and even distant gentle sounds set me on edge. Take that as a compliment to Neva.

And because Francine could not stop crying, I took her home and penetrated her from behind the way she said she liked it. Even when she was climaxing she kept her head down, sobbing into my pillow. Remembering what I had learned from worshipping Neva, I got myself to obeying Francine's cunt, being guided by the cunt, going in and out and climaxing only exactly as I was told. I think I fulfilled her; that could have been another beginning of sorts; but when I proposed a less short-term accommodation for mutual comfort, she said: Richard, you're a sweet guy, but I'm really into women.—Well, so was I.

As for the transwoman, I can only say that the retired policeman was wonderful with her. He walked all the way upstairs on his puffy aching legs, unlocked the door (because being who he was he had long since copied her key) and conducted a clean sweep of all her pharmaceuticals, even down to over-the-counter barbiturates, so that when she came staggering in, already huge-eyed like a space alien on God knows what, he was sitting on her bed with the confiscated items beside him in a double-strength paper bag from Save 'n' Shop. She was too high to scream; her mouth opened and she clutched between her legs.

Judy girl, he said, we're gonna have us a little puke party.

No!

One way or another, you're gonna sick that up. Now let's go. Right here. That's a good girl. Down on your knees. Lemme grab hold of your hair so it don't go in the toilet. Now get to work. I said do it. You gonna puke up those pills or am I gonna shove your head in the bowl and waterboard you like a goddamn raghead? Judy, I'm being super patient right now, but my legs are hurting from standing here and pretty soon I'm gonna get mean. Judy, are you listening? Honey, you just got to. Neva's gone, but you still have me. I'm not letting you go with her. You won't see her again. Now go ahead. You can't get out of this. I got your hair. Will you make this easy? Nod your head yes.

She shook her head no, of course. He sighed. He waited.

Cock . . . feather . . . , she whispered.

Glaring around, he found her ratty old faux-peacock feather boa hanging from, of all places, the showerhead. It was sodden and mildewed; she must have pissed on it or something and then tried to clean it. He yanked loose a feather (dyed chicken) and tickled the back of her hand with it.—There you go, honey. Now get this show on the road.

Obediently she took hold of the instrument. He resumed his guardian grip on her hair. Snivelling and whimpering, she bent lower, opened her mouth wide and tickled her tonsils. When the thick brown vomit came out, he almost got an erection, because this was a new kind of game.

Again, he said. Again. All right. Good girl. Here's your mouthwash. Rinse good. I'm gonna start the shower for you. Come on. Strip. Hurry the fuck up. Okay; that's good. You know something? I really love you, Judy. That's my girl. You're my very good girl. I'm gonna keep all your pills until you stop wanting to off yourself. Come on. Get in the fucking shower. Oh, me and my goddamn *life* . . . !

In the shower she kept crying so violently that the neighbors started kicking the wall, but when she came to him where he sat waiting in his underwear on the edge of her bed and his doubly pregnant paunch hanging down over the elastic, she gazed at him with something like the gently wide-eyed submission of the pretty girl in orange (aged thirty-six) who had strangled her mother for money, hid the corpse in the shed, then unexpectedly got visited by justice, the dark-uniformed bailiff now gazing down on her, perhaps compassionately, as she begins to rise and commence serving her sentence of *up to seventy years*, although it might be only fifty-three: *I choked her, strangled her, then I pulled her down to the shed. Then I told my boyfriend about what I did and he wanted to cut her up.* Sometimes the retired policeman wondered whatever happened to that bitch.

That night while he was snoring she tried to cut her wrist with that rusty box-cutter she kept in her purse, but it was what he called a *fake attempt*—in blander phraseology a *cry for help.* For three days and nights he kept her handcuffed to the bedposts, until she finally promised not to give her life for us as Judy Garland did.

2

December came, then a little rain, less than we used to get when I was young; and to me it now feels so long ago—even before Martina Navratilova defected from Czechoslovakia!—that we might as well have been figures on a buried Corinthian jar, dancing round the hydria; my memories keep listening with the uplifted ears of black horses, although all they hear is the rapid steady hissing of a police car up the otherwise unmarred greyness of Howard Street; if the lesbian were coming up to us through the dust my memories would hear her; the transwoman no longer listens, but lacks a need to, because unlike me she is as faithful as the headless woman from Miletua who holds a rock partridge tight against her stone breast. Desperate to rest down in the lesbian's darkness, she pulled down her panties and lay across the retired policeman's knees so that she could forsake the razor-edged burden of herself and sleep with Neva, yes; sleep with Neva: When he was beating her, she felt so happy to have been shaken out of herself, into the blissful darkness of freedom.

And Francine was always there. Alicia had been fired. Just as barren Wisdom, they say, is mother of the angels, so Francine who now had nobody nourished our dreams.

Sandra began again to envision mermaids out loud, and Judy to aspire to serving her. But as the saying went, why keep her eggs in one basket? Hence it was Erin whom Judy accompanied to Vallejo, so that after turning right and left and left and right among the Mission style houses they could visit the grave of her whom we wished had made us.

Judy said: Was she really that old? I don't believe it.

Erin took a cell phone photo of the lesbian's headstone. It looked as clean and shiny as candy, because early that morning Francine and Holly had come with ammonia and nail polish remover to scrub away the graffito instructing Karen to **SUCK DICK YOU BIG DYKE**.

Judy said: She might have been thirty at most . . . Erin? Erin, why are you so quiet?

Erin said: When I was little I wanted to live in tunnels underground and have a secret kingdom underground. I had a lot of fantasies about it. It would be really muddy and earthy. This was before I went to the Carlsbad Caverns or went to subways. I just wanted to be underground. I liked the smell of dirt; I liked playing with worms.

They stared down at Karen Strand's headstone, and Erin said: Now I think, no, I wouldn't like it anymore.

Judy eagerly said: I'll bet you had a little girlfriend you used to share those fantasies with—

Erin said: I didn't talk about that stuff with anyone.

Then they went away. That was when Judy realized that Erin would never become one of her *special friends.*

Once they were out of sight I slithered up to lick my darling's headstone. Closing my eyes, I seemed to see her bare marble breasts perfect, the tongue beginning to show between her marble lips, her shining wrist poised on her head. I might have given her the so-called melon hairstyle of Cleopatra . . . and I thought it for the best that she had died like this.

3

We were still clinging to the lesbian and hoping that she would raise us up. We had barely departed from the time when the lesbian was licking the inside of Sandra's ear; then Samantha draped her leg over the lesbian's shoulder in order to be entered with a sky-blue dildo; next the lesbian lay as limp as a feral kitten caught by sadistic children, while Shantelle happily fisted her. Strapping on her extra-long black dildo, the lesbian knelt, grasped Judy's ankles and penetrated her; after which Xenia, pulling aside the strap of her camisole so that the lesbian could grip a breast, closed her eyes and opened her mouth for a kiss.—Remembering Neva became nearly as much fun as retelling the death of Natalie Wood.

A punk T-girl with pink hair and red shoes came in one night in her short plaid skirt silkscreened with Betty Boop's image; she was as convincing as the original Judy Garland, and Xenia, who was high on goofballs and Old German Lager, approvingly shouted out: *She's a filthy whore!* but we withheld our worship, and the punk girl never came back. Xenia staggered off to the toilet. Half an hour later she was telling Francine: So the closest I felt to community with queer women was in Seattle with six, seven women who were all gay. I don't feel that yet.

Maybe you will someday, Francine said wearily. Three dollars.

Meanwhile the transwoman, who had inherited most of the lesbian's slips and dresses, found that they did still not fit, and rather than let some other woman use them she tore them to shreds.

She tried to go through the motions at the Pink Apple, without Xenia, telling herself: No, Judy, don't give up! You're starting to flower . . .—but there was no Neva to do it for—Neva, Neva, who had crushed her down with loveliness—no Colleen even (sometimes she dreamed of that girl's reddish-orange naked legs whirling around, and the girl saying: *Always* . . .), no one but the retired policeman, gazing up at her with pity, all the while admiring himself for bestowing use on that useless creature. (That was how she read him. The way he actually felt was how he used to feel in his first three months on the force, when he would hear a woman shouting and screaming in her holding cell; he got over that.) Sandra had promised: I'm *so* gonna be there on opening night!—but then she got sick . . .

Number One performed in a cheap curly wig and a skirt like a Mexican blanket, gesturing, crossing her legs, collecting dollar bills from eager men; her name was Synesthesia; Judy could have topped her, although I liked the way she kept swaying and flogging herself upside down, then pouting; she kept constantly opening and closing her long pink legs like nutcrackers. Her face was pretty enough. Tattooed and laced, she kept shaking off sweat and money. Suddenly I began to remember my baby daughter and her first smile. Cassandra had been a very sunny baby and used to laugh when she held my thumb in her tiny hand; in those days I often went to the toilet in order to burst into tears more happily and easily; once I had gotten my catharsis in there, I ran the faucet and reminded myself that even if I stayed with her and Michelle, Cassandra would change into someone else; then I felt relieved that I never had and never would need to do anything. I came out, and Synesthesia was onstage, hugging a happy sweaty lesbian; Judy still remained in the game . . .—but Number Two was Vulvalicious, the blonde in the red-checked suit-dress, who was vastly wide and pillowy, creased and bulging and quadruple-paunched, blue lipstick and eyebrows, whirling her tiny head as if it were a distant moon over a snowy landscape; Judy was no more than a shadow of a faraway planetoid against that lady's pallid flesh.—And unfortunately, Judy was Number Three.

Wicker-jickering on ultra-tall heels, she came onstage, raised her skirt and tried pretending that just now the retired policeman was sodomizing her while all these people watched and laughed . . .—but in truth she lacked the wherewithal to embrace her inner disgustingness anymore no matter how lewdly she wriggled, so she forgot her lip-synched lines and so her applause pattered away and turned into jeers as in the old days; she'd become a drunken crab creeping lethargically on the empty stage.—Well, they turned on Judy Garland, didn't they?

4

High as *fuck* on Concentrax and blue dolphins, Judy came swishing up the Hotel Reddy's carpeted stairs, trying to keep smiling, because the security cameras might be proof that she was starring in a movie. Then she remembered that Neva was gone. She banged on Catalina's door. No one answered.

5

She walked through night and wind all the way to Chinatown and came to the retired policeman's former haunt, the Buddha Bar. And there sat the retired dancer Helen, whom she had not seen in ever so long. And Helen was gracious again, and even remembered her!

It's Judy, isn't it? You're the one who hoped to perform in musicals. You look good; you've lost a lot of weight . . .

Oh, *thank* you, said the transwoman. You're one of the nicest people I ever met, except for Neva. You kind of remind me of Julie Andrews. But Neva just died. She was a real star for some of us, and . . . And we feel like, well, actually I can't remember when Marilyn Monroe died, but you're so pretty like her. Suppose you'd been in Marilyn's shoes, and everywhere you went people wanted to . . .

Oh my goodness, said Helen. I guess it would depend on whether you had a good support system.

Could I please buy you a drink?

No, thank you, Judy. I have to be running along pretty soon.

Did you ever hear of Neva?

I'm afraid not.

She was really just like a goddess. I . . .

You're upset, Judy; I can see that. You know, I think often when celebrities sadly die young, you kind of idolize them because they were at their peak and you can't fathom it. Michelle Pfeiffer is so beautiful, and I hadn't seen her in a movie in ages. How must she have felt to go on the shelf? I don't know, but you can get raised up and feel that you're super important and believe everything that you hear and then come crashing down. I mean in this business, the media doesn't allow people to grow old gracefully.

And the thing is, I'm already old! I never got to make it big, and now I see that if I'd only had more discipline or whatever—

Judy, said Helen, I can remember that when I lived in London I was at my peak. I felt confident. I never had that here. I could just tell that when I got here, I felt less comfortable. After *Wicked Frogs* I had one audition, and I thought, I just can't do this anymore. You know, you're used to taking rejection, but . . . Oh, my gosh, Judy, I have to go. It's been so lovely chatting with you—

But how do you stay happy once you—

My husband still works in the profession. There was a little bit for me of being envious of him in that world. You work at night, you're out on the town and it's fun. There's not really many jobs where people clap and cheer you. I think I kind of grieved. I watched the Golden Pussy Awards on television and I still wanted to . . . I mean, really, you train, and you slave at this job, and then, I mean, what am I now gonna do? And I know dancers for whom a lover and children never happened. One of my friends, she was not particularly successful, but she was really really good at getting to know people and she's the operations manager of a huge restaurant in London. No one has everything. So, Judy, make the best of it. Goodbye now.

6

And then the beautifully whitehaired old woman in the denim shirt sat with folded arms, looking into Judy's face.

Well, she said, we hold our meetings on full moon nights, and then we do get a lot of women who are like you in that way. So basically we tell them to take their time. Be in the community and see how it fits for you. You don't have to prove anything. If you hang out here in the community for awhile, you'll find out.

Oh, said Judy.

How old are you?

I . . . Forty-nine.

Well, some of my friends came out in their sixties. As for you, I personally don't have a problem with it, Reba reassured her. A lot of lesbians do. I see the need especially for women to be alone with women born as women. But I think in a general setting, when they are transitioning, if you identify as a woman, that's good enough for me.

Here Reba laughed; Judy thought of it as a sweet laugh, but wasn't she sentimental anyway? And Reba said: Who am I to judge?

How did you get that way? said Judy.

Because I'm kind of open.

But the other old woman, who so far had been silent (her name was Diane), now said: I don't understand it. I'm not comfortable. I live with women that are even less comfortable with it than I am. I tend to be a little softer, but I admit I don't understand it. I know that I wasn't comfortable living in my body when I was heterosexual, so how can I judge you for wanting to be a female? But transgender men still bring that patriarchy with them, and if they bring it into the woman's circle where we already feel oppressed . . . They're already a little more out there than women going into being men.

Judy said: That's not fair.

Diane said: Well, men who are transitioning to be women do bring along the male attitude. We can have a woman who's becoming a man talking normally, but a man transitioning to being a woman will try to take over the group. It's your shoving your male attitude into our faces that we won't stand. We talk about this in group, too—

Judy said: Well, Neva would have said—

They both laughed, and Reba said: Dearie, Neva was a special case.

She was the Goddess, said Judy, almost defiantly.

She might have been *your* Goddess, said Diane. You know, Judy, a long time ago I knew that I needed a feminine-based religion. I worship the Goddess. I see her in everybody. She's our Creatrix. We as women are the birth givers. We create. Patriarchy has taken that away from us. To me She's everything. I don't think of myself as a fanatic. I don't have to shove it down somebody's throat. I see a goddess in Reba, a goddess in all my friends, in everybody. We all fight patriarchy. We're all gonna die, but I don't believe in heaven or hell. Whenever something went wrong I used to always blame God. Never once since I have been studying the Goddess have I ever said, why have You done this to me?

Judy said: Here I am finally ready to join and be one of you, and you don't want me. So I want to know, why have you done this to me?

You're not ready. Anyhow, when we talk about loving everybody, it's not in a sense of your looking at them with starry eyes. In my sense, you're looking at all their faults. When the Goddess looks at us, She's not looking at us as perfect beings. Men are not allowed in our rituals. You know, I can still appreciate a good-looking man walking down the street. I can appreciate *you*.

No you don't, said Judy.

Reba gave her a little slap, even softer than she liked it, and said: You've got so much love in your life and you don't even see it. We *love* you, Judy. You won't remember this but we'll look in on you and maybe you'll come back to us . . .

7

Although Shantelle had repeatedly expressed extreme hatred for the lesbian in those last weeks, after that death she rapidly grew so lost and desperate as to sit sobbing at the Y Bar, begging everyone she met to kill her because she lacked the courage for suicide—at which the person of whom in the entire world she was most contemptuous, the transwoman, sat down beside her. Too aware of her own odiousness to make the mistake of hugging her, or indeed touching her in any way, knowing quite well that even the gentlest declaration of lovingkindness might meet with a punch in the face, the transwoman simply murmured: Shantelle, here's something for you.—The other woman jerked her head around, balling up her fists, but when the transwoman winked open a hand to show a tiny packet of aluminum foil, she snapped it up like a greedy turtle, then rushed weeping into the ladies' room. When she came out, her eyes were still red, but she wore the look of trustful hope, and in less than twenty minutes the relief she had thought impossible began to sweetly woo her; she smiled crookedly, with her eyelids half-lowered, and, slurring her words, began to mutter the lesbian's name. The transwoman paid for both their drinks, took her by the hand and, no longer fearing her, led her home. Shantelle kept searching for her ring of keys, which she was holding and then dropped onto the sidewalk. The transwoman picked them up and unlocked the gratinged gate for her. She said: Shantelle, here's my spare key. I'm going to give you all the drugs you want, to help you heal, because I . . . and then Shantelle slurred out: I love you, *too*, you stinking he-she *bitch.*

Sometimes Francine forgot to charge Shantelle for her Peachy Keen. She didn't even scold her when she vomited on the floor. (Throwing up on molly, it's like a great experience, a gorgeous young lesbian was assuring Sandra. By the way, did you feel my fingers in you at that party?)

What Shantelle wanted was marijuana wax.

She would creep into Judy's place at four in the morning and just take the wax, which was kept in the freezer behind the ice cube tray. Judy would wake up but never said anything; she knew it made Shantelle feel better to be stealing.

After three weeks she had to ask the retired policeman for a cash advance, and when that was gone she went to the Y Bar with the last shard of wax and said: Shantelle, honey, I don't have the money to keep buying this for you.

Shantelle said: Everything's gotta end sometime.—Then she said: Why did you do this for me?

Not knowing which reply might provoke her to rage, Judy told the truth: I just wanted to, that's all. As soon as my finances improve I'll get you some more.

Well, fantastic, said Shantelle, but what the *fuck* am I supposed to do until that happens? Answer me, bitch! What the *fuck* am I supposed to do?

Now you be nice, said Francine.

I'll try to make some money tonight, I promise! I'll really hustle! Shantelle, I'm really really sorry—

Just die, said Shantelle, hardly even angry.

The transwoman tried to reply with a silence as serene as the lesbian's smile. Then a flock of blonde girls rushed off to the ladies' room, where they stayed for half an hour.

8

One day the truth caught up with Shantelle, and she came to me.

Did you give Neva the stuff? she demanded.

Who's buying this round?

You are.

On the house, said Francine.

Answer me, said Shantelle.

Well, I asked, did I or did I not off myself?

She began breathing hard. I decided that if she were to attack me I would punch her face as hard as I could, by which time Francine would be on duty with the baseball bat.

Did you want me dead? I asked. Is that why you sold me the stuff?

I don't care shit about you.

I clinked glasses with her. To our left, three girls huddled around a single phone which showed a celebrity's image. Then the three girls held up the phone and took a selfie with it.

Well, she said then, maybe I wouldn't have done it if I'd had the time to think it through.

Done what? Sold me the stuff?

No, I would. I did it so you wouldn't suffer.

Do you think I wanted Neva to suffer?

So you did give her the stuff.

She never asked me for anything but that one time. You think I could have turned her down?

You know, I watch the TV news, she boasted. And they say when you give somebody the wherewithal to overdose, that's murder. You could get twenty years in prison for what you did.

I'll be sure and share the credit with you.

Why fuckin' *bother*? she said, rising with her glass in her hand.

Wouldn't you have given it to her? I asked.

If I had a gun, said Shantelle, I probably would have killed her earlier. That's why I didn't keep one around.

9

After a lonely while, a half-Chinese quarter-male TV actress named Xing walked into the Y Bar, seated herself on the barstool beside mine, and ordered a root beer and rye. Until then our heliotropic gazes had swung toward a slender young woman in a checked shirt whose keys and laminated identity card hung from a purple lanyard imprinted with the silhouettes of dogs and horses; but when Xing came in, the day grew as white as light in a wide Mexican doorway beyond some red awning that drooped like an old woman's eyelids. Faithful to Neva, Francine disdained her, but Xing reminded the rest of us of Natalie Wood at fifteen, posing naked-shouldered and naked-armed, with a slender string of pearls around her neck and everything airbrushed so angelically; so that was the end of the woman in the checked shirt. What were we supposed to do, but respect the moment? Back in 1769 a sage had informed Great Britain's restless colonies: *As to sovereignty itself, it is unsusceptible of destruction; and, like the sun, only sets in one place, that it may rise, with full splendour, in another.* So it was and will be, especially to us whom everyone had spat on. New customers sleepwalked in; sometimes lone men would shadowbox to the deep slow electronic music. Even the retired policeman was looking into Xing's eyes and sharing his troubles: I used to go out, answer calls, push a black-and-white, but that's not gonna catch the dope dealers, catch the prostitutes. What's the use? . . .—Thanks to Xing, there were more lesbians at the Y Bar than ever before, so the unknown owner finally fixed the catty pole.

Xenia was saying: Here, Francine. For you.

Thank you.

All right, dear. And then after a couple of pills, Selene gets a higher pitch, and it's that *tone* of hers, like an everlovin' drill goin' into my head . . . !

But they don't hear themselves the way we do. I don't hear myself.

No, Francine, insisted Sandra, I think that there's romance involved with mermaids that doesn't have to be incredibly sexual all the time. I think that there's a sense of adventure and communion with the natural world. And there's certainly a way to feel that your body is beautiful as a mermaid, just beautiful and free, without having to have sex right away . . .

And then Xing *smiled* on Sandra and they went home together, Sandra carrying her sweet, sweet narrow-lipped come-on smile; oh, how her brownish-green eyes were shining and her armpits shaved to perfect alabaster as she pulled her frilly white nightgown over her head and offered her redhaired vulva in memory of the lesbian!—How good was it? We had not entirely forgotten the way Neva could lighten her touch upon another woman's clitoris into something that barely existed (fragment of fresco like a faint stain of menstrual blood), in order to lead her up the knife-edge to orgasm—any firmer would abrade her while any lighter would be nothing at all—carefully spiralling in on that tiny delicate hardness, Sandra moaning yes yes yes, her mouth wide, the moment eternally new and perfect.—Was Xing that good? Well, she never picked me. (I'm not a fan, the retired policeman consoled me.)

On the following night Xenia, doing her best Greta Garbo, which is to say, powdering and overpowdering her face into something masklike, then flaring her nostrils, baring her teeth and narrowing her eye, attempted to impress Xing as follows: My lesbian friends are mostly highly professional. *Highly* professional working women.—And Xing picked her!

The next morning I inquired into how Xing compared to Neva, and she replied: No comparison. All of this undoing of genders, I'm not sure that I'm committed to it, but I *will* say that Xing is *hot*! And the thing about Neva (of course *you'd* never know this) was that she only wanted to use toys. You have toys, you have issues.

Shantelle, feeling nearly prepared to follow the lesbian's way to practice love and be infallible at it, wiped the sweat off her face, looked Xing saucily up and down, shot her a fuck-me grin, then submitted to rejection with a curse, feeling so humiliated that she might as well have been a naked girl alone on a red-glowing stage, slowly twisting, expecting nothing, not even a dollar; while I bowed my head—and our new adorable one *smiled.* Then we who had been dead arose with cries of joy.

Xing turned out to be nearly as considerate as the man who steals a couple of his wife's pills for his ex-mistress and her new boyfriend. Holly found her as good as the lesbian (she who had so many times taken my hand), and Samantha, who always lied, said she was even better, but I remember when the transwoman raised a glass to her, and Francine, who according to her own calculus had done everything right (it was only life that had failed her), stood smiling at her from behind the bar, while Xing looked indifferently sideways, watching her mirror image fix her hair.

I remember that slender girl pressing her knees together, never for me, and all those ladies whirling their skinny blue-white arms like spiders while I stood in the corner watching; Francine rolled her eyes at me.

With the help of mascara whose television praise ran as follows: *So effective, a panel of independent experts reported improvement in ninety-seven percent of all women,* Shantelle perfected her new look until she finally got selected to go home with Xing, who roosted in a grand one-bedroom in Tenderloin Heights. As soon as they were in the bedroom, Shantelle lunged to pull up Xing's nightdress as if expecting to discover between her breasts or thighs something to steal . . .—because Shantelle would always be the kind of person who, had she made the journey with the Chosen People to the Promised Land, nourished each day by manna from the Goddess, would still, preferring the unproved visible to the divine Unseen, have worshipped a golden calf. But all she found was what she already possessed. Already disbelieving in that slow and perfect intercourse of tongues in each other's mouths, so satisfying that it seemed (to her at least) that without hands, breasts or sex organs they both still would have felt fulfilled; already forgetting how she used to lay down her head between the lesbian's breasts, weeping easily, until she felt relief, she finally lay down alone, dreaming of cold black crocodile islands beneath the full moon.

How was it? inquired knowing Xenia.

A-one. A shitload better than Neva. Xing, now, she's my stud broad.

Seven dollars, said Francine.

Four lesbians stood at the bar, embracing one another. Francine washed glasses. A tall pale darkhaired lesbian (one of the four) started kissing Xing on the breast of her leather jacket, and the other three laughed *ha-ha-HA!* with their hands punching each other's shoulders. I still remember the knowing wrinkle at the corner of her eyes as Samantha swayed and wriggled. A bespectacled lesbian in plaid started tapping her long pale forefinger in a beer-spill, and the tall lesbian stripped down to her silver tights, swishing back and forth in hopes of alluring our Xing; Shantelle had selected "Happiness Is a Warm Gun" from the jukebox and we all loved it!—And then Xing was playing pool with the bespectacled lesbian.

And now, when everything pertaining to Neva had vanished, although I at least, and there must have been others like me, still awaited her, as if she had merely passed through a swinging door which went on vibrating, Judy came in, and I saw that for her there was no return.

Two nights later she swished into the Y Bar, ordered a bourbon and ginger ale, walked up to Xing's stool and offered herself, thinking: I'm only here to love; that's what Neva says . . .—Once she had been rejected she went peaceably home to instruct herself: Never mind; I'm not working that hard for it; I don't deserve it. I only love Neva, *Neva, Neva*! . . .—after which she played with herself, imagining that Xing had bought her a two-toned gauzy midi outfit with breast-peeps. Following two nights of this, the retired policeman, who had long since returned her pills, was looking bitterly at his darling and demanding: *Who are you fucking now?* But it never got serious, even though the novelty almost made it seem as if the lesbian were blooming or bleeding even more magnificently than before; Judy was already losing the memory of how it had been when she was inside the lesbian, how the lesbian had felt and tasted, but for awhile she held on to the unique topography of her lover's vulva.

If you bring forth what is within you . . . , she recited. But she forgot how the rest of it went.

If you bring forth what is within you . . .

She went home, got high and thought about it. How might she set out to find love for herself, now when there was none? Then she figured out a great joke. She went to the bathroom and chanted to the mirror: *If you bring forth what is within you . . .*

Then she bent over the toilet and tickled her throat.

(As for me, what did I have? I owned *if you don't stand for something . . .* and *listen to the cunt.*)

The retired policeman had given her back that much-faded snapshot of the braided young woman whose name we never knew, the one reaching out both arms from her bed and *Waiting for E., Stanford '74.* She tore it up. Then she flushed it down the toilet.

Late one night she strolled past the Women's Dream Center and into the wide parking lot she knew so well, following the inner side of the fence under the billboard and behind a car to the safely dark place where she had first blown the straight man, spitting his semen into a puddle. What had it been for? And now she continued up to Ellis Street, where she paused outside Glide Memorial to whisper three prayers for the lesbian, one for Shantelle, two for the retired policeman and six for herself. In the interest of cheerfulness she bought herself some five-dollar crystal-blue sunglasses, but they broke on the way home. She walked up Venus Alley, pressed the buzzer and clipclopped upstairs to her lord and master in his queen-sized bed. He was cleaning his ears. Squaring her shoulders, then widening her eyes at him in an expression which he always found idiotic, she said: I'm gonna go on loving you and pretending you love me, because what else do I have anymore?

What else? A whole garbage can's worth of johns.

She burst out laughing. They got shitfaced on Old Crow, and then to take her mind off her dead sweetheart he retold with added details the shining tale of one of his bygone triumphs; it involved an illegal immigrant, three grams of crack cocaine and a child's red dress with a bloodstain two and a half inches long on the left side of the underskirt toward the front; after the happy guilty verdict our transwoman, resting her head on his chest, licked her thumb and turned the coarse, moisture-sucking page of the *National Enquirer* to learn: **DOLLY IN LESBIAN PAYOFF SCANDAL! Singer pulled into GAY SISTER'S EMBEZZLEMENT case.**

10

Vacation time again: He took her to Hollywood!

Emerging from the rental car, they stood on the hot silent curve of Ivanhoe where the stairs went down and down the hill past Judy Garland's house; the gate was open so that they could look into the yard: unkept, with piles of brick. Later she would wonder whether she had mixed up that place with the house on Lakeview Terrace at Armstrong—a smaller house, actually, only a mile from the one on Ivanhoe, with a car in the garage; had she begged him to, the retired policeman might have even run a check on the license plate. In the cell phone photo she took, it had a boxy Frank Lloyd Wrightish look; at first she intended to crop out the limp palm on the corner, but it was so hot; she had gained back nearly all her weight and her slacks clung to her sweet plump thighs, which he kept pinching; it was already almost midday, so where was the traffic? So this was Silver Lake: so gentrified and jolly! . . . and nobody around but Latino gardeners walking from house to house (the kiddies all at school); the retired policeman said this might be the wrong address—Lakeview Terrace and Armstrong, right? They waved at the pink-clad joggerette who pounded toward them on the sandy path that passed for a sidewalk; she declined to wave back. At the next Judy Garland site, on McCadden, which Judy had written *McCaddan* with an "a" instead of an "e," they pulled in on the sidewalk and a man who was walking his dog glared and began pounding on the hood.—*Fuck* you, said the retired policeman; anyhow they couldn't find it amidst all the apartments; on the bright side, they had already learned from the studio tour that the noise of a kiss is added to the soundtrack by somebody lip-smacking his inner elbow, that the tornado in *The Wizard of Oz* was actually a big sock filled with dirt and tied to a revolving fan, and that the Wicked Witch of the West caught on fire when she fell through the trapdoor, after which the studio managers made her drive herself to the hospital. So they turned from Fairfax onto Fountain in hopes of approaching the next house; up on Sunset past Hillcrest it became all trees and hedges, with the houses set well back; Judy had never seen anything so *exclusive.* Around the wide curve with the green mowed median strip he drove them; they crossed Foothill Road and then Alpine Drive; finally on Ladera they saw the signs for movie star maps. Bel Air Road was all gate and no sidewalk, two-tiered hedges and mown grass, castles going up the hill and right on Bellagio Road. Judy was tremendously impressed.

They were high above the statewide drought, humming past green grass and hedges and trees, with gardeners kneeling worshipfully over flowerbeds. As they wound up Stone Canyon, the road narrowed, then dead-ended in a no trespassing sign and four gates; the security guard said he didn't know nothing about no Judy Gurrand. So they drove on into the shade of cool ivied trees. A blonde who was walking her dog alongside the lovely tree-ferns thrust out the palm of her hand so imperiously that they stopped in awe to let her pass. Their adventure continued into the raw arid hills behind it all; there was a bamboo grove behind a fence at number 1231, then they were on the other side of Sunset, swooping into South Mapleton Drive, Holmby Hills, by a driveway which ascended to a gate; it should have been number 144, but nothing remained between 130 and 200, the latter impressing both of them with gas flames in coach lamps on either side of an opaque gate, and lovely twisty trees with red flowers growing out of them, with a mansion beyond.—It's another world, said the retired policeman, struggling to be nonchalant; well, he was correct: Even the gardeners were slow and quiet, wandering from hedge to hedge with their leafblowers shouldered like ceremonial rifles.

11

As for Shantelle, her rendezvous with Xing might have been her last triumph. Although I do remember how through a narrow gap in the curtains the morning sunshine enriched her luxuriant reddish-blonde ringlets, which her hairdresser had already striped with long edge-strands of peach and of chestnut—half of her head remained in shadow, and there its most conspicuous hair-stripes were a pallid white, while the most noticeable parts of her sunstruck hair were the darknesses between curls—she had already begun to look old, and the booze jacked her up more than before. On certain midafternoons I would now catch her softly murmuring into the mirror: Goodnight, Neva . . .—In the last days of Xing our discussion of the fentanyl became a sort of disagreement, and Francine, the only one who ever paid attention, saw the transwoman's look of excitement when Shantelle punched me in the face. On my return from the hospital two days later, the retired policeman summarized the next chapter: Francine had risen up instantly from behind the bar and tapped her on the side of the head with a baseball bat, then dragged her away as lovingly as a crocodile. Shantelle got eighty-sixed for good. (No one believes me anyway, she said.) By the time the Y Bar closed in 2017 and Karen Strand's high school finally "updated" its mascot from an Apache Indian to some more progressive entity, Shantelle had gone positively sketchy. Now where was she supposed to do her business? Just after the Gay Pride parade of 2019, Xenia, who was amused by her and sort of liked her, claimed to have seen her in San Mateo alongside a tranny whore whose breasts had been installed in Tijuana and whose penis still functioned, but Xenia was sometimes a bullshitter and had told me a comparable story about herself; and the retired policeman now informed me that Shantelle got arrested both for an outstanding warrant, for which she was supposed to serve sixteen days, and also for a probation violation, for which she should have served thirty days, so that added up to forty-six days, which in the interest of fairness they rounded up to eighty-six, so that she lost her longterm hotel room with all her possessions, together with her security deposit, and accordingly became homeless. Here is what I know:

Once upon a time, an old black woman who wore a long dark blanket tucked around her face and dragging in the street behind her used to ask each person at the streetcar stop for matches or cigarettes. When they said no, she sometimes asked again and again. One day she boarded the L Taraval streetcar and sat down facing a young man who high-fived her. When the security guard came to check tickets, everyone but her had one.

The guard said: You'll have to get off here. Let's go.

The woman ignored him.

Get off, said the security guard. *Get off. Now.*

She sat there laughing. The man who had high-fived her laughed along.

The security guard spoke into his radio. Then he stood back, waiting. Nothing happened all the way to Van Ness station. The woman and her friend shrieked with laughter.

Then a policeman boarded.—Let's go, he said.

The woman ignored him. She told us all: There ain't no other woman in the whole wide world but Neva. Nobody.

The officer put his hand on her shoulder, and she screamed. Stepping back, he rolled on a pair of black rubber gloves, then jerked the blanket off her, presumably to make sure she carried no weapons. She began thrashing and hollering.

Let's not make an issue of this, he said.

He pulled her to her feet, while the slender, fragile young security guard stood triumphant. He marched her off the streetcar and sat her down on a bench. Another officer strode behind her, in case of trouble. Then our double doors closed, we hummed westward and that was the last I saw of Shantelle. *Thine enemy the Serpent hath been given over to the fire.*

12

Judy Garland once said: *I don't believe dying is the end,* which proved true—for the transwoman retained the lesbian's torn blouse that still smelled like her. The retired policeman smiled sadly whenever he saw her snuggling it; he wasn't jealous anymore.

And as for me, I never forgot that I had been nothing before her and I was nothing after, so what did I have to complain about? I did weep, if not as easily or copiously as the transwoman, who was expert at what she considered to be this important feminine skill. Then I drank down another rum and sodapop. Trying to remember the two of us, which is to say all of us, and the way that she used to suck the breaths out of our mouths and then breathe back in; longing to remember better than I could, I could almost see a naked man and woman, carved of whitestone, her hand on his arm, her breasts high and alert, their heads both gone.—Now as I lie here with my jacket zipped up to my chin, lurking like a lesbian who has not yet come out and shivering beneath the blankets while the fever blows flutetunes up and down my spine, loyalty insists that without her I shall never be warm again; but loyalty will also freeze to death. If it were truly revealed to me how many of us on this earth have been raped I would not believe it, because I could not bear to. And if I had it in me to look down into all the things that men and women do to each other, what then? Better to stare through the ceiling with my bloodshot eyes and pretend that I will never get over Neva.

In her way she was as successful as Nancy Kerrigan, who after winning her first bronze Olympic medal got commercial endorsements from Society Airlines and Smirchee's Tastee Soup. Moreover, she behaved well until the end. All the same, some of us now began badmouthing the dead lesbian. Why not? She was guilty for everything.

13

Let's keep it light!—as Judy Garland wrote in a letter to *Motion Picture*, right around the time she was preparing to kill herself.—I have many times been as lonely as the transwoman used to be when kneeling down in a stack of wet newspapers in a glaring humming laundry room and orally pleasuring a stranger for money or sometimes just for degradation; I too have gone over the hill and into quietude, listening to the rain on Powell and Clay, the cable car wires marking time, the round portholes of dryers dark and still in the laundromat at the Parker Hotel; all the while—*fuck*, yeah!—I've kept it light! When we lay out a dead girl's grave goods two thousand years after the fact, we're frequently lucky enough to collect a few of her lost memories which might as well have been lovely irregular coins with images of vulvas, insects and hydras; and these, or the hope of these, keeps it light, or something. So I tried hoping; I excelled at that. A nearly empty cable car came groaning up the tracks toward the horizon of blinking red lights, hesitated, then sank over the edge.

Why I should have ever gotten depressed, I certainly don't know. You people have proved to me that I've got thousands of friends the world over.

Judy Garland

AFTERWORD

This novel completes my "transgender trilogy," which also includes *The Book of Dolores* and a still unpublished tale entitled *How You Are.*

Most of *The Lucky Star* takes place shortly before and after the legalization of gay marriage in 2015. (For slatternly narrative purposes I have stirred in anachronisms from 2016 and 2017.) Some bars and apartment towers are imaginary; likewise certain streets and alleys. Despising product appellations of all kinds, I found cruel pleasure in coining appropriately idiotic brand names for liquors, junk foods, retail establishments and cars.

As for my characters, although they too are imaginary, I seem to have met several of them—for instance, the wise and helpful young lesbian in Seattle who told me that "consent is a huge part of our feminine culture," and that "there's never a time when you would not respect boundaries." (I awarded her an island and magic powers.) This is a tale about the violation of boundaries, and about those strategies, inspiring, pathetic, sacrificial, unhealthy and otherwise, through which the violated try to go on living.

Given my subject, how could *The Lucky Star* not address unluckiness? I believe that many of us lead sad lives without knowing it, and that our society is sick. "Celebrity idolification" and near-impossible standards for female beauty cause still more sorrow for those who feel saved from utter anonymity only by their own ugliness. The commodification of life has been further debased by an education in incuriosity. These American values color the thinking of all classes. The Hollywood actress, the showgirl in Las Vegas and the transgender streetwalker in San Francisco all seek to "sell themselves," performing allure in hopes of hooking the desires of others. Thus the ideal, and some people achieve it, for awhile. By definition, the majority fails. Judy Garland's adoring public can neither be nor have her; they can only yearn for her. As for Judy Garland herself, I wouldn't live her life for a million applause generators.

In short, *The Lucky Star* may be my most cynical book. Sexual abuse, street crime, poverty, illness, police violence and addiction saunter through its pages, dressed in the lurid livery of false consciousness.

But no matter how damaged we are, we can all aspire to love others and ourselves. This is why I sought out stories from women who perform their own versions of femininity, publicly and vulnerably: trannies, lesbians, showgirls. I found these research interviews to be quite simply uplifting. Like my characters, the interviewees deserve a far better world than they find. The bigotry, shame and self-hatred that so many of them have faced would have crushed me. In affirming to the world who they are and whom they love, they exemplify a beautiful female strength which occasionally moved me to tears. Two old women at the GLBT center in Las Vegas were so direct, self-accepting, funny and relentlessly defiant that I could not help but love them. Meanwhile a middle-aged retired dancer (now a housewife) shared with me the bravery, glamor and drudgery of her former life; a young activist trusted me with the tale of her first girlfriend; a women's studies professor described her experiences with puberty and shame. Without exception, these women implicitly or explicitly encouraged me to pursue the life-affirming question *how does one go forward?* The best compliment that I could pay them all was to allow a few patches of light into *The Lucky Star.*

And so nearly all of the female coming-of-age stories, straight or otherwise, and of course the accounts of sexual abuse, come straight from the lips of those who helped me with this book. To be sure, the characters are composites. For example, the biography of the transwoman Judy is partially constructed from memoirs in the archives of the GLBT Historical Society in San Francisco and partially from interviews, all seasoned with appropriations from Judy Garland's life.

Since my outlook is reliably dark, the matter of how to help Judy blossom in her new identity perplexed me. When I asked my genderqueer friends in Seattle what advice they would give this flamboyantly self-despising victim, they said: "We'd tell her to embrace her inner disgustingness." And this became a key to the novel.—I would be very proud if anyone who suffers the shame and isolation associated with nonconforming sexual identity were to gain any hope from *The Lucky Star.*

Of course it cannot be a *tremendously* hopeful book. Maybe I should have choked down Shantelle's fentanyl instead of writing it. But people can disagree in good faith as to whether Christ's story was happy or sad; so why not respect the ambiguity of my heroine Neva? In her I tried to imagine a sexualized female Jesus, who, like her original, must have been tremendously damaged, but radically powerful thanks to unstinting self-sacrifice.

Now let me tell you a secret: The real title of this novel is *The Lesbian.*

When I begin to write a book, its seed is nearly always a title which "just came to me." And this one came to me so fittingly! Here we have a parable about labeling and discrimination. Of course *The Lesbian*'s main character is not a lesbian, which is exactly the point. And every time she appears, the mock-portentous echo of her appellation with the title and the many homophobic epigraphs should have magnified the sad irony of her situation.

After more than a year of pressure from Viking, pressure which finally became, so I was told, unanimous, I capitulated, offering four second-rank titles from which the shadowy naming committee could choose. I gave in because I had already pushed this generous publisher to the limit by refusing to cut my last (and typically not very saleable) book. I did so with the urging of many who loved me, out of worry that my longterm stubbornness might destroy my career. I did so because, like Neva, I sometimes lose myself in putting up and shutting up. Most of all, I did so after gentle but remorseless requests from my friend and editor Paul Slovak, who has fought many battles for me, and, like me, is getting old and tired. Paul, I did it for you.

This little defeat is unimportant to anyone but me. Or is it? Why was Viking so insistent? Why should it be unacceptable for me to publish a book with the word "lesbian" in the title? Would I have gotten away with it had I been born with different equipment between my legs? What does my surrender say about our time? What will be forbidden next?

Paul, I did it for you. (Now I've come around to liking *The Lucky Star.* I can even tell myself I picked it.) But maybe, just maybe, I did it after inhaling a whiff of herd-fear, which weakened me. That is why whenever *The Lucky Star* meets my eyes I am going to feel sad and, what is worse, ashamed.

Reader, please do keep my secret. Don't tell anyone what the real title is.

WTV, Sacramento, Las Vegas, Los Angeles
and a few islands, 2014–19

NOTES ON SOURCES

EPIGRAPHS

ix "Since there are so many *literal* gaps in the tattered texts . . ."—Jane McIntosh Snyder, *Lesbian Desire in the Lyrics of Sappho* (New York: Columbia University Press, Between Men—Between Women ser., 1997), p. 3. [By the way, I have dropped in a few allusions to Sappho here and there. If you like, you may even find specific correspondences between us of the Y Bar and Sappho's lovers Irana, Atthis, Dika—how I remember the garlands in her hair!—Gongula, Kleis, Andromeda, Anaktoria and Brachea.]

ix "And that is how Madhavi was born . . ."—Prince Ilangô Adigal, *Shilappadikaram* (*The Ankle Bracelet*), trans. Alain Daniélou (New York: New Directions, 1965; orig. wr. *ca.* 171 A.D.), p. 27.

YOU WHO WERE LOVED ABOVE ALL OTHERS

3 Epigraph: "I, the servant of God, am thankful to Him . . ."—*The Perfumed Garden of the Shaykh Nefzawi*, trans. Sir Richard F. Burton, ed. Alan Hull Walton (New York: G. P. Putnam's Sons, 1964; orig. trans. 1886; orig. wr. betw. 1394 and 1433), p. 73.

6 Kathy Horvath *versus* Martina Navratilova—*The New York Times*, Sunday, June 4, 2017, sports sec. p. 6 (Cindy Shmerler, "The 1 in Navratilova's 86-1 Season"). According to Louise Allen, *The Lesbian Idol: Martina, KD and the Consumption of Lesbian Masculinity* (London: Cassell, 1997), Navratilova was "a lesbian star." Hence the sexualization of her persona, as when (p. 15) a certain young girl watched Navratilova on television and studied "where her thighs met the line of her underwear."

9 the anecdote about the studio writing Judy Garland out of *Showboat*—Information from *Judy Garland on Judy Garland: Interviews and Encounters*, ed. Randy L. Schmidt (Chicago: Chicago Review Press / An A Cappella Book, 2014), p. 175.

10 The straight man's ability to see underground—Actually, an attribute of Lynceus. Apollonius of Rhodes, *The Voyage of Argo* (*The Argonautica*), trans. R. V. Rieu (New York: Penguin Classics, 1971, rev. of 1959 ed.; orig. wr. 3rd cent. B.C.), p. 39.

17 "And the cloud of the hymen is like a shining emerald."—Willis Barnstone and Marvin Meyer, ed., *The Gnostic Bible* (Boston: Shambhala, 2003), p. 463 ("The Paraphrase of Shem": "Shem Ascends, In Mind, and Recites the Litany").

18 "the ancient lyric" of "long-dead Anacreon"—Somewhat after David A. Campbell, ed. and trans., *Greek Lyric II: Anacreon, Anacreontea, Choral Lyric from Olympus to Alcman* (Cambridge, Massachusetts: Loeb Classical Library LCL143, 1988), p. 235 (*Anocreontea*, 57).

21 Sandra's mermaid fantasies—Twenty years before he got bewitched by his true love, which is to say his daughter's young governess, the Russian poet F. Tyutchev advised us to *hide / your own dreaming* because *a thought expressed turns false.* Sandra now lived what some hacks would approve of as "a rich fantasy life" while other hacks would pronounce it neurotic. Within Tyutchev's nineteenth-century skull, secret feelings once rose in gemlike constellations where worms now patrol. He asserted that our selves were complete worlds—so stay in them and keep their contents quiet! What became of this philosophy once he said *I love you* to the beautiful Elena Deniseva? Fourteen years and three children later, she died. Did he then return to the starry nights within his head? And if so, how joyful was his solitude? I would submit that he found the darkness sad and cold. In the case of Sandra, dreamy images of mermaids were quite good enough for her time of life, but Neva might well spoil them forever.

CHILD STAR

22 Epigraph: "Association with women is the basic element of good manners."—Johann Wolfgang von Goethe, *Maxims and Reflections*, ed. Peter Hutchinson, trans. Elisabeth Stopp (New York: Penguin, 1998), p. 5 (no. 31).

22 Epigraph: "Well, Judy Garland isn't sophisticated . . ."—*Judy Garland on Judy Garland: Interviews and Encounters*, ed. Randy L. Schmidt (Chicago: Chicago Review Press / An A Cappella Book, 2014), p. 52 (James Carson, *Modern Screen*, January 1940).

22 "The Devil may shape a witch into a wolf . . ."—Johanna Sinisalo, ed., *The Dedalus Book of Finnish Fantasy*, trans. David Hackston, p. 12 (Aino Kallas, *Sudenmorsian* [Wolf Bride], 1928).

22 "What color was your daughter's hair?"—John G. Wilson, B.A., ed., *The Trial of Jeannie Donald* (London: William Hodge and Company, Limited, 1953), p. 68. This murder case informs several of the tropes in *The Lesbian.* The trial was July 16–19, 1934.

23 Judy Garland used to envy Joan Crawford for her *long, glittering fingernails*—Information and direct quote from Schmidt, p. 104.

23 "Her hair is a little lighter with just the right touch of gold . . ."—Information and direct quote from Schmidt, p. 32 n (199).

24 Attitude of Karen's mother—Samuel Johnson, *Selected Essays*, ed. David Womersley (New York: Penguin Books, 2003; essays orig. pub. 1739–61), p. 250 (*The Rambler*, No. 148, Saturday, 17 August 1751): "The unjustifiable severity of a parent is loaded with the aggravation, that those whom he injures are always in his sight."

25 that doublepage spread of Natalie Wood who in a dark outfit posed—Manoah Bowman, *Natalie Wood: Reflections on a Legendary Life* (Philadelphia: Running Press, 2016), p. 46.

25 Description of the woman who had bitten her six-year-old daughter—*Coal Valley News* (West Virginia), Wednesday, September 4, 2013, p. A1 (Fred Pace, "Bloomingrose woman arrested on felony child abuse charges").

26 "Now tell me this . . ."—Schmidt, pp. 4–5 (interview with Wally Beery, 1935, slightly abbreviated).

26 "Wait until you hear her sing . . ."—Schmidt, p. 6 (Wally Beery, "Shell Chateau Hour" interview, 1935).

26 "Judy Garland, child wonder of the screen . . ."—Schmidt, p. 7 (Victorial Johnson, *Modern Movies*, August 1937).

27 at eight years of age the daughter of the Dragon King became a Buddha.—*The Threefold Lotus Sutra*, trans. Bunno Kato, Yoshiro Tamura and Kojiro Myasaka, with revs. (Tokyo: Kosei Publishing Co., 1995 repr. of 1975 ed.; orig. mss. *ca.* 4th cent.?), pp. 212–13: "'. . . Behold me become a Buddha even more rapidly than that!' At that moment the entire congregation saw the dragon's daughter suddenly transformed into a male, perfect in bodhisattva-deeds." (For consistency I have capitalized the original "buddha" and "buddhas" throughout *The Lucky Star.*)

28 The tale of the Queen of Spain—Somewhat after *Italian Folktales*, selected and retold by Italo Calvino, trans. George Martin (New York: Harcourt Inc., 1980; orig. Italian ed. 1956), pp. 345–47 ("The Palace of the Doomed Queen," Siena).

28 and there was even the time when she took her to the beauty parlor to get turned into a blonde.—Other child stars' mothers did their respective best. Consider Natalie Wood's mother, who, they say, chauffeured the sixteen-year-old to the casting couch at Château Marmont, where the director, "old enough to be Natalie's father," after penetrating the girl became a good influence who "taught the actress to trust her own instincts" (Bowman, p. 43).

29 "That's how I see Hollywood . . . as the place that gives everybody a chance."—Schmidt, p. 22.

29–30 Memories of the Pacific campaign—Somewhat after Eric Bergerud, *Touched with Fire: The Land War in the South Pacific* (New York: Viking, 1996), pp. 413–14 (testimony of Bill Crooks, Australian Imperial Force), pp. 447–48 (testimony of Robert Kennington).

30 The tale of Shirley Temple and Santa Claus—Paul F. Boller, Jr., and Ronald L. Davies, *Hollywood Anecdotes* (New York: William Morrow & Co., 1987), p. 153.

32 Natalie Wood: "Woman of the Year" at ten and "Child of the Year" at eleven—Bowman, p. 39.

WHEN AN INNOCENT GIRL ABANDONS HERSELF

37 Epigraph: "When an innocent girl abandons herself . . ."—Frank S. Caprio, M.D., *Female Homosexuality: A Psychodynamic Study of Lesbianism* (New York: The Citadel Press, 1954), p. 144.

37 Epigraph: "Nobody ever taught me what to do on a stage."—*Judy Garland on Judy Garland: Interviews and Encounters*, ed. Randy L. Schmidt (Chicago: Chicago Review Press / An A Cappella Book, 2014), p. 182 (Michael Drury, *Cosmopolitan*, January 1951).

42 Lana Turner: "It's very difficult, growing up in public."—Schmidt, p. 142 (Adela Rogers St. John, *Photoplay*, April 1945).

43 "Christ Almighty, the girl reacted to the slightest bit of kindness . . ."—David Shipman, *Judy Garland: The Secret Life of An American Legend* (New York: Hyperion, 1992), p. 142 (Joseph Mankiewicz).

47 the Country Women's Festival in Mendocino—I am thinking of the one in 1974, mentioned in: Gay Lesbian Bisexual Transgender Historical Society, San Francisco (GLBTHS). Linda Welcome papers (2008-12), carton 1.

YOU SEEM A LITTLE SAD

51 Epigraph: "And Virgo, hiding her disdainful breast . . ."—Emrys Jones, comp. and ed., *The New Oxford Book of Sixteenth Century Verse* (New York: Oxford University Press, 1991), p. 139 (from "The Mirror for Magistrates").

51 Epigraph: "Ah, Catulla, dearest . . ."—Dudley Fitts, *Sixty Poems of [Marcus Valerius] Martial[is] in Translation* (New York: Harcourt, Brace & World, 1967 repr. of 1956 ed.; orig. wr. 1st cent. A.D.), p. 7, and facing Latin on p. 6 ("To Catulla," VIII:54]). Fitts translated the

original as "Ah, dearest, that you were less lovely or less vile." Since the Latin reads: "O quam te fieri, Catulla, uellem formosam minus aut magis pudicam!," I have inserted the woman's name in my "retranslation" and swapped out Fitts's period for an exclamation point.

52 Footnote: Zeus's abhorrence of murder and support of murderers—Information from Apollonius of Rhodes, *The Voyage of Argo* [*The Argonautica*], trans. R. V. Rieu (New York: Penguin Classics, 1971, rev. of 1959 ed.; orig. wr. 3rd cent. B.C.), p. 52.

53 "she had grown so accomplished at not feeling whatever pain inhabited her . . ."—Kristine L. Falco, Psy. D., *Psychotherapy with Lesbian Clients: Theory into Practice* (New York: Brunner/Mazel, 1991), p. 30: "Before long, a lesbian who is used to monitoring her every word and passing for what is acceptable will be unable to determine what her own feelings really are." I have heard a similar aphorism both from and about victims of rape and incest.

54 The Madonna could restore the sight to any princess . . .—Information (slightly distorted by WTV) from *Italian Folktales*, selected and retold by Italo Calvino, trans. George Martin (New York: Harcourt Inc., 1980; orig. Italian ed. 1956), p. 513 ("Serpent King").

55 "Don't worry, Karen. You're not a lesbian."—Falco, p. 43, quoting "Elena's" therapist: "Don't worry, you're not a lesbian."

THE ISLAND

57 Epigraph: "It is more than a coincidence that inverts have a fondness for islands."—Frank S. Caprio, M.D., *Female Homosexuality: A Psychodynamic Study of Lesbianism* (New York: The Citadel Press, 1954), p. 65. I probably should have set this chapter in Los Angeles instead, for as the same source shockingly reveals: "While visiting Hollywood, California, I learned that the incidence of male and female homosexuality in this area is relatively high and is attributed to the influx of persons with artistic temperaments." Who would have thought it?

57 Epigraph: "And from this moment on I shall strip myself . . ."—James M. Robinson, gen. ed., *The Nag Hammadi Library in English*, [3rd] rev. ed., trans. & introduced by members of the Coptic Gnostic Library Project . . . (San Francisco: HarperSanFrancisco, 1990 repr. of 1978 ed.; orig. Coptic codices wr. bef.-during 4th cent.), p. 36 ("The Apocryphon of James," bef. 314).

59 Judy Garland: "I'd like to have been part of that life where all women . . ."—*Judy Garland on Judy Garland: Interviews and Encounters*, ed. Randy L. Schmidt (Chicago: Chicago Review Press / An A Cappella Book, 2014), p. 133 (Judy Garland, *Movieland*, December 1943).

61–74 The magic doings on the island—Valerius Flaccus, *Argonautica*, trans. J. H. Mozley (Cambridge, Massachusetts: Harvard University Press / Loeb Classical Library, 1936 rev. repr. of 1943 ed.; orig. Latin ms. *ca.* 70–90 A.D.), p. xiii (introduction): "It is unfortunate from the modern point of view that the epic convention demanded, or at any rate permitted, the employment of supernatural machinery to effect anything so human as falling in love . . . ," p. 72+.

64 the girl would be a chosen instrument of hers to carry her love before woman and man . . . —Acts 9:15–16: "Go, for he is a chosen instrument of mine to carry my name before the Gentiles . . . ; for I will show him how much he must suffer for the sake of my name."

65 And the old lady cut away from her the things which should be cut from her.—Cf. *The Book of the Dead: The Hieroglyphic Transcript and Translation into English of the Ancient Egyptian Papyrus of Ani*, [trans.,] intro. and commentary by E. A. Wallis Budge (New York: Gramercy Books, 1999; orig. pub. 1895), p. 400: "And they have cut away from him the things which should be cut from him." [This source henceforth cited as *The Egyptian Book of the Dead.*]

66 whatever she could not cure in herself she must enlarge.—After Thomas à Kempis, *The Imitation of Christ*, trans. Leo Sherley-Price (New York: Penguin, 1987 repr. of 1952 ed.;

orig. Latin version wr. *ca.* 1413), p. 44: "Whatever a man is unable to correct in himself and others, he should bear patiently until God ordains otherwise."

66 "Grant what no woman has seen and what has not entered into any woman's heart."—After James M. Robinson, gen. ed., *The Nag Hammadi Library in English*, p. 27 ("The Prayer of the Apostle Paul," 2nd–3rd cent.): "Grant what no angel eye has seen and . . . what has not entered into the human heart . . ."

66 When the old lady had done away the offensive thing which had been on the girl—Somewhat after *The Egyptian Book of the Dead*, p. 404 ("The Third Arit").

69 "She shall have no inheritance . . ."—Slightly altered from Ezekiel 44:28.

69 Judy Garland: "I have a machine in my throat . . ."—Schmidt, p. xxiii. In those days most of us sought out love in the most crowded places—because while prowling for gemstones on that same cut in the mountain where rival rockhounds also pry decreases everyone's probability of finding a lovely specimen, love-hunters actually increase each other's likelihood of success. You see, most of us craved the same thing: ourselves, reflected in each other. One would think we could have won the prize by staying home and looking in the mirror—as I myself so often did, switching out the mirror for a rum and sodapop. But loving the lesbian taught me that self-love was too easy. As Judy Garland's mother explained to the world (Schmidt, p. 14 [Helen Champion]): *She's worked hard because she's so interested in getting ahead.* Meanwhile the transwoman toiled to look even three percent worth loving; while poor Francine was condemned to balance out the cash register, and every day the stage hands had to paint the Tin Woodman's face with ten dollars' worth of genuine silver. What a world, what a world . . . !—But what was love, and how could we know it if ever we found it? Some say that fire is neither matter nor energy, but whatever arises between them. That description satisfies me far less than the fantasies I get when altering the colors of the flames by sprinkling in this or that chemical salt . . . —and to say that love is something which flickers between two people is to describe it only from the outside. If I could only be one of those two . . . ! . . .—In the darkness of those places, the ones in need were frequently prepared to need one another, but when their needs failed to complement what their adorable rescuers gave them, love turned sad or even dangerous. Many began by lying out of hope or longing, then lied out of cowardice. They might go on pretending to love when they were bored, repulsed or worse. Any romance might end monstrously, after which both perpetrators blamed each other. (Daily cost of the Tin Woodman's facepaint—Schmidt, p. 44 [Judy Garland as told to Gladys Hall, *Child Life,* 1939].)

72 the stone Etruscan woman who contains human ashes within herself—Circa 400 B.C. Several tomb-tropes in this book derive from visits to the Museo Egizio di Torino in 2009 and 2012.

73 The assertion of Audre Lorde—Somewhat after *Sister Outsider: Essays and Speeches by Audre Lorde* (Berkeley: Crossing Press, 2007 rev. of 1984 ed.), p. 45 ("Scratching the Surface: Some Notes on Barriers to Women and Loving"). On p. 59 ("Uses of the Erotic: The Erotic as Power"), Lorde writes: "To refuse to be conscious of what we are feeling at any time, no matter how comfortable that might seem, is to deny a large part of the experience, and to allow ourselves to be reduced to the pornographic, the abused, and the absurd," which I have paraphrased in the old lady's admonition to "never forget your feelings."

IT'S ALL BEEN WONDERFUL

75 Epigraph: "It's all been wonderful."—*Judy Garland on Judy Garland: Interviews and Encounters*, ed. Randy L. Schmidt (Chicago: Chicago Review Press / An A Cappella Book, 2014), p. 216 (Roberta Orniston, *Photoplay*, October 1945).

75 Epigraph: "There is no law prohibiting a person . . ."—John P. Kenney, Ph.D., and John B. Williams, LL.M., M.S. and P.A., *Police Operations: Policies and Procedures: 400 Field Situations with Solutions*, 2nd ed. (Springfield, Illinois: Charles C. Thomas, 1968), p. 133.

75 Biographical details on the young Judy Garland—Schmidt, pp. xv, xvii, 3 (Wally Beery, "Shell Chateau Hour" interview, 1935), 7; (Victoria Johnson, *Modern Movies*, 1937), 14; (Helen Champion, *Screen Juveniles*, 1937), 21; (Gladys Hall, *Motion Picture*, 1938), 36–37; (May Mann, *Screenland*, 1939), 58; (James Reid, *Motion Picture*, 1940).

76 she had been well taught to take the wills of others for her own.—Thomas à Kempis, *The Imitation of Christ*, trans. Leo Sherley-Price (New York: Penguin, 1987 repr. of 1952 ed.; orig. Latin version wr. *ca.* 1413), p. 124: "Resolve to do the will of others rather than your own."

78 opener of all our locks—And here is an appropriate place to mention that a dozen-odd phrases concerning Neva have been looted, with and without further mutilation, from the "Accadian Hymn to Ishtar" in R. de Rohan Barondes, M.D., *Garden of the Gods: Mesopotamia, 5,000 B.C.* (Boston: Christopher Publishing House, 1957), p. 227.

78 Judy Garland: "I have a private instructor . . ."—Schmidt, p. 56 (James Carson, *Modern Screen*, 1940). Her name-switch was hardly unique. Natalie Wood, for instance, was formerly Natasha Gurdin, and before that Natasha Zakharenko (Manoah Bowman, *Natalie Wood: Reflections on a Legendary Life* [Philadelphia: Running Press, 2016], p. 13).

BUT I FEEL LIKE A TERRIBLE PERSON

80 Epigraph: "Dr. La Forrest Potter of New York believes . . ."—Frank S. Caprio, M.D., *Female Homosexuality: A Psychodynamic Study of Lesbianism* (New York: The Citadel Press, 1954), 146.

80 Epigraph: "What we're really scared of . . ."—*Judy Garland on Judy Garland: Interviews and Encounters*, ed. Randy L. Schmidt (Chicago: Chicago Review Press / An A Cappella Book, 2014), p. 216 (Judy Garland, *Coronet*, February 1955).

83 What she needed to do would happen even of itself . . .—This and several other such word-strings have been stolen from the testimony of Joan of Arc, then mutilated to fit my purposes.

NEVA

86 Epigraph: "She still takes her Teddy Bear to bed . . ."—*Judy Garland on Judy Garland: Interviews and Encounters*, ed. Randy L. Schmidt (Chicago: Chicago Review Press / An A Cappella Book, 2014), p. 20 (Gladys Hall, *Motion Picture*, January 1938).

86 Epigraph: "I never played with dolls . . ."—Schmidt, p. 84 (Judy Garland as told to Gladys Hall, *Screenland*, December 1940).

86 Epigraph: "Mom wants me to be safe . . ."—Kathryn Springer, *The Dandelion Field* (Grand Rapids, Michigan: Zondervan, 2014), p. 96.

86 Judy Garland: "I think women get themselves mixed up . . ."—Schmidt, p. 164 (Judy Garland, *Screenland*, October 1946).

WHO WE WERE

88 Epigraph: "And in my case there is no question of performance . . ."—Jean Stein, *West of Eden: An American Place* (New York: Random House, 2016), p. 191 (chapter on Jennifer Jones). The letter is undated, but the answering telegram is from 1953.

88 Epigraph: "It is natural that when one thinks of sex . . ."—Michele Eliot, ed., *Female Sexual Abuse of Children* (New York: Guilford Press, 1994 repr. of orig. 1993 British ed.), p. 85 (Hilary Eldridge, "Barbara's Story—A Mother Who Sexually Abused").

89 "She looks healthy and happy . . ."—*Judy Garland on Judy Garland: Interviews and Encounters*, ed. Randy L. Schmidt (Chicago: Chicago Review Press / An A Cappella Book, 2014), p. 84 (Judy Garland as told to Gladys Hill, *Screenland*, December 1940).

90 Judy Garland: "If she loses her sense of perspective . . ."—Schmidt, p. 162 (Judy Garland, *Screenland*, October 1946).

90–91 I remember that she stood just within our darkness as if she were waiting for her pupils to enlarge so that she could see us in . . . our various lonely self-tortures.—Cf. Serge A. Zhenkovsky, ed. and comp., *Medieval Russia's Epics, Chronicles and Tales*, rev. ed. (New York: E. P. Dutton, 1974; orig. ed. 1973), p. 154 (Anonymous, "The Visitation to the Torments by the Mother of God" [or, "The Descent of the Virgin into Hell"], 12th cent.): "And the Holy Virgin said: 'Let the darkness be dispersed that I may see the torment.'"

96 "Show yourself so submissive and humble . . ."—Thomas à Kempis, *The Imitation of Christ*, trans. Leo Sherley-Price (New York: Penguin, 1987 repr. of 1952 ed.; orig. Latin version wr. *ca.* 1413), pp. 110–11.

WHAT SHE DID TO US

97 Epigraph: "God, the magnificent, has said: 'Women are your field . . .'"—*The Perfumed Garden of the Shaykh Nefzawi*, trans. Sir Richard F. Burton, ed. Alan Hull Walton (New York: G. P. Putnam's Sons, 1964; orig. trans. 1886; orig. wr. betw. 1394 and 1433), p. 129.

97 Epigraph: "Unhindered by any ambiguity . . ."—Colette, *The Pure and the Impure*, trans. Herma Briffault (New York: New York Review Books, 2000 rev. repr. of 1996 ed.; orig. French ed. 1941), p. 97.

97 "I was born in Murfreesboro, Tennessee . . ."—*Judy Garland on Judy Garland: Interviews and Encounters*, ed. Randy L. Schmidt (Chicago: Chicago Review Press / An A Cappella Book, 2014), p. 22.

99 the gospel of truth is joy.—James M. Robinson, gen. ed., *The Nag Hammadi Library in English*, p. 40 ("The Gospel of Truth," 2nd cent.?).

THE STREAM OF PLEASURE

113 Epigraph: "And first, upon thee lovely shall she smile . . ."—Emrys Jones, comp. and ed., *The New Oxford Book of Sixteenth Century Verse* (New York: Oxford University Press, 1991), p. 60 ("Certain metres written by master Thomas More in his youth for 'The Book of Fortune,' and caused them to be printed in the beginning of that book").

113 Epigraph: "Authorities and investigators are not in complete agreement . . ."—Margaret Sanger, *Happiness in Marriage* (New York: Blue Ribon Books, 1926), p. 155.

113 What Judy Garland's ghostwriter saw—Schmidt, p. xv.

117 "UNSERE LÄCHERLICHE HUNDEFRAU KOMMT WIEDER!"—"OUR LAUGHABLE DOG-WOMAN RETURNS!"

119 Information on the Wicked Witch re: Judy Garland's amphetamines—Joan Beck Coulson, *Always for Judy: Witness to the Joy and Genius of Judy Garland* (Elmira, California: Yarnscombe Books, 2014), p. 55.

120 I felt as if everything were burning! . . . my thoughts glowed red and yellow with lust.—Cf. Paul Carus, comp. [and trans.?], *The Gospel of Buddha* (Guernsey, U.K.: Studio Press

Ltd. / The Guernsey Press Co. Ltd., 1995; orig. ed. 1915; n.d. given for original texts), p. 64 (the famous Fire Sermon): "Everything, O Jatilas, is burning. The eye is burning, all the senses are burning, thoughts are burning. They are burning with the fire of lust." (The Jatilas were a group of ascetic Brahmins.)

121 A Japanese asked Francine how he could buy a used pair of the lesbian's panties for fifty dollars.—Price information from an item on "Kokunbuncho, the largest sex industry area in Tohoku," in the *Asahi Shinbun*, n.d., trans. for WTV by Ms. Kawai Takako, *ca.* 2014. Called "Buncho," in Aoba ward of Sendai City, this "red-light zone where 60,000 people [including many decontamination workers] come and go on the weekends" employs a certain hostess. "To earn pocket money, she sold her underwear at 5000 yen [= about U.S. $50] and 20 nude photos at 10,000 yen. 'I didn't feel guilty. I felt secure to know that someone needs me' . . . After graduating from senior high school, she became a bus guide in Kyoto. 'I wanted attention from others.' But due to her health condition, she quit after 2 years." In Sendai a high school friend hooked her up with a "sex trade shop." "Soon she got used to be kissed by a middle-aged man who is a stranger to her and her breasts touched . . . 'From time to time I have a customer who I would hate but this is my job.' In half a year she became the No. 1 of the shop."

121 Judy Garland's lies to her psychiatrist—David Shipman, *Judy Garland: The Secret Life of An American Legend* (New York: Hyperion, 1992), pp. 142–43.

127 "Hostility is an emotion common to lesbians . . ."—Frank S. Caprio, M.D., *Female Homosexuality: A Psychodynamic Study of Lesbianism* (New York: The Citadel Press, 1954), p. 61.

127 a dangerous case of lesbian-thespian complex.—This is not Dr. Caprio's, but my own absurdity.

127 "The young aspirant to a career in the world of the theatre . . ."—Caprio, p. 132.

132 "Most of all, on a date I think a girl should be *herself* . . ."—Schmidt, p. 86 (Judy Garland as told to Gladys Hall, *Screenland*, January 1941).

134 "stream of pleasure rising up her arm . . ."—Gabriele d'Annunzio, *Pleasure*, trans. Lara Gochin Raffaelli (New York: Penguin Books, 2013; orig. Italian ed. 1889), p. 78.

140 "We called Neva the bodhisattva . . ."—Because we were religious. That religion can be practical has been proven long ago, by the Egyptian altar which is also a grindstone. We now re-illustrated that point: Worshipping Neva infallibly brought us five-star orgasms. I tried to remember her predecessor, the beautiful star called Letitia; compared to Neva she was nothing but a female mummy-mask with glass eyes.

152 "Near Jericho in Israel . . ."—World Pastor Tony Alamo, "World Newsletter: The Alamo Christian Nation," vol. 21200, April 2015, pp. 1 and (continuation) 7 (Tony Alamo, "Sodom and Gomorrah").

154 Marlene Dietrich's outfit in *Shanghai Express*—Information from Karin Wieland, *Dietrich & Riefenstahl: Hollywood, Berlin, and a Century in Two Lives*, trans. Shelley Frisch (New York: Liveright, 2011; orig. German ed. 2011), p. 197.

158 Alcman knew the tunes of all the birds—David A. Campbell, ed. and trans., *Greek Lyric II: Anacreon, Anacreontea, Choral Lyric from Olympus to Alcman* (Cambridge, Massachusetts: Loeb Classical Library LCL143, 1988), p. 425 (40, Athenaeus, *Scholars at Dinner*).

HER NAME IN LIGHTS

159 Epigraph: "Let me fly like a hawk . . ."—*The Egyptian Book of the Dead: The Hieroglyphic Transcript and Translation into English of the Ancient Egyptian Papyrus of Ani*, [trans.,] intro. and commentary by E. A. Wallis Budge (New York: Gramercy Books, 1999; orig. pub. 1895), p. 394 ("The Devourer and the Block of Slaughter").

159 Epigraph: "If I'm such a legend . . ."—*Judy Garland on Judy Garland: Interviews and Encounters,* ed. Randy L. Schmidt (Chicago: Chicago Review Press / An A Cappella Book, 2014), p. 394 (John Gruen, *New York / World Journal Tribune Magazine*, April 2, 1967).

159 "a natural born poison woman"—Christine L. Marran, *Poison Woman: Figuring Female Transgression in Modern Japanese Culture* (Minneapolis: University of Minnesota Press, 2007), p. 115.

159 Natalie Wood's mother on "the importance of cataloging her career . . ."—Manoah Bowman, *Natalie Wood: Reflections on a Legendary Life* (Philadelphia: Running Press, 2016), p. 14.

160 The Chu Era—Chinese, 4th through 3rd centuries.

162–163 Details on Tonya Harding, Kristi Yamaguchi and Nancy Kerrigan in competition, Minneapolis to Detroit—Keith Davidson, *Nancy Kerrigan* (New York: Scholastic Inc. / Sports Shots: Collector's Book 26, 1994), pp. 21, 30–32.

I GUESS I JUST LIKE NICE PEOPLE

164 Epigraph: "It does you no harm . . ."—Thomas à Kempis, *The Imitation of Christ*, trans. Leo Sherley-Price (New York: Penguin, 1987 repr. of 1952 ed.; orig. Latin version wr. *ca.* 1413), p. 35.

164 Epigraph: "Don't yield your leadership . . ."—*Judy Garland on Judy Garland: Interviews and Encounters*, ed. Randy L. Schmidt (Chicago: Chicago Review Press / An A Cappella Book, 2014), p. 215 (*Coronet*, February 1955).

164 Judy Garland's white party dress at the Academy dinner—Schmidt, p. 129 (*Movieland*, December 1943).

167 Garland's marriage to Minnelli so that "she could continue to have romantic flings with other men . . ."—David Shipman, *Judy Garland: The Secret Life of An American Legend* (New York: Hyperion, 1992), p. 169.

171 Four-paragraph dialogue beginning with "lesbian idolification"—Some phrases stolen from Louise Allen, *The Lesbian Idol: Martina, KD and the Consumption of Lesbian Masculinity* (London: Cassell, 1997), various pp.

177 "I guess I just like nice people and when someone has a lot of nice friends I'm sure to get along with them."—Schmidt, p. 34 (Robert McIlwaine, *Modern Screen*, August 1939).

CHAIN OF COMMAND

179 Epigraph: "What is known as 'G' . . ."—Courtney Ryley Cooper, *Ten Thousand Public Enemies* (Boston: Little, Brown, 1935), p. 231.

179 Epigraph: "How then ought ye to guard yourselves? . . ."—Paul Carus, comp. [and trans.?], *The Gospel of Buddha* (Guernsey, U.K.: Studio Press Ltd. / The Guernsey Press Co. Ltd., 1995; orig. ed. 1915; n.d. given for original texts), p. 94.

180 Nancy Kerrigan *versus* Oksana Baiul—Information from Davidson, *Nancy Kerrigan* (New York: Scholastic Inc. / Sports Shots: Collector's Book 26, 1994), p. 38.

187 Logic . . . can best be described as the orderly and sensible review of facts . . .—Verbatim from Charles P. Nemeth, J.D., LL.M., *Private Security and the Investigative Process* (Cincinnati, Ohio: Anderson Publishing Co., 1992), p. 15.

JUDY AT SCHOOL

188 Epigraph: "Without love, the outward work is of no value . . ."—Thomas à Kempis, *The Imitation of Christ*, trans. Leo Sherley-Price (New York: Penguin, 1987 repr. of 1952 ed.; orig. Latin version wr. *ca.* 1413), p. 43.

188 Epigraph: "Those whom nature has sacrificed . . ."—Radclyffe Hall, *The Well of Loneliness* (New York: Doubleday / Anchor, 1990; orig. pub. 1928), p. 146.

194 Shantelle: "Neva, Neva, can't you please help me? I wanna be less angry . . . And less proud . . . Because everything's empty"—Saint Basil [the Great]: "O our Lady, Mother of God, take away the pride and violence from my poor heart, lest I be exalted in the empty life by the vanity of this world," as quoted in Serge A. Zhenkovsky, ed. and comp., *Medieval Russia's Epics, Chronicles and Tales*, rev. ed. (New York: E. P. Dutton, 1974; orig. ed. 1973), p. 96 (Vladimir Monomakh, "Instruction to His Children," bef. 1126).

196 "In the movies, your face is magnified . . ."—*Judy Garland on Judy Garland: Interviews and Encounters*, ed. Randy L. Schmidt (Chicago: Chicago Review Press / An A Cappella Book, 2014), p. 161 (Judy Garland, *Screenland*, October 1946).

SOME NAMES ARE TRUE

200 Epigraph: "Self is an error . . ."—Paul Carus, comp. [and trans.?], *The Gospel of Buddha* (Guernsey, U.K.: Studio Press Ltd. / The Guernsey Press Co. Ltd., 1995; orig. ed. 1915; n.d. given for original texts), p. 67.

200 Epigraph: "Crime is intimately associated with female sexual inversion."—Frank S. Caprio, M.D., *Female Homosexuality: A Psychodynamic Study of Lesbianism* (New York: The Citadel Press, 1954), p. 302.

211 "A lesbian woman was assaulted by five people . . ."—Much abridged and somewhat altered [for privacy] from *Ebony*, November 13, 2017, Zahara Hill, "Lesbian Woman Brutally Assaulted in Los Angeles Hate Crime." Downloaded for WTV by Jordan Rothacker on February 20, 2018, from http://www.ebony.com/news-views/los-angeles-lesbian-couple-assaulted-hate-crime.

HUMILIATED IN SKIRTS

214 Epigraph: "I don't associate Frances Gumm with me . . ."—*Judy Garland on Judy Garland: Interviews and Encounters*, ed. Randy L. Schmidt (Chicago: Chicago Review Press / An A Cappella Book, 2014), p. 191 (Michael Drury, *Cosmopolitan*, 1951).

214 Epigraph: "This thing that you are is a sin . . ."—Radclyffe Hall, *The Well of Loneliness* (New York: Doubleday / Anchor, 1990; orig. pub. 1928), p. 202.

214 Judy's birthname Frank Masters—As mentioned on p. 75 of this book, Judy Garland's parents wanted a boy and at first called her Frank.

214–218 The transwoman's life story—A few incidents are stolen and variously modified from: GLBT Historical Society. Francine Logandice Collection (#2002-04). Carton 1. Folder containing Angela Douglas, "Triple Jeopardy" (78-pp. typescript), 1983.

214 Judy Garland: "I think I'm interesting . . ."—Schmidt, p. xvii.

215 Extracts from Dr. Morrow's circular: "To the typical female . . ." + "Don't be satisfied . . ."—GLBT Historical Society. Francine Logandice Collection (#2002-04). Carton 1. Folder with Angela Douglas autobiography. John Brown, M.D., "Sex Change" [typescript], February 17, 1977. According to another item in the Logandice Collection, until 1973 all the transsexuals got was a hole, not even labia.—Angela Douglas [born Douglas Carl Czinkski in 1943; named after General McArthur], "Triple Jeopardy" (78-pp. typescript, wr. 1983), p. 49. I have stolen from this source a few details of Judy's biography on the road and in prison, including Danielle's story of the vaginal dilator (p. 55) and Angela's happy night in jail (p. 40).

215 "a woman whose heart had been hurt"—David Shipman, *Judy Garland: The Secret Life of an American Legend* (New York: Hyperion, 1992), p. 40 (citing George Jessel).
216 *Time* magazine on Judy Garland: "one of the more reliable song-pluggers in the business"—Shipman, p. 130 (hyphen added by WTV).
217 *Fated for Femininity* and the other period titles here and in other Judy chapters of *The Lucky Star* are all genuine, taken from catalogues or from the items themselves, in various folders of: GLBT Historical Society. Francine Logandice Collection (#2002-04). Carton 1.
219 How Nancy Kerrigan's family financed her skating lessons—Information from Keith Davidson, *Nancy Kerrigan* (New York: Scholastic Inc. / Sports Shots: Collector's Book 26, 1994), p. 9.
219 Judy Garland's abortions—Shipman, pp. 128, 142, 139.
224 Judy gets her testicles punished by the Goddess—Logandice Collection. Folder: "Stories of Female Domination, 1997." The mistress was named Goddess Natasha.
224 "I would like to see women realize that the punishment we feel . . ."—Arden Eversmeyer and Margaret Purcell, *Without Apology: Old Lesbian Life Stories* (Houston, Texas: Old Lesbian Oral History Project, 2012), p. 176 (statement of Arden Eversmeyer).
225 Judy's exclusion from women-only spaces—About this matter the activist Erika Castro, whom I interviewed in Las Vegas in 2018, assured me: "I think there has been a change. With the new wave, being more inclusive to women of color, and the different obstacles that women of color have faced, have helped us to see that trans women are women. I think there's still more work to be done. I still hear from some people that as a trans woman is transitioning from male to female, you still hear these derogatory terms, but a woman is a woman whether she is born that way or not." I asked how the gatekeepers of a women-only space would deal with an evidently male-bodied claimant to femininity. Ms. Castro replied: "Most of the spaces that I am a part of, we say our names and our preferred gender pronouns and that's how we identify ourselves to each other. Do some of us have a penis? We can't ask those kinds of questions." And again: "If I were to be in a space like that, and a person like that identifies as a woman, I have to respect them. At the end of the day it goes back to how they identify themselves. It goes back to the conversation we have now about trans folks being able to use the bathroom they prefer."
225 "Don't you know that lesbians make love using their hands?"—After "lesbians make love with their hands."—Louise Allen, *The Lesbian Idol: Martina, KD and the Consumption of Lesbian Masculinity* (London: Cassell, 1997), p. 151.
230 "That's what I'm supposed to be, a legend."—Schmidt, p. xvii.
231 Description of the "Garland" ensemble—Information from Joan Beck Coulson, *Always for Judy: Witness to the Joy and Genius of Judy Garland* (Elmira, California: Yarnscombe Books, 2014), p. 220.

THE REPTILE SHEDS HER SKIN

232 Epigraph: "Therefore, you must be in want . . ."—James M. Robinson, gen. ed., *The Nag Hammadi Library in English*, p. 31 ("The Apocryphon of James," bef. 314).
232 Epigraph: "Only the most important things should be clothed in the honor of the symbol."—Wilhelm Stekel, *Sexual Aberrations: The Phenomena of Fetishism in Relation to Sex*, trans. Dr. S. Parker (New York: Liveright Publishing Corp., 1930; n.d. for orig. German ed.), vol. II, p. 325, apparently quoting Creuzer from Schlesinger, pub. 1912.
232 The FBI agent who "rewrites" certain passages of his notes—G. Daniel Lassiter, ed., *Interrogations, Confessions, and Entrapment* (New York: Kluwer Academic / Plenum Publishers,

Perspectives in Law and Psychology, vol. 20, 2004), pp. 215–17 (Vanessa A. Edkins and Lawrence S. Wrightsman, "The Psychology of Entrapment"), p. 218.

239–240 Description of the interior of the transwoman's skull—Slightly after a visit to the Basilica Santa Maria del Pi, Barcelona, 2014.

SHOW NIGHTS

242 Epigraph: "I'm terribly critical . . ."—*Judy Garland on Judy Garland: Interviews and Encounters*, ed. Randy L. Schmidt (Chicago: Chicago Review Press / An A Cappella Book, 2014), p. 167 (*Silver Screen*, December 1948).

242 Epigraph: "Today's women who have sex with other women . . ."—Kat Harding, *The Lesbian Kama Sutra* (London: Carlton Books, 2010 repr. of 2004 ed.), p. 28.

249 every religion even of love has to be unloving and cruel to unbelievers.—A Freudianism.

252 Neva's photos, rifled by Judy—Very loosely based (with embellishments, deletions and anachronisms, on photos in GLBTHS, Linda Welcome papers, carton 1.

255 Brief conversation on ovarian cancer—Information from Kristine Conner and Lauren Langford, *Ovarian Cancer: Your Guide to Taking Control* (Cambridge, Massachusetts: O'Reilly, 2003), pp. 55–62.

WITH SHANTELLE

258 Epigraph: "Things are the other way round . . ."—Bullhe Shah, *Sufi Lyrics*, ed. and trans. Christopher Shackle (Cambridge, Massachusetts: Harvard University Press / Murty Classical Library of Hindi, 2015; orig. lyrics bef. 1759), p. 15 (no. 8).

258 Epigraph: "Interest is seldom pursued . . ."—Samuel Johnson, *Selected Essays*, ed. David Womersley (New York: Penguin Books, 2003; essays orig. pub. 1739–61), p. 302 (*The Rambler*, No. 183, Tuesday, 17 December 1751).

WHAT THE CAT CAUGHT

263 Epigraph: "In the face of another's great excellence . . ."—Johann Wolfgang von Goethe, *Maxims and Reflections*, ed. Peter Hutchinson, trans. Elisabeth Stopp (New York: Penguin, 1998), p. 7 (no. 45).

263 Epigraph: "The conscious prayer of the inferior . . ."—George Bernard Shaw, *Saint Joan* (Baltimore: Penguin Books, 1951; orig. ed. 1924), p. 45 (introduction).

266 "she who for our sake hid her burning thoughts from us."—Somewhat after *The Egyptian Book of the Dead: The Hieroglyphic Transcript and Translation into English of the Ancient Egyptian Papyrus of Ani*, [trans.,] intro. and commentary by E. A. Wallis Budge (New York: Gramercy Books, 1999; orig. pub. 1895), p. 101.

266 Alcman: "Let no mortal fly to the sky . . ."—Gloria Ferrari, *Alcman and the Cosmos of Sparta* (Chicago: University of Chicago Press, 2014 pbk. ed.; orig. pub. 2008), p. 155 (*Partheneion* text and translation, slightly "retranslated" by WTV).

267 "Double Domination: Petticoat Punishment"—GLBT Historical Society. Francine Logandice Collection (#2002-04). Carton 1.

268 believing that Neva might have the power to lift him back up . . .—After Kathryn Springer, *The Dandelion Field* (Grand Rapids, Michigan: Zondervan, 2014), p. 285: "It's like saying I don't believe God has the power to lift me back up."

270 "Remember that you are a son of kings . . ."—Willis Barnstone and Marvin Meyer, ed., *The Gnostic Bible* (Boston: Shambhala, 2003), p. 391 ("The Song of the Pearl": "Remember the Pearl").

277 "I don't enjoy my troubles that much to dwell on them."—*Judy Garland on Judy Garland: Interviews and Encounters*, ed. Randy L. Schmidt (Chicago: Chicago Review Press / An A Cappella Book, 2014), p. 167 (Jack Holland, *Silver Screen*, 1948).

277 "I'm unscathed, unscarred, unembittered . . ."—Schmidt, p. 176 (Judy Garland, *Motion Picture*, September 1950).

279 "Police are offering a ten-thousand-dollar reward . . ."—Much abridged and somewhat altered [for privacy] from SFGATE: https://www.sfgate.com/bayarea/article/Richmond-police-seek-4-in-gang-rape-of-lesbian-3180025.php. [*San Francisco Chronicle.*] Elizabeth Fernandez, Chronicle Staff Writer Published 4:00 a.m., Sunday, December 21, 2008, "Richmond police seek 4 in gang rape of lesbian." Downloaded for WTV by Jordan Rothacker on February 20, 2018.

280 Nancy Kerrigan from Seattle to Lillehammer—Keith Davidson, *Nancy Kerrigan* (New York: Scholastic Inc. / Sports Shots: Collector's Book 26, 1994), pp. 20, 29.

285 Rosemary Strand "was a cervical cancer survivor"—Two days after her twenty-eighth birthday, Rosemary Strand was afflicted with a particularly painful menstrual period. As a rule her time of the month was merely inconvenient, and although her husband claimed that she got nasty-tempered a day or two before, Rosemary considered that he used her periods as excuses to blame their arguments on her, because she got along fine with everyone else. Her anemic friend Lily dreaded the onset of bleeding, and frequently had to call in sick at the office, where her position was accordingly becoming more precarious. Sometimes Lily had to stay in bed for a day or two; her pains were excruciating, and once or twice a year she had to go to the emergency room for a transfusion. Rosemary was grateful not to be Lily, whom she sometimes suspected of exaggeration. This period, while it annoyed her, did not prevent her from going to work. The flow was no heavier than usual, although the unpleasant sensation continued. She woke up uneasy. Her husband, wishing for a certain something, began to stroke her belly, and Rosemary flinched because her left side felt tender. Insulted, he thought she was losing her desire for him. After breakfast she decided to call Dr. Nisbet, her gynecologist, whom she rarely troubled and who therefore agreed to see her that day. Mr. Peterson, her easygoing boss, made no trouble when she asked to leave work an hour early.—Female trouble? he said with a wink. Dr. Nisbet asked whether everything was good at home. Rosemary said that it was. When he palpitated her left side, Rosemary almost screamed. He diagnosed irritable bowel syndrome. For the rest of that week the pills helped, but then it began to seem that she might actually be getting worse, so she went back to Dr. Nisbet, who appeared slightly annoyed. He referred her to a specialist. Rosemary had to wait three weeks for this appointment. The tenderness on her left side concealed itself unless she was touched. So Rosemary continued to be a star at work, and the only person whom she dissatisfied was her husband. There were dinnertimes when he sat staring at her, and twice he asked if she were seeing someone else. Once she convinced him that the problem was merely temporary and physical—the specialist would solve it—he bore up cheerfully enough. Rosemary felt embarrassed to have to ask Mr. Peterson for permission to leave early again. She promised to come in early on the following morning. He gazed at her for a moment, then nodded. This time he was definitely displeased, as she had known he would be; she had nearly cancelled her appointment, but then she remembered the other dissatisfied man in her life; the very thought of him on top of her almost made her side feel tender. The specialist said she had nothing to worry about. All the same, on the followup appointment he recommended exploratory surgery. Rosemary woke up after a surprise hysterectomy and her sexual

desire was gone forever. Her friends told her that she was lucky to be alive. Although Rosemary, who had seen her mother go that way, acknowledged the unpleasantness of ovarian cancer, she could not help but wonder whether the operation had really saved her. In her second year of remission, when she finally weaned herself from opioids, it turned out that the pain was mostly gone, but so was her pleasure. Although she thought that she wanted Kevin inside her, she could no longer get wet no matter what he did to her. Although she remained in possession of her clitoris, her orgasms felt unsatisfactory, for cervical contractions never come easy without a cervix. Kevin, who had been patient with her for a very long time, could not help but wonder whether, as he expressed it, *something psychological* might have happened. Rosemary spread her legs and lay there; it was hardly the same for him, either. Closing her eyes, she could see his face grown cold with disappointment. Another specialist, diagnosing vaginal atrophy, recommended estrogen-testosterone replacement therapy, and that helped a little, but even though his penis hurt her less and she could sometimes climax, she never felt satisfied; her frustrated desire built and built, and she began to get angry at him. They both pretended as long as they could, after which they avoided saying an ever increasing number of things. Just before their twelfth wedding anniversary, she was washing their clothes and found a lipstick stain on his underpants. Rosemary kept quiet. That night when he rolled over on top of her, she burst into tears. At first he tried to deny it, but when she reminded him that they had promised always to be honest with each other, he admitted that he was seeing another woman, and not the first. Seeing his shoulders stiff and his face averted as he sat there on the edge of the bed, the wife felt nothing. Then she heard their daughter tiptoeing past them to the bathroom. Karen must have been listening. Rosemary felt hatred and rage.

302 Details on the "calculating child killer"—John Glatt, *My Sweet Angel: The True Story of Lacey Spears, the Seemingly Perfect Mother Who Murdered Her Son in Cold Blood* (New York: St. Martin's Press, 2016), pp. 200–202, 218, 290–91, 308.

JUST KISS ME

324 Epigraph: "My only desire is to make love . . ."—Norman Johnston, Leonard Savitz and Marvin E. Wofgang, ed., *The Sociology of Punishment and Correction*, 2nd ed (New York: John Wiley & Sons, 1970; orig. ed. 1962), p. 474 (David A. Ward and Gene G. Kassebaum, "Homosexuality in a Women's Prison").

324–325 Tale of the "numerous sex acts" upon the fourteen-year-old girl—*Coal Valley News* [West Virginia], Wednesday, May 6, 2015, pp. 1A, 5A (Fred Pace, "Boone grand jury indicts 53 people").

327 "she's less simple." + "She's stretched awfully thin." + "Judy's finally losing weight."—David Shipman, *Judy Garland: The Secret Life of An American Legend* (New York: Hyperion, 1992), p. 175: "She was slim and talented but strung tight like a violin string—quite different from the happy little roly-poly who sang her heart out at Grauman's Chinese Theater" (Helen Rose, on Judy Garland, 1945).

329 The tale of Never Despise—*The Threefold Lotus Sutra*, trans. Bunno Kato, Yoshiro Tamura and Kojiro Myasaka, with revs. (Tokyo: Kosei Publishing Co., 1995 repr. of 1975 ed.; orig. mss. *ca.* 4th cent.?), p. 291.

337 rerun about an ingenuous young bride—Based, of course, on the plot of Daphne DuMaurier's *Rebecca* (New York: Avon / HarperCollins, 1971; orig. ed. 1938). The cited passage is on p. 271.

339 shall it ever be told of her that she would speak?—After Job 37:20.

THIRST

343 Epigraph: "Therefore, if I may not draw from the fullness of the Fountain . . ."—Thomas à Kempis, *The Imitation of Christ*, trans. Leo Sherley-Price (New York: Penguin, 1987 repr. of 1952 ed.; orig. Latin version wr. *ca.* 1413), p. 193.

343 Epigraph: "Jesus said, 'He who will drink from my mouth . . .' "—James M. Robinson, gen. ed., *The Nag Hammadi Library in English*, p. 137.

347 the more she could suffer for the lesbian's sake, the more pleasing would she become to her.—Thomas à Kempis, p. 86: "The more he can suffer for His sake, the more he will be pleasing to God."

349 Lynda Koolish's photograph of Margie Adam—Carol Ascher, Louise DeSalvo, Sara Ruddick, ed., *Between Women: Biographers, Novelists, Critics, Teachers and Artists Write about Their Work on Women* (Boston: Beacon Press, 1984), pp. 113–22 (Lynda Koolish, "This Is Who She Is to Me: On Photographing Women"). When I was interviewing lesbians for this novel, I was enthralled and inspired to hear in their testimony about the ladies they loved confirmation of Koolish's words (p. 116) that "what I depict as beauty in women is a kind of responsiveness—forthrightness, expressiveness, internal strength."

351 believing that the old lady had spoken all.—Willis Barnstone and Marvin Meyer, ed., *The Gnostic Bible* (Boston: Shambhala, 2003), p. 196 ("Three Forms of First Thought"): "Now I have come the second time in the likeness of a female and have spoken all."

351 healthy topless young women driving nails, & c.—Somewhat after an event in Albion, California, in 1972, as described in: GLBTHS, Linda Welcome papers, carton 1.

351 the faraway mother of a voice.—Barnstone and Meyer, p. 196: "I am alone and undefiled. I am the mother of the voice, speaking in many ways, completing all."

353 Judy Garland's nightmare—*Judy Garland on Judy Garland: Interviews and Encounters*, ed. Randy L. Schmidt (Chicago: Chicago Review Press / An A Cappella Book, 2014), p. 111 (Carol Craig, *Motion Picture*, June 1941).

NEVA AND THE BABY-KILLERS

357 Epigraph: "He shall come forth by day . . ."—*The Egyptian Book of the Dead: The Hieroglyphic Transcript and Translation into English of the Ancient Egyptian Papyrus of Ani*, [trans.,] intro. and commentary by E. A. Wallis Budge (New York: Gramercy Books, 1999; orig. pub. 1895), p. 433 ("The Judges in Nerutef").

357 Epigraph: "Then the female spiritual presence came . . ."—Willis Barnstone and Marvin Meyer, ed., *The Gnostic Bible* (Boston: Shambhala, 2003), p. 171 ("Three Forms of First Thought").

368 *The Gnostic Scriptures:* between us and the light above there is a veil . . .—James M. Robinson, gen. ed., *The Nag Hammadi Library in English*, p. 175 ("The Reality of the Rulers"): "A veil exists between the world above and the realms below, and shadow came into being beneath the veil."

371 the Grand Inquisitor improved Jesus's work, and the Prophet Muhammed later did much the same.—These comparisons derive from Peter Sloterdijk, *Critique of Cynical Reason*, trans. Michael Eldred (Minneapolis: University of Minnesota Press, Theory and History of Literature ser., vol. 40, 1997), p. 184.

373 "In almost every large city, one can find a particular tavern . . ."—Frank S. Caprio, M.D., *Female Homosexuality: A Psychodynamic Study of Lesbianism* (New York: The Citadel Press, 1954), p. 61. A page later comes an even more sprightly passage: "There are many

people who visit New York City and are curious enough to inquire from taxi drivers as to where they can go to see the 'female queers' that they have read or heard about. Many of the upper social circle refer to a tour of such taverns as 'going slumming.'"

ALMOST *FLAGRANTE DELICTO*

374 Epigraph: "Wanting-to-know is an offspring of the desire for power . . ."—Peter Sloterdijk, *Critique of Cynical Reason*, trans. Michael Eldred (Minneapolis: University of Minnesota Press, Theory and History of Literature ser., vol. 40, 1997), p. 179.

374 Epigraph: "Here, a barbed wire entanglement . . ."—Courtney Ryley Cooper, *Ten Thousand Public Enemies* (Boston: Little, Brown, 1935), p. vii (preface by J. Edgar Hoover).

374 a photograph from what must have been the 1970s—Somewhat after: GLBTHS, Linda Welcome papers, carton 1.

377 "Police say they are investigating an assault . . ."—Much abridged and somewhat altered [for privacy] from *Georgia Voice* (https://thegavoice.com), May 26, 2014, 10:54 p.m., Dyana Bagby (https://thegavoice.com/author/dyanabagby/), "Trans women brutally attacked on Atlanta's MARTA," downloaded for WTV by Jordan Rothacker on February 20, 2018.

378 "I can't help but feel like one of them T-girls was instigating the fight . . ."—Much abridged and altered from REPLY: *jem*, May 30, 2014 (https://thegavoice.com/trans-women-attacked-atlantas-marta/#comment-1684).

THE LUCKY STAR

379 Epigraph: "But I've always said that I was born under a Lucky Star . . ."—*Judy Garland on Judy Garland: Interviews and Encounters*, ed. Randy L. Schmidt (Chicago: Chicago Review Press / An A Cappella Book, 2014), p. 89.

379 "A woman's natural quality is to attract . . ."—Mrs. H. R. Haweis, 1878, quoted in Amy de la Haye, *A to Z of Style* (New York: Abrams, 2012 repr. of 2011 British ed.), p. 88.

379 the rarely fortunate case of a woman who is instructed by Truth Herself—Thomas à Kempis, *The Imitation of Christ*, trans. Leo Sherley-Price (New York: Penguin, 1987 repr. of 1952 ed.; orig. Latin version wr. *ca.* 1413), p. 30: "Happy the man who is instructed by Truth itself."

380 "Neva, don't forget how fucked up I am. I'm *lonely*! Please *help me all the time.*"—Thomas à Kempis, p. 119: ". . . I pray you remember the toil and grief of Your servant, and support him in all his undertakings."

384 "the conversation gradually assumed the tone best qualified . . ."—Sir Walter Scott, *Waverley, or, 'Tis Sixty Years Since* (London: Vintage Books, 2014 [w/ many misprints]; orig. pub. 1814), p. 423.

ONSCREEN

390 Epigraph: "In those days, I thought you achieved a state of loving . . ."—Manoah Bowman, *Natalie Wood: Reflections on a Legendary Life* (Philadelphia: Running Press, 2016), p. 220 (Wood's diary-memoir of 1966).

390 Epigraph: "We *have been* that mind, but we have never *known* it."—C. J. Jung, *The Undiscovered Self*, with *Symbols and the Interpretation of Dreams*, rev. trans. R. F. C. Hull (Princeton: Princeton University Press / Bollingen ser., 1990), p. 138 ("The Interpretation of Dreams," wr. *ca.* 1961).

390 Epigraph: "There may only be perhaps one . . ."—Bowman, p. 206 (Wood's diary-memoir of 1966).

DIVINGS OF A MERMAID

392 Epigraph: "Two women very much in love . . ."—Colette, *The Pure and the Impure*, trans. Herma Briffault (New York: New York Review Books, 2000 rev. repr. of 1996 ed.; orig. French ed. 1941), p. 119.

392 Epigraph: "We lose our identities quickly in what we're doing . . ."—*Judy Garland on Judy Garland: Interviews and Encounters*, ed. Randy L. Schmidt (Chicago: Chicago Review Press / An A Cappella Book, 2014), p. 218 (Judy Garland, *Coronet*, February 1955).

LIKE A SUSPECT WHO LOVES ONLY TO PLEASE

394 Epigraph: "You don't want a child bride . . ."—*Judy Garland on Judy Garland: Interviews and Encounters*, ed. Randy L. Schmidt (Chicago: Chicago Review Press / An A Cappella Book, 2014), p. 217 (Judy Garland, *Coronet*, February 1955).

394 Epigraph: "Thou knowest how like to flame our nature is . . ."—Valerius Flaccus, *Argonautica*, trans. J. H. Mozley (Cambridge, Massachusetts: Harvard University Press / Loeb Classical Library, 1936 rev. repr. of 1943 ed.; orig. Latin ms. *ca.* 70–90 A.D.), p. 85 (II.156).

395 "No star has been the subject of so many rumors . . ."—Schmidt, p. 166 (Jack Holland, *Silver Screen*, 1948).

396 Footnote: "In this relation we deal with one whom we respect . . ."—Henry David Thoreau, *Collected Essays and Poems* (New York: Library of America, 2001), p. 330 ("Chastity and Sensuality," wr. 1852; posthumous pub. 1865).

COMING DOWN

412 Epigraph: "The point is that it is impossible to retain equanimity . . ."—Plutarch [of Chaeronea], *Essays*, trans. Robin Waterfield, intro. and annot. Ian Kidd (New York: Penguin Books, 1992), p. 330 ("On Socrates' Personal Deity").

412 Epigraph: "United soules are not satisfied with embraces . . ."—Sir Thomas Browne, *Religio Medici* and *Urne-Buriall*, ed. Stephen Greenblatt and Ramie Targoff (New York: New York Review Books, 2012; orig. texts respectively *ca.* 1643 and 1658), p. 74 (*Religio Medici*).

419 Besides, what was she supposed to look for but troubles and crosses?—Thomas à Kempis, *The Imitation of Christ*, trans. Leo Sherley-Price (New York: Penguin, 1987 repr. of 1952 ed.; orig. Latin version wr. *ca.* 1413), p. 86: "You are greatly mistaken if you look for anything save to endure trials, for all this mortal life is full of troubles, and everywhere marked with crosses."

427 "If you bring forth what is within you . . ."—Willis Barnstone and Marvin Meyer, ed., *The Gnostic Bible* (Boston: Shambhala, 2003), p. 62 ("The Gospel of Thomas," verse 70). Cf. C. G. Jung, *The Red Book (Liber Novus): A Reader's Edition*, trans. Mark Kyburz, John Peck and Sonu Shamdasi, ed. Sonu Shamdasani (New York: Norton, Philemon ser., in arr. w/ the Foundation of the Works of C. G. Jung, 2009), p. 188: "If you do not acknowledge your yearning, then you do not follow yourself, but go on foreign ways that others have indicated to you . . . To live oneself means: to be one's own task. Never say that it is a joy to live oneself. It will be no joy but a long suffering, since you must become your own creator."

433 Procedure for nude shots of Natalie Wood—Manoah Bowman, *Natalie Wood: Reflections on a Legendary Life* (Philadelphia: Running Press, 2016), pp. 298–99.

WITHOUT SHAME OR LIMIT

443 Epigraph: "All my life I have tried to do whatever was expected of me . . ."—*Judy Garland on Judy Garland: Interviews and Encounters*, ed. Randy L. Schmidt (Chicago: Chicago Review Press / An A Cappella Book, 2014), p. 180 (Michael Drury, *Cosmopolitan*, January 1951).

443 Epigraph: "Not many of us have the names and identities . . ."—Schmidt, p. 192 (Michael Drury, *Cosmopolitan*, January 1951).

445 Paraphrase of Augustine in John Burnaby, *Amor Dei: A Study of the Religion of Saint Augustine (The Hulsean Lectures for 1938)* (Eugene, Oregon: Wipf and Stock, n.d. [probably 2007]; orig. ed. 1938), p. 30.

THE PARATROOPER

448 Epigraph: "By oneself evil is done . . ."—Paul Carus, comp. [and trans.?], *The Gospel of Buddha* (Guernsey, U.K.: Studio Press Ltd. / The Guernsey Press Co. Ltd., 1995; orig. ed. 1915; n.d. given for original texts), p. 131.

AUDITIONS

450 Epigraph: "You see, I'm so tired of reading articles . . ."—*Judy Garland on Judy Garland: Interviews and Encounters*, ed. Randy L. Schmidt (Chicago: Chicago Review Press / An A Cappella Book, 2014), p. 174 (Michael Drury, *Cosmopolitan*, 1951).

450 Epigraph: "First of all, I had grown up . . ."—Manoah Bowman, *Natalie Wood: Reflections on a Legendary Life* (Philadelphia: Running Press, 2016), p. 223 (journal-memoir dated 1966).

461 Marlene Dietrich's vomiting on the way to Paramount—Karin Wieland, *Dietrich & Riefenstahl: Hollywood, Berlin, and a Century in Two Lives*, trans. Shelley Frisch (New York: Liveright, 2011; orig. German ed. 2011), p. 199.

463 Applause: "the *most* beautiful music in the whole world!" (italics in original)—Schmidt, p. 86 (Gladys Hall, *Screenland*, December 1940).

465 Judy Garland's tears over *Pigskin Parade*—Schmidt, p. 117 (Gladys Hall, *Silver Screen*, November 1942).

465 When Natalie Wood lost the Oscars competition to Sophia Loren in 1962—Manoah Bowman, *Natalie Wood: Reflections on a Legendary Life* (Philadelphia: Running Press, 2016), p. 10.

476 "competing never gets in the way of our friendship."—Keith Davidson, *Nancy Kerrigan* (New York: Scholastic Inc. / Sports Shots: Collector's Book 26, 1994), p. 20.

477 "to be honest, I do wonder whether some readers will simply tire of, for example, all the climaxing . . ."—Paul Slovak to WTV, March 1, 2019, p. 1.

REHEARSALS AND PERFORMANCES

478 Epigraphs: "I must add that I washed my neck and the top of my bosom . . . ," and other three on same page—The Abbé de Choisy: A free translation of the *Memoires of the Abbé de Choisy Dressed as a Woman* (Vern Bullough and Barbara Burnett, privately printed, n.d.), unnumbered typescript. Pages 3, 7, 9 by my count.

SORRY I'M BLEEDING

484 Epigraph: "The love of pleasure begets grief . . ."—Paul Carus, comp. [and trans.?], *The Gospel of Buddha* (Guernsey, U.K.: Studio Press Ltd. / The Guernsey Press Co. Ltd., 1995; orig. ed. 1915; n.d. given for original texts), p. 134.

484 "She told me that she sleeps in a silk nightgown . . ."—*Judy Garland on Judy Garland: Interviews and Encounters*, ed. Randy L. Schmidt (Chicago: Chicago Review Press / An A Cappella Book, 2014), p. 55 (James Carson, *Modern Screen*, January 1940).

493 "the garment around us"—closely after *The Egyptian Book of the Dead: The Hieroglyphic Transcript and Translation into English of the Ancient Egyptian Papyrus of Ani*, [trans.,] intro. and commentary by E. A. Wallis Budge (New York: Gramercy Books, 1999; orig. pub. 1895), p. 411 ("garment which envelopeth the helpless one, which weepeth for and loveth that which it covereth").

496 The tale of Judy Garland and the MGM doctor—Information from David Shipman, *Judy Garland: The Secret Life of An American Legend* (New York: Hyperion, 1992), p. 129. She was nineteen.

THE OLD FAKE

502 Epigraph: "The Goddess who knew though I knew not hath caused darkness."—R. de Rohan Barondes, M.D., *Garden of the Gods: Mesopotamia, 5,000 B.C.* (Boston: Christopher Publishing House, 1957), p. 350 (Accadian Penitential Tablet, bef. 17th cent. B.C.).

502 Epigraph: "I believe you should be critical of yourself . . ."—*Judy Garland on Judy Garland: Interviews and Encounters*, ed. Randy L. Schmidt (Chicago: Chicago Review Press / An A Cappella Book, 2014), p. 159 (*Screenland*, October 1946).

502 "No one can defy the laws of our civilization . . ."—J. Edgar Hoover, *Persons in Hiding* (Boston: Little, Brown, 1938), p. 294.

505 "my daughter was always terribly unhappy . . . *pseudoadjustment to life*."—Here Mrs. Strand is parroting Frank S. Caprio, M.D., *Female Homosexuality: A Psychodynamic Study of Lesbianism* (New York: The Citadel Press, 1954), p. 180: "Lesbians are basically unhappy people. Many admit their unhappiness but others are deceived by their pseudoadjustment to life."

505 Mrs. Strand's descriptions of Natalie Wood—After photos and captions in Manoah Bowman, *Natalie Wood: Reflections on a Legendary Life* (Philadelphia: Running Press, 2016), pp. 34–37, 40.

508 Details on the mother who pillow-suffocated her four-year-old—Conflated from John Glatt, *My Sweet Angel: The True Story of Lacey Spears, the Seemingly Perfect Mother Who Murdered Her Son in Cold Blood* (New York: St. Martin's Press, 2016), pp. 283, 230. [My favorite post from this book's heroine (p. 233): "My Sweet Angel Is in the Hospital for the 23rd Time."]

514 Playing "Sardines"—David Shipman, *Judy Garland: The Secret Life of An American Legend* (New York: Hyperion, 1992), p. 137.

514 light-giver for life—Closely after *The Egyptian Book of the Dead: The Hieroglyphic Transcript and Translation into English of the Ancient Egyptian Papyrus of Ani*, [trans.,] intro. and commentary by E. A. Wallis Budge (New York: Gramercy Books, 1999; orig. pub. 1895), p. 417.

518 "For the second time this year, the same transgender woman . . ."—Much abridged and somewhat altered [for privacy] from https://sanfrancisco.cbslocal.com/2015/11/18/san-francisco-transgender-woman-attack-2nd-time-hate-crime/, November 18, 2015, at 9:43 p.m. Downloaded for WTV by Jordan Rothacker on February 20, 2018.

519 renamed so by her producer + "You try to find in yourself the essence . . ."—Bowman, pp. 214, 206.

SOME WARMTH THAT WASN'T THERE

522 Epigraph: "Most of them have never heard of the word Lesbian . . ."—John O'Hara, *Stories*, ed. Charles McGrath (New York: Library of America, 2016), p. 656 ("Natica Jackson," orig. pub. 1966).

522 Epigraph: "Alas, he knew not how dire a monster was she for whose marriage couch he yearned . . ."—Valerius Flaccus, *Argonautica*, trans. J. H. Mozley (Cambridge, Massachusetts: Harvard University Press / Loeb Classical Library, 1936 rev. repr. of 1943 ed.; orig. Latin ms. *ca.* 70–90 A.D.), p. 303 (VI.45–46).

522 Epigraph: "It works for a while . . ."—*Judy Garland on Judy Garland: Interviews and Encounters*, ed. Randy L. Schmidt (Chicago: Chicago Review Press / An A Cappella Book, 2014), p. 422 (Clive Hirschhorn, *Sunday Express* [London], January 16, 1969).

524 Judy Garland: "no more pills ever"—Schmidt, p. xvi.

525 Benzedrine and barbiturates for Judy Garland—Schmidt, p. 117. Shipman relates (*Judy Garland: The Secret Life of An American Legend* [New York: Hyperion, 1992, p. 77–78]) that when the MGM doctors put Judy Garland on Benzedrine to lose weight, Seconal to sleep and then more Benzedrine to wake up, the patient was fifteen years old.

531 The incident with Norma Shearer and Clark Gable—Schmidt, p. 10.

SHANTELLE'S MEDICINE

533 Epigraph: "The feminine faculty of anticipating . . ."—Colette, *The Pure and the Impure*, trans. Herma Briffault (New York: New York Review Books, 2000 rev. repr. of 1996 ed.; orig. French ed. 1941), pp. 173–74.

533 Epigraph: "Perhaps in most people's careers . . ."—Manoah Bowman, *Natalie Wood: Reflections on a Legendary Life* (Philadelphia: Running Press, 2016), p. 258 (journal, 1966).

NEVA'S SURPRISE

544 Epigraph: "I hope . . . that other girls who read Joan's bitter story will learn the folly of entering into a Lesbian relationship."—Frank S. Caprio, M.D., *Female Homosexuality: A Psychodynamic Study of Lesbianism* (New York: The Citadel Press, 1954), 269, quoting *Life Romances* (August 1953 issue), "Poignant Confession of a Lesbian."

545 "We demand the penalty of murder . . ."—Robert Zorn, *Cemetery John: The Undiscovered Mastermind of the Lindbergh Kidnapping* (New York: Overlook, 2012), p. 185.

546 The longhaired girl and her defense lawyer—*The New York Times*, Saturday, June 17, 2017, p. A11 (Katharine Q. Seelye and Jess Bidgood, "Young Woman Who Urged Friend to Commit Suicide Is Found Guilty").

547 Inhaling the entreaties which were made to her—Closely after *The Egyptian Book of the Dead: The Hieroglyphic Transcript and Translation into English of the Ancient Egyptian Papyrus of Ani*, [trans.,] intro. and commentary by E. A. Wallis Budge (New York: Gramercy Books, 1999; orig. pub. 1895), p. 410 ("The Pylons and their Doorkeepers"), with verb tense altered.

554–555 The tale of the Jewish wife's magic dress—Somewhat after Howard Schwartz, comp. and retold, *Leaves from the Garden of Eden: One Hundred Classic Jewish Tales* (New York: Oxford University Press, 2009), pp. 254–57 ("The Charm in the Dress").

555 Marlene Dietrich boasted of being able to fake orgasms [to Carl Zuckmayer]—Information from Karin Wieland, *Dietrich & Riefenstahl: Hollywood, Berlin, and a Century in Two Lives*, trans. Shelley Frisch (New York: Liveright, 2011; orig. German ed. 2011), p. 354. On p. 356 we read that Erich Maria Remarque, author of the famous *All Quiet on the Western Front*,

called Dietrich "someone who lies in bed like a fish afterwards." But she must have put on a good performance meanwhile, as evidenced (p. 238) by Elisabeth Bergner's telegram to her: "I EAT YOU I SMELL YOU I GREASE YOU . . ."

557 "the model, by remaining tacit . . ."—Antonio T. De Nicolas, *Powers of Imagining: Ignatius de Loyola: A Philosophical Hermeneutic of Imagining Through the Collected Works of Ignatius de Loyola with a Translation of These Works* (Albany: State University of New York Press, 1986), p. 72. I have slightly distorted the beginning of this proposition, which reads: "In the case of the model governing the Spirit . . ."

THE BLOODSUCKER

561 Epigraph: "I could beleeve that Spirits use with man . . ."—Sir Thomas Browne, *Religio Medici* and *Urne-Buriall*, ed. Stephen Greenblatt and Ramie Targoff (New York: New York Review Books, 2012; orig. texts respectively *ca.* 1643 and 1658), p. 35 (*Religio Medici*).

561 Epigraph: "The vampire is prone to be fascinated . . ."—J. Sheridan Le Fanu, *Carmilla* (London: Hesperus Press Limited, 2013; orig. pub. 1872), p. 100.

HOW FRANCINE AND I COPED

567 Epigraph: "Nothing had ever happened to me that a good piece of apple pie couldn't cure!"—*Judy Garland on Judy Garland: Interviews and Encounters*, ed. Randy L. Schmidt (Chicago: Chicago Review Press / An A Cappella Book, 2014), p. 121 (lifted from a longer sentence).

HOW SANDRA COPED

573 Epigraph: "You won't be a really happy person . . ."—*Judy Garland on Judy Garland: Interviews and Encounters*, ed. Randy L. Schmidt (Chicago: Chicago Review Press / An A Cappella Book, 2014), p. 163 (Judy Garland, *Screenland*, October 1946).

573 Epigraph: "At times I have been pretty much of a walking advertisement . . ."—Schmidt, p. 193. Citation continues: ". . . But some people have exaggerated the habit . . . and it is that sort of thing that gets a gal down . . ."

NARROWER THAN IT USED TO BE

575 Epigraph: "My body is the beloved . . ."—Bullhe Shah, *Sufi Lyrics*, ed. and trans. Christopher Shackle (Cambridge, Massachusetts: Harvard University Press / Murty Classical Library of Hindi, 2015; orig. lyrics bef. 1759), after p. 83 (no. 47).

575 Epigraph: "I am in the darke to all the world . . ."—Sir Thomas Browne, *Religio Medici* and *Urne-Buriall*, ed. Stephen Greenblatt and Ramie Targoff (New York: New York Review Books, 2012; orig. texts respectively *ca.* 1643 and 1658), p. 72 (*Religio Medici*).

575 Marlene Dietrich's attire in *Dishonored*—Karin Wieland, *Dietrich & Riefenstahl: Hollywood, Berlin, and a Century in Two Lives*, trans. Shelley Frisch (New York: Liveright, 2011; orig. German ed. 2011), p. 189.

579 hell "is the suffering of being unable to love."—Fyodor Dostoyevsky, *The Brothers Karamazov*, trans. Constance Garnett (New York: Modern Library, n.d. [bef. 1980]; orig. serial pub. 1879–80), p. 338.

579 Natalie Wood modeling Movie Star Bread—Manoah Bowman, *Natalie Wood: Reflections on a Legendary Life* (Philadelphia: Running Press, 2016), p. 83.

579 Judy Garland's three sets of false eyelashes—*Judy Garland on Judy Garland: Interviews and Encounters*, ed. Randy L. Schmidt (Chicago: Chicago Review Press / An A Cappella Book, 2014), p. 252 (information from James Goode, *Show Business Illustrated*, October 31, 1961).

THAT CERTAIN TONE

581 Epigraph: "But they that sometimes liked my company . . ."—Emrys Jones, comp. and ed., *The New Oxford Book of Sixteenth Century Verse* (New York: Oxford University Press, 1991), p. 87 ("Lucks, my fair falcon," wr. prob. 1540–41, pub. 1557).

581 Epigraph: "Lycóris, no woman used to be more darling . . ."—Dudley Fitts, *Sixty Poems of [Marcus Valerius] Martial[is] in Translation* (New York: Harcourt, Brace & World, 1967 repr. of 1956 ed.; orig. wr. 1st cent. A.D.), p. 16 (VI: 40), facing text on 17 ("Vicissitude"), "retranslated" by WTV. [Fitts's translation: "Lycóris, no woman was dearer to me in those days than you. Now Glýcera takes my whole heart." Original: *Femina praeferri potuit tibi nulla, Lycori: / praeferri Glycerae femina nulla potest.*]

581 Epigraph: "You must learn to let go . . ."—*Judy Garland on Judy Garland: Interviews and Encounters*, ed. Randy L. Schmidt (Chicago: Chicago Review Press / An A Cappella Book, 2014), p. 165 (Judy Garland, *Screenland*, October 1946).

582 "a rare nude portrait of Natalie . . ."—Manoah Bowman, *Natalie Wood: Reflections on a Legendary Life* (Philadelphia: Running Press, 2016), p. 267. I have added "Wood."

582 What befell in the temple of Ceres—Valerius Maximus, *Memorable Sayings and Doings*, Books I–V, ed. and trans. D. R. Shackleton Bailey (Cambridge, Massachusetts: Harvard University Press / Loeb Classical Library no. 292, 2000), p. 37 (I.1). My summary is somewhat after the Neopotianus version. In the Paris version, Ceres herself meets them "with a flame" and blinds them.

586 "His emotions become extraordinarily intensified . . ."—Robert Maynard Hutchins, ed.-in-chief, *Great Books of the Western World*, no. 54: *The Major Works of Sigmund Freud* (Chicago: Encyclopaedia Britannica, Inc. / William Benton / University of Chicago, 1975 repr. of 1952 ed.), p. 672 ("Group Psychology and the Analysis of the Ego" (1921), trans. James Strachey).

THE ABSOLUTE LATEST

588 Epigraph: "'Honestly, I'm in no hurry to grow up,'" Judy continued . . ."—*Judy Garland on Judy Garland: Interviews and Encounters*, ed. Randy L. Schmidt (Chicago: Chicago Review Press / An A Cappella Book, 2014), p. 32 (Robert McIlwaine, *Modern Screen*, August 1939).

588 Epigraph: "She doesn't want to grow up . . ."—Schmidt, p. 21 (Gladys Hall, *Motion Picture*, January 1938).

588 Epigraph: "But gosh, everyone who knows me . . ."—Schmidt, p. 32 (Robert McIlwaine, *Modern Screen*, August 1939).

591 Nancy Kerrigan's skating ensemble in Detroit—Keith Davidson, *Nancy Kerrigan* (New York: Scholastic Inc. / Sports Shots: Collector's Book 26, 1994), p. 30.

591 "Six months ago, I hadn't known my true love existed . . ."—Somewhat after Kathryn Springer, *The Dandelion Field* (Grand Rapids, Michigan: Zondervan, 2014), p. 224.

593 Allegation about Madonna's filler—This cruel claim appears in the magazine *In Touch*, December 5, 2016, vol. 15, issue 49, p. 47 ("Whoa! Stars Go Overboard with Filler"). The photos of Kimora Lee Simmons appear in the same place.

594 Judy Garland weeping all night because *Three Smart Girls* had made Deanna Durbin into a star—Information from David Shipman, *Judy Garland: The Secret Life of An American Legend* (New York: Hyperion, 1992), p. 63. This event occurred in 1937.

MORE TO TELL

598 Epigraph: "Do you think if she had lived . . ."—Quoted in Manoah Bowman, *Natalie Wood: Reflections on a Legendary Life* (Philadelphia: Running Press, 2016), p. 302.

598 Epigraph: "I used paint remover . . ."—Quoted in Bowman, p. 144. Kazan had instructed her: "Be bold, be brave, shock yourself . . . embarrass yourself."

RAISED AGAIN

603 Epigraph: "God raises Job again . . ."—Fyodor Dostoyevsky, *The Brothers Karamazov*, trans. Constance Garnett (New York: Modern Library, n.d. [bef. 1980]; orig. serial pub. 1879–80), p. 304.

603 Epigraph: "All these patients cry miserably for cure . . ."—Wilhelm Stekel, *Sexual Aberrations: The Phenomena of Fetishism in Relation to Sex*, trans. Dr. S. Parker (New York: Liveright Publishing Corp., 1930; n.d. for orig. German ed.), vol. I, pp. 82–83.

603 Description of Judy Garland's casket—Information from Joan Beck Coulson, *Always for Judy: Witness to the Joy and Genius of Judy Garland* (Elmira, California: Yarnscombe Books, 2014), p. 237.

603 as if we were all bearing her on our shoulders to the grave . . .—This extended trope is partially based on an untitled funeral scene by the Egyptian surrealist painter K. Yusuf.

604 "Oh, I'm so proud of you, Judy . . ."—*Judy Garland on Judy Garland: Interviews and Encounters*, ed. Randy L. Schmidt (Chicago: Chicago Review Press / An A Cappella Book, 2014), p. 6 (Wallace Beery, "Shell Chateau Hour," November 16, 1935).

604 "You could see something real inside her . . . Oh, she's *with* the angels now"—Somewhat after various online comments posted in memory of Judy Garland.

604–605 Deaths of James Dean and Natalie Wood—Information from Manoah Bowman, *Natalie Wood: Reflections on a Legendary Life* (Philadelphia: Running Press, 2016), p. 48.

607 Tale of the pretty girl in orange—*The Charleston Gazette* (West Virginia), Thursday, December 11, 2014, p. 1C (Rusty Marks, "Woman admits killing mother, gets up to 70 years"). I have altered or omitted the names of the protagonists.

615 "maybe I wouldn't have done it if I'd had the time to think it through." + "I did it so you wouldn't suffer." + "If I had a gun I probably would have killed her earlier."—Closely after David Adams, *Why Do They Kill? Men Who Murder Their Intimate Partners* (Nashville: Vanderbilt University Press, 2007), pp. 14 (Figure 1.1.: "Shooters' reasons for not using another weapon to kill their partner," p. 19).

615 Natalie Wood at fifteen—After a photo in Bowman, p. 43.

616 "As to sovereignty itself . . ."—Gordon S. Wood, ed., *The American Revolution: Writings from the Pamphlet Debate 1764–1772* (New York: Library of America, 2015), p. 516 (Allan Ramsay, "Thoughts on the Origin and Nature of Government," 1769).

620 "DOLLY IN LESBIAN PAYOFF SCANDAL! . . ."—*National Enquirer*, October 10, 2016, p. 5.

621 How it turned out with Xing—Xing left us; her replacement was a redhead in a shimmering turquoise blouse and turquoise eyeliner, who always waxed her legs; her long earrings glowed by association with her bright cell phone. She imparted a warm sensation in my

forehead, not quite a headache, much as when I had just popped a good strong dose of Francine's yellow serum and not even fifteen minutes had passed and I was already feeling it! All the same, I never dated her.

623 "Thine enemy the Serpent hath been given over to the fire."—*The Egyptian Book of the Dead*, p. 343 ("Hymn to Ra").

623 Judy Garland: "I don't believe dying is the end . . ."—Schmidt, p. 161 (Judy Garland, *Screenland*, October 1946).—More proof of immortality: For a surprise treat, with Judy lying next to him with her head on his chest, the retired policeman triple-clicked the remote control, so that dusty old television played hotel surveillance footage of the lesbian on the last day of her life, staring at the horizon in a long beige dress, while her husband, near but behind her, hung his head, standing with his hand in his pocket. The recording flickered, then skipped. Looking up from his neck almost slyly, her long hair gleaming like brown and golden snakes around his shoulder, the lesbian now gazed at two other women, as if she longed to awaken all who slept, but they ignored her. She let her face fall limply into the hollow of his neck and closed her eyes.—Judy, of course, sobbed. The retired policeman comforted her, and they lived happily ever after.

623 some of us now began badmouthing the dead lesbian.—Because we had made a new favorite for ourselves and because it distressed and perhaps even harmed us to remember the dead, I am not sure if we would have liked it had Neva come back again. *She was left there by the roadside as the old are left by the young.* So runs an old story. (Apollonius of Rhodes, *The Voyage of Argo* [*The Argonautica*], trans. R. V. Rieu [New York: Penguin Classics, 1971, rev. of 1959 ed.; orig. wr. 3rd cent. B.C.], p. 44. The person abandoned was a priestess of Artemis.) And from down the street we already spied the gilded bronze head of another unknown goddess, with dark flecks shining from her weary goldness. The lesbian was now as hateful as the black girl Letitia, who had once presumed to leave us.

624 "Let's keep it light!"—Schmidt, p. 176.

624 Judy Garland: "Why I should have ever gotten depressed, I certainly don't know . . ."—*Judy Garland on Judy Garland: Interviews and Encounters*, ed. Randy L. Schmidt (Chicago: Chicago Review Press / An A Cappella Book, 2014), p. 176 (Judy Garland, *Modern Screen*, 1950). Well, well; just in case you believe that more self-awareness would have benefitted her, let me quote what she said on p. 191: "In an effort to learn why I had never been able to get closer to people, I took a series of psychoanalytical treatments, and I have never regretted anything more . . . It just tore me apart."

ACKNOWLEDGMENTS

Unable to write like a woman or a policeman without help, I scoured, begged, stole and commissioned stories from others. The uses I have put them to in the sad world of *The Lucky Star* in no way reflect the real people they came from.

My great gratitude goes to Laura Michele Diener, Heidi Lehrman, Teresa McFarland (whose careful reading of the manuscript saved me from turning in an error-riddled pustulence), Lindsay Rickman and Mary Swisher (not to mention the Portland go-go dancer named Marley), and several unnamed prostitutes, for answering questions about various stages of womanhood. Their stories have much enriched this book.

Antonia Crane, experienced in love and sex with various genders, set aside an hour to answer both sweeping and personal questions. I have thankfully incorporated several of her tales and opinions.

In Las Vegas I would like to thank my friend and energetic fixer Mr. Dan Hernandez, and the performers past and present to whom he introduced me in June 2017: Ms. Zoe Deaton, Ms. Kathy Mckee, Ms. Kathryn Savage-Koehm, Ms. Cheryl Slader, Ms. Claire Tewalt, Wonderhussy and Ms. Natalie Walstead. A year later in the same city, with Dan's help, Erika Castro, Carlota Gonzalez, Cyntha Hall and Cynthia Patane did me the great honor of sharing intimate details of their lives with me. Their stories changed this book, and my life, for the better.

I am also grateful to my friend Joshua Schenk, the executive director of the Black Mountain Institute in Las Vegas, for his friendship and his help.

In Seattle, Jenny Riffles and her friend Colleen answered my alcohol-enhanced queries about lesbian and bisexual femininity, and helped me to place my S/M submissive transwoman character onto a happier narrative path. I was inspired by their optimism, openness and courage.

Without Greg Roden I would never have known anything about the Silver Fox bar in Bakersfield, not to mention several other sites. David Shook and his friend John provided me with much L.A.-based expert knowledge. Ditto to Chris Heiser and his beautiful Megan and Molly.

My dear friend Mark Merin shared with me some of his intake case files—grist for the retired policeman's mill. Officer Aaron Perez and the retired cop H. Lee Barnes (both interviewed in Vegas thanks to Dan Hernandez) gave me more stories and opinions. My P.I. buddy Chuck Pfister helped inform the retired policeman's investigation of Neva, suggesting specific procedures, databases and expungements.

Hillary Johnson was a perfect Vallejo reconnoitering and drinking companion. With her I discovered places transformable into Jingle's bar and Mrs. Strand's little house. I wish Hillary much happiness.

And thanks to my sweetheart of a sister-in-law, Laura Rhee Ryu, for driving me all day through Silver Lake, Los Angeles and Culver City in search of Judy Garland sites.

Father Brian Clary, who gave me Burnaby's book on Augustine, has been a fine pen pal over the years. I am lucky to know him.

Paul Slovak has been my friend and editor for decades now. Our business dealings have not invariably been smooth. My resistance to cutting sacrificed trees, and tested both of our patience. For my part, I gave way many a time on titles, covers, illustrations, charts, source-notes, etc. Paul has slogged thousands of extra miles in order to accommodate me where he could. This give and take between equals has been facilitated by memories of drinking together, of meeting each other's sisters and attending each other's weddings, of book-chats (and, from him, of book-gifts) and of a certain interesting hike in the Sierras. I will never forget the first time we discussed Thucydides, although I may not recollect our hundredth pint of Guinness. Now that I am oldish and in imperfect health, I cannot help but wonder how much farther we will travel together. Paul, when I look at the row of Viking books with my name on them, I think of you. I have not always been an easy author but I have always been grateful—and this time, I did actually cut *The Lucky Star*, by at least twenty or thirty words, so please pat yourself on the back.

Bruce Giffords remains the prince of production editors, and I feel very lucky to count him, too, as a friend. As my neurons die, I need him more than ever. And for his care, intelligence, tact and kindness, I value him more than ever. Thank you so much, Bruce. You have been very good to me.

I would also like to express gratitude to Jane Cavolina, Roland Ottewell, Lisa Thornbloom, and Bitite Vinklers for tightening sentences and saving me from typographical embarrassment. And I thank the designer, Meighan Cavanaugh.

Let me also remember Declan Spring of New Directions, whose kindness has on more than one occasion expressed itself in book-gifts—among them the *Shilappadikaram*, a passage of which helps open my novel. Thank you, my friend.